"I can make sure you'll never work on Broadway, or anywhere near it, again."

More defiantly than she felt, she snapped, "That's ridiculous. Hartman might have that much power, but you certainly don't."

"Oh, it's no threat, believe me. I can do it. If I choose, all I have to do is invoke the exclusivity clause you signed in your contract."

That stopped her for a second. "What are you talking about? Such a thing doesn't exist."

"Oh, doesn't it? Remember our little night of celebration in Philly when you signed it? No, I see by that blank expression that you don't. Well, let me enlighten you."

Suddenly, in one blinding flash, it came back to her. As if in a dream, she saw Nigel handing her a pen as she swayed drunkenly on the couch in his suite; she saw herself signing something with a flourish, laughing like a fool, guzzling more champagne to celebrate. What kind of fool had she been . . . ?

Also by Janis Flores
Published by Fawcett Books:

LOVING TIES
RUNNING IN PLACE
DIVIDED LOYALTIES
ABOVE REPROACH
TOUCHED BY FIRE

SIREN SONG

Janis Flores

FAWCETT GOLD MEDAL • NEW YORK

A Fawcett Gold Medal Book
Published by Ballantine Books
Copyright © 1993 by Janis Flores

Library of Congress Catalog Card Number: 92-97267

ISBN 0-449-14737-1

Manufactured in the United States of America

First Edition: May 1993

For my brother, Mark,
who left life as he lived it—
with dignity, courage, and a touch of humor.

And to Maria,
steadfast and loving—
thank *you* for caring . . . and sharing him with us.

CHAPTER ONE

"You're a fool to go, you know," a harsh voice said from the doorway. "You'll never make it as a *songwriter*, of all things, and not on Broadway, of all places. Never, not in a million years."

Keeley Cochran looked up from the suitcase she'd been packing and glanced toward the door. Her stepmother, Phyllis, stood on the threshold to the tiny bedroom Keeley had finally commandeered for herself three years ago, overriding the vehement protests of her half sisters, Jewell and Lila, because she was the oldest. Phyllis had one hip thrust out, one hand at her waist. In her pose, with her thin, frizzy blond hair hanging down on either side of her pale face, she looked—there was no other word for it, Keeley thought—just like a hooker.

Keeley didn't say anything, and they stared at each other for a long moment, Phyllis with a flat look of dislike in her pale eyes, Keeley trying to hide her contempt. It was Phyllis who looked away first. They both knew how she felt about Keeley's going, and it wasn't sad.

Keeley returned to her packing. She and her stepmother had been over it a hundred times—more. It was old ground, and she wasn't going to change her mind, not now, when she had finally made her decision, not now, when she'd dreamed about going for years.

Years, she thought, folding a blouse that had been washed so many times the cotton felt like fine lawn. She put it carefully in the suitcase, thinking that the time felt more like centuries. She was twenty-two years old, and she had wanted to be a musician, a songwriter, a Broadway *composer*, for as long as she could remember. If she waited any longer, she wouldn't go. She'd end up trapped here, as she had been ever since she graduated from high school. It was now or never; her pity had run out, and she had to go without looking back.

"If it hadn't been for your parasite of a family, you would

1

have been gone long before now," Keeley's best friend, Nina Calducci, had told her. That had been six months ago, when they were talking about it during a lunch break at work. She and Nina both worked for a car dealer here in Detroit, Keeley doing the books, Nina acting as secretary/receptionist. Nina was happy with what she was doing, but for Keeley it would never be enough. Good wages or not, she wanted more—much more than Detroit could ever give her. Broadway beckoned, and she'd denied herself long enough. If she failed, as Phyllis seemed to be so certain she would, at least she would have tried.

Tried? she thought. She wouldn't just *try*, she decided fiercely. She'd *succeed*.

"I just don't understand it," black-haired, dark-eyed Nina had said that day at lunch. They had known each other for years, and she knew she could say what she felt. "When are you going to stand up to your family? You never have a problem asserting yourself around here or anywhere else. But with *them*, you never say a word."

Keeley had pushed her half-eaten sandwich away. The stark lunch area at the dealership had always been unappetizing; the scarred Formica tables and drab gray walls and harsh fluorescent lighting made everything look half dead. "I can't say anything," she muttered. "You know how much they depend on me."

"Oh, pooh," Nina said with scorn. "They wouldn't depend on you so much if you weren't always there. What is it with you, anyway? Are you going to support them the rest of your life?"

"No, of course not! But my father's out of work—"

"Your father's *always* out of work," Nina pointed out with inexorable logic. "Why else have you stayed? If he'd have let you go to New York to study, instead of insisting that you get a job to help support him and his wife and all those kids of theirs—"

"It wasn't his fault," Keeley said, picturing her father, big and blond, who had once been the smartest, strongest man in the world to her. Since his remarriage, she had always felt so left out, waiting for him to *notice* her, but he never did. She hated herself for hoping things would change, but she couldn't seem to stop it. Would she never learn? Defensively, she looked at Nina. "No one predicted the plant would strike just then."

Nina wasn't sympathetic. "*Then?* What about afterward? What about six months ago? What about *now*? When is he going to get off his lazy duff and go out looking for a permanent job instead of expecting you to hand over *your* paycheck?"

"I don't just *hand* it over!"

"Close enough," Nina said flatly. This was her favorite subject, and she wasn't going to be diverted. She believed in Keeley; she'd heard her music, the songs she composed. Intensely, she leaned forward. "But even not counting your Dad, what about that lazy slut of a stepmother of yours?" Seeing Keeley's expression, she waved a dismissive hand. "Well, I'm sorry, but she *is*. Six kids in fifteen years. You'd think she never heard of birth control!"

Keeley couldn't argue the point. Sometimes she felt that what Phyllis did best was get pregnant. She certainly didn't work—outside the home, that was. Even in the leanest times—and there had been plenty of those over the years—she had never offered to go out and get a job herself to help support her growing family. Not even when Joe Cochran had been laid off for the umpteenth time and once again Keeley was the only breadwinner in the house. She had to stay home and watch the kids, she said.

Or more likely, watch her soap operas, Keeley thought resentfully. But she couldn't blame Phyllis entirely, she knew. Keeley's father, Joe, hadn't been much help; depressed about losing his job, he lay on the couch day after day, watching game shows and drinking endless cans of beer. It had been up to sixteen-, seventeen-, eighteen-year-old Keeley to rush from class to work at the diner, the only job she could find and stay in high school, so that she could make some money to help out. With her father's unemployment check and the salary and tips she made, they scraped by somehow, until the plant got going and Joe was called back to work, only to have it happen again, and again.

It was a cycle that had been repeated too often to count, and that day in the lunch area, she knew Nina was right. She had to make a break; she had to get out of the vicious circle she was in so she could finally do what she'd always wanted to do—go write the music. It was Nina's term, not hers, but it was what she'd wanted to do ever since she saw her first piano and asked her mother if they could buy it.

She'd only been about six at the time, but she remembered the day almost as clearly as if it had been yesterday. It was one of the last real memories she had of her mother, who had died only a few months later from a bronchitis that had swiftly turned into a fatal pneumonia. Eleanor Cochran had been beautiful, Keeley remembered, with thick, dark hair and the vivid green eyes that her daughter had inherited. Keeley could even remember how gaily her mother had laughed when Keeley saw the grand piano in the music store window and begged just to go in and look at it.

Thinking back, Keeley realized that the store's manager must have fallen under Eleanor's spell, too, for when she asked if her young daughter could just touch the beautiful instrument, he magnanimously lifted Keeley up onto the bench and smilingly suggested she entertain them all with a tune.

To everyone's astounded surprise, including her mother's, Keeley proceeded to do more than that. She never knew where the music came from, but without warning, it was just . . . there. She touched the piano with her baby fingers, and suddenly it was as if something magical occurred. She didn't know the full chords, of course; she wouldn't have been able to play them with her tiny hands, even if she had. But the melody was there, a lively tune that seemed to come out of nowhere. Like all the other music she had composed since then, the notes just poured forth as though the songs had always been at the back of her mind, waiting to come out and be recognized.

Even at such a young age, she was so enthralled by what she was creating that she didn't even notice other people, the shoppers, the salespeople, everyone in the store, stopping to listen to the six-year-old child with the solemn green eyes and the long, thick, dark hair. She'd been so small that her nose was barely even with the piano keyboard, but she had treated them to something they'd remember for a long, long time.

When she finished, she noticed the crowd for the first time. People were standing all around, and when she saw tears in her mother's eyes, she thought she'd done something wrong. Then Eleanor swept her up and gave her a fierce hug while the onlookers applauded, and she realized with wonder that her mother was proud of her. Even then, she hadn't thought of herself in the spotlight; to her, it was the music that was on center stage. But from that day to this, she had never taken for granted the exultation she'd felt at being able to entertain, to move people, to touch their hearts in a special way with what she created out of her own mind.

"You're right," she'd said to Nina, with a sigh. "You're absolutely right. I don't know why I haven't gone before this. It's just—"

"It's just that you're too softhearted, that's what," Nina said severely. But she put an affectionate hand on Keeley's arm to take the sting out of her words before she frowned. She had often visited the rundown old house where Keeley lived, and she shuddered as she added, "I don't know how you stand it there, Keeley. All the noise from those kids, Phyllis screaming all the time, the television blasting away even when no one's watching it." She shook her head. "It would drive me nuts!"

"It makes me crazy at times, I admit," Keeley said. Then she smiled. "You just have to learn to shut it out."

"By writing music, you mean?" Nina said meaningfully. "On the piano that you've wanted ever since you were little and never got?"

Again, Keeley had no answer. Nina was right: she had yearned for a piano at home for years. In the beginning, the excuse had been that her father couldn't afford such an expensive instrument; later, after all the kids started coming, and the house began to be stuffed to the gills, the reason was that there wasn't enough room. When she got older, she started using the piano at the high school. When she attended night school at the college to get her music degree, she'd had the use of the big music hall whenever she wanted. But she still had the cardboard keyboard she had made as a child—and sometimes even now, she used it when nothing else was available.

Fondly, she thought of her youngest half sister, ten-year-old Jewell, who had seen her with her fake keyboard recently. Always curious, Jewell had asked how she could write songs using a piece of cardboard that didn't make any noise, even if it did have piano keys drawn on it. Realizing it did seem strange, Keeley had tried to explain that she had never really needed to make sound; the music was always there, in her mind. Jewell still looked doubtful, but she didn't know what more to say about it. How could she explain something she didn't understand fully herself?

Aware of Nina's eyes on her, Keeley said, "You know there isn't room at the house for a piano, but even if there were, with all the other noise, I probably couldn't hear myself think."

"I don't deny it. Your dad and your stepmother are bad enough when they go at it, but Louis gives me the creeps. And the twins! If I could catch them, I'd wring their necks."

Nina was referring to Keeley's eight-year-old half brothers, the demon twins, Alfred and Harry. To her, they were no worse than other boys their age, but she agreed with Nina about Louis, who, at fifteen, was the oldest of Phyllis's six children. She didn't know if it was just a phase or not, but the past year or so, Louis had changed. He'd always been arrogant and rebellious and sly, but lately, he seemed . . . hard. Keeley was positive he was into something—maybe drugs, maybe not. Whatever it was, it was trouble. Phyllis had never disciplined any of her children, and Joe had always been too proud of his oldest boy, who took after him both in looks and personality, to make him toe the line. The result was that Louis came and went and did as he liked. The twins were about to follow in his footsteps, and Keeley was sure the youngest, Sid, would emulate them. She'd tried to talk to her father about it, but he just mocked her concern.

She didn't want to think about her half brothers, so she said teasingly to Nina, "You haven't mentioned the girls in the family. Have you suddenly taken a liking to Lila, or even Jewell?"

Nina wadded up the waxed paper she'd used to wrap her sandwich. "Jewell isn't so bad," she conceded, and paused. "But she's only ten—who can tell yet? But Lila . . ." She rolled her eyes. "If she doesn't get pregnant before she's fifteen, I'll kiss Larry Moffat—or maybe," she added slyly, "Russell Morley."

Keeley didn't want to talk about Russ. They had met at night school, and ever since, they'd been dating hot and heavy. She knew he was about to ask her again to move in with him. Come on, Keeley, we're practically married anyway, he'd say—and she regretted having to hurt him. She liked Russ; she did. She enjoyed his company, the time they spent together, the good sex they had. But he was happy with his job at the stereo store, and she knew she'd never be content here, not even if she failed on Broadway. She had to break it off; she just hadn't found the right way to do it yet.

Nina saw her expression, and her own softened. "I'm sorry, I shouldn't have said that. I know you have to break up with him when you leave." Remembering her subject, she added pointedly, "Of course, it's academic, isn't it, if you don't tell your family you've had it. Maybe you're just going to stay here like the rest of us."

"I said I'd tell them, and I will!"

Nina was nothing if not persistent. "When?"

"When the time is right," Keeley replied. Glancing at her watch, she was relieved to see that lunch hour was almost over. She stood, ending the conversation. "Right now, we have to get back to work."

"Keeley," Nina said warningly.

Keeley stopped collecting the lunch trash. Looking at her friend, she said, "I promised, didn't I?"

"When?" Nina said again.

Keeley sighed. "Soon."

Nina grabbed her arm, forcing Keeley to look into her face. "I hate to keep badgering you like this, but damn it! You're good, you know you are. Too good for this stupid town!"

"But what if I—" Keeley began, then stopped. Even she couldn't make herself say it. She did know she was good. But it wasn't much benefit if she didn't give herself the chance to prove it, was it?

Nina persevered. "And your night school drama teacher said she'd write a letter to a Broadway director she knows—"

"*She* doesn't know him," Keeley protested. "A friend of a friend of a cousin once removed is supposed to have talked to him once. He probably doesn't have the faintest idea who she is."

"Who cares?" Nina demanded grandly. "It's a way to get *in*! And just think—wouldn't it be wonderful to see your name up in lights some day? Imagine—splashed right across the marquee: Words and Music by Keeley Cochran!" Nina looked at her suddenly. "That's how it *will* read, won't it? You won't change your name when you're famous!"

Despite herself, Keeley laughed. "I think the time to change your name is *before* you get famous. But no, fame or not, I plan on staying just plain Keeley Cochran the rest of my life."

"But not after you get married!"

Keeley thought of her chaotic family life, all the people crowded into one tiny four-bedroom house, clothes flung all over, wet towels cluttering the bathroom, dirty underwear crammed into corners, used dishes always in the sink. Then she thought of her stepmother, always tired, with her stringy hair hanging down, defeated by all the mess, hiding behind the fascinating pictures of a tabloid—and her bleary-eyed father, lying on the couch while some game or another blared unnoticed from the TV. Without realizing it, she shuddered.

"It won't be a problem," she said, thrusting away the unsavory pictures of her home life. "I don't intend to get married."

Nina pooh-poohed the idea. "Oh, I know you've said that, Keeley, but you don't mean it."

"Yes, I do."

"No, you don't," Nina said firmly. "Someday you'll meet a man who will—"

"If you say 'sweep me off my feet,' I'll throw up."

Indignantly, Nina said, "Would I be so trite? I wasn't going to say that at all. I *was* going to say that someday you'll meet a man who makes you feel how everybody *else* feels when they hear your music."

"And how is that?"

"As though they've just fallen in love," Nina said dreamily.

Flattered despite herself, Keeley laughed. "You should be an actress. You're just that dramatic!"

It was time to get back to work, but as they left the lunchroom to go back to their desks, Nina stopped outside the door. Her brown eyes, usually so merry, were suddenly solemn. Intensely, she said, "Promise me, Keeley. Promise me that no matter what happens, you'll make the break and go to New York, as you've always said you'll do."

Keeley was about to make a flip remark, but when she saw how serious her friend was, she paused. She and Nina had been through a lot together; through the years, they had shared things they never would have told to another living soul. Best friends, they had laughed together, cried together, and planned the future together. She couldn't imagine a world without Nina, and when she felt a sudden chill, she gave Nina a fierce hug.

"What do you mean . . . no matter what happens? You'll be here to see that I do what I'm supposed to."

"But if I'm not—"

"You will be," Keeley said firmly. "Now, stop talking like that. You're scaring me."

But still Nina didn't seem satisfied. "Don't let anything stop you," she insisted. "You were meant for better than this. Everybody who knows you, all your friends, your teachers—everyone but that damned family of yours—knows it. Who else could have written all those original songs for the glee club in high school, not to mention our senior play? And what about the entire musical show you did for your college night school degree? It brought down the house. Even the dean, who's a theater buff, said it was good enough for a professional performance."

"He was just being complimentary."

"Complimentary or not, we can't all be wrong, don't you see? You're special, Keeley—you always have been. So you can't just . . . waste all your ability here, on ungrateful people who don't care how much talent you have. You've *got* to do what you were meant to do—no matter what."

"I will, I will, I promise," she said. Then, because Nina's urgency was making her uneasy, she laughed to dispel the tension. "Now, can we get back to work? I can't leave for New York this minute, you know. I still have the end-of-the-month books to finish up for Mr. Sandborn."

"You laugh, but I'm serious. I mean it, Keeley. You've got to tell them."

She didn't know why Nina was going on about it without pause, but she said, "All *right*. I'll tell them tonight, okay? Will that make you happy?"

To her dismay, Nina's dark eyes glowed, and she pounced. "You will? You promise?"

Now that she'd said it, she had to follow through. In a way, it was a relief. She'd been putting off making her final decision for months now, but she really didn't have a reason to delay any longer. She had enough money saved—or almost, and as Nina had pointed out, it would always be something where her family was concerned. If she didn't make the break soon, before she realized it, she'd be an old lady and all her opportunities would be past.

"Yes," she said, suddenly resolute where she'd only been half-serious before. She looked into Nina's anxious face and smiled. "Yes, I promise."

Nina looked relieved, as though a great weight had been lifted off her shoulders. "Well, hooray," she said fervently. "Now, I mean it, Keeley, I want you to call me tonight right after you tell them, and I want to hear word-for-word exactly what you said, okay?"

"Okay," Keeley said with a laugh as they went back to work.

But she never got the chance to tell Nina what she said to her parents. Unable to reach her by phone that night, she didn't find out until the next morning that her best friend in the whole world had been killed by a drunk driver on the way home from work. She had apparently died instantly when the big truck slammed into her little compact car, crushing it like a tin can, but for Keeley, it was small comfort. The horrible news seemed to make the world come to a stop. Even now, six months later, she couldn't think of Nina without wanting to cry.

If something ever happens to me, and you don't go to New York to write the music, I'll come back from my grave and haunt you, I swear it!

Nina had said it to her more than once, and as Keeley tried to finish her packing under Phyllis's staring eyes, she wished more than anything that Nina could carry out her threat. Even a haunting would be better than the acrid emptiness she'd felt since her best friend had died. Nothing, not even all her feverish

activity, or the songs she wrote in a vain attempt to comfort herself, or the music she had composed, had helped alleviate her
devastating sense of loss.

But she had kept her promise and told her family, and later,
she talked to Russ, who had been so upset he'd cried. The sight
unnerved her; for a moment, she faltered. She wanted to say
she'd be back, but it wasn't true; she wanted to say she loved
him, but that was a lie, too. In the end, she'd told him she would
never forget him and left before he could reply. She felt badly
about Russ, but there was no other way.

Phyllis spoke again, interrupting her sad thoughts. "You know
I've never liked you, Keeley, and it's for damned sure the feeling's been mutual. Oh, don't bother to deny it; I've seen the
look in your eyes. But this impulsive decision to leave your
home and your family, well, I really think you should reconsider.
You can't just go and leave everything behind!"

Keeley knew Phyllis didn't give a damn about her or her
well-being; what she was thinking of was how they were going
to manage without Keeley's paycheck. "What am I leaving behind, Phyllis?" she said. Pointedly she looked around the tiny
bedroom, so small there was barely enough room for the bed
and a dresser. "I'm twenty-two years old. It's past time I got out
on my own."

Phyllis sneered. "You can't be serious about going to New
York just to write *songs*! Do you know how many *talented* people there are who have tried what you're about to do and have
failed? How on earth do you think someone like *you* is going to
make it?"

"Someone like me?" Keeley repeated, slowly turning to look
directly into her stepmother's eyes. "What makes you so sure
I'm going to fail, Phyllis?"

"Oh, please! You always did think you were better than the
rest of us!"

Keeley took a tight grip on her temper. She'd always held her
tongue where Phyllis was concerned; she had discovered early
on that if there was a disagreement between the two of them, her
father would invariably take her stepmother's side. She had
learned to avoid quarrels that only emphasized how little notice
her father took of her, or her opinions. But now she was going,
walking out of this house—perhaps forever, judging from her father's reaction when he'd realized she was serious—and she
didn't want to be silent anymore.

"You're right about one thing, Phyllis," she said. "We never have liked each other. We haven't gotten along from the time my father first introduced us—when was it? Three months after my mother died? Fifteen years ago, and things haven't improved since."

Phyllis's pale eyes narrowed. "You always have been a little prig about that, Keeley. Tell me, what was your father supposed to do? He was a widower, with a seven-year-old child. How could he work and take care of you, too?"

Keeley didn't know why, but some demon seemed to take hold of her. Maybe it was because she'd been thinking of Nina, and how much she missed her friend; maybe it was the idea that in a few minutes, she was going to walk out of the only home she'd ever known. She wasn't sure what it was, only that she had to express her feelings, just once. After this, she need never mention it again.

"If you're trying to make me believe that my father married you so that we could be a family, you've forgotten that I've lived here all this time, too," she said. "The last thing *we've* been is family, Phyllis, so don't try to pretend otherwise."

"If you're accusing me—"

"I'm not accusing you of anything. Maybe it was your fault; maybe it was mine. I don't know, and I don't care anymore."

It wasn't really true. She had never forgotten the terror and confusion she'd felt after her mother died. She didn't understand what was happening, or why her mother was gone, or why Eleanor wasn't coming home again. Her father hadn't been any help; lost in his own grief, he shunted her off to a baby-sitter and was out every night—to bars, Keeley later found out, one of which was where he met Phyllis. The marriage came as a complete surprise, although to Keeley, years later, the "early" arrival of her half brother, Louis, explained a lot.

What it didn't explain at the time was why she had been left out. At seven years old, she was too young to comprehend the upheaval in her life, and her father and stepmother were too preoccupied with their young baby to pay attention to her needs. At a time when she missed her mother terribly and desperately craved attention and assurance that she wouldn't lose her father, too, she was all but ignored by the joyful new parents. Joe had always wanted a son, and at nearly thirty, the never-before-married Phyllis had been pining even more for a child than she had been for a husband. Together, they were a perfect trio, and Keeley was left out. To make matters worse, Keeley didn't even *look* like she belonged. In a new family of blue-eyed blonds, dark-haired, green-eyed Keeley stood out like a sore thumb.

Fifteen years and five more half siblings later, the differences were even more apparent. Maybe because she'd had to be, Keeley had always been a self-starter, self-motivated, ambitious, eager to learn. But except for Jewell, who had always been different from the others, and Lila, who already seemed a carbon copy of her mother, the four boys were just like their father, even young Sid. They were all lazy, self-centered, all of them only looking out for number one.

Of them all, Keeley thought distractedly, she would miss Jewell the most, but it couldn't be helped. As Nina had reinforced in her, she wasn't going to be someone who talked about a dream until it got so old it just crumbled to dust; she was going, and this time, nothing was going to stop her. Certainly not anything Phyllis said. She had waited too long already—*years* too long. Now it was November, and the latest forecast said Detroit could expect another storm before nightfall, with a new front gathering on the eastern seaboard, heading right for New York. It wasn't the best time to travel, she knew, but she didn't have a choice. If she didn't go now, something would stop her; it always had. If it wasn't family problems, it was other things. Six months ago, after Nina had been killed, she'd finally saved up enough to leave again—this time for sure—she'd been mugged on her way home from work. She had just cashed her paycheck, and of course the thief had taken every cent. People said she was lucky she hadn't been hurt, but all she could think of was the money he'd snatched. It had taken her this long to recoup, and now she was going to keep her promise to Nina and get out before it was too late.

"What did you mean, we haven't been a family?" Phyllis demanded. "If you're trying to blame me—"

Keeley didn't want to talk about it anymore. What purpose would it serve dredging up the past? Wearily, she just shook her head. "It doesn't matter."

"The hell it doesn't!" Phyllis cried. "I'm not going to have you blame me for something that isn't my fault! Do you hear me, Keeley? Do you hear me, girl?"

Keeley heard, all right; it would have been impossible not to, even with the television blaring from the living room, and three of the younger kids, the twins, Harry and Alfred, and Lila shouting at one another in the kitchen over the last piece of pizza.

"I heard you," she said, folding a sweater she had decided to take. She could only carry so much. With all her music, she couldn't take two suitcases, but what she was leaving behind was so old it didn't matter anyway. Without looking at her step-mother again, she packed the sweater. She was almost finished, and she glanced around to see what she'd missed. Arms akimbo, Phyllis stepped into her way.

"Well?"

Keeley sighed. "What's the point of arguing about it?" she asked. "If it hadn't been for the money I've brought in, you would have kicked me out years ago, and don't try to deny it. You've always said I didn't belong here, that I wasn't part of the family. I'd think you'd be happy now that I'm finally going to be out of your hair."

Phyllis's thin lips tightened. "Oh, no, you're not going to get away with that one! You're the one who's wanted to go. You couldn't wait, remember? You've wanted to desert us all from the time you turned sixteen."

Fourteen, Keeley thought but didn't reply.

Phyllis saw her expression, and her eyes flashed. "And don't give me that *look* of yours, as if you're somehow superior to the rest of us! You know we've tried our best, and if you go like this, you'll . . . you'll just break your father's heart!"

Keeley almost laughed. When she went, it wouldn't be Joe's heart that was affected but his wallet, and they both knew it. "Yes, well, I'm sorry," she said, "but it's not as if this is a big surprise. You've known what I intended for months now—for years."

"Oh, yes, that's right, you're off to be a Broadway star, how could I have forgotten that?" Phyllis said with a sneer. "Well, all I can say is, don't plan on coming back when you fail, my girl, because your bed isn't going to be here!"

"Fine," Keeley said. She'd known it would come to this. "I'm not going to fail, as you put it, but in any case, I won't be coming back." Their eyes met. "There isn't anything for me here but more of the same, and we both know it."

The pale eyes flashed—with anger . . . and fear. "After all we've done for you!" Phyllis cried. "And this is the thanks we get!"

The words were out before she knew it. "After all I've done for *you*, you mean," Keeley said, her voice tight. "If I'd kept accounts, I'd be flying to New York instead of taking the bus."

Phyllis looked ready to strike. "Oh, you horrible girl! We've never asked you for a dime, and you know it!"

Keeley couldn't believe it. Wondering how even Phyllis could say such a thing—Phyllis, who met her at the door every payday with her hand out—she wanted to laugh, but she felt too bitter. She and Nina had wanted to take an apartment together, but with what she had to pay to help here, she hadn't been able to afford it. And she hadn't been able to go away to college, either, because she'd had to get a full-time job right out of high school. She could still remember the terrible argument she and her father had gotten into the night of her high school graduation. She hadn't really felt trapped until that night, when he'd told her she couldn't go to college as she had planned. He had just lost another job, and with unemployment in his work so high, he'd informed her she had to get a job to help pay the rent.

"It doesn't have to be this way!" she'd cried, swamped by unfairness. "Why is it always up to me to help out?"

He'd shouted at her, his harsh voice loud and strident. "Because I say so, now don't argue with me!"

"But it isn't fair!" she'd shouted back. "If you want help, why don't you ask her? Maybe she can do something for this *family* instead of having another baby to drag us deeper into trouble!"

Before Keeley could get out of the way, Joe Cochran raised his hand and slapped her hard, right across the face.

"Don't you dare talk about your mother like that!" he'd shouted. "Phyllis is a good woman, and I won't have you criticizing!"

The slap had rocked her on her feet, but she wouldn't back down. Her green eyes blazing, she'd faced her father, shouting, "Phyllis isn't my mother! My mother's *dead*!"

The scene had taken place nearly five years ago, Keeley thought. She felt weary just thinking about it. All this time wasted here in Detroit when she could have been pounding on doors in New York. Why hadn't she gone? She wasn't sure of the answer; maybe she didn't want to know. The point was that, for whatever reason—guilt, obligation, duty, approval—she'd stayed.

But no longer, she thought, reaching for her coat. She had her bus ticket in her pocket, and she was going tonight. She'd tried to explain to people who didn't want to listen and who didn't care anyway; now there was nothing more to say.

"Good-bye, Phyllis," she said, lifting the suitcase.

Phyllis stayed where she was, making Keeley squeeze by. "You'll be sorry," she hissed, looking down with frightened eyes as Keeley was forced to sidle past her.

Keeley didn't reply. Taking a tighter grip on the suitcase, she went toward the living room, where her father lay on the couch. The newspaper was over his face, the television blaring away. Just for a moment, as she looked in at him, she faltered. Without warning, thoughts of happier times before her mother died flashed into her mind. She had a picture of him as he had been then, young and strong and happy, lifting her up to the sky.

But that man was gone, she realized, staring at the recumbent form; he had died the night Eleanor Cochran had died. He hadn't been the same since then, and if she'd stayed all this time in the hope that she would get him back one day, she'd been fooling herself. She had once believed he was her connection to the memories she had of happier times; maybe that was why she had stayed and worked so hard and given him everything she'd earned. What a fool she'd been to believe his taking it was proof that he needed her still.

She shook her head. Had she been the weak one, or had he? Maybe she would never know, she decided, tiptoeing across the gritty carpet to give him a kiss good-bye, and maybe it didn't matter anyway.

Gently, she pulled away the newspaper. Her father was fast asleep, his mouth slack, his breathing labored because he'd gained so much weight.

"Good-bye, Dad," she whispered, and leaned down to kiss his cheek.

He didn't stir.

Sighing, Keeley replaced the newspaper and turned toward the front door. The quarrel over the pizza was still going on in the kitchen, and Keeley didn't know where Jewell had gone. It didn't matter, she supposed; she'd already said good-bye in her own way.

"You'll be back, you know," Phyllis sneered as Keeley reached for the door.

Keeley didn't answer; turning the knob, she went outside. The cold air hit her like a slap, and she knew it would probably snow before she reached the bus stop. Somehow, it didn't matter. At long last, she was on her way. She was halfway down the walk when she heard a shout behind her.

"Keeley! Keeley!"

She turned. Jewell was standing in the doorway, the light from behind illuminating her slight figure, making her long blond hair look like a glowing halo. Her mother was holding on to her, so she couldn't come outside, but she gave a frantic wave.

"Good-bye, Keeley!" she cried. "Good luck!"

For the first time since Nina had died, Keeley felt tears coming into her eyes. Lifting a hand, she waved back.

"I left something for you on your bed!" she called.

"What?"

"You'll see," Keeley called, and smiled as Jewell gave one last hurried wave before dashing out of sight. She was just turning to head down the walk again when Jewell came back, hurling herself down the walk after Keeley despite her mother's attempts to hold her back. She was holding the cardboard keyboard Keeley had left behind.

"Oh, Keeley, it's your piano," Jewell said, looking up at Keeley with wide, deep-blue eyes. She was already shivering with cold, and she hugged the rectangle to her thin chest. "Don't you want to take it with you?"

Keeley bent and gave the girl a quick, fierce hug. Jewell always had been the best of the bunch, she thought, and tried not to cry as she said, "You keep it for me, honey—in case things don't work out and I have to come back and get it. All right?"

Before the child could say anything, Phyllis shouted angrily from the doorway. "Jewell, you come inside right his instant!"

Still Jewell didn't go. Looking up at Keeley with huge blue eyes, she said, "You won't forget me, will you, Keeley?"

Keeley squatted down. Their eyes were on the same level when she hugged Jewell again. "Never," she said fiercely.

"Jewell! This instant!" Phyllis shouted again.

Keeley glanced toward the doorway. The last thing she wanted was for her father to wake up now, so she reluctantly got to her feet and gently turned Jewell back toward the house.

"You'd better go, honey. It's cold out here, and you don't want to get sick."

"Jewell!" shouted Phyllis.

The little girl started up the walk, but after a few steps she turned. "You'll make it, Keeley," she said tearfully. "I'll never doubt it." She hugged the cardboard harder. "And I'll keep this for you, even though you won't need it. One day we'll see your name up in lights. I just know it!"

Before Keeley could reply over the growing lump in her throat, Jewell turned and ran up the sidewalk. Phyllis slammed the door behind her, and abruptly, Keeley was left alone, out in the dark, cold night. She stood there for a moment looking at the house she'd lived in all her life. Then, squaring her shoulders, she turned and headed toward the bus stop.

———&———

CHAPTER TWO

"You're a fool if you don't go," Edra Smits said sharply to her daughter from behind the counter, where she was marking soup cans on special, four for a dollar. It was Thursday night— "late night" at the store, and Valine had hurried home from her other job at the department store to help her mother. They were both down in the little corner grocery owned by Edra's mother, Evie, who this minute was lying upstairs in the tiny apartment they all shared over the shop. Lifting the metal stamp she was using, Edra jabbed it in Valine's direction. "You'll never get another chance like this, not in your lifetime, anyway. You can't give it up now, not when it's what we've been waiting for, working *toward* all these years!"

"I didn't say—" Valine began, but just then the bell over the little grocery's outer door tinkled, and a heavy-set woman came in carrying a string bag. Instantly, Edra's angry expression smoothed out, and she turned to her customer with a smile.

"Good evening, Mrs. Coleman," she said pleasantly, while Valine returned to what she had been doing before—wiping the glass doors to the milk refrigerator. Shaking her head at the transformation in her mother, she picked up her cleaning rag again.

"Good evening, Edra . . . Valine," Mrs. Coleman said, huffing slightly as she waddled up. Giving both of them a wide smile, she put her bag on the counter. Here in Allentown, Indiana, where the population was just nudging toward two thousand, almost everyone knew one another, especially in this neighborhood, where Lawrence Grocery had been a fixture for longer than many of them could remember, right here at the corner of Benson and Wood.

"I just this minute realized that I was out of dog food for my darling little Whistle," Mrs. Coleman said. "Be a good girl, Valine, and run and get me a few cans of Pampered Pooch, will you? Different flavors now!"

Glad of the reprieve, Valine obeyed quickly, moving off with a dancer's grace down the crowded aisles. With her wide blue eyes and delicate bones and long, silver-blond hair, she didn't resemble her mother in the slightest. Edra was tall and spare, with frizzy brown hair and gray eyes that could instantly turn as cold as the North Sea. Looking at Valine, it was hard to believe they were mother and daughter. It was harder still to realize such an ethereal-looking creature possessed such a powerful voice. Valine was twenty years old but seemed about fifteen—until she opened her mouth to sing. The voice that emerged then was meant for the stage: powerful and full-throated and clear as spring. Anyone who had ever heard her marveled at the glorious sound; she had a three-octave range and could sing anything, it seemed, the tone as true on the low register as it was on the higher. A phenomenon, her singing teacher had often ecstatically told her mother, who didn't need an expert to tell her what she had always known: that if anyone had been born, *meant*, to sing, it was Valine.

And there was nothing on earth that Valine wanted to do more. From the earliest she could remember, music had been more than a solace or a comfort; it was a real presence in her life, enabling her to express her feelings through song when she couldn't possibly have done it in words. Painfully shy and uncomfortable with strangers, even with people she knew, she became a different person when she was singing. The instant she opened her mouth and the first note rang out, it was as if she'd been transported to another place. She became so lost in the music, the melody, the sequences and cadence of notes, that everything else just . . . faded away. When she was singing, she felt she could do anything, *be* anything. It was the most powerful, ecstatic, wonderful feeling in the world.

And yet . . .

Aware that the argument with her mother wasn't finished, Valine hurried between counters. But when she came to the pet food section and began to select several cans of the Pampered Pooch at random, the two women's voices floated back to her from in front of the store, and she winced.

"Think it's the most exciting thing to hit Allentown in twenty years, Edra," Mrs. Coleman was saying. "To think! Your little girl off to New York to become a Broadway singing star! Isn't it wonderful?"

Edra's reply was lost as four of the six cans Valine had taken from the shelf slipped from her grasp and crashed to the floor. Stifling a cry, she dropped to her knees to collect them again, fighting the sudden sting of tears. She had to get a grip on herself before she went back, or Mrs. Coleman would think she was crazy.

Maybe she was crazy, she thought, swallowing hard over the growing lump in her throat. Why else did she seem to be the only one who didn't think going to New York was so exciting? Everyone who knew or who had heard about her chance to audition for the famous Broadway director, Cedric Abramson, had ecstatically told her what a splendid opportunity it was. They were all sure she was going to become a star.

Every time she thought of it, she felt almost faint, sick with anticipation and dread, sure that if she lasted that long, she was going to slink back in six months, a year at most, a complete failure. She had taken lessons, yes, from a woman who had coached two of the Metropolitan opera stars, but she had never studied anywhere, not really, and she cringed at the thought of auditioning with people who had sung in London's famous West End, or who had attended Juilliard. She had no chance against such talent and experience; if she didn't get laughed off the stage, she'd be pitied as a hick with stars in her eyes, which would be even worse. She'd come home with her tail between her legs, and what would her mother's enthusiastic friends and acquaintances say then? Worse yet, she thought with a shudder, what would her mother do?

Wincing at the thought, she found the last can and clutched them all to her chest. As upset as she was, she knew it wouldn't do for Mrs. Coleman to see her cry—or for her mother to notice her tears, so she brushed quickly at her face before standing again. Wondering how she was going to get through the rest of the evening until nine when the store closed, she headed back to the front, holding tightly to the pet food cans. She'd been so upset at the thought that this was her last night home that she'd been dropping things all day from sheer nerves, tripping over her own feet. Relieved when she reached the counter safely, she deposited the cans on top before they could get away from her again.

"Well, Valine, thank you," Mrs. Coleman said, smiling. "And how are you tonight, my dear? Excited about your big trip?"

"Oh, yes," Valine said, avoiding her mother's eyes. She knew that as soon as this customer left, Edra would start in on her again. Forcing a smile, she asked, "Did I get the right flavors?"

"These are fine—just fine," Mrs. Coleman said, beaming. Still on the subject of Valine's exciting trip, she playfully shook her finger in Valine's face. "Just think, soon you'll be too famous to wait on people in the store. You'll be a Broadway star!"

Valine didn't know what to say. She felt tongue-tied, as she always did, whenever she encountered someone she didn't know very well. "It's a little too soon for that, Mrs. Coleman," she said faintly. "After all, I haven't even left yet."

"To be sure," Mrs. Coleman said comfortably. "But those of us who know you haven't any doubts. We've heard you sing, and God couldn't have given a more beautiful voice to an angel." She laughed suddenly, her heavy jowls quivering with amusement. "Why, I think your being in the choir is the reason half the people come to church on Sundays! And you've sung at all the weddings and anniversaries and club meetings in town since you were just a tot. That says something, doesn't it?"

Aware that her mother was glowering, Valine said, "It says that you've all been very kind, Mrs. Coleman."

"Oh, pish," the woman said. "You've always been far too modest, my dear, but I suppose that's to your credit. Still, what I wouldn't give for a voice like yours! You don't know what a talent it is."

"She's going to find out," Edra put in, with a quelling glance in her daughter's direction. She was anxious to get rid of the Coleman woman so she and Valine could settle this once and for all. "Now, will that be all, Beaulah? Or would you like something else tonight?"

Successfully diverted, Mrs. Coleman turned back to the counter. "No, I think that's it. If I don't get this food home soon, heaven knows what revenge Whistle will take." Her eye fell on the soup Edra had been marking. "Now, that's a good bargain, isn't it?" she said, distracted again. "Why don't you wrap me up four of those cans there. I don't think you can beat that price anywhere." She glanced around, missing the brief tightening of Edra's thin lips. "And while we're at it, maybe I should get some eggs . . . and a loaf of bread or two. Oh, and do you have any of those packaged crumb cakes? Violet Slade was telling me she got some here, now where might they be?"

As the two women moved off, Edra reluctantly leading the way to the bakery shelf, Valine stood still. She wanted to turn and sprint for the door that led to the apartment upstairs, but she knew that if she did, it would be postponing the inevitable. It was better to stay here and get it over with, she thought with a sigh, and was reaching for her cleaning rag when the outer door bell tinkled again. Resigned to waiting on this customer herself, she looked toward the door. To her surprise, no one was there. Then she saw the face at the window outside and looked quickly in her mother's direction. Fortunately, Edra and Mrs. Coleman were still over by the bakery shelves and couldn't see who was outside.

Go away! Valine mouthed, pantomiming frantically so that her mother wouldn't hear. *Go away!*

The young man waiting outside shook his head. He mouthed back: *Come out, talk to me.* Valine shook her head. He gestured again, more firmly. Valine shook her head again. When he indicated he would come in if she didn't come out to him, Valine knew he'd do it. He'll never leave if I don't go, she thought, and with another desperate glance in her mother's direction, she headed quickly toward the front door. She'd get rid of him as soon as possible.

Long ago, she had learned to come in and go out without causing the bell over the door to tinkle; her skill stood her in good stead tonight. Another quick glance back at her mother as she opened the door reassured her that Edra hadn't heard, and as she slipped out and closed the door carefully behind her, the November cold hit her like an Arctic blast. She hadn't thought to bring a coat, and as she shivered outside in her sweater, she turned accusingly to the young man waiting on the walk. His name was Ned Kowalski, and he'd been courting her—there was no other word for it—for years. They'd known each other since kindergarten, and he'd wanted to marry her since fifth grade. Tall and blond, with blue eyes and a scattering of freckles across his nose, he worked as a mechanic at the local garage. Aside from marrying Valine, all he'd ever wanted to do was work with cars.

"Ned, I told you—" she began.

"I'm sorry, Vallie," he said miserably. "But I had to see you."

She wanted to send him away, but when she saw his unhappy face, she fell silent. She was fond of Ned, and sometimes she thought that if her mother had allowed her to consider anything other than singing, she would think about marrying him. Heaven knew he'd asked her enough times—the latest just the other night, when she had crept over to his apartment for the last time. They'd been secretly carrying on for some while now, and if her

mother even dreamed she and Ned had slept together, there'd be
hell to pay. But Ned had been so kind and gentle the first time,
back in the summer, and at twenty, she'd been so ashamed of
still being a virgin that she had given in to him one night. By
then, she had wanted him as much as he wanted her, and the result had been heaven.

Of course it had been a mistake. *Good* girls didn't sleep
around; hadn't she heard that since she was tiny, from everyone
she knew? And now she felt even worse, so guilty about leaving
him.

Feeling worse than ever at the sight of his unhappy face, she
said desperately, "Ned, you can't just come around here. You
know I'm working, and I thought we agreed—"

"*We* didn't agree about anything," Ned said. "It was you who
wanted to run off, to do your singing."

"But it's my life, Ned—"

She shivered again, and he suddenly seemed to realize how
cold it was. Taking off his heavy jacket, he made her put it on,
ignoring her protest. Now he was in shirtsleeves, but he didn't
seem to care. Taking both her cold hands in his, he said passion-
ately, "Valine, are you *sure* you want to go to New York?"

Ned's jacket was denim and sheepskin and far too big for her.
But it was still warm from his body, and as she pulled it closed
in front of her, it smelled like him—clean and masculine. He
might work in a garage, he'd often told her, but it didn't mean
he had to look or smell like a mechanic. Even his hands were
clean, no grease or dirt under his fingernails or grime in his
knuckles. As Valine looked up at him, she realized once again
how good-looking he was, and she felt a pang. If only, she
thought . . . and wouldn't allow it to go further.

"Yes, I'm sure," she said, trying to extricate her hands. She
didn't want him to touch her because she was afraid she might
weaken. Ned had made her feel things she hadn't known existed, and the feeling was growing in her that she was making
a mistake about him. He'd make a good husband, she thought,
and ruthlessly shut her mind to the fantasy. She couldn't think
about Ned; she was leaving for New York tomorrow.

"I'm sure," she repeated, although she wasn't at all. "This is
what I've planned to do all along. You know I've always wanted
to sing professionally."

"No," he said, holding her eyes and forcing her to look at
him. "You said yourself that your mother was the one who al-

ways wanted you to go. You told me long ago that you'd be happy staying here and—"

"My mother only wants the best for me," she said quickly. "She wants what I want. I told you!"

His eyes seemed to look into her very soul. His hands tightened on hers. "Does she?" he said quietly. "Would she want what you want if you said you were going to stay here and marry me?"

She stiffened. She couldn't admit she wasn't sure of the answer. "That's beside the point. I've told you again and again I don't want to marry you! Why can't you let it be?"

"Because I can't, that's why. Because I love you, Vallie—"

A look of pain flashed across her pale face. "Don't, Ned—"

"I have to, don't you see? I might never get another chance, not after tonight. You're supposed to go tomorrow, and . . . Oh, Vallie, you're the most beautiful woman I've ever set eyes on. I've loved you for years, you know it. I want to take care of you, protect you . . . love you. Is that so hard to believe?"

It wasn't; it never had been. She had always known that Ned loved her. And in her own way, she knew she loved him, too. Who wouldn't love a man like Ned, who was so gentle and generous and just? As cold as it was, he'd given her his jacket without complaint. Over the years, he'd done other things for her, too many to count. When she thought of it . . .

But she couldn't let herself think, or she'd lose all resolve. "I'm sorry, Ned," she said unhappily. "It just wouldn't . . . work out."

His handsome, open face tensed. "Because of your mother—or because of you?"

"Because of me," she said, unable to meet his eyes. She forced herself to go on. "I've worked hard for this chance, Ned. I've practiced for years. Now I have an opportunity to go to New York and maybe sing on Broadway. Would you deny me that? Would you ask me to stay here and give up something I've dreamed of all my life?"

She could see the indecision in his eyes, the pain, the unhappiness. She knew she had hurt him, and she wanted to call back the words, but she couldn't do it. It was better this way, she thought. She knew it, and if he were honest, he knew it, too.

Ned didn't reply for a long moment. Then, reluctantly, he shook his head and dropped her hands. "No," he said, his voice so low she could hardly hear him. "No, I guess not. I'm sorry, Vallie. I had no right to . . . to ask."

Now she felt worse than ever. Glancing through the store windows, she saw her mother and Mrs. Coleman back at the counter. Edra was counting out change, putting things in the woman's string bag. She didn't have much time; if Edra saw her talking to Ned, there'd be trouble.

"I'm sorry, Ned," she said, shrugging out of his heavy coat. She felt close to tears, reluctant to part with it. Before she could say something she'd regret, she thrust the jacket back at him. "I'm really sorry. I mean it."

Ned took the coat from her, but he didn't put it on. "So am I, Vallie," he said quietly.

"Look," she said impulsively, knowing it wasn't enough, but not wanting to leave it this way, "when I come back, I'll give you a call. We can go out and . . . have coffee."

He looked at her a moment, such a look of deep hurt in his eyes that she knew she'd never forget it. Then he said something that stabbed her right to the core. "Don't you know, Vallie, that once you go, you can't come back?"

"No, Ned, that's not—" she started to say, but it was too late.

"Good-bye, Vallie. And good luck. I hope you find what you want."

He turned and walked away. Left alone, Valine didn't know whether to go after him or not. She was still standing outside indecisively when the bell tinkled behind her and Mrs. Coleman emerged from the store.

"My goodness, dear," the woman said. "You shouldn't be standing out here. You'll catch your death of cold!"

Valine was so distracted she hardly heard what the woman said. Quickly she glanced in the direction Ned had gone, but he had already disappeared into the dark night. Feeling close to tears again, she turned back to the woman standing beside her. Mrs. Coleman was peering out into the darkness, too, wondering what they were looking at.

"Yes, you're right," she said. "Well . . . good night."

"Good night, dear—oh, and good luck in New York. What's the saying? Break a leg, is that right?"

It was for dancing, but who cared? Feeling as if her heart were breaking instead, Valine managed a forced little smile, and watched the woman waddle away. Mrs. Coleman was going home to feed her dog and eat her crumb cakes, and, wishing that she could do the same, Valine shivered again and went inside the store. Warmth from the heater hit her with a blast, and she was standing there, rubbing her arms, when her mother turned and saw her.

"You were out there talking to Ned, weren't you?" Edra asked. "Oh, don't bother to deny it, I saw you. I hope you sent him packing, as he deserved."

Valine couldn't answer. Staring down at the red glow of the heater, she was seeing the pain in Ned's blue eyes.

"Well?" Edra demanded.

Slowly, Valine looked up. "Yes, Mama, I sent him away, just like you ordered."

Her mother's eyes narrowed, but suddenly Valine didn't care. It was almost nine, time to close the store. Before Edra could object that it was a little early, she turned and locked the door, pulling down the shade and putting the CLOSED sign in the window. It was her job to close out the cash register, but she had already decided she'd leave it when Edra put her hands on her hips and glared at her.

"I don't understand you, Valine. You heard Mrs. Coleman just now. She's as excited as everyone else is. You're the only one who's moping around. What's the matter with you? If I didn't know better, I'd think you didn't want to go!"

Valine didn't answer. She felt so torn. For years now, the plan had been that, as soon they saved enough money, Valine would go to New York to become a singing star on Broadway. At least, it had been Edra's plan, and Valine had gone along with it because she loved to sing. She had never admitted it to anyone, not even her voice teacher, but she only felt alive and vital and important when she *was* singing. When she was on stage, she became someone else, someone who could admit she loved the applause and the adulation and the performance. When she was singing, she wasn't Valine Smits, a shy, awkward girl from Allentown, Indiana; she was a *singer*, someone who transported her audience by the medium of her voice to another place for a while, to somewhere they hadn't been. It was a heady feeling, a delight, something she couldn't explain. It was why she had sung at weddings and anniversary parties and club functions; it was why she had belonged to the choir, and had sung in the Christmas pageant, and at Easter, and for school plays. Singing wasn't just something she did; it was what she *was*, and whenever she thought of herself on Broadway—*Broadway*, of all places, the feeling was too ecstatic to imagine.

But it was frightening, as well. For the plan to work, she had to leave home—alone. Edra couldn't go with her; she had to stay here and take care of her mother—Valine's grandmother—along with the store, which would now be their only income until Valine found a job. Valine had to go alone, to be on her own, as she'd never been before. Worse, she had to leave the protective atmosphere of her small town and go to New York, which loomed in her mind like a malevolent monster filled with terrors. It was small comfort that Edra had carefully researched a place for her to stay: a women's hotel just off Forty-ninth Street and Broadway. She'd be safe there, close to the theater district, able to get around easily. The money they'd saved would last for a time, and of course, if she was hired to sing, she wouldn't have to worry about finances because she'd be getting a salary. Once she was on her way, the sky was the limit, according to Edra, who was positive that any director who heard the first golden note out of her mouth would make her daughter a star.

It had sounded wonderful and exciting all the years they had been planning, but now that the actual departure day was tomorrow, Valine felt paralyzed with doubt and fear. What did she know about New York? What did she really know about the theater? How would she find her way around? Suppose no one would hire her?

Part of her wanted to go—the part that loved the applause and the attention. But another, much bigger part, was afraid to leave. What if she failed? What if she wasn't any good?

"But of course you're good!" her mother had said to her once when she had finally managed to give voice to her fear. To Valine's dismay, she had immediately brought up the subject with her voice teacher.

"Is she good?" Antoinette LeDuc—*Madame* LeDuc—had repeated, when she heard. In her day she had been a coloratura soprano who had sung with the Metropolitan Opera. After retiring, she had coached several other singers to stardom, and while her fees were outrageous, and she was contemptuous of anything other than opera, she had taken Valine on after hearing her sing. Valine had learned more—and suffered more—at her hands than she could ever have imagined, but she had control of her voice now, and she was grateful. At Edra's question, Madame had fixed her with an intimidating glance and sniffed. "If she didn't have *possibilities*, do you think I would have wasted my time all these years?"

Valine was frightened of Madame LeDuc, but Edra wasn't. "Yes, but do you think she's good enough for Broadway?" she pressed.

"Broadway!" Madame spoke the word like she'd just stepped in something. "With her range, her depth, her *control*, she should be in opera, not singing on some two-penny stage!"

"Broadway is *hardly* two-penny!" Edra exclaimed. She didn't like anyone denigrating her dream, not even a famous singer, as Madame had once been.

It was like a clash of the Titans. While Valine closed her eyes and shrank back, Madame drew herself up haughtily. "Mrs. Smits, I don't think you quite realize just what a . . . a *voice* your daughter has," Antoinette LeDuc declared. "A talent like hers comes along once in a lifetime!"

"My point exactly," Edra had replied grimly. "*My* lifetime. And since Valine is my daughter, I know what's best for her. Now, I don't want you filling her head with opera, Madame—do you understand?" Pointedly, she glanced around the cluttered apartment, at the furniture that had clearly seen better days. "Otherwise, I will be compelled to find another teacher, and I don't think you would like that, now, would you?"

Nothing more had been said, but for weeks afterward, an angry expression on her face, and her eyes fierce, Madame had drilled Valine to the point of collapse during her weekly lessons. But she learned. She learned.

And now, tomorrow, she was leaving for New York. Seeing her mother's set expression, Valine sighed. She couldn't try to talk her mother out of it just because she was scared; she knew how Edra felt about her going. She'd heard the story so many times she could have repeated it word for word, and tonight she couldn't bear hearing it again. In Edra's youth, before an unplanned pregnancy, and a husband who walked out one night, leaving her with no money, no marketable skills, and a two-year-old child to care for, she had possessed a decent singing voice. Decent enough, she'd always said, to enable her to dream of singing on stage herself. Years of bitter unhappiness and a two-pack-a-day cigarette habit had long ago taken care of her fantasies; now it was up to Valine to carry on in her place.

"I told you, Valine," Edra said tonight. "Nothing was going to stand in our way—not haughty voice coaches," her own voice hardened—"nor love-lorn garage mechanics."

"Mama, I—"

She was interrupted by a shout from upstairs. "Edra! Valine!" Evie called. "It's past nine—are you coming up or not?"

Relieved, Valine slammed the cash register shut. "Coming, Granny!" she shouted in return, starting to run up the staircase, only to be stopped forcibly on the bottom step when her mother grabbed her arm and jerked her back.

"We haven't finished this discussion yet, miss!"

The last thing Valine wanted was to go over it again. "Oh, Mama, not on my last night, okay?" she pleaded. "I said I was going, and I will. Let's just leave it, all right?"

"No, we're not going to leave it!" Edra said sharply. "After all these years, all the skimping and pinching, just to save enough to send you to New York, I'm not going to feel as if I have to push you out the door. Isn't this what you've always said you wanted, Valine? Isn't it?"

No, Valine thought, it isn't. It's what *you* always wanted. But with Edra staring at her, she couldn't say it.

"Yes, Mama," she said meekly. "It's what I always wanted. It's just—"

"If you didn't want to go, you should have said something before now. *I* could have had a life, then, too. But nooo"—she drew the word out, making Valine flinch—"I suppose it was to be expected that I forfeit my own happiness for no good reason at all, is that it?"

"No, Mama, no—of course not. It's just . . . this is going to be a big change for me. I've never been away from home, you know, and it's a little scary."

It was the wrong thing to say. Angry color flooded Edra's sallow cheeks, and she shook Valine's arm again. "Don't you think *I* was scared all those years ago when your father left me in a strange city, with no money and a baby and no place to go? How do you think *I* felt? But I managed, didn't I? And so will you. And you're luckier than I was, you silly girl—you have me to support you. I've sacrificed for years to get you this far. How can you be so ungrateful?"

Feeling more desperate by the second, Valine tried to explain. "I'm not ungrateful, Mama, really I'm not. I do appreciate everything you've done for me. But—"

"Your grandmother has been talking to you again, hasn't she?" Edra interrupted harshly. She gave Valine's arm another shake. "What has she been saying to you? I want to know!"

Close to tears, Valine tried to extricate herself from her mother's grasp. "Mama, please, you're hurting me!"

"It's nothing compared to what I'll do if I find out that your grandmother's been going behind my back, trying to convince you to stay here!"

Valine was shocked. "She hasn't done that! Granny only wants what's best for me."

"The hell she does," Edra said flatly.

Valine was silent, feeling guilty and torn again. She knew how hard her mother had worked since they had come to live with her grandmother; she had seen for herself and didn't need to be reminded.

Once she was older and learned what had happened so many years before, she could understand her mother's bitterness. Who wouldn't be bitter, left alone with no resources and nothing to fall back on? Edra had been forced to come home again, to the little apartment her parents lived in over the grocery that was their only source of livelihood. Even though the apartment was cramped for two, Evie and Sol Lawrence had made room for their daughter and their granddaughter, trying to make them feel welcome. The problem was that Edra had never gotten along with her parents, and the crowded conditions only exaggerated their differences. Valine could remember the shouting and loud quarreling that constantly went on between Edra and her father, but for her, those two years were the happiest she could remember. She was only about four when Sol had died of a heart attack while wrestling a case of crackers into place downstairs, and, sixteen years later, the things she remembered most about her grandfather were his booming laugh and how he'd put her up on his shoulders and carry her around like she was special. Her father she didn't remember at all, and it was no use asking. She didn't even have a picture of him, and, after all this time, Edra still couldn't speak of him without becoming livid.

Evie called again, interrupting Valine's thoughts. "Granny hasn't said anything to me, Mama, honest," she said pleadingly. "Now, let go, will you? I still have to pack, and . . . everything."

Edra gave her a hard look. "You'd better be on that bus tomorrow."

"I will be, I promise."

"All right, then. Go and pack. I'll be up in a few minutes."

"Thanks, Mama," Valine said, and took the steps two at a time up to the landing that led to their living quarters.

The apartment the three women shared was at the head of the stairs. The staircase opened onto a postage stamp–sized living room, made to look even smaller by the heavy, dark furniture crammed inside. The busy rose-and-lattice pattern of the thin carpet covering the floor added to the cramped feeling, and the gloomy prints on the walls made everything seem even more closed in. The only real spots of color were the antimacassars Evie had crocheted for the two chairs and the sofa before she became too crippled to work yarn anymore, and the vases of dried flowers Valine had put out to lighten the room.

There were only two bedrooms, one that Evie and her husband, Sol, had shared until his death, and which Evie had kept for her own; the other for Edra, who had taken it again when she moved back home. For years now, Valine had slept on the foldout couch, her "closet" a makeshift screen at one end of the room, her few personal things in a Chinese-red lacquered trunk she kept out on the service porch. Since turning twelve she had dreamed of her own room, but now that she was about to get her wish, all she could think of was how much she would miss this place.

The kitchen was minuscule, half-hidden under an archway, barely large enough for a stove and refrigerator, a few cupboards, and one chipped counter. Evie, who always tried to make the best of things, often joked that because the kitchen had no storage space, it was lucky they didn't have far to go to the market. Edra never thought it was funny, but Valine always laughed, no matter how many times Evie said it. She'd always been closer to her grandmother than to her own mother, and as she ran into Evie's bedroom tonight, she gave the wizened little woman in bed a quick but affectionate hug.

"Did you think we'd abandoned you?" she teased, plumping her grandmother's pillows.

Evie Lawrence, seventy years old last May, lay back on the pillows. Her hard life showed in the deep lines of her face and in her crippled, arthritic fingers on the counterpane, but her eyes were still bright, and her mind was—to Edra's annoyance and dismay—still sharp as a tack.

"No, I thought you'd taken all the money we took in tonight and went out on the town," Evie shot back, her eyes sparkling. "It wouldn't surprise me, knowing what gadabouts you and your Ma are."

"Oh, Granny! The things you say!" Valine said, teasing her back. "Everyone knows you're the one who can't stay home!"

Evie laughed before she noticed that despite her efforts, Valine looked almost ready to cry. Instantly, her twinkle vanished, and she reached for her granddaughter's hand.

"Sit," she commanded, painfully making room for Valine on the edge of the bed. "What is it, child? Are you having second thoughts?"

Valine had never lied to her grandmother. Swallowing, she admitted, "Second and third and fourth thoughts, I'm afraid."

Evie studied her face. "But I thought you wanted to go," she said softly. "It's all settled, has been for months. Did you change your mind?"

Valine looked away. "No," she said uncertainly, wishing she knew how to express what she felt. "It isn't that."

"What then? Cold feet?"

Sighing, Valine picked at the colorful quilt covering the bed. "I guess," she said. "It's just that New York seems so . . . big."

Evie was silent a moment. Then, quietly, she said, "Plenty of room to fail, is that it?"

Her grandmother had always known her better than she did herself, and with a sob, Valine threw herself down. "Oh, Granny," she said, her voice muffled by the quilt. "What am I going to do?"

Tenderly, Evie stroked her granddaughter's bright hair. "Well, you'll never know till you try, isn't that right?"

A shudder went through Valine. "But what if I don't make it?"

Calmly, Evie continued to stroke Valine's hair. "What if you don't?" she said reasonably. "It won't be the end of the world."

"It will be for Mama!" Valine lifted her tear-streaked face. "She'll never forgive me!"

Something flashed across Evie's face, and her mouth tightened briefly. She took Valine's chin in her gnarled fingers and looked into her eyes. "Is that what concerns you the most, child? Because if it is, you shouldn't go. If you're going to do it, you should do it for yourself, no one else."

"But—"

"No buts about it, child. It should be your decision, your choice. Your mother's had hers to make, and no matter what you think, you can't make up for her mistakes."

"But if she'd only had a chance—"

Evie's glance hardened. "She had her chance, child, we all do." Her grip tightened on Valine's chin. "We make our luck in this world, Valine, don't let anybody tell you it isn't so."

Valine wanted to believe it more than anything in the world. "But New York is so big, Granny," she repeated weakly.

Evie smiled and pulled her close. "Not big enough for the talent you've got, child," she said over her head. "Not big enough for you . . ."

"Oh, Granny! I hope it's true."

Her eyes bright, this time with unshed tears, Evie held her
granddaughter away from her again so she could look into her
face. "Trust me, child," she said. "Have I ever lied to you?"

"No, Granny," Valine said mournfully. "But then, you're prej-
udiced, aren't you?"

Evie laughed. Turning to her crowded bedside table, she
searched for something and a moment later held out a little box.
"This is for you," she said. "For good luck."

Valine was surprised and touched. Her grandmother never left
the apartment anymore; not even Edra, as strong as she was,
could carry her down the stairs, and together she and Valine
couldn't maneuver the wheelchair outside anymore. "Where did
you get it?" she asked, her eyes wide.

Evie's glance was faraway. "I've had it a long, long time,
child," she said. "I've been saving it for you. Go ahead—open
it."

Her hands shaking slightly, Valine obeyed. When she saw
what was in the little box, she gasped. "Granny, your locket!"

When she had been small, she had loved playing with the
locket, which was made of heavy gold in the shape of a heart.
She hadn't seen it for years, and when she'd been about ten, she
remembered asking her grandmother what had happened to it.
She looked up at Evie, the locket warm in her palm. "You said
you'd lost it!"

Evie smiled. "I found it again," she said. "Go ahead, open it."

Holding her breath, Valine obeyed. She had expected to find
a picture of her mother inside, but instead what she saw made
her gasp. On one side of the heart was a picture of Evie as a
young woman. She was smiling, youthful, happy—and why not?
On the other side was a picture of Valine's grandfather. She
knew it was Sol; he was laughing in the photo, and she could
practically hear an echo of his great booming laugh coming to
her down through the years. Instantly, her eyes filled with tears.

"I didn't know you had this," she said, her voice choked.
Then, emotionally, she threw her arms around her grandmother
and hugged her tight. "Oh, Granny, I'll treasure it forever."

Evie had to wipe her own eyes. "Your granddad always loved
to hear you sing, even when you were so small," she said. "He
used to say you had a voice that could charm the fish from the
sea and the birds out of the trees."

"Oh, Granny!"

"I want you to take this locket with you, and when you feel
sad or depressed or blue, look at your granddad's picture—

remember how he could always make you laugh? And think of how proud he'd be of you."

Valine was so overcome she didn't know what to say. "Thank you, Granny," she said, getting up. She was clutching the locket so tightly that the point of the heart bit into her palm. "I'll try to make you both proud."

Evie smiled wearily. The scene had tired her, and she lay back, her eyes almost closed. "I'm always proud of you child," she said, starting to fall asleep. "No matter what happens, you remember that."

The next morning, Valine left for New York. Her mother went with her to the bus station and, just before her bus was called, gave her a quick, hard hug.

"Now, you write," she said.

Valine was trying not to cry again. "I will," she promised, "every week."

"And you call once a month, without fail."

"I will."

"And you let me know immediately when you get a part."

Valine smiled shakily. "I will. But Mama—"

"What?"

She had to say it. "It might be awhile."

"Oh, no, it won't," Edra said positively, and handed her a package just before Valine boarded the bus. Surprised, Valine looked down.

"What's this?"

"Something for you. Now, don't open it until you get there. And call me from that women's hotel. I want to make sure you arrive safely."

The driver was motioning impatiently for her to get on. Suddenly afraid and apprehensive all over again, Valine threw her arms about her mother for the last time.

"I love you, Mama," she whispered.

Edra hugged her again. "I love you, too," she said brusquely. "Now, go on, they're waiting."

Tears blurring her eyes, Valine stumbled in. Somehow she found a seat, and as the bus pulled out of the station in a cloud of black smoke, she pressed her face against the window, trying to see her mother. She saw Edra lift her hand to wave, and raised her own, but just then the bus gave a mighty lurch, and she fell back against the seat. By the time she regained her balance, they'd turned a corner and her mother was gone. Taking a shaky breath, she looked down at the package she was holding.

Edra had told her to wait until she arrived, but she desperately needed something more from home right now, so she pulled the string that held the box together.

When she saw what her mother had given her, she sat back. There, nestled in the box, was a blue flannel nightgown, plain and simple, without decoration. It was so like her mother she had to laugh.

———————— ✑ ————————

CHAPTER THREE

"What are *you* doing here?" Gabe Tyrell's brother, Frank, said in surprise, when Gabe walked in the door.

Gabe had been wondering himself. In fact, he'd driven around for twenty minutes before deciding to enter the house. Then he realized he was being ridiculous; after all, he'd driven down from Washington State to Southern California—to rarefied Holmby Hills, in fact—to talk to his family. He was here, so he might as well go in and get it over with. But as he sat there, in that exclusive enclave of wide streets and ancient trees arching overhead, with estate-sized homes set so far back off the road that they were guarded in many cases by electronic gates, the whole thing had begun to feel surreal, and he had to ask himself if this was just another of his escapes. Was he was running off again to find something he wouldn't be able to find once he got there?

His older brother, Frank, had accused him so often in the past of being a dabbler, a dilettante, a dreamer without substance. As he entered his parents' big Georgian-style house, with the elegant, columned front porch and the wide patch of perfectly manicured grass, he wondered if Frank was right. If he was, it was too late to worry about it. Frank might be a good businessman, an excellent administrator, the perfect son and husband and father, but he wasn't right about everything, Gabe decided, pausing in the wide entry and taking a deep breath. Frank had been trying for months again to get him to come to work for the family company; he'd even used the inducement that if he signed on, Gabe could travel as much as he liked. Tyrell Industries had long since reached the lofty stage where it had clients and customers all over the country, enough travel to warrant owning a company plane. Frank's latest promise had been that if Gabe came to work for them, he could live out of a suitcase as much as he liked. Knowing his restless nature, he'd thought to tempt him by saying he wouldn't have to stay in one place for long. Amused and irritated at the same time, Gabe had told him no . . . again. Frank wouldn't believe it; he insisted Gabe give it a try.

He knew then that he had to talk to the family in person. So tonight, he'd come to tell Frank and his father that he couldn't take the job, that, in fact, he had decided on something else. He had to let them know; his mother, for one, would never forgive him if he went to Africa and didn't tell them. But he was sorry that he had to make his announcement the night of his parent's anniversary.

The family was in the dining room having dinner when he looked in. They all glanced up at his entrance, his parents at either end of the long rosewood table, Frank on one side with Sarah, his elder daughter; Amy, Franks wife, on the other with their younger girl, Melissa. As soon as the little girls saw him, they jumped up from the table and ran to him with shrieks of joy. He had always enjoyed his nieces, and with a laugh and a joke, he gathered them up, one in each arm, giving them both resounding raspberry kisses. At the table, Amy pursed her lips, but both girls screamed with delight.

"Uncle Gabe, what did you bring us?" demanded Sarah, the older. Like her sister, she was small for her age, with honey-colored hair that swung almost to her waist and wide amber eyes. She was already a beauty; Gabe knew she was going to be a knockout when she grew up.

"Yes, what did you bring us?" Melissa lisped. Held so high aloft, she smiled shyly at Gabe, all brown curls and big brown eyes. He never would have admitted it, but Melissa was his favorite; there was something compelling about someone so innocent and in need of protection, and he had the feeling that she'd need it all her life. Smiling in return, he set the little girls back on their feet.

"Go into the hallway and see for yourself," he told them, and then laughed again when they both ran off, petticoats flying under their party dresses.

"Well, we certainly didn't expect *you*, Gabe," Frank said, sitting down again with a thump after the surprise had shot him to his feet.

"I know," Gabe answered, determined not to get into an argument. He went to the foot of the table to give his mother a kiss. Smiling at her, he murmured, "I came to wish you and Dad a happy anniversary."

"Thank you, darling," Audrey Tyrell said, turning pink. She was a small woman turning plump in her fifties, always pleased when her younger son came home, even for a brief visit. Taking his hand, she gave his fingers a squeeze. "I'd hoped you would. See, I set a place for you."

Turning, he saw with a stab of guilt that despite his telling her earlier in the week that he might not be able to make it, she had indeed set a plate for him. The empty chair was on her right, the silverware and china and crystal gleaming under the light from the chandelier. Chagrined because he had nearly chickened out, he put a hand on her shoulder.

"Thanks, Mom," he said. "But I told you—"

"I know, dear," Audrey interrupted serenely. "But you always manage, no matter what excuses you make." She smiled. "Besides, it never hurts to be prepared."

"Not where Gabriel is concerned, obviously," Ellis Tyrell said heavily from the head of the table.

Gabe looked fully in that direction for the first time. His father returned his look aggressively. Nearing sixty, Ellis had become portly with his prosperity, and his hair—what was left of it—had turned silver years before. With increasing weight and girth, his face had become round and smooth, with a ruddy undertone to his complexion that made his doctor and his wife nervous. A workaholic who still thought nothing of putting in eighteen-hour days, he bore little resemblance to the passionate youth who had courted and then married Audrey Walker thirty-five years before. The only thing age hadn't altered were his eyes, which were as blue and sharp as they'd always been, and which were fixed on his younger son right now.

"Good evening, Dad," Gabe said calmly. "Happy anniversary."

He started toward his father to shake his hand but halted again when Ellis nodded coldly and pointedly lifted his fork. With a shrug, Gabe changed course and sat down at the place Audrey had saved for him. Amy was directly across from him, and he smiled. She colored and looked quickly down at her plate.

"What a surprise," she murmured, mimicking her husband.

"Yes, well, I don't get down from Washington State all that often."

Frank looked at him. "But that's going to change, isn't it?" he said, obviously referring to Gabe's coming to work for the company.

Gabe had hoped to postpone the moment a little longer, but he couldn't ignore the opening, and he sat back, wishing he hadn't given up smoking a few years ago. He could have used a cigarette now, he thought. From the moment he'd come in, he'd felt the rise in tension—not only in himself, but throughout the entire dining room. He hated to be the cause of dissension, but he couldn't help it tonight.

"As a matter of fact, that's what I came to talk to you about," he said mildly.

Frank straightened with a wary look. "Oh?"

It was now or never, Gabe thought, glancing apologetically at his mother. "Yes. I took another job—"

It was all he had time to say. Throwing down his napkin, Frank looked at him disbelievingly. "The hell you say!"

Ellis slowly returned his fork to his plate. His tone low and ominous, he asked, "What kind of job?"

Gabe looked down the table at his father. "It's with an outfit called—"

Frank still looked shocked. It was obvious he'd thought he had finally talked Gabe into coming to work for them. "I don't care what it's called! You said you—"

"Why don't we listen to what Gabe has to say, Franklin?" Audrey said quietly.

His jaw tightening, Frank sat back. "Go ahead, then. Tell us what this wonderful new job is. I'm sure it's much better than anything Tyrell has to offer!"

"Excuse me," Amy said faintly. She put aside her napkin and rose. Conflicts always made her nervous, and she looked pale. "I think I'd better go see what the girls are doing."

As she disappeared quickly from the room, Gabe looked at his mother. Their eyes met, and when he saw the resignation in her expression, he felt even worse. Long ago, he'd given up hope that his father would ever understand or approve of anything he did, and Frank was just like Ellis. But Gabe cared what his mother thought, and he didn't want to hurt her. As though she instinctively understood, she made herself nod encouragingly. It didn't make him feel any better, but he had to get it over with, so he turned back to the table again.

"I'm going to Africa to film a wildlife documentary about elephant poaching," he said.

For a moment, there was silence. Not even his family, who was more or less accustomed to, if not approving of, his peripatetic wanderings, could have expected this. Finally, Audrey said weakly, "Africa, Gabe?"

"I know it's a surprise—"

"A surprise!" Frank exclaimed.

"But, darling," Audrey said, "how did you ever get involved in something so . . . far away? I thought you were happy working for the police department in Washington."

"I was—I am," Gabe said, trying to brace himself for the explosion he knew would arrive momentarily. His father hadn't said anything, but he knew from experience that Ellis was just gathering strength. "But the last time I was in Spokane, I happened to meet some people from an organization called the International Zoological Foundation, and we got to talking, and . . . well, one thing led to another, and when they said they wanted to stir up public interest and support to stop elephant poaching in Africa, I said I'd be glad to help."

"To help!" Frank repeated incredulously. "Just what does that mean?"

Gabe had obtained his pilot's license when he was eighteen. "It means that I'm the one who's going to be flying in, filming what's going on, and then flying out again." He'd nearly added *before I get caught*, but didn't want to worry his mother any more than she already was.

"Oh, Gabe!" Audrey exclaimed, her hand at her throat. "It sounds so dangerous!"

He wasn't going to admit that it could be. He'd always felt protective of his mother, who was dear and sweet and innocent, and he reached out and took her hand.

"Not any more dangerous than anything else," he said, his eyes on her face, willing her to believe it. "And think of the good it will do—"

Ellis reacted finally, slamming his hand down on the table so hard that the cutlery jumped. Audrey was so surprised that she cried out, and even Frank was startled.

"The *good* it will do!" Ellis exclaimed. "And what about the *good* you're supposed to be doing as one of my executives?"

"Ellis," Audrey gasped.

Her husband swung his big, round head toward her. Glaring, he said, "What?"

Cringing at his expression, she said weakly, "Shouting won't help."

"The hell it won't!" Ellis shouted, red in the face as he turned to his younger son again. "What in the blue bloody hell is going on here? Elephant poaching? I never heard anything more ridiculous in my entire life!"

"It's not ridiculous," Gabe said, trying to hold on to his temper. "You don't understand—"

"You're damned right, I don't! You have a commitment to me, and I'll hold you to it, by God, or know why! This is outrageous! Trust you, Gabriel, to come up with a hare-brained scheme like this! No, it's out of the question. I won't let you do it!"

"Won't *let* me?" Gabe repeated; then he caught his mother's eye. With an effort, he controlled himself. Tightly, he said, "I'm sorry, Dad, but I think the time for your telling me what to do is long past."

"The hell it is!" Ellis shouted again. "For once in your life, I'm going to hold you to something you said you'd do! You're going to report to Tyrell Industries at the end of the month as you promised, or else."

Something dangerous leapt into Gabe's deep-blue eyes. "Forget the fact that I never promised to take the job," he said. "Let's get to the 'or else' part, all right?"

"Ellis!" Audrey said, her voice sharp with anxiety. Intuitively, she guessed what was coming and wanted to stop them from saying something they'd always regret.

Frank looked from his brother to his father, a strange expression on his face as he reached for his wineglass. He was just taking a sip when his mother turned to him for help.

"Frank, say something!"

"What do you want me to say?" he asked. "You know neither of them ever listens to me."

Gabe barely heard him. His entire attention was on his father. In a way, he thought, he was almost glad things had finally come to a head. He would have preferred it to be at another time, but what time was ever right for what had to be said now? He and Ellis had never gotten along, and from the time he was small, he had always felt he could never please his father no matter what he tried. It was obvious that he would never measure up to Frank, who did what he was supposed to do, seem-

ingly without effort, certainly without complaint. He had tried;
he had, but he just couldn't fit into the mold his father set out
for him. He couldn't help it. With his restless nature, he felt stifled and bored at the thought of going to an office all day; even
the prospect of flying around for the company didn't entice him
because it meant he would be at someone else's beck and call.
Uncharacteristically bitter, he had long ago decided that Ellis already had the son he wanted in Frank; why start something he'd
never be able to finish?

Gabe didn't know why he had always craved adventure and
excitement, but he only felt alive when he was doing something
dangerous—challenging the gods, trying to beat the odds. As
sappy as it sounded, he'd always felt the need to do what he
could to make the world a better place. He despised people who
complained, but never tried to effect change, and more than anything else, he wanted to be where the action was.

Put your money where your mouth is.

His father had told him that, and from a very young age, he'd
accepted it as a maxim. It had held him in good stead; his first
lesson had been when, at sixteen, he'd told his father he wanted
to learn to fly. The man who was president of a company that
owned a plane had refused to pay for his son's flying lessons.
"If getting your pilot's license means so much to you," Ellis had
told him, "you'll find a way to get it yourself."

He had.

But it was pointless to get into an argument about it now, especially when the real issue was his decision not to come to
work for that same man.

Audrey saw Gabe's expression. She guessed what was coming, and she said hastily, "What your father means, dear—"

Ellis stiffened. "What I mean is what I said, damn it!" Turning fiercely to Gabe, he added, "You've defied me for the last
time, Gabriel. I'm warning you, if you don't come to work for
me now, you'll never be asked again!"

"Fine," Gabe said. Before he could lose his temper, he pushed
back his chair and stood. "You never wanted me at the office,
anyway, so let's save ourselves a lot of grief, all right? You don't
need the two of us with you, we both know it. We're all aware
that you only have one son, and he's where you want him to be,
at your right hand."

Frank stirred. "Gabe, wait a minute—"

"Shut up, Frank," Gabe said, without looking at him. His eyes were only for his father. "Let's get to the bottom line, shall we? Why don't you go ahead and say what you really mean?"

Like an angry bear, Ellis lumbered to his feet. "Don't you dare speak to me in this manner!"

"How would you like me to speak to you, then? Bend my knee and tug at my forelock? Would that make you happy?"

"Oh, dear," Audrey murmured, her napkin at her lips.

Gabe glanced at her. "I'm sorry, Mother. I didn't mean for it to happen this way."

"The hell you didn't!" Ellis said, red-faced with fury.

Gabe looked at him again. "Don't push me, Dad. I'm warning you."

"And I'm warning you, you arrogant pup! You come back here right now, and—"

"And? What will you do if I don't? Disown me? Well, fine, do it, I don't care. Maybe it's just as well."

Ellis's face was crimson. "Don't tempt me!"

"Ellis!" Audrey gasped. "You don't mean it!"

"The hell I don't!"

Gabe was about to fling down a final challenge, but then he looked at his mother again and felt ashamed. It wasn't worth it, not when she looked so distressed. "I'm sorry," he said again to her. "I really didn't mean for this to happen. I . . . I just have to get some things I left behind in my old room, and then I'll be on my way."

Audrey looked pleadingly at him. "Please don't leave, Gabe!"

Briefly, he pressed a hand on her shoulder. "I think it would be best, don't you?"

She didn't answer; no one did. He stood there a moment longer, regretting how things had turned out but not knowing how to make them right again; then he left the dining room and went upstairs. He stopped briefly in his parents' room to leave his anniversary present behind on his mother's pillow; then he went to his old room. He was staring at something on the wall when Frank appeared.

"Well, Gabe, I didn't think you could top yourself," Frank said, from the doorway of the bedroom. "But this time I actually believe you have."

Gabe had been staring at a picture taken long ago. It had been snapped by a fellow fisherman during one of the rare fishing trips he and his brother, Frank, had taken with their father. The photo showed the three of them after four days on the American River, unkempt, wet, and dirty—but smiling proudly into the camera. They were all holding a fish aloft along with their poles, and when he saw the grins on his and his brother's faces, he felt a stab of regret. He'd been ten at the time. Frank had just celebrated his fifteenth birthday, and it was the last real vacation they had with their father. Tyrell Industries, Ellis Tyrell's fledgling electronic research and development company, was just taking off in the escalating Vietnam war, and the years since had occupied the elder Tyrell even more. Staring at his father's smiling face, he wondered what had gone wrong between them. With a sigh, he turned away from the photo and looked at his brother.

"Somehow I knew you'd feel that way," he said. "You never have approved of anything I do."

"That's not true." Glancing quickly over his shoulder, Frank came in and shut the door behind him. The room looked the same as it had when Gabe lived at home—something he hadn't done since leaving for college. Frank thought it was ridiculous, but Gabe was amused that their mother insisted on leaving their rooms as they had been. But Frank's room was filled with scholastic awards and certificates, while Gabe's held school flags, a baseball mitt, some bats in the corner, and the basketball signed by his high school team when they had won the state championship. Gabe had always been a natural athlete; in a special bookcase on one wall were all the trophies he'd ever earned in sports. Much to his brother's disgust, for the bespectacled Frank could barely stretch to five-ten and couldn't see beyond that without his glasses, Gabe had reached his present height of six-foot-two long before he left high school. He had gotten good grades—when he was interested—but he was more involved with being the captain of the basketball and baseball teams.

To make matters even worse for Frank, who thought himself disgustingly *average*, Gabe was blond and blue-eyed and extremely good-looking. Devil-may-care, girls used to call him.

Frank's only comfort—if he could call it that—was that Gabe didn't seem able to commit himself for long to anything, especially a relationship. Whether it was because he was too arrogant, or too unstable, or just too independent, the same women who flocked to him in droves ran the other way after a time—mainly in tears, because he was incapable of settling down. Gabe admitted it was true. At twenty-five, he was single and unattached . . . and likely to stay that way. Frank knew that Gabe wasn't perfect, as so many seemed to believe; his younger brother hadn't even finished college, while he had gone on to get his business degree at Stanford. He went to work soon after for his father at Tyrell Industries and was now a valued executive, responsible for generating millions of dollars for the company. He had married Amy, his high school sweetheart, and they had two beautiful daughters, now four and three. He had everything a man was supposed to want. Then why did he feel so jealous of his brother?

Thinking of his daughters made him frown. The girls adored their uncle—and why not? Tonight was no exception; they always reacted the same way when they saw Uncle Gabe. Like a knight on a charger, he would suddenly appear, bearing gifts and forbidden candy and taking them, despite their mother's protests and his own objections because they were too young, to exciting places like Magic Mountain and Disneyland. They always came home overtired and overexcited, but chattering for days afterward about what a good time they'd had with his wonderful brother. Frank didn't understand his feelings. He should be *glad* Gabe took such an interest in his girls. He hated this rotten envy he felt.

Increasingly grim, he stared at Gabe for a moment, trying to decide what to say. He'd come to talk about the scene downstairs. How like Gabe, he thought irritably, to *appear* when he hadn't been expected, then to announce that he was leaving soon for Africa to film a documentary. A *documentary*, when he was due to come to work at Tyrell Industries at the end of the month. Remembering that, Frank started to feel angry.

"Well, I hope you're happy," he finally said. "You succeeded in ruining the party Amy's been planning for months."

It was a stupid thing to say, not what he had intended at all. As soon as the words were out of his mouth, he regretted them. He was sure Gabe would be amused, but to his surprise, his brother looked regretful instead.

"I know, and I'm sorry," Gabe said. "I'll apologize before I leave."

"It's not that simple," Frank snapped.

"I'm sorry I ruined the party. I just didn't know how else to tell everyone."

"That's the trouble with you," Frank said. He hated it when his brother was like this; it was so much more difficult to stay angry with him. "You never think. You just rush right in."

Turning away, Gabe picked up a baseball that had been lying on a shelf and hefted it. Frank found himself following its trajectory—up and down, up and down. Suddenly picturing Gabe sliding into home plate, Frank glanced quickly away again. Naturally, it had been Gabe's home run that had won the championship game.

"Will you stop playing with that and look at me?" he demanded. "I think you at least owe me an explanation."

With a sigh, Gabe returned the baseball to its place. "All right. What do you want to know?"

"I want to know about this new . . . job of yours, if that's what we can call it! Don't you have any feelings at all? How could you do it? Do you realize how disappointed Dad is?"

Something flashed across Gabe's handsome face, so quickly gone that Frank couldn't identify it. Then Gabe infuriated him even more by shrugging as if it didn't matter. "Dad will get over it," he said. "My coming to work for you wasn't a good idea anyway."

"How can you say that? Dad's been wanting you to come into the company for years. I thought I'd found the perfect solution—"

"What you're really angry about is that I made you look bad in front of Dad."

Frank took a grip on his temper. "No, what I'm angry about is this damned irresponsibility of yours. It's always this way. You've never been able to settle down to anything for longer than five minutes."

Gabe had himself under better control than Frank did. "Not true," he denied mildly. "I've been a police photographer for three years, haven't I?"

Frank looked at him witheringly. "Oh, please. The only reason you stayed that long was because someone handed you a camera and gave you license to run around like someone demented to murder scenes and accidents." He drew himself up angrily. "Do you know how Mother felt about that? Do you? Do you even care?"

"Of course I care. But what I was doing was necessary—"

Frank didn't want to listen to anything Gabe had to say. He was still too annoyed. "Necessary? You just took advantage of it because one of the courses you took before you *dropped out* of college was photography!"

Gabe's jaw tightened. "Not that it matters," he said, "but the course was filmmaking."

"Oh, *excuse* me," Frank said sarcastically. "How could I have forgotten? It was just that the filmmaking seemed to pale so quickly, I guess. The next thing any of us knew was that you were jumping out of planes into forest fires because—what was the reason you gave? Oh, yes, I remember: it was exciting."

"It *was* exciting," Gabe said. He didn't mention how dangerous it had been as well.

Frank still wasn't finished. His face flushed, his expression increasingly outraged, he went on, unaware of the painful images that flared behind Gabe's deep-blue gaze.

"Then, as if you hadn't aged everybody ten years with your antics, you got a job working for the police department," Frank said. "Before we knew it, there you were—dashing off to all those murders and accidents, taking pictures as if you were on a Sunday picnic!"

"Well, I wouldn't describe it as a *picnic*, Frank. But it did have its interesting moments, I agree."

Frustrated, Frank briefly shut his eyes. "How like you to poke fun. I don't think you've ever been serious in your entire life."

Into Gabe's mind leapt the image of the little girl who had died in his arms at the scene of an accident just two months ago. She'd been about four, he recalled, delicate and doll-like—like one of his nieces. He couldn't tell that night if the little dress she wore was pink or white; by the time he got there, it was covered with dirt and grease and gore from the accident. Two adults— her parents, he supposed—were lying dead in the street beyond him, and the drunk driver who had caused the accident was sitting on the curb, holding his head and telling everyone within earshot that he needed an ambulance. Noise and confusion and traffic were all around, bystanders trying to get a closer look, some policemen shouting at everyone to stay back. Two fire trucks had arrived and roadblocks and flares were being put out, and in the distance more sirens screamed, announcing the approach of the paramedics.

Gabe didn't know the child, of course, but as he gazed down at her, he realized he never would. Her long blond hair was matted with blood and brains from the wound at the side of her head, but she didn't whimper as the sirens came wailing up, winding down to a gasp of a stop. As though they were alone on that bloody, grimy street, she just looked trustingly up into his face and held on to his hand until the light faded from her eyes. He didn't realize he was crying until the ambulance attendant tried to take the child from him, when he felt her small bones crunching under his hands and he realized how crushed her little body had been. Oh, he'd been serious at times, he thought; he had, indeed.

"And now police photography seems to have paled," Frank was saying. "So you're onto something else. Filming a wildlife documentary, of all things, flying off without a thought to take pictures of elephants."

"Elephant poachers," Gabe said, still trying to shake off his memories. He looked at Frank, but he wasn't really seeing him; the memory of the accident site wouldn't fade. Distantly he added, "And it's not that dangerous."

Frank looked at him quickly. "Not *that* dangerous? Are you out of your mind or what? I've read about what's going on down there. People getting maimed, killed—disappearing without a trace. For God's sake, Gabe, think what you're doing. Poaching's big business!"

Something hard and determined appeared in Gabe's eyes. He hadn't been able to make a difference here, but he hoped that in Africa, he could do some good. "That's exactly why I want to do it," he said. "Someone's got to stop the slaughter."

"But why you?" Frank demanded. "Don't you think you've caused this family enough grief? Don't you ever think of anybody but yourself?"

Gabe had listened long enough. Frank always thought he knew best—and worse, what was right. "Of course I do. I told you I was sorry it had to be this way—"

"Oh, sure you are," Frank said angrily. "You could have chosen a better time, you know. You didn't have to ruin Mom and Dad's anniversary."

"There wasn't a good time, and you know it." Meeting Frank's eyes, Gabe shrugged. "Besides, it was long in coming, and now it's over and done with."

"Is it?" Frank asked, his eyes hard behind his glasses. "Is it? What exactly have you accomplished, Gabe, except to hurt Mom and make Dad mad?"

Glib again, Gabe shrugged it off. "It's what I seem to do best, isn't it?"

Frank didn't say anything for a long moment. Then, a muscle bunching along his jaw, he said, "God, I despise you sometimes."

Gabe looked at him. "Sometimes I feel the same way myself," he said, and left.

*   *   *

Two hours later when Audrey wearily went up to the big master bedroom after Frank and Amy and the girls had gone, she saw a box on her pillow. She knew instantly it was from Gabe—his anniversary present. Biting her lip, she sat down and opened it.

Frank and Amy had given them an elaborate and very expensive silver punch bowl, engraved with their names and the date. Audrey appreciated the thoughtfulness behind the gift and had made a big fuss. But she had secretly wondered where she was going to put the thing; she already had two, and anyway, she and Ellis rarely entertained—on such an elaborate scale, at least.

But Gabe hadn't given them so predictable and safe a gift. When she opened the little box and saw what was inside, tears came to her eyes. Carefully, she lifted the exquisite little carving out. It was made of jade, a rich, deep green, with a base of coral that was like delicate lace. She'd never seen anything like it, and as she stared in wonder at the freeform sculpture, she realized that one moment she was seeing a bird in flight, and in the next a graceful dancer executing a pirouette. It was anything the viewer wanted it to be, she realized, and she marveled anew at the skill of the designer, who had executed such a beautiful piece.

"Oh, Gabe," she murmured, closing her eyes. She had just realized that coral was traditional for this anniversary, jade the more modern gift. How like her younger son to have found the best of both in one present, she thought. Then, stifling a sob, she bent mournfully over the sculpture.

"Please, God," she whispered, "keep him safe. . . ."

CHAPTER FOUR

It took Keeley about five seconds to decide she didn't like anything at all about New York City's Port Authority Bus Terminal. At ten o'clock at night, the place was cold and unwelcoming, and when the bus finally arrived from Detroit after a mechanical breakdown compounded by weather delays, Keeley was stiff, hungry, and out of sorts.

To make matters worse, the terminal was chilly and dank. Buses pulled in and out of the cement parking bays, sending out foul-smelling exhaust and generating so much noise that the headache she'd been fighting the past hour suddenly blossomed into fierce life. The acrid smell made her feel a little ill when she stumbled off the bus with the other passengers, and as she lined up to wait for her suitcase, she longed for a hot bath and about two days of sleep.

As awful as it was, though, this was New York, and despite the fluorescents overhead that made everyone look pale and pasty and sick, she forgot her headache and stiff muscles and glanced around with rising excitement. She had waited a long time to be here, and now that she had finally arrived, she couldn't wait to see the rest of the city and get started.

Reminded of why she was here, she touched the big purse over her shoulder like a talisman. She hadn't trusted her precious demo tapes to her luggage; they were in her bag, so close she could put her hand on them any time she chose. She could lose everything in the battered suitcase—all her clothes, the few mementos she'd brought, even the sheet music she'd written out— and still survive. But if something happened to the precious tapes she'd brought to send around to directors in the hope of landing a job, she might just as well pack it in and go home again. It wouldn't matter that her music was in her head, and always would be; now that she was here, she couldn't waste the money making additional cassettes. She had planned everything down to the last cent, and she had no room for error. It was do or die, and she hadn't let the purse out of her sight the entire time she was on the bus. She had allotted herself six months—a year, if pressed. If she didn't make it then, she was convinced she never would.

But I will make it, she thought determinedly. *I will.*

Just then her eyes met those of a young black man—a teenager, really—who was lounging against one of the massive pillars that presumably held the ceiling up. He was wearing a leather jacket that had seen better days, skin-tight jeans that bulged suggestively between his thighs, and massive black running shoes with the laces carelessly untied. A soiled leather cap covered hair that had been shaved practically to the scalp, and as their glances met and held, he smiled arrogantly, running his tongue over his lip.

Catching her breath, Keeley quickly looked away. The feeling of menace he exuded made her uneasy, and unconsciously, she moved closer to the knot of people who were still waiting for the bus driver to empty the luggage compartment. She could feel him still staring at her, but she didn't look at him again. Suddenly she was glad she wasn't alone.

She certainly wasn't by herself. Her bus was slotted into one of a vast array of concrete parking bays, hot exhaust from its still-running engine competing with a pervasive cold that made her shiver even inside her coat. People came and went; even at this time of night, the place was a hub of activity. She saw by those coming in that it was still raining outside, and all the cement made the air seem even more chill. Shivering again, she pulled her coat closer to her, trying not to think that she was being stared at.

Maybe it was the look in the young man's eyes that made her feel so cold, she thought. She had planned on taking a street bus to the nearest cheap hotel, but now she wondered if she shouldn't part with a few precious dollars and hail a cab instead. She didn't know what she would do if he followed her onto a bus, and at least a cab was safe—she hoped. She was still trying to decide what to do when she heard a shrill cry, the sounds of a scuffle, and then a high-pitched wail. Startled into looking around, she gasped.

The teenager who had been staring at her a few moments earlier had obviously grown bored with his game and started looking for other prey. To Keeley's horror, he had moved in on a young blond woman and was trying to take her purse. As fragile as she looked, the girl seemed determined to prevent the theft, and when Keeley turned to look, they were engaged in a bizarre tug of war. The more the teenager jerked at the purse, the harder the girl held on. She was actually leaning back on her heels, clinging hysterically to the strap when Keeley unconsciously took a step forward. Transfixed, Keeley stared for a moment before she realized no one was running to help.

She didn't stop to think. "Hey!" she shouted. Several people in line with her glanced at her curiously for shouting but quickly looked away again. Other travelers, passing near where the two were struggling, didn't even look up; they just hurried by, averting their eyes.

"Hey!" Keeley shouted again. "You stop that!"

The girl would not let go of the strap. She had obviously been carrying a suitcase, for one was on its side by her feet, abandoned in the struggle for the purse. Additionally, she had a box of some kind under her arm, which she wouldn't drop. It was awkward for her to hold, and it kept slipping, causing her to list to one side to keep it in place. But she was starting to lose the battle on all counts, and she looked scared and desperate.

"Please!" she cried. "Oh, please!"

Keeley didn't think of the danger. She didn't know if the mugger had a weapon of some kind, but she didn't stop to consider what she'd do if he did. She couldn't just stand by; she had to do something—anything, she thought, starting forward. Only seconds had passed since the teenager had tried to grab the purse, but she knew the girl couldn't hold on much longer. She was too slender, too delicate; every time her attacker yanked at the purse, her long blond hair flew out behind her. Several times he had almost jerked her off her feet, but she still wouldn't let go.

"Hey!" Keeley shouted a third time, running up behind the mugger. Without thinking, she swung her own heavy purse, crying, "I said, stop that!"

She had a lot in her bag—her demo tapes, her wallet, a couple of books to read on the bus, a notebook in case a snatch of music occurred to her, a flashlight, a makeup kit, and various other collectibles that females everywhere carried. She hadn't intended it, but she timed her attack perfectly; the purse hit the assailant right smack in the spine, knocking the breath out of him and pitching him forward. Uttering a startled cry, the blond girl leapt out of the way, and he stumbled over the fallen suitcase. He couldn't catch his balance in time, and he sprawled to the cement floor, cursing vividly.

Now that she had felled him, Keeley wasn't about to let him get away. "Police!" she screamed at the top of her lungs, and then she hit him again as hard as she could with the heavy bag. He was still trying to get up, and the second blow knocked him off his feet again. This time when he went sprawling, he turned and looked at her with a murderous expression.

Keeley wasn't afraid; the adrenaline was running too high. "Just try it!" she cried, reaching into her purse, her fingers scrabbling for the flashlight.

She didn't get a chance to use it. Before she could find the thing in the bottom of her bag, the teenager had scrambled to his feet. "I'll get you, you fucking bitch!" he shouted, but instead of coming toward her, as she had expected, he turned and saw the blond girl, who was bent over, trying to catch her breath. The girl still had the box under her arm, and in one swift movement, the mugger reached out and jerked it away from her. Obviously used to quick getaways, he turned in practically the same motion and started running the other way.

"You—!" Keeley cried. She would have gone after him, but the girl reached out and grabbed her arm.

"Let him go," she panted, holding her chest. "It's not worth it."

"But—"

"No, it's okay, really," the girl gasped. She went white. "I think . . . I think I . . ."

Keeley knew she was about to faint. "Here," she said quickly, shoving the girl down onto the fallen suitcase. "Just put your head down and breathe. You'll be okay."

Sweat broke out on the girl's face, but she obeyed. Keeley knelt beside her, holding her head, wondering what she was going to do if the girl passed out. No one seemed inclined to help; despite her shouting just now, there wasn't even a policeman in sight. People made little eddying lines around them, averting their eyes.

After a few tense minutes, the girl looked up. She was still pale, but she seemed better. "Thanks," she said, shivering with fright. "I don't know what I would have done if you hadn't helped." Shakily, she held out her hand. "My name's Valine. Valine Smits."

Now that the incident was over and the danger past, Keeley was having a hard time catching her own breath. Shaking Valine's hand briefly, she said, "Keeley Cochran."

Valine smiled tentatively. "It's nice to meet you."

"Yeah, likewise," Keeley said vaguely. Suddenly she realized what could have happened. Frightened at the thought, she gave the girl a sharp, accusing look. "You should have let him have the damned purse."

"I know," Valine said, her smile faltering. She had beautiful eyes, wide-set and aquamarine blue. She shook her head, still trying to catch her breath. "But I just . . . couldn't. It had all my money in it."

Keeley was still angry. Completely forgetting that she would have fought to the death herself to protect her precious demo tapes, she said, "So what? It wouldn't have done you much good if he'd pulled a gun . . . or a knife."

Valine seemed to shrink. "Yes, you're . . . right," she said faintly, putting her hand to her chest again. "I . . . I guess I just didn't think."

"Yeah, well," Keeley muttered. Now that it was over, she was feeling a little weak herself, and she rubbed at her face. "Well, it's over now, and nobody got hurt." She glared again at Valine for good measure. "No thanks to you."

"I'm sorry," Valine said. Then she looked bewildered. "I don't know why I didn't let go, you know? I ... I've never fought anyone like that, never in my entire life." She shivered. "I didn't even know I was capable of it."

"Right," Keeley muttered.

They sat in silence for a few minutes, relieved that the danger had passed, glad to realize they'd come out of it relatively unscathed. Suddenly, despite herself, Keeley started to smile. She was remembering the kid's amazement when he grabbed Valine's purse and she fought him back. If Keeley could have taken a picture of his face at that moment, it would have been a prizewinner.

Valine saw her smile. "What's so funny?"

Keeley chuckled. "You should have seen that guy when you wouldn't let your purse go. He couldn't have looked more surprised than if you'd turned into a gorilla right before his eyes!"

Valine thought about it for a moment, then, slowly, she started to smile, too. Putting a hand over her mouth, she giggled. "You think that's funny? You should have seen his face when you came up behind him and hit him with *your* bag! What do you have in that thing, anyway? A couple of bricks?"

Keeley giggled, too. "He went down like a shot, didn't he? Two times, no less! I'll bet he thinks twice before trying that again!"

They grinned at each other; then Valine sobered. "I really don't know how to thank you," she said, her voice low. "If you hadn't helped when you did, I don't know what I would have done."

Embarrassed, Keeley shrugged. "Well, it turned out for the best," she said, before she remembered the mugger had gotten away with something after all. "Except—he did steal the box you had. I hope it wasn't anything valuable."

Valine's eyes danced. "It was a present my mother gave me before I left."

Keeley didn't understand. "But you're not upset?"

"Upset?" Valine shook her head. "No, I'm thinking how upset *he's* going to be when he finds out what's inside!"

Keeley couldn't imagine what was so funny. "What was it?"

The more she thought about it, the more Valine started to laugh. "It was a blue flannel nightgown," she said merrily. She looked at Keeley with glee. "Do you think he'll look good in it?"

Keeley started to laugh, too. Soon they were holding on to each other, unable to control their mirth. People glanced at them as they hurried by, and that made them laugh even harder. When a policeman appeared and started toward them, they practically screamed with hilarity.

"*Now* he shows up!" Keeley said, holding on to her sides.

"Where are they when you need them?" Valine cried, tears running down her face.

The cop approached cautiously, obviously not sure if they were crazy or not. His hand on his nightstick, he said, "You ladies all right?"

"*We* are," Keeley said, trying to control herself. "But somewhere around is a black guy carrying a blue flannel nightgown who might need help."

Valine went off into another fit of giggles at that, making the cop look at her suspiciously. Deciding they'd sat here long enough, Keeley struggled to her feet. Reaching down, she grabbed Valine's arm and hauled her up, too. Trying to control herself, she looked at the policeman and said, "It's okay, really, officer. We just got mugged, but we're not hurt."

The cop looked around. "You want to tell me about it?"

"Nothing to tell," Keeley said. "The guy didn't hurt us, and we ran him off."

He didn't seem convinced. "Are you sure you're all right? Maybe we should go down to the station and—"

Keeley didn't want to get involved in all that. "No, really, there's no point," she said. She looked at Valine. "Unless you—"

Valine shook her head. Now that it was over, she just wanted to put it behind her, too. "No, I'm okay." She smiled at the cop. "I just got in. I'm from Allentown, Indiana."

The officer grinned. "Indiana, no kidding? I'm from Indianapolis, myself."

"Really?" Valine exclaimed. "Well, my goodness—"

Seeing a chance to escape, Keeley said, "You two don't need me for old-home week, so if it's all right with you, officer, I'll just be on my way."

"Wait, I'll go with you," Valine said. She looked up at the cop. "If it's okay."

He touched his hat. "If you've got someplace to go, it's fine by me. This place isn't safe to be wandering around alone at night."

"You're right about that," Keeley agreed. As he moved off, she turned to Valine. "Well, it was nice—"

"Oh, please, you can't go yet!" Valine exclaimed. She thought quickly. "At least let me buy you a cup of coffee or something. I really am grateful for your help."

Keeley didn't want to go for coffee. It would make something more of this encounter than it already had been, which was nothing more than a chance meeting between strangers. Coffee meant being *involved*, getting to know each other, and she didn't want that. She wanted to be on her way—alone and unencumbered. But when she saw Valine looking at her with her big, blue eyes, she suddenly wondered, despite the way she had tried to fight off the mugger, how she would survive in this city. She looked like such an . . . innocent, Keeley thought irritably, and told herself firmly it wasn't any of her business. It was going to be hard enough for her to get along here, she knew, and she was used to taking care of herself. She certainly didn't need to worry about anybody else.

"No, I don't think so—" she started to say.

Valine took her by the arm. "Oh, please," she begged. "I . . . I don't know anybody here, and . . . and it would mean a lot to me." Her beautiful blue eyes with their long honey-colored lashes seemed to grow even brighter. "I . . . I know it's presumptuous, but I'd sort of hoped we could be . . . friends."

"Friends?" Keeley repeated, unconsciously drawing back as if the word were contaminated. She didn't want to become friends with anyone, not until she got her bearings, and maybe not even then. Hedging, she said, "But you don't know anything about me."

"Yes, I do," Valine said earnestly. "I know that you put yourself in danger to help a stranger. That's something, isn't it?"

"Look, it's something that just happened," Keeley said, immediately feeling guilty when she saw a look of hurt on the other girl's face. *Oh, damn it to hell,* she thought. She didn't need this complication in her life, not when she wanted to concentrate on her career. If she'd thought when she went to help that she'd feel bound to this girl in some way, she would have turned her back like everybody else. Now that she had done what she had, she could just walk away. Make some excuse, say she was sorry, but . . .

While she was debating, a painful flush had appeared on Valine's pale cheeks. "I'm sorry," Valine said miserably. "I just thought . . ."

Dejectedly, she began to turn away. Cursing inwardly again, Keeley reached out before she thought. "Wait."

Hopefully, Valine turned back. Her expression made Keeley feel even more annoyed. *A cup of coffee won't bind you for life,* she told herself, and said, "All right, we'll go find a café or something. Just let me get my suitcase."

"And I'll get mine," Valine said, delight transforming her face. She added ingenuously, "And you can have anything you want, okay? Anything. After what you did, the treat's on me."

Keeley frowned at the generous gesture. "All I want is coffee," she said. "Nothing more."

"Fine," Valine said happily. "Whatever you say."

They found a coffee shop up the street, a little hole in the wall of a place that to Keeley's surprise offered fresh apple pie. She hadn't realized until she ordered how hungry she was; relief that the mugger hadn't waited outside the terminal to attack them had made her ravenous. She was glad the café had been close by; as it was, she'd practically dragged Valine up the street while throwing fearful glances over her shoulder, expecting him to leap out and attack. What an introduction to New York!

"Thank God," she muttered, when they went in. The place was brightly lit, and once inside, she felt safe. Condensation from the coffee machine and the grill misted the front windows, making it seem cozy and inviting after the raw wet cold outside, and a little bell over the door tinkled when they entered. Shrugging out of her coat, Keeley noticed that Valine looked up at the sound.

"Something wrong?" she asked.

Valine shook her head. "No, the bell just reminded me . . . never mind. It's not important."

NELLIE's, the sign outside had read, and a large woman with an apron tied around her ample middle was behind the counter. Wearing a name tag that said "Belle," she was measuring something into a can when they arrived, but she stopped what she was doing and smiled at them.

"Sit anywhere you like," she said, gesturing with a pudgy hand. "As you can see, the place ain't exactly jumpin' tonight."

Keeley debated about sitting at the counter so she could make a quick getaway when she wanted, but then she looked at the half booths lining the walls and opted for one of those instead.

Despite all the hours sitting on the bus, she was tired, and now that the excitement was over, she felt like collapsing. How she was going to find a place to stay tonight, she didn't know; maybe the waitress would know of something, she thought hopefully, and glanced up as the woman approached with a carafe of coffee.

"You two look like somethin' the cat dragged in," Belle commented, smiling. "How 'bout a cup of coffee?"

Keeley accepted at once. "Thanks."

Valine put a delicate hand over her cup. "None for me," she said apologetically. "Coffee hurts my throat. May I have tea instead?"

"Comin' right up," Belle said cheerfully, pouring Keeley's coffee. She looked expectantly from one to the other. "Now, what'll it be? I got some good meatloaf I made just this afternoon—or there's always apple pie."

Keeley had already realized how hungry she was. "I'll take the pie," she said, and added for good measure, "With ice cream, if you got it."

"Is New York called the Big Apple?" Belle said with a wink, and she looked at Valine.

"Nothing for me," Valine said with her tentative smile. "Just the tea."

"Whatever you say," Belle said doubtfully. "But you look like you could use somethin'. Otherwise, you're likely to blow away in a light wind."

Valine smiled faintly. "I'm sorry, but I'm just not very hungry right now."

Belle was back in a few minutes with the tea and a plate with Keeley's pie à la mode. As she set the things down, Keeley said, "Excuse me, but would you know of a nice, cheap place to stay around here?"

Belle laughed. "Nice *and* cheap? You don't want much, do you, sweetie? You must be new here."

Keeley flushed. "As a matter of fact, I just got in. I thought a hotel somewhere, just until I got my bearings."

"Why don't you come and stay where I'm going to be?" Valine interrupted eagerly. "It's called the Hudson Arms Apartment Hotel, and it's on Forty-ninth—"

"I know the place," Belle said, nodding. "It's not bad. About the cheapest you'll find up this way—and it's clean, or so I hear."

Delighted, Valine looked at Keeley. "You see?"

Keeley decided to dig into her pie. She felt as if with every passing second, she was being drawn further into Valine's life. "Well, I don't know," she said, as Belle moved away again.

Valine leaned forward. "You heard her say—"

Impatiently, Keeley put down her fork. "So what? We don't even know the woman, for God's sake!"

Valine flushed. "Yes, I know. But . . . would you believe my mother?"

"What does your mother have to do with it?"

"My mother found the place. She looked up in all sorts of guide books, and—"

"And you always do what your mother says?"

The flush deepened on Valine's cheeks. "Not always," she said, but Keeley knew it was a lie, for Valine added quickly, "Don't you? Always do what your mother says, I mean?"

"My mother's dead," Keeley said flatly.

Valine looked shocked. "Oh. I'm sorry."

Feeling guilty about stating it so baldly, Keeley tried to make amends. "So was I. But it happened a long time ago, when I was seven."

"Oh," Valine said. She was silent a moment, then she leaned forward again. For some reason, she seemed eager to know. "And your dad? What about him?"

Keeley's face tightened. "My father remarried a couple of months later," she said curtly, and then brushed it aside. "Look, it doesn't matter," she said, impatient again. "The point is, I'm not going to stay at the Hobson—"

"Hudson," Valine said in a small voice. "It's called the Hudson Arms Apartment Hotel."

"I don't care if it's called the Good Ship Lollipop! The point is—"

"The point," Valine said quietly, but persistently, "is that you don't have a place to stay, and I know of one." She glanced down at the tabletop, took a deep breath, and then raised her glance again. "But you don't want to stay there because you're afraid I'll want to be friends, isn't that right? You think—"

"Look," Keeley started to say uncomfortably. "It's not that I don't—"

Valine held up a small hand. In an even smaller voice, she said, "No, please, it's all right. You don't have to explain. I just thought it would be nice, you know? I mean, we're both new here, and—"

Keeley couldn't stand to see the hurt look in Valine's eyes.

Wondering what in the hell she was doing, she said irritably, "Oh, for Christ's sake! I'll see what the place looks like, all right?"

"You don't have to—"

"I know I don't *have* to," Keeley said, frowning fiercely. She shook her finger to make her point. "I'm not making any promises, okay? And don't ask me to share a room, I'm warning you. I like my privacy."

Like the sun coming out from behind a cloud, Valine smiled. "I understand," she said, and then added so earnestly that Keeley gritted her teeth, "But if I promise not to bother you, do you think we can get rooms side by side?"

"Okay, *fine*," Keeley said, wondering why she didn't just get up, collect her stuff, and leave. Why was she doing this? Who was Valine Smits to her? Impatiently, she noticed that all the ice cream had melted into her pie. Shoving the plate away, she asked, "What did you mean, coffee hurts your throat? That's the silliest thing I ever heard. Are you a singer or something?"

"Yes, I am," Valine said. Suddenly, she looked nervous and fearful again. "It's why I came to New York—to sing on Broadway."

Keeley couldn't have been more surprised if Valine had said she was a mud wrestler here to compete in a championship contest. The last thing she'd expected was for Valine to admit she was a singer, and she leaned forward. "You're kidding me, right?"

"No, really, I am."

She still couldn't believe it. "You've really got a voice?"

Valine blushed again. "Well, I'll find out, won't I?"

Keeley shook her head. "I'll be damned."

Valine misunderstood. "I know I might not look like it—"

"No, it's not that," Keeley said, starting to smile. "You won't believe it, but that's why I'm here, too!"

Valine's eyes widened. "*You're* a singer?"

"No, no—a songwriter, a composer," Keeley said, patting her bag. "I've got my demo tapes right here. Tomorrow I'm going to start taking them around to every director in town." She grinned suddenly, confidently. "*Someone's* got to want a composer—especially one as good as I am."

Valine looked as if she didn't doubt it for a minute. "I bet you are good," she said. "Do you . . . do you think I could hear your tapes sometime?"

"Sure. Whenever you like. Maybe we can even collaborate on

a song together," Keeley said expansively, not sure she really believed it. "I'll write it, and you sing it."

Valine clasped her hands together under her chin. With anyone else, the gesture would have looked precious and coy, but somehow it seemed right on her. "Oh, I'd love it!"

Wondering how anyone could be so ingenuous, Keeley leaned back. She was getting more involved here than she'd intended, and she said, "No promises. We'll see."

Valine looked dismayed. "You won't change your mind, will you?"

"You don't even know if I'm any good or not."

"Oh, but you said you were, and that's good enough for me," Valine said. Then she added shyly, "In fact, I can't imagine you not being the best at whatever you did."

"You don't even know me!"

"Oh, yes, I do," Valine said with such quiet conviction that Keeley was taken aback. "I know you're kind and strong and brave, and that you came to the rescue of a perfect stranger. If you can do that, there's nothing you can't do."

Keeley looked at her for a moment; Valine gazed directly back. Then Keeley said something she'd never told anyone before, not even Nina. The words were out before she knew it, and with wonder, she heard herself say, "One day, I'm going to direct my own musical on Broadway."

Valine didn't look surprised at all. Instead, nodding as though she didn't doubt it for a minute, she said, "I bet you will."

Keeley didn't know what to say. Even Nina, she thought, would have laughed and teased her about her dream; the fact that Valine believed she could do it—believed without even really knowing her—made it suddenly seem more possible than it had ever seemed.

"Come on," she said quickly. "I'll spring for a cab to this Hobson Hotel of yours."

"Hudson," Valine said, smiling as she obediently gathered her things. "It's called the Hudson Arms Apartment Hotel."

"Whatever," Keeley said. But she gave Valine another thoughtful look as they paid the bill and went outside. It was still raining, but by some miracle when they came out a cab was just cruising by.

"The Hudson Arms on Forty-ninth and Seventh," Valine said, when they climbed inside. She smiled shyly at the cab driver. "Is that the right way to say it?"

The cabby grinned back. "You can say it any way you like,"

he said. Then he stomped on the gas and proceeded to treat them to one of New York's famous taxi rides. Thrown back against the seat by the sudden acceleration, Keeley looked at Valine, and suddenly they both laughed. At long last, they were finally on their way.

CHAPTER FIVE

TWO months later, Keeley and Valine were sharing a tiny second-floor apartment near the hotel where they'd stayed the first week. Things looked bleak. Neither of them had a job on Broadway, although the inexhaustible Keeley had found work as a cocktail waitress at a bar nearby. The job left her days free to make the rounds of producers and directors, and she was determined to convince someone, anyone, to listen to one of her tapes—or better yet, give her two minutes to play a medley of the songs she had written. Even after eight fruitless weeks of pounding on doors, begging for a chance, she was convinced that all she had to do was get just one person to listen, and she'd be on her way.

How does she do it? Valine wondered dismally one day, as she stood by the apartment's front window, staring down at the depressing street below. She was waiting for Keeley to come home so they could eat, but she wasn't really hungry. Her mother had called again today to ask about the new show she was in, and she'd had to lie again. She'd never in her life lied before she came to New York, and the thought depressed her even more.

She was just turning away from the window with a heavy sigh when she heard Keeley's quick footsteps on the stairs outside. She knew it was Keeley; no one else moved with so much energy, even after a hard night at work.

How does she do it? Valine asked herself again, heading toward the tiny kitchen to turn up the stove on the stew she was cooking. She contributed to the running of their little household with the money her mother sent, but since Keeley was the only one bringing in any real income, she had volunteered to do the housewifely stuff. After all, she thought bitterly, she wasn't doing anything else; she might as well put her cooking talents to use. She was just checking the burner when Keeley flung open the back door and sailed in. She was working a split shift tonight—four to seven, then ten until two. Normally she hated the split; she got more tips working the evening shift, and it was easier working straight through than going back and forth. If anything could put her in a bad mood, it was this shift, so Valine was surprised to see her looking excited and happy. She came in, practically dancing around the four-foot kitchen space.

"You'll never guess what happened!" she said.

Valine dropped the spoon she was using to stir the stew. "You got a job!"

Some of the excitement vanished from Keeley's expressive green eyes. "Well, no," she admitted. When she saw how disappointed Valine looked, she grinned determinedly again. "But it's the next best thing! Come on, get your coat, I'll tell you on the way."

"On the way to what?" Valine asked, bewildered.

"We're eating out!" Keeley announced.

"Eating out! But we can't afford it!"

"We'll get pizza up at the Square."

Valine wanted to groan. Keeley was forever dragging her off to Times Square. No matter how many times they toured the theater district—an area, she had learned after hours of sore feet, that roughly bounded Forty-second to Fifty-seventh streets west of Sixth Avenue, Keeley never seemed to tire of it. Valine would have liked it, too, she had long ago decided, if just one person behind all those doors had given her a real job—one she could honestly write home about.

"Keeley, I don't want to go," she said. "Dinner's almost ready, and—"

Keeley glanced at the pot bubbling on the stove. With one of her quick, incisive gestures, she turned off the gas flame underneath, slammed the lid on the pot, and grabbed Valine's hand, dragging her into the minuscule living room.

"You're going," she said firmly, reaching into the tiny closet for Valine's coat. She had already changed out of the detested low-cut, short-skirted costume she was forced to wear while waitressing before she left the bar. She might have to put on the sexist thing while she was at her job, she said, but she wouldn't be caught dead in it on the street. The only reason she agreed to wear it at all was because she needed the job, but she had adamantly refused to stuff her bra with tissue to make herself look bigger, as the manager had initially suggested. In fact, his ears were still burning from her reaction—as was his crotch. When he had first held out the wad of tissues to her and made his suggestion about her bust, she had grabbed the tissues and proceeded to stuff them down his pants.

"How do you like it, bud?" she'd demanded, her eyes flashing. He hadn't said anything since, and he hadn't fired her. Despite her hands-off attitude, Keeley had already become one of his most popular waitresses. He knew when to cut his losses, when to keep his mouth shut, and how to keep his hands to himself. He hadn't made any suggestive remarks after the tissue incident. When she had heard, Valine had been horrified and fascinated. She could never, in a million years, have done something like that.

"Why can't you tell me here?" Valine grumbled, catching the coat Keeley tossed to her. She knew it wouldn't do any good to suggest it, but she tried anyway. "If we have to go all that way, can't we at least take the bus?"

Keeley never rode when she could walk, and she never walked when she could run. As Valine, who was much more sedentary, had already learned, Keeley had energy to burn. "If we save on fares, I'll buy you an egg cream," Keeley said slyly, mentioning a treat that Valine had never heard of until she came here, but which now she found hard to resist.

"You really know how to hurt a gal," she muttered, but she followed Keeley out.

The cold air hit her like a slap, but before she could even button her coat, Keeley was down the stairs and practically halfway up the street. "Wait for me!" she cried, and as always had to hurry to keep up.

Keeley didn't tell her what the great news was until they had almost reached Forty-second Street, where Broadway becomes Times Square. This was the heart of the theater district, the place where all the contrasts of the city seemed to converge into one giant pulse of neon light.

"God, I love this place!" Keeley exclaimed, her eyes as bright as all the flashing lights. She turned to Valine. "Isn't it wonderful? Can't you just *feel* the beat?"

Valine was feeling a little overwhelmed, as she always did, whenever she saw the place at night. She had often heard the theater district referred to as the Great White Way, but she'd never been able to figure out why. Everywhere she looked was color and radiant light and billboards and traffic and noise and people and movement. It was so gaudy and raucous and filled with vivid life that she felt as if all her senses were overloaded.

"I feel something, all right," she said. Seeing Keeley's flushed and happy face, she teased, "I think it's the subway under our feet."

Keeley shook her head and laughed. She knew how Valine felt, but this was her territory; she'd known it the instant she set foot on the street two months ago, fresh off the bus. She'd felt such a deep thrill of excitement and anticipation that night, and despite the disappointments along the way, she felt it even more keenly now.

"It's like something out of a circus," she said, laughing again in sheer joy.

"Or a bazaar," Valine added, wincing as a wino lurched across their path and disappeared into an alley.

"Come on, let's walk," Keeley said, taking her arm.

Valine held back. "Do we have to? I thought we came for pizza—and so you could tell me your wonderful news."

"Don't you want to see a movie first?" Keeley asked mischievously, pointing to one of the many porno houses lining the streets. The one she indicated was right across the street, a movie theater called the Big Apple. Tonight, it was advertising a triple-X-rated film experience entitled *Pussy in Boots*.

Valine decided she'd been gloomy long enough. Although much of what she had seen since she came to New York shocked her—and even Keeley could startle and dismay her at times—she was tired of sounding naive. "No, I think I'd rather catch that one," she said pointing to another theater down the street. The marquee there said something about hot girls and hotter sex. "Or maybe," she added, getting into it, "we should check out one of the lingerie shops. I've heard they've got the latest in edible panties. What do you think?"

"I think you're light-headed from lack of food and drink," Keeley said, laughing and dragging her across the street toward one of the fast-food stands. Next door was a pinball and shooting gallery, and with all the noise they couldn't hear themselves think, so after getting their pizza and soft drinks, they started down the street again, munching as they went.

"I can't stand it," Valine said, wiping sauce from her mouth with the back of her hand. She was holding a Coke in the other and couldn't get to her napkin. "If you don't tell me what happened, I'm going to make a scene."

Every few feet along the street was a woman who was obviously a prostitute, sashaying out to the curb occasionally looking for a trick, or standing around, one hip thrust out on impossibly high stiletto heels. Between them was a mixed bag of other derelicts and eccentrics. Grinning, Keeley said, "I don't think anyone would notice, do you?"

"Keeley, please! If you've got a job—"

"No, it's not a job," Keeley said. But her eyes sparkled, and she couldn't keep the news to herself any longer. "Guess who I met tonight!"

Valine took another bite of pizza. "Bob Fosse. Hal Prince," she said, mentioning two of Broadway's most famous choreographer-directors. Then, unable to bear the suspense, she said, "I don't know, Keeley. *Who?*"

Keeley paused dramatically. "Barry Archer, that's who," she announced. "*The* Barry Archer. Can you believe it? Well, can you? Come on, Val—say something!"

Valine swallowed. "Who's Barry Archer?"

Keeley stopped in the middle of the sidewalk. "*Who's* Barry Archer! You're kidding, right? Tell me you're kidding, Val. Everyone in the *world* knows who Barry Archer is!"

"I don't," Valine said, finishing her pizza and her Coke. She looked around for a trash can, but finding none, stuffed the napkin inside the paper cup, folded it, and put it in her coat pocket. Keeley was still looking at her in shock. "Are you going to tell me or not?"

"I'm not! You don't deserve to know! Oh, I can't believe this! And you call yourself a singer, a musician!"

Deciding it was time to stop teasing, Valine smiled at Keeley's indignant expression. "Of course I know who Barry Archer is," she said. "In his heyday, he was one of the most talented composers on Broadway." She shrugged. "It's just that I thought he was dead."

"No, he's very much alive."

"So, tell me about him!"

"I met him, isn't that enough?"

"Why do I sense a 'but'?"

For the first time, Keeley glanced away. "No buts. It was just that when I met him, he was a little . . . drunk."

"A *little* drunk?" Valine groaned. "Oh, don't tell me you met him at the Olive Pit!"

The Olive Pit was the cocktail lounge where Keeley worked. It was a tiny bar off Broadway that catered to ... well, not the best clientele, Valine thought. She was always worried about Keeley when she was at work; she'd been there once or twice and didn't like the place at all. Despite the fact that she knew Keeley always carried a steel nail file for protection, and didn't doubt that she'd use it, she was concerned for her friend—especially when she worked a late shift.

Looking curiously at Keeley now, she said, "Why would someone like Barry Archer go to the Pit?" It was what they called the place—an apt description as well as a nickname, Valine had always thought.

"I don't know," Keeley said, some of her elation disappearing at the reminder. "I couldn't believe it at first, but there he was."

"You recognized him?"

Keeley looked at her scornfully. "Well, of course I did. You'd recognize Shirley Jones, or Angela Lansbury, wouldn't you?"

"I guess," Valine said, starting to feel depressed again.

"You *guess*?"

"Oh, I don't know! I'm beginning to wonder if I know anything. Maybe famous people are all around me, and I don't recognize one of them. Maybe it's why I can't get a job."

"That's the most ridiculous thing I've ever heard!"

"Well, it's one explanation, anyway," Valine said, thinking of her first audition, the one that had taken place the very day after she had arrived. She had discovered then that the real Broadway, the one behind all these doors, was even harder and tougher and more uncaring than the street outside. It had been a bitter lesson.

To this day, she didn't know what she would have done if it hadn't been for Keeley. Keeley had been the one who helped her through the disappointment and disillusion and self-disgust; Keeley had been the one who suggested they share an apartment. And Keeley had been the one who *found* the apartment—by reading the obituary notices and tracking down the landlord before anyone else did. It was Keeley who kept her going because she herself refused to give up. If it hadn't been for all her help, Valine sometimes thought she probably would have left town and disappeared.

Even now she squirmed when she thought of that first audition. It was an opportunity that Madame LeDuc had obtained for her through her fading connections—the audition with the famous director upon which her mother had pinned all her hopes.

She had been determined to do her best, but the worst disaster possible had occurred.

She'd been too nervous; it was why everything had gone so wrong. Despite all the public singing she had done—the birthdays, the anniversaries, the church socials, the parties—she had never stood upon a stage as big as the one seemed at that audition; she had never felt so *pinned* by a spotlight. The light was so bright she couldn't see beyond the edge of the apron, but it wouldn't have mattered anyway; the entire cavernous theater was dark, and to make matters worse, there was only a ghostly, disembodied, impatient voice to concentrate on.

"Ready when you are, Miss Smits," the voice had said.

She was as ready as she would ever be under such stressful conditions. She knew how important this was, and she wanted the job more than anything she could think of. The stage manager's assistant, or whoever he was, had handed her a photocopy of the song she was supposed to sing, and despite her nerves, she had memorized it in a few minutes. She'd never had trouble learning music, and she didn't really need to hear it; she had always been able to sight-read, and the instant she looked at a sheet of music, she could hear it in her mind. So she was ready. The problem was that the piano wasn't.

She knew the instrument was off by half a note the moment the pianist began the intro. She might have been desperately unsure of herself that day, but she still had perfect pitch. She stood there, frozen for the first opening bars, wondering what to do. Should she say something, or shouldn't she? She couldn't believe that these people, who were auditioning singers for a Broadway musical, couldn't hear the flat note; for a horrible second or two, she wondered if she was mistaken. Thinking they knew more than she did, she was so upset she missed her cue.

The disembodied voice floated out from the darkness again, this time with obvious impatience.

"We don't have all day, Miss Smits."

Should she say something or not? She was still trying to decide when the pianist resignedly began the intro again. Again, she almost winced. Couldn't they hear it? Maybe it was a test, she thought frantically. Maybe she was *supposed* to say something, to prove she really did know what she was doing.

She didn't get a chance to say anything at all. Before she could open her mouth, either to complain or to sing a single note, the voice came at her again.

"Thank you, Miss Smits," it said with finality. And then, to her absolute horror, "Next?"

"Wait!" she cried, but it was too late. Broadway waited for no man—or woman—and she didn't even have time to beg for a second chance before the next hopeful came out on stage and practically shoved her out of the spotlight.

Just like that, it was over and done with. Her big chance, gone forever, and all because of a flat. She didn't know how to explain what happened; she didn't know what she was going to say to Keeley, to her mother. Oh, God, her mother! At the thought of what Edra would say, she burst into tears and stumbled into some stage props as she left the stage. The assistant came to help disentangle her from the scenery, but before she could collect herself enough to ask him for another chance, he'd jerked the photocopied pages from her clammy hand and handed them to someone else.

"Sorry," he said briefly, and then seemed to notice how awful she felt. "Hey, look," he said kindly, briefly. "These things happen. You just froze up, that's all. It happens to everyone sometimes."

"I didn't freeze up," she said mournfully. "It was the piano. It's out of tune. . . ."

But he didn't hear; the damned disembodied voice of the director was calling him back to the stage, and the only thing she could do was run the gauntlet of the other hopefuls waiting in line in the hallway outside. Wondering if she had courage enough to step out in front of a bus, she kept her head down so no one would see her tears and somehow got back to the hotel in one piece.

"Are you going to tell your mother?" Keeley asked, after she had sobbed out the whole awful story.

"I can't!" she wailed.

"Well, then, I guess the thing to do is keep trying, isn't it?" Keeley said, going to her own room to finish what she'd been doing.

Like a sad little puppy, Valine followed. They hadn't even discussed getting an apartment together yet, and Keeley wasn't too pleased when she knocked timidly on her door, but she was too miserable to care. "Please, I'll just sit here and not say a word," she begged. "It's just that I . . . I don't want to be alone right now, okay?"

Keeley gave her the look she already recognized as exasperated impatience, but she opened the door wider. "All right," she agreed, heading toward the little table by the window where she'd been working. "But I'm trying to write something, so don't interrupt, or back you go."

Dabbing at her tears, Valine nodded and sat down on the sagging sofa. Trying not to think how she was going to explain this to her mother, she glanced around, but there wasn't much different to see in Keeley's room at the hotel than there was in hers. They both could only afford a single, and each room was about twelve by fourteen, with a tiny kitchen beyond one door, a bathroom behind another, and a three-quarter size Murphy bed that came down from the wall. Each apartment had a thin India rug covering the floor; hers was in blue and mustard, Keeley's was scarlet and faded cream. Curtains hung limply at the windows, but at least, Valine thought, the place was clean. Wondering how much longer she could afford the room without a job, she glanced at Keeley, who already seemed to have forgotten her. Dark head down, her competent hand flying across the paper, she seemed oblivious to anything but what she was doing.

Valine sniffed again, wishing she'd brought a handkerchief. The only thing she had was her sodden Kleenex, and as she wiped her nose, she studied her friend and wished she were more like her. Even in the short time that they'd known each other, Valine thought that nothing seemed to faze Keeley—not a mugger, nor the great, noisy city outside that already terrified her. From her short dark hair, to her intense green eyes, to her determined stance, everything about Keeley exuded confidence, and even dressed, as she was today, in old jeans and a baggy sweater, she had a . . . a presence that Valine wished desperately she possessed. There was something electric about Keeley, something vibrant and vital and so dynamic that Valine fancied all she had to do was touch Keeley's shoulder to feel the energy crackle.

She's going to be a star, she thought, and suddenly knew, without a doubt, that it would happen. It might not take place today or tomorrow, but as sure as she was sitting in the dingy little hotel apartment, with rain starting to fall drearily outside, and no real prospects at present for either of them, she knew it would happen. For Keeley, at least, the dream would come true.

And what about me? she wondered, and immediately felt like crying again.

"What's your range?" Keeley asked suddenly, from her place by the window.

Startled, Valine looked over. "Three octaves, a tad more."

Keeley sat back. "For real?"

"For real," Valine said. She nearly began crying again, thinking of the chance she had just muffed. "Not that it's doing me any good right now. Why?"

But Keeley just shook her head and bent over the table again. Curious now, Valine stood and tiptoed over. She'd thought Keeley was writing a letter, but when she saw the sheet music, she drew in a breath.

"You're writing—"

"Shhh," Keeley commanded, holding up a hand. "I've almost got it."

"What?"

"I said, quiet!" Keeley snapped.

Valine subsided. But she couldn't prevent herself from peering over Keeley's shoulder, sight-reading and singing the music in her mind, as Keeley rapidly changed and rearranged what she had composed so far. When she saw that Keeley had penciled in the verses to a song below the music, she couldn't help it. Unconsciously, she started humming what she was reading. Before she got to the end of the first quatrain, Keeley's hand had slowed and then stopped. Her expression strange, Keeley looked up at her.

Valine immediately stepped back. "I'm sorry," she said. "I didn't mean—"

"No, no, it's all right," Keeley said. She grabbed the paper and thrust it at her. "Here, sing it again, use the words this time."

"But I thought you didn't want to be interrupted."

"Just do it!" Keeley commanded, and then paused. "You don't need a piano, do you? Because if you do, there's one down in the lobby."

She shook her head. "No, it's not necessary."

"Then, go ahead!"

She looked down at the music in her hand. It was a deceptively simple arrangement, but rich in complexity, requiring a trained voice with good control to do it justice. But even as she glanced over the first few bars, marveling at Keeley's talent, she could hear the melody rising like a phoenix in her mind, demanding expression. When she began to sing, it was as if she'd opened the cage door and freed the imprisoned bird, so that it rose on wings of sound and soared into the sky. Lost in the music, she didn't notice Keeley's expression until she sang the last note and it dwindled into a sigh, exactly as it had been written.

She'd never sung anything like it, and she was feeling a little dazed when she finally looked at Keeley again.

Her face pale, Keeley stared at her. "When you said you could sing, I didn't . . . I mean, I wasn't . . ." She shook her head. "I've never heard anyone sing like that," she finally said, and sat down again with a thud.

But that had been months ago, and since then, except for a few short breaks, one dismal day had followed the next, Valine thought, and nearly stepped out into the street against a red light.

Grabbing her arm, Keeley hauled her back. "What's the matter with you?"

Slowly, Valine focused again. "I'm sorry," she said. "I . . . I was thinking of something else."

"What?"

Valine looked out at the traffic. "About how . . . how hard it's been. We've been here two months, and nothing's happened."

"That's not true," Keeley said, carefully taking her arm so they could cross the street with the light. "You, at least, got a part off-Broadway, remember?"

Valine winced. "It doesn't count. The show folded the first night."

Keeley wasn't going to be deterred. "But you got another—"

"It didn't last a week," Valine said, and then added, "And don't forget the show that never even opened, or that last one that I had to quit."

"You shouldn't complain, not when you left."

"But the director fondled my breast!"

"Oh, yeah, that's right. Well, I hope you grabbed his balls and gave them a hard squeeze to show how it felt."

"Keeley!"

Keeley flapped her hand. "Don't sound so shocked. It's the only way to teach a man like that to keep his hands to himself."

Valine thought about it. "I suppose you're right," she said doubtfully. "Well, I'll remember it—if I ever get another chance. Oh, Keeley, what are we going to do? It's been months, and neither of us has found any real work!"

Good spirits immediately restored, Keeley stopped her under the statue of George M. Cohan that dominated Times Square. They'd made a circuit and came back to where they started. Sounding excited again, she said, "That's what I've been trying to tell you! Barry Archer might have been drinking a little too much, but he took one of my tapes—"

"You had one of your tapes with you?"

"I *always* have a tape with me," Keeley said, grinning before she went quickly on. "Anyway, he took one of them, and then—" She was so excited her voice practically shook "—and then he told me to come to see him tomorrow where he and Nigel Aames are reworking their new show, *Dan Tucker*."

Valine couldn't believe such good luck. "Tomorrow!" she exclaimed in delight, only to look immediately doubtful again. "But Keeley, you said he'd been drinking. Do you think he'll remember?"

"He'd better remember," Keeley said grimly. "I'm not going to lose a chance just because he was a little sloshed."

Valine thought of something else. "Did you say Nigel Aames?"

"Yes, now I know what you're going to say, but don't."

An article on producer-director Nigel Aames, once the toast of Broadway, but for the past decade one of its fading stars, had appeared just the other day in *Variety*, the bible of the entertainment industry. Among other things, it had panned the Boston opening of Aames's new show and questioned whether the director's time had come—and passed. "Steadily losing his grip on what makes an involving show" was the kindest thing the article had said about him, but Keeley brushed it aside. She looked at Valine. "I know what you're thinking—"

But Valine knew what she thought, and on impulse she gave Keeley a hug. "I think it's wonderful!" she said excitedly, meaning it. "Oh, Keeley, at *last* you're going to get the chance you deserve. You write wonderful, beautiful music, and now the whole world will know it! I couldn't be more thrilled if it had happened to me!"

"Hey!" Keeley protested, embarrassed. Quickly, she moved out from Valine's enthusiastic embrace, but she was grinning from ear to ear. "You really mean it?"

"You know I do!" Valine couldn't prevent herself from giving Keeley's arm a joyful squeeze. "Oh, this is wonderful! I can't wait to hear all about it!"

"Well, if you're going to be home tomorrow, I'll call you from the theater and let you know the minute I know anything myself."

"You'd better! I'll never forgive you if you don't!"

Determinedly thrusting aside her own depression, Valine tried to be excited at Keeley's news. To prove how delighted she was at her friend's good fortune, even if she couldn't celebrate in like manner yet herself, she dug into her pocket and produced enough money to buy them both a treat.

"Egg cream!" Keeley said. "If you don't watch out, you're going to turn into one yourself!"

But she proceeded to demolish it with gusto, and as Valine joined her, she thought how glad she was to know Keeley and how lucky she was to have found such a good friend.

"Race you home!" Keeley cried, after they'd been around the Square a second time.

"Oh, Keeley!" Valine protested. "Don't you *ever* sit down?"

But they ran home arm and arm, and when they arrived, flushed and gasping for breath, Valine didn't feel quite so down. With a friend like Keeley, she couldn't stay depressed for long.

CHAPTER SIX

The next morning, Keeley presented her "pass"—the signed napkin Barry Archer had given her in lieu of a business card—to the old man behind the desk at the stage door entrance. The January day was gray and gloomy and bitingly cold, but she didn't notice; she was too nervous. Just being allowed to come backstage was exciting; after all the rejections and refusals the past two months, she'd begun to think that she'd never even get this far. Holding her breath while the guard peered at the napkin, she wondered what she'd do if he didn't let her in. She had already decided that after getting this far, he wasn't going to throw her out again.

"Well, I don't know," he said finally. "It looks like Mr. Archer's signature, but—"

"Look," Keeley said, forcing herself to be patient when she felt like grabbing him by the lapels, "he said he didn't have a card, but he was sure you'd recognize his signature and let me through."

The old man squinted. "It sounds like Mr. Archer, all right, but I don't know about this writing here." He scratched his head. "Why don't you tell me what he looks like."

She'd tell him anything, she thought, as long as she got inside. "He's slender, about five-foot-ten, with sandy hair and blue eyes and he ..." She thought quickly, trying to remember if he'd had any scars or tattoos or anything. Then she thought of something. "And he's ambidextrous!" she said triumphantly. "See?" She pointed to the napkin. "He showed me. He signed his name twice—first with his right hand, then his left."

The old man bent again to peer at the napkin. "Ambidextrous," he muttered to himself. "I didn't know that."

If he didn't let her in, she was going to jump over the counter and shake him senseless. "You can see where he signed—"

"I see it, I see it," he said irritably. To her relief, he waved his hand. "Well, you might as well go on in, then."

"Oh, thank you, thank you!" she said, turning away as he muttered, "Damndest thing. Ambidextrous. Why doesn't anybody ever tell me anything?"

Keeley hardly heard him. While she'd been standing there trying to convince him to let her in, sounds of rehearsal going on had tantalized her. She started down the labyrinth of hallways toward the stage, but as she got closer, she began to realize that things weren't going well.

"Oh, great," she muttered under her breath. She paused for a moment, but then she went on again. She hadn't come this far only to leave and wait for a better time; she'd brought more tapes with her, and she also had her sheet music in her bag. She was prepared for anything. This was her chance, and she wasn't going to let it get away.

A young woman holding tightly to a clipboard, with a pencil stuck in her hair and a pale, strained face turned toward her as she ran up the steps to the area behind the stage.

"Who're you?" she asked in a shrill whisper.

"My name is Keeley Cochran, and I'm here to see Barry Archer," Keeley said boldly. Then, for good measure, she added, "I have an appointment."

The woman checked her clipboard. "I don't see your name here."

"Well, I'm sorry, but—"

They were interrupted by sounds of someone shouting downstage. The woman was so nervous that she actually jumped, and she shut her eyes briefly when someone called, "Linda! Linda, where in the *hell* are you?"

"You'll have to wait," she said hurriedly. "Our director, Mr. Aames, is—" Shaking her head, she rushed off.

Keeley had no intention of waiting. Following in the direction the young woman had gone, she paused behind the curtains, shaded her eyes against the glare of spotlights that had been directed toward the stage, and peered into the theater's darkness. From the orchestra section, she could see a desk with a single lamp on it. The dim light from the desk lamp illuminated the faces of a few people sitting nearby, and Keeley figured it was as good a place to look for Barry Archer as anywhere else. She was just trying to figure out how to get down there without disturbing anyone when the music started again. One of the people sitting in the orchestra leapt to his feet and began waving his arms before the five dancers on stage could move two steps.

"No, no, no!" the man cried. He looked to be in his forties, but to Keeley, it was hard to tell in the dim light. He was about the same height as she remembered Barry to be, but he wasn't quite as lean; he had a bit of a paunch, black hair, and dark eyes. At the moment, he didn't look too happy.

"It's face *upstage*," he shouted from where he was. "Chin *up*, pop the heel on the downbeat, *then* snap, reverse directions, and . . . five, six, seven, eight . . . Is that so hard? Am I not making myself clear here? Can't you hear me? Just what *is* the problem? Oh, never mind! Take five and give us all a break!" As the dancers disappeared quickly in relief, he glanced around. "Carlotte! Where's Carlotte?"

Another woman appeared on stage. Watching, it was difficult for Keeley to guess her age because of the heavy makeup she was wearing. She was dressed in a pink leotard with gray tights and a short black skirt, and she seemed much more at ease than the dancers who had just vanished. Shading her face with one hand, she peered into the darkness.

"What is it, Nigel?"

"Take your mark and give me the 'Leaving Home One Last Time' number from the first act," Aames said, wiping his brow. "Let's see if we can make it work this time, all right?"

"You're the boss," she said nonchalantly. Turning, she took her place, snapping her fingers at the backup singers hovering behind her. They came out and took their places quickly; at another snap of her fingers, they all struck a pose. Glancing over her shoulder, she said, "We're ready."

"God, I hope so," Aames muttered, throwing himself down in his seat. Wearily, he pulled out a lighter and lit the cigarette that had been dangling, unlit, from his lips. Taking a puff, he turned to the man who was sitting beside him, holding his head in his hands. "I can't take this anymore, Barry," he said plaintively. "If it doesn't work, I'm going to slash my wrists."

"If I had the energy I'd join you," Barry muttered. "God, I've got the grandmother of all hangovers! Is there any whiskey around here?"

"We're in the theater, not one of your sleazy bars," Aames said impatiently. He lowered his voice. "For God's sake, pull it together, will you? This is hard enough without—" He stopped, spying Keeley, who had slipped down off the stage during the shuffle and who was waiting in the aisle. He looked at her in surprise. "Who are you?"

"My name is Keeley Cochran—" Keeley began.

"I don't know you," he said, obviously thinking she was a stage groupie. "How'd you get in here? Whichever way it was, please take the same way out."

"But I have an appointment—"

"Not with me, you don't."

"No, it's—"

But the music had already started, and the singer and her backup group weren't to the third bar when Aames leapt up, arms flailing. "No, no, *no*!" he shouted. Pushing Keeley aside, he strode up the aisle toward the stage, shouting directions the entire way.

Keeley couldn't spare any time for the woman named Carlotte and the other singers; she figured she had about two minutes with the composer before the director came back. Threading her way between the seats, she sat down next to him and said, "Mr. Archer?"

Her only response was a groan. On stage, Aames was explaining, "This is a girl who's just sailed all the way from England in *steerage*—in *steerage*, remember—to be with her husband, only to find out that he hasn't come to meet her. What does she do now? She doesn't *gambol* over the stage in delight; she's worried, she's depressed, she's *tired*. She doesn't know what happened to him; she doesn't know how to find out. She's *unhappy*, people! Now, show it will you?"

Keeley knew there wasn't much time. She turned to Barry again. He seemed to have passed out. Dismayed, she heard him snore; in desperation, she shook his arm. "Mr. Archer!"

"Now, try it again, Carlotte, and make me believe it!" Aames was saying from the stage. The music started again, but Barry didn't move.

"Mr. Archer!" she hissed. Suddenly, she was reminded of her

father, who had often passed out just this way in the middle of a conversation—in the middle of a word, in fact. Her face tightened. She wasn't going to let a little thing like the composer having too much to drink deprive her of her chance. Now that she was here, she intended to make the most of it. On stage, Carlotte began the song again, and Keeley took Barry's arm and practically jerked him out of his seat.

"Wha . . . ?" he muttered, looking blearily at her.

At least she had his attention—such as it was. She spoke hurriedly, before he could pass out on her again. "Mr. Archer, we met last night—Keeley Cochran, remember? At the Olive Pit. You took a tape of my songs, and—"

He frowned, trying to focus. "A tape?" he repeated, and then he brightened owlishly. Reaching into his pocket, he took out a cassette. "A tape, right?"

Keeley wanted to groan. She hadn't realized until now that he was wearing the same clothes she'd seen him in last night; it was obvious that he hadn't been to bed, much less listened to her recording.

"Mr. Archer—" she began, but there was another interruption on stage. The singers had managed to get through the first two stanzas of the song and into the refrain before the director stopped them again.

"No, no, no!" he said, sinking dramatically down onto the stage floor, his head in his hands. The music cut off abruptly.

"I'm sorry, Nigel," Carlotte said nervously. She looked at her backup. "They were a beat late, and—"

"It's not the backup, Carlotte," Aames said. He glanced heavenward, as though silently asking what he had done to deserve this. He looked at Carlotte again. "It's you. What in the *hell* is wrong with you today?"

Carlotte put her hand to her neck. "It's my throat," she said. "I think I've got a cold coming on."

He gave an exasperated sigh. "If you have a cold coming on, maybe I'd better get someone else to sing the song."

Carlotte dropped her hand. Anger flashed in her eyes. "Oh, no, you won't! I'm going to sing the song, or no one is!"

"Are you threatening me?"

Keeley stopped paying attention; from the look on Carlotte's face, she could fight her own battles. Right now, Keeley had enough problems herself. "Mr. Archer, if you would just give me a—" she started to say, but the music had started again, and when Carlotte tried to hit a high note, it sounded like metal screeching on slate.

"My God!" Nigel cried, clapping his hands over his ears. "What in the hell was that?"

Carlotte had grimaced herself at the sound she'd made. But when she saw the smirks of her backup group, she turned furiously to the director, as though it was their fault. "I can't sing with these people, Nigel!" she cried. "I can't! And the damned song is all wrong for me! Can't you see that? Can't you?"

Keeley's nerves were already stretched to the breaking point. The constant interruptions and the argument now escalating on-stage were making her even more tense. She'd pinned such hopes on Barry Archer, only to have trouble keeping him awake, much less convince him to listen to her music, and she could feel herself getting angrier and angrier. When Carlotte started yelling again, she couldn't help herself. Without even realizing what she was doing, she stood up.

"She's right, it is the song!" she cried, her hands clenched. "It's all wrong!"

There was dead silence. Nigel Aames couldn't have looked more astounded if the theater had suddenly erupted into green flame right before his eyes. Slowly, he turned. "Who said that?"

Well, she'd ruined any chance she might have had, so she might as well confess, Keeley thought, stepping recklessly forward. "I did."

Aames shaded his eyes with his hand and peered into the darkness. Impatiently, he said, "Charlie, cut the damned Q2-48. I can't see my hand in front of my face!"

Instantly, the brightest light bearing down on the stage dimmed, and abruptly the rest of the theater seemed a little lighter. Aames slowly came forward. Keeley could see a muscle jumping in his jaw. It was obvious he was annoyed, and she couldn't blame him.

"And who," he said, enunciating each word precisely, "are you?"

Keeley decided to throw caution to the wind—as if she hadn't already. Figuring she could hardly be in worse trouble, she lifted her chin and said boldly, "I told you. My name is Keeley Cochran, and I'm a composer. A songwriter."

"Is that so," Aames said, gazing down at her. "And I suppose *you* know more than Mr. Archer there, who has won two Tonys, a Grammy, who was nominated for an Oscar—" his voice was rising with every word now, and Keeley winced "—and who *wrote* the song you just said was all wrong!"

"Well, no," Keeley said, glancing quickly at the composer. To her alarm, he suddenly seemed alert. He was sitting up in his seat staring at her. *Now he comes alive,* she thought, turning back to the director. "Of course not. I just meant—"

"Get out," Aames said flatly. "Get out before I have you thrown out!"

"Wait a minute, Nigel," Archer said.

Surprised, Nigel turned to him. "Wait for what?"

Wearily, Barry Archer rubbed a hand over his face. "I've been telling you for months now the song was all wrong for the spot. Maybe she's got something."

Aames gave him a look of sheer disbelief. "Maybe she's *got* something?" he echoed. "What's the matter with you, Barry? We don't even know who she *is*!"

"True . . . true," Archer muttered. He looked at Keeley. "What would you do with it?"

Keeley didn't hesitate. As anxious as she'd been trying to make the composer listen to her, she was too talented, too able, not to have been listening to the music. She knew what was wrong; better, she had an idea how to fix it.

"Yes, *do*—Miss Corcoran, was it?" Aames said, unable to hide his sarcasm. "Please enlighten us. Tell us what *you* would do with the number."

"It's Cochran," Keeley said. "The name is Cochran." But she said it absently, for already the song was taking shape in her mind. She could hear it, the melody, the lyrics, and she knew it was right. She didn't know how she knew; she just did. During the "discussion" on stage, Nigel had inadvertently given her the setup for the number. She already knew the "book" for *Dan Tucker*; she'd seen the review in *Variety*, which she'd avidly read before coming to the theater today. It was now or never, she thought, and looked up at the director again.

"May I use the piano?" she asked.

Aames couldn't have been more elaborately polite. Bowing deeply, he swept an arm in the direction of the instrument. "Please. Be my guest."

Keeley hardly noticed; running up to the stage, she went to the piano, an idea already forming in her mind. Hoping her idea would work, she sat down at the piano and flexed her fingers.

"Any time you're ready, Miss Corcoran," Aames said mockingly behind her.

"I'm ready now," Keeley said, and after stopping a moment to think, closed her eyes and began to play.

As always when she was composing, she immediately lost herself in the music. As soon as her fingers touched the keys, she pictured the lonely dock, and the girl who was waiting for the husband who hadn't come to meet her. She could smell the salt air and see the waves at her feet and feel the woman's desolation at having come so far only to discover she was alone after all.

She was so involved that she didn't notice what was happening behind her; she didn't realize Barry Archer was sitting up straight in his seat and didn't see the sudden change in Nigel Aames. She didn't see Carlotte's expression, or Linda's, or notice the dancers who had been drawn back to the stage at the sound of her inexpressibly sad and haunting music. The unforgettable melody floated out and took center stage, holding everyone transfixed until she finished playing the song. When she took her hands off the piano keys, there was utter silence.

It always took Keeley a moment to come back from where the music had taken her, but when she looked around, she was startled to see the little crowd.

"That was—" Nigel started to say, and couldn't find the words. Shaking his head, he turned to the show's composer. "Barry?"

Barry Archer was already out of his seat and moving toward the stage. "Where did you get that?" he demanded.

Keeley looked at him. "I just . . . wrote it. Right now."

"That's impossible! It's a finished piece!"

She shook her head. "No, I think it still needs some work. I moved it through several different keys trying to get the right effect, but now I think that maybe a contrapuntal version would be better. What do you think?"

"I think we could use you on the show, that's what I think," Barry said. He turned to the director. "What do you say, Nigel?"

Nigel looked like he didn't know what to say. He obviously hadn't expected what he'd just heard; he still looked a little taken aback. Giving Keeley a quick glance, he collected himself and spoke to Barry. "Melody we might have here, but what about the lyrics? It's obvious you'll have to write an entire new—"

"I've got the lyrics," Keeley said. Both men turned to stare at her.

"You can't possibly—" Barry started to say.

Keeley knew she was taking a terrible chance. He seemed to be her only ally at the moment, and if he thought she was trying to upstage him, all she might get was the door on her way out. "I can write them out right now, if you like."

Nigel obviously thought she was making it up. "Now, look—"

"No, I mean it," Keeley said.

The director had had enough. Flatly, he said, "I don't believe you can do it."

"If I prove it, will you give me a job?"

Looking like a mongoose with a snake—or was it the other way around? Keeley wondered; she never could remember—Nigel was clearly trying to make up his mind whether to throw her out or not. "If you prove it," he said cautiously, obviously wondering what he had here, "I'll think about it." He glowered at her. "But you'd better be quick. We're trying to rehearse."

"Yes, I know. And I'll give you the lyrics as soon as I make a phone call."

"A phone call?" Barry looked at her as if she were out of her mind. "What for?"

Her heart starting to pound, Keeley knew she couldn't back down now. Only Valine could do justice to the song she had in mind; she'd thought of Val as she was composing it just now. "I have a friend—" she began.

"Oh, no, you don't!" Nigel said.

She turned to him. Trying to ignore Carlotte's face, she said, "She can sing this song, Mr. Aames."

"I've already got a singer."

"Couldn't you at least give her a try?"

To her surprise—and relief—Barry Archer came to her rescue. Glancing at her with amusement, he said, "I think we should at least give her a chance, Nigel. If she's as good as this girl is, we might have quite a team."

Nigel looked at him in amazement. "Are you crazy? What's the matter with you today? We can't allow—"

"You liked the music, Nigel," Barry pointed out. "You can't deny it. And if the singer is as good as this girl says she is . . . Can you afford *not* to audition her?"

The director suddenly exploded. "Yes, I damned well can! In case you've forgotten, Barry, this isn't an audition; it's a rehearsal! I'm not—"

Barry's quiet voice overrode him. "In case you've forgotten, we're into trouble here," the composer said quietly. "*I* can't fix the damned spot; I've told you so. And if she can—" he indicated the avidly listening Keeley with a flick of his hand "—I'm for it."

Carlotte obviously thought it was time to defend her position. Elbowing her way forward, she said aggressively, "Now just a minute! In case either of *you* have forgotten, *I'm* the one who plays Emma in this show! You can't seriously be thinking of—"

Nigel turned to her. It was obvious he didn't like being dictated to, especially by his own cast. He said, "This isn't your decision."

"The hell it isn't! Damn it, Nigel, I won't put up with this!"

"Fine," he said, turning red and holding on to his temper with an effort. "We'll just replace you."

"Why, you—"

Dismissing her before he said something he'd regret, Aames turned to Keeley. "You've got five minutes to give me those lyrics."

"Will you audition my friend?" Keeley asked.

Nigel looked at her in amazed disbelief. "Are you always so brazen? Do you know how many people would give their right arm for a chance like this?"

"Yes, I do," she said recklessly. "I'm one of them. But I also know my friend, and you won't be sorry if you just listen to her sing, I promise!"

"I don't believe this! Are you actually . . ." Catching Barry's eye, he controlled himself. Just when Keeley was sure he was going to have her thrown out, he turned away, gesturing sharply with his hand. "Write out the first verse for me. If I like it, we'll see. If I don't, you'll get out and not come back."

Keeley had to fight to keep her hand from shaking as she wrote out the first few lines of the song. She knew that everything, perhaps her entire future, depended upon how well the director received what she wrote, and she held her breath as she handed him the paper and watched him read. He didn't say anything, but when she saw the gleam in his eyes, she knew she'd bought her chance.

"May I call my friend now?" she asked.

He glowered at her. "She'd better get here in fifteen minutes—in time for you to finish the second lyric *and* the refrain. You got it?"

"I've got it!" Keeley cried, leaping up to find a phone.

To her relief, Valine answered on the first ring. Excitedly, Val asked, "Well? What happened? Did you get the job?"

"Never mind that," Keeley said hurriedly. "Just get yourself over here—*now*—and be ready to sing."

"What?"

"I don't have time to explain. But we're auditioning—right now!"

"But Keeley—"

"Take a cab and don't argue with me, just get here!"

Valine arrived in a flurry ten minutes later. Her face flushed, her scarf flying out behind her, she rushed in, skidding to a stop when she saw the little crowd on stage. Before she could even take off her coat, Keeley shoved sheet music into her hand. She'd written out the words and music to the song while they were waiting, and as Valine looked bewilderedly down at the page, Keeley whispered fiercely in her ear, "If ever there was a time for you to sight-read, it's now. Sing like you've never sung before!"

Valine glanced covertly at the group standing tensely on stage. A woman in a pink leotard was glaring murderously at her, and a good-looking man with black hair didn't seem too happy, either. She thought he looked familiar, but she was too unnerved to remember where she'd seen him. Grasping Keeley's sleeve before she rushed back to the piano, she hissed, "What's going on?"

"Never mind. Just sing!"

Valine didn't know why Keeley wanted her; she thought it was because Keeley was auditioning and needed her to sing. Eager to help her friend land the job, she gave it all she had. She knew Keeley's work, and she sensed from the moment she read the first note how the song should be sung. With Keeley playing piano, as they had so many times at home, Valine sang the melancholy song of a woman left alone, without the husband she'd loved, after leaving the only home she knew to be with him. It was a song of loneliness and helpless longing, and as Valine's voice rose like a wounded dove, even Carlotte paused to listen. Whether they wanted to be or not, everyone on that stage was touched in some way, and when Valine's bell-like voice finally faded away on the last lingering note, no one moved or spoke for a full minute. Then, as though unable to help themselves, the group burst into spontaneous applause. Even Carlotte looked stunned.

Nigel was the first to move. Unable to prevent a quick, wondering glance at Keeley, he said hoarsely, "Okay, you convinced me. You've got a job."

Then, looking just as surprised, he looked at Valine. "You, too. What's your name?"

Before Valine could answer, Keeley got up from the piano bench. She had known, as she was playing, that Val had never sung so well, and she thought fiercely, *We did it. We're really on our way now!*

"Her name is Valeska Szabo," she said, willing Valine to keep still. "That's Szabo, with an s-z."

"Szabo," Nigel repeated, frowning. "Is it Polish or what?"

Startled, Valine turned to look uncomprehendingly at Keeley. She hadn't the faintest idea where Keeley had gotten the name, but when she saw her friend's fierce expression, she suddenly realized why. The name was exotic and foreign-sounding, unforgettable—just like she intended to be when she was on stage. On Broadway.

"It's Hungarian," she said, turning back to Nigel. Then, for good measure, she added, "But please don't ask me to change it. It's very well known and respected in Europe, and my family would be devastated if I didn't keep it."

"Fine," Nigel said. He thought a moment. "It does have a certain ring to it, I agree. All right, then, rehearsals at ten tomorrow, standard contract."

Keeley managed to contain her elation until they were out of the theater and safely down the street. But once they were far enough away, she gave a great whoop of glee and proceeded to dance Valine around the sidewalk.

"It worked!" she crowed. "We're finally going to do it!"

Valine was breathless, so thrilled she could hardly express it. Things had happened too quickly; she still wasn't sure whether to believe it. "Oh, Keeley, I don't know how to thank you! It's all due to you!"

"What do you mean, to me? If you hadn't sung the way you did—"

"If you hadn't written like you had—"

"If Barry Archer hadn't gotten drunk—!"

"Oh, this is wonderful!" Valine cried. She stopped suddenly right there on the sidewalk. Her eyes dancing, she hauled Keeley back. "I just want to know one thing—"

"What's that?"

"Valeska *Szabo?*" she said, laughing. "Where in the world did you come up with a name like that?"

Keeley laughed, too, giddy with delight. "I don't know. It just came to me. Don't you like it?"

"I love it!" Valine—now Valeska—declared. She grinned. "It's just that if you were going to change my name without telling me, the least you could have done was find one I could spell!"

"It's easy!" Keeley said with a glorious shout as she grabbed Val's arm and they began to race toward home. She laughed, a sound of sheer, delighted triumph. "You spell it S-U-C-C-E-S-S!"

Keeley and Valine—Valeska—discovered during the following weeks that success wasn't quite so easily achieved. When the cast moved over to the six-hundred block of Twelfth Avenue, even a change of place didn't ease the strain of fixing a wounded show. The new rehearsal studio was one of a long street of featureless brick buildings, with an occasional streetlight to break the monotony, but Keeley was often so tired when she left at night that she wouldn't have noticed if the pavement had suddenly started blooming with roses. As the days went on, sometimes she thought that if she heard Nigel say, "No, no, no, that's not right!" one more time she was going to start screaming.

Then came the morning when Nigel announced that he had agreed to allow a television crew to film rehearsal. The spot was going to profile "A Broadway Musical in the Making," and because such exposure could do great things for the show when it opened again, he wanted everyone to do their part.

"That means everybody, including you, Barry!" Nigel commanded.

Barry had come in late, as usual, popping aspirins and demanding gallons of black coffee; he didn't care what kind, as long as it was strong and hot. He had another hangover, and he was sitting to one side of the big rehearsal room in a metal chair, leaning his head against the mirror, looking miserable. When Nigel singled him out, he opened one eye and said, "Fuck you, Nigel," before going back to sleep. Someone in the assembled crew giggled, and Nigel whirled fiercely around.

"You think it's funny?" he demanded. "In case you're interested, it's your livelihood, too. If the show closes, you're going to close with it, and believe me, you'll never work for *me* again!"

"Who'd want to?" someone muttered, but fortunately Nigel didn't hear. He was telling them that the television crew was due that afternoon and what work he wanted done before they came.

"We're going to rehearse all numbers for the first act so I'll be certain they'll play well for the cameras," he dictated, pointing to Austin Cherry, his second in command. "You, Austin, work with the dancers. I want to go over a couple of songs with Barry." He glanced at his composer, who was still asleep by the mirror. "Barry!" he shouted. "Goddamn it, if you can't stay awake, I'm going to kick you from here to Cleveland!"

"It wouldn't be the first time," Barry said, without opening his eyes. "Would you mind keeping your voice down? I've got a bitch of a headache."

"You've got another goddamn hangover, that's all!" Nigel declared as everyone else but Keeley filed out of the room. "Now, get out of that chair and tell me what you've done with the trouble spot in the second act."

"Spot?" Barry said, opening one eye again and frowning. "What spot?"

Nigel looked like he wanted to smash something. Even Keeley, who normally sided with Barry, felt some sympathy for the director when Nigel said incredulously, "I've got a film crew coming here in two hours, and you ask me what *spot*? Damn it, Barry, you were supposed to be writing another song for that bridge! Don't tell me you don't remember!"

"Well, to tell you the truth—"

Nigel clenched his hands into fists. It was obvious that he'd had it. "If you don't have that number to review for me right now, *right this instant*, you're fired, Barry, do you hear me? I've put up with enough! If you want to drink yourself to death, it's your affair, but you're not going to do it on my time! Barry! Do you hear me?"

With a tremendous effort, Barry sat up. Wearily, he said, "Threats again, Nigel? Come on, be a—"

"I mean it!" Nigel shouted. "If you don't produce that song in two seconds, I'm going to—"

Grabbing another aspirin, Barry popped it dry. "All right, all right. Jesus, you don't have to yell."

"You haven't heard yelling! Now, do you have that song or not?"

Keeley felt she had to interrupt at that point. She'd been acting as Barry's assistant, so she knew what the trouble was—and that he hadn't fixed it yet. Val—or Valeska, as she was now supposed to call her friend—had been thrilled when, after joining the show, she'd been singled out for two solos. One was Keeley's song, "Alone at the Dock" that Nigel had immediately added to the show; another was a number of Barry's called "Wishful Thinking" that Keeley had always thought could be improved. She and Barry had been working on the problem for days now, but he couldn't seem to come up with something that would work, and until now, Keeley hadn't wanted to introduce something she'd done herself. Now she thought it might be time.

"Uh ... Mr. Aames," she said, with a quick look in Barry's direction, "we've got the number for you, sir."

Nigel raised his eyes heavenward in thanks. "Where is it?"

Mentally crossing her fingers, hoping Barry wouldn't interrupt until she could explain, she said, "I just finished copying the music. I've got it right here."

It wasn't the whole truth; she had copied the music after she had written it the night before. Holding her breath, she handed Nigel one of the sheets. He glanced down and turned red.

"This isn't what I want! This is something called—" he frowned ferociously when he saw the title"—'Guilty, But I'm Goin' Anyway.' " He looked up. "What kind of title is that?"

"If I could just explain—" she started to say.

Dryly, Barry interrupted. "Yeah, go ahead, Keeley," he said. "Explain."

She could feel herself flushing. She and Barry both knew she had written the song and hadn't told him. She glanced at the piano in the corner. "I think you can get a better idea if we play it for you, Mr. Aames," she said with another quick look in Barry's direction. "Uh ... what do you think, Barry?"

Indulgently, Barry waved a hand. No one would have guessed he'd never seen the song when he said, "Go ahead. You play it better than I do."

Keeley practically ran to the piano. She sat down immediately to play and actually got to the chorus before Nigel interrupted.

"Are you both out of your minds?" he demanded. Incredulously, he turned to Barry. "Is this your idea of a joke, or what? *Dan Tucker* is a tragedy, not a farce! We can't have a rollicking little number here! It'll destroy the continuity of the entire show!"

Barry's expression had changed while Keeley was playing; he sat up a little straighter, and even before Nigel interrupted, he was nodding. Throwing Keeley a look of thanks, he lit a cigarette and faced the director. "The show's going to be a flop if we don't add a couple of light moments, Nigel," he said, waving a hand. "All this angst! People are going to stay away in droves if it's such a downer. After all, if they want to be depressed, all they have to do is read the newspaper. We're supposed to be entertaining them for a few hours."

"And this song is going to achieve the purpose? It doesn't even make sense!"

"I bet the lyrics will. Just listen, will you?" Barry said, turning again to Keeley. "Go ahead, sing him the lyrics."

But before Keeley could obey, they all heard the sound of new voices in the hallway outside. The television camera crew had arrived, and Nigel was immediately distracted. When he left to deal with them, Barry took Keeley aside.

"Thanks, kid," he muttered. "I owe you one."

She didn't want his gratitude, not when she was so grateful for the chance of working with him. Shaking her head, she said, "You don't owe me anything."

"Yes, I do. You pulled my little chestnuts out of the fire—again. I want you to know I won't forget it."

Embarrassed, she replied, "I'm just glad it worked."

"It worked, all right. You've got a knack. I don't deny it."

"Not like you."

He dismissed the compliment with a weary wave of his hand. "I used to, I guess. But that's the operative word, I'm afraid," he said sadly. His bloodshot eyes held hers. "I'll tell you, kiddo, if you never learn anything else from me, learn this: don't ever let what happened to me happen to you."

She didn't know what to say. She knew he was referring to his obvious drinking problem, but they had never discussed it before, and she didn't want to now. She wasn't one to give advice to a man like Barry, who had won more awards and written more songs and collaborated on more Broadway hits than she could ever hope to in her entire life. It saddened her to see him boozing his talent away, but she just nodded.

Barry saw her expression and tried to smile. "Take five," he said, giving her a little push. "God knows, you earned it. And Keeley," he added, as she obediently turned toward the door. She turned back, and their eyes met. "I won't forget all your help. I mean it. Now, how about letting me look at those lyrics. . . ."

It took Nigel less than an hour to get completely wound up about the camera crew. With the bad reviews from Boston, he was aware that the show was in trouble, and it made him even more anxious to see that everything went right. He was so manic that by the end of the first hour, everyone was on edge; by the end of the second, nerves were raw. Dancers missed simple combinations; singers suddenly went hoarse. Barry went home with a thunderous headache, leaving Keeley alone to try and please Nigel, who at one point demanded frenziedly that she completely rewrite the lyrics to the second verse of the opening number. He changed his mind five seconds later, turning his frantic attention on another hapless cast member. Long before the day was a wrap, everyone was close to a nervous breakdown.

Keeley managed to escape from the overheated, suffocating rehearsal room where she'd been working—and reworking—the lyrics to yet another song sometime after five P.M. It occurred to her as she headed toward the battered coffee machine in the office that she'd completely forgotten about lunch. Now it was coming up to dinnertime, it looked as if she wouldn't have time for that, either. Nigel was like a madman, careening from one rehearsal room to another, trying to be everywhere at once, and no one ever knew where the TV camera crew would show up next. Keeley knew if she felt on edge, everyone else must be sick.

When she got to the office, about an inch of black sludge was left in the coffeepot. Since there wasn't anything else, she poured a cup. Grimacing at the acid taste, she looked around the office for something to eat, but the usual crackers and doughnuts were long gone, and there wasn't a crumb. Impatient and irritated, she decided to take the coffee back to the piano room and continue working. Maybe if she could get the lyrics changed to Nigel's satisfaction, she could go home.

She was just coming out the office door, gingerly carrying her music, along with the hot coffee in a paper cup, when someone came down the narrow hall. She didn't have time to stop; before she even realized anyone else was there, she had run smack into him. Coffee sloshed over her hand, but it wasn't the burn that upset her. In her other hand was the sheet music she'd spent all afternoon revising. When she saw the spilled coffee running the ink, she lost her temper. She was tired and hungry, and the thought that she was going to have to write everything all over again enraged her out of all proportion.

"What the *hell* do you think you're doing?" she cried. The cup was empty, and she threw it down, futilely trying to brush away the black flood that was ruining her music. "Why don't you watch where you're going?"

"I'm sorry, but you were the one who ran into me."

"I did not!"

She jerked her head up, halted momentarily by the sight of the man standing there with her. He was tall and good-looking, in a Viking sort of way, with thick blond hair and a prominent nose and deep-set, intense eyes as blue as the North Sea—but not nearly as cold, she realized abstractedly, suddenly feeling a little warm inside without knowing why. He was dressed in jeans and loafers and a sheepskin-lined denim jacket, and he was carrying what looked to be camera equipment. He must be with the television crew, she thought, and wondered why she didn't remember seeing him. She certainly couldn't have missed him, not the way he looked!

It was the *way* he was looking at her that made her lift her chin. "I didn't run into you," she declared. "It was all your fault! What are you doing here, anyway?"

He seemed to find her amusing, a fact that annoyed her and distracted her from his handsome good looks. "I came to meet a friend who's filming here today," he said, in a deep voice that held laughter. "And I disagree. If you'd been watching where you were going, this wouldn't have happened."

"And if you were any kind of a gentleman, you wouldn't be accusing me!" she retorted. Suddenly, she realized that her coffee had splattered over the expensive-looking camera case he carried. Grudgingly, she said, "Maybe I can find something in the office to wipe all this off."

"That would help," he agreed.

She looked at him sharply, but he stared back innocently. Her head high, she led the way into the office. Unfortunately, the only thing she could find was an aged box of Kleenex in one of the desk drawers. It wasn't any use for her sheet music, and he'd already taken out a cloth from the camera bag he was carrying and was carefully wiping the case. When she saw a monogram on the corner, the letters "G.T.," she couldn't resist.

"A monogram? How fancy."

Looking indulgent rather than embarrassed, he stuffed the cloth back into the bag. "Thank my mother," he said. "She still thinks I'm off to camp."

She couldn't help it; she smiled. "You're a little big, aren't you?"

He smiled, too. He really did have a nice smile, she thought, as he said, "Well, you know how it is. Once a mother, always a mother."

Keeley thought of Phyllis at home, then brushed the image

away. Deciding he wasn't so bad after all, she held out her hand. "My name's Keeley."

After a moment's hesitation, he took her hand in his. Despite the cold day, and the obvious fact that he'd just come in from outside, his fingers were warm. When she looked down, she saw that her hand had almost disappeared in his. "Gabriel—Gabe—Tyrell," he said.

Again, she couldn't resist. Maybe it was the look in his eyes; maybe it was . . . something else. But her own eyes sparkled as she said, "Gabriel? As in the angel?"

He laughed. "Keeley?" he teased. "As in Smith?"

She couldn't seem to look away from his face. They were nearly on the same level now, for he had perched on the edge of the desk. She took a step back. "Keeley," she said, lifting her chin. "As in Cochran."

His eyes held hers. "And do you—"

She never knew what he was going to say, for just then, there was a noise at the door. "Gabe!" a new voice exclaimed. "You made it after all!"

Disappointed at the interruption without being sure why, Keeley turned toward the newcomer. She recognized him as Pat Jarman, one of the crewmen from the television studio, but before she could say anything, Pat came in and started pumping Gabe's hand. "How are you?" he said, clearly delighted. "God, it's been a long time! How long can you stay? I couldn't believe it when you called. Is it really true that you're off to Africa?"

Laughing, Gabe stood. "Whoa," he said, glancing in amusement at Keeley. "It's true, if I survive New York first."

Keeley knew he was referring to their encounter in the hallway. She didn't think the comment was funny—or maybe she just didn't want to think it was funny, she thought—and she decided it was time to leave. As though he sensed her intentions, Gabe moved a step or two toward the door, effectively blocking the way.

"Man, what an opportunity!" Pat said enthusiastically. "You're going to have to tell me all about it!"

"I don't have much time," Gabe said, his eyes on Keeley. "My plane's leaving in a couple of hours. I just stopped by to say hi."

"Oh, man!"

"Hey, I'll be back," Gabe said. He was still staring at Keeley. Their eyes met and held for a few seconds, and something—she wasn't sure what—passed between them before he turned back to his friend. Clapping Pat on the back, he asked, "How're things?"

"Aw, we're just taping the making of a Broadway musical, real corny," Pat answered before he remembered Keeley was in the office with them. Reddening at the slip, he turned to her. "Sorry. It's just that director of yours . . ."

When he shook his head dolefully, Keeley had to smile. Nigel might have put his cast through its paces, but he'd made sure the television crew hadn't been far behind.

"I understand," she started to say, but just then Valeska came rushing down the hall, calling her name.

"Keeley! Where are you?"

"I'm in here!" Keeley called.

Valeska skidded to a stop in the doorway. Uncertainly, she looked from one to the other. "I didn't know you had company."

"It's not company, we just met," Keeley said, wondering why she felt the need to explain. Aware of Gabe's amused glance on her, she added, "Valeska Szabo, meet Gabe Tyrell. You already know Pat, from the camera crew."

Valeska smiled shyly up at Gabe. "Hi," she said. "It's nice meeting you." Then she looked at Keeley again. "I'm really sorry to interrupt, but Nigel has been calling you for the past ten minutes. I think you'd better—"

"Yes, I think so," Keeley said hastily. Grabbing her smeared sheet music, she tried to get by. "It was nice meeting you," she said to Gabe. She made herself look up into his handsome face again. "And I'm sorry about the coffee."

His intent stare made her nervous. "It's okay. No harm done."

Keeley couldn't seem to look away from him. Awkwardly, she said, "Well, good luck."

"You, too."

She wanted to say something else; she couldn't imagine what. But she could feel his glance on her as she left the office, and it was an effort not to look over her shoulder. What had happened back there? Usually, she didn't react like this, but there had been something about him that made her pause. Something . . . but what?

"Who was *that*?" Valeska asked as they hurried toward the rehearsal hall.

"Just some guy," Keeley said. For some reason, she didn't want to talk about it.

"Some guy, all right," Valeska said admiringly. "I wonder where *he* came from."

"He's a friend of Pat's."

"I wish he were *my* friend," Valeska said slyly. "Don't you?"

"Don't be silly. The last thing I have time for right now is a man in my life."

"Even one as good-looking as that?"

But it wasn't just his good looks that held her, Keeley thought as they entered the suffocatingly hot studio again. She avoided Valeska's keen glance as she sat down at the piano, but despite her attempted nonchalance, she realized that it would be a long time, if ever, before she forgot the way she'd felt at the look in Gabe's intense blue eyes.

CHAPTER SEVEN

Gabe lay in the meadow grass, his binoculars trained on a stout sausage tree a hundred yards away. In a fork twenty feet above the wildflowers at the tree's base lounged a perfectly camouflaged leopard. Minutes passed before the big cat stretched its neck. Then, with lazy grace, it sat up, extended an elegant foreleg and abruptly flowed down the trunk, vanishing into the grass as though it had never existed. The only sign it had been there at all was a flurry from a cloud of yellow-and-white butterflies disturbed by its passing. Bemused by the sight, Gabe lowered the binoculars just as someone approached him from the rear.

"We go tomorrow," a voice like rich velvet said.

Turning to look over his shoulder, Gabe saw a tall, haughty-looking African standing behind him. The man's name was Mhoja Lombongo, and he was a member of the Masai. In the old days, he would have been a warrior carrying an iron spear as tall as he, adorned in bloodred cloth and leather, with bands of tiny multicolored beads on his neck and wrists. Today he wore khaki. The warrior days were long past, and now Mhoja was one of Tanzania's small cadre of game wardens, assigned to be Gabe's guide.

Gabe would never forget his first sight of the Masai people. He and Mhoja had been in a truck heading toward the Crater

Highlands when they had come across a tribe. Bells around the necks of the cattle driven by the boys tinkled in the hot air; shaven-headed women in bright clothes and beads walked alongside the truck for a while, smiling. Forever after, he would always associate the day with the almost overpowering scent of crushed herbs underfoot—and with Mhoja saying, tight-lipped, that the tribe was moving to seek better grazing. It had always been so, but now these wanderings by his people were becoming more and more compressed. Due to modern medicine, human and beast populations alike had expanded, a double-edged sword. Soon all the pastureland would be overgrazed, and then both would starve.

Mhoja had been Gabe's guide since he arrived, and they had been waiting a week to meet Dr. Delmont Smith, one of Africa's leading experts on elephants. For two days now they had been trying to reach Dr. Smith by radio at his compound north of Seronera, here in the middle of Serengeti National Park, but they hadn't been able to get through. One explanation for their failure to communicate was the rumor of fighting between rangers and poachers in another section of the park called Lobo. Both had been hoping it wasn't true.

Shoving the binoculars back into their case, Gabe stood up. "You managed to contact Dr. Smith, finally?"

Mhoja gave his solemn nod. "Yes. We fly to Seronera, but from there we must make our way by Land Rover. I hope it is satisfactory."

It was more than that, Gabe thought, pleased. He hadn't expected that Mhoja would be able to wangle the plane—an aging Cessna that had seen better days but that still managed to stay aloft somehow. In the entire area, it was the only aircraft available for ranger use, and since no private planes were procurable right now, he was grateful that Mhoja had been able to pull strings. He'd been waiting for the opportunity to meet Dr. Smith, and the plane would save a lot of travel time. "Thanks," he said. "I appreciate it."

Gabe was tall, but the Masai topped him by at least two inches. Gravely, Mhoja inclined his head. "I am glad to be of assistance."

"Assistance? You're being modest, and you know it. I would have been lost from day one without you, and believe me, I'm aware of it." He grinned. "In fact, I'm so used to your watching out for me that no doubt I'll be helpless when I return to the States."

Mhoja had an excellent command of English—as well as a break-through-the-clouds smile that transformed his face. He used both now, displaying a mouthful of perfect white teeth as he said, "Maybe I should go with you, to act as your body-guard."

"Maybe you should," Gabe agreed. "I could certainly use you when I take my film and the pictures to the powers that be in New York."

"New York," Mhoja repeated, his smile disappearing. "It is a long way from here."

"I'm afraid so. But that's where the foundation's headquarters are."

"But you will be back?"

Gabe hesitated. When he'd taken on this job, he had figured it would be a onetime thing—fly in, get the film and the pic-tures, fly out, just as the sponsors at the International Zoological Foundation—the IZF, he called them—had said. But that was before he got here, before Africa took hold of him, before it did something to his head. He'd heard it said that once you came, you never really left. He could understand it now; despite him-self, Africa seemed to have gotten into his blood. It had changed him in some way he didn't yet comprehend, and things didn't seem so simple after all. New York and California—the entire United States—all seemed very far away. In fact, about the only thing he could remember clearly from home was a pair of deep green eyes.

Keeley, as in Smith? he'd teased.

Keeley, she had replied, her gaze direct, her chin lifted, as in Cochran.

She had said it defiantly, almost challenging him to forget it. Remembering the meeting with Keeley in New York before he left, Gabe shook his head. He wouldn't forget. Her face had flashed into his mind a hundred times since, and he didn't like it. In some inexplicable way, she had gotten to him just as Af-rica had done.

Reminded for some reason of the fierce and graceful leopard he had seen, Gabe turned to look back the way he had come. He had seen some unforgettable things in his life: the fearsome sight of ten thousand acres of burning forest consuming itself and ev-erything else in its path; the roaring of a mighty river reaching a terrifying flood crest. But never had he felt the immensity of nature so forcefully as he did here on the Serengeti—and he had never appreciated more the creatures that gave it life. It was awesome, grandeur beyond belief.

Seeing it laid out in front of him in all its majesty, it was hard to believe that on a map, the Serengeti looked about the size of Vermont back in the States. There, of course, any resemblance ended. Before him now stretched a vast tree-fringed meadow that could reverberate with the thunder of millions of hooves and the snarls of the predators after them, or it could be so quiet that he could hear a calf sucking milk from its mother, or even imagine the sound of stars blinking in the velvet black night sky high above. In the space of a heartbeat, the scene in front of him could erupt from picturesque serenity to a flurry of deadly menace; then it could be still as a pond again, with only gentle ripples to indicate that something dangerous had passed.

It was an ecosystem onto itself, Gabe mused, with a pulse that beat to the rhythm of migration: impala, wildebeest, zebra, and gazelle grazed the southeastern plains during the wet season, from December until May. Then, with the outriding lions and hyenas, wild dogs and jackals, the great mass moved west into the woodlands, later spreading as far north as the Mara. With the end of the dry season in November, the exodus returned to the plains, and the eternal rhythm began anew. So it had been since the beginning of time, Gabe supposed, and so it would go on, until finally destroyed, utterly, by man.

This morning, three months after he had arrived in Africa, he had awakened early, in time to watch the sun turning the sky from ink to lavender to pink to the flame blue of day. Dressed in the shorts and T-shirt and heavy boots that had become a sort of uniform since he had arrived, he had left the campsite with his binoculars and headed toward the nearest *kopje*, one of the huge tree-tufted piles of boulders that rose like islands here and there in the sea of grass. It had been occupied by three female lions today, who looked at him lazily as he made a wide detour. When he passed the site, he saw why. The attention of the lionesses was all for a bigger male than he, one with a black-tipped mane and tail who happened to be nearby.

Gladly leaving the big cats to their own preoccupations, Gabe went some distance off and threw himself down beside a yellow fever tree. Already, even though it was early morning, he could feel perspiration prickling him, and he knew it was going to be another searing day. He'd never felt heat such as he had in this country; even the ever-present wind brought no relief. Breeze or gale, it seemed to blow as hot and as fierce as everything else.

Mhoja said it was a matter of becoming accustomed to the heat, but Gabe sympathized with the lazy lions. No wonder they weren't interested, he thought, amused; it was too hot to do anything but lie around and breathe. Smiling to himself, he'd put his binoculars up to his eyes.

He had just focused on the leopard and the sausage tree when he heard Mhoja coming up behind him, and now as they returned to camp, Gabe felt an even greater reluctance to leave. Two crowned cranes, feathery bonnets bobbing, were leaping and twirling beside the creek near where they'd pitched the tent, and when Gabe approached, a family of warthogs emerged from the bushes, snorting before trotting away like little roasts, their tails held high. An ostrich had happened by the battered ranger truck; it was staring curiously at the mirror on the side, almost as though it were preening. Startled by their appearance, the big bird took off, body seeming to balance unmoving between the two windmills of its long legs.

Watching the scenes unfolding around him, Gabe remembered the first few times he'd camped out on the plain with Mhoja and two other rangers right after he'd arrived. Elephant carcasses had been spotted in the area, and they'd gone out to see, but by the time they arrived, the only evidence remaining were skeletons covered with stiff, darkening hides. Gabe had seen how efficient Africa was in reclaiming its own, and the sight had remained with him that night. Unable to sleep, he'd decided to take a walk and had gotten the shock of his life. Unthinkingly, he'd emerged from his tent and practically tripped over a lioness who had come into camp. His startled shout had brought everybody running, but the cat wasn't in any hurry. Lumbering to her feet, she meandered through the camp, disappearing soundlessly without a ripple into the night.

"Breakfast," Mhoja called just then, interrupting his thoughts.

Breakfast on the plain was a mush made out of a local grain that tasted to Gabe almost like oatmeal and honey. They finished the last of the jerky they'd brought and had coffee—a strong, black mixture made by throwing grounds into boiling water, cowboy style. The result was a drink with enough caffeine to keep one going for days, Gabe thought, on a single cup.

"Ah, that's good," Gabe said, taking a sip.

Mhoja shot him an amused look. "You say it now, but it has taken you this long to appreciate my cooking, has it not?"

Gabe smiled, remembering his first taste of Mhoja's coffee. It had been worse than drinking white lightning straight, and he had nearly choked. "You're right. What a greenhorn I was!"

"I do not know this 'greenhorn,' but if it is what I think it is, it does apply." Mhoja laughed, a deep, rich sound. "Remember the elephants who came into camp?"

Gabe reddened. "How could I forget?"

The incident had taken place on his first trip up to the magnificent Ngorongoro Crater, a place where mornings were filled with mist and afternoons with black rainstorms that quickly passed. One day two storms had met head to head. The result was a double rainbow when the rain passed, a sight that Gabe had never seen before or since. He was still awed by the beauty of it. They had gone to observe elephants, and he'd gotten much more than he'd bargained for.

It happened when Mhoja and two of the other rangers who had gone with them were setting up camp. He had been checking his cameras, for a herd of about forty elephants had been spotted nearby, and he wanted to go out in the morning to film them. Preoccupied with what he was doing, he had absently looked up to ask Mhoja something, and never got the words out. He hadn't heard them come, but there they were, right in front of him: two of the biggest elephants he'd ever seen. It was as though they had just . . . materialized.

The beasts were so close he could see the stiff hairs on their trunks, the cratered skin of their flanks. Transfixed, he had totally forgotten the camera he was holding. He was about five feet away from the water tap that had been set up in camp, and as one of the elephants headed toward him, it was all he could do not to turn and run. He had never seen anything so massive in his life. It was like watching a house lumbering forward. He didn't know why it was coming his way, but he was afraid to move in case it hadn't seen him. Would it attack? he wondered, sweat starting to pop out on his back. Would it step on him, knock him down and walk right over him—what?

It hadn't done any of those things. While he stood there like someone transfixed, it sauntered up to the water tap right next to him, reached out with its prehensile trunk, explored the faucet, turned the tap on and took a drink. The second elephant ambled up then, and when it had drunk its fill, they both turned and left, walking into the mist at the edge of the campsite.

Sometimes Gabe still wasn't sure it had really happened; if he hadn't seen it with his own eyes, he never would have believed it. He'd been so unnerved that he hadn't taken any pictures, a lapse that Mhoja delighted in ribbing him about for days afterward.

"Oh, I remember," he said, aware of Mhoja's amused glance. "I always thought that the least they could have done was turn off the tap before they left."

Mhoja laughed and poured more coffee.

They were almost finished when Gabe decided to broach a subject he'd been wondering about ever since they met.

"Can I ask you something?" he said, as they started to break camp.

Mhoja was squatting by the tiny fire, carefully putting out the last of the few coals. The Masai used fire to burn away the ticks that caused east coast fever and other cattle diseases, but a runaway blaze was feared by everyone, and he was always meticulous about dousing every last spark, often with urine, since water was precious. "Anything you wish, my friend," he said, with his innate courtesy. He grinned. "Of course, I may choose not to answer."

"I was just wondering why you became a ranger," Gabe said. "The hours are long, the equipment—what there is of it—is so old half of it is falling apart, and the pay is lousy. You said yourself that it's less than a hundred bucks a month, and sometimes weeks late at that. Why risk your life for a job like this?"

As always, Mhoja gave careful consideration to the question. Sitting back on his heels, he stared thoughtfully at his hands for a moment before he said, "It is not the money, my friend. It is that when the animals are no more, our turn is next."

"You think that man will become extinct, too?"

Mhoja raised his dark glance to Gabe's face. The Masai were a tribe of handsome people, tall and lanky, with liquid dark eyes and smooth chocolate skin, who had shared this land with all other life for untold generations. Living in huts of cow dung thickened with straw, clustered in fenced compounds called *engangs*, the tribes moved from one place to the next, seeking good grazing for their cattle. But "progress" had altered the time-honored process of natural selection, and now, along with other endangered species, the Masai way of life was in jeopardy as well.

"It is all a balance," Mhoja said gravely. "And when the balance is disturbed, every living thing is affected by the change. We are all one, my brother, whether we live in modern cities or out on the plains. What comes to us will come to you, and finally, only the wind will remain."

"So in the meantime, you do what you can, is that it?" Gabe asked quietly.

Mhoja met his eyes. "As do you, my friend."

They packed up and headed back to the ranger station a little while after that, both occupied with their thoughts, stopping only to allow a black rhino, another increasingly rare and poached species, the right of way. Mhoja gestured at the curiously graceful animal as it lumbered across the track and disappeared into the distance. "One day he will be gone, too—and not so far into the future, it seems."

Gabe, aware that the animal was being slaughtered for its horn, which wasn't really a true horn at all, but hard-packed hair and other fiber, nodded grimly. In Asia powdered rhino horn was widely believed to possess medicinal value, while in parts of India, it was used as an aphrodisiac. To his surprise, he had learned that the greatest demand for the horn was North Yemen, where it was made into ornate, highly polished handles for the *jambiyya*, a curved dagger worn as a badge of manhood and class. When he'd heard that, Gabe had found himself wishing that just one of those macho men would come out here and challenge a rhino face-to-face. After an encounter like that, he had no doubt they'd switch to something else for handles for their knives. He hadn't been here a week before they had surprised a rhino out here in the bush. It had been one of the most frightening experiences in his life. He'd had the presence of mind to get the camera out, but he hadn't had a chance even to focus before the maddened beast was charging the Land Rover. The impact when it hit the heavy car had nearly thrown the vehicle over, and everyone had to hold on for dear life. The only reason they'd escaped unscathed was because Mhoja, who was driving, had floored the gas. Even then, they'd had a tight time trying to outrun the beast. Gabe shook his head. Africa was many things, he thought, not one of them boring.

They arrived in late afternoon at the ranger post at Naabi Hill, where they were to take the plane. Gabe had been surprised and relieved that Mhoja held a pilot's license—or what passed for one in the bush: he knew how to fly. With Mhoja at the controls, he could film from the air, something he'd done on more than one occasion when they spotted something interesting. He hadn't expected to be using a camera until they reached Dr. Smith's research compound, but when they spotted the carcasses out on the plain, he immediately reached for the one by his hand.

"Is that what I think it is?" he said to Mhoja, who was piloting. He pointed, but the Masai ranger had already seen and looked grim.

"Do you want me to take us down so you can film?"

Gabe tightened his jaw. He was beginning to hate this job, he thought. "Might as well," he said, putting the viewfinder up to his eye. "It's what I'm here for."

Mhoja took them down to about 350 feet. At their low altitude, the elephant carcasses seemed to surge up at them as they approached, and Gabe's face tightened as the zoom lens brought the carnage into larger focus. There were four, sprawled where they had been felled, in this day of modern weaponry, by automatic rifles. All four trunks had been hacked off and callously flung aside; what remained of the faces was a mass of blood and tissue and bone, cut away and discarded when the tusks had been taken. As though making a final pitiful stand, the elephants lay side by side, silent testimony despite their size and power to their helplessness in the face of walkie-talkies and high-speed bullets. Only the hands of man could have committed such an atrocity as this, Gabe thought. Not even a natural enemy would have been so bestial.

Gabe had seen gruesome scenes, but this sight made him feel ill. He could understand hunting for food—or killing for protection. But on the parched plain below, what had these beasts done, except exist?

The answer was obvious, he knew: they provided ivory that was becoming more valuable and scarce as the slaughter progressed. Gritting his teeth, he readied the camera again as Mhoja brought the plane around, calling over the engine noise, "Let's make this pass lower. Then we'll land and get closeups, all right?"

Mhoja nodded. Gabe wasn't the only one affected by such sights, and Mhoja kept his eyes on the instruments. They were just turning to make the second pass when the radio crackled to life.

"Alpha-One, this is Lobo, do you read me?"

Mhoja reached out immediately for the microphone and brought it up to his lips. Lobo was the location of another ranger station to the north, the place where the recent trouble was reported to have occurred. "Alpha-One here," he said. "You have a problem?"

They did, indeed. The problem was that dead elephants had been seen in their area, and the head ranger, another Masai named Alfred Men'goriki, was worried that the poachers were still around. If they were, the herd of about sixty elephants roaming the section was in danger. He was trying to put together a posse of sorts, and he asked if they could help.

Mhoja looked at Gabe when the warden made his request, and Gabe knew they didn't have any choice. Even though they were due to visit the elusive Dr. Smith tomorrow, he nodded.

"Tell them we'll be there as soon as we can."

They landed late afternoon in the fierce heat, using the crater floor as a landing strip. Silver-mauve meadow grass rippled in the hot wind, and as they left the plane, a hyena ran right in front of them, carrying something bloody in its jaws. Obviously startled by the noise of the plane, it wasn't going to leave dinner behind. Alfred met them in front of the fly-specked ranger post, his dark face worried.

"I tried to call before, but you were out of range," the warden said when the introductions had been made. The situation was so serious that he didn't waste words. "You have heard about the recent gunplay?" he asked. When they nodded, he went swiftly on. "Early this morning, my men shot and killed two poachers."

That was news, and Gabe glanced quickly at Mhoja, whose dark face was impassive. "Tell us what happened," he said.

"I had heard of poachers in this area," Alfred said, "so I sent some men to investigate. They were going up a hillside when they stumbled upon a large herd of elephants—at least fifty, it seems. The herd was nervous, and they didn't know why, until they saw the poachers, hidden in trees, watching this post through binoculars. Someone must have seen my men, for a gun battle broke out."

"And your men?" Mhoja asked.

"They were sensible enough to retreat, but not before killing two of the poachers. Unfortunately, the others escaped, and it is those we are going after now. The chief warden is coming tomorrow to seize the evidence—"

"Did your men bring back the bodies?" Mhoja asked.

Alfred regretfully shook his head. "No, they had to leave them because they feared an ambush. But we will return tomorrow—"

"Tomorrow may be too late," Mhoja interrupted.

"That is so, but what can I do? My men were two against twenty, and as always, the poachers were well armed. My men brought back some of the weapons they left behind in their flight."

"May I see them?" Gabe asked curiously, and then whistled when they went inside the tiny post and Alfred displayed the guns that had been seized. One was a well-oiled .404 rifle with a homemade sling; another was a much-used, old-model Mannlicher elephant gun. But the crowning glory was the Soviet AK-47, and Gabe looked up into the troubled faces of the two rangers.

"You are fighting assault rifles," he said quietly.

Alfred nodded. "And all for this," he said, his face sad. He brought out some other evidence that had been quickly gathered: four small tusks stuffed with green grass and bundled in old rags. The tusks, from a female or a young bull, weighed not more than eight or ten pounds each, and from the condition, were probably the result of previous kills.

"In the old days," Mhoja said, staring somberly down at the plunder, "one could still find many big bulls carrying sixty to seventy pounds of ivory in each tusk." He reached out with a dark finger and touched one of the larger tusks, pitifully small in comparison. There was pain in his eyes. "Now we're reduced to this."

The chief warden, a man named Martin Kapela, arrived early the next morning. He was a compact, powerful-looking man who led the little group up to the ridge where the killing had taken place. But when they arrived at the scene of battle, much of the remaining evidence had disappeared: hyenas had eaten the dead poachers.

Gabe thought it was a fitting end and was relieved when it seemed that the raid had foiled the poachers' original plan to drive the herd to an even more remote region near the isolated border and there to slaughter the entire group.

"So, we will all live to fight another day," the warden said, smiling grimly at his men before he departed for Nairobi again. "I am proud. You have done well."

Gabe got it all down on film—from the weapons and confiscated tusks back at the station, to the elephant carcasses out in the woods, now stained with droppings from the vultures who had already begun to move in. Then he and Mhoja left to visit Dr. Smith.

This was the final leg of Gabe's journey; after interviewing the elephant expert, Gabe would leave for the United States, taking all the film back and making his report in person. Mhoja was aware of this, and they were both quiet on the drive through the dark and silent Manyara forest. Gabe was deep in thought, thinking of all he'd seen these past months, when his last encounter with an elephant came. It was a spectacular finale, a fitting end to the trip.

Gabe had just turned to say something to Mhoja when, suddenly, a huge gray mass *appeared* on the track right in front of the battered Land Rover.

"Jesus Christ!" Gabe exclaimed, bracing himself as Mhoja instantly hit the brakes. The vehicle rocked to a halt barely ten yards away from the huge beast.

"Don't move," Mhoja said quietly. "It's a female, and she's warning us away from her family. The group must be nearby."

Gabe couldn't have moved if he'd tried. He felt frozen to the seat, all his blood draining to his feet. Not even the elephants who had come into camp the first night had seemed so . . . big. The female's appearance was so sudden and unexpected and menacing that he couldn't even think. His lips stiff, he whispered, "Is she going to attack?"

Mhoja didn't answer. The elephant was moving toward them, ears flapping like giant sails in slow motion, seeming to *flow*, as if on water, until she came to a halt directly in front of the car. As scared as he was, Gabe noticed that she didn't stop suddenly; she just seemed to . . . *sway* to a halt, a disorienting and somehow strangely beautiful move in a creature so powerful. For a few seconds all was silent except for the wild pounding of Gabe's heart. Then the elephant lifted her trunk and shattered the quiet with a thunderous trumpet blast that raised the hair at the back of his neck. If he hadn't been so paralyzed with fright, he would have jumped out of the truck.

It was fortunate he didn't. For when he and Mhoja remained motionless, she seemed satisfied that they were no threat. To Gabe's great relief, she gave them one last suspicious warning look, then moved off with the same flowing grace.

Now that he could breathe again, he noticed other elephants standing nearby; some of them went with the old matriarch, while others remained, watching. Keeping a wary eye on those who had stayed behind, he muttered, "I guess we passed."

Mhoja seemed as relieved. Now that the danger seemed to be over, he wiped a quick hand over his sweating brow. "And a good thing," he said, with an almost grin. "Because in a contest,

I think we would have been dreadfully overmatched, don't you?"

They had rifles in the back of the truck, and a Beretta automatic in case things got dicey, but if the elephant had actually charged, Gabe doubted anything would have made a difference. Thankful he hadn't been put to the test, he nodded. "I'm glad it didn't come to that," he said, exhaling a long breath. "For more reasons than one."

"I am, too," a man said, suddenly appearing much as the elephant had, but this time by the side of the truck. He was dressed much as they were, in shorts and sandals and a faded T-shirt, but Gabe was so unnerved that he nearly jumped. Realizing that he had startled them, the man smiled underneath his bushy beard and held out his hand. "I'm Dr. Smith," he said. "Didn't mean to come up on you like that, but I wanted to make sure that Cassandra didn't hurt you."

"Cassandra?" Gabe repeated, with a quick glance at Mhoja.

Dr. Smith nodded toward the departing matriarch before he jumped into the back of the Land Rover and introduced himself to the Masai ranger, who looked a little wary himself when he shook the man's hand.

"I think it's safe to go on now," the doctor said. "My compound is just ahead."

With a covert glance at Gabe, who shrugged slightly, Mhoja carefully put the Land Rover in gear. They started off but hadn't gone a hundred yards before Dr. Smith asked them to stop again. Before they realized what he intended, he'd slipped out of the vehicle and was moving cautiously toward an elephant with one tusk who was standing in a small clearing. This was his territory, and he obviously knew what he was doing, but even so, Gabe felt himself tense all over again, especially when Smith was about two steps away from the elephant and she turned on him.

Suddenly, everything went quiet. Even the ever-present buzz of the insects seemed to disappear. Still unnerved by their previous encounter, Gabe realized that this elephant wasn't the one who had challenged them on the track, and he nearly called out a warning when the elephant lifted her head, her ears outstretched. Smith was so close, she only had to fling her trunk out to smash him down, but to Gabe's amazement, the doctor spread out his arms and stood his ground. Elephant and man looked at each other, and then slowly, as if in silent agreement, Smith lowered his arms, and she lowered her ears. Smith stretched out a hand. Hesitantly, she touched it with her trunk. It was a fleeting moment of contact, but Gabe, watching, forgot his fear as a lump came into his throat. This was quintessential Africa, he thought: the land of contrasts.

"That was Ianthe," Dr. Smith told them when he returned to the Land Rover and got in. "It's taken me nearly three years to get that close to her. In a few more months I'll be able to stroke her."

Gabe looked over his shoulder at the peaceful little group as they started off. The elephant Smith called Ianthe was watching them, and he nearly lifted his hand in farewell. When he looked at the doctor again, Smith's eyes were sad and bitter.

"This poaching business has got to stop," Smith said intensely. He leaned forward and put his hand on Gabe's shoulder. "It's got to stop."

Gabe left for the States a week later after an emotional good-bye at the airport with Mhoja. The aristocratic Masai's dark eyes—eyes that to Gabe seemed to hold the wisdom of the ages—held his as their hands clasped one last time.

"Thank you, my friend," Mhoja said solemnly. Neither of them had seen all the film or the stills yet, but his glance went to the precious case Gabe had slung over one shoulder, and he nodded. "Your pictures will bring the eyes of the world to bear on what is happening here. Maybe then, it won't be too late."

"I hope so, Mhoja," Gabe said fervently. He took a firmer grip on the case. "I'll do everything I can to make things change."

The tall Masai looked at him gravely. "If anyone can, you will," he said. "You are unique, my friend. I saw it on the plains, in the bush. You can see things that others don't see; you feel things that others don't. With your film and your pictures, you can focus what needs doing in a way that few can. In your talent is our hope."

Gabe hadn't answered; just then his flight was called. But as the plane lifted off from Nairobi Airport and he looked down one last time at the modern, bustling city, and the grandeur of the ancient African landscape beyond, he was somber. He already knew that the footage he'd shot, the stills he'd taken, were everything the International Zoological Foundation had wanted; he was sure they wouldn't be disappointed. He'd gotten what he'd come for—and more. Why, then, did he feel as though he'd left something behind, something unfinished?

You are unique, my friend, Mhoja had said. In your talent is our hope.

"May I get you anything, sir?"

The flight attendant interrupted Gabe's reverie, and he turned from the window. The decision had been coming upon him for quite a while now, without his even realizing it. Mhoja's words had somehow crystallized it, put everything into place, and when he saw the attendant smiling at him, he suddenly grinned in return.

"Yes, thanks," he said. "I'll have champagne."

The attendant was a beautiful young woman in her early twenties, with vibrant red hair and light blue eyes. Her answering smile was slightly more personal than professional this time, as she asked, "Are you celebrating something, sir?"

"You could say so," Gabe answered. He thought suddenly of his father. What would the old man say, he wondered, when he found out that his ne'er-do-well younger son had found his calling at last?

"Well, then, congratulations," she said, smiling again before she moved away to attend to her other passengers.

Gabe's glance briefly followed her, automatically noting the shape of her calves, the slight swell of hips under her straight skirt. This flight had a stopover in Amsterdam, he remembered, and he wondered . . .

Then an image of another face flashed into his mind, and he sat back thoughtfully. The foundation's headquarters were in New York, he mused; perhaps he should make plans to stay an extra day or two. Those green eyes had haunted him for three months now; maybe it was time to get to know their owner.

"Keeley, as in Cochran," he murmured to himself with a grin.

"I beg your pardon, sir?"

He looked up. The flight attendant had returned with his champagne. She made sure their hands touched as she handed him the glass, but alas, with Keeley in mind, a liaison in Amsterdam with a redhead had lost its allure.

CHAPTER EIGHT

The reviews on the new Aames musical, *Dan Tucker*, weren't good. One critic wrote that the staging didn't so much glide in places as stumble; another smugly asserted that the lighting was deliberately murky in an effort to obscure other obvious flaws. Valeska, eagerly searching the trades and any other newspapers she could find, was feeling depressed despite herself as she read; she had been determined to find *something* good. Then she came upon one last item. Her eyes widened, and she straightened from her slumped position on the lumpy couch.

"Keeley!" she cried, jumping up. "Did you see this? It says, and I quote: '*Dan Tucker*, the new off-Broadway musical mounted by fading producer-director Nigel Aames would be a night at the theater to forget if it weren't for two stand-out numbers—the desolate "Alone at the Dock" and the rollicking, delightfully mocking "Guilty, But I'm Goin' Anyway." Both songs were sung by golden-voiced newcomer Valeska Szabo . . .' " Valeska looked up, her eyes aglow. "It's the first time I've seen my name in the paper," she said, and giggled. "My new name, I mean! Oh, isn't it wonderful?" She looked down at the item again, her face still alight, taking up where she'd left off. " '. . . and were written by famed lyricist and composer, Barry Archer. Archer, who hasn't done much lately—' "

Valeska stopped abruptly, frowning as she quickly scanned the rest of the article. She looked up again. "Keeley, it doesn't say anything about you!"

"Did you expect it to?" Keeley asked absently. She was sitting by the window, scribbling rapidly into a notebook. Preoccupied, she didn't look up.

Valeska was shocked. "Yes, I expected it to! You wrote those songs, everybody knows it! You should have gotten credit!"

"It's too early for that," Keeley replied, her eyes on her notebook. She bit the end of her pencil a moment, then resumed writing again, apparently dismissing the subject.

Valeska looked at her in disbelief. She knew how Keeley hated to be interrupted while she was composing, but she couldn't let it go. "Too *early*? What do you mean? How can it be too soon to take credit for songs you wrote yourself?"

Keeley made a few more rapid notations in her book. "It doesn't matter," she said, looking critically at what she'd just written. She closed her eyes a second, obviously running the melody in her mind; then she changed a note or two on the paper. "Besides, Barry needs the credit more than I do. The only thing that matters to me right now is that I have a chance to write music."

Valeska stared at her, unable to understand. Keeley was always so strong, so determined, so ... self-confident about everything she did. Hadn't she brazenly worked her way into an audition for both of them—with a song she'd composed herself, right on the spot? If she could do that—something Valeska couldn't have done herself, not in a million years—how could she not want credit for those two songs? "Learn?" she echoed. "From whom?"

"From Barry, of course," Keeley said, sounding surprised. She finally looked up. "Who else?"

Valeska was beginning to think she'd never understand her friend. "But Barry hasn't been a teacher," she protested. "If anything, he's leaned on you!"

"No he hasn't."

"Yes, he has," Valeska insisted. She pointed to the article she'd just read to prove it. "Whose songs were the only ones praised in here? In *any* review, I ask you? Answer me that, Keeley. If Barry is so good, why didn't someone mention his title song to the show, 'Dan Tucker, That's Me!' Or what about his 'Blessing in Disguise,' or his supposed love song, 'A Side of Heaven'? Do you know why no one's mentioned them? I'll tell you! It's because they're awful. Awful! And you know it, too!"

"Look, do we have to talk about it now?" Keeley said impatiently. "I don't know if you noticed, but I'm trying to work here."

Valeska flounced around, her feelings hurt. "I don't know why, since you don't want credit for anything you do, anyway."

Her eyes narrowing, Keeley slammed the notebook shut. "That's not true," she said. Despite herself, her tone turned bitter. "Besides, what does it matter now? You've seen the reviews. We'll be lucky if the show lasts a month."

Still injured, Valeska muttered, "Sometimes I'm surprised it opened at all."

Keeley had worked hard on the show; despite her pretended disregard, she felt fiercely protective about it. It was her first project, after all, and she and Barry had spent many long hours going over lyrics and musical passages, trying to smooth over some of the more awkward transitions. Or, at least, *she* had worked hard, she thought, remembering how many of those nights she'd slaved on a particular sequence while Barry snored, unaware, somewhere nearby.

"I don't know how you can say that," she said defensively. "There are a lot of good moments in the show."

Valeska was still piqued. "And there's a lot wrong with it, Keeley. Even you can't deny it."

Keeley couldn't deny it. Aggravated, she said, "If we'd had more time, we could have fixed it."

Valeska tossed her long hair back. It looked like a pale gold waterfall. "All the time in the world isn't going to turn *Dan Tucker* into a hit," she said flatly. "The show couldn't be fixed if God Himself came down and gave us a hand."

Keeley exploded. "I can't believe you're talking like this! It's your problem, too! After all, you *do* play Emma!"

"Only because Carlotte was too old," Valeska flashed back. "If she'd had her way, the closest I would have gotten to performing in *Dan Tucker* was cleaning out the rest rooms backstage."

Keeley knew that was true, too. She'd seen the black looks Carlotte gave them both, and she knew they'd made an enemy. She felt badly for a second or two, but then she became indignant. It wasn't *her* fault Carlotte was too old to play Emma. Carlotte had only herself to blame for still thinking of herself as an ingenue.

"It doesn't matter what Carlotte thinks," she declared. "Besides, given a chance, I could fix the show. I know I could."

Valeska turned to look at her. "You're talented, Keeley, I'll be the first to say it. But I don't think even you can save *Dan Tucker*."

In her heart, Keeley knew Val was right. But she wasn't ready to give up on her first show. She'd thought about doing it, dreamed about it, fantasized about it for years, and now that she was finally here in New York, working on Broadway—well, off-Broadway, but close enough—a member of the privileged few who could go up to a stage door and just walk right through to another world, she couldn't admit failure.

"Yes, I can," she said stubbornly. "With Barry's help—"

She stopped, realizing her mistake too late. Valeska pounced. "Aha! You see? Even you know, deep down, that Barry Archer isn't what he used to be!"

"He is, too!" Keeley said sharply. "He just needs a little time to—"

"To what?" Valeska said. She looked at Keeley knowingly. "Dry out?"

Keeley started to answer, but what was the point? Not even she could deny the extent of Barry Archer's drinking—not when he came to rehearsal every morning, or at least the mornings he bothered to show up, reeking of booze. Too many times to count before the show opened, he'd spend the entire day in the prop room, sleeping it off. Opening night, he'd arrived late, handsome as could be in a tuxedo but sloshed to the gills—so drunk that Keeley couldn't even hold him up. Already tense and irritable about the opening, Nigel had taken one look at his head songwriter and turned away in disgust, but Keeley couldn't abandon Barry. She'd spent most of the first show—the exciting first night that she'd looked forward to for weeks—trying to force black coffee down Barry, only to have him throw up all over her good shoes before the end of the first act. She'd given up at that point, covering him with a cape she'd found in costumes, running out just in time to hear Valeska sing the first of her two songs in the show.

When she thought of Valeska on stage, Keeley forgot about Barry for a moment. She'd heard Val sing that song hundreds of times, it seemed, in rehearsal, but she had never heard her sing as she had that night. It was as though, performing before a live audience, something hidden in her had burst into vivid and vital life. The transformation had been amazing, inspiring. Listening in the wings, Keeley could hardly believe it was Val.

She wasn't the only one who had been affected. The audience, restless and impatient before Valeska's first number, had instantly quieted when she opened her mouth to sing. From the first note, she'd cast a spell. Alone under a single white spot, with her delicate appearance and her pale blond hair cascading down her slender back, she had looked like a spirit, an angel, a creature from another world. Golden notes poured out of her throat, and the audience had been . . . spellbound.

"Well?" Valeska said, dragging Keeley back to the present.

Keeley waved her hand impatiently. "I know Barry has a drinking problem—"

"Barry Archer is a drunk," Valeska said, forcing herself to be blunt. "Why can't you admit it?"

Keeley couldn't explain her almost mystic reverence for Barry Archer. Her feeling went beyond admiration and regard. At the top of his form, Barry was not only a great musical talent, a genius in his own right, he was the first person of any real accomplishment who had actually sat down with her as an equal and shared things with her no music school or professor could have taught.

It wasn't true what Valeska had said, she thought defensively, that Barry couldn't teach her anything. In the few months she'd known him, she had learned more about lyrics and composing and staging than she could ever have imagined. Sure, she knew Barry had a problem with alcohol; she would have been a fool not to see it. But Barry Archer drunk was so much more a creative force than any other abstinent composer that she could put up with his blackouts and his passing out and his unexplained absences just for the chance of working with him. Barry Archer sober was a musical genius such as she'd never imagined.

"You know, I don't like you when you're this way," she said to Valeska. "Since when did you become judgmental and cruel and unfair?"

"Since I became your friend," Valeska said. Then her face crumpled. Criticism, even the mildest kind, hurt her to the quick, and she burst into tears. "I'm sorry. I know you like Barry. I just don't want to see you get hurt."

Keeley steeled herself against the tragic look in Valeska's blue eyes. She was angry, and she wanted Val to know it. "Barry would never hurt me," she declared.

It wasn't like Valeska to pursue something Keeley didn't want to discuss, but this one time, she couldn't help herself. Over the months they'd known each other, Keeley had become more than her roommate, her friend; she had evolved—at least Valeska felt it was so—into a sister, the one she'd always longed for and never had. They'd been together only a short time, but Keeley would have been appalled to realize how much Valeska knew about her that she didn't want anyone to know. So sensitive herself, Valeska knew how susceptible Keeley was despite her tough exterior. She knew how deeply Keeley felt about things . . . all things. Her passionate nature, carefully hidden from the outside world, revealed itself in her music—music that Valeska with her own special talent and all her training, knew was superior to anything Barry Archer had ever composed. Keeley would scorn the notion, but Valeska knew she was right. She loved Keeley enough to try and make her see it.

"Barry already has hurt you," she said quietly, "by taking credit for those two songs himself."

Keeley flushed. The blush did wonderful things to her complexion, heightening her already vivid coloring, deepening the green in her eyes. Valeska was the traditional beauty, to be sure, but when Keeley looked like she did now, people stopped and stared.

"I let him do it," Keeley said, lifting her chin. "And I told you, it doesn't matter."

Valeska was naive in many ways, too eager to please, too anxious for approval, but she wasn't stupid. "It should," she persisted. "One day when you're famous, it will."

"By the time I'm famous, I'll have forgotten all about those two songs, and so will you," Keeley said with a toss of her head. "Why does it matter so much to you, Val? You'd do the same for a friend. You'd do it for me, I know you would."

"That's different."

"Tell me how."

"I'd never try to take advantage of you, that's how."

They were back to where they'd started. "Look," Keeley said, impatient again. "I'm sorry if you think—"

But just then the phone rang. Eager to end the argument, they both leapt for it, but Valeska was closer, and she got there first. With Keeley glaring at her, Val snatched up the receiver.

"Hello?" she said. She paused to listen, frowning slightly. Then, she said, "Yes, this is the right number. Keeley? Sure, she's right here. Who's calling?"

The answer startled her, for her light brows shot up. "Who?" she said. Then, quickly, "Yes, of course, I remember you. Uh . . . just a minute. I'll get her."

Whenever she was upset, Keeley worked. She was hunched again over her notebook when Valeska, her eyes wide, put her hand over the receiver and hissed, "You'll never guess who it is!"

"Ask me if I care," Keeley said mulishly. She was annoyed with Val and didn't look up, so she didn't see Valeska's wide grin.

"It's that guy you met at the studio, that's who!" Valeska was too excited to carry on the argument. "Remember, the day the television crew came, and we'd just started with the show? He came to—"

Keeley wouldn't look up. "I don't remember any guy. Tell him I'm busy."

"I can't tell him that! I already said you were here!"

"Well, tell him I can't talk to him, then," Keeley said impatiently.

"*You* tell him," Valeska said, and put the phone up to her ear again. "She'll be right with you," she said sweetly. Ignoring Keeley's fierce look, she placed the receiver on the table and went into the kitchen.

Expelling an exasperated breath, Keeley got up and snatched up the phone. "Hello?" she said. Then, without giving the caller a chance to say anything but a quick hello, she rushed on. "Look, I'm really busy right now, so if you—"

"Is this Keeley?" the voice said. "As in Cochran?"

Keeley would never forget that voice. As soon as she heard it, she pictured Gabe Tyrell, tall and blond with those intense blue eyes she was sure could see right into her soul. They'd only met once, and it had been months ago now, but ever since, she'd found herself thinking of him when she least expected to. A snatch of music would remind her of him for some reason, and she'd remember the way he smiled; she'd hear a joke and think of the way he'd looked when he laughed. She didn't know why she thought of him so often; she didn't even know the man.

"How . . . how did you get my number?" she asked. She felt off balance, out of kilter, annoyed, and irritated. She couldn't imagine why she didn't just hang up on him.

He laughed. Against her will, she remembered the flash of his white teeth when he smiled. "Simple. I called information for it."

She flushed hotly, feeling like a fool. Of course, how else? she asked herself scathingly, and tried to pull it together. She didn't do very well. "What do you want?" she asked.

He laughed again. "Straight and to the point. Just like I remembered."

She didn't want him to remember her. Deciding the best thing was to end the conversation as quickly as possible, she said pointedly, "I've found it saves time that way."

"It certainly does," he agreed, still sounding amused. "So *I'll* get right to the point. I called to ask if you would come to an IZF—sorry, that's the International Zoological Foundation, the folks who pay me—benefit tomorrow night. I'd really—"

"I'm sorry," Keeley said, interrupting him before he could finish. She had an irrational impulse to slam down the phone. "I can't go."

He paused. "I know it's short notice, but I just found out about it myself."

She didn't know why, but she didn't want to go out with him. Even from their single brief meeting, she'd sensed . . . what had she sensed? That he could create complications where none existed? She didn't want to think about it. "Well, that's too bad," she said rudely. "You'll just have to call somebody else."

"Just the point, I don't know anybody else in New York."

She didn't believe it for a minute. "What a shame."

"It is, I agree. And I wouldn't prevail upon you, not at the last minute like this, if it weren't kind of important."

She didn't know why she asked; she couldn't stop herself. "How important?"

He sounded offhand, almost embarrassed. "I didn't want to mention it, but I'm sort of the guest of honor at this shindig. I thought it would look a little strange if I didn't have a date. What do you think?"

She didn't know what to think. She didn't like the uncertainty she felt, a sense of shifting sands under her feet. She rarely felt unsure of herself, and she didn't like it. She decided to be rude again to get rid of him. "I can't help you. You'll just have to go alone, brazen it out. Something," she added sarcastically for good measure, "which I'm sure isn't at all foreign to you."

To her annoyance, he laughed. "You see? And here you said we had nothing in common. Look how well we already know each other."

"We don't know each other at all."

"You're absolutely right. But we could, if you'd give me a chance. Come on, if you're bored, I promise we'll leave early. I can't be more fair than that, can I?"

"Look—"

He went blithely on, as though she hadn't spoken. "I'll pick you up at seven-thirty. That'll give us plenty of time. Oh, and one more thorn, I'm afraid. It's semiformal, they say. I guess it means—"

It meant she would have to wear a party dress, something she didn't have and never intended to get, especially on her meager salary. "Semiformal means fancy," she said. "And I—"

"Oh, you don't have to get too dressed up," he said, as though she hadn't spoken again. "I'm supposed to wear a tux, but I'll just wear a tie over my T-shirt if that'll make you more comfortable. What do you say?"

She couldn't help it; she laughed at the mental picture he'd made. The laugh was her mistake, for he instantly caught her up on it. "You're weakening, I can hear it. Listen, I'll tell you what we'll do. We'll just put in an appearance and slip out the back way. You can help me out that much at least, can't you?"

She didn't know how he'd done it, but she heard herself agreeing to be ready at seven-thirty. Feeling as if she'd been finessed, but not knowing exactly how, she hung up the phone.

Valeska was leaning in the kitchen doorway, an avid expression on her face. Keeley took one look at her and shook her finger. "Don't start."

"I wasn't going to say a word," Valeska said loftily, and immediately ruined her pose by giggling. Going to the closet, she took out both their coats and threw one to Keeley.

"What's this for?" Keeley said, still wondering what had happened.

Valeska turned and grinned at her. "Well, since you don't have a thing to wear, and I don't have anything appropriate to loan you, we'd better go shopping, don't you think?"

Beginning to think she was a fool, Keeley put on her coat and went anyway.

Gabe was right on time the next night, arriving by cab, ringing the doorbell precisely at seven-thirty. Keeley, who had never believed in artifice or pretense, answered the door herself, and as soon as Gabe saw her, his face lit up.

"I didn't think it was possible, but you're even more beautiful than I remembered you," he said gallantly.

For once, Keeley had taken pains with her appearance. She never bothered with her hair or makeup when she was working, but tonight, with Val's help, she'd curled her short hair, sweeping it up and back on one side with a jeweled clip in a style that was feminine and sophisticated at the same time, and she had even applied two kinds of eye shadow, mascara, lipstick, and blush. She'd found the perfect dress in a secondhand consignment shop—a simple black sleeveless sheath with a V-neck, covered with black sequins that shot sparks when she moved. The sequins eliminated the need for jewelry she didn't have anyway, and with a hem that just skimmed her knees and high heels that showed off her legs, even she hardly recognized herself. Pleased at his expression, she opened the door and gestured for him to come in. To her annoyance, she was having trouble maintaining her composure. He was wearing a tuxedo and looked so handsome he took her breath away.

"Come in," she said. She didn't realize that Valeska was right behind her until she nearly stepped on her. Giving her friend an exasperated look, she said, "You remember my roommate, Valeska, don't you?"

"I do, indeed," Gabe said. "How are you?"

"Oh, I'm just fine," Valeska said, coloring. "Can I get you anything? We don't have any liquor, but I could offer you a Coke, or something."

"No, thanks. I've got the cab waiting, and Keeley and I had better be on our way. I'll take a rain check, though, if it's all right."

"Oh, sure. Whatever you say."

Since they were all standing awkwardly in the tiny entry, Keeley said quickly, "I'm ready. I just have to get my coat."

The coat had been a problem; neither she nor Valeska had anything remotely appropriate, and even though the dress had been secondhand, she couldn't also afford a wrap. But she had to have something, and after a desperate search through their closets, she had finally remembered something she'd seen in the costume room at the theater. They'd rushed down and unearthed a black velvet cape that was perfect, and as she took it from the chair where she'd put it earlier, she prayed Gabe wouldn't guess where she'd found it.

"Here, let me," he said, coming up behind her and taking the cape from her hands.

Despite herself, she tensed when he went to put the velvet on her shoulders. But he wasn't so gauche as to take advantage of the opportunity; deftly he tucked the garment around her and then turned toward the door. Grinning at Valeska, who was staring openly, he said, "I'll have her home early, I promise."

Valeska smiled shyly back. "Oh, I wasn't planning on staying up, honest. You're both adults."

"Good night, Val," Keeley said, glaring. "You've been a big help."

The benefit was being held at the Plaza, near one of New York's famous landmarks, Central Park. As they drove up, they passed a hansom cab—a horse and buggy—another equally famed sight. Reminded of the romantic rides through the park—or anywhere else in town—that she'd never taken, or had time to take, Keeley swallowed nervously. By the time the taxi came to a stop by the curb, and Gabe came around to help her out, she was fighting the urge to tell the cabby to drive away. She didn't want to go in; she didn't belong here.

"What is this IZ . . . whatever foundation, anyway?" she muttered, as Gabe took her arm and they went inside.

"It's a wildlife foundation dedicated to—" he started to say, but they were interrupted by a bald man in a tuxedo that looked too small for his wide girth. He saw them before they reached the entrance to the room where the benefit was being held, and he rushed forward to pump Gabe's hand.

"Gabe! How nice to see you again!" the little man exclaimed, beaming.

"Thank you, Lawrence," Gabe said, taking Keeley's arm. Politely, he introduced them. "Keeley, I'd like you to meet Lawrence Levitt, the head of the IZF. Lawrence, this is Keeley Cochran."

Levitt beamed at her, too. "Pleased to meet you," he said, shaking her hand. He looked at Gabe again. "We're all so grateful for what you've done, Gabe. Did you see the write-up in the paper this morning?"

"No, I'm afraid not."

"Well, it was just what the foundation needed! We've been fielding calls all morning, and donations are pouring in. We ran trailers for the film on several stations last night before the actual showing on public television, and, as we hoped, people were moved. Moved!" The man smiled happily and thumped Gabe on the shoulder. "We've got a proposal for you, my boy, one I'm sure you're going to like. We'll talk tomorrow, all right?"

"If you like."

"Got to run now. Duties as president, right?" the man said. Smiling at Keeley, he rushed off again.

"Well, he was brisk," Keeley commented, amused despite herself.

Gabe grinned as his glance followed the stout man up to the dais. "Larry's usually not so frantic. Maybe he's nervous about tonight."

Keeley could understand his feelings, she thought, as she glanced around the big room. She and Gabe hadn't been here five minutes, and already she wanted to leave. She didn't belong with all the ritzy people, the men in their tuxedos, the women in gowns that she knew hadn't been bought secondhand. She saw more diamonds flashing than there were lights on Broadway, and more jewels and gems than she would have believed possible, and she looked covertly at Gabe to see if he felt out of place, too. But no; he seemed at ease, as though he fit right in, and she suddenly wondered what kind of a family he came from. It had to have been money, she thought, since he was so comfortable with these people who obviously had it. Wishing she'd never accepted the invitation, she wondered how soon she could leave.

"Don't panic," Gabe murmured in her ear. It was as if he'd read her mind. "I don't like it either. We'll leave as soon as we can."

Surprised that he'd seemed to know what she'd been thinking, she looked at him sharply. But he just smiled, took her arm, and propelled her farther into the room. She lost count of all the people who came up to Gabe to congratulate him, to praise him for furthering the cause, to admire his talents, or perhaps, where some of the women were concerned, just to admire him. Even she had to admit he was one of the best-looking men in the room; the contrast between his sun-bleached blond hair and the black of his tuxedo was noticeable, especially because he was so tall. Tanned, clean-shaven, his shoulders broad under his jacket, he inclined his head politely when someone spoke to him, and he never forgot Keeley, drawing her into the conversation constantly, keeping his hand circumspectly on her elbow. Keeley caught the envious glances thrown her way by some of the women and started to enjoy it despite herself.

"You should have told me you had so many fans," she teased when there was a small lull and they were alone for a second. "I could have brought forms for everyone to fill out so we could start a club."

Gabe laughed. But before he could respond, Lawrence Levitt had stepped to the microphone up at the dais and was asking for everyone's attention.

"If you'll all find your seats now, we'll show the film—the reason we're here tonight," Levitt said. He waited a few moments until the high decibel level began to go down before he went on. "I don't intend to give a speech before the presentation; the film speaks for itself. But our guest of honor, the man who brought us such an eloquent plea on behalf of the African elephant—Gabe, where are you?" Levitt spotted Gabe just taking his seat and insisted he stand again so that everyone could applaud. Looking slightly embarrassed, Gabe waved and sat down.

"Don't say it," he murmured to Keeley when he saw her amused expression.

"I wasn't going to say anything," she protested, but she laughed at the look on his face before turning to listen to the IZF president again.

"As I was saying," Levitt said, "Gabe Tyrell is here tonight himself and will be happy to answer any questions you might have after the viewing."

A screen was being lowered behind the dais as he talked; quickly, he wound up his speech. "All of us here have dedicated some portion of our lives, our resources, our talents, to wildlife. And we are all aware of the atrocities, the carelessness, the waste, and the cruelties perpetuated by man. Therefore, some of the things you will see in the film tonight will come as no surprise. However—" he paused briefly "—however, what we will be viewing is strong stuff, so I want you all to be prepared. If anyone must leave during the film, please feel free to do so. I've worked for the foundation nearly thirty years, but even I, when I first viewed the rough cut, felt stunned. Then I was more outraged than I ever have been. I hope you will feel the same way. As Dr. Delmont Smith says, in his eloquent prologue, the atrocities have . . . got to . . . stop." And with that, he solemnly signaled the projectionist to begin.

Like the rest of the audience, Keeley was instantly transported to the African veldt with the opening montage. She could feel the heat, hear the buzzing of the insects, almost smell the particular odor that was solely Africa. The film had been shot in color, too graphic at times, vivid and horrible at others. But no matter what was showing, it was so compelling that, like everyone else, she couldn't take her eyes away from the screen. From the air, from the ground, through the trees, or between the blades of grass, the tale of the slaughter for ivory was laid bare. Without warning, as she watched, she could feel the music inside her growing.

The soundtrack included an instrumental with the narrative, but Keeley created her own sound. Transported by the melody growing within, she didn't hear the music from the film; in her mind, she was hearing instead what she would have composed.

There! she thought: instead of the violin, that sequence needed the blaring of a bassoon to mimic the hoarse challenge of the bull elephant turning to fight. And instead of brass, they should have used a cello to underscore the stark reality of elephant carcasses strewn across the plain. She would have had drums rolling like thunder across the Serengeti as an elephant fled from poachers in trucks; she would have brought in the brass ... to underwrite the blaring of car horns and the spatter of the automatic weapons fire that brought the great beast to its knees.

She heard it all in her mind, creating the music as the film unwound, a powerful theme that underscored the tragedy she was seeing on the screen. She didn't realize how tense she had become until Gabe took her hand and shook it a little to bring her out of her trance.

"Are you all right?" he whispered, leaning toward her.

Dazzled, she looked at him. Flickering images from the film moved across his handsome, lean face, and suddenly she felt a surge of ... what? It couldn't be *love*, she thought, dazed.

Quickly, she looked back at the screen. Gabe had caught on film what had moved her to music; that she couldn't deny. They used two different mediums, but after seeing this tonight, she knew without doubt that, somehow, they both felt the same rhythm of things. He was filmmaker, she was musician; but they were linked in a way she couldn't yet explain. Like a magician, he'd made the audience see tonight what he had seen; he had shown them the agony of the beasts as they fell—or were wounded, or turned in a last pitiful and futile stand.

She understood because, like a sorceress herself, *she* could make people feel with her music, make them experience what they were seeing on stage, on film. She had never felt this way before, but as she looked into Gabe's eyes, she suddenly felt as though she had known him all her life—she, who had only met him twice.

She couldn't answer his question. How could she say what she was thinking? He'd think she was crazy, and maybe she was.

"I'm fine," she said. She didn't understand what was happening to her. Did he feel it, too?

"I know," Gabe said. Smiling, he reached for her hand.

And suddenly, she knew he did understand. Their eyes held in the flickering images from the screen, and as she searched his face, she was aware that something had happened to her tonight. She didn't know how, or why, but she knew she would never be the same.

She was quiet in the cab when Gabe took her home again, but so was he. They both needed to be alone with their thoughts, to examine what had taken place so unexpectedly between them, to decide how it felt.

With the taxi waiting, Gabe walked her up the stairs to her door, and she didn't protest. She didn't know it, but her eyes were brilliant in the light from the streetlight nearby as she looked up at him.

"Gabe, I . . . I don't know what to say," she murmured. "The film was . . . magnificent."

Gabe didn't want to talk about his film. He was having trouble breathing, and as he stared down at this woman he hardly knew, he felt something tighten in his gut. It was all he could do not to reach out and pull her into him; his arms ached to hold her, and he wanted to bury his face in her hair. Her lips were parted, and he thought that never had a woman's mouth looked so desirable to him. It was an effort to concentrate on what she was saying.

Keeley didn't know what was happening to her. The entire night had been an experience she wouldn't forget; stark and vivid images of Gabe's film still burned behind her eyes. But it wasn't the film that was making her feel this way now; as she looked up at Gabe, the longing to move into his arms was almost unbearable. She wanted to pull his head down to hers, to feel the warmth of his lips, to see if the hard beating of his heart matched the pounding of hers. Gabe had touched something, some hard little knot inside her, and it was melting before her eyes.

"Forget the film," he muttered. Tentatively, he reached up and touched her face. Her skin was so soft. . . . With an effort, he jerked his thoughts away. "I want to see you again," he said hoarsely, his voice sounding as strange as he felt himself. "But Larry is offering me another assignment, and I'll be leaving as soon as I take care of some business in California." His eyes searched her face. "Can I call you?"

Keeley wanted to say no, to tell him she didn't have time for him—for anyone. But she couldn't make herself say the words, and she knew, suddenly and without equivocation, that if Valeska hadn't been home, she would have invited him in.

What's happening to me? she asked herself in a panic. *I don't even know him!*

But it wasn't true, she knew that even as she thought the words. She did know Gabe; she had always known him.

"Yes," she whispered, unable to take her eyes from his face. She wanted with all her heart to reach up and put her arms around his neck, but she knew that if she did, she'd no longer be balancing on the precipice; she'd fall right off. "You can call me . . . anytime."

Gabe looked as if he wanted to say something more, but like her, he didn't trust himself either. "Good," he said awkwardly. He stood there a moment longer, then he lifted his hand slightly and turned to go down the stairs.

Gabe went down four steps before he turned back. Keeley stood at the head of the landing, holding her breath. In two steps, he was back again, reaching out to pull her fiercely to him. She met him halfway, and when they kissed, Keeley could have sworn she heard two cymbals meeting, a clash of triumphant sweet sound that was almost as sweet as the taste of his lips on her mouth.

Gabe was breathing harshly when he pulled away; his eyes looked dazed. Staring down at her, he muttered, "I thought I could leave without kissing you. What a fool I was." He searched her face. "Don't forget me," he said, and was gone before she could answer.

Keeley waited until the taxi disappeared before going inside. Locking the door behind her, she rested her hot forehead against the wood for a moment, still feeling shaky.

Forget you? she thought. She'd sooner forget her own being.

CHAPTER NINE

When the phone rang early in the morning, Nigel rolled over and jammed the pillow over his head. The bedroom draperies in his fourth-floor apartment on Sixty-fourth Street had been pulled tight, and the room was nearly black as night. He had no idea what time it was, but it had to be an ungodly hour, not fit for man or beast. He had no intention of talking to anyone, and he was just falling back asleep when the phone rang again, jarring him to the bone.

"Answer that, for God's sake!" he implored the woman sharing his bed. "Tell whoever it is that I'm not here!"

Mercifully, the ringing stopped. Dimly, he heard her answer, then, just as he was drifting off again, she poked him in the ribs.

"I think you'd better take it," she said. "It's Manfred Rosser."

Manfred Rosser was one of his backers, a businessman whose secret dream had been to be a Broadway star. But since even he admitted that he was much more talented at making money than he was as a song and dance man, Rosser had resigned himself to financing shows instead. He and Nigel went back a long way, and he rarely interfered unless things were serious. If he was calling now, it had to be important. Muttering, Nigel rolled over, jerked his eye mask off his face, and took the phone from Carlotte's hand.

"What do you want, Manny?" he said hoarsely. He was never at his best in the morning, and when he glanced with one eye toward the luminous dial on the bedside clock, he wanted to curse. It was only ten o'clock; no one in his right mind was up at this hour.

"Good morning, Nigel," Rosser said calmly. He knew Nigel's habits, and he apologized. "I'm sorry to be calling so early, but I have some . . . bad news."

"Bad news?" Nigel sat up, trying to clear his head. He'd had a hunch this was coming; he just hadn't expected it so soon. Frowning fiercely, he made a terrible grimace to wake himself up. "What kind of bad news?"

"I think you know," Manny replied. "Look, the group is meeting at two, and I'd like you to be here. I know it's short notice, but Raleigh just got back into town, and he has to leave again tonight for his home in California. Something about a movie deal. Do you think you can make it?"

It sounded like a question, but Nigel knew it was more a summons. Raleigh Quinn was a real estate developer in Southern California who, like Manny, had always had a yen for show business. He'd been another of Nigel's backers, but lately he'd turned his attention more and more toward Hollywood. Things must be serious if Quinn had made a special trip. Usually it was just the two of them, old friends Nigel and Manny, going over expenses. If the big guns were being called in, he must have gone farther over budget than he'd realized. Deciding he couldn't deal with all the inevitable recriminations right now, he tried to stall. "I don't think so, Manny. Two o'clock is inconvenient as hell. We've got rehearsal this afternoon."

Rosser was his neutral best. "Another item we have to discuss," he said smoothly, giving Nigel no room for argument. "I promise it won't take long. Shall we expect you at two, then?"

Nigel didn't like being backed into a corner, especially when his internal alarms were ringing all over the place. "If I *must*!" he exclaimed, feigning impatience when what he was starting to feel was fear. "Whatever it is, I might as well get it over with."

"Thank you, Nigel," Manny said mildly. "I knew we could count on you."

Rosser broke the connection with a tiny click, but Nigel wasn't so cavalier. He slammed the receiver into the cradle with such force that the entire instrument jumped out of his hand, falling to the floor. It landed with a discordant ring, making him feel both foolish and furious.

"Carlotte!" he shouted. "Carlotte, where are you?"

As soon as she had handed over the phone, Carlotte had gotten up and wandered, naked, into the luxurious master bath. She'd started to run a tub and didn't hear him over the roar of the water.

"Damn it to hell!" Nigel exclaimed in frustration. Leaning forward, he saw her standing in front of the sink, staring at herself in the mirror, and at the sight he paused. The bank of lights flanking each side of the big bathroom mirror pinned her mercilessly in a bright spotlight.

She looks old! he thought, as though seeing for the first time the growing bags under her dark eyes and the lines creeping up around her mouth. At forty, she was five years younger than he, and her figure wasn't as tight as it had once been. Her waist had thickened, and she had developed—there was no other word for it, he thought with alarm—a paunch. Fat dimpled her thighs, her breasts had begun to sag, and she looked, Nigel thought, like a hag. They had been lovers for five years, a record in this business, but as he stared at his mistress, he felt fear rise like an acid tide. Do I look like that? he wondered, and cringed.

A face flashed into his mind. His first thought was, She's too young, even for me. But the more he thought about it, the more enticing the idea came to be. He hadn't realized it until now, but he'd been wanting a change. It would make him feel younger; it would help him forget the disappointments of the past few years. He could leave it all behind and start again.

Thoughtfully, he sat back among the pillows to ponder the idea of taking a new mistress. Picturing the show and the two songs from it that brought the house down every night, he knew the one he was thinking of definitely had talent; there was no doubt about that. Every time Valeska sang either of the numbers, the audience changed; he could feel it. He'd been in the business a long time; he could read audiences like a book. As *Dan Tucker* limped along, he'd thanked his lucky stars every night that at least the show had those two songs.

He'd also been in the business long enough to realize that what *Tucker* needed was more of the same. He'd changed everything he could think of, and it still wasn't working. He closed his eyes. Barry wasn't much help these days, buried at the bottom of a bottle when he was most needed, apparently not giving a damn that he was pissing whatever was left of his talent right down the drain. But that was about to change, too, Nigel decided. It had to, if either the show—or, more eloquently, its director—was to survive.

Throwing back the black satin comforter, Nigel got out of bed. Now that he had decided, he had to think of a way to implement his plan. He straightened proudly. At forty-five, he still had the old charisma, the charm that had stood him in such good stead. He had always been a ladies' man, and even he couldn't deny that when he wanted to, he could still summon the touch. It wouldn't exactly be child's play, and the girl was only in her early twenties, but so what? She was talented, and under his direction, she'd go far. He wasn't taking advantage; it would be to their mutual benefit. For the first time in days, he laughed in delight. Yes, indeed, this could be the solution to all his problems. He could hardly wait.

"What are you laughing at, Nigel?"

Calling from the depths of her bubble bath, Carlotte interrupted his thoughts. He reached for his robe at the end of his bed, but he turned at the sound of her voice. He'd forgotten Carlotte, he realized. He had to think of what to say to her. He was just starting for the bathroom when he caught sight of his reflection in the cheval mirror.

Frowning, he leaned closer to the mirror. Would he need surgery soon? he wondered, peering intently at his face. He lifted his chin and stretched his throat before deciding he still looked okay. Not like Barry, who seemed old now, used up. Barry was two years younger than he, but he looked like an old man. It was all the drinking, Nigel thought. It marked a person, and it had marked Barry—in his blood-shot eyes, in lines in his forehead and around his mouth. He'd known Barry a long time; they had been through a lot together, but lately the conviction had been growing in him that they'd come to a parting of the ways.

He didn't want to think about Barry. Stepping back, he pulled in his gut. He'd never had a weight problem, but lately, he had to admit, Carlotte wasn't the only one developing a paunch. So far it wasn't too bad, but if it got any worse, he definitely would consider a nip and tuck.

"What did Manny want?" Carlotte called from the bathroom.

The question reminded him of his summons this afternoon, and he frowned. "He wants me to meet him at two."

Carlotte had been around a long time, too. In the old days, she'd been his lead singer, but lately he'd had to relegate her to minor roles and bit parts. He hadn't said it was because of her age or her declining voice, but they both knew it was just a matter of time before she'd be out altogether. Like Barry, though, she was a part of his clinging past that he had to decide about sooner or later.

"Is it trouble?" she asked.

Taking his time to answer, Nigel belted his robe around his middle. He didn't want to discuss it with her, not until he'd seen Manny and Raleigh and heard what they had to say. It might not be as bad as he anticipated, and the last thing he needed to deal with today was Carlotte in one of her moods.

"Nothing I can't handle," he said nonchalantly, and went to see if his housekeeper had remembered to plug in the automatic coffee maker.

Alone in the bathroom, Carlotte slowly stood up in the tub. Foamy bits of bubbles from her bath salts clung to her body. Fifteen, twenty years ago—was it that long? she wondered dismally—she'd been the toast of Broadway. They were doing all the great musicals then—*Oklahoma, Carousel, Gypsy, Fiddler on the Roof.* What glory days those were! she thought, climbing out of the deep tub and reaching for a towel.

Her reflection in the wall of mirror opposite caught her eye again and she turned quickly away. When had she stopped looking *young*? she wondered, feeling tears sting her eyes.

An image of Valeska Szabo flashed into her mind just then, and she grimaced. Not a line in *her* face, Carlotte thought savagely, scrubbing at herself. No bags under her guileless blue eyes!

Tossing the towel aside, she reached for the silk wrap she'd brought in with her. The robe was too small; it wrinkled around her hips and emphasized her protruding stomach when she belted it around her waist. She thought of Valeska again, whom she had hated from the moment of her first audition and realized she was jealous. Well, she had good cause. Once *she* had sounded like that; once *hers* was the voice that had enthralled. Now she was getting old, past her prime. The ingenue roles that had become her trademark were getting harder and harder to come by, and soon she wouldn't be able to manage it even with all her stage makeup expertise—not when a silken-voiced, ethereal young thing like Valeska Szabo was waiting in the wings. Before long, not even the fact that she was Nigel's mistress could keep time at bay. Something had to be done, but what?

Fearfully, she glanced in the direction of the bedroom. She and Nigel had been lovers for a long time now, and she understood him well. He would never have admitted it, especially to her, but she knew he was feeling the pinch of years, too. Barry wasn't helping these days, either, soused to the gills all the time. Sometimes she didn't think he even knew what month it was, not to mention the day, and she couldn't remember when he had last written anything really good. He left it to Keeley Cochran now; everybody knew it, but with the show in trouble—and it was, she had to admit it—no one dared complain.

Carlotte's face changed again when she thought of Keeley Cochran. She disliked both Valeska and Miss Butter-would-melt-in-her-mouth Cochran, but of the two, she had to admit she feared Keeley the most. She had seen right through that ambitious little bitch the day she manipulated the audition, so petite and innocent, with her green eyes and expressive face. Carlotte had been furious at the way Keeley had taken over.

But she'd been forced to accept the situation, and now they were at this sorry state. She knew that Rosser's call this morning couldn't mean anything good. The others in the cast, the dewy-eyed, eager young wonders, who didn't want to know, and some of the old-timers who preferred to look the other way, might not accept it, but she'd been around too long not to know when they were dying. And if ever a show was in its death throes, it was *Dan Tucker*. She was only surprised that it had held on this long.

"But it's not my fault!" she said fiercely, turning to the mirror with her hands clenched. The strangest thing happened. Instead of seeing herself reflected there, she suddenly saw Valeska Szabo. Young and beautiful and so talented, Valeska's face seemed illuminated, as it always was when she sang; her long, pale blond hair falling like liquid gold nearly to her waist. In that odd moment, Carlotte had the weirdest feeling that if she just listened for a moment, she would hear Valeska's voice, as clear and pure as a mountain echo, right here in the bathroom. With a cry, she squeezed her eyes shut.

Nigel met with two of his backers—men who distinctly lacked vision—he fumed as he took a cab downtown, exactly at two. The taxi had barely come to a stop before he was out and striding into the forbidding gray-brick building on Lexington, and he was in such a state that he elbowed someone out of the way so he could get into the elevator first. As the conveyance bore him upward to the tenth floor, he felt like murdering the first person he came across. He knew what Manny and Raleigh were going to say, but on the way down he had decided he wouldn't give them a chance to complain about expenses. He had to make them understand that art had no price, and if they didn't agree, he'd walk out and do another show for someone else. This town didn't lack for people who made up with money what they lacked in artistic talent, he told himself haughtily. He'd find another backer before the day was out.

But to his dismay, four men, not two, were sitting around Manfred Rosser's football-sized conference table when he was ushered in by the secretary. He was so surprised to see them that he stopped a moment to assess the situation. Manny was at the head of the table, as always, Raleigh by his right hand. But across from Raleigh Quinn was Wayne Abscott, the backer from Texas, and next to him was that most dreaded of all creatures, Manny's accountant, Albert Sparks. Mustering all his composure, Nigel came into the room with a smile.

"Gentlemen," he said, as the secretary silently closed the door behind him.

"Hello, Nigel," Raleigh said. Nigel didn't like the look in his eye.

Wayne coughed.

Albert looked down at the ledgers in front of him, but Manny took charge. "Sit down, Nigel," he said. "There's no sense wasting time. We all know why we're here."

"Do we?" Nigel said, feigning innocence until he could get a feel for the group. "Perhaps you'd better enlighten me, then, Manny, because I really have no idea."

"Oh, come on, let's not play games here," Raleigh said impatiently. He glanced toward the head of the table. "You haven't told him?"

"Told me what?" Beginning to hear the clang of doom despite himself, Nigel looked from one to the other.

Manny nodded to his accountant, who cleared his throat. "As you're no doubt already aware, Mr. Aames," he began, "*Dan Tucker* has gone quite a bit over budget—"

"Yes, I'm aware of a dollar or so deficit," Nigel said. He'd decided just to brazen it out. What could they do to him, except close the show? He doubted they'd take such a drastic step. They'd already spent too much; it wouldn't make sense not to recoup the investment.

"It's more than a 'dollar or so,' " the accountant said severely. He glanced at his employer, who nodded for him to go on. "First, there is the matter of the time sheets—"

"A matter easily explained," Nigel said smoothly. "Things weren't going well, so we had to extend rehearsals slightly."

"Slightly? You're over three months on a four-month schedule. If the show was in trouble—"

"The show wasn't in any trouble!" Nigel said sharply. "We just needed more rehearsal time!"

Sparks intercepted another slight signal from the head of the table. Nodding, he said, "Very well, we'll leave the matter of the time sheets for moment. Why don't we go over the other expenses?"

"Fine," Nigel said, his voice clipped. He didn't like the way this was going at all. He'd expected trouble, but he'd never anticipated he'd be nickeled and dimed to death.

Sparks ignored his tone. "First, there's the matter of design—eight thousand. Then costumes, another eight thousand. Electrical *before* performance, four thousand; scenery construction at an appalling seventy-five thousand. We won't even go into expenses for the director—" Sparks glanced briefly up at Nigel, who glared back "—or cast, stage manager, musicians, etc. I will point out that the press agent—who, judging from the receipts, hasn't been doing his job—has received nearly two thousand. The script was fifteen hundred. With rehearsal hall and auditorium nearly ten thousand, along with twenty thousand for advertising and printing, and another ten thousand for orchestration, not to mention author's advances, equity bonds, rehearsal salaries, musicians, security, legal and audit fees, we're running close to—"

"Stop!" Nigel commanded. Imperiously he glanced around the table. "If I'd known that this meeting was going to turn into a grubby little penny-pinching session, I never would have come! Since when do we put a price on art?"

"Since you started running nearly three-quarters of a million dollars over budget," Manny said. He spoke calmly, but there was steel underlying his tone. Holding Nigel's eyes, he went on. "Now, we could probably absorb it if we thought there was a chance in hell that *Dan Tucker* would eventually be a hit. As you always say, sometimes a show just needs to find its audience. Well, I'm sorry, but I'm afraid this is one show that isn't going to have the luxury of doing that anymore. We called you here to tell you that we've decided to close it. Today."

Nigel couldn't believe it. Slowly, he rose from his chair. "You . . . you . . ." He was so outraged he could hardly speak. "Since when do you decide when to close a show, *especially* without discussing it with your director first?"

"I'm sorry," Manny said calmly. "But that's why we're here."

"To discuss it? It sounds to me that you've already decided!"

For the first time, Manny dropped his glance. Raleigh Quinn took over. "I'm sorry," he said, too. "But we're afraid your judgment was a little off in this case."

Nigel whirred toward him. "My judgment? What the hell do you know about my *judgment*?"

Reddening angrily, Raleigh started to tell him, but Manny lifted his hand. "I'm sorry, I think it would be best just to leave it. We all make mistakes—"

"*Dan Tucker* is not a mistake!"

Wayne Abscott, a big bull of a man who had made his money in Texas oil, interrupted in a drawl that—in Nigel's heightened state—made his skin crawl.

"It is from where ah'm sittin'," the Texan said. "And only a fool keeps puttin' good money down a rat hole, which is what that danged old show of yours is. Now you're just gonna have to accept it, Nige. We're gonna cut our losses and get out while the gettin's good. As my old daddy used to say—"

"I don't give a flying fuck what your *daddy* used to say!" Nigel shouted, beside himself. Turning his back on Abscott, he faced the head of the table again. Of all the men in the room besides himself, only Manny knew what it would really mean to him to close the show this soon. He didn't like to admit it, even to himself, but he'd had a string of failures these past ten years, and one more would . . . He didn't want to think about it. "Look, Manny," he said, trying not to sound as desperate as he was beginning to feel, "I know the show has a few problems—"

"A *few* problems?" Abscott snorted.

Nigel ignored him. "I can work it out. I just hired some new talent, and—"

"Ah, yes," Raleigh said. "The new singer, what's her name? Valeska Sawbo—"

"Szabo," Nigel said, dismissing Raleigh and Valeska with a brief motion of his hand. He looked at Manny again. "I wasn't talking about her. I was talking about a new songwriter named Keeley . . . Keeley Cochran. She's good, Manny, she really is. Even better than Barry, I think."

"Barry today, or Barry in the old days?" Raleigh asked.

Nigel wasn't sure how to phrase it. They all knew what Barry's problem was, and how it had affected his work, but only Nigel knew why. "Barry in any day," he said coldly. He could say what he liked about Barry, but that didn't mean anyone else could. Making a quick decision, he turned to Manny again. "If you want the truth, Keeley's the one who wrote the two hits from the show: 'Alone at the Dock,' and 'Guilty.' Now, I know—"

Raleigh leaned forward. "If she wrote those two songs," he said, "why did Barry get credit for the entire score?"

"Because she's a nobody, all right?" Nigel exclaimed, thinking that if Quinn interrupted him once more, he'd take him by the lapels and throw him against the wall. "Because she just came out from Hicksville, USA, and doesn't know her ass from a hole in the ground, all right? Because—"

Raleigh interrupted. "Or maybe it's because she's young and talented, and you decided to take advantage of her, could that be it?" He sat back disgustedly. "Somehow, it doesn't surprise me."

Nigel was furious. "Oh, don't come off all high and mighty with me, Quinn! We all know what *you* are, don't we? Raped any more meadowland for a new parking lot lately? Torn down some more old trees to build another mall?"

Raleigh half stood. "Now, that's—"

"Gentlemen, gentlemen," Manny said sharply. "Let's not allow ourselves to be distracted from the real issue, shall we?"

"We *shall* if the real issue is closing the show without cause," Nigel declared.

"The cause," Manny said with finality, "are the cost overruns balanced against receipts. The difference simply does not justify continuing on at this time with *Dan Tucker*."

There wasn't any more to say. Manny had spoken, and Nigel left the meeting in a rage that lasted all the way down in the elevator to the street, where he immediately broke into a cold sweat. Now what? he wondered, trying not to panic. Crowds of people swirled and eddied around him, everyone seemingly in a hurry, with purpose and someplace to go. As he looked about, he hated every person he saw. How could they all go about their puny little business, when he felt like slashing his wrists?

Like a beacon, a yellow taxi appeared on the street, and he was just lifting his hand to signal it when a matronly woman carrying several bags stepped out in front of him, hailing the cab herself. Nigel was so infuriated that he practically pushed her aside when the taxi swerved over toward the curb; reaching for the handle, he opened the door and jumped in himself.

"You son of a bitch!" the woman yelled.

Nigel hardly heard her. He had more important things to worry about than being rude to some stranger. He needed the cab more than she did, and when the driver turned around, he surprised himself by giving Barry's address.

At the moment, Barry lived in a loft in SoHo, over one of the many cast-iron row houses that dated from the early nineteenth century. Nigel, whose own apartment uptown was luxurious and cozily crammed with knickknacks and bric-a-brac and memorabilia from all his years on Broadway, had never been comfortable at Barry's; all the empty space, so prized by artists willing to ignore the noise of trucks and loading docks in the low-rent neighborhoods, seemed cold and sterile to him, the cast-iron columns and pressed-tin ceilings—a survival from warehouse days—more prisonlike than avant-garde. But then, Barry didn't really care where he lived, as long as he had a bottle for company.

The thought made him angry again, and his expression was grim as he paid the cab and went up to confront his songwriter. Predictably, these days, Barry was hung over, but at least he was home when Nigel banged on the door.

"Hold your horses, I'm coming," Barry called from the other side when Nigel kept pounding. His face pinched, he opened the door. When he saw who was there, he just looked at Nigel for a moment, then he said, "Oh, it's you." Leaving Nigel standing outside, he turned and staggered away.

Nigel came in, slamming the door behind him. "Are you sober?"

Barry had gone to one of only two or three pieces of real furniture in the entire loft—the couch. Throwing himself down, he put his arm over his eyes. "Why?"

Nigel stared at him for a moment, trying to control himself. When Barry was like this, he felt like lifting him up bodily and shaking him until his teeth rattled. Not trusting himself to answer, he went toward the kitchen—or what passed for the kitchen, a line of countertop surrounding the seldom-used stove—and reached for the coffeepot. Viciously, he thrust it under the tap to fill it with water, then he opened all the cupboards one after the other, searching for the coffee. After he'd slammed the fourth cupboard door shut, Barry hauled himself to a sitting position and peered over the back of the couch.

"What are you *looking* for?" he said, holding his head. "Jesus, every noise is like a cannon going off behind my eyes!"

"That's *your* problem," Nigel said pitilessly, spying a jar of instant coffee hidden behind an empty fifth of vodka. It wasn't what he'd been looking for, but it would have to do. He wanted Barry sober for this—or as sober as he was going to get—and after he made the coffee, he took it over to the couch. "Here," he said, shoving the cup at his composer. "Drink it."

Barry glanced down, made a horrible face, and tried to push it away. "I don't want it," he whimpered. "What I need is a little hair of the dog—"

"What you need is a kick in the ass," Nigel said in a rage. The urge to pick Barry up and throw him out the window was almost overpowering; he couldn't reconcile the disheveled, stubble-faced, bleary-eyed Barry Archer today with the eager young talent who had composed and created such memorable songs as "Mystified" and "Cold Winter Nights." Where did it go wrong? he wondered, just for a moment. Then his expression hardened again. He knew where it had gone wrong.

"Drink it," he said again, forcing himself over to the window to stare down at the busy street below while Barry—hopefully—pulled himself together.

He was still there when Barry cleared his throat. "They closed the show, didn't they?" he asked.

Nigel turned around. "What made you guess."

Barry flinched at his tone. "You blame me, don't you?" he said plaintively.

"No," Nigel said coldly, "I blame myself."

"What?"

"I blame myself because I hired you on in the first place," Nigel said, his rage growing again with every word. "I knew you were down in the bottle again, but like a fool, I went ahead anyway." He stopped to control himself. When he went on, his voice had become cruelly mocking. " 'Just give me a chance, Nigel—for old times' sake. Just a chance. I promise I won't let you down.' "

Barry dropped his eyes, but unable to help himself, Nigel went on. "Remember who said that to me, Barry? Do you remember? 'Just give me a chance, Nigel. I'll write a score that'll put *Dan Tucker* right over the top.' Now, who said that to me, can you think? I thought it was you, but it must have been someone else."

"It was me, but Nigel—"

"No buts!" Nigel shouted so suddenly that Barry cringed back against the couch. "No more excuses, no more nothing! As far as I'm concerned, you've had it. You're finished, washed up. Of no use to yourself or anybody else."

"I can fix the show, Nigel, I know I can. All we need is a little more time."

"We don't have any more time!"

"But you can talk to the backers," Barry said desperately. "They'll listen to you—they always do."

"They didn't today," he said flatly.

"But if I promise to stay away from the booze—"

"You? Don't make me laugh. You sang that old tune before, and I believed you, but not anymore. Besides, I've got Keeley now, and we both know she's as good—probably better—than you ever were. So, good-bye, Barry, and don't come around again. I won't be so kind next time."

Nigel started toward the door, but Barry got up shakily from the couch. "So," he said. "Now that you've found someone to take my place, you're going to throw me away like an old sock, is that it? You and I go back a long way, you know." Nigel turned, and their eyes met. "A long way," Barry repeated.

"That was then," Nigel said, after a moment. He broke eye contact, and his voice turned harsh. "And this is now."

"So it's every man—or woman—for himself, is that it?"

"Something like that."

Suddenly Barry's brave facade crumpled. "You can't mean it, not after all we've been through together," he said desperately. "Remember *Torchlight*? And how about *Miss Fortune*? Those were both hits, Nigel, and we had a string of others. How can you forget—"

"I haven't forgotten anything," Nigel interrupted angrily. He'd said what he'd come to say, and he just wanted to get out of there. "But those shows are gone now, and I'm thinking of the future."

Barry looked at him bitterly. "A future with a new songwriter, right?"

He went to the door. "You said it, I didn't."

As if impelled, Barry took a step forward. "Just remember I know who you really are, Nigel, and what you've done to get there."

Slowly, Nigel turned around again. Holding Barry's bloodshot eyes, he said, "Don't threaten me, Barry. You spoke of *Torchlight* a moment ago. Well, I remember what happened during the running of that show, just like you do. Do you want to talk about Leo Sargeant? Is that it?"

Barry paled. Clutching the back of the couch, he said, "You . . . wouldn't."

"You don't think so? I will if you try to carry out your puny threat, Barry. *You* don't have any proof—"

"Don't be too sure of that."

Nigel felt a flash of fear before he caught himself. He forced himself to laugh. "Good old Barry, I'll give you *A* for effort on that one. You had me going for a minute, I'll admit, but we both know there's no proof. It was stolen, remember? You told me so yourself, after the break-in." His face hardened. "But what *I* have on *you* wasn't. And I'm sure I can find one or two people who would like to know what happened to old Leo. So, you tell me. Is that what you want?"

Their glances met again, but Barry couldn't hold the stare. His shoulders slumping in defeat, he said, "No. It's not what I want."

"All right, then," Nigel said, reaching for the door once more. He opened it but turned around to say one final thing. "I'm sorry it turned out this way."

Barry looked at him acridly. "Yeah, sure."

He was already reaching for the bottle he'd left on the coffee table as Nigel walked out.

Out on the street again, Nigel decided to walk a few blocks before he caught a cab home. It was unusual for him, for he loathed walking anywhere, but he was too agitated to sit in a taxi right now. He didn't want to think about the scene with Barry, but it kept running in his mind like a bad play until he thought he'd lose his mind. Cursing aloud, he caught the startled glance of someone passing by and knew he had to get a grip on himself.

All right, he told himself, *Dan Tucker* was dead; he had to go on. The show hadn't been right for him. It was obvious now, but he wasn't finished, not by a long shot. There were other projects more suitable to his talents; all he had to do was look around.

He'd find new backers; he always had. On Broadway, there were always would-bes and hopefuls who fulfilled their stage dreams by funding shows. So he'd had a few flops these past few years, so what? Everyone hit slumps now and then; the point was, now that he'd finally had it out with Barry, he'd be like a new man. It would be like starting over again.

And best of all, he had new talent to choose from. Which would it be? he pondered. Keeley or Valeska? He couldn't have them both; he had to select carefully. Carlotte's face flashed into his mind, but he thrust the image away. He'd brush the slate clean, get rid of her, too. He had to, if he wanted to survive. And he did want to; he always had, hadn't he?

He still hadn't decided exactly how to go about staging his new plan when he finally hailed a cab at the end of the block. But as he climbed in and gave his address, he felt better than he had in months. The future spread out before him, he thought, and the past was just that. Of his lifelong friend and partner, Barry Archer, steadily drinking himself into oblivion in a SoHo loft ... well, he'd tried his best. And as for Carlotte, waiting anxiously back at his apartment, she'd just have to understand things had changed. He'd known for a long while what he needed to do; the closing of the show had given him the impetus he needed. It was time to move on, and once he took care of a few loose ends, he intended to do just that.

CHAPTER TEN

Dan Tucker closed without notice not long after its New York opening. Barry Archer disappeared the very next day, leaving his loft and all his possessions behind. Keeley didn't know which event distressed her more. When a week passed, and then another, and another, without word from him, she went to Nigel. As she'd tried to explain to Valeska, Barry had been more than her mentor; he was her friend and she was concerned about him.

"Where could he have gone, and why hasn't he come back?"

she demanded of Nigel, who denied any knowledge. "Why didn't he let anyone know where he was going?"

"How should I know?" Nigel said impatiently, dismissing her concern with a wave of his hand. "Why should I care? Barry walked out on the show, remember? He left before we closed, so to hell with him."

"But—"

"Look, I've got enough problems. In case you've forgotten, we're all out of work right now. If you're so worried, go check his apartment. I don't care, just get out of here."

But Barry wasn't at the loft; Keeley already knew it. It had been almost a month since he'd left, and she had gone there every week to see if he'd come back. No one had heard from him—not his neighbors, nor the owners of the little café down the street, where he'd gone to eat, nor even his landlord, who would have tossed all his stuff into the street if she hadn't pleaded with him to let her put it in storage. She was so worried by then that she went to the police.

The police weren't much help, either. All they did was put Barry's name on a missing persons list. But with the history she'd been forced to give them about his drinking, they didn't hold out much hope.

"If he's not on vacation—" the sergeant started to say.

"He wouldn't leave, not without telling someone," Keeley insisted.

The policeman shrugged. "Then he's either bumming around somewhere, or he's de—I mean, well, you know what I mean," he said. Seeing Keeley's stricken expression, he shrugged. "It's the times, you know. I'm sorry, but this is a big city, and things . . . happen."

She didn't want to believe something so awful had happened to Barry, but as time passed, she had to accept that, for whatever reason, he was gone. When she wasn't worried, she felt hurt. She was sure he'd had a compelling reason to disappear, but if something hadn't happened to him, why hadn't he said good-bye to her? She'd thought they were close; they had spent a lot of time together during *Dan Tucker*, and he'd taught her so much. She wanted to learn more, but more than that, she missed him—missed his dry wit when he was sober, missed all the little nuggets of information he casually tossed off even when he was sloshed.

"A songwriter has to stage each number to the last detail," he'd said once. "We have to be able to tell the director and the choreographer exactly where the character is when he starts the song, what he does by the second quatrain, where he goes when he sings the third quatrain, and where he ends up in the fourth. Plot every detail, Keeley, even though they may not use it."

"But I'm not a stager," she had protested.

"Then learn," Barry had said. "There's nothing worse than having a choreographer complain that he or she can't choreograph a number because it's too long or too short. What are you going to do if they say something has to have eight more bars? Or six less? Suddenly there's a hole in the middle of your song where everybody just stands around looking awkward."

"So, what do you do?"

"Allow for every single thing that's going to happen on the stage," he'd said. Then he winked. "It took me years to learn that, but I'm giving it to you for free 'cause you're such a nice kid."

He'd helped her again one night when they were working late and the subject of collaboration came up. Curious, she had asked him why he rarely collaborated with anyone.

"Because I believe that when music and lyrics are done by different people, the best way for the lyricist to collaborate with the composer is by being in the same room with him," Barry had answered, then he laughed. "And no one has ever wanted to be alone with me that long."

She laughed with him, but then she turned serious again. "I mean it, Barry. Stop joking for once."

Shrugging, he'd assumed his "teaching" stance, one hand on his middle, the other on his hip. "All right, let me tell you a little inside stuff. I learned from Oscar Hammerstein and Cole Porter that when I'm writing a lyric, I have to get a rhythm even if I don't have a melody in my head. Sometimes I make one up for the moment, if I have to, just to get the thing going. Now Hammerstein, as you may or may not know, almost always wrote to well-known tunes—" he grinned "—he just wouldn't tell Rodgers what they were. But Cole Porter, on the other hand, was able to think up melodies, and he always wrote knowing exactly what the rhythmic structure of the melody was, even if he didn't know the notes yet. That's generally what I do when I'm working on a lyric." He smiled. "Until I ran into you, I found it easier to do by myself."

Embarrassed and pleased by the compliment, Keeley had blushed. "Tell me more," she had begged, not realizing how it sounded until he laughed.

Now, months later, she had begun working with Nigel on another musical, this one with a rollicking libretto and an even
livelier score, called *Out on the Klondike*. Keeley remembered
every word Barry had said, all the help, all the advice. As time
went on, she found she missed him more, not less.

To her dismay, she also missed Gabe Tyrell. Months ago, he
had called her from California to tell her he had accepted a permanent position with the wildlife foundation. He hadn't had
much time; the IZF wanted him to leave immediately for a new
assignment in Spain, and after that, he was on his way to India.

"It sounds so exciting," she'd said, too aware of the rapid
beating of her heart while talking to him. She'd felt a little
breathless when she realized it was Gabe on the phone and despised herself for it even as she eagerly reached for the receiver.
Even then, she couldn't prevent herself from asking when he'd
be back in the States.

"Why?" he asked teasingly. "Are you going to miss me?"

She could feel herself blushing. Damn it, she thought, she
would miss him. "Not really," she made herself say nonchalantly. "I'll be pretty busy myself."

"I read in *Variety* about the show closing. I'm sorry, Keeley.
I can imagine what a disappointment it was."

She was surprised. "You read the trades?"

She could hear the laughter in his voice. "Only since I met
you. I have to keep up on what's happening to you, don't I?"

"Do you?" The words were out before she knew it.

The laughter vanished from his voice. Quietly, he said, "I always want to know where you are and what you're doing,
Keeley. I knew from the moment I met you that you'd go far,
and I intend to keep track of you. I won't let you get away, and
that's a promise."

"Then you'll have the advantage, Gabe, because with your
new job, I'll never know where you are."

"Oh, you'll know," he answered softly. "I'll make sure of
that, believe me."

Now it was September, and Gabe was God knew where.
Keeley often wished she'd gone with him out into the bush, for
working with Nigel on the new show was exhausting. He had
terrorized no less than four songwriters and composers, and now
she was the only one left. As everyone had always told her, she
had confidence to burn, but she was keenly aware what a big
difference there was between assisting a composer like Barry
and taking on the writing of an entire score herself.

"Look, you've already written six songs and the overture, you'll do just fine," Nigel had assured her.

She didn't want to do *fine*; she wanted to be a success. But even *she* knew she didn't have enough experience yet. "Will you be able to find backers, with an unknown composer doing the score?" she asked Nigel one day.

Smiling, he touched her cheek. He was making quite a few of those gestures lately, she realized. She wasn't sure what to think about it. "Why don't you write the music, and leave all the other grubby details to me?" he told her indulgently, and went out to lunch.

Wondering if she'd ever be so blasé, Keeley went back to the keyboard. After months of hard work, they finally had a professional group together, and with Keeley playing the songs she'd written, the actors read the script. Now all that remained before the go-ahead for casting and rehearsal was the backers' audition—a formality, Nigel said, since he already had the commitments.

The thought of attending a backers' audition as the show's sole composer struck terror even into Keeley's confident soul, and she worked harder than ever.

"You're going to make yourself sick," Valeska said worriedly, after Keeley had again worked all night. "Please, please, stop and get some rest."

But she couldn't rest, not until the backers' audition was over. She didn't sleep for weeks before the fateful day, for even though Nigel had only requested half a dozen songs that would cover all the colors of the show, she still didn't have a choral piece.

"Don't worry so, Keeley," Nigel had said, indulgent as he seemed to be with her lately. "I never believed a backers' audition should go beyond forty-five minutes, and we'll have talk between the songs so they have a chance to absorb them. We won't need a choral piece yet. Trust me."

But in her exhaustion, she reflected that the only person she had really trusted was Barry, who had vanished out of her life. Barry would know what to do here . . . and here . . . and here . . . she'd think mournfully, studying the script, the score, Nigel's cryptic notations, the choreographer's notes.

But Barry wasn't here to help her, and just when she thought she was going to lose her mind, Gabe called from Bangkok. The connection was terrible; she could hardly hear him. But even the sound of his voice made her feel weak, and she clutched the phone as though it were a lifeline.

"Oh, Gabe, it's wonderful of you to call!" she exclaimed, when she realized it was he. "It's been a long time!"

"Did you miss me?" he asked, his voice warm and teasing even so far away.

She was so happy to hear from him that she laughed gaily. "I haven't had time to miss you, you conceited thing! I've been working my fingers to the bone while you've been gallivanting around the world having the time of your life."

"Well, I have to admit, it has been fun. But I did ask you to come with me, remember? You were the one who insisted she had a show to do."

"Yes, more fool I."

He laughed at her desolate tone. "You can't tell me you don't love it. How's it going, anyway? Are you knocking 'em dead yet?"

Immediately, she felt deflated. "Not yet," she said. "We've got a backers' audition soon, and that will tell the tale."

His voice sounded rich with promise. "Well, like the rest of the world, I have confidence in you, Keeley. I know you'll be a success."

Remembering with what confidence she'd said those exact words only a few months ago, she said plaintively, "Thanks, but at this point, I'm just hoping to get through the audition without making a fool of myself."

"You'll never do that, darlin'," he said. "I'll make book on it."

"Thanks," she said gratefully. Then, before she knew it, she was adding, "And Gabe, be careful, will you?"

"Always," he agreed. "You, too."

Two days later, Keeley went to the backers' audition with her heart in her throat.

The audition was held in a rehearsal hall down on Nineteenth Street. She and Nigel and the two singers he'd hired arrived first, but they were just taking off their coats when four men with suits and big wallets arrived. Keeley just had time to glance at the metal chairs surrounding the battered piano in the corner of the room before Nigel was introducing her, and somehow she made herself smile and nod. She had no idea what she said to the men, but it must have been all right because they nodded politely in return. On shaking legs she made it over to the piano, and she even managed to prop her music on the stand without dropping it before she began. Things seemed more ominous when she caught a quick glance between two of the men as they took their places. It was plain to see that they thought she was a little young and much too unknown to be carrying the entire music for the show on her inexperienced shoulders, and for an instant, her courage faltered.

Then she recalled something Barry had said. "Don't let them intimidate you," he'd told her. "Backers' auditions are hell, but remember: if they could write the music, they would. Since they can't, they have to pay you to do it. So you go out there and do what you do best."

The memory restored her confidence. Reminding herself that she had worked long and hard on the music, and that Nigel had faith in her, she took a deep breath and began.

Almost before she knew it, the ordeal was over. Between the first and second songs, the solemn faces of the backers relaxed; by the third and fourth numbers, they were glancing approvingly at one another. By the time Keeley played the last note, they were all smiling. Even Keeley knew they were a success. That night, she took Valeska out to dinner—a real dinner, in a real restaurant—to celebrate, and not even the later run-through for the dreaded 'theater-party' ladies, the women who book the shows and sell the advance tickets, scared her. By then, she told Valeska with a laugh, she was starting to feel like an old hand.

After a month of rehearsal, *Out on the Klondike* opened in Philadelphia. Carlotte Basile played the role of Sophie, the woman who goes to Alaska in the early 1900s to find a husband for her daughter. But it was Valeska who won the juicier role of Garnett, the rebellious daughter who was having too much fun, in a country overrun by men, to settle down in marriage.

The reviews weren't good; they were fabulous. Once again, Valeska's singing and Keeley's music took center stage. Keeley got credit this time, and she was walking on air.

"Sings like a nightingale" said one review of Valeska. "A new Jenny Lind," rhapsodized another.

And of the music, a famous critic for the *New York Times* said it all: "Once in a decade, or two, or three, a composer comes along who knocks us all out of our complacency. Cochran's score is sheer delight, unexpected, delicious, and oh, so alive. I haven't taken a turn around the floor in years, but tonight she made me want to dance in the aisles."

Of Carlotte there was, mercifully, little mention. Reviews for her Sophie ranged from kind to condescending, and Keeley was

worried as she and Valeska got ready for the preview party a
week after the show opened. Until she had realized that Nigel
and Carlotte were lovers, she hadn't understood why he continued casting the older woman as his star.

In the role of Sophie, the woman who was desperately—and
comically—trying to marry off her daughter, Carlotte could have
made the transition to more mature parts easily—if she hadn't
tried to overshadow Valeska, who was on stage with her for almost the entire show. Fortunately, Valeska's performance and
those of the other actors diluted Carlotte's overacting and shrill,
strident voice; in fact, Keeley was relieved the first night, and
thereafter, that the audience seemed to believe Carlotte was playing it that way on purpose. But they were treading a fine line,
and she wondered if Nigel would reconsider his casting and give
the role of Sophie to someone else.

"Oh, I hope so," Valeska said with a shudder, when Keeley
mentioned it as they left for the party. "She pulls my hair so
hard when we do the scene in the second act. And did you notice that she stepped all over me vocally when we sang our duet
tonight?"

Keeley had heard it, and she was already trying to work out
a way to change the song so it wouldn't happen again. "Yes, I
noticed," she said grimly, as they caught a cab. "But don't
worry. I'm going to rewrite the song."

Valeska was a vision in blue sequins tonight. Her mother had
sent the dress for her first preview party and as Keeley looked
down at her own black velvet—purchased from a department
store this time, instead of a secondhand shop, she felt a little
drab. Then she smiled. Valeska should shine, she thought. After
all, she was a star tonight.

Impulsively, as the cab pulled up in front of the hotel, Valeska
grabbed Keeley's hand and gave it a hard squeeze. "I'm so
proud of you, Keeley!"

"Me!"

"Yes, you, silly. Oh, don't look so surprised, of course I'm
proud. None of us would be here tonight if it weren't for your
music!"

Keeley smiled as she paid the cab driver and they got out. "I
think Nigel and the librettist and the rest of the cast and crew,
not the mention the backers, and God knows who else, might
have something to say about that."

Valeska tossed her long, blond hair as they went inside. "Say
what you like, but *I* saw how hard you worked on the score.

Without your music to drive us forward, we'd just be so many lumps on the stage."

"Thanks," she said, "but—"

She didn't have time to say more. The noise drifting out into the corridor from the ballroom increased as they approached, and they paused in the doorway, agog at the sight of the cast and crew and a host of other people in party dress milling about inside.

"Do you know any of these people?" Valeska asked, her eyes wide.

Keeley glanced around. Then she saw Nigel, and beside him, Tommy Snyder, the choreographer, and Bert Banks, the lighting director.

"Yes, there's Nigel," she said.

Valeska straightened. Eagerly, she asked, "Where?"

Keeley pointed before she realized she'd heard something in Val's voice. "What—"

"There he is!" Valeska exclaimed, spying Nigel at last. Hurriedly, she turned to Keeley. "Excuse me, I've got to—" She stopped when she saw Keeley's face. "What is it?"

"I don't know," Keeley said. Slowly, she looked from Valeska to Nigel, and then back again. An idea was forming in her mind, and she didn't like it. "Why are you so interested in Nigel?" she asked.

To her surprise, Valeska blushed furiously. "I'm not." She saw the look in Keeley's eyes. Sighing, she said, "Oh, all right. You're going to guess anyway, so I might as well tell you."

But Keeley had already guessed. Incredulously, she exclaimed, "You're not in love with Nigel!"

Valeska's blush deepened; embarrassed and flustered, she put her hands up to her face. "Now, Keeley, I know what you're thinking—"

"No, you don't! You don't have the slightest idea what I'm thinking!" Realizing they were still standing in the doorway, she quickly drew Valeska to one side, behind a potted palm. "Are you crazy? Nigel Aames is twice your age! But even if he weren't—"

To her dismay, Valeska wasn't in the mood to face facts. Dreamily, she said, "Yes, I know, but things like that don't matter when you're in love."

"In love!" Keeley couldn't believe they were having this conversation. When had this happened? Why hadn't she seen it? Accusingly, she said, "Why didn't you tell me?"

Valeska glanced away. "Well, you've been so busy—"

"That's not it," Keeley said. Grabbing Valeska's arm, she looked her in the eye. "You didn't want to tell me because you knew what I'd say! *That's* it, isn't it?"

Valeska tried to pull her arm away. "As a matter of fact, it is," she said petulantly. "And I was right, wasn't I? Look how you're acting right now, Keeley. You'd think that I—"

Struck by a sudden awful thought, Keeley clutched her more tightly. "You and Nigel haven't—"

"No, no, of course not!" Valeska said, reddening again. Then she lifted her chin defiantly. "But if we had, I don't think it's any of your business!"

Keeley controlled herself with an effort. "This is crazy, Val. You don't have any idea what you might be getting involved in."

"Oh, I get it. You want him yourself, right?"

"No!" Keeley was horrified even at the idea. She was even more appalled at the expression in her friend's eyes.

"You know, now that I think about it, you've been spending an awful lot of time with Nigel," Valeska said accusingly. "Maybe you're not all that innocent yourself!"

"What!"

Valeska suddenly became angry. Blue sparks shot from her eyes, competing with the glitter of sequins on her dress. "Despite what you think, Keeley, you don't know everything," she said furiously. "Just butt out, all right? This is none of your business."

Before Keeley could collect herself enough to reply, Valeska turned and walked into the ballroom. Staring after her friend, she felt as if she had just been slapped. What was wrong with her? she wondered. Valeska never acted like this!

Her eyes went to Nigel, handsome and charming in his evening clothes. Flushed with success, he looked like he was having the time of his life. Keeley's eyes narrowed. She had never been attracted to Nigel herself, but when he looked like he did tonight, she could see why Valeska might be. Surrounded by people, he looked every inch the successful Broadway director, and she suddenly realized that, seen in this new light, he could be father figure, mentor, teacher, and guide. He seemed to be all things tonight, and she had a difficult time looking away.

The noise in the ballroom seemed to have increased while she was pondering the change in her friend. She couldn't stand here all night, so she went inside. In one corner, Valeska was already surrounded by admirers of her own, and Keeley's eyes narrowed again. Val was laughing and smiling as though they hadn't quarreled, and she was so aggravated at the sight that she snagged a waiter bearing a tray of champagne as he went by. The first glass tasted so good, she promptly took another. And another. She rarely drank because she hated the feeling of losing control, but every time she thought of the fight she'd had with Val, she felt angry all over again. Damn it, she reflected boozily, this was supposed to be her night of triumph. With all the praises for her score, and four of the songs in the show already being singled out, she'd felt she was finally on her way. It was what she had been dreaming about all her life, and after another quick glance in Valeska's direction, she decided that no one was going to spoil it.

Determined to have a good time, she lost track of how much she had to drink; congratulations seemed to flow like the champagne, each one making her feel a little more giddy. Waves of people came and went; the noise level rose and fell and rose again; the music they'd taped from the show seemed to surround her; despite Valeska's defection, Keeley was having the time of her life. After months of nonstop work, letting go was a relief, and she went farther than she intended. Some time during the early hours, a man came up to her and introduced himself as Raleigh Quinn.

Despite her increasingly intoxicated state, she recognized the name and managed to pull herself together enough to smile and say, "How do you do, Mr. Quinn. I've heard so much about you."

Raleigh cast a glance over her shoulder at Nigel, holding forth for a group in the corner. He smiled, a little grimly. "I can imagine," he said, over the noise.

She glanced Nigel's way, too. Feeling more bubbly than she could ever remember because of what she'd had to drink, she laughed. Then she remembered how Nigel had cursed Raleigh Quinn after *Dan Tucker*'s closing, and said, "No, despite what you might think, it wasn't from Nigel . . . er . . . Mr. Aames. You have a reputation of your own, Mr. Quinn." She looked at him owlishly. "As an astute judge of talent."

Raleigh was a tall man, and spare, with a crew cut that didn't look out of place even in his tux. Bowing slightly, he looked amused as he said, "Thank you, Miss Cochran. In fact, that's what I wanted to talk to you about."

Despite her efforts, she was having a hard time concentrating.

Wishing she hadn't drunk so much, she peered at him. "I don't understand."

"I admit that when I heard Nigel was going with an untried composer for his new show, I thought there wasn't a chance in hell he'd succeed," Quinn said. "I'm glad to know I was wrong. After hearing your score tonight, I wanted to introduce myself and say that if you ever decide to come out to California, I've got a few contacts in Hollywood."

"Thank you, Mr. Quinn, but Broadway is home." She laughed again, high with champagne and success. "Or, it's going to be, from now on."

He smiled again, too. "I understand. But if you change your mind, here's my card. I mean it, now. From the success you've had tonight, I've no doubt we'll be running into each other now and again. But if you ever want a change of scene, all you have to do is call."

She'd brought a tiny, useless beaded bag that was just the right size for holding his card. Taking it, she tucked it inside. "Thank you," she started to say, but just then someone came up behind her. His expression changing, Quinn bowed slightly and moved away.

"What did he want?" Nigel asked, in her ear.

She wasn't sure why she didn't want to tell him, but she said, "Oh, just to congratulate us on the show."

"That's all?"

If she'd been her usual, sober self, she would have wondered at his interest; as it was, with the room starting to spin and the chandeliers beginning to look like roman candles, she swayed slightly and had to clutch at him.

"Are you all right, Keeley?" he asked in sudden concern.

She wasn't sure. "I think I need some air. . . ."

"I think you need to lie down," he said, taking her arm. "Look, I've got a room in the hotel, why don't we go there, and you can rest for a while?"

She wasn't *that* drunk. "No, I think I'd better—"

"Oh, don't be silly," he said persuasively, his grip tightening on her elbow. "You really think I'd take advantage of my new songwriter-composer?"

She realized how he'd gotten his reputation as a ladies' man. With that look of worry in his eyes, and his hand comfortingly holding her up, he really was hard to resist. Without quite understanding how it happened, she found herself leaving the ballroom with him and taking the elevator to his suite upstairs.

"Just for a few minutes," she mumbled, as he unlocked the door to his room. All she wanted was for things to stop spinning. She felt hot and sick and dizzy; she could hardly stand up. No celebration was worth this; she felt terrible now.

Nigel couldn't have been more chivalrous. His suite was large, with one door presumably leading to the bedroom, another to the living room. When she saw the couch, she made a beeline toward it and sank down. Grateful to have made it this far, she closed her eyes. It was a mistake. The spinning sensation seemed worse, and she immediately sat up again, wondering if she was going to be sick.

Nigel came to sit beside her. "I think what you need is a good, hot cup of tea."

She groaned. Hiding her head in her hands, she thought that the last thing she wanted was anything else to drink. "I don't think so, Nigel," she moaned. "Oh, I feel awful!"

"Let me get you a cloth for your forehead."

Somehow she managed to hold on until he returned with a cool, wet washcloth from the bathroom. By this time, she was lying down, and as he put it across her forehead, she cautiously opened her eyes. "Thanks."

To her woozy astonishment, he took her hand and kissed it. "Don't look as though I'm going to eat you," he said, smiling. "That was just to show you how glad I am that I found you. We're going to make quite a team, Keeley. Oh, yes, quite a team."

As long as she lay still, she didn't feel so dizzy. Smiling weakly, she said, "They liked the show, didn't they?"

He kissed her fingers again. "Yes, they did. And they liked the score, too." His eyes held hers. "But you already know that."

"I wasn't sure until the last act—"

"Oh, nonsense, of course you were. We're two of a kind, Keeley, you and I. We both know what we want, and we both know how to get it. Together, there's nothing we can't do."

She wasn't sure where this was going, but she felt too sick to care. "I know," he said, getting up so abruptly that she winced and closed her eyes against the sudden movement. "I think we need to seal the bargain with a little champagne."

She never wanted to drink champagne again. "No, Nigel, I don't think—"

But he was already back, with two crystal flutes. "Here," he said, holding one out to her. "It will make you feel better, I promise."

Cautiously, she sat up. She felt so horrible she was willing to try anything. She took a sip. Then, at his encouraging nod, she took another. "You know, you're right," she said, marveling. "I do feel better."

"In that case, I think we should have some more. After all, this is a night to celebrate, isn't it?"

He went away and returned in an instant, carrying an ice bucket in which was nestled a bottle of champagne. She immediately protested. "I can't drink all that!"

"You won't have to," he said, filling her glass again. "We'll split it. After all, it's not every night you become a star, is it?"

"I'm not the star—"

"You are to me. So here—a toast! To you!"

"Oh no," she said, holding up her glass. "To . . . writing music to remember!"

He liked the toast and clinked his glass with hers. Then he toasted her again, and she thought of another, and another. . . . Somewhere along the line, he brought out a pen and paper, and they both signed their names with a flourish to seal their new partnership. By then, she thought everything was funny, and she nearly fell off the couch laughing. He helped her up, and before she realized what he intended, kissed her.

She didn't know why, but it seemed the most natural thing in the world to put her arms around him and kiss him in return. As their kiss deepened, she felt his hands at the zipper at her back and knew she should stop him. Bemused by it all, she suddenly thought that she didn't want to. She'd been so busy lately, so preoccupied and strained and tense, that she couldn't remember how long it had been since she'd taken any time for herself. She certainly hadn't taken time for a man, and as Nigel gently pulled her dress down to her waist, exposing the wisp of a strapless bra she wore, and then removing even that, she thought briefly of Gabe Tyrell, so far away in India now, on the other side of the world. Strangely, when Nigel leaned down to nuzzle one nipple, then the other, it wasn't Nigel's mouth on her breasts, it was Gabe caressing her, Gabe who was arousing her, Gabe who was making her want him. Without realizing it, she moaned.

The room spun again as she put her arms around Gabe's strong neck, and as he carried her into the bedroom, she thought—she couldn't be sure—that she whispered his name. It was the last thing she remembered until—an indeterminate time later—she heard a door slam.

* * *

The noise was so loud that Keeley immediately came awake. She started to sit up, but she fell back with a moan. Her head felt as though it were about to split wide open, and she was trying to open her eyes when the overhead light came on. The sudden illumination was blinding, and she squeezed her eyes shut and cried out.

"What are you doing?"

"The question, I think," came the shrill response, "is what *you're* doing!"

Keeley recognized the voice; how could she not? She'd heard it every day for months now. But hung over and disoriented as she was, she couldn't imagine what Carlotte was doing in her room.

Someone was lying beside her; she felt the body before she turned to look. "What's going on?" Nigel muttered.

Keeley looked at him in horror. What was he doing in her room? What was he doing in her *bed*? Appalled, she looked down at herself and realized with utter shock that she was completely naked. Quickly, she grabbed the sheet and covered herself. She looked at the furious woman still standing in the doorway and realized then where she was, and just what Carlotte thought.

"Now, Carlotte—" she started to say.

"Never mind, you little bitch!" Carlotte screamed. "Oh, I should have known it was you, sneaking around my back like this!"

"No, wait!" Keeley said desperately. "You don't understand. This is all a mistake—"

Nigel was awake now, too. Sitting up, he glanced at Keeley, then at his mistress. "I know how this looks, Carlotte. But I can explain. Keeley and I did get carried away last night, but—"

Keeley looked at him in fresh horror. What was he talking about? Fragments of memory flashed into her mind. She remembered the party, and coming up to Nigel's suite. . . .

Had she been that drunk? She couldn't believe that she had actually gone to bed with him. Putting a hand to her head, she tried to think, but the evening was a complete blank after she'd talked to . . . what was his name? She couldn't remember right now.

Carlotte was still standing in the doorway. Realizing she had to say something, Keeley looked at her again. "It's not what it looks like, but—"

"Will you stop saying that!" Carlotte screamed. She turned to

Nigel. "And you! This is the last time you pull your monkey business on me, you . . . you two-timing slime! Keep your part of Sophie, keep your new mistress, see if I care!"

"Carlotte—"

"Don't you Carlotte me!" she shrieked. She looked at both of them, her face contorted. "You'll be sorry, I swear. Do you hear me? You'll be sorry!"

Keeley winced as the door slammed behind Carlotte again. She didn't look at Nigel but quickly got out of bed, pulling the bedspread with her to cover her nakedness. She didn't know where her clothes were; oh, what a mess!

"Now, Keeley," Nigel said. "Surely you aren't upset about Carlotte. You know what a hysteric she is."

"I don't want to talk about it." She looked around quickly for her clothes. How could she have done such a thing? she asked herself with a groan. She was aghast.

Nigel got out of bed, too. Wrapping a towel around his middle, he helped her find her cast-off garments, but before she headed to the bathroom, he took her hands and stopped her for a moment.

"Don't worry about Carlotte," he said. "She'll get over it."

"I'm not worried about Carlotte," she said, trying to free herself. "I'm wondering how this could have happened!"

"Are you sorry?" he said reproachfully. He was being his charming best, but Keeley had weakened once, and she had no intention of doing so again.

"I don't have anything to be sorry for!"

"No, of course not."

"Don't patronize me, Nigel!"

He looked at her in dismayed amazement. "You don't remember, do you?"

"There's nothing to remember! We both know nothing happened! I was drunk last night, but I wasn't *that* drunk, and don't try to tell me I was!"

Looking as though she'd slapped him, he stepped back, his hands raised. "All right, Keeley, if that's the way you want it."

"That's the way it was!"

"Okay, okay, whatever you say."

"Stop saying that!"

"I don't know why you're so angry."

"I'm not angry! I just know what happened—what *didn't* happen! Don't look at me like that! You know what I mean!"

"Yes, I do," he said, smiling. He reached out and touched her face; she jerked back. "We make such a good team."

"A good team!" She was so unnerved she didn't know what to say. Any composure she might have had was fast deserting her. The longer she stood here with the bedspread awkwardly wrapped around her, the more ridiculous she felt. Her head was pounding, her stomach was roiling, and she couldn't even think.

"Nigel," she said, trying to speak over the roaring in her ears, hoping she wasn't going to be sick, "I really don't think we should have a personal relationship."

"It's a little late for that, don't you think?"

"Nigel, please!"

He studied her for a moment. Then, with a sigh, he stepped back. "Perhaps you're right," he said regretfully. "And if you want me to say nothing happened, I will."

"Nothing *did* happen!"

He lifted his hands again. "Fine, whatever you say."

She knew it was futile. Without answering, she rushed into the bathroom, slamming the door behind her and locking it for good measure. When she turned around, she saw herself in the mirror. Her hair was sticking up; her makeup was smeared. She looked like a wreck. Oh, what a night! she thought, and was running cold water over her hot face when she suddenly remembered Valeska. She straightened. Valeska! What was Val going to think?

She needn't have worried. By the time she rushed back to their hotel, Valeska had already moved out. It was obvious that Val had figured out what had happened, for she hadn't left a note.

CHAPTER ELEVEN

Valeska moved out of the little apartment she and Keeley shared as soon as the show came back to New York. Tearfully, she timed it so that Keeley wasn't there when she came to collect her things. She was so hurt by what Keeley had done in

Philadelphia that she wouldn't speak directly to her during their entire two-week run. She was polite, if Keeley spoke to her; she sang the changes in the songs she was given. If someone wanted her to do something, she did it; beyond that, she wouldn't go.

"At least let me explain," Keeley had finally said.

It was obvious that she felt badly about what had happened, but Valeska couldn't forgive her. Keeley had *known* how she felt about Nigel, and every time she thought of seeing Keeley leave the party with him, she felt hurt all over again. She did it on purpose, she thought, and refused to give in.

"There's nothing to explain," she said coldly. But then, because she couldn't understand why Keeley had done it, because she was still so angry and upset, she ruined it all by blurting, "I thought you were my friend!"

"I am your friend!"

"A friend wouldn't have done what you did," she'd said, and turned away. She wanted it all to go back the way it had been, but she knew it would never be the same again. As much as she mourned the death of their friendship, she felt betrayed. She had never had a friend like Keeley, with whom she had shared her innermost thoughts and problems; until the incident with Nigel, she had believed that if anyone could, Keeley could be trusted utterly with a confidence.

Well, obviously, she'd been mistaken. She didn't blame Nigel; clearly he, too, had been taken in. After all, Keeley wasn't only talented, she was beautiful, too, with her expressive eyes, and her straight nose, and the way she had of carrying herself that made her look much taller than she was. What man wouldn't be captivated if Keeley chose to turn all her effortless charm and assurance on him?

After she'd snubbed her, Keeley hadn't approached her again, and somehow she managed to get through that horrible time until they came back to New York. Everyone in the cast and crew knew how close she and Keeley had been; it was obvious they'd had a fight, and it contributed to the strain. When she just wanted to go home, away from Keeley and all the prying eyes, she had to force herself out on stage every night to play Garnett. Only the thought that so many people were depending on her to continue in the part stopped her from packing up and leaving on the first train.

She hadn't decided what she was going to do by the time the show moved back to New York; the only thing she was certain of was that she had to move out of the apartment. With things so tense between her and Keeley, living together would be impossible, but she had no place to go. She was desperately contemplating trying to live alone when one of the backup singers, a girl named Skye Reeves, told her she needed a roommate because hers had moved out. Valeska didn't need to be asked twice; thinking it was a godsend, she moved right in.

Skye was a party girl, always out, scouting work or fun, so they were rarely in the apartment at the same time. The arrangement suited Valeska, or so she tried to convince herself. She didn't want company; she needed time alone to get herself straightened out. It wasn't like living with Keeley, who was forever dashing in and asking her to sing the lyrics to a new song she was working on, or demanding that she listen to something else she'd written, but it had to do.

The cast of *Klondike* hadn't been back a week before new problems arose, difficulties that didn't have anything to do with Valeska's new living arrangements. After a rocky start, she had finally begun to believe the show would last more than a month, when the trouble began. It started, of course, with Carlotte.

Keeley had never been frightened of Carlotte, but Val had always been terrified of the temperamental woman with the fierce eyes. Every time Carlotte turned her way, she started to shake. She almost believed that Carlotte knew how to put a curse on someone, as the rumor went; she had a ferocious temper, and for the run of the show, she had decided to stay out of her way as much as possible. It was difficult, for they were on stage together so much of the time, but she gritted her teeth and hung on—for Nigel's sake.

Nigel. Even the thought of him gave her goose bumps. The night she had blurted out her feelings to Keeley was the first time she had admitted she was in love with him. She knew he didn't love her—not yet—but as time went on, and she watched him dreamily from afar, she became convinced that one day the miracle would happen, and he'd see her the way she saw him. She was aware of his relationship with Carlotte, and of course she knew now how Keeley had . . . *inveigled* him. But that only made her more determined to show her loyalty and love. She was sure that if she just waited long enough, he'd come to see what she had to offer him.

She knew it was stupid, infantile, naive to be fantasizing about a man twice her age—a man who hardly seemed aware of her existence except when she was on stage—but she couldn't help herself. To her, Nigel Aames was not only a famous Broadway director, he was the father she'd never had, her tutor, her mentor. He knew more about directing than most others had forgotten, and when he turned those dark eyes of his on her, or briefly touched her arm to give her some stage direction, she almost felt like swooning. She didn't know what it was; other men were more handsome, more powerful, more consuming, but when he chose to, he could make whomever he was talking to feel like the only other person—the only other *woman*—in the world. In those precious moments when his sole attention was on her, she could almost forgive Keeley for surrendering to the passion he aroused; she could understand why Carlotte was so fiercely protective.

She still hadn't told Nigel how much she loved him the night she met Sidney Thomas, a Broadway producer, at a party. She hated these parties, which she was required to attend, but she went because Nigel asked her to—because it was good for business. Why that should be, she didn't know, but she was drinking a glass of wine to hide her nervousness at being in such a crowd when Sidney Thomas came up and introduced himself. He had two friends with him, and they all complimented her on her performance that night.

As always when someone said something nice to her, she blushed. For some reason, they seemed delighted at her reaction, and because they were all so nice, so interested in what she had to say, it seemed, she found herself telling them things she rarely told anyone else. Maybe it was the wine she'd been drinking; maybe it was because Keeley was there, and she was feeling the strain of ignoring her friend. Maybe it was because she finally had a second lead in a show off-Broadway. Whatever the reason, she was more gregarious than she ever was, and when she thanked them for the compliment, they asked her how she'd feel if she had a really big hit.

"I don't know," she said, wide-eyed. "I'm having so much fun playing Garnett that I haven't thought beyond that. It's wonderful just being able to sing."

"And you are able to do that," another of the men said approvingly.

She could feel her cheeks reddening again. "I didn't mean that I *could* sing," she said quickly. "I meant that it's wonderful being *allowed* to go out on stage and sing. I know it's not Broadway yet, but still, it's like a dream come true."

"What if it *were* Broadway, Miss Szabo?" Sidney asked curiously.

Valeska thought of her mother and how ecstatic Edra would be if she were actually to appear on Broadway. Her eyes shining, she clasped her hands together. Fervently, she answered, "If I ever got a chance to appear on Broadway, I'd never ask for anything again!"

The three men smiled at each other. Then Sidney said, "Tell me, have you signed a long-term contract with Nigel?"

She shook her head. "Nigel doesn't believe in them. The way he explained it, a short-term contract, for the run of a show, or the end of the season, whichever comes first, is for our own protection." She smiled dreamily. "He's so considerate, don't you think? He said he doesn't want to tie anyone down, in case something else comes along. Isn't that thoughtful?"

"Yes, indeed," Sidney said. He looked significantly at his companions, who smiled into their glasses.

Valeska saw the look that passed among the three men. Wondering what she'd said, she frowned slightly. "Why do you ask?"

"Just nosy," Sidney said, patting her arm. Then, smiling, he called the waiter over for champagne.

"Oh, I shouldn't," she protested. She'd already had one glass of wine, and she wasn't sure she should have more. As Keeley said, she didn't have a head for liquor, and she didn't want to make a fool of herself.

She didn't want to think of Keeley, for it had been at another party just like this when she realized the woman she'd thought was her friend was really a traitor in disguise.

Now, weeks later, she still wasn't talking to Keeley, and she felt worse than ever.

"Miss Szabo, is something wrong?" Sidney Thomas asked, bringing her back from her reverie.

Guiltily, she focused on him again. "I'm sorry, Mr. Thomas," she said, seizing on the first excuse she thought of. "But I'm very tired, and I'm afraid I'll have to excuse myself."

"Of course, I understand. After a performance like yours tonight, I'm surprised you're here at all. You must be exhausted. May I take you home?"

"Oh, no, that's all right. Please, stay and enjoy the party. It was so nice of you to come."

"It was nice meeting you, Miss Szabo," he said. "If you don't mind, I'll be in touch."

She wasn't sure what he meant, but she smiled anyway as she excused herself. By the time she got back to the apartment she shared with Skye, she had a splitting headache, and she was just throwing herself on the bed when the phone rang. Crawling across the bedspread, she grabbed for the receiver and mumbled a hello. To her dismay, it was her mother.

"Valine? Valine, is that you?" Edra said. Then, her voice muffled, as though she'd turned away from the receiver, she said, "I don't *know*, Mother. It sounded like Valine, but I can't be sure. I don't think we have a good connection." Edra's voice became clear once more as she spoke directly back into the phone again. "Valine? For heaven's sake, Valine, will you answer? Is something wrong? Are you there?"

"Yes, Mama, I'm here," she said. Wishing she had an aspirin handy, she sat up and took a deep breath. "Nothing's wrong. Everything's just fine. In fact, I just got in."

Edra's voice rose. "At this hour? Valine, what are you doing out so late?"

"I'm not doing anything, Mama. I just came back from a cast party. We were celebrating *Klondike*'s first month in New York."

"Why do you sound like you've been crying, then?" Edra demanded suspiciously.

"It must be this awful headache."

"Headache, you say? Valine, are you getting enough rest?" Edra's voice became muffled again as she turned to answer something Evie had said in the background. "Just a *minute*, Mother! I'm trying to find out!" She came back on line again. "Valine—"

Valeska didn't know why she said it; maybe because she was so upset about Keeley, or still overstimulated about the performance, or giddy from the wine she had drunk. Whatever the reason, she asked before she thought.

"Mama, will you call me Valeska from now on?"

"What? What do you mean, call you—what did you say?"

She had told her mother about her stage name when she was first hired, but she had never asked to be called by it before. Now she wanted to be known by that name; it made her believe that her success and good fortune would continue.

"I said, would you call me Valeska, Mama. Valeska Szabo. Remember, I told you it's my stage name."

There was an ominous silence. "Mama?" she said faintly after a moment. "Are you still there?"

"Yes, I'm here," Edra said. Valeska couldn't tell from her voice whether she was angry or not. Abruptly, Edra asked, "Just what's the matter with Valine?"

"Nothing, Mama. It's just—"

But Edra was speaking away from the phone again. "She wants to be called by her *stage* name, Mother!" she said, obviously speaking to Evie. She came back on line. "Your grandmother wants to know how you thought of a name like that."

She didn't want to talk about Keeley now; maybe not ever. Edra knew about her roommate—her *former* roommate, she amended mournfully, but she decided it was simpler just to make up a story. "The director thought Valeska Szabo sounded more . . . exotic than Valine Smits," she said, and hesitated. "Are you angry, Mama?"

To her surprise—and relief—Edra said, "No, I'm not angry. But why didn't you say something before now?"

She didn't know how to explain. "I don't know, Mama. I guess I just didn't believe it yet. But it does sound more like a Broadway star, don't you think? I mean, people will remember the name Valeska Szabo, won't they?"

"They will when you finally get to Broadway. When do you think that will be?"

Valeska closed her eyes. Would it never end? she wondered. "I don't know, Mama. *Klondike* is still running—"

"*Off*-Broadway," Edra reminded her heavily.

"Yes, but it's close, isn't it?"

"Not close enough," Edra said flatly. "Well, this is costing us money, so I'll say good-bye."

"Wait! Can I talk to Granny for a minute please?"

"No, I'm afraid we don't have time for that. As I said, this is costing us money, and your grandmother hasn't been feeling very well lately."

Alarmed, she sat up. "What's wrong?"

"Nothing, nothing," Edra answered impatiently. "It's just the arthritis flaring up. We can handle it." She added pointedly, "But it means that I have to stay here and take care of her, and since neither of us can travel, we won't be able to come and see the show."

Valeska was too worried about her grandmother to be concerned about it. "There's plenty of time for that," she said quickly. "The important thing is for Granny to get better."

"Oh, yes, it's all very well for you to say that. Let's just hope that *I* don't get sick, too. *Then* who would support us?"

Valeska closed her eyes. "I'm sending you as much money as I can, Mama," she said desperately. "And when I get better parts, I'll be able to bring you both here."

"There? I don't want to live in New York! Whatever put such a foolish notion in your head?"

"But I thought—" Valeska started to say. Her voice trailed away. Beginning to feel nothing would ever please her mother, she asked, "If you don't want to come here, what do you want, Mama?"

The reply was swift in coming, straight to Valeska's heart. Edra said flatly, "I want you to be a star."

And, incredibly, six months later she was. Valeska was starring in a production of *Florentina*, in a role that Sidney Thomas, the producer she had met at the cast party, insisted had been created just for her. The show was directed by none other than the highly respected George Gideon, the second of the three men with whom she had spoken that night, with a score by the hot team of Banks and Jasper. Valeska was on her way to being a star, all right, but it hadn't been without heartache and sacrifice. She never knew what Thomas had done to free her from *Out on the Klondike*, but when he asked if she'd audition for him and she reminded him she was under contract to Nigel, he made a phone call or two, and suddenly it was done.

Valeska thought she'd be glad to leave the show. By then, everyone was feeling the strain, not only she and Keeley. Jealous of all the attention Valeska was getting as Garnett, Carlotte had become an evil-tempered shrew, but Nigel . . .

Sadly, Valeska remembered that Nigel didn't even seem to care that she was leaving. When she told him about Sidney's offer and asked him what she should do, he'd indifferently told her to do as she wished.

"But I thought you were pleased with my performance," she'd said, hurt and bewildered. "I mean, I've gotten such good reviews—"

"The show doesn't revolve around you, Miss Szabo," he'd said coldly. She didn't know at the time that Sidney had already spoken to him personally. "There will be other Garnetts, I guarantee you."

She couldn't believe he could be so cruel. It was all Carlotte's fault, she decided pitifully. Carlotte, who was so demanding her poor, darling Nigel didn't know what to do.

Unable to bear the thought of leaving him, she'd said, "I'll stay if you like."

"Do as you please," he'd answered. "And now, if there's nothing else, I've got something to do."

She'd never felt so hurt, not even the night Keeley had betrayed her. She was sure he was acting like this because Carlotte had convinced him that she had to go. Carlotte always had been envious of her; she must have convinced Nigel that anyone could play the role. It seemed she was wrong, for three Garnetts later, the show closed. It was cold comfort to Valeska, who didn't want to be vindicated, who wanted only to be noticed by the man she loved.

In the meantime, she had to deal with her feelings about Nigel. Lost and alone, not sure what to do, she was so lonely that she contemplated giving it all up and going back to Allentown. She was walking in the neighborhood park the next day, trying to decide what to do, when she came across an old woman who seemed frightened and confused. With her stooped posture and white hair, the woman reminded Valeska of her grandmother, and despite her preoccupation, she stopped to ask if she could help.

"Oh, could you, my dear?" the little old lady asked gratefully, clutching her arm. "I went for a walk, and I can't seem to find my way back."

"Where do you live?" Valeska asked.

"At the Hildredth Convalescent Home," she said. "Oh, they're going to be so *angry* with me. I wasn't supposed to be out by myself, but I just couldn't help it. The day was so pretty, and all I wanted was some fresh air."

Valeska smiled. "I don't know how anyone could be angry with you for that."

"Oh, but they will, I know it." The woman looked at her hopefully. "Will you take me back and explain? They won't be upset with me then; they'll think I was with you."

Valeska doubted the ruse would work, but she couldn't refuse such a simple request. The nursing home was only a few blocks from where they were standing, and she had the time. "Of course I'll go with you," she said. "What's your name? My name is . . ." She nearly said "Valeska Szabo," but she caught herself in time. She wasn't sure why, but she wanted this gentle old woman to know who she really was. So she said, "My name is Valine. Valine Smits."

"Valine," the woman repeated. "Why, that's a beautiful name. I'm Bettina. Bettina Gregory."

"I'm pleased to meet you, Mrs. Gregory," Valeska said gravely as Bettina held out her hand.

Bettina laughed, a girlish sound. "Oh, please, call me by my given name, won't you? *Mrs.* sounds so old!"

With a laugh, Valeska agreed. Bettina was so pleased that Valine had taken the time to escort her back to the home that she insisted on introducing her new friend. Her circle of friends was in the recreation room when they arrived, and they all crowded around.

"Oh, you naughty girl!" one silver-haired old gentleman scolded the old woman. "You shouldn't have walked out like that and worried us all."

"I know, I know, Jeffrey," Bettina replied serenely. She drew Valeska forward. "But just look what I found! This is Valine Smits. Isn't she lovely?"

There were murmurs as Valeska was introduced. She had always been good with older people, and when she saw a guitar by one of the easy chairs, she asked if they had been singing.

"Do you play, my dear?" Bettina asked.

Valeska thought of the guitar she'd once owned. She'd loved to play it while singing folk songs, but her mother had made her give it up because she was "wasting" her time. She hadn't played in years, but when Jeffrey brought it to her and handed it over with a shy smile, she took it and strummed a few chords for practice.

"Oh, that's beautiful!" Bettina exclaimed. "Please, play something for us, Valine!"

That was how Valeska, who would soon be starring on Broadway in the smash hit *Florentina*, came to be a regular visitor at the Hildredth Convalescent Home. Every Thursday, or as many as she was able, she stopped by to conduct the weekly singalong. And as she looked around the circle of new friends, many in their eighties, with their bright eyes and beaming faces, their vibrant falsetto voices raised with her own in such old Kingston Trio favorites as "Sloop John B." or "Sail Away," she came to think that not even the wild nightly applause she received as Florentina meant as much to her. The Hildredth became her haven, and even though they all told her over and over again how grateful they were to her, Valeska felt that she was the one who truly benefited. Away from the world, they never did realize she was Valeska Szabo, Broadway star, and although she had many opportunities to tell them, she never mentioned it. To them, she was Valine Smits . . . herself.

*   *   *

Rehearsals for the new show began almost immediately after Valeska's introduction to her newfound friends at Hildredth. Sidney didn't have to tell her about the trouble he had convincing his backers to take a chance on her in the starring role of *Florentina*; she found out right away. When the money men found out Sidney had cast her, they requested a meeting. To her dismay, Sidney insisted she go, too.

"Oh, Sidney, I can't!" she exclaimed, when he told her he wanted her there. "I won't know what to say! I won't know what to do!"

"Just be yourself, my dear," Sidney had said confidently, and despite her protests, off they went.

"I'm sorry to be so blunt, miss," one man had said to her while she sat, trying not to cower, to one side during the meeting. He turned to Sidney, at the head of the conference table. "Sidney, have you lost your mind? What makes you think people will come to see Valeska Szabo? She's not a star, she's not even a *name*."

"She will be," Sidney had replied positively. He winked at Valeska, and she forced a faint smile.

"That's all very well for you to say, Sid," someone else commented. "But we have to think of the bottom line here."

Sidney was a businessman, too. Leaning forward, he said, "No one is more aware than I that the show is going to stand or fall on Valeska in the title role. We all know that the book isn't very good and will never be great. The score is fine, but it's not *Carousel* or *Oklahoma*, and we know it." He turned to smile at her, but this time she was so nervous she couldn't even smile back. "We have a nova, here, gentlemen," he went on, "and we're about to witness the birth of a star. If we can explode Valeska in the Broadway sky, we'll have a hit."

He obviously convinced them, for rehearsals started soon after. She fell in love with her director, the short, round George Gideon, who seemed anxious to make her feel as much at ease as possible. He complimented her at every turn, even taking time to ask if she had everything she wanted. Unlike Nigel, who even she had to admit had a tendency to be sarcastic when he was under pressure, George was unfailingly kind. Even when one day she kept flubbing one scene, no matter how she tried to get it right.

George gave everyone five, then he came over to where she had collapsed side stage, sweating profusely and near tears. As she wiped her dripping forehead with her arm, he smiled down at her.

"You're doing just fine."

"I'm not!" she said despairingly. "I know I'm making a mess of it. I just can't get it right!"

Squatting down beside her, he looked into her eyes. He had directed some of the greatest actresses in the musical theater, and she had to believe him when he said, "Now, listen to me. If I'd told an experienced singer like Shirley Jones or Angela Lansbury that she'd have to do this terrific song, and then three choruses of dancing, and then another chorus of the song, and then a dramatic scene, she'd immediately say she couldn't do it because she'd be out of breath. But you're doing it, aren't you?"

She hadn't imagined that anyone would object. "Well, I'm *trying*, anyway," she said, and then, despite her frustration and weariness, she smiled shakily. "You didn't tell me I could protest."

"You can't," he said, grinning. He got to his feet, called the cast together, and they began again. This time she got it right.

All through rehearsals for the demanding role, Valeska surprised even herself. She knew she looked too delicate and fragile to do anything but break, but she'd always been strong, and she had great stamina from all her dance lessons as a child. She had never been a fighter, but as rehearsals went on, something happened to her. Little by little, she began to realize that the show depended on her and her performance, and with so many changes being made, she began to assert herself, to trust her instincts, to tell George when she didn't think something was right. Almost without realizing it, she began to understand that she could no longer be the wide-eyed innocent and survive. If she were going to be successful in the business, she had to know what was right and stand up for herself.

The first thing to go was the microphone. She knew she could easily fill any theater with her voice, and when she learned that the sound director wanted to strap a microphone to her thigh, she protested loudly.

"I don't need it, George," she declared, stopping rehearsal right in the middle of a scene. "I don't need it, and I won't have it. It'll make me self-conscious, and I won't be able to move right."

"Trust me, angel," Gideon said soothingly.

"No! You trust me!" she commanded. "Now, listen—"

And she proceeded to belt out a tune that could be heard up in the rafters and beyond. The microphone was removed with little fuss, and the show prepared to go to Boston the following month.

Florentina had its first public performance there on January 13. The curtain fell at 1:45 A.M. The show had started late because a storm was raging, but even allowing for the delay, it was at least an hour too long.

"I don't believe it!" George moaned, holding his head in his hands. "We've wrought the musical version of *The Longest Story Ever Told!*"

They were all sitting around a large table in a restaurant, and Valeska was so exhausted from excitement, nerves, and the demands of her performance that she hardly cared what anyone said. All she wanted to do was go to bed, especially when Sidney read the reviews. Among the best was one from Boston's *Herald-American* stating that the show had a limp libretto and that the lead characters were energetic if nothing else. Valeska couldn't say anything; she was too depressed. Unfortunately, no one was allowed the luxury of feeling sorry for him- or herself, especially not the star. The very next day, they were back in rehearsal.

George was like a man possessed. With all the discarded scenes, props and arrangements, the costs were steadily rising, and only Sidney's powerful personality—and his track record—persuaded his investors not to pull out. Any other musical in similar straits would have closed long before, but then Sidney had the brilliant idea of having Valeska record one of the songs in the show, the haunting "Ever Again."

Valeska had never recorded before, but to her delight—as well as everyone else connected with the show—the song broke out as a tremendous hit. It was a natural for her, an unforgettable ballad that went straight to the heart. Curiosity about the artist who had recorded it became so strong that not even rumors of an impending fiasco could stop the show. It started selling out in Boston, and soon had a million-dollar advance in New York. With all the radio play, people were recognizing the tune and applauding it even in the overture. Every time she sang it, it stopped the show, something that rarely happened with a ballad. Before long, they even had to have an encore for it.

But all too soon, it was time to move back to New York for a week of previews before the critics came. During the run in Boston, an incredible twenty-two songs had been eliminated, and more than twice that number of scenes. Even on the very last day of rehearsal on Broadway, things were still being changed. The curtain was set for seven-thirty, but at ten minutes to seven, George was rehearsing a new version of the last scene. Valeska was a nervous wreck; she and her leading man had just learned the latest version at six, and she finally told George that if he changed it one more time, she wouldn't be able to go on.

"You're going to be just fine," George soothed, as she stood in the wings waiting for her entrance. She was so tense she nearly cried out when he touched her arm. "Look at me, Valeska. Look at me!"

Her head felt as if it were turning on a rusty screw. At the moment, she couldn't remember any of the songs, much less her opening scene. "George!" she said in panic.

He took hold of both her arms. "You're going to be brilliant," he said, staring hard into her eyes. "Do you hear me, Valeska? Brilliant! By the time the curtain comes down for the final time, you're going to be the newest star on Broadway."

"Oh, George!" she moaned, but there wasn't time to say more. The curtain rose at that moment, and, suddenly, she was on.

Months later, after she had moved into her new apartment in the East Sixties, near Central Park, Valeska thought about that night and smiled. She'd been so nervous, but now, with nearly two hundred performances behind her as Florentina, she felt like an old hand.

Her life was so different, she reflected, staring out the window at the distant greenery of the park. Pushing the lace curtain aside, she watched as a couple strolled along the sidewalk. How long had it been since she'd walked like that? she wondered, and then realized, sadly, she couldn't remember. Her life in Allentown seemed very far away; she could hardly recall her old boyfriend's face. Would he still like her if she went back? What would she think of him? She felt she'd changed so much since she left. Sometimes she thought that her only real comforts were her visits to her friends at Hildredth. Despite the demands of her new career, she hadn't forgotten them, even if she didn't drop in as often as she once had. But whenever she did, she was known simply as Valine, and for a few hours, she could forget all this.

Dropping the curtain, she looked around the elegant room. She'd come a long way, she thought, and wondered why she felt like crying.

"Oh, stop it," she muttered. She had no reason to cry; her life was like a fairy tale. She was a success, doing the very thing she loved best. People recognized her everywhere she went; she, who had been an anonymous nobody before, not only got the best tables in restaurants, but was attended to like she was a princess. She rarely took taxis anymore; whenever she needed to go somewhere, a limousine picked her up. If she lacked for anything, it was company. Her mother still refused to leave Allentown, and of course, Evie wouldn't come without her. But that wasn't why she felt this vague sadness, a sense of unhappiness that never quite left her these days. It was something else; something she didn't want to identify.

On impulse, remembering the couple she had seen strolling just now, she left her luxurious apartment and went down to the street. With her engagement tonight, she didn't have time to go to see Bettina and her friends, so she decided just to walk for a few minutes. The doorman leapt to attention when she appeared; holding the door for her, he touched his cap. She smiled at him, but for once she didn't really see him; she was thinking of someone else instead, and as she turned and started walking in the direction of Broadway, she felt even more dejected. She was due at a dinner for some theater patrons at eight, and she had to get ready. They expected Valeska Szabo, and that's what they'd get.

But as she reached the corner and stood there, staring into the distance, she wasn't thinking of how she'd look tonight, elegant and sophisticated, her long, blond hair done up, jewels at her wrists and throat. She wasn't thinking of her mother or her grandmother or the people at Hildredth. In that moment, she was thinking of the person she used to be, and wishing with all her heart she was back at the old place, getting ready to go out for hot dogs and sodas, walking arm and arm up Broadway with Keeley.

CHAPTER TWELVE

Gabe had never seen anything in his life to approach the grinding poverty and chaos of New Delhi, India. When his guide, Rajesh Singh, met his flight at Palam International Airport and apologized for the fact that they were going to have to detour to Shahjahanabad—the old walled city—before they met with the Indian representative of the IZF, he didn't understand. A few minutes later, as they passed Delhi Railway Station, he knew why Rajesh had been so apologetic.

He had never seen such a mass of humanity in his life. Amid noise, clutter, and endless confusion, belching steam locomotives pulled into the station, their grimy carriages depositing hordes of travelers from the far plains of the south. With their baskets and bundles, goats and chickens and other animals, the endless throngs spilled into the crowded streets, making a Los Angeles freeway jam, or a New York gridlock, look almost uncluttered by comparison. The clamor and bedlam were exhausting but somehow exhilarating at the same time, for as he and Rajesh joined the milling crowd, they had no choice but to be swept along.

The whole city was vivid, riotous, enervating, and stimulating. Beneath the towering walls of the Red Fort as they pushed their way past, the air resounded with British tunes of empire as a dozen brass bands drummed up trade for the wedding parades that were their livelihood. Gabe's ears were still ringing when Rajesh plunged them into the broad thoroughfare called Chandni Chauk. Grinning, his dark-skinned, dark-eyed, turbaned guide told him that once the Mogul lords had made a grand procession there along tree-lined waterways. Gabe didn't believe it. On this day, as on every other, the place was choked with the traffic of the cloth and garment industry, a major source of India's foreign wealth. Bicycles, carts, wagons, and hand trucks piled high with grain sacks competed with a sea of pedicabs—rickshawlike conveyances used as cabs. All vied for space in the street, while on foot, people with bags, bundles, boxes, and God knew what else, were crammed everywhere. The din and dust and turmoil rose like a smothering blanket, making Gabe feel almost claustrophobic. On one street corner alone, small entrepreneurs sold stationery and books, cigarettes and candy, tinsel garlands, fried breads, antique reproductions and silver. Here and there in a warren of tiny shops off the main thoroughfare, Gabe saw what Rajesh told him were prospective brides examining lustrous saris of silk and gold while all around dirty children begged or panhandled. Rajesh had already warned him not to give in to the beggars or they would be instantly mobbed, but it was hard to resist. So many were so poor that Gabe felt rich.

He decided not to visit the street of brothels, where, according to Rajesh, teenage country girls were still sometimes sold into bondage for two hundred dollars—half the price of a bullock. Instead, they wandered down the Street of Stuffed Chapati, peeked into the Street of Silver and Gold, passing perfume shops fragrant with patchouli, sandalwood, and oily musk. When they finally made their way out, Muslim pilgrims were surging up the steps of Jama Masjid, India's greatest mosque, to utter prayers "worth a thousand said elsewhere."

"My God," Gabe said, when they had left the worst of the street traffic behind them. "Is it like this all the time? I've never seen so many human beings crushed together in one place in my entire life."

Rajesh grinned, showing white teeth against his dark skin. "You think New Delhi is crowded, or Shahjahanabad?" he asked. "Wait until you get to Calcutta."

"I'm not going to Calcutta," Gabe said with a shudder. Even on the fringe of the city, the road was still packed. Instead of an ocean of pedicabs like they'd left behind, turbaned men on ancient motorbikes and bicycles, and pedestrians, men and women alike, competed here for space with cows, which were protected by India's constitution. To Gabe, it was all a little surreal, and he was just starting to say something else to Rajesh when there was a commotion up ahead. The street was so crowded that he couldn't see what was going on, but something was causing the bottleneck, and when he and Rajesh made their way to the place where a crowd had congregated, Gabe stood rooted to the spot.

An ancient man dressed in moldy pants and a turban and nothing else, was flogging an exhausted bullock who was trying to pull an overladen cart up the slope of the street. It was an impossible task; the cart was too heavy, and one of the wheels canted alarmingly, acting as an even greater drag. The struggling animal heaved against the harness, the old man beating it mercilessly with a heavy pole, but the cart wouldn't budge. Finally, the bullock just stopped, sides heaving. It stood, head down, as the cart owner screamed and beat it again and again with the pole.

Gabe wasn't overly sentimental, but he couldn't just stand by and watch an animal being beaten to death. He was just starting forward when Rajesh, sensing what Gabe was about to do, put a restraining hand on his arm. "It is better not to interfere," the guide said.

Gabe's eyes were on the cart driver, who, in sheer frustration, was jumping up and down with rage. In the split second before it happened, Gabe realized with horror what was about to take place; he was just starting forward again when the old man took the pole he was using to beat the bullock and rammed it straight into the animal's rectum, impelling it forward. The bull roared in agony and half collapsed in the traces just as Gabe reached the man and jerked the pole from his grasp.

"That's enough!" he shouted, flinging the instrument of torture away. He towered over the wizened old man, and they stood glaring at each other as Rajesh came rushing up.

"Oh, no, oh, no," Rajesh moaned, behind him.

Gabe didn't hear him; his entire attention was taken up with the cart driver, who looked ready to attack. He wasn't worried about his safety, but he didn't like the idea of having to subdue an old man in front of the growing crowd. The sight of the tall, blond American entering the fracas had drawn even more eager onlookers, and now there was quite a throng. Gabe's eyes met Rajesh's, and reluctantly the guide stepped forward. Still bawling with pain, the bullock had gone to its knees in front of the cart, and Gabe was sure it was dying.

Rajesh and the driver began a rapid conversation in Hindi. The old man's voice rose with every word until he was screaming again, and after a moment, Rajesh turned to Gabe.

"I told him you were sorry—" Rajesh began.

"Sorry!" Gabe's blue eyes blazed, but he restrained himself. Reminding himself that he was in a foreign country, he said, tight-lipped, "Ask him how much he wants for the bullock."

Rajesh looked at him in disbelief. "You . . . you want to *buy* the animal, Mr. Tyrell?" he asked, shocked. "But . . . but what will you do with it?"

Gabe hadn't thought that far. "I don't know; I'll think of something. Ask him."

There was another rapid exchange. Gabe noticed a sly look in the old man's eyes, and he prepared himself. Rajesh shook his head several times, but the driver persisted, and finally Rajesh turned back to him.

"He says—" Rajesh obviously didn't want to relay the request. At Gabe's impatient gesture, he reluctantly went on. "He says he wants one thousand."

"Dollars?" Gabe said, his voice rising. Even he knew it was much too much. He glanced at the old man, who stared right back and grinned. His own expression became grim as he reached for his wallet. "Tell him I'll give him five hundred."

Rajesh turned to the cart driver. But before he could relay the
amount, Gabe added, "Five hundred—and I won't do to him
what he did to the bullock."

Humor gleamed in Rajesh's eyes as he began to relay the
message. There was another rapid exchange in Hindi, during
which the driver quickly glanced at Gabe, as if assessing how
serious he might be. Gabe stared neutrally back, and the driver
looked quickly away. The deal was hastily concluded, money
exchanged hands, and as though by magic, the crowd, including
the old man, faded away. Gabe didn't notice until everyone was
gone that the cart with the goods had somehow disappeared as
well. But the bullock had been left behind, and Gabe glanced at
Rajesh.

"*Jai Hind!*" Rajesh said with a smile. "All hail to India."

Gabe didn't think it was funny. "Any ideas?" he said, glancing at the animal he'd just bought.

Rajesh just grinned.

After his introduction to New Delhi, Gabe was glad to leave
the city behind. The bullock safely in the care of Rajesh's delighted farming relatives, Gabe and his guide set out for Kanha
National Park, in central India.

It was late February by this time, when chital fawns were
finding their legs, and the peacocks were coming into full plum-
age. The wild boars were in full rut, and swamp deer and
bisonlike *gaur* grazed unafraid in the meadows. The first morning out, with the mahout, Sabir, steering the elephant Gabe was
riding with practiced ease, they saw a tiger—a handsome female with four cubs. She let them approach close enough to see
a bright red flash, evidence of a fresh kill, before she vanished
into a bamboo lair. It happened so quickly Gabe barely had a
chance to lift the camera to his eye. He vowed he'd be more
prepared the next time.

At midday, they heard a tiger roaring in the distance. With Sabir guiding the elephant toward the sound, they soon found fresh
tiger footprints along a sandy ravine. The prints led into a dense
forest, and despite himself, Gabe felt his skin tighten as they entered the shadows. Taking out the Nikon, he pulled his black
Temba bag closer so he could reach it quickly. He'd practiced
with the arrangement of the lenses inside until he could put his
hand on what he wanted without looking. He preferred the 800
mm when he was in control of the situation, but today he had
the 20-mm-wide angle attached since he didn't know what

they'd run into. Rubbing his sweaty palm down his pants leg, he gripped the camera firmly.

Rajesh, riding behind them on another elephant, spotted the tiger first. "There he is!" he whispered.

At first Gabe couldn't see anything, but then the tiger moved, an awesome vision in fierce orange and black stripes gliding through the green bamboo. Suddenly, he stopped in his tracks. Thankful that the tiger hadn't stopped to stare at *them*, Gabe followed the direction of the big cat's glance. The animal had seen a herd of spotted deer browsing on bamboo at the edge of a small clearing.

Gabe looked back at the tiger. The animal was motionless, no tail twitch, no ear movement, not even a quiver of a whisker. As though painted on canvas, he stood in the partial cover of a small patch of grass. As long as he remained motionless, the deer couldn't see him. There was no breeze, so he couldn't be scented.

Under the direction of the mahouts, the patient elephants halted. Holding his breath, Gabe focused the camera. Praying that the tiny click it made as he advanced the film wouldn't disturb the tiger, he began bracketing—three f-stops over, three under—to make sure that whatever happened, he had the picture.

For a half hour or more, they remained in position. The tiger watched the deer, the humans watched the tiger. Gabe took several rolls of film, the elephants slept. Then, not making even a crackle in the dry leaf litter, the tiger suddenly moved. Carefully placing one foot in front of the other, he began gliding from bush to bush. To Gabe, it seemed as though his heart had stopped beating.

Suddenly, the quietly grazing deer seemed alerted to something; one doe sniffed the air, and another stamped a forefoot, a sign of mild alarm. Their companions lifted their heads, ready to run. It was so quiet Gabe was sure everyone could hear his stiffened muscles screaming.

The tiger was rigid in a crouch, his powerful hind legs gathered under him when the deer stamped her foot again. Raising her tail, she uttered a bell-like alarm call just as the tiger burst from cover. In unbelievably fast bounds, he rushed the deer, and they scattered.

Gabe was ready with the camera. Changing the motor setting from single to continuous to catch the running animal, he focused on the tiger as it closed on one of the deer. With a giant leap that Gabe caught center field in perfect focus, he surged into the air and . . .

Missed. Snarling, the tiger roared and threw himself down in a pool of sunlight as the deer disappeared.

"Now what?" Gabe whispered.

Rajesh grinned. "The show's over. He won't hunt again for a while. We might as well go back."

With jabs of their sticks, the mahouts awakened the sleeping elephants, and they moved away. Gabe felt elated at what he'd gotten on film. Moving inch by inch, so as not to disturb the tiger, he'd managed to maneuver the eleven-foot tripod to steady the camera so he could film from the height advantage atop the elephant. Next time, he planned to get a different perspective, from the ground.

The opportunity came a few days later, when Gabe caught something on film that would win him an award and seal his partnership with the IZF. It happened deep in a forest with pools of clear water. Gabe was the first to spot the tiger this time, a beautiful female who seemed restless and discontented as she paced the stream.

"What do you think it is?" Gabe whispered, after he and Rajesh had quietly canvassed the area and settled down in a concealed spot that had the best view.

Rajesh considered. "I think she wants to mate."

It seemed to be so. The tigress couldn't keep still; anxiously, she lashed her tail and moaned, alternately throwing herself down and then standing up to pace. Gabe was using the 800 mm this time, with two tripods, one for the camera body, and one for the lens, which by itself weighed around twenty pounds. He didn't know what was about to happen, but whatever it was, he'd be ready—unless, of course, she saw them and charged. It was a sure bet he wouldn't be ready for *that* possibility.

Abruptly, the tigress pricked her ears and stared down the nullah. Hidden in the bushes to one side, with the elephants and their mahouts waiting at the edge of the forest, Gabe and Rajesh followed her gaze. When Gabe saw what she was looking at, he tensed. A magnificent male tiger, athletic and powerful, was slowly walking along the streambed. Hardly daring to move in case he caught either animal's attention, Gabe put his eye to the camera. No matter what happened, he wasn't going to miss this, he thought, and nearly cringed when he turned the video camera on. He'd set it up earlier because he wanted film as well as stills, but the almost-inaudible *whir* sounded like a helicopter hovering overhead, and he was sure every animal within ten miles could hear it.

The tigers obviously had other business in mind. When the male came to within twenty feet or so of the female, he threw himself down. The female, tail no longer lashing, did likewise. Even Gabe could see that this was no casual meeting, and he started to feel excited himself. Was this a prelude to mating? He couldn't be sure; they'd just have to wait and see.

Tigers have unlimited patience, it seemed. Gabe and Rajesh waited almost an hour while the tigers snoozed. Then, suddenly, the female got up, yawned, and stretched. Head low, she walked over to the male who actually purred in pleasure—a sound that raised the hair on Gabe's arms. It was the sound a domestic cat makes, but louder, more resonant, fuller. He'd never heard anything like it.

The two tigers touched faces. Then the tigress lay down with all four feet under her, head on the sand of the streambed. Without further ado, the male got up, walked over, and straddled her.

The mating was spectacular, rough, and quickly over. Astride, the male bit the female's neck fiercely and growled. She turned her head, curled her lip, and roared right into his face. He roared back, and for a moment the forest resounded with the deep-throated cry of animals in full heat. After waiting so long, it was over too soon. The male climbed off, walked a few paces away, and flopped down again. The tigress rolled sensually onto her back and all was quiet. Carefully collecting the camera equipment, not daring to make a sound, Gabe and Rajesh crept away and went back to camp.

Camp was a two-room cabin deep in the forests and bamboo jungle of the park. To Gabe, it was an idyllic spot, far from India's crowded cities and towns. At this time of year, the only people there were park officials and those who looked after the park's six trained elephants. When he'd first come, he'd been surprised that elephants were used to track tigers, but as Rajesh explained, they were necessary because of the terrain and the distances involved. Because elephants had been used so much over the years, the tigers in the park had become accustomed to them—as well as to the strange sight of their human cargo. The familiarity enabled Gabe to work in closer than he normally would have, and over the following months, both his expertise and his ability to catch tigers in revealing close-ups grew.

But as he had in Africa, out here at Kanha, and then later at Rajasthan and Ranthambhor, he came to see things differently.

The rhythms of nature are sharply perceived in India, and Gabe soon understood that nature was its calendar—the coming of winter, the dry season, the monsoon. The precise year, even what century it was, seemed less important than the endless changing of the seasons in the bush. Sometimes, camped in the hills, it was possible to imagine that the years had passed India by. He could almost believe that, as Rajesh said one time over a supper by campfire light, the Hindu gods still rode their favorite mounts, the swan, the kite, the bull; and that Mogul emperors rode forth with hooded hunting cheetahs selected from a stable of hundreds. With the crackling of their campfire lighting the night, and the stars blazing overhead, he could see a time when the forests and hills still teemed with so much game that British colonials, bored with shooting, had turned to hunting with matched bulldogs and a knife.

When he had met with the IZF representative before leaving New Delhi, the man had told him a story. "Forty or fifty years ago," the representative had said, "when you traveled by train from Bombay to Ahmadabad, there was hardly a time after you left the settled areas when you didn't see herds of black buck. At that time, everyone shot. In a morning, you could easily bag three or four black bucks.

"But every hunter with any ambition wanted a tiger," he'd gone on, regretfully. "Some shot five, ten, even thirty or more. I remember once, about 1960, when I was doing some fieldwork in Madhya Pradesh, I met the Maharaja of Surguja. He was an old man then, shaking with palsy. 'I am very happy today,' he told me. 'And why is that?' I asked him politely. Demonstrating how he'd braced his rifle on a stick, he'd answered. 'Because today I have shot my eleven hundredth tiger.' "

The IZF man had looked a little sick. "He ended up with eleven hundred fifty-seven."

Gabe hadn't forgotten the story or the others he'd heard since. Now that he'd been so close to these magnificent beasts, he could understand the fascination for tigers. Rajesh had felt it, he admitted. Before he became a protector of wildlife, he'd had his days with a rifle, too.

Gabe couldn't believe Rajesh had hunted.

"Yes, it is true," the guide admitted, ashamed.

"But you have such . . . reverence for the tigers," Gabe said. "I've seen your admiration. I can't imagine you killing one."

"Not now," Rajesh answered, his eyes downcast. He looked up with a strange expression. "But even now, as repulsed as I am at the thought of it, I can still remember how ... stirring it was to compete with an animal before whom every other beast of the forest trembles." He glanced unhappily at Gabe. "I am not proud of it, but there it is."

Gabe realized that he'd been wrong before. The years had not passed India by, as he'd wanted to believe, but had ravaged her instead. From what he had seen himself, the once mighty forests had shrunk under the ax and the plow, and the vast herds that had once roamed freely had diminished to scattered numbers. Worst of all, the predators had become the hunted. The Indian cheetah was now extinct, the tiger gravely endangered. Wondering if mankind would ever learn, he renewed his efforts. With his cameras and his eye for detail, he could make people understand what was happening, not only here, but all over the world.

Then came word of a man-eater on the loose in Kanha. He and Rajesh heard the terrible news one night as they sat on the veranda at the cabin base. It was after dinner, and Rajesh had drifted off to sleep, but Gabe sat in the quiet, listening to the calls of the owls, the stone curlews, and the nightjars. He could identify them now, and for some reason, the musical chorus reminded him of Keeley. Smiling at the thought, he sat back, wishing he had a cigarette.

He'd been trying all this time not to think of Keeley, who was so far away, but now that her face had flashed into his mind, he seemed doomed. Something stirred inside him, and an ache began in his loins. At the moment, he knew just how the male tiger had felt coming up the streambed in search of his female.

What was it about Keeley, he wondered, that made her so unforgettable? He'd met other women who were more beautiful, more sophisticated, more educated, more ... cultured. Why was it Keeley he couldn't forget? What had she done to him with her great green eyes and her expressive face? Right now he could remember how clean her hair had smelled, how he'd wanted to run his hands through it, just to touch it.

He laughed at himself. He wanted to do more than touch her hair, he thought, picturing Keeley's slender, compact body with her economy of movement. Keeley didn't just come into a room; she burst into it, immediately filling it with her energy. Remembering how she had looked the night of the fund-raiser, a vision in black sequins, he felt the ache become a pulse, and he cursed what a woman could do to a man with just a look. Helpless, he wondered why he was thinking of her out *here*, miles away from any sort of female companionship. Now he felt hot and restless, and he didn't know what to think. It wasn't fair; did this happen to women, too? He was sure it didn't, and if it didn't, it wasn't right. If men had to suffer this way, women should, too.

At least he had talked to her before he disappeared into the wilds of India; that was some comfort, he thought—or was it? When he remembered how musical her voice had sounded to him, how delightful her laugh, he wanted her here with him. She'd love India, he thought. The endless rhythms of nature in this ancient place would appeal to her. He smiled. Knowing Keeley, she'd sit right down and write a symphony.

Hi, he'd said teasingly to her the last time they'd talked, separated by endless miles of land and sea from New York to Bangkok. Did you miss me?

Her laugh had done something to his insides. Miss you? she'd teased right back. I've been too busy to do that.

But he could tell she was glad to hear from him, and that was good enough. He hadn't wanted to take this assignment so far away from her, but he knew she was busy, and it was for the best. He knew instinctively that if he wanted this budding relationship of theirs to grow, he couldn't crowd her, or it would never work.

Thinking of it, he laughed at himself. Listen to him! Wouldn't Frank be amazed if he could hear what his little brother was thinking now! He'd spent most of his adult life running away from entangling relationships, and here he was, wondering how best to nurture one. He wouldn't have believed it himself a couple of months ago, but it was happening now. Amazing, wasn't it, how a woman could change a man's life around. Without even trying, she had him thinking of her, wanting her, *longing* for her, from halfway around the world.

Remembering her surprise when he'd told her he was sorry that the show had closed, he smiled. You read the trades? she'd asked in astonishment.

But of course he did, he mused now. Right from the beginning, he'd wanted to know everything there was to know about Keeley Cochran.

But why? she'd asked, sounding pleased despite herself.

It was a good question. But how could he tell her then, when he didn't even know himself, that the reason was because he was falling in love?

Tonight, months later, and thousands of miles away from Keeley, Gabe thought of the night he'd kissed her. Remembering the feelings that had surged up in him that night, he closed his eyes. He'd felt passion before, and desire and need. In fact, he thought he had experienced every emotion possible with a woman, but that kiss proved him wrong. He hadn't been prepared for the emotion that erupted within him when his lips touched hers. Blood surged through his head, and for an insane moment, he wanted to rip off all their clothes and make love to her right there on the step. It was a miracle that he had held himself back.

He wouldn't leave next time, he thought. And there *would* be a next time. He'd see to that.

The distant bark of alarm from a sambar deer brought him out of his reverie with a snap. The warning sound suggested a tiger on the prowl, and beside Gabe, Rajesh stirred in his chair and sat up. "What is it?"

Before Gabe could answer, the radio inside crackled to life, and Rajesh got up and went inside to answer. When he came out, he looked tense, and Gabe sat up just as a full-throated roar resounded across the meadow. They glanced at each other as the tiger roared again. Gabe had heard many tiger calls during his months in India, but he'd never heard anything approaching the ferocious savagery of this. He could feel the hair lifting on his arms.

"What is it?" he asked Rajesh.

Rajesh's dark eyes scanned the darkness. A muscle jumped in his dark jaw. "That was Salim Ali on the radio," he said, still looking anxiously out at the night.

Salim Ali was the chief wildlife warden for the area. "What did he want?" Gabe asked.

Rajesh looked ready to jump out of his skin. "To tell us that a man-eater is in the area."

Gabe was sure he hadn't heard right. "A . . . man-eater?" he repeated. Involuntarily, he turned to look at the inky darkness beyond the veranda. He wanted to joke that man-eating tigers only appeared in movies, but he knew better. He'd heard stories about the three man-eaters that had roamed once in Uttar Pradesh. One had taken five lives, while the other two had two kills each. Feeling his gut tighten, he turned to Rajesh again.

"What do we do?"

"A senior forest officer has been delegated to destroy it," Rajesh said. He was still scanning the darkness beyond the porch. It was making Gabe nervous. "Apparently, he's an old *shikari*, and a good shot. He's on his way, but it's possible he won't get here in time."

"In . . . time?" Gabe felt a stab of fear shoot through him at Rajesh's words. "What do you mean?"

Rajesh looked at him, his dark eyes burning. "Before the next human kill."

The tiger roared again, closer this time, and Rajesh and Gabe both jumped. "The *next?*" Gabe repeated. He seemed to be echoing everything Rajesh said. "You don't mean that the tiger has already killed someone here!"

"Yes, to the north." Rajesh looked at him again. "There are other rangers out right now, looking for him. The hope is that they'll be able to herd the tiger in the direction the *shikari* comes."

Gabe didn't want to ask. "And if they can't?"

But before Rajesh could answer, a sound came out of the night that Gabe had never heard before and hoped never to hear again. It was a scream torn from a human throat, cut off in midflight, shattering the night into a thousand pieces.

Without another word, he and Rajesh leapt off the porch and ran for the Jeep. They both knew, because they had discussed it only that afternoon on the way in from a day's filming, that the Jeep's battery was almost dead. They had planned to recharge it during the night, so they could be on their way in the morning. Now it was a luxury of time they couldn't afford. Rajesh knew the territory better than Gabe; he leapt into the driver's seat. As they roared away from the cabin toward the sound of the scream they had heard, they were both aware that the only things between them on the seat were a single rifle and a flashlight.

The tiger bellowed again as they set off but abruptly fell silent. Coming to a screeching halt out in the meadow, they stopped to listen. Gabe had never felt more vulnerable in his life, not even when the elephant had charged him and Mhoja in the Manyara forest. Rajesh cut the engine so they could hear, and they both got out to reconnoiter. The silence was deadly, almost palpable with danger. Gabe imagined he could feel the tiger's breath at his neck and had to force himself to keep going forward. Only the stars, blazing in the inky sky, gave any light, but running on adrenaline as he was, Gabe imagined he could see as well as if it were day.

They heard rather than saw the tiger at first. Before he and Rajesh had gone five paces, the beast roared with full force only forty or fifty feet away—a thundering sound that made Gabe's blood run cold and his hair stand on end. It was all he could do not to bolt for the puny safety of the Jeep. His pounding heart was about to choke him; he could hardly breathe. He'd never been so afraid in his life. Menace was thick enough to cut with a knife—if he'd had one.

As suddenly as it began, the roar stopped. In the silence, his senses heightened to an unbelievable pitch, Gabe could hear the faintest cricket chirp. An owl calling softly overhead startled him so much he almost dropped the flashlight he held. Rajesh, more experienced, had the rifle, and they whispered a quick plan. As soon as they caught a glimpse of the big cat, Gabe would switch on the flashlight and Rajesh would fire. One shot was probably all they'd have a chance to get off; a charging tiger was like lightning, swift and merciless. It was no comfort at the moment that they missed nine times out of ten.

The crackling sound of padding feet on dry leaves nearby turned Gabe to stone. In his fright, the light he'd imagined was bright enough to see by only seconds before turned instantly to utter blackness. Even though he was straining with every fiber of his being, he almost missed the sight of the immense animal emerging from the underbrush. Slinking low, the beast advanced steadily and purposefully, the gleam of his murderous eyes like twin beams. Feeling impaled in the starlight, wanting nothing more than to turn tail and run, Gabe forced himself to stand still. His hand shaking, he turned on the feeble flashlight when the tiger was about twenty feet away. At the same moment, Rajesh raised the rifle to his eye.

Whether it was the gleam of light on the rifle barrel, or Rajesh's sudden movement that caused it, the massive cat launched himself in an attack. Five hundred pounds of sinew and muscle charged toward them, and before Rajesh could get off a shot, the tiger was airborne, straight at him. With a mighty roar, the beast swatted the rifle from Rajesh's hands and landed heavily right on top of him. Screaming, Rajesh went down. The tiger went with him.

On the other side of the Jeep, Gabe leapt for the rifle. He lost the flashlight in the process, but with every sense electrified, he didn't need it. His scrabbling fingers touched the steel of the rifle barrel. Without giving himself time to think, almost without taking time to aim, he whirled and fired.

The tiger screamed as the bullet went through one of its massive haunches. Snarling with pain, it whirled, batting at itself, as though to slap away a bee.

"Get out of there, Rajesh!" Gabe yelled, just as the animal, realizing where the sting had come from, rounded on him. With

Rajesh scrambling for cover under the Jeep, Gabe aimed the rifle. Almost at the same time, the beast hurled himself right at him. Gabe felt fire blossom in his cheek as a claw ripped into his face, but he didn't have time to respond to the pain. In sheer terror, he looked into the maddened eyes of the cat as it charged again, and he fired one last time.

As though in slow motion, Gabe saw the tiger slow, falter, then impel itself on through sheer fierce will. His back was to the Jeep; he couldn't raise the rifle to fire again. It seemed to take forever: the tiger falling through the air, the deadly claws missing him again only by inches. Then, with one last snarl, it crashed to the ground by his feet and was still.

Rajesh scurried out from under the Jeep. Battered himself, he managed to catch Gabe just as he fell. "Aieee," he wailed, when he saw the blood on Gabe's face and the deep gash in his cheek.

Gabe only had time to make sure his friend was all right before he passed out.

CHAPTER THIRTEEN

Keeley waited months before going to see Valeska in *Florentina*. Long before then, the star of the show was getting raves, and *Variety* and *Theatre Arts*, two bibles of the industry, declared every performance a sellout. Valeska's face appeared on billboards, in magazines, even on television a time or two. She had cut an album of the show; two songs, a ballad called "Ever Again" that Keeley privately thought only Valeska could have made believable, and the bitter, "Yesterday, Long Ago" that worked because of her exceptional voice control, constantly played on the radio.

Keeley had always known Val would be a star, and she wanted to see the show. The only reason she stayed away so long was because she still felt guilty about what had happened in Philadelphia. The months since hadn't made her feel any better about it, especially after Val had moved out.

She had stopped wondering how Valeska could have fallen in

love with Nigel. When he wanted to be, Nigel could be quite a charmer. If he chose, he could make a woman feel that she was the only woman on earth, that she was the most beautiful, the most talented, the most sensuous. She had been too preoccupied to notice before, but now that she had worked with him so long and spent so much time in his company, she was beginning to understand why some women found him irresistible. Unfortunately, she wasn't one of them; that's why his marriage proposal had been so completely unexpected.

Every time she thought about it, she felt the same sense of shocked astonishment as she had the night he'd asked her to marry him. As she entered the theater where *Florentina* was playing and found her seat, she was still taken aback as much by the idea as by the thought that he had actually proposed. She couldn't imagine why he had; in her mind, except for that one drunken night in Philly when *nothing had happened*, they were just colleagues, co-workers—maybe, friends. The whole thing had taken her completely by surprise, and she wished she had someone she could talk to about it. Someone like Valeska. But Val was no longer her friend, she thought sadly, and she had only herself to blame.

Valeska had walked out of Keeley's life, right into the middle of a smash hit. As Keeley arranged her coat on the back of her seat, she listened absently to the orchestra tuning up and wondered why she had really come. Now that she was here, she wanted to get up and leave, but just then the overture started and the show began. Valeska was the first one on stage, and from the moment she appeared, Keeley, like everyone in the audience, forgot everything else.

Keeley tried to be professional about it, to analyze the music, the performance, the acting. But all she could think was that Val had never looked or sounded better. The young woman who had once been too shy and withdrawn even to speak up for herself took immediate charge of the stage and her audience; in seconds, she had everyone on the edges of their seats. From the opening bars of the poignant hit song "Ever Again," to the final, jubilant, "Sittin' on Top," she was in control—of the show, the music, the cast, herself. She made everyone in the theater believe she was Florentina, the girl who overcomes her humble beginning to achieve her dreams. The story was a simple one of rags to riches and rags to riches again, but Valeska made it fresh and new that night. No one would have guessed that she had played Florentina two hundred times by then; from what she put into the performance, it could have been opening night. Keeley, who knew how difficult it was to keep a role fresh while doing it over and over, was impressed. When the curtain came down, she was on her feet like everyone else, and she thought the dozen curtain calls weren't nearly enough.

When the lights finally came up, she knew she had to go backstage. She hadn't planned on it, but after what she'd seen, she couldn't leave without saying how much she had enjoyed the show. How far she's come from our first night in New York! she thought. She paused. And how long ago now was that first audition.

Reminded of so many things, she had to tell Val how she felt. She *was* sorry about what had happened, and while she knew they could never go back to the way they had been, she hoped enough time had passed to be forgiven. But most of all, she thought, she wanted to tell Val how much she had missed her.

A crowd had gathered around the backstage area by the time she made her way there; eager theatergoers were trying to convince the guard that they were sure Miss Szabo would see them. Keeley recognized the big man in uniform as someone she had worked with; he let her in.

"How's it going, Jimbo?" she asked, over the protests behind them.

He grinned. "You can see for yourself."

She smiled back. "Valeska's done pretty well, hasn't she?"

"She has, indeed. Did you see the performance tonight?"

"I did. It's why I came backstage. I wanted to congratulate her."

"Sure, go ahead. She's got some people in there with her now, but I'm sure it will be all right."

"People?"

"Some friends of hers. From some convalescent home, I think. Anyway, they're all old codgers, thrilled as hell to be back here with the star."

Keeley didn't remember Val knowing anyone from a convalescent home, and she frowned slightly as she started toward the dressing room door with the star. Two of the dancers in the show passed her; they were still in makeup and looked at her curiously before they disappeared into the common dressing room farther down the hallway. As she approached, Keeley could hear a delighted hubbub from inside the dressing room. The door was open, and she paused on the threshold, wondering if she should go in.

Half a dozen elderly men and women were crowded into the small, cluttered room. They were all wearing what looked to be their Sunday best, the men in old-fashioned suits and carefully knotted ties; the women in dresses with lace collars and sensible shoes. Every wrinkled face was alight, and they were looking around as though they'd entered a different dimension.

Keeley couldn't blame them. Costumes from the show were scattered over every available surface, and, as in all theater dressing rooms, the mirrored table was cluttered with bottles and jars and brushes and pots and paints and all the other accoutrements of stage makeup. Valeska sat in front of the mirror, looking pleased at all the company, but a little tired around the eyes even as she graciously entertained her guests.

"But why didn't you *tell* us you were a Broadway star?" one little old woman with bright blue eyes and fine white hair was asking when Keeley stopped in the doorway. "If we'd known, we'd never have *dreamed* of taking so much of your time."

Reaching for the woman's hand, Valeska gave her fingers a fond squeeze. "That's just the point, Bettina, don't you see? I love coming to Hildredth. It's the only place in New York where I feel I can be myself." She shook Bettina's hand warningly. "And if my inviting you tonight is going to make a difference, I'm going to be very put out. I mean it!"

An elderly man in an immaculate suit and vest that was so old the creases shone turned toward Valeska. "You mean you still want to come?"

Valeska turned to him. "Of course I do. Don't be silly, Jeffrey. Why, if I didn't have my friends at Hildredth, I don't know what I'd do!"

"But—"

"No buts about it," Valeska said firmly. "Now, I invited you all tonight to be my guests for the show only because I thought you might find out who I was by accident. I didn't want you to feel hurt I hadn't told you. But you know better than I do that this—" Valeska waved her hand "—is just make-believe. Out there is the real world." She fixed them all with a stern glance. "And out there, my name is Valine, and I'm the girl who comes on Thursdays to play the guitar and lead the sing-along. Okay?"

There was a chorus of agreement, and in the doorway, Keeley felt a little bemused. She had never seen Valeska like this, and she was charmed just like Val's guests.

"We did enjoy the performance tonight, Valine," another of the little white-haired women said. "You were splendid!"

"Thank you, Gerda, I—" Suddenly, Valeska spied Keeley standing there. Without realizing it, her face lit up and she got to her feet. "Keeley!"

"Hi, Val," Keeley said, coming into the room. Everyone turned to her and she smiled. "Hello," she said to them. "I see you came to congratulate Valeska just like I did."

"Oh, yes, did you see the performance? Wasn't it wonderful!" the woman named Bettina asked.

"Yes, I did," Keeley said. Her eyes met Valeska's over the crowd. She had expected Val to be smiling as she had been when she came in, but to her dismay, Valeska's first flush of pleasure at seeing her unexpectedly had disappeared, and her expression had turned cold.

Because she was looking at Keeley, Bettina didn't notice the change that had come over Val. "We had the most delightful time!" she exclaimed. "It's been ages since we've been out this late, and we are so grateful to Valine for inviting us tonight."

"Yes," Keeley said, still gazing at Valeska. "It was a lovely thing to do."

"She sent a limousine for us and everything!"

"Did she?" Keeley jerked her eyes away from Val's face and looked at the elderly woman. "Well, she always has been generous."

That was enough for Valeska. "Speaking of the limousine," she said to her guests, "I think the driver is waiting to take you back to Hildredth. I did promise to get you back before midnight, you know. Thank you all for coming, and I'll see you . . . as soon as I can."

Somehow, she managed to shepherd them all out on another chorus of thanks and congratulations. But as soon as the door closed behind the little group, she went back to her dressing table and sat down. Grabbing a tissue, she started wiping the stage makeup off her face. "So," she said. "You saw the performance tonight."

Keeley looked around for a place to sit, decided she wasn't going to be here that long anyway, and stayed where she was. "Yes, you were brilliant."

Valeska didn't reply. Grabbing another tissue from the box, she continued what she was doing. The glow Keeley had seen in her face and eyes when the old people were here had disappeared.

"You're still angry with me, aren't you?" Keeley asked, when the silence had gone on too long.

"Angry?" Valeska's eyes met hers in the mirror. She had taken most of the makeup off now; without it, she looked much younger, more vulnerable despite the hard look in her eyes. "Why should I be angry?"

Keeley hadn't intended to get into it—or maybe she had. Why else had she come backstage, if not to explain? If what she'd wanted was to congratulate Valeska, she could have sent a note; there had been no need to come in person and see the accusation and coldness in her friend's face.

"Oh, come on, Val," she said, tired of fencing. "We both know why you're angry. I'm not denying you had a right to be when it happened, but don't you think you've carried it on long enough?"

Slowly, Valeska wadded up the last tissue she'd used. Taking up a jar of cold cream, she dipped a finger into it and began carefully applying it to one cheek.

"I hear you and Nigel are doing another musical," she said, without acknowledging the question. "Something called . . . *Bangles*, is it?"

"*Sequins*," Keeley said. She could feel her jaw getting tight. She knew Val was aware of the show's title; it had been in *Variety* for weeks.

"Oh, yes, that's right," Valeska said, dipping her finger into the cold cream again. "Well, congratulations. It seems that you and Nigel are quite a team—" her eyes briefly met Keeley's in the mirror again "—in more ways than one."

Keeley had always hated sparring; it was a waste of time. "I told you before, Val, what happened in Philadelphia was a misunderstanding."

"Oh, is that what you're calling it now?"

Clenching her fists, Keeley said, "Nothing *happened*, Val."

Valeska raised a delicate, blond eyebrow. "You could have fooled me. Maybe you're just using him, is that it?"

"I don't need to *use* anybody!"

Valeska capped the cold cream. "I'm sorry, Keeley, I've got to meet some people for dinner. Will you excuse me now?"

"That's all you have to say?"

"What more is there?"

Frustrated that she couldn't reach her, Keeley said, "I don't know why you've changed so much, Val. You never used to be this way."

"And what way is that?"

"Cold, hard. It's not you."

"It is now," Valeska said. Suddenly she became angry. "You always told me I was too naive, too gullible, and that night in Philly I finally realized you were right. I've learned a lot since then, Keeley, and you taught me all of it. Because of you, I'm not *nearly* so trusting. I've grown up a lot, and I have you to thank."

Keeley lost her temper at last. "For Christ's sake, Val, I said I was sorry! What more do you want?"

Valeska seemed unmoved. "I don't want anything, nothing at all," she said. "Now, get out. Get out before I call the guard to throw you out!"

They glared at each other, breathing hard. Then Keeley reached behind her and jerked open the door. "You don't have to go that far," she said. "I'm leaving."

"Good!"

"But not before I tell you what I think."

"I don't want to know what you think."

"That's too bad, because I'm going to tell you anyway. You've come a long way since the days in our little apartment, all right. You're a big star on Broadway, you've even got your own little crowd of admirers. It's too bad you've developed an ego to match."

Val's eyes flashed. "*You* talk about egos?"

"At least I don't treat my friends like dirt!"

"You don't *have* any friends! They all know you for what you are—a two-faced, conniving little bitch!"

Keeley was so angry she nearly came forward and slapped Val right across the face. "Enjoy your fame," she said, her voice shaking with fury.

Keeley slammed the door hard behind her, and then stood out in the hall for a second or two, gasping for breath. She was just starting angrily away when she heard a crash on the other side of the door. Out of control herself, Val had thrown something after her, and whatever it was, broke.

Good, thought Keeley savagely as she walked away. She hoped it was the face cream, and that it was all over the goddamned floor.

Keeley was still in a black mood when she arrived at rehearsal the next morning. She had awakened to a gray and gloomy day, and to make matters even worse, it started raining before she got to the studio. She hadn't brought an umbrella, and she was soaked when she came in, only to discover that

Linda Swan, the choreographer, was having trouble staging one of the songs they had changed just yesterday.

"What's the problem?" she asked, trying to keep in control. She'd just arrived, and she already felt like screaming.

"The problem is the stairs," Linda said tentatively. She could see the mood Keeley was in, and she wanted to tread lightly.

Keeley threw her heavy briefcase down on the desk in the cubbyhole of an office she had commandeered. There was barely enough space for the desk, a chair, and a mock-up of the stage with the offending staircase; she and Linda were practically jammed against the wall, trying to talk.

"What about them?" she said, struggling out of her coat. The garment was dripping, and she hung it on the doorknob before brushing back her wet hair. She wasn't going to think about Val, she told herself fiercely, and willed herself to concentrate on what Linda was saying.

The choreographer pointed to the model of the staircase. "With the changes . . . er . . . we made yesterday, the number doesn't work," she said apologetically. "Because of the six bars you had to take out, now there's not enough time for anyone to get down the staircase and into position on the stage. I've tried it both ways—having them run down, which looks like they're trying to escape a fire, or having them sing the entire number on the stairs, which looks like they don't have any other place to go. What do you want to do?"

At the moment, Keeley wanted to reach out and wipe the staircase out of existence. She was furious at Nigel for demanding the changes; it had worked perfectly well the way she had composed it before.

"I don't know what I want to do," she said, feeling a headache coming on. "Let me have some coffee and think about it."

Still Linda hesitated. Warily, Keeley looked at her. "Anything else?"

"No, it can wait," Linda said, hurrying out and closing the door behind her.

Keeley didn't call her back. She'd had enough bad news for the moment, and she jerked the chair out and flung herself down in it. Already tired, she put her head back against the wall and closed her eyes. At times like this, she wondered if the struggle was worth it.

Nothing was going right. *Sequins* was scheduled to open next month, but the whole show had too many problems to count. Things that should have been settled weeks ago were still simmering; obstacles kept cropping up. Already Nigel had hired and fired two sets of dancers, and in addition to everything else, they were auditioning more late this afternoon. She and Linda had been working like demons trying to get the dance sequences together so they could rehearse the newcomers, but nothing meshed yet, and now with the opening number to rewrite and restage, she was feeling murderous.

Adding to all the difficulties, she thought angrily, was Nigel himself. She had never seen him so evil-tempered; he always seemed close to a boil these days, and she could just imagine how he'd react if she tried to point out the problems with the opening number. Even so, it couldn't be helped; she had to tell him when he came in.

"Oh, why did I ever agree to do this?" she muttered to herself, her head in her hands. *Sequins* had turned out to be much more balletic than anyone had realized; because of it, she'd had to create a greater amount of music than they had originally planned. She had already rewritten two of the best songs in the show, the comical, "I'm Esme, The Rarest of Gems," and the somber, "Tomorrow Is All Night Long." Now the staircase number wasn't right because Nigel had asked for changes in a fit of pique yesterday. Her face grim, she looked up. If he tried to change anything else, she vowed, she was going to quit.

Nigel arrived an hour later. Keeley collared him as soon as he came in. "We have to talk about the opening number," she said tersely when he entered the office where she was waiting.

"There's nothing to talk about," he muttered.

He wasn't at his best in the morning, and he looked on edge already. Thinking she was feeling a little tense herself, she said, "Oh, yes, there is," and took him out front to demonstrate. Linda and the dancers were already waiting; everyone sprang into action the moment they appeared.

Sequins was about the rise to fame of a singing trio comprised of two sisters and another shy singer named Rhoda, their best friend. In the book for the show, the plot turned on Rhoda's role as peacemaker, mother figure, ally, and supporter; when Rhoda is offered the chance to go solo, the trio not only falls apart, but the two sisters turn on her and each other. The opening number showed them at the height of their fame, when the world was at their feet. The grand staircase they came down during the opening was a symbolic as well as a dramatic entrance, but when Linda and the dancers did the run-through for Keeley and Nigel with the new changes, the problem was obvious. If they tried to get down the stairs before the song ended, they *did* look like they were going to a fire; if they stayed on the steps while singing the song, it looked like they were stuck and couldn't decide whether to go down or up.

"So put back the six bars," Nigel said, when the song finished. He seemed preoccupied, intent on something else.

Keeley stared at him in disbelief. "Put back the six bars?" she repeated. He'd almost had a fit about it just yesterday, demanding they be taken out. "Just like that?"

"Just like that," Nigel said. He was looking over his notebook.

"But yesterday you said—"

He looked up impatiently. "I'm not worried about the opening number, it's the suicide scene that concerns me."

"The suicide scene? What's wrong with it?"

"It's not scary enough," he said, while she looked at him, openmouthed. "During that scene, I want the music to be unsettling. Gothic, maybe. You know, with lots of organ sounds and maybe something electronic."

She was horrified. The scene didn't play that way at all. "But it's not a horror movie, it's a moving scene about a girl thinking about taking her own life! We don't want to scare the audience, Nigel. We want them to feel her pain!"

"No, we don't!" he shouted at her, right in front of Linda and her dancers and anyone else who happened to be around. She was so shocked she just stood there. "And how dare you contradict me, anyway? *I'm* the director here! All *you* do is write the damned music, so go and do it!"

She couldn't believe he was treating her this way. Shock gave way to anger, and she said furiously, "Obviously, I can't write the kind of music you want! If you want something *Gothic*, you can damned well do it yourself!"

Turning on her heel, she stormed off the stage and headed back to the office. She had just slammed the door behind her when Nigel followed, looking apologetic. She hadn't become accustomed to his quick changes of mood lately, and she was angry enough to glare at him as she went to sit down.

"I'm sorry, Keeley," he said, coming up behind her as she sat stiffly at the desk. He put his hands on her tense shoulders and began kneading persuasively. "I know I was a monster just now. Can you ever forgive me?"

"No," she said sullenly. The massage felt good, but she

twisted out from under his touch. She'd had enough of his temper tantrums; right now, it would take one more word and she would quit.

He reached for her again, this time bending down to kiss the back of her neck. "Come on, darlin'," he whispered. "You know you can't stay mad at me for long, now, can you?"

"Yes, I can, especially when you act like this!"

He'd been an ogre before; now he was at his charming best. "I said I was sorry, didn't I?" he wheedled. "Come on, Keeley, you know what kind of pressure I've been under lately."

Angrily, she got up and moved away from him. "Well, so have I!"

"I know, I know, and I'm sorry I yelled at you like that," he said. His eyes, as they sometimes could be, were mesmerizing. "Please forgive me, will you?"

"I don't know," she said curtly, but she already had. When he looked at her like that, she couldn't help feeling that somehow *she* was in the wrong. Besides, he *was* right. They had both been under intense pressure lately to get the show in shape, and she could hardly blame him for losing his temper when she was always so close to losing hers. And she couldn't stay angry with him for long; despite everything else, she was grateful to him for the opportunities he'd given her. She had learned a lot from him during their association, probably more than she would have with anyone else. He gave her responsibility and creative space and almost more latitude than she could have wished. And in those times when they were casting, or staging, or choreographing a number, she could see why he'd once been on top.

Ashamed of the treacherous thought, she turned to look at him. He was right behind her, and before she could move back, he'd put his hands on her waist.

"You still mad?" he murmured.

She sighed. "No, I'm not still mad." She pointed a finger at him. "But I don't like it when you yell at me like that."

He smiled that charming smile that seemed to melt some women's hearts. "I'm sorry. I won't do it again."

"Yes, you will. You can't help yourself." She put her hands on his, trying to free herself. "Come on, we'd better go—"

"We have a few minutes," he whispered, bending down. His breath fanned her cheek, and she pulled back. He immediately looked hurt. "What's wrong?"

She couldn't help glancing toward the door. "Nothing's wrong. I just don't want anyone to misinterpret—"

He returned to nuzzling her neck. "No one's going to think anything, especially if you give me the right answer. I did ask you a rather important question the other night, remember?"

Oh, she didn't want to talk about that now! "Of course I remember," she said, trying to stall. "But this isn't the time—"

"If now's not the time, when is?"

Briefly, she closed her eyes. She hadn't intended to tell him like this, but he was giving her no choice. Deciding just to get it over with, she said, "I'm sorry, Nigel. I did think about it, but I just can't marry you."

He didn't believe her. "You don't mean it. We make a great team, don't we? We—"

She didn't want to tell him she didn't love him; it sounded too cruel after all he'd done for her. "That's just it, we *do* make a good team," she said. "A professional team. You direct, and I write the music. I don't want anything to jeopardize it."

He looked at her reproachfully. "And what makes you think marriage will do that?"

"I think marriage jeopardizes everything. Long ago, I vowed never to get married. So can't we leave it like this?"

"It's the age difference, isn't it?" he asked. Shoulders slumped, he turned away. "It is. I knew it."

"No, it isn't that. Age has nothing to do with it. I just don't like the idea of marriage—to anyone. I saw the problems it could cause in my own family, and I decided long ago I didn't want any part of it."

He turned back eagerly. "Then we can live together!"

Why was he pushing it like this? Feeling a little desperate, she said, "Live together? Why? Oh, Nigel, why can't we just leave things as they are? Why complicate everything at a time when we're having all these problems with the show? The opening of *Sequins* is only weeks away, and that's all I can think of right now."

Hurt, he said, "You're obsessed, Keeley."

She couldn't give in now. "That's true. Would you have me any other way—especially at this point?"

He thought about it. "All right, I'll agree to table this—for now. But we're going to talk about it again, I swear it."

She didn't want to ruin their relationship, but she had to warn him. "I'm not going to change my mind."

"Don't be too sure," he replied, staring at her with those deep-set dark eyes. Softly, he added, "I do love you, Keeley."

"And I love you, too," she said. *Like an uncle, or a brother, or a director who holds my future in his hand.* She dredged up a smile. "Now, will you leave me alone so that I can write the new number? If I start right now, maybe we can begin staging it by this afternoon."

He looked at her a moment longer before shaking his head ruefully. "I don't know why I let you do this to me. Here I bare heart and soul and ask you to marry me, and all you can think of is the damned show."

"I'm sorry, Nigel."

He raised his hand. "Don't apologize. I always knew how ambitious you were, so it's my own fault that I keep coming back for more."

"We do make a good team, Nigel."

"Yes, and that's the hell of it, isn't it?"

She didn't know how to respond, or to interpret the strange look on his face as he went out. Just then, the phone rang, and without thinking, she picked up the receiver.

"Keeley Cochran."

"Well, hi," said a deep voice she remembered all too well. "Did you miss me, darlin'?"

Instantly, Keeley forgot about Nigel and all her other problems. "Miss you?" she repeated. Even she could hear her voice quivering with delight. "I told you, I never have time to miss you. How long have you been gone, anyway?"

"Too long," he said, in a way that made her feel weak. "I had some ... business ... to take care of, but it's out of the way now, and I wondered if we could get together. Soon."

"You're back in town?" Her heart started pounding so hard she was sure he could hear it. Then she realized what he'd said, and she straightened. "You've been here for a while and haven't called me?" she demanded. "What makes you think I'd want to see you now?"

He laughed. She thought it the warmest sound in the world. "If you don't agree to see me, I'll camp outside the theater until you do. How about dinner?"

"Tonight?" She looked at the mountain of notes and changes and music sheets and other paraphernalia on the desk and closed her eyes. She couldn't possibly. "Oh, Gabe, I'm sorry, but we're right in the middle of rehearsals. I don't have a spare minute until ... next February."

He laughed again but was undeterred. "I understand. But you have to eat, don't you?"

She could feel herself weakening. She had thought about him

too often since the last time they'd met, and his voice alone was enough to bring back all the longing she'd been trying to deal with. Too many nights, helpless, she lay in bed, aching with the memory of his kiss, yearning to feel his arms around her.

Her fingers tightened involuntarily on the phone. She glanced again at the mound of work on her desk. She had so much to do; she couldn't ask him to come all this way just for a few minutes. It wouldn't be fair; it wouldn't be enough!

"Gabe, I really am busy," she forced herself to say. "I'd be pressed even to go out for coffee, and I'd hate for you to go to so much trouble when I wouldn't have much time."

"It's no trouble at all," he said cheerfully. "Five minutes will do. I just want to see you."

She gave up. She wanted to see him, too. Oh, she did—even for five minutes, five seconds. But not here, she thought quickly. She didn't want him coming to the theater, where there would be too much noise and confusion and interruptions even to talk—if that's what they were going to do.

She said, "I have to go back to my apartment to pick up some music, but maybe if you meet me there about seven, we could have a sandwich or something before I come back here. Would that be all right?"

"More than all right. Do you want me to bring something from the deli?"

"Would you?"

"No problem. I'll see you at seven."

He already had her new address; she'd given it to him the last time he'd called—right before she had moved out of the apartment she had shared with Val. The place held too many memories, and once she started making some good money at last, she had decided to make a clean break. Now she had a walk-up near the Village that suited her just fine. She even had a new roommate of sorts, she thought with a smile—one who had just walked in and made himself at home as if he owned the place. She called him Tuxedo, and she'd found him outside the building one night, battered and bloody, one ear half torn off as though he'd been in a fight. Naturally, she couldn't just leave him there, so she had taken him in—and the next day to the vet. Two hundred dollars later, the big black cat with the white fur bow tie was a permanent fixture, even if he'd never really forgiven her for having him neutered when he was under anesthesia for surgery to fix his ear. He was very independent, standoffish, not grateful at all to her for what she'd done for him. He gave

Keeley space, and she returned the favor, but she had noticed that whenever she sat down to write music, he'd come to sit by her and purr.

Thinking of writing music reminded her that despite this red-letter day now that Gabe was back in town, she still had problems to solve here. Sighing, she went out to get Linda, and they spent the afternoon staging the new number. By six, when she headed back to her apartment, she felt drained. Tux wasn't there when she arrived; he had his own schedule and had gone out the cat window she'd put in to explore around town. Putting food out for him in case he came home later, she hopped into the shower and managed to get herself together by seven. She had just finished dressing in fresh jeans and sweater when the doorbell rang. Gabe was exactly on time, and she didn't care: she ran to the door to greet him.

"Well, you're on ti—" she started to say brightly as she threw open the door. Despite herself, she choked when she saw him. "My God! What happened?"

Ruefully, he touched his cheek, where an angry red scar was still healing. "Gee, and here I thought it was hardly noticeable now," he said. "Maybe a little more makeup?"

Horrified, she practically dragged him inside. Slamming the door, she turned to look at him. "Are you all right? Were you hurt?" she demanded, and then laughed hysterically. "Of course you were hurt, what am I saying?" She put both hands to her cheeks, staring at him in dismay. "Oh, Gabe!"

Smiling, he took her hands and held them. "I know it looks pretty awful, but it's just a scratch, really."

"Just a scratch!" Her eyes followed the jagged line on the right side of his face from above his temple, down the side of his eye, over his cheekbone, until it finally disappeared under his jaw. "Oh, Gabe! You could have lost your eye!"

"Yes, but I didn't," he said, staring at her as if nothing else mattered. "I admit it was a close call, but these things happen."

"Not to anyone I know!" she exclaimed. "Oh, Gabe, you have to tell me about it!" Reaching out, she touched his face. When she realized what she was doing, she snatched her hand back. "I'm sorry. Does it hurt?"

He smiled again, clearly delighted that she was worried about him. "Not anymore. But it did when I got it. Let's just consider it a love pat from a tiger I met in India."

"You were attacked by a tiger?"

"Yes, but in the end, I got the best of him."

She forgot all about her time schedule; quickly she dragged him over to the couch and sat him down. "Tell me all about it," she commanded, sitting beside him.

"I thought we were going to have something to eat."

She noticed that he'd brought a bag from the deli. Taking it out of his hand, she tossed it on the coffee table. "We can eat later."

"But don't you have to get to the theater?"

"Gabe!"

"All right, all right," he said with a laugh. "But first, I want to say I like your new place."

"Great." She didn't want to talk about her apartment; she wanted to know about him. "Go on."

"It looks just like you."

"Like me, it needs work. Now, if you—"

"What made you decide to move to the Village?"

She was ready to throttle him. "The fact that people can commit murders here and get away with it. Now, are you going to tell me what happened, or not?"

She learned more from what he didn't say than what he did tell her. City girl she might be, but she wasn't fooled about his casual mention of going out to hunt a man-eating tiger. He made it sound like something one did every day, but she knew better.

"Oh, Gabe!" she said, her head in her hands. Despite herself, she was hearing it all musically—the menacing tympany of the drums as the tiger padded forward, a vibrating cello as it crouched to attack, a quick, shrill slice of a violin string, abruptly cut off, indicating hair-trigger danger. Her face pale, she looked up.

"You could have been killed," she whispered.

"Yes, but I wasn't," he said, grinning. "And I got some spectacular film."

"You were *filming* while the tiger attacked you?"

"No, I'm not *that* nerveless," he said, laughing again. "I meant, before, and after."

"Then the foundation was pleased? Oh, I'm so glad. But I'm sure it would have made bigger headlines if you'd gotten a picture of the tiger *while* it was slashing at you!"

Smiling at the sarcasm, he said, "No, they were satisfied with what I gave them. But in a few days, I'm off to South America."

"So soon!"

"Well, I've been here awhile, having this damned plastic surgery," he admitted. "I couldn't go home like I was; my mother would have taken one look and fainted."

"You've been home to California?"

His face changed, his expression turned inward. "No, not yet. If there's time, I might stop in before I leave."

"Well, that will be nice," she said. She was trying not to feel hurt that he'd been here awhile and hadn't called her.

With his disconcerting habit of seeming to read her mind at times, he took her hand. "I would have called you before, but the surgery was a little more complicated than I expected. Besides, I didn't want to see you while I was in the hospital; it's much nicer seeing you here."

They were still sitting on the couch, and at his touch, her heart stuttered a little and then began racing. Looking into his eyes, she could feel herself tremble. Now that she was used to it, and knew he was all right, the scar made him look quite . . . dashing.

"So tell me, Keeley, as in Cochran," he said, "what's been happening with you."

He knew Valeska, too, and she felt she had to explain. But she didn't want to go into the whole story, not while they had so little time, so she made up a tale about how they'd agreed to go their separate ways.

"That's too bad," he said, his eyes on her face.

"Yes, it is," she agreed, thinking of the scene with Val backstage. Unconsciously, she sighed. "I miss her."

"I bet you do," he said quietly. "It's always difficult when friends . . . part." His fingers tightened on hers. "So she's doing well in *Florentina*, and you're about to wow them with a new show called *Sequins*."

Dismissing the show and the number of people who were waiting for her at night rehearsal, she laughed gaily. "You've been reading the trades again."

"Only since I got back."

"Oh, Gabe!" She couldn't stop herself. "I missed you!"

His face changed. "I missed you, too."

He reached out, and she threw herself against him, raising her face for his kiss, wrapping her arms fiercely about his neck. She had missed him, more than she had realized, for as his mouth closed on hers, and she drew in the sweet, masculine scent of him, something erupted inside her. He slid his hands under her sweater, and as he touched her bare skin, she gasped.

"Oh, Gabe!" she said softly.

In answer, he leaned back on the couch, pulling her with him. She could feel the hard beating of his heart under her chest as she lay on top of him, and when he put his hand in her hair and drew her head down to his, she opened her mouth and their tongues met. She felt on fire, every nerve, every sense on overload. Her head was spinning, and all she could think of was to get their clothes off and make love. His breathing was a harsh rasp in her ear, he held her so tightly she could hardly breathe.

"Gabe, let's—" she started to say, but just then there was a thud on the back of the couch, the sound of a hiss, and then a sharp *Me-errow!* Startled, she looked up.

Tuxedo had come home. The sounds they were making, their passionate clinch, had made him suspicious, and he was perched menacingly on the back of the couch, looking ready to attack.

Gabe looked up, surprised as well. When he saw the big black cat with the white bow tie glaring down at him, he glanced at Keeley, then back at the cat. He started to laugh. "I don't seem to be having such good luck with felines these days, do I?" he said wryly. "Who, may I ask, is that?"

Sighing, Keeley sat up. Moving off Gabe, she gave the cat a dirty look. "That's Tuxedo," she said, glaring while the cat gazed back with narrowed eyes. He still wasn't sure this was all right. Darkly, she added, "Soon to be out in the street."

Straightening his clothes, Gabe sat up. Running a hand through his disheveled hair, he took a deep breath. "Well, I guess that takes care of that—for the time being, at least. When did you adopt him?"

"I didn't," she said, wishing she had a cat swatter. "He adopted me. I think he was sent to torment me, because tonight he's certainly doing a fine job."

Laughing, Gabe reached for her and pulled her into his side. "How about that sandwich?" he suggested. "I know you're in a rush."

She glared over her shoulder again at her cat. Nonchalantly, now that he'd done the damage, Tuxedo jumped lightly off the back of the couch and stalked into the kitchen. "I wasn't in that much of a rush," she muttered.

But he was right. The mood was gone, and when she looked at the clock and saw how late it was, she felt defeated. They ate quickly, Gabe tempting the suspicious Tuxedo out of the kitchen with the last of his sandwich and earning a feline friend for life. But as they were cleaning up, Keeley turned to him seriously.

Reaching up, she gently touched the still-healing scar on his face.

"Promise me, you'll be more careful next time, will you, Gabe?"

With sandwich papers and napkins in his hand, he started to say something frivolous and glib, but at the look on her face, he became serious, too. Reaching for her hand, he held her gaze. "As long as you're here to care about me, I'll be careful, I promise."

"I do care about you, Gabe," she said softly. "In fact, I—"

She didn't get a chance to finish the sentence. The phone rang just then, sounding like a firecracker in the quiet. She jumped, then reached for it automatically. It was Nigel, and he was mad.

"Where in the *hell* have you been?" he demanded when she said hello. "We've been waiting a half hour. Do I have to send someone down for those arrangements, or what?"

Her eyes on Gabe, she sighed. "No, no, I'll be right there."

"You'd better be!" Nigel declared, and slammed down the phone.

"Trouble?" Gabe said, as she slowly replaced her own receiver.

"No, everybody's just waiting for me. I have to get back."

"I'll take you."

"No, you don't have to."

"I'll take you," he repeated firmly.

They rode in a cab back to the theater. Gabe asked the driver to wait while he walked her to the stage door. It was cold out, and she shivered, and he pulled her briefly to him to warm her. She put her hand on his chest and felt an answering rise in his pulse. Her eyes bright, she looked up at him in wonder.

"You see what you do to me?" he said softly.

In answer, she took his hand and put it over her own heart. "You see what you do to me?" she murmured.

Gabe closed his eyes at the softness of her breast. He wanted to crush her to him right here on the stairs, but he didn't dare. Opening his eyes, he looked down at her. Clearly wishing he didn't have to go, he said, "I'll be back."

"You'd better," she replied, trying to smile, Then, not trusting herself, she turned and went into the theater.

Sequins opened the following month in Boston to good reviews—about the score, the songs, the choreography, everything but the direction. Keeley only managed to calm Nigel down by reminding him that he'd never played to good press in Boston; she assured him that by the time they took the show back to New York, the critics would be raving.

And they did—about Keeley's score. After previewing to the critics there, the show sold out. The lead singer was no Valeska Szabo, but she did a credible job, and the new song Keeley had added during their Boston run, the sensually charged, "Can't Get Enough of Him," that she had written, known only to her, with Gabe in mind, was recognized and applauded in the overture. Nigel had his pride; he went to the backers' party with his head held high. Once there, he proceeded to get utterly and absolutely drunk. Wishing Gabe were there, Gabe, who was somewhere in South America this night—Keeley took a cab home by herself. As she unlocked the dark apartment, only Tuxedo was there to greet her. He rubbed against her legs, purring mightily as if trying to chase away her loneliness, and as she bent to pick him up and hold him close—a gesture he allowed for once—she thought of the accolades that had come her way tonight, the compliments, the praise. She had come a long way, she thought. She should be delighted, ecstatic. Instead, as she buried her face in Tuxedo's thick black fur, she felt like crying.

Then, for no reason she could really fathom, she thought of Valeska. And wondered if she, too, went home alone at night.

———— ❧ ————

CHAPTER FOURTEEN

Keeley spent the night of the Theater Awards dinner home alone. She had planned to go with Nigel, but he called an hour before they were to leave to beg off.

"I'm sorry, Keeley," he said. "I'm really not feeling well tonight, and I think it's best if I just stay home and go to bed. You don't mind, do you?"

Normally she wouldn't have minded; as she'd told anyone who would listen, she hated dinners and parties and awards ceremonies. But this ritual was held only once a year and she had never been before. It was almost as prestigious as the Tony

Awards, and she had been looking forward to it. But she said, "Of course I don't mind. You can't help it if you're sick. I hope it's nothing serious."

"No, just a flu bug, I think," Nigel said. "I'm really sorry for letting you down, but you can always go alone, you know."

"No, no, it's okay." He was the one who had been invited. She forced a smile into her voice. "There's always next year."

"Sure there is. And we'll be there."

Disappointed, she hung up the phone. It didn't occur to her until then that his coming down with the flu might have something to do with the fact that their new show, *Sequins*, had just closed. Resolutely trying not to think that Valeska would be at the dinner because she was up for an award for *Florentina*, Keeley put on sweats instead of an evening dress, rejected the idea of an unappetizing TV dinner, and decided to get some work done. Settling on the couch, she began to plan the lyrics to a new song.

Half an hour later, she tossed the notebook aside. She had been using a technique Barry had taught her, employing separate pads for each section of the song: three pads for the A, B, and C sections, then three more for A Prime, B Prime, and C Prime sections, but she couldn't concentrate. She had never used this shorthand method of composition until she met Barry, but she could still hear him saying—his eyes closed, one hand to his aching head—If you don't keep them separate, everything jumbles together, and before you know it, you'll be stealing ideas from the third quatrain and putting them into the first. Then what will you do with the hole you suddenly find in the second?

Frowning at the memory, she got up and went to the window seat under the front window. Impatient with her restlessness, Tuxedo had abandoned her and curled up on a pillow here; he opened one sleepy eye as she approached, and she stroked him absently. He began to purr, something he did only for her. It was a comforting sound that acted as counterpoint to the soft stereo in the background, and she sat down beside him, watching a man across the street walking a huge dog that lumbered from side to side.

Now that she had started to think of Barry, she couldn't get him out of her mind. He'd been gone for so long now—almost two years. It was hard to believe. But she still missed being able to go to him for advice, and she had valued his opinion, whether he was drunk or sober.

Maybe what she wanted was for someone to tell her what to

do. She couldn't remember ever feeling so confused and uncertain about her future, and now that Valeska was out of her life, too, she had no one to talk to.

Sighing heavily, she turned away from the window. Her glance fell on the framed picture Gabe had given her before he left the last time, and she picked it up. It was a magnificent study of a tiger, like none she'd ever seen. The shot had been taken with the animal hidden in dark shadows; instead of its own stripes, bamboo shoots formed a pattern over its face, and the eyes that looked out from behind the fronds seemed to burn. As Gabe had intended, every time Keeley looked at it, she found herself drawn to that deep gaze. The beautiful cat seemed to hold the secret to life itself.

"She went her way and allowed me to go mine," Gabe had written at the bottom of the photo. "But I'll never forget the look in her eyes. It reminded me of you at times. . . ."

She knew the inscription by heart, and she shook her head slightly when she put the photo back on the table. She hadn't forgotten how horrified she'd been when Gabe last visited and she had seen the scar on his face. Every time she realized he could have been killed, she felt faint.

He'd made light of it, but the scar made her realize just how dangerous his work was at times. When she had asked him what made him do such hazardous things, he shrugged. "I'm doing something I love. And, fortunately, I seem to be good at it, too. At least the foundation says my films and pictures are making a difference, so whatever danger I face is worth it, don't you think?"

She didn't know how to answer. The red slash across his face seemed to have called something up inside her, something passionate and protective and wholly out of place.

"I don't know," she had said, unaccustomed to feeling this way. "I'm not sure what I think."

That's when he'd given her the picture of the tiger. It was so beautiful that she'd drawn in a breath. With a smile at her reaction, he'd said, "Wouldn't you rather know something this magnificent is free instead of decorating a trophy hunter's wall? If what I do can wake the public up to what's happening out there, then any price is worth it."

She couldn't argue, but she couldn't stop herself from asking him to be careful, at least. Ruefully touching his face, he'd promised, "I can definitely tell you I'll be much more prudent in the future."

She wanted to believe him, but she didn't. He had a passion for his work just like she had for her music. He'd go where he had to go and do what he had to do for it. Because they were so much alike in that aspect, she had no right to ask him not to take chances. If someone had told her that the only way she could compose was while sitting atop the Empire State Building on a one-legged chair, or while balancing on her head over a board thrown across the Grand Canyon, she wouldn't have given it a thought. So how could she ask less of him?

But the knowledge didn't stop her from worrying about him, and she wondered where he was tonight. Probably hacking his way through a jungle riddled with poisonous snakes and deadly plants, she thought, and without warning, as sometimes happened, she heard a musical accompaniment in her inner ear—an ominous, sliding sound of cymbals being caressed by a drummer's brush. It sounded so much like the slithering of a snake that she shivered. Before she could begin to orchestrate an entire musical jungle scene in her mind, she turned away from the tiger picture.

Remembering that she hadn't had dinner, she went to the kitchen to make a cup of tea. While the water was heating, she thought of Gabe again. He'd liked her apartment, she recalled. He had complimented her on how warm and cozy it was. It should be, she thought. When she had found the place, it had almost nothing to recommend it except the location, close to the subway, and a view of a small park across the street. It was the sight of the park that decided her; she had always loved trees and plants and grass and flowers; just being able to glimpse a bit of greenery outside her front window exerted a calming effect when she was tired or upset.

Debussy had been a bad idea, she thought, going to the stereo to change the music. He always made her feel melancholy, and sad was the last thing she needed tonight. But as she searched through her collection for another record, she suddenly remembered something else Barry had said.

"Listen to the great composers, Keeley," he had told her. "Beethoven, Tchaikovsky, Mozart, Rimsky-Korsakov, Prokofiev, Straus. The list is endless, and so are the possibilities. You can learn from the masters, derive inspiration from them. Even pop tunes take from the old-timers, if you're careful to listen.

"Study the great lyricists as well: Oscar Hammerstein for warmth, Frank Loesser's bite, the simplicity of Irving Berlin. Through them, you'll expand upon your own style."

Wishing she could stop thinking about Barry and worrying about him and wondering where he had gone—and why— Keeley shook her head and put another record on. The dramatic four-note "fate" theme from Symphony No. 5 in C minor by Beethoven leapt into the room. It seemed appropriate. Da-da-da-dum, da-da-da-dum ... Those four notes had been likened to fate knocking at the door, and she had the strangest feeling that might be happening to her tonight.

Slowly, she went back to the couch and sat down. A program from *Sequins* on the table caught her eye, and she picked it up. The show's producer, Lionel Hartman, had breezed into town the other day; she could still hear the yelling and shouting that had gone on between Nigel and him behind the closed office door. Everyone in the cast had heard; for all the noise the two men made, they might as well have been standing center stage.

Keeley had met Hartman before. He was one of the most feared and hated producers on Broadway, and after their initial meeting, she had tried to stay out of his way. It wasn't that he was so physically commanding; in fact, at five-foot-eight, he wasn't even a big man. He only seemed big because he was so ferocious. Like Nigel, he'd had a string of flops the past few years—a situation that aggravated his already legendary temper. Loud, rude, and obnoxious, he entered the theater like a pit bull on the rampage, actually shoving aside the stage manager and yelling for Nigel as he went down the hallway. Apparently he'd seen the latest gate on the show and had come to find out why the receipts had dropped off so dramatically.

"It's not my fault!" Nigel had claimed, after listening to Hartman harangue him for five minutes in the office. The entire cast had stopped to listen. Everyone knew they were about to be canned, but they couldn't help themselves. Nigel had a temper at times, but Hartman could out-shout him.

"You're the goddamned director!" Hartman had yelled. "If you couldn't stage the goddamned show, you should have said so. I would have found somebody else. Francis, the talking mule, for instance. Ed, the wonder horse. Even Lassie would have done a better job!"

Nigel was enraged. "You don't understand the problems—"

"What problems?" Hartman's voice rose in fury. Standing in the hallway, Keeley was sure she could hear him pounding on the desk to make his point. "Just in case you've forgotten, or never learned, there are only a few reasons why a show doesn't work. One: the director can't direct it. Two: the choreographer can't put a button on it—"

A "button" was the closing moment in any song that led the audience into applause. Listening intently because she had no choice, Keeley knew that the most common reason for a number not working was lack of a button. She'd tried to tell Nigel about two of the songs in the show, but he wouldn't listen.

"Three," Hartman roared, "are the songs and the score—which are two of the only things remotely redeemable about this entire mess, I might add—and four is the goddamned book, which in this case is not only about forty-three minutes too damned long, but confusing as hell to boot!"

"The book doesn't make a musical good!" Nigel shouted back. "No one comes out humming the *book* in a musical—"

"No, goddamn it, but if the book is confused, no musical number is going to save things, and I'm telling you, *nothing and no one* is going to save this one! You've fiddled and fiddled with it until it's not even recognizable as the show that opened in Boston!"

Keeley could just picture Nigel's apoplectic face. She had told him all these same things, to no avail—as had the choreographer, the stage manager, the production manager, the lighting director. Everyone who could, had put a word in. Nigel hadn't listened to any of them, and since Hartman had been away, busy attending to all the other projects he had all over the world, he hadn't been here to ride herd. Keeley, along with the rest of the cast and crew, had been forced to stand by and watch the show's "fixable" problems become insurmountable because of Nigel's capricious and inexplicable changes. A song that had fit a scene was out of place when Nigel moved it, so the writers had to be called in to change the dialogue. Those changes made other numbers awkward to stage and sing and those had to be changed as well. It went on and on, a vicious circle with no end until Hartman appeared.

When the producer emerged from Nigel's office, angrily slamming the door behind him, the cast didn't have to be told they'd given their last *Sequins* performance. No one wanted to face Nigel, so they scattered for home. Drained and unsure about her own future, Keeley had followed.

Now she had to decide what to do next.

In a way, she thought, the cancellation of *Sequins* couldn't have come at a better time. She hadn't been happy working with Nigel for a long while now, and it wasn't only because of the strain of their personal relationship. She had told him she wouldn't marry him, and while he seemed sure she would come around in time, it wasn't that. The more problems that cropped up with the show, the more Nigel began acting like a drowning man, panicked. One minute he was the most charming, attentive man in the world, praising her talents as songwriter and composer, listening intently to her suggestions; the next, he was like a Mr. Hyde, demanding change after change without explanation, becoming sarcastic and inexplicable as could be. He'd throw pages of music at her, insisting she give him what he wanted *now*, and when she angrily protested such treatment, he'd act hurt and wounded, as if she were at fault for criticizing. She didn't know how Carlotte had put up with him so long, but then, she guessed that some women liked men who acted like little boys needing to be loved.

Well, she didn't want a little boy, she knew, thinking of Gabe, who was so much a man. And right now, she wasn't even sure she wanted to continue a business relationship with Nigel. The only reason she had stayed on so long was because she had been so absorbed in her music. Nigel had allowed her all the space she needed to compose, and because of the opportunity he'd given her, she felt she owed him her loyalty. But he had become so capricious lately she wasn't sure she could continue working with him. Nothing she did was right, and if he didn't know what he wanted, she couldn't tell him.

Still feeling indecisive, she picked up her notebook again. The stereo began the second movement of the symphony, and she lifted her head to listen. She'd always thought there was something soothing about this movement; the music was so peaceful, with a lovely, slow melody that was repeated several times, but suddenly, without warning, the sounds from the stereo faded, and she was listening instead to her own internal music, the opening notes of a musical she had been planning and thinking about and dreaming of for years. It was her own creation, based on the fairy-tale story of the Beauty and the Beast and, even though she knew it was much too soon for her even to contemplate, she planned one day to bring it to life herself on Broadway.

The music wasn't completed for it yet, far from it, but over the years she had composed a half-dozen songs and polished them until they gleamed. She had planned who the characters were, and what the book should be, and too often to count, she had amused herself by staging it from beginning to end.

But the time wasn't right yet for something so ambitious; she still had her immediate future to contemplate tonight. Unable to concentrate on her music, feeling too unsettled to go to bed, she decided to watch television—something she rarely did. One of the local channels carried theater news, and she switched the set on, hoping it would have something on the awards dinner.

It did. The ceremony was apparently over, and people were streaming out of the place where it had been held. A reporter outside was recapping the night's events, and she waited to hear if Valeska had won for *Florentina*. It seemed everyone else connected with the production had won something; the commentator was listing an impressive array of awards for the musical when he stopped in midsentence and turned to a couple just emerging. Before Keeley was prepared, there was Valeska, in full-color and floor-length mink, looking more radiant than Keeley had ever seen her. She was carrying the award she'd won, and when she turned to the man on her arm with a luminous smile, Keeley froze. Right beside her, looking healthy and fit, was Nigel Aames, who was supposed to be home sick.

"You bastard!" she exclaimed. She couldn't believe it.

Nigel turned to the camera, apparently answering a question from the reporter that Keeley had been too surprised to hear.

"Yes, we're all delighted—*delighted*—that Miss Szabo won for *Florentina*," he said, charm oozing like syrup. "But there really wasn't any doubt, was there? Such stage presence, such a glorious voice! I knew the instant I saw her she'd be a star, and tonight I've certainly been proved right."

"You and Miss Szabo know each other well?" the commentator asked.

Nigel's smile broadened. He put an arm around Valeska, who laughed breathlessly and nestled closer to him so she could look lovingly up into his eyes. Watching, Keeley wanted to throw up. How can she look at him like that? she wondered. Then she remembered that Valeska had told her that she loved Nigel. Keeley hadn't dreamed she still had the same feelings after all this time. Was it possible?

"Yes," Nigel was saying modestly, "I was the one who gave Miss Szabo her start. She first appeared on stage as Emma in *Dan Tucker*, a couple of years back."

"*Dan Tucker* . . ." the reporter repeated, looking blank.

"Yes, it was off-Broadway," Nigel said smoothly, glancing down at Valeska, who smiled adoringly back. "But we aren't here to talk about that, are we? The big news tonight is the award this darling girl just won for her performance in *Florentina*, am I right?"

"Indeed you are," the reporter agreed, congratulating Valeska again before stepping back and allowing them to move on. He began to interview someone else coming out, but Keeley had seen enough. Feeling a little sick herself, she switched off the set.

Keeley didn't see Nigel for several days after the awards dinner. She tried to call, but his service would only tell her he was out of town, so she had no choice but to wait. She knew he would eventually have to come back to the theater to clear out his desk, and she made sure she was there the day he finally dropped in. They looked at each other as he entered the office, and she decided to wait him out.

"Keeley," he said finally, coming in and closing the door behind him. "What a . . . surprise to find you here."

"Not as much of a surprise as I had when I saw you on television the night of the Theater Awards dinner," she said evenly. "What happened, Nigel? Did you experience a miracle cure, or weren't you sick in the first place?"

He flushed at her tone; he didn't like being put on the spot. Well, too bad, Keeley thought. He'd sure as hell put her on one.

"Look, I don't owe you anything," he started to say.

"Oh, is that so?" she said, her eyes beginning to flash, a warning sign that despite her vow to remain in control she might lose her temper after all. It wasn't so much that he had lied about the awards dinner; it was her growing feeling that she had been duped about nearly everything else. He probably hadn't even been sincere about his marriage proposal, she thought, and decided it was time to find out.

"You do owe me something," she said. "You asked me to marry you, remember? What if I told you I've decided to accept?"

"But you didn't," he pointed out. "Was I supposed to wait forever?"

"Not that I believed you, or dreamed of holding you to it, but you were the one who said you would."

Anger flashed in his eyes. "I really don't have to explain my actions, Keeley, but since you ask, it's very simple. Valeska called me at the last minute to say she didn't have an escort. She wondered if I could oblige. I didn't think you'd mind—"

"You didn't ask. You made up a story about being sick. Why didn't you just tell me the truth?"

"Because I knew you'd be angry, just like you are now," Nigel said. "Now, can we drop it? I only came by to collect some papers and things, not to get into an argument about something that is, after all, none of your business."

"Your breaking a date made it my business," she said. "Perhaps this is your idea of marriage, too—doing what's convenient for you. If so, I'm glad I turned you down." Her eyes narrowed. "Let me ask you something, since obviously it doesn't matter anymore. *Were* you serious, Nigel? Or was it just another game with you?"

"Oh, I meant it, all right, at one time," he said, beginning to search through the desk drawers for something. He had his briefcase with him, and he began stuffing things inside it. Glancing up, he added, indifferently, "As you said yourself, it doesn't matter now, does it?"

"No, I guess not, now that you've moved on to other prey," she said.

He looked up sharply. "What do you mean?"

"We both know what I mean, Nigel," she said coldly. "The only reason you asked me to marry you was because you wanted to tie me to you, to make sure I wouldn't leave and take my music with me."

Flushing angrily, he snapped, "Well, you think a lot of yourself, don't you, Keeley? You're not the only composer in town."

"You're right, Nigel. I'm not the only one. I'm just the only one stupid enough to work with you."

Furiously, he slammed his hand down on the desk. "I have a reputation!"

"Oh, indeed you do," she flashed back. "You have a reputation, all right—as a director with a string of flops behind him! What kind of reputation is *that*?"

"Don't you dare speak to me that way!"

"Why not? It's true!" She was really angry now, but with herself or him, she wasn't sure. How could she have been so stupid? she wondered. How could she have gone blithely on, so preoccupied with her music, with being involved in a show, with her ambition, that she hadn't stopped to wonder what was going on? Everyone else must have known, she thought, writhing with shame. What were they thinking? That she was so consumed with her desire for success that she'd do anything to achieve it?

Lifting her chin, telling herself she'd think about what her ambition had done to her later, she said, "I might have been willfully blind, Nigel, but even I know the situation. I know what you've done and what you haven't."

Despite his anger, he suddenly turned pale. "You don't know anything. Nothing at all!"

She wasn't sure what he was talking about, but she wasn't about to give up any advantage to him now. "Don't be too sure of that."

Before she could pull back, he came around the desk and gripped her arm so tightly she winced. Before her startled eyes, his face changed. "What did Barry tell you before he left?"

"Barry?" she repeated, trying to free her arm. Despite herself, she began to be alarmed at the look on his face. What had she said? "What's Barry got to do with this?"

"You tell me."

She was determined not to let him scare her off. "Or else what?" she demanded, jerking her arm away from his grasp at last. Looking down, she saw red marks where his fingers had been. Angrily, she looked up at him again. "Why are you so concerned about Barry after all this time?"

He didn't answer directly. "You'd better tell me," he warned. "If I choose, I can make sure you'll never work on Broadway, or anywhere near it again."

More defiantly than she felt, she snapped, "That's ridiculous. Hartman might have that much power, but you certainly don't."

"Don't try me, Keeley."

"And don't threaten me!" she said sharply.

"Oh, it's no threat, believe me. I can do it. If I choose, all I have to do is invoke the exclusivity clause you signed in your contract."

That stopped her for a second. "What are you talking about? Such a thing doesn't exist."

"Oh, doesn't it? Remember our little night of celebration in Philly, when you signed it? No, I see by that blank expression that you don't. Well, let me enlighten you."

Opening his briefcase, he took something out. Smirking, he handed it to her. It was a copy of something, and he said, "Here. Read it and weep."

Keeley looked down. She was about to tell him that she'd never seen it before, but when she saw her scrawled signature across the bottom, she paled. She had tried for months to remember what had happened the night of the preview party for *Out on the Klondike*, and suddenly, in one blinding flash, it came back to her. As if in a dream, she saw Nigel handing her a pen as she swayed drunkenly on the couch in his suite; she saw herself signing something with a flourish, laughing like a fool, guzzling more champagne to celebrate. This had to be what she had signed—or a copy of it. She couldn't deny the fact that the signature was hers. What kind of fool had she been?

The worst kind, apparently. With growing horror, she read the quickly written words that guaranteed Nigel Aames exclusive rights to whatever she composed while working in New York. Wondering how such a thing could have happened, she looked at him again. "You'll never make it stick."

"No? You want to try it to find out?"

"I'll get a lawyer."

"Go ahead."

He was too sure of himself. Quickly, she glanced down at the paper again. It seemed to burn in her hands. She looked up. "You've done this before, haven't you?"

To her revulsion, he almost preened. "Successfully, too, I might add. So go ahead, Keeley. Give it your best shot. You won't win, and in the meantime, you'll be tied up in litigation for years—assuming you can afford it, that is. Wouldn't it be better just to give in gracefully and continue doing what you do best?"

"I won't write for you, Nigel," she said, her voice shaking despite herself.

He was too confident by far. "If you don't write for me, who will you write for? No, I think after you've had a chance to think about it, you'll realize where your best interests are and come crawling back."

Her eyes flashed. "I'll never crawl!"

He shrugged, unimpressed. "A figure of speech, my dear."

"You used me!"

"Did I. And what were you doing to me? I might have put your talents to good advantage, but you're no innocent, Keeley. If I hadn't taken you under my wing, how did you expect to get your songs on Broadway?"

"I would have done it without you!"

"Don't be too sure. As you've discovered—or are about to, I fear—this business eats people alive. You might have been a success; you might not have been. But in any event, it would have taken you a lot longer without my guidance and expertise."

She wanted to deny it, but she felt too mortified and repulsed to argue further with him. How had she allowed this to happen?

she asked herself, and suddenly thought of Valeska. Remembering how Val had clung so adoringly to Nigel the night of the awards dinner, she looked fiercely at Nigel.

"I'm going to warn Valeska about you," she said.

He actually laughed. "*Warn* her! About what?"

"About what an opportunist you are, about how you'll do anything to get what you want," she said.

Carlotte's face flashed into her mind, and suddenly she knew what had happened to *her*. Carlotte wasn't around anymore, and the last Keeley had heard of the aging singer was that she had gotten a minor part in some experimental off-off-Broadway production. Now Nigel was courting Valeska. It was obvious why. Val's star was rising; her success in *Florentina* was only the beginning. Keeley had read in *Variety* that Valeska was about to cut another record, and with her current success, appearances on television, maybe even parts in films, weren't outside the realm of possibility. There didn't seem to be anything Val couldn't do; right now, the world was waiting to welcome her no matter what she chose.

He'll destroy her, Keeley thought with a chill. She was strong herself, and Nigel had used her. Val was so trusting, so naive, so eager to please. What would he do to her before he was through?

She couldn't let it happen. Somehow, even though they weren't even speaking anymore, she'd make Valeska listen to her. No matter what had occurred, they were still friends, sharing a bond that had been forged that night at the Port Authority when they had fought back against the mugger.

Reminded of their first night in town, she looked at Nigel with loathing. "I'm not going to let you crush her, Nigel," she said. "I'm going to tell her—"

But she never got a chance to say what she planned, for the office door opened and Valeska herself came in. "Nigel, darling," she said brightly, "I got tired of waiting, so I came in to see what was taking . . ."

Valeska's voice trailed off when she saw Keeley. For a moment they just looked at each other. Then Valeska said, "Oh, it's you. What are you doing here?"

"Not to worry, my dear," Nigel told her. "Keeley was just leaving."

"Not before I say what I have to say," Keeley said. She looked at Valeska. "I'd like to speak to you . . . privately."

"I've got nothing to say to you, Keeley."

"It's important. I wouldn't ask if it weren't."

Valeska glanced at Nigel, then back to Keeley. Her blue eyes haughty, she said, "Whatever you have to say, you can say in front of my husband."

For a few seconds, Keeley didn't realize what Valeska had said. Then comprehension dawned, and she said, "Don't joke, Val. It isn't funny."

Calmly, Valeska removed her left glove. Even from across the room, Keeley could see the flash of a diamond. It was like a sword stabbing her in the heart, and she flinched.

Smirking, Valeska held out her hand for Keeley to see. "We were married in Las Vegas two nights ago," she said, obviously pleased by Keeley's stunned reaction. "Right after the awards dinner. Of course, we've been seeing each other for some time, but even so I was surprised when Nigel proposed. I couldn't say no, so we took the first plane out. It was *so* romantic."

Keeley tried not to believe this was happening. Not even the glint of the diamond made it completely real until she looked into Valeska's face and saw her triumphant expression. She knew disaster was ahead, but she couldn't stop it. It was too late to change things, to do anything for her friend.

"Oh, Val," she said. She didn't trust herself to say more. Her throat working, she reached for her coat. She didn't cry until she was out on the sidewalk, but once the tears came, she couldn't stop.

Keeley's answering machine light was blinking when she finally arrived home, drained, feeling as though someone had died. Her steps dragging, she walked over to the phone, but it was a long moment before she could make herself press the button that rewound the messages. She felt exhausted; she didn't know where to turn or what to do. As though he sensed her despair, Tuxedo appeared and rubbed against her legs, purring like a little engine. With a sob, Keeley picked him up and buried her face in his fur.

All their bright plans, she thought: gone. She and Val had been so enthusiastic and excited and hopeful not long ago. What was to become of them now? Valeska was married to that evil man, while she . . .

Remembering the contract she had signed, granting Nigel exclusive rights to her work while on Broadway, she sobbed again. How could she have done such a thing? Was it legal? Maybe she should see an attorney. But even if she took Nigel to court over it, the process would take months, and in the meantime, what? The idea of composing another note to help Nigel Aames was unbearable, but if she couldn't write music, what would she do?

She couldn't think about it anymore; her head was spinning and she was running around in circles, feeling increasingly panic-stricken. Hardly knowing what she was doing, she put Tuxedo on the table and reached for the rewind button on the answering machine. There was only one call, and she didn't care who it was until she heard the name Raleigh Quinn.

"Hi, Keeley," Quinn said, after identifying himself. "I hope you remember me; we met at your opening in Philly. The reason I'm calling is because I'm heading up a film project that I'm sure has your name on it. I know you said you'd never leave Broadway for Hollywood, but I'm hoping that if the offer is good enough, I might entice you out here just for a look. Before you decide you won't come, will you at least call me back? I'll come to New York to talk to you in person, if you like, but we really need your kind of music for this film, and I'm hoping you'll at least think about it. I'll give you my number. Please call anytime. I'll look forward to hearing from you." He laughed, a warm laugh that she needed to hear at the moment. "I promise, I'll make it worth your while. . . ."

As she took down the number, she looked around her apartment. She had put a lot of work into it; until a short while ago, she had felt she'd put down roots. Now it seemed foreign and strange to her, a place she wouldn't mind leaving. Gabe's picture of the tiger caught her eye, and she would have laughed derisively if she weren't afraid she might cry. How fierce did she feel now?

Her hand to her head, she wondered what to do. She felt so trapped, so confused. She wished Gabe were here, then was glad he wasn't. She felt too mortified, humiliated, and ashamed to face him and tell him what had happened. Did everyone she worked with know what Nigel had done? Did they all look at her pityingly behind her back? Would she ever be able to hold her head up again in this town?

Close to tears, she looked down at the phone. She had scribbled the number Raleigh Quinn had given her on the pad beside the machine. Staring at it, she made her decision. Right or wrong, she wasn't sure at the moment; she only knew she had to get away for a while, to think things out, to decide what to do about the mess she'd gotten into here. The contract she had signed didn't say anything about Hollywood, she thought, and smiled a bitter smile. Slowly, she lifted the receiver and dialed.

---------⊘---------

CHAPTER FIFTEEN

Gabe was in French Guiana finishing a documentary on jaguars when he received a telegram reminding him about his mother's birthday. With two native guides and a mound of camera and film equipment piled carefully in the middle of the canoe, he was heading back along the Sinnamary River, not far from the Courcibo, when he saw another craft swiftly coming toward them. On both sides of the river the vegetation was so thick it looked impenetrable; it had been so long since he'd seen any signs of life other than an occasional white egret, that he was startled. Shading his eyes with one hand, he waited while his guides stood and waved.

This part of the expedition hadn't been a spectacular success. After trekking for months through the jungle, Gabe could understand the jaguar's elusive reputation. In this area, they had seen only one, a magnificent creature sighted quickly and gone so soon that he'd barely had time to film it disappearing into the thick underbrush. He wasn't pleased at his results here and had been in a bad humor since they started back to Cayenne, the capital of this godforsaken place. Thank God, he'd gotten some good film before.

He'd be glad to leave this part of the jungle behind. His guides didn't seem to have a problem, but for him it had been sheer torture trying to carry his share of the equipment and watch where he was going at the same time. Two steps into the forest from the river, the jungle closed claustrophobically around him, and he couldn't have found his way out alone if he'd had a string to guide him. In the riot of greenery, with tree boles half-buried under moldering leaves and vines snaking all over the place, they'd had to hack their way through. The constant chattering of the birds and the screams of the monkeys high in the trees overhead got on his nerves, and with sweat rolling down his face and into his eyes and his shirt sticking to him wherever it touched, he was glad to come out to the river again. Even out on the water, the air was only slightly less suffocating, and he'd been thinking longingly of a drink when they spotted the other canoe.

His two guides began pointing and chattering about the newcomers. At least, he guessed that's what they were doing. Both were native men who spoke a mixture of French, Creole, and English that was almost impossible to understand. The guide in the prow, a tireless, squat man named Henri, shouted a greeting as the second canoe neared; one of the other paddlers waved back, calling out something that Gabe couldn't have translated if his life had depended upon it.

"What is it?" he asked the guide behind him. Jean-Louis was practically a clone of his friend; each had the square, powerful frames of the natives here, with thick, straight black hair and eyes like ink. Gabe had already learned that of the two, Jean-Louis had the better command of English, but out here, that was relative, too.

Jean-Louis jerked his chin in the direction of the other canoe. "They have . . . massage, M'sieu," he said.

"Massage?" Not understanding, Gabe found himself thinking longingly of Mhoja, his Masai guide in Africa, or Rajesh Singh, who had guided him through crowded New Delhi into the wilds of India. Both spoke better English than he did, and since coming here, he'd wished there was a universal sign language. It would make things a lot easier.

Jean-Louis jerked his chin again. The other canoe was coming up beside them, the man in the prow waving a grubby-looking envelope. *"Pour vu, M'sieu,"* he said, gesturing.

Gabe took the envelope while two of the men steadied the canoes. It was a telegram, and as he ripped it open, he felt a bolt of fear. It had to be his father. The old man had had a heart attack or something.

It wasn't his father. Annoyed, he read the terse message.

MOTHER'S BIRTHDAY COMING UP STOP WE'RE EXPECTING YOU STOP LET ME KNOW TRAVEL ARRANGEMENTS STOP FRANK STOP

Impatiently, Gabe crushed the yellow paper in his hand. *Damn it, Frank*, he thought. He'd been imagining all sorts of horrible things, and it was just a reminder of a birthday party. How like his brother, he thought, exasperated. Wait until he got hold of him!

Abruptly, he realized that all four natives were watching him with frank curiosity. Putting the crumpled telegram in his pocket, he gestured. He knew it would be useless to try to explain, so he just said, "We go to Cayenne. Now."

The next day, *as he had already planned*, he thought heavily, he was on his way back to the States for his mother's birthday.

"Well, I'm amazed that you actually came," were the first words his brother, Frank, said when Gabe's plane finally landed at Los Angeles International. It was two A.M., and after going through several time changes, an aggravating delay in Trinidad because of some mechanical difficulty with the plane, and a customs search when he finally got to the States, Gabe wasn't in the mood to defend himself. He had been traveling nearly twenty hours, his eyes felt gritty, and his temper was on a hair trigger. He hadn't been able to sleep on the plane; he hadn't eaten. Telling himself it was just Frank's unfortunate way of phrasing things at times, he went to collect his luggage and the camera equipment he'd brought with him without replying.

"Hey, wait up!"

Gabe had himself under better control when he looked back at Frank, but he had to ask. "What was all that business with the telegram? I was out in the bush, and when they came to bring it, naturally I thought something terrible had happened."

Panting, Frank caught up. "Well, I wanted to make sure you didn't forget."

Gabe stopped so suddenly that Frank nearly bumped into him. "When have I ever forgotten, Frank? What's the real reason?"

Try as he might, Frank couldn't hold Gabe's eyes. "I told you. All right, maybe I shouldn't have sent it. But I . . . I just know how much Mom's missed you," he said. Then because Gabe had put him on the spot, he became angry. "She worries about you, you know. You never have been a letter writer, and—" Suddenly, he noticed the scar on Gabe's face. "What in the hell is *that*?"

"What?"

"What! Your face, that's what! Where did you get that scar?"

Gabe had forgotten all about it. The scar still showed, but it wasn't an angry red, like it had been. He shrugged. "A slight miscalculation on my part."

Frank looked appalled. "Miscalculation! Good lord! It looks terrible!"

"Thanks," Gabe said dryly. "You should have seen it before the plastic surgery."

"Surgery? When did you have that? What happened?"

"All right, if you must know, I got into an argument with a tiger."

Frank was still inspecting the scar. "Human or animal?"

For the first time, Gabe smiled. "Only you would ask that. Come on, let's get this luggage together."

By the time he had collected everything, Frank was looking around for help. "Do you always travel with so much stuff?" he asked. "I think we should call a porter to help. I'm parked way to heck and gone out there."

"We can manage," Gabe said, grabbing the lion's share.

Left with several boxes and a duffle, Frank looked down at the pile and sighed. "You're worse than Amy and the girls put together."

"How are the women in your family?" Gabe asked, as they trudged out to the car. Los Angeles International was right on the beach, and tendrils of fog clung to the halogen lights in the parking lot, giving the whole place an ethereal look. For Gabe, who had spent months in the jungle, the mild Southern California night seemed chilly, and he shivered as they shoved his gear into the trunk of Frank's Mercedes.

"They're fine," Frank grunted, trying to stuff the last box in. He glanced at Gabe. "Naturally the girls are excited about their uncle Gabe coming. They wanted to wait up for you tonight, but for once Amy and I managed to overrule them."

"I'll stop and look in on them if you like."

Frank looked horrified. "You don't mean *now*! It's three o'clock in the morning!"

Gabe grinned. "I'll pretend I'm Santa Claus."

"You'll do no such thing. You've already spoiled them beyond belief. They're still talking about that last box of goodies you sent from India. Silk *saris* for children, no less. When will you ever learn?"

"Never, I hope," Gabe said cheerfully. He reached for the car door. "Do you want to drive, or shall I?"

"I'll drive, thanks. The last time you drove one of my cars, you dropped the transmission all over the street, remember?"

Gabe looked at him, wounded. "I was sixteen, Frank. Are you going to hold that against me forever?"

"Yes. Now, get in the car."

At this time of night, the drive to elegant Holmby Hills took just over an hour. As soon as they were on their way, Gabe put his head back against the seat and closed his eyes. He was so tired that he fell instantly asleep and didn't awaken until he felt the car slowing. He sat up, rubbing his face.

Frank glanced across the seat at him. "Man, you were out like a light."

"Jet lag, I guess," Gabe said, yawning. "Where are we?"

"Almost to the house. That is where you're staying, isn't it?"

Gabe grinned. "I had thought of getting a hotel, but I knew Laveda would never forgive me."

Laveda Grange was the Tyrell family's housekeeper—and had been as far back as Gabe could remember. Tall, big-boned, "handsome" more than pretty, she had been the rock that anchored them all. With no children of her own, she had mothered both Gabe and his brother from the time they were small.

Frank laughed. "That's true. She probably would have sought you out and strung you up by your heels."

"Yeah, I figured it was easier this way."

As they spoke, Frank had turned onto the quiet, tree-lined street where the Tyrell house stood at the end of a cul-de-sac. As they passed estatelike homes set well back from the street, protected by ancient, towering old trees, and in some cases tall fences with silent alarms and electronically operated gates, he couldn't help but contrast the scene with others he had witnessed in his travels. He couldn't forget the crowded streets of New Delhi, with its masses of humanity packed like sardines in so little space, or the Great Rift Valley in Tanzania, where he had camped with Mhoja for a few days in his native village. There the tribe still lived in traditional ways, a once-proud people reduced to poverty, their land overgrazed, with illiteracy rampant and the children diseased. From far away, the *boma*—the village—looked intriguing and mysterious, with symmetrical rings of molded mud huts and stick fences. But up close, the reality was filled with flies and undernourished babies crying in the dust. Looking around at the perfectly manicured streets and homes and trees under the streetlights tonight, Gabe thought of Mhoja and his people and closed his eyes. He didn't belong here anymore than the Masai did, he thought, and suddenly he couldn't wait to leave.

Frank had a house key, which he handed to Gabe when they pulled up in the driveway.

"Don't you want to come in?" Gabe asked.

"At this hour? No, thanks. I'll be back with my women tomorrow."

"Well, thanks for coming to get me. I could have rented a car, you know."

"I know. But I wanted to make sure you got here in one piece."

They got out, and after they'd piled Gabe's luggage in the entry, he went out to the car with Frank. "Thanks again. And Frank . . ."

Frank was just getting into the car. "What?"

"No more telegrams unless there's an emergency, all right?"

Frank raised his hands. "All right, but it wasn't my fault. I sent it to the hotel. How did I know they'd go out and beat the bush for you?"

"Well, next time—"

"Let's hope there won't be a next time, all right?" Frank said, yawning himself. "G'night."

Gabe locked up the house but was too tired to drag all his stuff up to his old room. By now, it was after four, and he was so tired he threw himself down on the bed, fully clothed, and slept without moving until a morning shaft of sun fell across his eyes. He sat up, feeling wearier for some reason than he had even last night, gritty, and in need of a shave. Rolling stiffly off the bed, he went to take a shower.

When he came downstairs to the delicious smell of perking coffee, Laveda was in the kitchen. As soon as she saw him, she held out her arms and gathered him unprotestingly to her ample bosom.

"Gabriel Lee," she murmured, hugging him hard. "Oh, it's so good to see you. It's been too long—and you're thin as a stick!" Holding him away from her, she looked up at him more fully and was horrified. "Your face—!"

He was tired of talking about it. "A swat from an unhappy tiger," he said. "It'll go away."

"Oh, lordy, lordy," she moaned. "What next?"

Gabe smiled, giving her a hug, thinking it was good to be here, after all. Laveda seemed so much a part of home that he couldn't imagine the house without her, and it was a pleasure to watch her bustling around the kitchen. She ran the household with tireless efficiency, going home each night to her husband, who worked as a chauffeur, to their little house in Studio City. Pushing him into one of the kitchen chairs, she poured him a cup of coffee.

"Pancakes coming up," she promised. Pancakes had always been a favorite of his, and she turned eagerly back to the stove.

"No food for me, Laveda," he said. She looked at him in surprise, but he shrugged. "I guess I'm not on California time yet. I'm sorry, I'm just not hungry."

"And no wonder," she said tartly. "Running all over the world like you do, I'm surprised your body has any kind of clock at all."

He grinned. "Same old Laveda. Always harping on something."

Raising a pancake turner in mock attack, she said, "I'll harp on you if you're not careful. Now, are you *sure* you don't want any of these?" To tempt him, she put a pile of fluffy buttermilk pancakes, each as big as a dinner plate, on the table.

Gabe looked down. "Well, maybe I can force myself to eat one or two."

Laughing happily, she turned back to the stove. "It's good to have you home again, Gabriel Lee. Your mama's been waiting—"

Abruptly, she broke off. She was busy with something else at the stove when Gabe looked up.

"Laveda?"

She shook her head. "Never mind. I wasn't supposed to say anything."

Abandoning the pancakes, Gabe stood up. "Anything about what?" Reaching for her arm, he turned her gently to face him. "Talk to me, Laveda," he said.

She looked distressed. "Oh, me and my big mouth! Elmo always says I talk too much, and he's right."

"Laveda," he warned.

Her warm brown eyes met his, and she sighed. "Oh, all right, it's no secret, anyway, is it? You know how much your mama misses you, how much she worries about you. And it's been so long since you've been home even for a visit that she was starting to worry you'd never come home again. There," she said, almost defiantly. "I've said it." She looked up at him again, shaking her finger in his face. "And if you say one word to your mama that I told you, I'm never coming here again myself, you understand, Gabriel Lee? I wasn't supposed to say anything in the first place, so don't you go getting me in trouble, you hear me?"

Gabe didn't know whether to laugh at her indignation or feel guilty about what she'd said. "I hear you. And I won't say anything, I promise." He looked down. "I'm sorry she felt like that. I really did intend to visit. It's just that Dad and I—"

He stopped. There was no point going into it; Laveda knew as well as he did what his relationship was with his father.

Laveda patted his arm. "Yes, well, you're here now, and that's what counts," she said softly. She looked at him again. "You can stay awhile, can't you?"

He thought of the next assignment he already had waiting. He thought of the ranch he'd just purchased in Montana. He had always loved it there, and his work with the foundation finally enabled him to afford it, but so far he hadn't had much time to visit. He thought of Keeley and how much he wanted to be with her. She was here, in California, he thought with a little rush; some time ago, she had called the IZF and left a message in case he got in touch. He'd called her as soon as he found out she'd moved, and he couldn't wait to see her. But he had obligations here to take care of, so he said, "I can stay awhile, Laveda." He met her eyes. "But not forever."

Laveda nodded. "Well, that's just fine, just fine. I know your mama will love having you here—as long as it is. She's been looking forward to a little visit from you for a long time."

Gabe's little visit lasted two days. Long before then, he and his father weren't speaking again; that same morning, they got into another disagreement almost as soon as they saw each other.

"Have you come to your senses yet?" Ellis asked when he came downstairs.

"About what?" Gabe asked, knowing full well what his father meant.

"About coming to work for me, that's what."

Sighing, Gabe said, "I told you, Dad. I work for the foundation now."

"You're wasting your life, boy. Do you hear me? Just wasting your life!"

Gabe took a grip on his temper. "I'd appreciate it if you wouldn't call me 'boy.' I'm twenty-eight years old, and—"

"And still acting like an irresponsible teenager. Do you know how worried your mother is by all your gallivanting around? If you had any sense, you'd come home where you belong."

A muscle leapt in Gabe's jaw. "Then I guess I don't have any sense."

"I guess not," Ellis said flatly. "What happened to your face?"

"I got hit by a beer bottle in a bar fight."

Ellis grunted. "Doesn't surprise me at all."

It was Saturday, but Ellis left soon after that for the office.

Gabe was out in the backyard, trying to compose himself, when his mother came out.

"Gabe, darling!" she exclaimed, rushing up to give him a hug. "Oh, it's wonderful to—"

She saw the scar just then, and gasped. "Gabe, your—"

He sighed. Grasping her hands, he gave her a kiss. "It's nothing, Mother. Don't worry about it."

"Nothing! But—" She saw his face and subsided, but not before a murmured, "Oh, dear."

"Now, don't go saying you knew something like this was going to happen, Mother. It's old stuff, and we have more important things to discuss, such as how young you look today. No one would guess that this is your birthday. How old are you? Let me see. I'm—"

Audrey laughed. "Didn't I raise you better than this? You know you never ask a lady how old she is. We females are supposed to be ageless."

"Well, you certainly are," he replied, giving her another kiss on the cheek. Somberly, he looked into her eyes. "How have you been, anyway?"

She touched his face. "Worried about you. But then I always am. It seems to be a permanent state of mind for me."

"I wish you wouldn't worry."

She sighed. "You might as well tell the birds not to fly."

They were on the patio; there were chairs scattered around under a huge umbrella. He sat down with her. "Do you want me to quit, Mom?" he asked quietly.

She gazed at him sadly for a long moment before she answered. With a sigh, she shook her head. "No, no, I don't . . . not really. I've seen pictures of your work, darling, and I really think that this time you've found your niche. The International Zoological Foundation had a big write-up in *Life*, and some of your photos were featured. I was so proud. Your pictures were so . . . moving." She looked at him mischievously. "I took them to my club, and we all pledged a contribution."

He laughed. "Maybe I should get you a job there as fundraiser. We need all the help we can get."

"With you taking such beautiful photos, I'm sure contributions are flooding in."

"Thanks, Mom. You always did know how to make me feel . . . worthwhile."

She looked at him reproachfully. "I don't need to make you feel something you already are."

"It's too bad Dad doesn't think so."

"Oh, Gabe," she said with a sigh. "Your father is proud of you. He just doesn't know how to . . . to show it."

He couldn't help sounding a little bitter. "Really? You could have fooled me."

"Now, Gabriel . . ."

She rarely called him by his full name; he knew he'd upset her. "I'm sorry," he said contritely. "I shouldn't have said that. What's between Dad and me is . . . between Dad and me."

She searched his face. "Has he . . . said anything to you?"

Gabe knew that if she were aware of the quarrel he and his father had just had about it, she'd be upset, so he shook his head. "No, not recently," he lied. He forced a smile. "But it's early days yet. Give us time."

Audrey smiled, but there was a sadness in her eyes. She put her hand on his arm again. "Promise me . . ."

"What? Anything."

"That you'll do what makes you happy."

"Oh, I—"

Her fingers tightened on his arm. "No, I mean it," she insisted. "I need to know that no matter what happens, you'll follow your heart."

She was making him uneasy. "What do you mean, no matter what happens? What's going to happen?"

"Promise me," she said, gazing into his eyes. "I know what your father wants. I know what I'd like for you, darling. But it doesn't matter what either of us would like. It's your life, and it's up to you to decide."

She was so intense, so insistent and concerned, that he had to do as she asked. "I promise," he said, loving her more in that moment than he could remember. Smiling, he added softly, "And now you must promise me something."

"What?"

"That you'll take care of yourself if I go. I won't be able to take any more of those photos and films you're so proud of if I'm worrying about you worrying about me."

She had laughed, but she had promised with an indulgent shake of her head. Gabe knew that she had talked to his father, for that night at the birthday party, Ellis was civil to him, at least, and there were no more barbed references to his wasting his life. The party was a success, and Audrey's mother was so happy to have her family around that he couldn't tell her he'd talked to the foundation that afternoon and learned that the re-

search team he was supposed to meet for his next assignment
was already waiting in Nepal. The schedule had been moved up,
and they apologized for the rush, but he had to go. He was packing when Frank came in and realized he was leaving.

"So soon? Damn it, Gabe, you just got here."

Gabe was sitting on the bed, sorting through film and lenses
and various camera equipment. "I'm sorry, but it can't be
helped. A team is waiting for me, and I've got to go."

"But I thought you said you could stay a week."

"I thought so, too." He picked up a big 400-mm lens, used for
filming long distance. It was heavy, and he hated to carry it
around, but it had proved invaluable in the bush. Except where
jaguars were concerned, he thought, and set it aside. He glanced
up and saw Frank looking at him strangely. "I know you're upset, but I can't—"

"It's not that," Frank said. He shook his head. "I was just
wondering how you do it."

"Do what?"

"Just . . . pick up and go."

"I have to. The foundation is paying me, and I—"

"No, I don't mean that."

"What, then?"

"You really don't feel any obligation to Dad, do you?"

Slowly, Gabe set aside the camera equipment. "You're not going to start in about me coming to work for the company, are
you?"

"No, I realized long ago that that was beating a dead horse.
I just wondered . . ."

Gabe tried to hide his impatience. "If you're got something to
say, just say it, Frank."

Frank made up his mind. "Okay, I will. Did it ever occur to
you that *I* might want to do something else with my life?"

Gabe was honestly surprised. "No. Did you?"

"Oh, what do you care? You only think of yourself. You always have."

"And you haven't?" Gabe asked, stung. "Don't kid yourself,
Frank. You like to think of yourself as the self-sacrificing mar-
tyr, but the truth is that you've gotten your needs satisfied here.
Otherwise, you wouldn't have stayed."

"Dad needed one of his sons!"

"And so you were the one."

"Only because you wouldn't join him."

"You can't be saying that you think Dad favored me!"

"Why not? It's true. He did."

"No, he didn't," Gabe said flatly. "In addition to the fact that we've always fought about every single thing I ever wanted to do, I was never suited for the company, and you know it. But you were. You were perfect for it, and it worked out perfectly. I would only have been in the way if I'd stayed."

"Well, how convenient for you to leave then," Frank said nastily. "You had an excuse to go out and have your fun. Not that you ever needed one."

Gabe could feel himself getting angry, and he didn't want to fight. "I did what I wanted to do—what I felt I had to do. And whether you want to admit it, so did you."

Frank was getting angry, too. "But Dad—"

Gabe wasn't going to buy into it. "Dad had his own life, his own choices. You can't make yours doing what you think he expects you to do."

"*You* certainly haven't, that's for sure."

"If I'd tried, I knew I'd never measure up, so what was the point?"

"*I* measured up, why couldn't you?"

"Because," Gabe said evenly, "it wasn't as important to me as it was to you."

Angry color flared in Frank's face. "You'll never understand, will you?"

"Sure I understand. I just never needed what you needed from the old man."

"You selfish bastard!"

Gabe went back to packing the camera equipment. "This isn't getting us anywhere, Frank," he said quietly. He looked up. "You've got no reason to be jealous of me."

Outraged, Frank tried to deny it. "I'm not—"

"Yes, you are. You always have been. But there's no need. You've got a wife, two beautiful daughters, a good job ... a place in the community. I never would have fit into that lifestyle."

"How do you know? You never tried."

"No," Gabe agreed. He looked at his brother as he gathered his stuff and put it by the door. "But then, you've never tried to fit into mine, have you?"

Gabe called Keeley before he left for the airport. He knew he shouldn't delay; the team was waiting for him, and he had an obligation to get on the first plane. But he couldn't leave town without seeing her; it would have been easier to cut off his right arm.

After dialing her new number, he waited with tense anticipation, wondering what he was going to do if she didn't answer. An article from *USA Today* was on the bed, and as he counted the rings at the other end, he looked down at it and smiled at the sight of Keeley's picture.

She hadn't sent it; she wouldn't. So he'd had to get a copy of his own. But every time he looked at her, as beautiful as ever, smiling at him over a headline that read, "Hollywood's newest songwriting team walks away with major award!," he felt as proud as if he were responsible for it.

One ring. Two. He tightened his grip on the phone, wondering if a damned answering machine was going to pick up instead of her, reading the article again, although he already knew it by heart.

"Keeley Cochran and Fitz Cowan, Hollywood's hottest new songwriting team, won the first of what we're sure will be many awards last Thursday night, when the Film Industry's Music in Film Awards was held at the Forum. Tinseltown's newest songwriters waltzed off with the award for best score, for the epic *I Will Fight No More Forever*, the story of the Nez Percé Indians' last fight for survival. Since her arrival in town, Cochran has made quite a splash at Charbonne Films. Before the latest coup, and with her new partner, the hot song-and-score writing team had already written the hit title song from the newest superspy Jason Cross series, *Spies Never Die*. Charbonne's president, Raleigh Quinn, is delighted with his songbirds. To quote, 'I hope they'll both be around for a long, long time.' "

Three rings. Four. There was a click in Gabe's ear, and he steeled himself against the disappointment of some recorded message telling him she couldn't come to the phone. Instead, to his delight, it was Keeley herself, brisk as always, right to the point.

"Hello. Keeley Cochran here."

Gabe closed his eyes. Why was it that even the sound of her voice could send reverberations right through his body, all the way up to his heart?

"Hi, there," he said, calm as could be when he felt like shouting, singing, dancing on air. "Is this the Keeley Cochran who's become a Hollywood songwriter?"

CHAPTER SIXTEEN

When Keeley arrived in Southern California, she felt as if she'd landed on another planet. The freeway system alone was enough to strike terror into her soul, and if she'd thought the Port Authority Bus Terminal in New York was busy, it was the eye of the storm compared to Los Angeles International. But, unlike Nigel, Raleigh Quinn knew how to treat people: an emergency prevented him from coming to meet her himself so he sent a chauffeured limousine instead. As she sank back into plush upholstery, her single suitcase stowed carefully in the cavernous trunk by the solicitous driver, with classical music coming in crystal clear on the excellent stereo system, and an array of drinks from bottled water to French champagne in a little refrigerator, she looked around and decided maybe she would like to live out here after all.

Raleigh convinced her it would be a good move. He wanted her to come to work for him at once, but she had loose ends to tie up back East, so it took longer than she wanted to get there. When she did, she went right to work next to Universal at Charbonne Films, Raleigh's production studio in Burbank.

California was an eye-opener. Palm trees were everywhere, and sun-tanned natives went around in shirtsleeves no matter what time of year. Back home it could be coat and scarf weather, but people in Los Angeles rarely had to bundle up unless the Santa Ana winds came to town. The Pacific Ocean was much calmer than the Atlantic, and even on the rare cold days, surfers could still be seen bobbing far out, waiting for the right wave. No matter what the season, it seemed the beaches were always crowded, especially on weekends.

Hollywood itself was a disappointment, she thought. In the land of the stars and the home of the dreams, the famous walk of fame was trod upon not only by tourists, but by prostitutes and hucksters who hawked everything from maps to stars' homes to cocaine and crack. The famous street corner, Holly-

227

wood and Vine, was host to porno theaters and adult book shops, and even though the two places were a continent apart, at times it reminded Keeley of Broadway. It didn't have the same humming rhythm she'd had always felt there—California was much too casual for that—but the old movie city had an electricity of its own.

Keeley didn't want to think of Broadway; it reminded her too much of painful memories she wanted to leave behind. She wanted to forget her last scene with Valeska, but it stayed with her, like the remnants of a bad dream. She'd been so angry with Val that day, but as the months passed in her new home, she was able to view what had happened with some objectivity, and she realized Valeska wasn't entirely to blame. After all, she had been taken in by Nigel, and she hadn't even been attracted to him. What a fool she'd been! Every time she thought of it, she wanted to cringe.

Raleigh's call couldn't have come at a better time; after that horrible episode, she needed a change of scene, and by moving all the way across country, she certainly got it. Los Angeles was about as different from New York as Mars was from Earth, and it wasn't only the climate, it was the place itself. In Manhattan, the buildings seemed as crowded as the people waiting on street corners or filling the subway stations, but even in downtown L.A., there was a sense of openness. In New York, people still walked; in Los Angeles everyone drove to the corner market. Streets were wider and more spacious, and the freeways, once she got used to them, stretched out eternally, connecting one part of the endless city to another, weaving in and out of all the canyons and beaches and valleys. The "wide open spaces," as an amused Fitz had said when she mentioned her impressions: "The New Old West."

Keeley smiled when she thought of Fitz Cowan, her partner and collaborator. Raleigh had introduced them at a party shortly after she had moved out to California, and very quickly they had become not only partners but friends. Fitz inspired confidence, Keeley thought; he wasn't threatening in any way—and it wasn't because he was gay. It was—as corny as it sounded—because he was kind and considerate, a true good friend. And talented, she thought, remembering the party where they had first met.

Newly arrived, not even unpacked yet, Keeley had never been to a Los Angeles/Hollywood–type party, and she didn't know what to expect. What she got was an eyeful. In a town of Beautiful People, where fame and fortune and money generated an entire subculture, a gathering wasn't a party, it was an event. Stature and power depended upon seeing and being seen at all the "right" places. The party where she'd first met Fitz was different. She had liked him right from the start, and after learning that their mutual interest was music, they had immediately become involved in a detailed, technical discussion of their craft. Their rapport was instantaneous; they forgot everyone and everything, even Raleigh, who was watching in the background with a satisfied smile.

The next day, Raleigh called her into his office. Fitz was already there, and he asked them if they would like to work together on his nearly completed epic film about the last stand of the Nez Percé Indians. Naturally they jumped at the chance. They were just completing scoring when Raleigh had a falling out with a songwriter assigned to the new Jason Cross superspy project and asked them to compose the title song for the film. It was going to be the first of a series of James Bond–like spy films—updated, of course, in the new era of *glasnost*—starring Noel Harrington as the spy, Jason Cross. Keeley and Fitz wrote the song, and the result was the megahit *Spies Never Die*. They were still basking in their success when the Music in Film Awards were announced. When the great night came, she and Fitz won Best Original Score for Raleigh's Indian film, *I Will Fight No More Forever*.

Keeley knew that if she lived to be a hundred and ten years old, she would never forget the thrill of the awards ceremony. She was so excited when their names were called for Best Score that she couldn't even get up. She started shaking, and she felt faint; when she looked at Fitz, she could see that he was in the same state. His eyes shining behind his round glasses, he grabbed her hand and gave her a loud kiss. Then, smiling and laughing like fools, they ran up on stage together to accept the coveted prize. She hadn't the faintest idea what she said: something about being grateful both to Raleigh and Fitz for giving her the opportunity to do what she'd dreamed of doing since she was a kid. Then it was Fitz's turn. Grinning from ear to ear, sweating profusely from excitement and the hot lights, he said a few words and they were hustled off stage for pictures. Dazzled by the flash bulbs, Keeley couldn't believe success had come so fast. It was more than she had ever dreamed, and she couldn't ask for more . . . except for the chance to do it again and again.

Next time with a Tony Award? a little voice whispered. As she drove to work one day a week after the awards ceremony, Keeley frowned. She tried not to think of what she had left behind, but every now and then, Broadway beckoned like a siren's song. As busy as she had been since moving out here, learning a new craft, forming a satisfying—and profitable—partnership with Fitz, getting settled and trying to fit in, she hadn't forgotten the goal that had kept her going since she was young. She still wanted to create, compose, and direct her own Broadway musical. Even though it wasn't complete, the music for *Beauty and the Beast* was never far from her mind. Some day she would finish it, and when she did, she would bring it to life on the stage.

But that day was still in a distant, misty future, and as she pulled into the studio lot, she thought how different her life was here from the one she had led before. Writing for film was so unlike composing on Broadway that it was almost a different world. Back there, she'd had a piano in a rehearsal room, with access to performers acting or singing or dancing out their roles. Here in Hollywood—Burbank, to be exact—most often the performers had already done their bit by the time she and Fitz were called in, and it was their job to make the music and the action fit.

Thinking of how little she had known about the craft when she started, she shook her head. She hated feeling ignorant and unsure of herself, so she had submerged herself in intensive instruction. She learned orchestration so she could identify every instrument; she sat with other scorers while they "spotted" a film until she could do it herself. She worked with film editors at the moviola machine to learn how they synchronized the music, and she studied conducting, taking a class at UCLA to analyze the scoring of public television, cartoons and commercials, even army and navy films. She still had a lot to learn, she knew, but she'd come a long way.

Fitz had helped immensely, and the more they worked together, the more she realized what a master he was at building a musical scene. Effortlessly, it seemed, he could spot empty moments in a film that needed help, and he knew instinctively when full orchestration was called for, or when a four-piece combo would do. He never gave a scene away by telegraphing dramatic moments in advance—except when the effect was deliberate, as John Williams had done with *Jaws*, for instance. Williams had done such a clever job of composing in that film that Keeley was sure there wasn't a person in the entire world who didn't feel a tingle when they heard the now-famous *dah-dah-*

dah-dum . . . dah-dah-dah-dum. The back of her neck prickled whenever she thought of it herself.

Fitz helped in other ways, too, channeling her own tendency just to let the music flow into more productive areas. From him, she learned to supply what actors called "subtext"—the use of strident music when a character is laughing but is really panicked inside, for instance. He also taught her when to play the music against the action, and to realize that sometimes, as when suspense is building, silence was the best tool to create a sense of horror and doom.

As she drove up to the gate and waved at the guard, who tipped his hat, Keeley felt bemused at the changes that had taken place in her life. The car was only one, she thought. She had never owned a car before; in Detroit, a city built on cars, she couldn't afford one, and no one in their right mind drove in New York. But California was a land of drivers, and with public transportation nonexistent or still in the dark ages, she had to have a vehicle to get her back and forth. The red Mustang convertible was a sinful luxury, but she had always wanted a sporty red car, and since she had to have *something*, she decided it might as well be something she liked. At first she had felt self-conscious and unsure of herself, but after a year driving the freeways, she was amused to discover she could hold her own with the rest.

But the car was only one outward sign about how different her life was. At the studio, she not only had her own parking place, but her own office, with Fitz, of course. And most exciting of all, she had recently bought a house. It was in Benedict Canyon and had a yard and a pool and a gazebo of all things. Even with what she was making now, the mortgage was still high enough to make her gasp, and she wondered constantly if she'd made the right decision. If she hadn't, she thought, smiling, she could blame Fitz. He'd been the one to talk her into it.

"Now that you're going to be famous, you're going to need something more befitting your enhanced status," Fitz had declared a while ago, right after the Music in Film Award nominations were announced.

"Oh? What's that?" she asked absently. She wasn't really paying attention. With a sheet of music in front of her, she was absorbed in what she was doing.

"Well, for one thing, you need a bigger place to live."

"What for?" She couldn't get a certain passage to flow.

Maybe if she changed a few bars ... yes, that was right. "I'm happy where I am."

"That tiny little studio apartment?" he scoffed. "You don't even have room for a piano in there. No, you need your own house."

He finally got her attention. "A house?"

"Yes, a house. You've heard of those, haven't you? It's a place with four walls and a roof and usually a bedroom or two and a couple of bathrooms and maybe a pool—"

"A *pool*!" She was scandalized. "I don't have time to take care of a pool. Besides, I wouldn't know how."

"That's just the point. You don't have to know how. You pay someone to do it. With 'Spies' going platinum, and with what you're going to earn if we win that award, you can have an army of pool cleaners."

"Why would I want to pay someone to take care of something I don't want in the first place?" Keeley asked.

Sorrowfully, Fitz shook his head. "I can see you definitely aren't California-oriented yet. We're going to have to do something about that."

He contacted a real estate friend of his, and before she knew it, she was buying a house. The thought still amazed her. The colossal mortgage aside, she was so used to living in cramped quarters that she hardly knew what to do with all the room. Neither did Tux. They both rattled around like two peas in a tin can. But Fitz had been right about one thing: she had more than enough space for a piano. In fact, she could have housed an entire orchestra if she wished. A Grand stood against the windows in the living room alcove, and right now, besides her bed and a few other paltry pieces scattered around, it was the only thing in the house. She'd been so busy she hadn't had time—or energy—either to unpack or to shop for furniture. Maybe she wouldn't, she thought with a grin, knowing what Fitz would think. Now that she was getting used to it, she liked all that empty space. Oh, she'd come a long way from the cardboard keyboard back in Detroit; sometimes when she looked in the mirror, it was hard to believe she was the same person.

I wonder what Val is doing, she thought suddenly, and felt sad again. Even though it hadn't been entirely her fault, she still felt badly about what had happened between her and Val. They'd been through a lot together, and to have it end the way it had left a bitter taste. Since coming to Los Angeles, she had picked up the phone a dozen times to call, but each time she had put the phone down again. As much as she wanted to talk to her, to smooth things over and try to be friends again, she didn't want to take the chance of having to speak to Nigel. She had heard through the theater grapevine that he had become very protective of Valeska; it seemed he had not only appointed himself her manager, but he screened her calls as well.

Keeley didn't like the sound of it, but she was more concerned about the other bit of gossip she had heard concerning Val's performance in a new production called *Maggie the Cat*. The show had opened out of town a couple of months ago to lukewarm reviews, but Valeska had a tremendous following in New York, and, based on her performance in *Florentina*, advance ticket sales had been in the gratifying million-dollar bracket. On the surface, the show looked to be a solid hit, but Keeley knew the ins and outs of the business herself, and with so much on the line, she suspected Nigel must be pushing Val pretty hard. She had no other explanation for Valeska taking on the role; from what she had read, Maggie wasn't really her kind of part. The character was too strident, too hard, too shrill. Val had a powerful voice; she couldn't deny it. But if it wasn't right for her, it wouldn't work, and from what she had heard, Maggie wasn't the kind of role to advance either Val's career or her voice.

She'd been concerned enough that she called a mutual friend, a costumer they'd both worked with, named Angela Saber, back in New York. Angela had been surprised to hear from her—and immediately sounded guarded. She knew it was because Angela was working on the show and didn't want to jeopardize her job, so she had quickly reassured her.

"I'm not calling to get anyone in trouble, Angie," she'd said. "I've just heard . . . things . . . about Valeska, and I'm concerned about her."

"I know, Keeley," Angela said unhappily. "But if this gets out, you know, my head's going to be the one to roll."

"I won't say anything, I promise. Come on, Angie. You know me. For old times' sake?"

"All right, but you didn't hear it from me, okay?" Angela said with a sigh. "One of the problem's been this laryngitis. She's been out a lot with it, and just when it seems to be going away, here it comes back again. She's missed a lot of performances, and people aren't happy."

"All singers get laryngitis," Keeley said uneasily. "Usually it's from strain and overwork. Maybe she just needs a break. She did go right from *Florentina* to rehearsals for *Maggie*, didn't she?"

"Yeah, but that's not the only thing," Angela said, her voice low. "I shouldn't tell you this, Keeley, but you were her friend. The problem is her drinking. . . ."

For a second, Keeley thought she hadn't heard right. "Drinking! Val?" She laughed. She knew what a teetotaler Valeska was. One drink, even a glass of champagne, and she was out on her feet. "Oh, no, Angie, you're mistaken. Val isn't a drinker; she never has been."

"She is now," Angela said stubbornly. "I dress her, and I know. I can smell it on her."

Keeley stopped laughing. "That's not funny, Angie."

"You're telling me? There's been more than once when we weren't sure she could go on, she was that stinking drunk."

"I can't believe it!"

"Yeah, well, it's true. And you know what I think? I think it's Nigel, that's what. He's always on her case. If it was me, and *I* had a husband like him, God knows, I'd turn to drink!"

Keeley didn't know what to say.

"You won't say anything, will you," Angie begged as they ended the conversation. "If there's trouble, and it gets back to me—"

"Who am I going to tell?" Keeley said, feeling chilled. "I left all of it behind when I moved out here."

Distressed, she hung up. When she'd heard there was trouble, she'd never dreamed it would be this. Valeska drinking? She'd sooner believe Val had tried out for a porn film. She looked at the phone again, then reached out and picked it up. Valeska had made it quite clear that she didn't want any interference from Keeley in her life, but she couldn't sit here and not *try* to find out what was wrong. Before she could change her mind, she dialed Val's number. She had memorized it long ago, but this was the first time she had actually called. She let it ring ten times, then twelve, before she replaced the receiver. Either Valeska wasn't home, or she was letting it ring. Thrusting away an image of Val too drunk to get to the phone, Keeley forced herself to get back to work.

But her uneasy feeling didn't go away as the days passed, and after trying to reach Val five more times and listening to the phone ring endlessly, unanswered, at the other end, she plunged into work to ease her worry about her friend. Fortunately, she was busy. She had a new life-style, more work than she could handle, and, before she knew it, she was involved in a . . . fling.

Keeley squirmed when she thought of the episode with Noel Harrington. She had first met him on the set of *Spies Never Die*, where he'd been Raleigh's new superspy, Jason Cross. Even now, she didn't know what had happened. One minute she didn't even know a Noel Harrington; the next, it seemed, they were in bed. It had happened months ago—just twice, thank God, but it had been enough. Her only excuse, if she could call it that, was that she had been so lonesome. Back then, she'd been unsure of herself, missing New York and Val, still wondering if she'd made the right decision . . . and wanting to see Gabe more than she realized, maybe more than she wanted to admit. They had tried to get together for so long; the entire time *Sequins* was running, in fact. But one thing after another kept interfering, and finally he'd been sent to South America for months and months, just when she decided to leave New York.

Talk about a long-distance romance, she thought, and sometimes wondered bleakly if they'd *ever* get together. She'd been in one of those hopeless moods the night she and Noel had run into each other at a party of Raleigh's, and somehow one thing had led to another. She wasn't proud of it, but with his dark hair and gray-green eyes, and a broad-shouldered physique he kept in fabulous shape, Noel was a handsome man, and he had women everywhere falling all over his feet. It was mortifying to admit, but for a short time, she had been one of them. Their brief affair had been intense and passionate and wholly unplanned, and she was still embarrassed when she thought of it.

It's all your fault, Gabe Tyrell, she thought, as she pulled into her parking space at the studio lot. *Noel was around, and you weren't.*

It was a nice excuse, but she knew that Gabe wasn't to blame, not really. And at least she'd broken it off with Noel before she made a complete fool of herself. He didn't like it when she told him she didn't want to see him anymore, but he didn't have any choice. And it wasn't that he didn't have an entire smorgasbord of willing women to choose from, she pointed out—a reminder that instantly restored his good humor. In fact, now that she thought about it, she'd been a little miffed that he took it so well. The least he could have done, she'd thought, was *pretend* to be crushed.

Fitz was already at the office when she arrived, deep in a

copy of *The Hollywood Reporter*, one of the film industry's two bibles. He'd already been through *Daily Variety*, for it was scattered in heaps all over the floor, and she smiled at the sight as she came in and shut the door.

"I'm glad to see that you've been working hard this morning," she said, dumping the pile of music she'd been carrying, along with her briefcase, on the cluttered desk.

Fitz looked over the top of the paper with a beatific grin. "Nothing you can say to me is going to dampen my mood. Not with that baby up on the shelf."

The "baby" was the Music in Film Award, a gold-plated depiction of a treble clef mounted on a polished walnut base. Their names were inscribed on the gold plate at the bottom, along with the month, the year, and the name of the film that had contributed to their success. Keeley still felt a thrill of pride when she glanced at the prize in its place of honor. With a grin, she looked back to Fitz.

"You're going to rest on your laurels, eh?" she teased.

"Not at all," he murmured, bringing up the paper to cover his eyes again. "I'm just going to enjoy it for a while."

"While you're enjoying yourself, maybe we'd better think about scoring this film, don't you think?"

Slowly, Fitz put the paper down again. He was a small man, barely five-foot-six, and slight, with receding light brown hair. Round wire-rim glasses made him look owlish, especially because the lenses were so thick they magnified his brown eyes. No matter what the season, he always wore corduroy—pants and jacket. He would have worn the same baggy clothes to the awards ceremony if Keeley hadn't told him he had to wear something appropriate or she wouldn't go with him. She claimed that if she had to get a dress for the occasion the least he could do was rent a tuxedo. Muttering, he said he'd take her cat, but at her look, he'd decided to rent one after all, even if he did spend the night—at least until they were called up on stage to collect their award—looking like he was strangling on something.

Staring at her now from behind his thick lenses, he asked, "Don't you ever think about anything but work?"

Smiling again, she sat down at her desk, right across from his. "Writing music isn't work."

"Yes, it is. It's the most agonizing thing to do that I know."

She laughed. "You don't mean that."

"Yes, I do," he said earnestly. "People who don't do it think it's easy, but it's not. Even with a simple song—six bars of C, two of G, four of F, two of C again, you still have to add dashes of color now and then, or listeners will go to sleep." He made a mock shudder. "It's those occasional bars of color that terrify me. What if I can't think of any? What if the music just . . . goes away?"

Keeley looked at him indulgently. Fitz often went off on such tangents; at first it alarmed her, but now she knew it was just his way of warming up. "The music won't go away," she stated. "It's always been there, and it will always be."

He leaned forward. "But how can you be sure?"

They'd had the same discussion before. "Because I can't remember a time in my entire life when I haven't had a snatch of something running through my head," she said. "I *think* in terms of music, and so do you, and you know it. I've had artists tell me they think in terms of color—their day is red or green or pale blue. Writers I've known say they think in terms of words or phrases—describing what they're doing in their own minds at times, not just *doing* it, like everybody else. Composers—that's you and me, Fitz—think in terms of music. Right now, for instance, I'm thinking of the opening bars of the funeral march—*dum . . . da . . . dum-dum. Dum . . . da . . . dum-dum.* It means we'd better get to work or we'll be attending our own funeral, you got it?"

Fitz sighed. "You know something, Keeley? It's just dawned on me that you aren't much fun."

"Thanks a lot."

"No, I mean it. There's more to life than music."

"There is? What's second?"

"I'm serious here."

She grinned. "So am I."

"You must want *something* else."

"I have everything I want."

"Well, lucky you."

"Are you being sarcastic? Come on. I *do* feel lucky. Don't you?"

"Yes, I do. We worked hard for that award, but Keeley, I have a *life*, too. Is this all you want?"

"No," she said promptly. "I want the chance to compose—anything and everything, as much as possible, as long as I can."

Fitz sighed. "No, I mean aside from that."

"There *isn't* anything but that."

"Yes, there is," he insisted. He came and sat on the edge of the desk. "You need something more," he said earnestly. "Someone to come home to."

Gabe's face flashed into her mind. Dismayed, she became flippant. "Isn't that the title of a song? If it isn't, it should be."

"I mean it, Keeley. Can you be serious for once?"

"I'm always serious about music."

"Keeley!"

It was her turn to sigh. "Look, you're just saying that because you found Lindsey."

Diverted, as she had known he would be, Fitz beamed. He had met Lindsey Grosvenor in a bar several months before. What had begun as a casual relationship had quickly blossomed into something more, and Fitz had invited Lindsey to move in with him. He was in love and didn't care who knew it. To Keeley's amusement, he had changed overnight from a gadabout to a devoted homebody, and because he was so happy in his new life-style, he had begun, maddeningly, to advocate it for everyone else.

"That's not the *entire* reason," he said. "You're young—"

"And getting older every minute."

This time he wasn't going to be distracted. "And you're beautiful—"

She laughed. "Flattery isn't going to get you out of working on the new score."

He shook a finger in her face. "I mean it, Keeley, these things are important—home, hearth ... maybe children someday."

She thought of Phyllis and her father, with their six children, and shuddered. "I don't want children," she said.

"You don't mean it."

She didn't want to get into a discussion about it. A child was an option she planned on exploring when she had time. Right now, she didn't. "I haven't decided yet," she said, looking down at all the work on her desk. "Look, Fitz, can we leave the Home and Hearth Show and get down to business? We've got a lot to do here, and they want us in the studio at two."

"Okay, okay," Fitz sighed. He got off her desk and went to his own, a twin to hers. But before he sat down, he shook his finger at her again and said, "But the subject isn't closed, you know. If nothing else, we're going to get you a decorator for your house. If you won't furnish it yourself, we'll just hire someone to do it for you."

"Oh, no, you don't," she said instantly. "I'm not going to have a strange person swarming all over my house, claiming I need some *motif* that's going to nauseate me every time I walk in. If I want to decorate, I'll do it myself."

"Oh, I can just see it! Early tin can! No, no, I've got a call in to someone this morning. She's supposed to call me back—"

The phone rang at that moment, and he looked at it in surprise. "Maybe that's her," he said, lifting the receiver. "Hello?"

Keeley had already decided she wasn't going to waste time talking to a decorator, no matter what Fitz said. Taking up her work, she debated about the thematic score they had used for the first Cross film. There was a danger that it was too superficial, and she was playing around with another idea when Fitz put his hand over the mouthpiece of the phone and gestured.

"It's for you," he said.

Keeley didn't even look up. "Take a message, will you? I want to work this out."

Obediently, Fitz relayed the request. He listened a moment, then put his hand over the mouthpiece again.

"He says it will only take a minute."

Impatiently, Keeley glanced up. "For crying out loud—"

"He says his name is Gabe Tyrell," Fitz went on. "He's just in from South America, but if you're too busy—"

Keeley nearly fell off her chair reaching for the phone. She was so excited that she barely noticed Fitz's smile when he handed the receiver across. Snatching it, she said breathlessly, "Gabe? Gabe, where are you? Are you in New York? When did you get in?"

The voice she knew so well was tinged with amusement. "Which question do you want me to answer first?"

Realizing that Fitz was grinning at her like the Cheshire cat, she made a face at him and turned away. "The first. Where are you?"

"I'm in Los Angeles. I came for my mother's birthday, but I couldn't leave again without seeing you. By the way, congratulations again on the award. Do you take every town you're in by storm?"

"It wasn't just me," she said, embarrassed and pleased by the compliment. "My partner, Fitz Cowan, and I won it together."

"It must have been exciting. I wish I could have been there."

"So do I," she said fervently. "We were thrilled. But you should talk. That photo spread of yours in *Life* was wonderful."

"Since we're so talented and special, maybe we should celebrate together," he said, a smile in his voice. "Could you manage it?"

Could she? She'd been longing for months to see him, and if she had to leave now and drive out to the airport, she'd do it. Catching sight of Fitz grinning into his hand, she frowned fiercely at him. "I'd love it," she said. "Are you going to be in town long?"

"Only overnight, I'm afraid."

Dismayed, she exclaimed, "You're leaving so soon?"

"I'm supposed to be on my way to Nepal right now, but I figure the team can wait another twelve hours. I'll understand if you have other plans. I know it's short notice."

Thinking that she would have canceled a command performance before Queen Elizabeth for the chance to see Gabe again, she laughed so gaily that Fitz looked up with another grin. Ignoring him, she said, "I don't have any plans but seeing you. What would you like to do?"

When Gabe hesitated a fraction, she knew what he was thinking and she turned pink. After a moment, he said, "We can go out to dinner if you—"

"No, no," she interrupted quickly. She wanted him all to herself. Glaring again at Fitz's knowing glance, she said, "Why don't you come to my place? I know you don't believe it, but I really did buy that house. We'll christen the kitchen. In fact, in honor of the occasion, I'll even cook dinner."

"Talent and you cook, too?" Gabe teased.

"Well, it's been a long time," she said, feeling light and giddy and happier than she'd felt even on awards night. "But if I've forgotten how, there's a fast-food place not too far away. We'll have hamburgers."

"I don't care what we eat, just as long as I get to see you," he said, making her heart take off in full flight. "What can I bring?"

"Just yourself."

Fitz was pointedly staring at something on his desk when she hung up. Aware of the gleam in his eyes, she said defensively, "He's an old friend."

"Did I ask?" Fitz protested.

"No, but you were thinking it!"

"Whatever it was, I wasn't, I swear," he said. But he laughed and gave her a thumbs-up sign. "Whoever he is, he's got to be better than Noel Harrington."

Thinking there was no comparison, she reached for something to hide her red face. "He's just an old friend," she muttered again.

Fitz gave her a few minutes; then he calmly reached out and took the pages she'd been staring at. Turning them right-side up, he held them out to her again with an innocent look.

"Think that will help?" he asked.

"Never mind," she said, snatching them back. She couldn't look at him. "Let's just get to work, all right?"

"Whatever you say," he agreed, and proceeded to carry her the rest of the day. So eager to see Gabe again, she thought it would never end.

CHAPTER SEVENTEEN

For the first time since she'd started working at Charbonne Films, Keeley left the office early. On the way home, she rushed through the market buying what she had planned for dinner. It had been a long time since she had bothered, but she was sure she remembered how to fix chicken and rice, and with a salad on the side and maybe poached pears for dessert, hopefully she would acquit herself well in the kitchen. Paying for it by running her credit card through a slot at the checkout stand—another California innovation—she dashed home.

It wasn't until she was pulling into her driveway that she wished she'd taken Fitz up on his idea of a decorator. As she ran inside with the groceries, she looked around at the empty rooms, the walls bare of pictures or paintings, what little furniture she had arranged where she'd pushed it, and decided she had to do something in a hurry. She wasn't without imagination, she told herself; if she was quick, she could throw some floor pillows around, hang up a few posters she hadn't unpacked . . . at the least, pick up the bedroom. She could put candles around in place of missing lamps, and with enough candlelight blinding him, maybe Gabe wouldn't notice that she lived like a hermit.

Two hours later, the chicken roasting in the oven, the rice on the counter, and the salad crisping in the refrigerator, she wiped her face and stood back to appraise her handiwork. Even she had to admit that she had wrought a miracle in a short time. Instead of an abandoned derelict, her house looked like a home now.

Trying not to think too much about Valeska, she had even put up a poster or two from past shows they'd done. There was one for *Dan Tucker* and another for *Out on the Klondike*, when Val had played Emma. She had hesitated over the *Florentina* poster. Valeska was prominently featured on the front, her eloquent face with the big blue eyes shining as she stared up at something only she seemed able to see. The pose had been taken from one of the hit songs in the show, the unforgettable, wistful, "Ever Again," and as she took it out and gazed at her friend, she felt tears sting her eyes.

"Oh, Val," she whispered, and knew she couldn't look at it for long. Choosing one from *Sequins* instead, she put it up, staring at it critically for a moment before she changed her mind again. Taking the *Sequins* poster down, she put *Florentina* up in its place after all, and then went to check on the chicken.

By the time Gabe came, she had the dining room table set with place mats and linen napkins, with candles for the centerpiece. Soft lights in the living room added to the luster, and as she looked around, she was satisfied with what she had done.

Then the doorbell rang, and her composure vanished like mist. She'd been so busy with the dinner and the house that she'd completely forgotten about herself. Looking down, she wondered if she could run and change, but the doorbell rang again, and she knew she'd run out of time.

"Oh, swell," she groaned. She'd wanted to look her best for Gabe, but now all she could do before answering the door was tuck her blouse into her jeans and smooth her hair with her hands. Wishing she had at least remembered to put on lipstick, she switched channels on the stereo as she went by. Beethoven's Emperor Concerto floated out into the room, reminding her poignantly of Barry, who had drilled her in the classics, insisting she listen and absorb the music as a base for her own compositions. He had even tested her a few times, playing snatches of music for her to identify.

"The Emperor Concerto," she murmured. "Better known as Beethoven's Piano Concerto No. Five in E flat major." She smiled sadly. "See, Barry? I haven't forgotten."

But Gabe was waiting, and she hurried toward the door, her heart pounding. As she reached for the knob, she took a deep breath. It had been so long since she had last seen him; with his growing reputation as a documentary wildlife photographer, he was kept so busy by IZF that he rarely got back to the States, and he was usually on the way through to someplace else when he did. They spoke frequently—or as often as he could get to the phone from the back of beyond—but she also kept track of him through his pictures that appeared in magazines, and his IZF films on public television.

Before heading down to South America, he'd gone to Canada to film polar bears, and while there, he had done something very few photographers had managed before. Fearlessly climbing inside a flimsy metal cage, he'd used himself as bait to entice the curious bears closer. No matter how beautiful, she had cringed when she saw the shots he'd taken: the great furry beasts were so close even she could imagine their hot breaths in her face. From Canada, he'd gone to the Alaskan wilderness to film an award-winning documentary on the elusive white wolf. With one other man, he had insinuated himself into the tightly knit pack, gaining their confidence to the point where the alpha female actually let him film her den and the birth of her three pups.

After Canada, it had been this long stint in South America. It's been so long, she thought. Had he changed? There was only one way to find out, so she opened the door.

He hadn't changed, physically at least—except to become even more good-looking. His blond hair was longer than when she had last seen it, more sun-streaked, but his eyes were still the same intense blue. Tanned and fit, he was wearing slacks and loafers and a sportshirt under a dark blue corduroy sportcoat, and the grin he was wearing with it made her instantly feel weak.

"Hi," she said.

Gabe didn't say anything for a long moment. In one hand, he was carrying a huge bouquet of white lilacs; he had something else in the other. She never got a chance to see what it was.

"Lord, I've missed you," he said hoarsely.

She didn't think. The longing in his voice mirrored the yearning she had felt herself, and the next instant she was in his arms, the forgotten flowers crushed between them, his mouth hot on hers. The blissful contact after such a long separation was like spontaneous combustion. A coldness she hadn't even known existed inside her instantly melted, and she clutched at him fiercely, not wanting to let him go. Her entire body strained toward him, holding him so tightly to her she could feel the hard hammering of his heart. With his lips on hers and their tongues meeting, she felt as though the earth had come to a complete stop, propelling her like an arrow straight to the stars.

"The bedroom," Gabe whispered huskily into her ear. "Where's the bedroom?"

"Upstairs," she gasped.

He nodded, his eyes like blue fire. Reaching behind him, he kicked the door shut. Clinging to each other, they headed toward the staircase.

At the door to her bedroom, he paused with his hands on her shoulders. Suddenly, he didn't seem so sure of himself. Now that they had come this far, he looked almost reluctant. They both knew that once they took this step, they couldn't go back.

"Keeley—"

She put her finger over his lips. She had no doubts. She had dreamed of this, longed for it, *burned* with it almost from the time they'd met. She wanted him so badly she felt light-headed and dizzy. "Don't say it."

"But I have to ask—"

"Don't," she said, opening the door to the bedroom. Reaching out, she took the hand of the man who had hunted elephant poachers and fought man-eating tigers, who had tracked polar bears and trekked into the jungle after jaguars. Smiling, she pulled him into the bedroom after her.

The master bedroom overlooked the landscaped backyard, with the built-in barbecue and gazebo. She had switched on the pool lights before Gabe came, and a silvery aqua light flickered on the bedroom ceiling when they entered. She had kept the drapes open as she always did, and the movement of the waterfall at the deep end of the pool caused the light to change pattern as it reflected up into the room. The effect was eerily beautiful, and as Gabe paused a moment to look dazedly around, he murmured, "It's like being underwater. . . ."

"Better," Keeley whispered.

The phenomenon was one of the reasons she had decided to buy the house. The effect of the constantly changing light pattern was soothing, almost mesmerizing, and many a night when she couldn't sleep for one reason or another, she had lain in bed just watching the designs it made on the ceiling. She hadn't realized until she turned to look at Gabe again how incredibly romantic it could be. The play of the aqua light on the angles and hollows and planes of his face made her breath catch. He looked like Poseidon, she thought, the god of the sea. A snatch of music floated through her mind at the thought—a flare of trumpets followed by a deep rumble of bass; she could almost picture him rising dramatically from the ocean, trident in hand.

"What are you smiling at?" Gabe asked, pulling her close to him.

She didn't know how to tell him. Lifting her hand, she touched his face, gently tracing the whitened scar from the tiger, down to his cheek.

"I was thinking how handsome you were," she answered. "Like a Greek god."

He laughed. Taking her hand, he pressed her palm against his lips. "You're the beautiful one," he murmured, his glance holding hers. Then he closed his eyes briefly. "If you only knew how many times I've dreamed of this moment," he said. "Out on the Serengeti, in India, Alaska, the jungle—" He looked down at her again. "You were always there with me, Keeley, a part of me I couldn't leave behind. . . ."

She wanted to tell him that he had been with her, too, in every note she had put to paper, in every song she had created. But her heart was too full to say what she meant. She could only whisper, "Me, too."

He pulled her into him again, and as he bent down to kiss her, part of her marveled that they fit so well together. She couldn't understand it; he was so much taller than she, but it was as if they had been made for each other. Slowly, while kissing her, he began to unbutton her blouse, as she pushed his jacket off his shoulders and then unfastened his shirt. There was only one catch to her bra, and as it joined her blouse on the floor, he pulled back a moment to look at her.

"I knew you would be lovely," he murmured, touching one breast and then the other, almost with a sense of wonder. Tenderly, he bent down and put his mouth over a nipple. Sensation seared through her, and she grabbed his hair with a moaning sound. His lips moved to her neck, her shoulder, and then her lips again, and, mouths locked together, they pulled off the rest of their clothes and then fell on top of the bed, wrapped tightly against each other. Silvery blue light played over their bodies as they rolled back and forth. Feeling the play of Gabe's taut muscles under her seeking hands, Keeley couldn't touch him enough. She wanted him inside her, but they had waited a long time for this moment, and even with desire tearing at her, she wanted to prolong the anticipation as long as she was able. Gasping, she sat up and pushed her hair out of her face.

"What is it?" Gabe asked. His voice sounded hoarse, and he

was having trouble controlling his breath. His chest heaving, he reached for her again.

"Wait," she said, staring down at him. Wonderingly, she touched his powerful shoulder, ran her hand over his broad chest, down to his flat belly. He looked strong and fit and every inch the man she had pictured, but better.

"You're just like I imagined," she whispered, marveling as she ran her hand over the muscles in his thigh and felt them quiver at her touch. "I can't believe it."

Gabe didn't answer. When she looked at him, what she saw in his expression made her feel faint. He was staring at her with a look of wonder, as though . . . as though she were the most beautiful thing he had ever seen.

"Come here," he whispered, holding out his arms. Willingly, she came to him and let him pull her down to his chest. The sensation of her breasts against his bare skin felt exquisite, and she knew she couldn't prolong the moment much more. Her body was betraying her, demanding release, wanting to feel him explode inside her while she cried out in bliss. Lifting her head, she looked down into his eyes and started to speak. He didn't give her the chance. Desire was riding him, too, and he put his hand in her hair and guided her mouth to his. Pulling her fully on top of him, he spread her legs with his and then rolled over so she was underneath. His breath was hot against her face, his hands demanding a response she was only too willing to give. She took him inside, deeper and deeper, until he uttered a moan and put his head back. Balancing on powerful arms, he looked down at her, and the look in his eyes made her tremble.

With his mouth on hers and his hands caressing her wherever he could touch, Keeley put her hands on his strong back, wrapped her legs around him, and gave herself up to sensation. Her hips began to move in the unconscious, ancient rhythm of all living things in the throes of passion, and when Gabe groaned again, an animal sound deep in his throat, as though it had been wrenched from him, Keeley responded with a sound of her own, arching upward so his hands could come under her, cupping her buttocks. Together, they moved as one in a dance as old—older—than time itself.

"You're incredible," he gasped, but Keeley hardly heard him. Her body was no longer her own; she was possessed by him, filled with him, swept away by such a flood of sensation she could no longer hold back. Pleasure began as a pinpoint, expanded swiftly to encompass her entire body, and then exploded without warning into sheer bliss.

He cried out hoarsely at the same time, his own body straining as he went with her, shuddering with the force of explosive release. They clung together as feeling swept them up and away, until finally, like two leaves coming to rest after the whirlwind passed, they collapsed.

An endless time later, when Keeley was nearly asleep, Gabe lifted his head. He was still on top of her, and he asked anxiously, "Am I too heavy for you?"

She opened her eyes. His face was only inches from her own. "What do you think?" she whispered. Reaching up, she ran her fingers through his hair, tightening her grip when he tried to slip off. "Don't you dare," she said. "I'll pull out every strand."

"Whatever you say," he agreed without protest. "I've got no energy left to fight you even if I wanted."

"Good," she said, when he lay down again. Nestling her head into the hollow of his shoulder, she breathed deeply and closed her eyes.

"Are you asleep?" he asked, some time later.

"I was."

"You can't be."

She opened one eye. "Why not?"

"Because I'm hungry, that's why," he said, lifting himself off her before she could stop him. "We . . . er . . . bypassed dinner, in case you don't remember."

She grabbed part of the bedspread and pulled it over her. Warm inside her nest, she closed her eyes again. "How can you be hungry at a time like this?"

"Easy," he said, and got up. "Up, woman," he ordered. "It's time to eat."

In answer, she snuggled deeper under the covers. "Chicken's in the oven, rice is on top of the stove. Help yourself."

There was a rush of cold air as he jerked the bedspread off. She shrieked and tried to grab it, but he held it out of reach. "I'll count to three," he warned. "By then, you'd better be up. One."

"And if I'm not?" she demanded, trying unsuccessfully to wrest the corner of the bedspread out of his grasp.

"You'll see. Two."

She nearly giggled. He looked so funny standing there, stark naked, trying to keep the bedspread away from her. Then, when she pictured herself, crouched on the bed in the same bare fashion, fighting him for a scrap of cover, she had to laugh. "I don't believe you," she said.

"Take your chances," he said, grinning wolfishly. "Three!"

He reached for her, but she sprang off the bed. Laughing and snatching a short robe from the closet, she tossed him the one-size-fits-all terry-cloth robe she used on cold nights. "Here. Let's go see if the chicken has turned to jerky by now."

"I don't care if we end up scrounging peanut butter and jelly," Gabe said, shrugging into the robe, which, despite its size, looked too small for him. "Let's just get something to eat." He grabbed her from behind as they left the bedroom, almost lifting her off her feet as he kissed the back of her neck. "This is what you do to me, woman!" he claimed, throwing her over his shoulder despite her shriek of protest. Ignoring the pounding she gave him, he ran downstairs with her in that ignominious position.

As Keeley had feared, the chicken was dry, the rice a gluey mess. Deciding it had been worth it, she made chicken salad sandwiches instead of the elegant dinner she had planned, and they went into the living room to eat. On the way, carrying plates and a soft drink for her, a beer for him, Keeley saw the crushed bouquet of flowers still on the floor of the entry, and she exclaimed in dismay.

"Here, take this," she said, shoving her plate and glass at him. "I've got to put those in water."

"It's a little late, I think," he replied, trying to juggle what she had given him. Seeing her expression, he said consolingly, "Don't worry, I can get more."

"But these are my favorite, and they only bloom a short time each year!" She looked up at him. "How did you know I liked lilacs, especially the white ones?"

Grinning, he kissed the tip of her nose. "I don't know. You just looked like a white lilac kind of woman." He held her eyes. "After tonight, I'll never see one without thinking of you."

She smiled, burying her nose in the fragrant bouquet.

She couldn't just leave them there; the perfumed blossoms were crushed and bent, but she went to put them in water, anyway. When she came back into the living room, Gabe was sitting on one of the chairs, staring forlornly at his plate.

"Why didn't you start?" she asked, curling up on the couch.

"My mother taught me to wait for my hostess. Is it okay if we eat now?"

Laughing at his expression, she said teasingly, "You sound like you're starving to death."

"I am," he replied, reaching for the sandwich and taking a huge bite. "Hey," he said, around the big mouthful after he'd chewed a moment, "this is really good."

"Unfortunately, it's not how I expected to serve it."

"It suits me. Better than some of the culinary delights I've come across in my travels."

He had told her once about the Masai in Africa, and what they used in place of water to put out campfires, and after he'd returned from India, he had regaled her with stories of what some of the delicacies were there. On his trip to Alaska, he'd learned from the natives not to eat polar bear liver, which contained enough vitamin A to kill a human, but to go ahead and feast on the heart because it was rich in iron as well as the spirit of the animal.

Seeing her expression, he swallowed and grinned. "But we can spare the grisly details if you like."

"Thank you," she said dryly, taking a dainty bite of her own sandwich.

Gabe gave her an evil smile. "One of these days, I'm going to tell you about one hundred and one ways to cook snakes that I learned in French Guiana."

"I can hardly wait," she said. "I think I'll have some coffee now. Would you like some, too?"

"That's fine, unless you want champagne."

An image of a champagne-soaked night flashed through her mind, and she winced. She'd learned her lesson the hard way, she thought, and said lightly, "I think I'd prefer the coffee."

"That's fine. Do you want me to get it?"

She looked at him, astonished. "You would?"

He seemed surprised at the question. "Why not?"

She thought of her father, and how, even when he wasn't working, he had never offered to lift a hand to help with the housework or in the kitchen. Even if he had been lying around the house all day, he expected to be waited on.

"Well, I don't know," she said, confused. "I guess I just never thought that men could—"

"Help themselves?" Gabe grinned. "You mean you thought we were big useless lugs, good for just one thing?"

"Well, maybe two," she said, with her own smile. "Changing the oil in cars and fixing washing machines they don't know how to run."

"You have a pretty poor opinion of my sex, I see. I think I'm going to have to change it."

She could feel herself responding again to the look in his eyes. Before she could succumb, she jumped up to get the coffee. "I'll be right back," she told him hastily, and composed herself before she returned with the tray. Pouring a cup for him from the carafe she'd brought in, she said, "I saw that photo spread you had in *Life*. It was wonderful, Gabe. You made me feel—"

He took the cup from her hand, his eyes intent on her face. "Let's not talk about me," he said. "I'm more interested in you."

"Oh, but your life is so much more exciting," she protested.

"My life has more action, that's all. I think it's more exciting to do what you do. I can't imagine sitting down and creating music, much less something so beautiful that wins an award."

"But I didn't do it by myself. My partner and I did. I think Fitz is the best in the business. I'm very lucky we're able to collaborate."

"I think he's the one who's lucky."

Blushing at the compliment, she said, "Thank you, but he's taught me an awful lot."

"You already knew an awful lot," Gabe said, his glance going to the posters she'd put up earlier. "Those are proof, aren't they? His eyes went to the poster from *Florentina*. "That one of Valeska is beautiful."

"Yes, it is."

Sensing something in her voice, he looked at her again. "You two still aren't speaking?"

He knew about the estrangement between them, about Val's marriage to Nigel. "No," she said sadly.

"That's too bad. I know how close you were."

Feeling close to tears, she took a sip of coffee to distract herself. "Yes, we were. But not anymore."

Gabe didn't pursue it. Instead, he said, "So, tell me what else is new. Now that you've conquered Tinseltown, are you going back to the Big Apple?"

One thing she hadn't told him was what Nigel had done to her. The idea that—drunk or not—she could have signed that contract was still too humiliating to admit. Hoping to divert him, she laughed. "Well, even though you spend all your time out in the bush, you've still got the lingo down pat. But to answer your question, I think I'll stay here for a while. I've got the house now, and—"

Just then there was a thud from the direction of the kitchen. They both heard it, and Keeley smiled when she saw Gabe's expression. She knew it was Tux coming in his cat door, and she laughed as Gabe said, "I recognize *that* sound. Don't tell me the cat from hell is still around."

"He is," Keeley said, as the feline in question sauntered into the room. Tux saw Gabe and stopped to stare for a moment. Then, independent as always, he sat down and disdainfully began to wash himself.

"And here I thought we were friends," Gabe said reproachfully.

"Oh, you still are," Keeley told him. "He's just telling you he's upset that you haven't been around for a while."

Gabe's eyes met hers. "Well, we know what his opinion is. What about yours? How do you feel?"

Keeley hesitated. Then she said, "I'm not sure. After all, *you're* the one who's been in town for a while without calling me."

"It hasn't been a *while*, it's only been two days, and I wanted to get my family out of the way first."

"Out of the way?"

"You know what I mean. I wanted you all to myself. I thought we'd have the better part of a week then—not that I really expected *you* to have so much time free, I might add. I never expected the foundation to call and tell me the time schedule had been moved up."

"And now with hardly a by your leave, you're off to the Himalayas," she said, trying not to sound wistful. "How long will it be this time?"

"I don't know. As long as it takes."

She gave him a meaningful look. "Great. That's a *big* help."

"Don't make it sound like I'm the one who's always rushing off while you pine at home," he shot back. "You can't tell me you won't be busy."

She abandoned her haughty pose. "Well, as a matter of fact, Fitz and I are working on a new film right now," she had to admit. "And we have commitments lined up for the next two years or so."

"Aha!"

"Aha, nothing! At least *you* know where to reach *me*. If I want to get in touch with you, I have to send up a smoke signal or something."

He laughed. "I think Hollywood's rubbing off on you."

"What do you mean?"

"You're so melodramatic."

"I've always been melodramatic," she said with a toss of her head. "You've just never been around long enough to notice."

His eyes glinted. "Maybe I should rectify that."

Suddenly alert, she parried, "And maybe we should get off this subject before we get ourselves into hot water."

He looked a little relieved himself. "Speaking of water, why don't we go for a swim?"

"A swim!" She looked at him in disbelief. "At this time of night?"

"You've got pool lights."

"But we just ate!"

"We'll stay in the shallow end."

"But you don't have a swimsuit," she protested. She thought about it. "Come to think of it, neither do I."

"You have a pool, and you don't have a swimsuit?"

"I just moved in. Besides, the pool came with the house. It wasn't anything I planned."

He looked at her curiously. "You haven't even gone in once?"

"Don't make it sound like a cardinal sin," she said testily. "Besides, I haven't had time."

He stood, hauling her up with him. "Then come on, it's time to get your feet wet."

She hadn't wanted to tell him, but as he pulled her outside, she had to confess. "I can't, Gabe," she said, trying to hold back. "I can't swim."

He looked at her in astonishment. "Everybody can swim. It's a natural instinct."

"Well, it's not one of mine. And I never learned."

He stood there a moment, nonplussed. Then he grinned. "No problem. I'll teach you. Just follow me in."

Before she could stop him, he had stripped off his robe. She couldn't help it; as he stood for a second, poised on the coping before he dove in, she drank in the sight of him—his lean, powerful body, his undeniable masculinity.

"Gabe," she started to say, but he had already launched himself toward the water. His naked body cut the surface without a splash, and he swam underwater the length of the pool and halfway back before he surfaced again. Treading in the middle of the pool, he called out, "What are you waiting for? The water's great!"

"I told you."

He swam to where she was standing, hugging her short robe around her. Placing a hand on the coping, he looked up at her. Even at night, she marveled, his eyes looked more blue than the water. "I'll teach you," he said, no longer teasing. "Come on, just jump in. Trust me, I'll catch you—always, I promise."

As she looked down at him, she suddenly knew he was talking about more than teaching her to swim. Gazing into his eyes, she saw something there she felt herself, but, like him, wasn't quite ready to admit yet.

"*Can* I trust you, Gabe?" she asked softly. She didn't hear the longing in her voice.

Gabe heard it and held out his hand. His glance never leaving her face, he answered, "Yes, you can, Keeley. Always, I swear."

She had never really trusted any man—Fitz had come the closest, but that was friendship. It wasn't this . . . this deep kinship she felt with Gabe. All other men she had kept at an emotional distance, afraid to let anyone get too close because betrayal hurt too much. But as she looked from Gabe's face to the hand he was holding out, she knew, deep down, he *was* one man she could trust, not only with her life, but with her heart.

Slowly, she reached down and untied her robe's sash. Posing on the edge of the pool for a moment, she grasped his hand and jumped in.

Gabe left reluctantly the next morning, disappearing out of her life once again, to return . . . when?

"I'll call you as soon as I can," he promised, as they were saying good-bye at the front door in the predawn darkness.

Keeley didn't know what she felt. The past hours had gone so quickly, and she never had learned to swim. Instead, she had discovered the joys of making love in a pool, where the water added an element of buoyancy that made everything even more erotic than being nude to begin with.

But now it was time for him to go again, and as she kissed him good-bye and hugged him for the last time, she whispered, "Be safe, Gabe."

Tenderly he touched her face. "I always am."

She looked up. "No, you're not. You—"

"Yes, I am," he said, pulling her tightly against him. Kissing her once more, he looked into her eyes. "Because now I have someone I want to come back to."

Tearing himself away, he was gone before she could reply.

She didn't find the photograph he had left behind until it was too late to thank him. Without telling her, he had left it propped against one of the lamps in the living room. When she saw it, she felt a surge of love for him that was almost a physical pain.

The picture was of two polar bears, the most fearsome animals in the arctic wilderness. As incredible as it seemed, even for a talented photographer like Gabe, he had caught them *sitting* together on an ice floe, backs to his camera, looking as though they were admiring the spectacular sunset. In what photographers called "magic light," the few moments after dawn or just before sunset when the light was perfect, the mauve and fuschia rays of the dying sun had tinted the bears' thick white coats a deep pink—a beautiful sight in itself. But most astounding of all was the way Gabe had shot them. In the picture, the fierce-looking male had a protective arm around the smaller, equally fierce female.

Like couples did the world over, in that pose they looked like lovers.

CHAPTER EIGHTEEN

Music Design in midtown Manhattan was one of the best recording studios in the business. At one time it had been a church, so the high-vaulted ceiling provided room and resonance for a full-string section although it was used mainly now for rock stars and rock bands. Even at rental prices of five hundred dollars an hour, the facilities were in great demand because of the quality of the state-of-the art equipment. A first-line recording studio's apparatus had to combine a violin's sensitivity with the durability of a Peterbilt truck—if the equipment wasn't delicate enough, it wouldn't capture the music's nuances; if it wasn't sturdy enough to run at full capacity for eighteen to twenty hours a day, which it did, even at such exorbitant rental prices, malfunctions occurred, at great cost.

One cold winter night, Valeska was standing under the boom mike in one of the studios, earphones on, sheet music on the stand in front of her. She'd been here since seven that morning.

It was now two-thirty A.M., and despite the advanced technology, the best "sidemen" in the business, top-notch backup singers, a talented sound engineer, and her own inimitable voice on the line, the best they had managed were marginally acceptable versions of just two of the eight songs they had planned. Out in the control booth, Nigel was furious, the sound engineer looked ready for a drink, the guys in the band were exhausted, and the backup singers looked ready to walk out.

But worst of all, Valeska thought, trying not to panic, was her realization that she was losing her voice. Only her control had made it last this long, but she knew she wouldn't be able to hold out much longer. Her throat felt raw, her neck muscles were tired, and with every note, she could hear a hoarse tone creeping in that soon she wouldn't be able to hide.

"Okay," came the tired voice of the sound man. "Let's try it again, shall we? Valeska, you were behind the beat on the last section. Wait until it's right before you come in again, okay?"

She wanted to say she couldn't do it again, but with the cost of studio time, she didn't dare complain. Nigel had arranged the session because he thought an album of songs from the show would boost ticket sales. She knew *Maggie* was in trouble, too, so she couldn't refuse. Nigel had invested a lot of his . . . her . . . *their* money in the show, and she had to do everything she could to help. He was already angry at her, as he was so often these days, and she didn't want to make him lose his temper, especially in front of everyone. Trying not to think how tired she was, and how much her throat burned, she obediently adjusted the headphones, waited for the downbeat, and came in right on cue.

Nothing happened. When she opened her mouth, no sound came out. At first she didn't know what was wrong. It had never happened to her before, and she tried again, with the same result. By this time she was behind the beat again, and she glanced toward the darkened control room with approaching dread. Making a slashing sign, she waited until the sound man's voice came over the intercom again.

"What's the problem, Valeska?" he asked wearily.

"I . . . I don't know," she managed to gasp. Her voice sounded coarse to her, strange in her own ears. Frightened, she fought back tears. "I think . . . I think I need a doctor."

"Oh, for Christ's sake!" she heard Nigel exclaim.

The sound engineer leaned over his microphone. "Let's take ten, shall we?" he suggested, looking at the backup singers and the men in the band. Nigel had hired three guitar players, a piano man, steel, bass and drums for the session. Valeska had argued in vain for a traditional four-piece combo, but Nigel wouldn't listen. It was time, he declared, for her to develop a "pop" sound.

Horrified, she'd exclaimed, "But I'm not a pop singer!"

"Maybe you should be," he'd replied nastily. "You sure aren't bringing them in the way you're singing now, are you?"

As always when he criticized her, she had felt herself shrinking inside. Still, she tried again. One thing she knew, and that was her voice. "I told you before, the role of Maggie isn't right for me. It won't change by recording an album this way."

He gave her the cold look he used more and more. "I thought you were a professional. Pros can sing anything."

Weak tears came to her eyes. She hated to cry; he became even more cruel. But she couldn't help it. It was her voice, her career. Oh, where was Keeley? she wondered, before she caught herself. Thrusting away the thought that Keeley had always known how to compose for her, she said pleadingly, "But Nigel, the arrangements are all wrong for me."

"For someone who has your range, the arrangement shouldn't be a problem," he said flatly.

She'd been so upset, she had said the unforgivable. She'd been thinking of Keeley, and her name just came out. "If Keeley were here—"

He had turned on her so fiercely she took a step back. "Don't mention that name to me! Keeley Cochran was a little bitch who was nothing but trouble!"

Valeska hardly knew what she was saying. "She was the best. She always knew—"

"She knew *nothing*! I don't want to hear her name again. The best day of my life was when she went away!"

"Well, it wasn't mine!" she cried, and burst into tears.

Disgusted and enraged, Nigel had slammed out of the apartment and been gone for two days. Valeska was glad he was gone; she spent the time mourning what had happened between her and her friend. She had always been sorry for the way she had treated Keeley the last time they'd seen each other. Whenever she recalled how she had flaunted her ring in Keeley's face, taunting her with the fact that she and Nigel were married, she wanted to cringe. How cruel she had acted—and how unnecessary it had been! She had always been ashamed of herself for that scene. Keeley had been trying to help; she should have listened.

But it had been too late even then, she realized. As her mother always said, what was done, was done, and she had made her own bed. As the months went on, and things got worse—first with the show, and then with Nigel, she had wanted to call Keeley and apologize. So many times she had picked up the phone, but she hadn't been able to follow through. She didn't know why, exactly; she thought it was because she felt conscience-stricken and ashamed.

Or perhaps it was something else, she thought guiltily. Maybe she just couldn't admit to Keeley that she'd been right. Or maybe, by not admitting it, she could avoid for a while longer the growing knowledge that she had made a terrible mistake.

She had tried, but she couldn't put her finger on when her drinking started, or why. She couldn't understand it; before she married Nigel, she had never even liked the taste of liquor. But soon she was reaching for a glass of vodka with her toothpaste in the morning, feeling as though she couldn't get through her day without that first jolt. And the second and the third, she thought with a grimace. Soon, she had a glass in her hand all day—then far into the night. She knew she had to stop; it was getting out of control. There were days now when she could hardly see straight by noon. It was a miracle that she'd been able to continue with the show; half the time she didn't even remember going on.

And now Nigel was insisting that she develop a new sound for the album. On the way to the studio, she had tried to persuade him again. She knew the style he wanted was a mistake, especially in this case. The songs from *Maggie* were either loud and strident or low and sultry; it was theater all the way, and it just wouldn't work trying to force a sound that wasn't right.

"For Christ's sake," Nigel exclaimed angrily. "Recording techniques have become so sophisticated that almost no sound gets on tape without being electronically modified anyway, so what difference does it make?"

She didn't know how, but she found the courage to say, "It makes a difference to me, Nigel. It's my voice."

He gave her the look that meant she was being tiresome and childish in the extreme. With obvious patience, he said, "You'll see when we get to the studio. I'll have the sound engineer explain things in a way even you can understand!"

He sounded so annoyed that she lapsed into silence, slumping down on her side of the car. True to his word, when they arrived, Nigel took a man aside and asked him to give her some background. The engineer's name was Chuck, and he was the sound man for the day. With a smile, he took her to the control room to show her around.

Despite her feeling that this was all wrong, she was impressed with what he called his office. Facing a wall of glass so that he could see into each individual recording booth, he sat at a twelve-foot console studded with a bewildering array of dials, gauges, switches, and push buttons. A confusing tangle of what Chuck called patch cords looked to her like an old-fashioned switchboard.

Chuck laughed when she told him. "Maybe in the 'old days,'" he said kindly. "But not now. All sound is picked up and transformed into electrical impulses by the mike, and the impulses are channeled through this control board, then put onto magnetic tape. When the tape is played back, the electronic patterns are retranslated into sound. Because of the way sounds are altered during recording, and because of the changes we can make after the musicians leave, the final version is generally something different, and ideally better than what was actually played."

"But isn't that cheating?" she ventured.

"Is it cheating to dress fashionably instead of walking around naked?" Chuck asked her. "Is it cheating for a man to shave every morning, or a woman to put on makeup and do her hair?"

There was a flaw in the argument, but she couldn't see where. "No, I guess not," she said. "But somehow, it doesn't seem like the same thing."

"But hair and clothes are enhancements—just like this. All we do is improve on what we hear. The equipment makes sound louder, or adds echo, or positions it in various places along the stereo spectrum. Even when an entire band is performing together, we can put each sound onto a separate channel of the tape. That way, we can erase one instrument's errors but leave something else that sounded fine. This is vital to modern recording, because it allows instrumentalists and vocalists to add solos to basic tracks that the rest of the band may have recorded days or weeks earlier."

The technology was brilliant and impressive, but she still wasn't sure it was right for her. Smiling faintly, she said, "With so much equipment and all you can do, it makes me wonder why you need me at all."

He laughed. "If I didn't have the singer's sound to move

around, this fancy console of mine would be pretty useless, don't you think?"

Nigel came back just then, and before she knew it she was in one of the booths, big earphones on, trying to get the right sound. Why, she wasn't sure, if they could change it to make it what they wanted.

That had been nineteen hours ago, when she still had a voice. She didn't know why she'd missed this last cue in, and cautiously, she tried to clear her throat. No sound came out. Trying not to panic, she looked up as Chuck spoke over the intercom to the band again. It seemed as though eons had passed since she'd failed to come in on the beat, but he was still talking to them about what was wrong. No one seemed to be paying attention to her at the moment, and she had to clamp down on an irrational impulse to hurl herself against the glass. Didn't anyone notice she'd lost her voice? Was she so unimportant to all this modern technology that no one cared? She could feel herself getting hysterical and tried to control herself. Maybe it was a temporary thing, she thought, and decided to wait a minute to find out.

"Guys, the places we're in trouble are the two fives—" Chuck was saying, identifying the chords by number rather than letter, as recording studios did. "And now you're also out of tune with the piano. During the break, everybody either walk over to the piano and tune, or we'll respec the strobe."

Chuck turned to say something to her, but Nigel reached down and jerked the mike in his own direction. "Valeska, what in the *hell* are you doing?" he demanded angrily. "I know you're tired, but this business about a doctor is ridiculous. We're not leaving until we have some basic tracks, at least, then we're going to do some overdubbing. Your voice needs—"

By some miracle, she managed to speak. She sounded hoarse, her voice fading in and out, but at least she could talk. "I need a doctor," she insisted. "Please, Nigel, something is—"

She never finished the sentence. Just like that, her voice completely vanished. It was as though someone had plucked the words right out of her throat. Her mouth moved, but nothing came out. Jerking the headphones off, she bolted for the soundproof door.

Nigel met her outside the glass booth, grabbing her arm and jerking her to a stop. "What are you doing?"

She tried to speak and couldn't. Terrified that she had completely destroyed her voice, she managed to rasp one word out. "Muelrath . . ."

Martin Muelrath was the throat specialist she'd been seeing for her laryngitis. She'd never told Nigel, because she knew he'd be angry, but Dr. Muelrath had warned her that she was straining her voice playing Maggie every night. He had urged her to take a rest, and she had promised she would, but it hadn't been possible. The advance sales had been so good, but they weren't generating any new interest, and she was afraid Nigel would blame her if the gate fell off again—or worse, if the show folded when the advance ran out.

I never should have let him talk me into playing Maggie, she thought frantically. *I knew it was wrong from the first. Why didn't I say something? Why didn't I stand up to him?*

She knew why, but she didn't want to think about it now. Besides, it was too late. Continuing to play Maggie wasn't the problem, not when she couldn't even speak. Pleadingly, she looked at Nigel again.

"This is ridiculous," he said fiercely. He kept his voice low, in case anyone was listening, but his grip on her arm tightened, and she winced. "Do you know how much we're paying for studio time? Not to mention all the people here on overtime? It's costing me a fortune, and I won't allow you to act like a prima donna and walk out because of a little problem with your throat!"

She could hear the words she wanted to say in her mind, but she couldn't say them aloud, no matter how she tried. When Nigel saw her throat working, the apprehension in her face, he stepped back.

"Stop it," he commanded, but now there was a flash of fear in his own eyes. "You're just doing that because you want to leave."

She tried to answer him and couldn't. Shaking her head, she pointed to her throat. Now she was afraid even to try to speak. She didn't know what was wrong. Was it a return of laryngitis or something much worse? Maybe it was nodes, she thought, in terror. Nodes were caused by strain, and she couldn't deny she'd been straining her voice for months. If it was a node, she'd have to have surgery, and if she had to have surgery . . . What if it was cancer? she thought, in full panic. She nearly fainted from fright.

*   *   *

It wasn't cancer. Dr. Muelrath dragged himself out of bed and met them at his office at four in the morning, not long after Nigel called from the studio.

"Thank God," Nigel said, when the doctor told them. Then he saw Muelrath's face. Sharply, he asked, "What is it?"

It was a swelling on a capillary in her throat, a tiny flaw, something called a hemangioma. Valeska had never heard of it, and neither had Nigel. "It's not serious, is it?" Nigel asked.

Dr. Muelrath looked grave. "I won't kid you, it could be quite serious. It's not cancer, but a hemangioma can be fatal to a singer if it gets big enough. The swelling can interfere with the production of sound, and then—" he hesitated, but then decided they had to know the worst "—it can rupture."

As Valeska involuntarily grabbed her throat, Nigel exclaimed, "She won't lose her voice!"

"Not if I can help it."

"What can be done?"

"If it doesn't absorb, we can take if off surgically, but I wouldn't want to do that," Dr. Muelrath said. He saw how pale Valeska was and patted her arm. "Let's wait and see what happens," he suggested. "In the meantime, I want you on a complete vocal rest. No singing, even talking at a minimum. In fact, I'd prefer if you wouldn't use your voice at all. Understand?"

Mournfully, she nodded her head. After what the doctor had said, she was afraid even to utter a sound. Mutely, she looked at Nigel, begging him to understand.

"I'm sorry," Muelrath said. "I know how disappointed audiences will be, but it can't be helped."

"Of course not," Nigel agreed. He put his arm around Valeska, a show for the doctor. She knew he was furious. "The important thing is for my baby to get well, right?"

The doctor seemed relieved as he went to write out some prescriptions. When they were leaving, Muelrath patted Valeska's arm again. "Come back and see me in ten days," he told her. "And remember—in the meantime, rest that lovely voice. The time will go by quickly, I promise." He glanced over her critically. "You look like you could use the rest. You've been working too hard, I think. This might be a good time for a vacation, in fact."

"We don't have time for a vacation," Nigel said impatiently. "Valeska has commitments."

The doctor looked at him evenly. Valeska was one of his favorite patients; he was a fan, as well. "At this point, it's only a suggestion," he said. Pointedly, he added, "I'd hate to have to make it a medical request."

"Well, this is just great." Nigel fumed in the car on the way back to the apartment. "Ten days! What does that old fool think we're going to do about the show? Just put a sign up, telling everyone to come back when you're ready to sing again?"

Automatically, she opened her mouth to answer, but he looked at her sharply. "For God's sake, don't talk! I don't want the ban on speaking extended any longer than it has to be. We're already in a big enough mess."

Valeska stared unhappily at her hands, clenched tightly in her lap. She debated about saying it—especially after what the doctor had ordered—but she thought now was the time. She'd been thinking about it for months. "Maybe I should take some time off," she said hoarsely. "This might be a good time to start a family—"

Nigel was driving; he jerked his head toward her. "A *family*! Are you out of your mind?"

"But—"

"Enough! I don't want to be a father, and you don't have time to be a mother, so the subject is closed."

"But—"

He glared at her angrily. "Let's just get through these next ten days, all right? We'll have other decisions to make if this business with your throat doesn't clear up."

Alarmed, she rasped, "Decisions?"

"Let's just wait," he repeated tightly. "And for God's sake, stop using your damned voice! Do you want it to disappear forever on us?"

Valeska subsided at once, shrinking into her corner of the seat. Without warning, a vision of herself in happier days, months ago, flashed into her mind, and she closed her eyes. She remembered the day so clearly, she thought miserably. She had been holding her box of birth control pills in her hand, wondering whether to start a new cycle or not. She wanted a child so badly, someone to hold, to cherish, to take care of. She longed for a child, *yearned* for one; boy or girl, it didn't matter, just as long as she had a baby of her own to love.

Nigel had said they'd talk about a family one day, but she knew if she left it up to him, they never would. She had stared at the little pink box for a long time, trying to decide. In the end, she had thrown the pills away.

She hadn't told Nigel; she assured herself she was waiting

for the right time. He was so tense about the show, so busy with plans for the new album, so preoccupied with all the details of managing her career that she decided to wait until she got pregnant. She was sure he'd come around then; she knew there were many husbands who didn't want to be fathers until after the fact, and she was positive it would be the same with Nigel. Once he knew a child was on the way, he'd change his mind. Wouldn't he?

She was glad to get home. She had never felt so weary; it seemed as if every bone in her body ached. She had a terrible headache, and her throat was raw. Feeling as though this had been the longest day in her life, she went upstairs and fell wearily into bed.

Two hours later, the phone rang. Jerked out of an exhausted sleep, Valeska reached for the phone before it could ring again. Nigel hated to be disturbed when he was sleeping, and a glance at the clock told her they'd just gotten to bed. Feeling as if sand had been thrown in her eyes, she reached out quickly and pulled the phone under the covers before rasping a hello.

"Valeska?" her mother's voice said. "Is that you? I can hardly hear you. This must be a bad connection or something." There was a fraction of a pause; then Edra's voice sharpened. "You don't have a cold, do you?"

Restlessly, Nigel shifted position. Valeska looked quickly over her shoulder. She didn't want to wake him. If he knew her mother had called so early, he'd have a fit. Taking the phone, she slipped out of bed and went into the bathroom, closing the door behind her. She didn't want to go into what was wrong with her voice, so she said, "No, I'm all right, Mama."

For once Edra had other things on her mind than her daughter's voice. "Well, I'm sorry to be calling so early, but I'm afraid I have some bad news."

Valeska felt as though someone had punched her in the chest. The only thing it could be was her grandmother, she thought. Completely forgetting she wasn't supposed to be talking, she said, "It's not Granny! She isn't sick, is she?"

"Your grandmother died an hour ago at the hospital," Edra said. "I thought you should know."

For a moment, Valeska couldn't comprehend the awful news. Her granny dead? It couldn't be. She'd just been home—no, that wasn't right, she thought. The last time she'd gone home to Allentown had been months ago, and then only for a night. She'd wanted to stay longer, but there never seemed to be enough time. She always had a show to do, commitments, responsibilities, demands. She missed her grandmother, who had been so proud of her; she hated to be parted from Evie, but no matter how she'd begged and pleaded for them to come to New York, Edra refused to leave home. Now it was too late.

"Oh, Granny!" she said, tears coming into her eyes. "What happened, Mama?"

"She had a series of strokes several days ago that put her in the hospital—"

Valeska sat up. "*Days* ago?" she croaked. "Why didn't you call me?"

"Well, what could you have done?" Edra said impatiently. "Even the doctors said she'd never come around. There was no point in you coming home. It wouldn't have done any good."

Feeling numb, Valeska leaned against the bathroom counter. In the lights around the mirror, her face looked pale and sick. She couldn't believe her grandmother had been in the hospital and her mother hadn't told her. Edra *knew* how much she loved Evie; she knew how close Valeska and her grandmother had been. Not to tell her seemed so cruel that for a moment she couldn't even speak. How could her mother treat her this way? Why would she?

Her voice hoarse, she said, "I'll take the first plane out."

"You don't have to—"

"I'm coming," she said, and hung up.

"You've changed," Edra said when they were getting ready for the funeral. "And I'm not sure I like it."

Valeska felt too weary to argue about it. Lately it seemed she couldn't get along with anybody about anything. She didn't want to do this, to say good-bye to her grandmother the final time with everyone looking on; she was so tired, all she wanted to do was lie down. It was an effort to get dressed; when she looked in the mirror, her eyes were shadowed, and she was so pale she looked sick.

"I'm sorry, Mama," she said, knowing she should make an effort with her hair, but unable to force herself to care. She left it down, falling over her shoulders and down her back like a pale gold veil. Her grandmother had always liked her hair loose, she thought, and had to brush quick tears away again.

Edra was already dressed in severe black, with a black hat and veil. The veil looked like a spider web over her face, and when she saw it, Valeska glanced away. She had left her gloves and the prayer book Evie had given her a long time ago on the table, and she went to get them.

"You're just not the same sweet girl you used to be," Edra accused.

Despite herself, Valeska tensed. "I don't know what you mean, Mama."

"I mean that you've changed. You used to be so thoughtful, but you've hardly said a word since you got here. People have been waiting just for a chance to talk to you, but you haven't put your nose outside the apartment since you came."

"I'm sorry, Mama," she said wearily. "I haven't felt like socializing."

"Well, whether you feel like it or not, you have an obligation. You're a Broadway star, Valeska. You should act like one. You're famous now, and you have—" Edra drew herself up haughtily "—a public to think of."

She couldn't believe her mother was worried about what the neighbors would think at a time like this. Instead of answering, she asked slowly, "Why didn't you tell me Granny was sick?"

Her lips tight, Edra said, "Because there was nothing you could have done."

"I could have been here," Valeska said quietly. "Why didn't you let me?"

"Because you had other . . . obligations."

"Other obligations?" she repeated. "Nothing was more important than Granny—"

Edra looked at her angrily. "Oh, really? Well, you certainly proved it since you left, haven't you? I don't think you've been home half a dozen times in the entire time you've been gone."

"That's not fair! Except for that first year, I was always involved in one show or another. I couldn't just walk out! Besides, you know I wanted you and Granny to come to New York. I asked you and asked you." She couldn't hide her bitterness. "Maybe if you'd come when I asked you, this wouldn't have happened!"

Edra had started toward the door. At the accusation, she stopped and turned around again. "So that's what this is about. You're feeling guilty for abandoning us, and now you want to put the blame on us!"

"I didn't abandon you! What are you saying? I *begged* you to come and live with me!"

"We didn't belong there," Edra said flatly. "You know it, and so do I. Besides, it's what *you* always wanted, not us."

Valeska looked at her in openmouthed disbelief. "I never wanted to go to New York!"

"Indeed you did. You wanted to be a Broadway star."

"*I* wanted it! Broadway was always *your* dream, not mine!"

"Don't be a fool, Valeska," Edra snapped. "You wanted to sing on Broadway ever since you were a little girl."

Valeska couldn't believe her mother was saying such things. Had the world gone mad? Had her mother? Had she? How had things gotten so turned around? Now she didn't know what was the truth.

"No," she said desperately. "I did it for you, Mama. I wanted to sing in the choir and get married and—" despite herself, her voice broke "—and have children. *You're* the one who always wanted me to have a career!"

"I only wanted what you said you wanted. You said you loved to sing. You said you'd *die* if you didn't sing."

"I did, that's true, but it didn't have to be on Broadway! You pushed me and pushed me until I couldn't stand it anymore. I had to go, just to stop you from nagging me to death!"

Edra stiffened. "Well! This is the thanks I get? You have fame and fortune, all the money you could want! You're married to a famous Broadway director, people fall all over your feet. Now all you can do is accuse me of forcing you to do something you said you wanted yourself! Oh, I never thought I'd live to see the day when you blamed me for helping you to fulfill your dream. I'm glad your grandmother isn't here to hear this! She'd be ashamed of you, just as I am!"

"No, she wouldn't! Granny understood! She always did!" Despite her precarious throat condition, her voice rose in an agonized cry. "Oh, Mama, how could you have let her die without me?"

Edra stared at her a moment, her face tight. "She wouldn't have known you."

"She would have known I was with her!"

"No," Edra said flatly. "She wouldn't have."

"Then *I* would have known! Oh, how could you do this to me? Granny died, and I wasn't even here!"

"Well, what's done is done," Edra said. "It's senseless going on about it now."

Valeska felt something break inside. She looked at Edra with loathing, not seeing her mother, who had always worked hard, but a cruel, vindictive woman who had always been jealous of the warm relationship between her mother and her daughter. She realized now that Edra had always felt left out, but she was too angry and betrayed to feel pity—or guilt. Now all she could think was a cold: it's her fault.

"I'll never forgive you for this, Mama," she said, her voice shaking with anger. "Never!"

"Don't be ridiculous," Edra replied. But a look of fear flashed through her eyes. "Forgive me for what?"

"You know what, Mama. After the funeral is over, I'm going back to New York. I never want to see or talk to you again, do you understand? Never!"

"Valeska!"

"No, it's done between you and me, I mean it. Now, you go on ahead. I'll meet you at the funeral parlor. Don't worry, no one will know. I don't know why, but maybe I owe you that." Her beautiful mouth twisted; she flung back her long golden fall of hair. "After all, you're responsible for my career."

As soon as her mother left, angrily slamming the door behind her, she went to the suitcase she'd brought. It was standing by the fold-out couch, and she dropped to her knees beside it and snapped the locks. Knowing her mother never kept liquor in the house, she had hidden a flask in one of the side pockets, and she took it out and unscrewed the cap. Her hands were shaking so badly she nearly dropped it before she got it to her mouth. She took one swallow, then another. The sharp bite of the vodka going down felt good, and she took a third swallow for good measure before reluctantly replacing the flask. As much as she might need it to get through the service, she didn't dare take it with her. Wondering how she was ever going to get through this day, she put the suitcase back where it had been, ran into the bathroom for a swallow of mouthwash, and then went to join her mother at the funeral parlor.

Evie Barstow Lawrence was buried in the pouring rain, with half the town of Allentown at the grave site. The minister spoke eloquently of how valued a member of the community she had been, how loved and beloved, while Edra, tall and gaunt and stark in black stood stiffly, staring straight ahead, her daughter sobbing beside her.

"Stop that!" her mother hissed at Valeska at one point. "As you pointed out yourself, you're a celebrity now, and everybody's watching!"

But Valeska couldn't hold back her tears; misery threatened to overwhelm her. She didn't care who saw her cry; they all knew why. Scores of people had come to pay their respects; Evie had been loved by everyone it seemed, not least of all the grand-daughter who mourned her the most. At the funeral parlor, where she'd sat alone with her grandmother before everyone came, she'd been swamped with memories when she saw Evie's face, at peace now, without the pain that had marked it so long. Visions of sugar cookies and strawberry tarts, stories at bedtime and rag tails on kites, came to her, making her cry even harder. Evie had made her childhood a magical time of love and delight and laughter; she had chased away nightmares and scolded taunting little boys; even when her arthritis nearly crippled her fingers, she still created wonderful toys from scraps of things: green velvet frogs with big bulging eyes, checked aprons with crocheted edges, pillowcases with such fine embroidery it was a shame to use them. It was painful to think of Evie locked in her coffin, buried deep in the ground, lost to her forever. Valeska couldn't stop sobbing all through the service.

People she knew, and strangers she had never seen before, came up to her when it was over, to offer sympathy and congrat-ulate her on her success.

"I know it's not appropriate now," someone said, "but when your time of grief is past, you could come back and we'll have a parade for you. . . ."

"We wanted to have a town holiday in your honor," another person told her. "We're so proud you came from here."

"The keys to the city—"

"A picnic—"

"A speech—"

"A dinner—"

She wanted to scream at them all to go away. Didn't they un-derstand she wasn't thinking of her celebrity? She was famous, but all she wanted was another chance to tell her grandmother she loved her.

At last, all the mourners and fans had gone by; only she and her mother and a few close family friends were left. Hands clasped around his Bible, the minister stood under the awning by the grave, obviously waiting for them to leave, so he could sig-nal the attendants to finish their work.

Edra grasped Valeska's arm. "It's time to go," she said.

Valeska couldn't bear the thought of going back to the house after their quarrel, but she didn't know what else to do. Blankly, she looked around. The minister was still standing under the aw-ning with them; two men dressed in dungarees and holding shovels were standing discreetly some distance away in the rain. It was still pouring, but she hardly noticed.

"You go ahead," she said, disengaging her arm from her mother's hard grasp. "I'll meet you back at the house."

"What? If we leave, how are you going to get there?"

"I'll bring her back," said a voice behind them.

Startled, Valeska looked around. Ned was standing there, and for a moment she almost didn't recognize him, he'd changed so much. No longer the gangly boy he'd been when she left for New York, Ned Kowalski had matured into a self-assured young man. His hair was longer, but his eyes were still a kind blue. For the occasion, he had dressed in a dark suit and somber tie.

"I was so sorry about your grandmother, Vallie," he said softly. "Is there anything I can do—besides take you home, I mean?"

Edra looked from one to the other. She was about to say something when Ned glanced her way. Tightening her lips a moment, she muttered, "Don't be late. We have food back at the house and Valeska is expected to be present."

"Yes, ma'am," Ned said, but he was looking at Valeska again, who was still marveling at how much he'd changed. Then she realized they all had. No one was the same, especially she. The ugly argument with her mother this morning proved it.

So did the vodka bottle buried in her suitcase, she thought, and glanced away from Ned's kind blue gaze.

Edra waited a moment, but there was nothing more to be said. "Well, then," she sniffed, and went to the car on the minister's arm.

Ned had brought an umbrella; unfurling it, he held it over Valeska's head. Nodding at the two men still patiently waiting, he said, "I can tell them to come back if you'd like a moment alone."

Without warning, Valeska's eyes filled with tears again. The rain was coming down so hard the flowers on the casket were starting to droop. Impulsively, she reached out and took one of the pale pink roses for herself. She shook her head.

"No, I already said good-bye."

"Would you like to be alone, then?"

She looked up at him. A moment ago, she had. Now more than anything, she wanted his company. She felt so lonely. Nigel had refused to come for the funeral, saying he wasn't in the mood to be ogled by a bunch of hicks. She hadn't pressed him; he'd been angry enough.

"I know it sounds silly," she said softly, "but I'd like to walk for a while, if you don't mind." She hated to ask him, but she didn't want to go back to the apartment yet; it would be hot and crowded, with people milling around, everyone saying what a blessing it was, Evie had been in so much pain. She couldn't endure being told how to deal with her grief.

Ned didn't point out that it was raining or that he had a car close by. Saying he didn't mind at all, he led her away from the grave site. "I loved Evie," he said simply, when they had walked in silence for a few minutes.

"I did, too," she said mournfully, knowing she was going to cry again.

He stopped and turned so that he was looking down into her face. Putting his hands on her shoulders, he said quietly, "She was proud of you, Vallie, so proud. You were the light of her life."

"Oh, Ned," she said, and couldn't help herself. Putting her hands over her face, she began to sob. "I miss her so much!"

Ned, who had turned a talent for fixing car engines into an import car business that he had later expanded from backyard beginnings all the way to Cincinnati, gathered her gently into his arms and let her weep against his silk tie. He didn't talk about how successful he had become or how famous she was; he simply held her until she'd cried herself out. Then, his arm around her, and her head on his shoulder, he led her to his car. Tenderly he tucked her into the seat; then he drove her home again, as he had dozens of times before, when they were young and didn't know what was before them.

Two weeks later, Valeska counted the days since her last period. Her eyes shining, she looked up. She'd been trying not to talk, but her throat still felt tender and inflamed. But this was enough to make her forget all about it. She counted again, to make sure, then she called and made dinner reservations at Tavern on the Green. It was one of her favorite places: during the day, the glass walls made the park seem to come inside, and at night, the lights sparkled and glowed. It was the perfect setting to tell Nigel the news about the baby. She just knew that once he got used to the idea, he'd be thrilled, too.

CHAPTER NINETEEN

High above Langu Gorge in Nepal, Gabe had been watching the goatlike *tahr* for an hour or more. Tethered to the ground in an alpine meadow, it was grazing peacefully, and the scene was so serene he felt like going to sleep. The other two members of the team, Gail Marchuk and her husband, John, had baited the trap for the snow leopard while Gabe set up his camera in a blind. They were crouched behind a rock outcropping, waiting. The plan was to snare one of the world's most elusive cats, dart it with a tranquilizer so they could fit it with a radio-tracking collar, film the sequence, and then let the leopard loose just as the tranquilizing drug wore off.

"It'll be a piece of cake," Gail had promised. John had rolled his eyes. The snow leopard had a reputation for being unaggressive toward humans, but that didn't mean it could be taken for granted. The cats preferred a solitary existence, but they had big teeth and sharp claws, and they could seriously wound, even kill, if cornered. Since even the most primitive medical facilities were a hundred and sixty miles away, on foot, it paid to be cautious.

Gabe had been lying in the same position the entire time, propped awkwardly behind the camera, which was aimed at the little goat. The nagging sensation in his thigh had become a cramp that was turning into something that demanded he move soon, or go into spasm. He was just about to chance a tiny shift to the right when the goat jerked its head up. Instantly, the hairs on the back of Gabe's neck stirred; Gail and John became alert, too. They all watched intently as the goat sniffed the air, then looked right and left. Anxiously, it took a step or two forward, hit the end of the tether and moved back again, dancing on tiny feet.

"It's here," Gail whispered, barely making a sound. "Get ready, everybody."

Hardly daring to breathe, Gabe tried to spot the creature only

Gail and the goat seemed to see. The *tahr* was pulling frantically on the tether now, bleating piteously with each tug. Gabe could practically feel the menace in the air, and he reached ever so slowly for the camera. He had completely forgotten about the cramp in his leg.

Suddenly, there was a rush of wind, a blur of dense smoky gray fur dappled with black rosettes, and without warning, the leopard appeared, bounding up the slope toward the panic-stricken goat. Gathering itself into a streak of energy, it exploded up from the ground, intent on taking the little *tahr* down. Bleating in renewed terror, the goat had only seconds to live. The cat reached the apex of its leap, about to descend. Then, it seemed to jerk in the air. With a surprised snarl, it came crashing down.

"Got him!" John cried jubilantly. He scrambled to his feet, Gail not far behind. Gabe leapt up with them, his camera already on his shoulder, recording the whole thing. They all rushed to where the cat now crouched, ears flat, eyes a compelling icy green such as Gabe had never seen, its jaws opened wide in a murderous snarl. For a cat supposed to be nonaggressive, even docile, it looked to Gabe like it was prepared to do as much damage as possible. Hissing, it lunged in his direction, prevented from escaping by a harmless loop snare two feet long wrapped around a huge hind paw. The snare had looked sturdy enough to Gabe when they had set it earlier, but now it seemed as fragile as a cobweb, especially when the cat snarled at him again and slashed out with a front paw, claws fully extended.

"Isn't it gorgeous!" Gail exclaimed.

"Unbelievable," John muttered. His job was to aim a four-foot jab stick holding a dose of immobilizing tranquilizer into the cat's flank, but the leopard kept moving, spoiling his aim.

"Here, let me go around," Gail said. She had about a two-and-a-half-foot space to maneuver, and John jerked his head at her.

"Don't you dare," he commanded. "You don't have enough room. Wait for Puchang."

Puchang was their Sherpa guide who was supposed to be keeping watch on the other side of the slope. Since he hadn't appeared yet, Gabe figured he'd gone to sleep. He was about to suggest that he maneuver to the cat's other side when Puchang came up over the hill. Distracted by movement behind him, the cat whirled, and John seized his opportunity. With a quick thrust, he injected the tranquilizer into the leopard's flank. Breathing hard, they all retreated back to the blind to wait for the drug to take effect.

The respite didn't last long; as soon as the cat went down, eyes wide and dilated, they crept back. They didn't have much time: the drug was designed to immobilize only for a few minutes; any longer, and there was a danger the animal would feel the effects. With Gabe filming the entire procedure, John and Gail went to work, first removing the snare from the hind foot. Holding up the foot so Gabe could get a clear shot, they marveled at the huge, fur-covered paw that looked soft until John squeezed the pad and vicious claws extended out.

"Wouldn't want to meet *that* in a dark alley," John commented. "Did you get the close-up, Gabe?"

"I got it. Don't worry about me, just do your thing."

The two researchers covered the leopard's head against the bright sun—and the stress of being around humans—and then, while Gail measured vital statistics, length, height, teeth, jaw, head and paw size, as well as estimating the animal's weight, John fitted the radio collar and tattooed a tiny "l" in the cat's ear, in case the collar was lost and the cat retrapped.

Filming the entire time, Gabe checked his watch when the leopard began to recover, muscles rigid and straining against John's hands. It had been about ten minutes since the drug had taken affect, and it was obvious that soon the leopard would regain mobility. He was almost sorry, in a way. To be so close to such a magnificent creature took his breath away.

"Come on, let's get out of here," John commanded, quickly packing up his equipment with Gail as the cat rolled to its feet and began moving unsteadily away. It didn't go far; as though its legs refused to hold it, the cat threw itself down in the shade of a wild peach tree.

"He'll be all right," John assured them. "He just needs to get his bearings again."

In awed silence, they all returned to camp. Gabe felt almost as though he had witnessed some spectacle of creation, privileged to experience another of the many rhythms of nature so seldom seen by humans. Divesting himself of his equipment, he went to where John was crouched over some complicated-looking electronic components. Smiling, John pointed. On a screen in front of him a tiny light pulsed, accompanied by a beep. The world's first radio-collared snow leopard was on the move, already beginning to give the Marchuks valuable information about its almost unknown habits in the wild. Gail came over and stared at the screen, too; Puchang appeared. They all gazed in wonder at the moving, beeping dot for a few minutes, then, as one, they looked at each other and grinned.

They celebrated that night, supplanting their usual meal of bread and rice—with a little dried meat mixed in—by adding fruit cups from army rations, and a small bottle of wine John had carried in his pack all the way from Nepalganj, their final jumping off place.

"To *Panthera uncia*," John toasted, honoring the snow leopard with its full name. He raised his metal coffee cup with the inch of wine.

"Long may she reign," Gail chimed in.

As Gabe lifted his cup, he thought suddenly of Keeley and wished she could have shared this experience. *She would have written a symphony,* he thought, remembering how she had told him she thought in terms of music. Like no one else, she could have brought to vivid musical life the essence of the cat they'd seen, and through it, even those who had never glimpsed a snow leopard would have experienced the feel of the dense fur, heard the heart-stopping snarl, marveled at the fluid stride, and smiled at the flattened ears. He took pictures to capture on film such power and grace, but Keeley . . . Keeley used music to touch a chord deep down that all could experience.

"Whatcha thinkin'?"

Gabe was crouched by the campfire. When he looked up, Gail was smiling down at him, looking curious. Tall and thin with fine blond hair, Gail was in her thirties somewhere, with sharp gray eyes and more courage than was good for her. Even her husband, John, acknowledged that she was the leader of the group; he claimed that he just tagged along to make sure she ate and slept and was rescued if she got hurt. From what Gabe had seen, he could almost believe it. In the weeks he'd been with them, she'd taken chances that made him cringe.

"I carry the heavy equipment," John had said with a wink. "Gail's the brains of the team; I just lift."

Gabe had laughed, knowing it wasn't the entire truth. No one besides John was better with the complicated electronic gear they carried, and John was no coward either. Still, Gabe couldn't deny how dedicated Gail was to the research. She was the one who had insisted that they establish one of the tracking camps high up here in Dhukyel Cave, nearly fifteen thousand feet above Langu Gorge. Gabe had to admit the view was spectacular, but the climb had been a greater test of endurance than he'd bargained for. Gasping himself, John had told him when they finally hauled themselves into the cave—where Gail had been waiting a good ten minutes—that only a few mountaineers had visited the gorge since it had been mapped in 1964. Collapsing at the cave's opening as he tried to catch his breath, Gabe understood why.

Still, it was beautiful, and as Gail insisted, now that they could begin tracking the cats, the signals from the collars wouldn't be deflected by valley walls, as they would be, if the camp were lower. All they had to do, she'd said blithely, was adjust to the monotonous diet, the excruciating terrain, and the isolation. Other than that, they'd have a great time.

"I was thinking about the cat we collared today," Gabe said, when Gail sat down beside him, her tin mug in her hand. He smiled. "It was quite an experience."

She grinned, her eyes glistening. "Yes, it was, wasn't it? I was shaking the entire time."

"You didn't look it. You seemed cool as could be."

"So did you. But then, this is what you do, so maybe you're used to it."

"I don't think anyone ever gets used to something like this. Seeing the leopard up close . . ." Words failed him, and he shook his head.

"I know, I feel the same way," Gail said. She put the empty cup down and clasped her hands around her pulled-up legs. "So, tell me about yourself, Gabe. In all this time, you've never mentioned anybody special back home, but I know a good-looking guy like you can't have gotten completely away. There must be *someone*."

Reaching out, he used a stick to poke up the fire. In the leaping flames, his eyes took on a faraway look. "There is," he admitted. "Sort of."

"Sort of?"

He grinned at her. "It means there's someone I . . . see when I get a chance."

"Well, she must appreciate *that*."

Laughing, he explained. "She's got her own career. Sometimes it's touch and go whether she'll have time for *me*."

"What's her name?"

"Keeley. Keeley Cochran."

"Keeley," Gail repeated. "It's an unusual name."

"She's an unusual woman."

"So, tell me what your Keeley does for a living."

"She's a musician."

"She is!" Gail looked intrigued. "Is she with a band?"

Gabe laughed, trying to picture Keeley as a member of a band. The only image that came to him was one of her standing on a podium in a tuxedo, conducting a full symphonic orchestra.

"No, she's not with a band," he said, smiling at the picture. "She writes music. For a while, she was writing for Broadway, but now she's in Hollywood, writing scores for movies. She and her partner won a big award a while ago for Music in Film."

"Wow," Gail said, impressed. She leaned toward him. "Tell me more."

"Gail," John said, from where he was still fiddling with his equipment. "Leave the man alone, will you? You don't need to know about his private life."

"Yes, I do," Gail said. "Besides, what else are we going to do? Watch reruns on the portable TV?"

Her husband ignored her sarcasm. "We can hit the sack," he said, switching off some of the equipment. "We've got a lot to do tomorrow. You and Gabe have to set the camouflaged camera and the pressure pads, and I have some tracking to do with Puchang. So come on, say good night."

"He thinks he's the boss," she muttered to Gabe, but she got to her feet and went.

Puchang had already retired to his tent, and when the Marchuks entered theirs, Gabe was alone by the fire. He knew he should climb into his sleeping bag, too, but he sat on for a while, staring into the dying flames. The conversation with Gail had conjured up thoughts of home, and he frowned as he remembered another "discussion" he'd had with his father. Except for emergencies, he knew he'd be incommunicado for months once he and the Marchuks trekked into the Himalayas, so he'd called from Nepal before they left, to make sure everything was all right at home. Ellis had answered the phone, and he'd been curt.

"Your mother is fine," his father had said, when Gabe asked. "Except for being constantly worried about you. If you're really concerned, Gabriel, maybe you should give some thought about giving up this photography business and coming to work for me."

He didn't want to get into a battle over a long-distance call. "I thought we had settled that, Dad," he'd said, trying to keep his cool. "Some people think my work is important, and so do I."

"You always have been self-centered," Ellis said. "If you won't think of your mother, you might devote a moment to your brother."

"Is something wrong with Frank?" Gabe was surprised by the comment, more so by the jab of fear he felt.

"Nothing that a vacation wouldn't cure," Ellis replied. "But of course he won't take any time; he feels responsibility far too strongly."

The rebuke was clear, but then, it always was, Gabe thought. "Well, that's his problem, Dad," he said, and couldn't help adding his own thrust. "Besides, you haven't taken a vacation in years—no matter how much Mom begged. So I'd say that Frank's just following in your footsteps, wouldn't you?"

He'd wanted to talk to his mother, but she'd been resting. Unhappily, he'd said good-bye. As always, it seemed he and his father just couldn't communicate; sometimes he wondered why he bothered trying.

"Stupid," he muttered, stirring up the fire again. He'd intended on going to bed like everyone else, but thinking about his father always agitated him, and he looked around to see if they'd finished all the wine. There was a swallow in the bottle when he found it, and on impulse, he made a silent toast to Keeley.

"Here's to you, darlin'," he thought, remembering despite himself their lovemaking the last time he'd been home. Instantly, his groin began to ache—not a good sign ten thousand miles away from relief. But the more he tried not to think about Keeley, the clearer a picture he had of her in his mind. Without even trying, he could feel her small body under his hands, her smooth skin, her small waist and rounded breasts. Closing his eyes, he pictured them both in the pool that night, water cascading off her face and shoulders as she stood up in the shallow end, looking like a young Aphrodite.

No woman should be so sexy, he thought, and shook his head. He couldn't believe sometimes that any woman had taken such a hard hold of him. She was beautiful, to be sure; she was supremely talented, there was no doubt. She was also intelligent and quick and sure of herself, and she knew where she was going and how to get there. But best of all, he thought, she expected to live her own life, and she wanted him to live his. He'd never thought to find a woman like that, and sometimes he didn't know if he were blessed or cursed.

"I don't want a permanent, steady relationship," she had told him earnestly the last night they were together. "I'm married to my music, Gabe, to my career. I'd never ask any man to wait around until I had time for him—" her eyes held his, her glance so direct it made his heart ache "—just as I wouldn't want any man to ask me to wait around until he had time for me. Can you understand?"

He understood perfectly, and he loved her for it. Now that he had found his niche, so to speak, he couldn't imagine trying to fit into a regular nine-to-five job, clocking in and out, doing the same thing day after day. Just thinking about it made him feel claustrophobic. Whether he was baking in the African veldt, or freezing in the high Himalayas, he felt more alive than he ever had before, he realized. The bonus was that through his pictures and films, people who otherwise might never be aware of what was going on were able to experience a rhythm of nature that was growing more and more precarious. He couldn't give it up, not for anyone. Maybe he was a selfish bastard, as his brother, Frank, had said; maybe he was egotistical and ungrateful and a host of other uncomplimentary things his father had claimed the last time he was home. If he was, it was too bad. He was making a difference, he knew, and no matter how sappy it sounded, it gave him a satisfaction he'd never felt anywhere else. For the first time in his life, he was really proud of what he was doing.

He thought suddenly of his ranch in Montana. He'd always loved the place, and the first chance he had, he'd bought a chunk of land there. He hadn't had much chance to visit yet, but the next time he went back to the States, he planned to stay for a while. Silly, but he'd thought of Keeley when he first saw it. The brilliant blue sky, the distant mountain ranges, the wind cool against his face, and the endless vistas had a power of their own that reminded him of her, and he wanted her to see it. He sensed another rhythm there, untamed but not so wild as the places he'd been; it was a point to come home to, a place to take shelter in.

Wondering if that's how he thought of Keeley, he smiled as he banked the fire before going to bed. One of these days, he vowed, he was going to take Keeley to Montana. She'd love it, he thought; once he got her there, they could write a concerto all their own.

Then he sighed. It would be some time before he got back to the States, much less to Montana. Right now he had work to do, and if he didn't get to bed, he'd be sorry in the morning. Gail got everyone going before dawn. If he wasn't out of his tent when she was ready, she was perfectly capable of pulling it down around him.

Smiling again at the thought, he hit the sack. But as the cold stars of the Nepalese night blinked icily away in the endless black sky overhead, and the snow leopards, unlike other big cats who spoke in roars, called to each other occasionally with their high-pitched yowls, Gabe didn't dream of the work he loved. He dreamed of Keeley and how her face would look the first time she saw his ranch.

In the morning, fortified with a breakfast of the usual rice and dried meat, but treated this time to an addition of biscuits with raisins, everyone set off to work. Puchang and John went up, while Gabe and Gail started the precarious climb down to the place where they would set the camouflaged camera. They were each carrying a backpack filled with equipment, the load equally divided. Gabe knew better than to say he'd carry the heavier pack; one look from Gail stifled his automatic, gentlemanly protest.

Earlier in the week, they had gone down to mark out the trail they would use, and Gail had made drawings to preserve the area. The plan was to install a camouflaged camera and flash, activated by a pressure pad similar to the ones used for security systems, so that a cat coming by would take its own picture.

It wasn't as simple as it sounded, but Gabe had talked to an expert to get his ideas before they left Nepal, and he knew what he wanted to do. The place he had selected was a trail crossing a riverine terrace next to the Langu River. The trail had been marked by scent sprays, droppings, and scratchings, so they knew it was used frequently. The danger, of course, was that the cats would sense something had changed and would avoid the place, so he and Gail worked carefully, placing a pressure pad in the center of the trail, then carefully feeding wires back to the camera assembly, which Gabe prefocused at fifteen feet. The power source for the assembly was a six-volt solar-powered battery, which they placed behind the camouflaged tripod, attaching the flash to a nearby shrub. When they were finished, they put everything back the way they had found it, using the drawings Gail had made to make sure every pebble and leaf was in the same place. Retreating cautiously, they headed back up to camp.

They had almost reached the meadow near the cave when they came upon a herd of *bharal* feeding off the alpine grass. Startled, humans and sheep looked at each other, but before Gail and Gabe could begin skirting around the little group, a male sheep suddenly appeared over the top of the slope, plunging directly toward Gail.

"Look out!" Gabe shouted, sending the herd scattering. He grabbed Gail and jerked her back, nearly pulling her off her feet as the ram bounded past.

"What—" Gail started to say, and then blanched. Hard on the ram's heels came a large snow leopard, traveling at top speed. The big cat flashed right by them, so close they almost felt the brush of its fur. Intent on its prey, it didn't see them, but charged after the sheep, who veered sharply and ran off to safety. Suddenly, the cat became aware of the two frozen humans. Pulling its ears back so tightly they seemed to disappear into the sides of its head, the cat dropped instantly into the low vegetation. Motionless, it was nearly invisible.

"Don't move," Gail murmured, barely moving her lips.

Gabe wasn't going to. Even though he had seen the cat drop to the ground, the leopard blended so perfectly into the grass that it was difficult to see, even looking straight at it. But he could feel the fierce stare of the big cat, and his skin prickled. Would it attack? It was so damned close. As he stood there, hardly daring to breathe, he tried to remember if he'd ever heard of a substantiated report of a snow leopard killing a human. He was sure he hadn't, but with the one facing him now, it was cold comfort. Trying to tell himself that a smart cat like this would never mistake a human for a sheep, he waited tensely with Gail to see what it would do.

For an endless fifteen minutes, they stared in the direction of the cat; the cat stared back. Gabe was just beginning to wonder if they were all going to freeze in permanent position when suddenly the leopard looked away. Then he looked back. He looked away again, as if debating what to do next, while the two petrified humans held their breath. Finally, he made his move. Barely lifting its belly off the ground, it began to creep away through the low vegetation as though it had found wheels. With a final glance back, it stood and broke into a full run, disappearing over the crest of the meadow with a flick of its thick, black-tipped tail.

Left disdainfully behind, the humans could breathe again. "Whew," Gail said, running a hand over her sweating forehead, even though by this time it was nearly dark and starting to get cold. "That was a close one."

Gabe couldn't have agreed more. His only regret was that he hadn't been able to get to his Nikon, trapped in his backpack.

He could see in his mind's eye how magnificent a frame-by-frame sequence shot at high speed would have been as the cat bounded off.

They told John and Puchang about the incident when they got back to camp, Gail trying to make light of it while John's face darkened more with every word. After making sure they hadn't been hurt, John gave them both a lecture about being more careful. Winking at Gabe behind her husband's back, Gail solemnly promised to watch it, but in the end, it was John who had a much more serious run-in with one of the cats.

It didn't happen until the last of the season. By then, they had been out eight months, and Gabe had shot almost three hundred rolls and countless feet of film. They had collared four leopards and collected reams of data about the elusive and solitary cat, and they were beginning preparations to start the long trek out the following week when they ran across a skinned carcass abandoned near a riverbed. It was a gruesome sight, the remains desiccated, the limbs curled into rigid contortions, the tail spiraling grotesquely straight up. Gabe never went anywhere without one or more cameras; while he set up shots of the grisly find, John and Gail stood around, looking somber. It was the first time Gabe had seen Gail remotely near tears, but he was feeling emotional himself. The contrast between the skeletal remains they'd found, and the magnificent, *living* creatures they had seen in action, on the hunt, and more rarely, at play, seemed like desecration.

"It was obviously skinned for the pelt," John said finally, when Gabe was finished and he and Gail had examined what was left of the carcass. "And since there are no major wounds, I'd venture to guess it was killed with poison."

Gabe had seen the native hunter's way of killing the big cats. Three-foot-long bamboo spears were sharpened to deadly points, then tipped with a concoction from the poisonous monkshood plant. Placed at an angle along ledges, the spears were set to impale any cat leaping down to follow a trail. The poison was so lethal that even a superficial wound could kill.

Feeling sick inside, Gabe packed away his cameras and film. "I thought poaching for pelts had declined."

"It has," John said sadly. "An international convention has restricted trade, but coats are still sold, even on the open market. This hunter might get ten, twelve dollars for a skin, but a pelt in good condition will fetch a couple of hundred dollars when it's sold in the city. From there, the price climbs quickly as it passes through the hands of all those middlemen, and coat makers and dealers."

Gail looked up. "We found one coat at a government tourist store in China one time that was on sale for just over a thousand dollars," she said. "It was made from three snow leopard pelts."

"Three?" The waste was beyond imagining.

She shrugged, but there was sorrow in her gray eyes. "It's the tip of the iceberg, Gabe. To make a coat of really high quality, a furrier will take the best parts of as many as a dozen pelts. Of course, a coat like that would cost a great deal more—over sixty thousand on the black market."

Gabe looked at the carcass. In his mind, he could see the cat coming over the hill, after the ram. It had passed so close, he could almost have touched it. When it saw them, it could have attacked . . . and hadn't. "It's hard to understand."

John shook his head in disgust. "I've given up trying."

In silence they headed back to camp. The only good thing about the day was discovering that during the night something had tripped the camouflaged camera again. Gabe would have to wait to develop the film to see if the prized picture was a self-portrait of a leopard—or something else—but even so it was a great find. During the time the camera had been in place, the flash had only been activated twice. Gail and John were pleased with the results, but Gabe felt the setup hadn't been much of a success.

The next day, one of their last on the gorge, they went out to try to trap the new arrival that had been wandering the area for the past few weeks. Either the cat was phenomenally lucky, or it was more crafty than the others, because so far, despite their best efforts, it had eluded all of the traps they'd set to capture it. Gail had excitedly identified it as a newcomer because the paw prints it left behind were different from the others she had studied; this one had a missing toe on the left front. They speculated that the injury might have made it even more cautious than usual, and no one had faith they'd capture it at this late date. In fact, with a hundred-and-sixty-mile hike down precipitous cliffs in front of them—not to mention having to rig a cable and sling seat just to get over the river—John wanted to start packing up to go. While Gabe wouldn't be back the following season, the Marchuks would be. John insisted they'd have time then to track the elusive upstart.

"No, we're going to do it today," Gail said stubbornly. "After all this time, we've only collared four cats. Five would make a nice round number to finish out the season."

"Four is a better round number," John pointed out, but Gabe could see that even he was reluctant to leave without at least trying once more.

Resigned, Gabe went to select his camera equipment. With so little time, they all knew the chance of finding the cat was slim. It was difficult, in fact, to locate the cats they had collared, even with the radio gear to track them. Easily upholding their reputation as secretive and shy, the leopards could conceal themselves even in areas of sparse vegetation. He and Gail and John had spent hours—with the radio giving them a cat's exact location— trying to spot a tiny movement of a tail, or even more obvious, the distinguishing black tips on the ears, only to realize when they finally gave up, that it had been sitting practically in front of them the entire time. Puchang thought it was funny, but even he couldn't spot the big cats all the time.

That morning, they were lucky . . . or so it seemed at first. Gail was standing at the cave's entrance, looking around with the spotting scope when she drew in a sharp breath. "We got him!" she exclaimed, excitedly handing the scope to John, who came rushing up. Sure enough, high up the steep embankment, half-hidden behind a boulder, crouched a beautiful leopard—a prime specimen, it was obvious even from a distance. He'd been caught in the loop trap Gail had set earlier, and as they all scrambled up to the place, Gabe struggling with his precious cameras, they could hear hissing and snarling as the animal fought to free itself. The snare had been designed to hold, not to hurt, so they weren't worried it would injure itself. In fact, when they were finally face-to-face with the beautiful creature, Gabe wondered if it was they who might end up getting the worst. The cat was a magnificent male, obviously in no mood to cooperate, and despite Puchang's and Gail's help, John had a hard time getting it tranquilized.

Even to Gabe's eyes the leopard didn't seem to react in the usual way; it seemed only lightly sedated as Gail and John quickly went to work, measuring and placing the radio collar. Uneasily, Gabe said, "Is it my imagination, or is this cat waking up a little sooner than the others?"

Working at high speed, Gail had finished taking her measurements and had stepped back, but John was still adjusting the radio collar. Without looking up, John said, "He is, but I don't want to give him another injection. I'm almost fin—"

He never got the chance to complete the sentence. With a snarl, the cat came to life just as John was tightening the collar. Before anyone could react, least of all John himself, the cat sank its teeth into his hand.

Fortunately for John, he yelled with pain, startling the cat so badly that the animal lurched to its feet and tried to run off. It was still groggy with the tranquilizer, and its hind legs wouldn't work properly, but it managed to move off a short distance before it fell.

No one noticed. Swiftly, they gathered around John and his bleeding hand. "Let me see," Gabe said, kneeling down. As soon as he saw white bone glistening in the wound, he knew it was bad. His expression tense, he looked at Gail.

"This is beyond what medicine we have," he said. "We're going to have to take him down."

Gail had no color in her face; even her lips looked white. But she took charge, both of herself and the situation, saying, "You go back and pack what we need to take. Puchang and I will help John to the river, and we'll all go on from there."

John's eyes were dark with pain, but he said, "Don't be ridiculous. There's time to pack up. It's late enough in the season that we don't need to come back."

"But—"

"No buts," he said firmly. "Here, Gabe, help me up. We'll go back, I'll wash this out as best I can, take a hit of morphine, and we'll set out."

Gail didn't like the plan. "I don't think—"

"Look, Gail," John said in a tone he seldom used, "I can't just head back with my hand like this. I've got to take care of it, and besides, I'm not going to leave all that equipment behind. Puchang, can you get us some help from your village?" He tried to smile, wincing with the effort. Apologetically, he added, "I don't think I'll be up to carrying my share this trip."

It was obvious Gail wanted to argue further; her lips were tight as she looked at Gabe, who shrugged. He didn't like it, either, but he couldn't argue. John knew his limits, and his injury, while serious, wasn't life-threatening . . . at least, not yet. He agreed with the reasoning about not leaving the equipment and all the research behind. They had spent months collecting valuable data, and with antibiotics and painkillers inside him, John should make it back to Jumla, the nearest medical facility, before things got serious.

The trip was a tough one, Gail pushing them all the way.

They set off that afternoon because she wouldn't wait, and eight days of hard walking got them back to some degree of civilization. But in Jumla, they were advised to fly on to Kathmandu, where there were facilities for surgery. John's hand was in good shape, but no one wanted to take the chance of permanent tendon damage.

In the narrow, winding streets of Kathmandu, they were directed to a Nepalese surgeon, who examined John minutely and assured him he would heal just fine with a month or so of rest. Relieved, Gail smiled for the first time in days and even gave Gabe a kiss on the cheek before he packed up his own gear and reluctantly left for his next assignment. From the high Himalayas, he was going back to the rain forest of French Guiana to take up where he had left off, tracking the jaguar.

Gabe's snow leopard photos were given a special showing at galleries in New York, Washington, and Boston. The show got rave reviews; the crowds of people who came were entranced, awed, and impressed, especially by the highlights of the show, the only two self-portraits of snow leopards in existence. Gabe's diligence with the camouflaged camera had paid off: in one picture, the lens had captured a leopard full on, the glare of the flash making the cat's eyes glow with a deep green hue. In the other picture, the cat was slunk down, seeming to reach out to slash at the camera just as the flash went off. It seemed startled, surprised, but even at that, very sure of itself, ready to attack.

Only Keeley knew there was a third self-portrait.

She received it in the mail one day, and when she saw what Gabe had sent, she gasped. It was the third shot, one Gabe had kept from the public, even from the IZF itself, an outstanding, never-before-seen photo of a snow leopard on its nightly rounds. With its head low, and its icy green, kohl-rimmed eyes mesmerizing and intent, the big cat padded along the trail with power and grace, one huge deadly paw spread out in front, its glance fixed on something only it could see in the dark. The prized coat, luxurious silver gray dotted with black rosettes, stood out in gorgeous relief to the black coldness of the Himalayan night behind and around it. Ice crystals, caught in the flash, sparkled like jewels, giving the photo an ethereal quality that made it an even more extraordinary sight. It seemed the perfect setting for one of the world's most elusive and splendid wild cats.

The accompanying note, written in Gabe's bold hand, read:

"Fierce, quick, independent, legendary. Sort of reminds me of you, Keeley."

CHAPTER TWENTY

"You owe me, Keeley," Noel stated. Riding the success of his newest movie, he had barged into her office that morning without warning. The big money people had turned him down on a project he wanted to do; Raleigh Quinn wouldn't back him, so—on the strength of what he called their past "relationship"—he had come to her. He'd been after her for the past ten minutes, wheedling at first, cajoling, then finally demanding that she help him. She knew she should just say no, but she felt guilty. After all, they *had* briefly been lovers, once.

"Listen, Noel—"

He sensed what she was going to say and looked at her bitterly. "I can't believe it! After all we've been to each other, you can refuse me, just like that!"

She wanted to say that they hadn't *been* that much, but decided to take a different tack. "I haven't refused—"

"You haven't said you would, either!"

The famed gray-blue eyes that had entranced millions of women from his ten-foot-high image on the movie screen didn't seem so seductive at the moment; the handsome face wasn't quite as perfectly good-looking. Noel Harrington was an attractive man under most circumstances, but right now he looked exactly like the product of the Chicago slums where he had grown up. Sullen and resentful, his sensuous mouth an ugly slash, he glared at her, and as she stared back, she wondered why she'd ever found him attractive.

"I don't *owe* you anything, Noel," she said evenly. "And if you can't be civil, I think you'd better leave."

"What are you going to do if I don't?" he demanded. "Call security? Get Fitz to throw me out, the little—"

"Let's leave Fitz out of this, all right?" she said, her eyes flashing. "This is between you and me."

"Damn right it is," Noel agreed. He leaned forward, over the desk. "What is this shit you're trying to hand me? You promised your support, Keeley. You said if Quinn wouldn't go for it, you'd help me."

"No, I said I'd try. And I *did* try. But if the head of the studio won't commit to financing your project, what do you think I can do?"

"You can back me."

"I don't have that kind of money!"

"I don't believe it. You've got more money than you know what to do with—all successful songwriters do. And it just keeps coming, what with all the attention you've gotten—hell, the word is that you and Fitz are going to be up for Best Song at this year's Oscars. Even if you don't win, we both know what it means."

"What it *means*, Noel, is that I'm not going to celebrate until the nominations are in and I see Fitz's and my name down in black and white."

"Well, fine, be that way. But you're still rolling in dough."

It was true, to a point. Even Keeley couldn't deny that her success had brought her more money than she'd ever dreamed. To deal with financial matters, as well as a host of other problems that came with it, now she had an accountant and a financial adviser. Sometimes she thought it was all a fantasy from which she would awaken and find herself still making up tunes on the old cardboard keyboard she'd left behind in Detroit.

But money had always been too important for her to take lightly; growing up hand-to-mouth with too many babies underfoot and a father who was out of work more often than not had taught her the value of saving, and she doubted she'd ever feel secure no matter how much she had in the bank. Her accountant applauded her thriftiness, her investment man threw up his hands because he thought she was too cautious. But at least, she thought, she could sleep at night now, without worrying about how she was going to make the house payment.

Since she wanted to keep it that way, she said to Noel, "It wouldn't matter if I were as rich as Croesus. Financing a picture is enormously expensive, as you should know, and besides, you're not a pauper yourself."

"Yes, but I have expenses."

Keeley had a good idea what those expenses were. Noel was an eligible bachelor, quite the man-about-town, especially since the release of his last film, *Minus the Midas Touch*, the second in the Jason Cross series.

"Look, Noel," she said reasonably, "even if we *both* wanted to, together we couldn't come up with the money to finance what you have in mind. You're talking about a major motion picture, not a home video."

"But it's a picture that's going to make me a star!"

"You're *already* a star."

"No, I'm Jason Cross, superspy extraordinaire," he said, sounding frustrated over something countless other aspiring actors would have given their eyeteeth for. "I want to be known as Noel Harrington. I want to be known as an *actor*, goddamn it. I don't want to be typecast!"

Thinking it was a little too late now, Keeley tried not to glance at her watch. She didn't want him to be here when Fitz showed up; her partner had made it very clear that he thought she'd been crazy to get involved, however briefly, with Noel in the first place. Thinking she agreed, she said patiently, "I don't know where you got the idea that I was going to invest in your—"

"I don't want you just to invest, Keeley. I thought you'd produce."

Now she did believe he was out of his mind. Bursting into laughter, she said, "In the first place, I don't know beans about producing a film, and in the second, as I already pointed out, it takes a lot more than I've managed to save."

Stubbornly, he said, "We can find other money. I never expected to do it ourselves."

Keeley was all too familiar with the financial backer concept. It was how shows came to Broadway, especially these days when just mounting a production could cost several millions. It was the route she would have to take if she ever brought *Beauty and the Beast* to life. She still dreamed about it at times—although lately those moments were fewer and farther between. She'd been so busy, and had so many commitments, that she wondered sometimes if she ever would go back to New York and Broadway. The longer she stayed in California, the more entrenched she became.

But it wasn't Broadway Noel was talking about; it was Hollywood and *his* dream. Jason Cross had been good to him; the role had brought him fame and fortune and a lot of attention—mainly from the female half of the population. In the process, it had also given him an inflated sense of his own importance to the film industry. Now, despite his limited acting ability, he claimed he wanted to expand his range. To Raleigh's annoyance, Noel wanted to abandon Jason Cross and play another kind of hero entirely: Marshal Wyatt Earp of the Old West.

Keeley knew that Raleigh had already vetoed the idea. Correctly, he had pointed out that not only were Westerns notorious for running over budget, but the vast majority never even made back their original investment, not to mention any kind of profit. But more important to Raleigh was the fact that Charbonne Films had spent a lot of money and a great deal of time and effort and publicity building up Noel as the suave Jason Cross, and the studio didn't want anything to detract from the image they'd so carefully manufactured. Unmoved by Noel's eloquent plea for artistic and creative expression, Raleigh had also curtly pointed out that he was still under contract to star in two more Cross films—one of which was scheduled to begin filming as soon as the monsoon season ended in Malaya. Incensed at what he perceived to be Raleigh's callous disregard, Noel had angrily assured him he had every intention of fulfilling his commitment to Charbonne Films, even if he'd never heard of Kuala Lumpur.

"Good move," Keeley had said dryly, when Noel furiously related what had taken place in Raleigh's office. "It saves you from a little something called breach of contract."

"But that doesn't mean *we* can't get started," Noel said persuasively.

She leaned back. "We?"

He changed before her eyes. Gone was the belligerent, demanding, outraged actor; in his place was the charming man who had first attracted her. "Come on, Keeley," he wheedled, coming around the desk to put his hands on her shoulders. Despite herself, she tensed. He felt it and began kneading her tight muscles. "You know I'm a good investment, don't you?" he murmured, massaging away. "My name alone—"

She didn't know why, but she couldn't refuse him outright. Shrugging out from under his grasp, she stood and went to the file cabinet. "I'll think about it," she said.

He grinned. "I knew—"

Seeing his satisfied smile, she shook her finger at him. "I'm not promising anything. All I said was that I'll think about it."

"That's all I can ask, darlin'."

"Don't call me that," she said curtly.

He looked surprised at her tone, then shrugged. He'd gotten

what he wanted—half of it at least. She'd said she'd think about it, and that was good enough for him.

Feeling like a fool, she muttered, "Why you need me, I don't know. You should just ask one of your innumerable fan clubs for financing. You'd get all the money you wanted in a minute."

He laughed, good humor restored because he was sure—despite her warning—that eventually she'd come around. "It wouldn't be the same."

Exasperated, she said, "Why not? According to you, money's money, isn't it?"

Surprising her, he said, "People respect you, Keeley. You've made a name for yourself in this town, and you've done it on your own. I think if people find out you're on the team, they won't be so quick to dismiss my film as crackpot nonsense." He laughed, never serious about anyone or anything but himself for long. "Does it matter?"

She refused to be swayed by this innocent approach. Glancing away from his blue-gray eyes that were the best at faking sincerity that she'd ever seen, she said, "It does matter, to me. Tell me the truth. Why are you so determined to do this film?"

Without warning, his face changed again, and she was startled to see through his mask to the little boy he was underneath. She knew his background—the hard, mean streets of tenement house Chicago—but he'd always hidden his hunger so well that she'd never been aware of it until now. She knew that hunger; having grown up sustained at times only by her own dreams, she knew how it felt to want something so bad no price seemed too high to attain it.

"I've dreamed of playing a cowboy since I was a little boy," he said simply. "Not just any cowboy, mind you—but a real hero, one of the men who helped civilize the Old West." He colored, embarrassed at his confession, but in too deep not to go on. "I used to dream of riding into town on my white horse and saving the people from the bad guys—me, who had never been on a horse in my life." He paused. "Silly, isn't it?"

Touched despite herself, she said, "Not so much. I used to dream of hearing my music played on Broadway—I, who never owned a piano until I went to New York."

His glance met hers. "Then you know what I mean."

"Yes," she said quietly. "I know what you mean."

He seemed relieved. "I don't know why this means so much to me, Keeley. Maybe it's the kid in me, still. But I remember how I felt about those men—Wyatt and Buffalo Bill, and all the rest, and I think kids need heroes today. Someone to balance out the Terminators and the Rambos and the Lethal Weapons." He looked down at her and smiled. "I think Old Wyatt might just do that, don't you?"

She didn't answer for a moment. She wanted to believe him, but she had seen him turn on the act dozens of times, only to revert to a spoiled little boy behind closed doors when he didn't get his way. She knew he meant what he said now, but would he still be so determined if the going got rough? Self-indulgent and pampered, would he act like one of his heroes, or himself?

He saw her uncertainty, for he came over and put his arms around her waist. Drawing her gently to him, he looked down into her face. "You had a dream, Keeley, you can't deny it. And you've achieved it. How can you deny me the chance to know the same satisfaction?"

"I said I'd think about it," she repeated, moving away from Noel. She put the file she'd taken from the cabinet between them as a sort of shield. "Now, will you leave me alone so I can get some work done?"

He left with a smile and a backward glance that just missed being a smirk. As she watched him head down the hall—*swagger*—down the hall, with the strut of a man who knows he has only to snap his fingers for women to come running, Keeley shook her head. Had she imagined the little boy behind his smile just now? Surely not, she thought, and slowly closed the door when he disappeared around the corner.

Fitz came in two minutes later. Flopping down into the chair behind his desk, he said, "I just saw supersleuth in the hallway, looking like the lion whose mate has brought him the kill. Since he was obviously coming from this office, was he here on private business, or to tell you about the shouting match with Raleigh this morning? From what I hear, they're going to meet out on the quad at high noon, six-shooters strapped on."

Despite herself, she laughed. "Where'd you hear that?"

"Which—the rumor about the duel, or the even more incredible story about our boy challenging his nonexistent acting ability by going back to the Wild West to play Wyatt Earp?"

Her arms akimbo, she glared at him. "What are you, a fly on the wall? He just talked to Raleigh about it not a half hour ago, and you already know. How many spies do you have, anyway?"

Fitz grinned. "Oh, I had a thing going once with Raleigh's office boy. He told me on the sly."

"Clever. What else did your office boy say?"

"Not much," he replied. Then, carefully, he said, "I know it's nobody's business, certainly not mine, but . . . you aren't going to back Noel, are you?"

"Who told you that?"

"Nobody, but it wasn't hard to figure out. After all, you were . . . er . . . close once, and he needs a name for cachet."

She didn't like to be reminded of that brief liaison. "Well, he certainly doesn't need mine. He's the star, not me."

"He's the star of the Jason Cross films, which was stretch enough, as you know."

Wondering why she was defending Noel to Fitz, of all people, she said, "Well, if he's such a rotten actor, why has Raleigh invested so much in him? He must have faith—"

"Oh, but that's different. Raleigh knows he's got a sure thing in the Cross films. Take a man as handsome as Noel and surround him with the latest in special effects, tie them together with beautiful women and a plot that doesn't exist but promises a lot of excitement, and bam! It's a winner. Women come to see his sexy body and those smoldering glances, and men are drawn by the newest gadgetry. Everybody goes home happy—including the studio."

Keeley crossed her arms. She knew he was right, but it didn't make her happy. "I see you've got it all figured out."

"So does Raleigh. Any other questions?"

Keeley had been too preoccupied to notice before now, but suddenly she frowned. "Are you all right?"

Fitz had gone to hang up his coat at the rack behind the door. Surprised at the question, he glanced over his shoulder. "Sure. Why?"

"Because you don't look right."

"Well, thanks a lot. I know I don't look my best in the morning, but you don't have to be cruel."

"No, I mean it, Fitz. You look pale, and . . . you've got circles under your eyes. Are you sure you're feeling well?"

He thumped his chest. "Never felt better. But you look like you could use a rest."

She wasn't going to be diverted. "We're not talking about me. Come to think of it, you look like you've lost weight, too." She looked at him anxiously. "Have you seen a doctor?"

"What for?" he said, coming back to his desk. "I told you, I feel fine."

"Then why—"

"And as for the weight—" He patted his stomach. "I have

been on a diet, I confess. Lindsey thought I was getting a little rotund, so I decided to lose a couple of pounds."

She wasn't convinced. Why hadn't she noticed it before? "You look like you've lost more than that. Fitz, don't you think you should see—"

"I'm fine," he said, startling her with the note of anger she heard in his voice. "Now, can we let it go and move on to something a little more important? As I recall, we have a meeting with the new arranger this morning, and I want to go over the whole first section of the score again. I was listening to it last night, and . . ."

He kept talking, but Keeley wasn't listening. She'd never seen—or heard—Fitz like this; it was almost as if he were hiding something. Worried, she thought that he really didn't look well, but before she could panic, she decided he was coming down with the flu, maybe catching a cold. If he didn't feel well, she reasoned, he wouldn't have come in to work.

"Will you stop looking at me like I'm going to fall over in a dead heap?" Fitz demanded, looking up. "I said I was all right, so let's get to work."

"Sure," she said stiffly, her feelings hurt. She withdrew to her side of the desk. "I didn't realize I was staring. I'm sorry."

Fitz slumped. "Oh, damn it. I'm sorry, too." He took a deep breath. "Look, I guess I should just tell you—"

"What?"

Uncomfortably, he said, "I lied about Lindsey."

"Lindsey? What do you mean, you lied?"

"I mean about him saying I needed to go on a diet. The truth is, Lindsey . . . left me."

"Oh, Fitz!" It was the last thing she had expected. "I'm sorry. I don't know what to say. Do you want to talk about it?"

"Yes . . . no . . . I don't know. I just can't understand it. I thought we . . ." He paused, swallowing painfully. "Maybe he met someone more attractive. Maybe he wanted someone younger, who knows? But he took all his stuff and split a couple of weeks ago."

"Oh, Fitz, I'm sorry," she said again. She was hurt, too. "Why didn't you tell me?"

"I don't know. I guess I was . . . embarrassed."

"But we're friends!"

He finally looked at her, his eyes moist behind his round glasses. "We are, aren't we?"

"Yes, we are. Now, what can I do?" Feeling badly about it,

she wanted to help. "I know! You can stay with me for a couple of days. We'll send out for pizza—" she knew it was his favorite meal, breakfast, lunch, or dinner "—and we can rent dozens of videos and watch them all until our eyes cross. What do you say, Fitz?"

Smiling wanly, he said, "Thanks, Keeley, I appreciate the offer—really, I do. But I'm afraid I wouldn't be such good company right now."

"I'm not asking for your *company*! Come on, pack up a few things and come over and let me spoil the hell out of you."

"You'd really do that?"

"Sure, of course I would. You have to ask? You'd do it for me, wouldn't you?"

"In a minute, though not that I'd have to. You're always so . . . so fierce and independent. I can't imagine anything getting to you."

Fierce, quick, independent, legendary. Sort of reminds me of you, Keeley.

The words Gabe had written at the bottom of the snow leopard photo leapt into her mind, and she colored. "Don't believe it," she said. "Sometimes I hate myself for missing Gabe so much."

Fitz had never met Gabe in person, but he'd seen the pictures, and of course he'd heard a lot about him. Nodding, he said, "Yeah, I know. You've got it bad, Keeley."

"Bad?"

He grinned. "Don't play innocent, it doesn't suit you. You're in love with the guy, you might as well admit it."

She went from pink to red. "Love? I don't know—"

"Oh, please. The question is when you're going to get married?"

"Married! Gabe and me?"

She sounded so horrified that Fitz laughed. "Well, Keeley, it's not exactly an improper thing to do, you know."

"I'm not so sure. From what I've seen, marriage ties you down, destroys your freedom, takes away your independence, and stifles creativity."

"Whew. You've rather a jaundiced eye, don't you think?"

"I only know what I've seen firsthand."

"But it wouldn't be that way with Gabe, would it?"

"Maybe not," she admitted. She thought about it. "If I were going to consider marrying anyone, it would be Gabe." Then she looked at Fitz. "But take my word for it, it's better this way."

Fitz suddenly looked bleak again. Sadly he said, "You know, I think you're right. Getting involved just hurts too much when someone leaves."

"Oh, Fitz," she said. Getting up from her desk, she went and put her arms around him. "Lindsey was a jerk," she muttered. "And if I ever see him again, I'll tell him so right to his face."

Fitz made a sound somewhere between a laugh and a sob and patted her arm. "You're one in a million, Keeley," he said, his voice muffled. "I'm glad you're my friend."

"That makes two of us," she replied, and she held him until he looked up with a shaky, sad little smile.

Feeling drained, Keeley went home that night alone. She still hadn't decided what to do about Noel, and she was worried about Fitz, who had gently but firmly refused her offer to come to stay for a few days, insisting that he'd be better off at his own place. Wondering how to cheer him up, she let herself into the house, absently sorting through the mail she'd gotten that day. Nothing interested her, so she threw it on the hall table and switched on her answering machine as she headed toward the kitchen to make a cup of tea. When the first message came on, she stopped cold in her tracks and turned to stare at the machine.

"Hi, there, Keeley," said a voice she knew all too well. "Bet you're surprised as hell to hear from me. Never did get the hang of these machines, so I don't know how long I've got to talk. Wanted you to know we're comin' over to see you. Would have called before, but I—" embarrassed cough, with noise in the background "—forgot. See you soon, all right?"

There was a click. Another message cycled on, but she didn't hear it. She was staring, wide-eyed at the machine, frozen in disbelief. "It can't be . . ." she muttered, rushing over to play the tape back.

She'd hoped she had heard wrong, but the message was the same as it had been before. When it finished playing a second time, she switched it off without going through the rest of the tape. Shakily, she went into the living room and sat down.

"I don't believe it," she muttered. It had to be a joke. The voice on the tape had belonged to her father, whom she hadn't heard from in years, since she'd left to go to New York. Thinking of what he'd said, she shook her head violently. He couldn't be thinking of coming here; it didn't make sense! Even though he'd never set foot in the state, he hated California; he'd always called it the land of fruits and nuts. Wincing, Keeley started to get up from the couch, only to sink back again. *We*, he had said. Did he mean he was bringing the entire family?

"Oh, lord," she said, groaning at the thought. It couldn't be. It had to be a bad dream. Hoping she was right, she got up again and called home. She let it ring sixteen times, but when no one answered, she slowly put back the receiver. "It doesn't mean anything," she muttered. "Phyllis probably didn't want to cook again so they all went to a hamburger place for dinner."

Reminded that she hadn't eaten herself, she tried to put the horrible thought of her family's coming to visit out of her mind by fixing a sandwich for dinner. She forced herself to eat half of it, then gave the other half to Tuxedo, who had come in for his meal and liked what people ate more than cat food. Worried about Fitz, and indecisive about Noel, exasperated and annoyed about the call from her father, she switched on the stereo and tried to be soothed by Brahms's Symphony No. 4 in E minor, when inside she felt like the 1812 Overture. Restlessly, she tried to get some work done, but for once the notes that came so effortlessly eluded her, and she was about to toss the notebook aside when she heard a commotion on the porch. As Tux got up and streaked for his cat door, the bell rang and someone began pounding on the front door.

"Keeley! Keeley, I know you're home!" her father called. "Come on, open up!"

When she heard his voice, she had an urge to switch out all the lights and pretend she wasn't here. But that was ridiculous; they knew from the lights that she was home. She had to let them in, but her steps were dragging as she went toward the entry.

"Why now," she muttered. Steeling herself, she opened the door.

"Finally!" her father exclaimed, when she let them in. He was wearing a loud Hawaiian shirt and was loaded down with paper bags and suitcases and boxes under both arms. The rest of the family pushed into the house, an irritable-looking Phyllis in the lead, barely acknowledging Keeley as she went by, the kids fanning out in all directions without saying hello, except for Jewell, who gave her a quick hug and a look of apology.

Hugging Jewell in return, Keeley looked at Joe Cochran. "Why didn't you let me know you were coming?" she asked, when everyone had trooped inside. Her throat felt tight; she could hardly speak.

"I did," he said, his teeth clamped around a cigarette. he was acting as if they'd seen each other yesterday, instead of years ago. "I called, didn't I?"

"Tonight! Did you really think that was notice?"

His eyes narrowed, and he took a breath that puffed out his unshaven cheeks. "Don't matter now, does it?" he said.

She wanted to rip the dangling cigarette out of his mouth and grind it under her heel. "How long do you plan to stay?" she asked curtly.

"I haven't decided yet. It depends."

"On what?"

He lost patience. "Look, are you going to keep me jawin' out here on the porch all night, or are you going to let me in?"

Silently, she stood aside. But as he edged by her, loaded down with what he was carrying, he shifted the cigarette again and said, "Oh, by the way, the car broke down somewhere down by the beach, so we had to take a couple of cabs. Pay the guys, will you, Keeley? This stuff is killin' me, and I need a beer bad."

She hardly heard the last remark. Turning stiffly, she watched him toss his load down in the entry. Disbelievingly, she said, "You took two *taxis* from the beach?"

"Well, what did you expect us to do—walk? Go on, now, you're a rich Hollywood songwriter, you can pay them for me. Give the second guy a good tip," he called as he started off to find the kitchen. "He put up with a lot of shit from the kids."

Left by herself in the entry, Keeley counted to ten. In the living room, she heard one of the twins exclaim about the great stereo. Before she could call out, Brahms disappeared and strident hard rock took his place. Instantly, the whole house seemed to throb with the beat of the bass as the volume was turned up full blast. She cringed at the sound. Fortunately, the neighbors weren't close, but she was sure someone would hear the noise and call the police.

Deciding to deal with the cab drivers first, she grabbed her purse and went out to pay them. "Good luck, lady," one of the drivers said, as she counted out his money and added a tip. He shook his head. "Jeez, what a horde."

Despondently, Keeley agreed. Steeling herself to go back inside, she marched into the living room, intending to take charge. The twins were gyrating to the music when she came in; she hardly recognized them. At thirteen, both boys had grown inches and pounds, and she shouted at the nearest, Alfred, to turn down the noise. Trying not to feel overwhelmed already when he ignored her, she was just starting across the floor to do it herself when she saw a girl she didn't recognize. Sprawled on the couch, the girl was holding a grubby-looking baby about a year old and switching channels on the TV as fast as she could, using the remote.

"Man," she said, when she saw Keeley looking at her. "You sure got a lot of channels out here."

"It's cable," Keeley told her, forced practically to shout because of the loud music. She couldn't get to the stereo; the twins were in the way, oblivious to everything as they stomped to the heavy beat. She looked at the girl again. "Who are you?"

The girl, a blond with stringy hair, gestured toward Louis who was stretched out nearby. The oldest of the clan—now twenty, Keeley realized—he looked to be just as much of a punk as he always had been.

"That's Debbie," Louis said, taking a swig from the beer he'd found. "She's my girl. Oh, and meet Pearl," he added, taking another swig. "She's my kid."

"You're married?" Keeley couldn't believe it.

"Nah," Louis yawned. "You think I'm stupid, or something?"

Keeley didn't want to tell him what she thought. She had never liked Louis; she liked him even less now, with his booted feet up on her coffee table, looking as though he owned the place. "Get your feet off the table," she said coldly, and started to tell the twins one last time to turn down the stereo when Lila emerged from the kitchen.

Keeley's older half sister had obviously helped herself to what she wanted from the refrigerator: in one hand was a huge sandwich, dripping with mayonnaise and mustard and probably the last of the cold cuts; in her other hand was a huge bowl of ice cream. Glimpsing Keeley looking at her, she grinned slyly. "Can't help it," she said, nodding down at her stomach. "I'm eatin' for two these days."

Keeley didn't trust herself to respond. Instead, she asked, "Where's Phyllis?"

Lila jerked her chin in the direction of the stairs. "Upstairs, trying to figure out where everybody's going to sleep, I guess. Why?"

Why? Keeley thought, taking the stairs two at a time.

As she'd suspected, she found Phyllis in her bedroom, glancing around appreciatively. When her stepmother heard her at the door, she turned in Keeley's direction. "Nice," she said. "I think this will do just fine."

"For what?" Keeley asked. She was holding on to her self-control by a thread. She couldn't believe she was related to these people. Who did they think they were, coming in as though they owned the place, making themselves at home without even being invited?

"Now, Keeley," Phyllis said. "We're family, remember?"

Family? Keeley almost laughed. "Look, Phyllis," she said evenly. "You can't stay here. I'm not equipped to put up so many people. I've hardly moved in myself—how did you know where I lived, anyway?"

"It wasn't from you, that's for sure," Phyllis said, brushing back her lank hair. Keeley saw she hadn't changed in five years, except to look older and grayer. "We had to look it up in the phone book when we got here."

"I see," Keeley said. "Well, then, how long are you going to be in town? If you're on vacation, I could help you find a motel. . . ."

"Vacation!" Phyllis laughed as though Keeley had told a joke of some kind. "Didn't your dad tell you?"

Feeling a hard knot growing in her stomach, Keeley made herself ask. "Tell me what?"

"We're staying, Keeley! We've left Detroit for good!"

Keeley stared at her. It was her worst nightmare coming to life. "I don't believe it," she choked. "Dad would never move out here. He hates California."

"He used to. But when he realized how well *you* were doing, he decided this is the place for us!"

Keeley couldn't imagine what the connection was. "I see," she said. Well, that's very nice, Phyllis, but as I said, you can't stay here. . . ."

"What do mean, we can't stay here?" her father demanded, behind her. He startled her, and she turned quickly to look at him. He'd found the beer, too, and he took a long swallow from the one he was carrying before crushing the can in one hand. "What kind of shit is that, Keeley? Now that you've made it, you're going to turn your back on your family, is that what you're trying to say?"

"I'm not. . . ."

"You owe us, Keeley," he said, his expression turning ugly. She knew that in another second or two, he'd erupt into shouting, trying to intimidate her as he had when she was a child. He took a menacing step toward her and despite herself, she stepped back. He was so close, she could smell the beer on his sour breath. "You've got this big empty house," he said, leaning down. "It wouldn't hurt you to share it with us, now, would it?"

With an effort, Keeley controlled herself. She wanted to grab their stuff and throw it all out into the front yard and everyone here with it. But suddenly, behind her father, she saw Jewell, her eyes wide and frightened. Jewell was fifteen now, obviously turning into a young woman. Could she toss Jewell out on the street without thinking?

She knew she couldn't. No matter how little the rest of the family meant to her, she had always been fond of her younger half sister. "All right," she muttered, glaring at her father. "You can stay—for a while. But only until you get a job, Dad, I mean it. After that—"

He drew himself up, shoving his paunch into place over his falling-down trousers. "After that, we're out of here," he said nastily. "I can see that you don't want us, and we sure don't want to stay where we aren't welcome. Don't worry, Keeley, my loving daughter. We'll be out of here in no time."

No time was almost a month later, much longer than it took to ruin Keeley's house, her life-style, and her sanity. With so much noise and confusion at home—the television blaring, the stereo blasting, even her bedroom usurped—"because the bed is so much more comfortable, and your father has a bad back, you know," Phyllis had said without apology—Keeley bunked down with the agitated Tuxedo in the den until finally she couldn't stand it. Wondering why everyone—except Jewell, she thought—seemed to feel she owed them, and worse, why she hadn't questioned it, she decided one morning that she wasn't going to put them up anymore. Her father blustered, her stepmother was shrill, but she stood firm. She would pay for a hotel for a week while they looked for an apartment. She was sorry they thought she was coldhearted, but she *wanted her home back*.

With grumblings and mutterings and dire warnings for ungrateful daughters who didn't appreciate all that had been done for them, her family finally moved out and she and Tuxedo were by themselves again. She spent three nights cleaning up the mess they had left behind, and contrary to her usual custom, didn't turn on the stereo for a week. The silence after all that noise was sublime.

She had barely gotten rid of one problem before she had to deal with another. Noel kept pestering her about investing in his picture deal until finally she relented. She couldn't forget the time he had bared his soul to her about his dreams, so against her better judgment—and the advice of her accountant and her financial investor—she loaned him a huge sum and became a partner.

Noel couldn't have been more charming or grateful. He sent flowers and wine—not champagne, he knew how she felt about it—and he took her out to dinner.

"I won't let you down, Keeley," he promised, his handsome face sincere, the famed blue-gray eyes ingenuous.

But he did let her down. Barely three weeks into the shoot, he had a violent disagreement on location in Arizona. Keeley didn't know he had walked off the picture after a fistfight until she heard it one morning at the studio. From his bed in a hospital, where he was confined with a broken jaw that had to be wired, the director had issued a statement and an ultimatum. He'd see that the picture never got made by suing everyone connected with it, he claimed. Furthermore, if he had anything to say about it, Noel Harrington would never work in the industry again.

When Keeley heard the news, she knew she had only herself to blame. Everyone, including Fitz, had advised her against it, but she'd gone ahead because she believed Noel had meant what he'd said. She hadn't forgotten the look on his face when he'd told her he'd dreamed about being a Western hero since he was a kid; she knew how it felt when a dream was all you had to hold on to, and she'd hoped that by helping Noel, someone would come to her aid when the time came for her to bring *Beauty and the Beast* to life. She'd believed that Noel was as dedicated to making his fantasy come true as she was, but she'd been wrong. When disaster came, she knew her financial problems were just beginning, but by then she was more worried about Fitz. He never had recovered from losing Lindsey, and he looked so wan and pale that she was seriously concerned about him.

She was still digesting the news about Noel when Fitz came in one morning. He looked so awful that she immediately forgot her own problems. Jumping to her feet, she helped him to his chair behind the desk. She had never seen him look so pale; his eyes were like large bruises in his face.

"What is it?" she asked anxiously, kneeling beside his chair. "Fitz, what's happened?"

He looked at her as though he didn't see her.

"Fitz!" she said, shaking him a little. She thought he must be having some kind of attack or something; jumping up again, she started to call for help. His hand shaking, he stopped her.

"I . . ." He started to speak but couldn't finish. Something was obviously horribly wrong. She knelt by his chair again, taking his hand and holding it tightly. But as hard as her grasp was, she couldn't stop his trembling.

"Fitz, what is it?" she asked again. She was beside herself with worry. If he didn't tell her, she would call 911.

He managed to look at her this time. "I just came from the doctor," he said, his voice hoarse.

"And?" she prodded. She thought he had cancer or something, a brain tumor; she didn't know what. "And what?" she said. She felt like screaming.

Fitz looked at her. His eyes were hollowed, his face leached of all color, the bones standing out in stark relief. Like a . . . a skeleton, Keeley thought, grasping his hand tighter. She was very afraid, but it was nothing compared to the fear she saw in his face.

Stark terror flared in Fitz's eyes. "He told me," he said, "that I have AIDS."

CHAPTER TWENTY-ONE

"So," Carlotte said to Nigel as they were lying in bed one afternoon, "does your sweet young wife know about me yet?"

Sated after a bout of sex with his old mistress, Nigel had been almost asleep. Frowning at the question, he rolled over and reached out to the bedside table for a cigarette. Lighting it after the scratch of a match, he inhaled, blew out a series of smoke rings that drifted toward the ceiling of Carlotte's bedroom, and said disinterestedly, "I don't know. Does it matter?"

The satin sheets rustled as Carlotte moved closer. Her breasts pushed against his chest as she propped herself up to look into his face. "Not to me." She smiled slyly. "Why should I care what your child bride thinks?"

Glaring, he took another drag off the cigarette. "I wish you wouldn't call her that."

"But why not, darling? She is so much younger than you."

Impatiently he pushed her away. "I know what the age difference is. I don't need you to point it out every time we see each other. Now, go, get me something to eat. All this activity has made me hungry, and I won't have time to stop for something now."

"Oh, so now that you're satisfied in bed, you expect me to perform in the kitchen, as well?" Flouncing around, she hauled herself to a sitting position against the padded headboard and crossed her arms. "Find yourself something to eat. In fact," she added, abruptly throwing off the covers and heading toward the bathroom, "go find your way out. Be sure to lock the door behind you."

"Now, Carlotte—"

"No! There was a time when I allowed you to treat me badly, but no more. This time *you* came to me, remember?"

The bathroom door slammed shut before he could reply. Alone in the rumpled bed, Nigel exclaimed angrily and stubbed out his cigarette in the ashtray on the table. Briefly, he debated about following Carlotte and trying to make up, but then he decided the hell with it. He really didn't have time, and it wasn't worth the trouble anyway. Telling himself that she would come around—she always did, didn't she?—he hauled himself out of bed and got dressed. Before he left, he paused outside the still-closed bathroom door. He knew from experience that it would be locked, so he didn't even try to go in. Leaning close, he said, "I'll see you on Tuesday."

To his surprise, Carlotte opened the door. She was dressed in a short black silk robe, loosely belted at the waist.

"Not Tuesday," she said, brushing her hair back with her hands. "George will be home from Europe, and I will be occupied with him."

George Sanger, the other man in Carlotte's life, was the lover who paid for the apartment. Nigel didn't know how she'd talked Sanger into it, but he had been supporting her ever since what was left of her career dried up on Broadway. In return, Carlotte was available whenever George came to New York from his many trips abroad. He was in the import-export business, but what he sent out or brought in, Carlotte didn't know. George was very rich, so Carlotte felt he could do as he pleased. The only drawback was that he didn't want to marry again. After five tries, he'd had enough of marital bliss. He was tired of an endless parade of empty-headed girls with their minds only on his money; as he'd told Carlotte, he was getting too old for stellar sexual performances with nubile young things. As strange as it might seem, he'd said, there were times when he preferred intelligent conversation with a woman.

But he also, Carlotte had confided to Nigel, liked her to sing to him wearing nothing but high heels and a rose in her hair. It was a small price to pay for being kept in luxury, she believed, especially since George was always thoughtful enough to call ahead to let her know when he was coming into town.

Carlotte had agreed to the terms, such as they were, and she and George had been together for several years now. She had been surprised when Nigel had called her one evening last spring; she hadn't heard from him since his marriage. As though it were fate, George had been out of town, so she had invited Nigel over for old times' sake. It had been quite a reunion. Months later, they were still seeing each other; since the first call, if George was away, they usually met twice a week.

Carlotte stood in the bathroom doorway, studying him. Seeming to make up her mind, she said, "Come into the kitchen. I have something I want to tell you."

"If it's about Valeska, I don't want to hear."

"It's not about the child," she said, irritating him as always with her description of his wife. She glanced at him idly over her shoulder as she moved off. "Although there has been gossip . . ."

"Gossip," he sneered, dismissing whatever it was with a wave of his hand. He was much more interested in the movement of Carlotte's buttocks under the silk robe. Because of her new status, she was taking better care of herself, and it showed.

"This has substance to it," Carlotte said, dragging his attention back to what she was saying. They came to the kitchen and she paused to look at him. "Is it true that the prodigy is about to burn herself out?" She paused. "Or has she already?"

"Where did you hear that?" Nigel demanded, forgetting his preoccupation with Carlotte's body. He looked at her angrily. "Just because she had something wrong with her throat—"

"Had?" Carlotte echoed. "Past tense, darling?" She smiled her sly smile. "That's not what I heard."

"Then you heard wrong," Nigel said flatly. "After the rest the doctor ordered, Valeska is singing better than ever now."

"Oh, really? Then why did she drop out of *Maggie*?" They

were on either sides of the counter, and as she fiddled with the coffee maker, she glanced at him. "Perhaps you're going to try and blame it on her so-called miscarriage?"

"What do mean, 'so-called'? Everyone in the theater knows how devastated she was when she lost the damned baby."

"And so was the father, as well, I see." Carlotte got down two cups and put them carefully on the counter. "You don't have to get angry. I'm just repeating the rumors."

"Fine. But I'm telling you that what you heard—whatever it is—is wrong! Valeska is just fine." Even he couldn't get away with it; glancing away from the quick look she gave him, he gestured with his hand. "Well, she will be, when she gets over this damned depression."

"I see," Carlotte said. The coffee maker finished the cycle, and she poured two cups and pushed one toward him. "Is she on medication?"

He looked at her in exasperation. "Yes, she is, not that it's any of your business. I suppose you've heard something about *that*, too!"

Calmly, she added a spoonful of sugar to her coffee, and stirred. Lifting the cup, she gazed at him over the rim. "I hear a lot of things," she said. "Just because I no longer perform doesn't mean I don't keep up with what goes on, Nigel."

"And?" he said dangerously. He knew there was more. "What else?"

She shrugged. "Well, this is old news, but the word is that little Valeska was released from her *Maggie* contract because of her voice . . . and her drinking." She met his eyes again. "Is it true?"

Nigel stiffened. "No, it is not! For Christ's sake, Carlotte, where do you hear such things?"

Shrugging again, she said, "Around. But as you pointed out, it's none of my business, anyway."

"Is this what you wanted to talk to me about?"

She wasn't intimidated by his temper; she'd seen it too often. "No, but come to think of it, I did want to say that you'd better get the child to shape up, or people will think you've hitched your wagon to the wrong star." She smiled blandly at him. "It is a pity, though, that you chose Valeska over Keeley Cochran. I hear she's doing very well out in California."

Flushing, Nigel snapped, "Only if you ignore the fact that she prostituted herself instead of remaining true to her art!" He looked her up and down. "An action that isn't so foreign to you, either, I might add."

Carlotte's cheeks reddened, but she controlled her temper. "Nor you, darling," she replied. "You've been known to cut a few corners yourself, haven't you?"

He drew himself up. "I did what I had to."

"The show's the thing, right?"

Their eyes met. To his annoyance, Nigel was the first to look away. "Are you finished?" he asked sullenly. "I didn't come here to be insulted."

"No, we both know what you came here for." Lifting a hand to stifle his angry protest, she added, "Let's not fight—about that, anyway. I didn't realize you were so sensitive about the little Cochran bitch."

"I'm not sensitive. She's nothing to me."

"So you never were serious about marrying her."

"What do you think?"

She shook her head. "I should have known. To think I was jealous! It was all a ploy, one of many you use to make people dependent upon you."

"It worked, didn't it?"

"For a while. Long enough for you to tie her up with one of those contracts of yours. You did do that, didn't you?"

"Well, of course. You didn't think I was about to let a talent like hers get away, did you?"

"But it happened anyway, didn't it, poor darling," she said with false sympathy. "How chagrined you must have been when Raleigh Quinn stole her away."

"A miscalculation on my part, I agree," he said, frowning fiercely. "I never dreamed she'd go to California. She laughed at the idea when I asked her about it once."

"What a pity you didn't foresee her defection. If you had, you could have tied up her composing rights from coast to coast. Now you'll just have to wait until—if—she comes back here. Oh, my, what a shame. You almost had it made."

"I might have known you'd find it amusing."

"I'm not laughing," she denied, her eyes glinting. "But I wonder sometimes. How did you ever let it happen? You usually anticipate all contingencies."

"I was in a rush that night," he said irritably, seeing no point in not telling her the truth. They had few secrets from each other now, anyway. "I never dreamed I could actually get her up to my hotel room, so when I did, I wasn't prepared. I had to scribble out something in a hurry, and I'd had a little champagne myself by that time. It didn't occur to me to control anything outside the theater, because she had such scorn for anything but Broadway."

"What a blow it must have been when she changed her mind."

"Yes, well, it happens," he said with a dismissive wave of his hand that didn't fool her at all. "Besides, the game's not lost yet. If she ever does come back, the contract will still be in effect." He looked smug again. "I'll not only have creative control, but sixty percent of gross."

Carlotte arched an eyebrow. "You certainly didn't cut her any slack. That's more than you usually levy, isn't it?" She leaned forward suddenly. "Tell me, Nigel, how did you get her to sign? I've always been curious. I might dislike the little bitch, but even I have to admit she was no dummy."

"No one thinks straight on champagne mixed with a mickey."

She didn't look surprised; she had been around Nigel a long time. "I see. I'll bet you never really went to bed with her, either, did you?"

"Of course not. Don't be absurd."

"You really are a cruel bastard, you know that? For years, you let me think—"

"Does it matter?" He wasn't paying attention anymore; seeing the curve of a heavy breast peeking out from the V of her loosely held robe, he reached out and pulled her toward him with the sash, untying the knot as she came to him. Pushing the silk off her shoulders, he began to fondle her breasts.

"You've grown more luscious with the years, my dear," he said, closing his eyes at the sensation of the soft weight in his hands. He rubbed his thumbs over her nipples, satisfied to feel them coming erect under his touch; then he opened his eyes and smiled. "I always did prefer women to girls."

"A preference you've kept well hidden," she replied. "Since you're married to one at the moment."

"Yes, but that was just for convenience," he said, bending to kiss behind her ear. "Valeska is a frozen, sexless stick compared to you, Carlotte. You have the body and the emotions of a real woman. You know how to satisfy a man. . . ."

Before he could move lower with his caresses, Carlotte pushed him away and fastened her robe shut again. "And Valeska doesn't?" she said, trying despite herself to catch her breath. Nigel always had been an expert, experienced lover. "After all, you *did* get her pregnant, so you must have gotten together at least once."

"Don't be vulgar, my dear. The pregnancy—" he looked revolted just saying the word "—was an accident."

"Or a convenient excuse," Carlotte remarked, picking up her coffee cup again. The coffee was cold, and she looked at it distastefully before pouring it into the sink.

Nigel had reached for his own cup. "What do you mean—convenient?"

"Well, you have to admit, Valeska's pregnancy couldn't have come at a better time. Her voice was going, and she needed a re—"

Slamming the cup down onto the counter, he exclaimed, "Damn it, Carlotte! I told you there was nothing wrong with her voice!"

"Yes, so you did," she agreed, unperturbed. She had made her point. She had seen the fear he couldn't hide and was satisfied. "Anyway," she went on, "I didn't want to talk about Valeska. I had something else I wanted to say."

"Get on with it, then," he growled.

She hesitated, then took a deep breath. "I saw Barry."

For a long moment, Nigel said nothing. Then he asked tightly, "Where?"

"Here."

He stiffened. "He came to the apartment?"

"No. It was . . . at a coffee shop. He asked me not to tell you where."

His face darkened. "Why not?"

"Because the two of you didn't exactly part on good terms."

"We didn't part on any terms at all!" he snapped. "Like the coward he was, he just . . . disappeared."

"Yes," she said slowly. "So you always told me."

"And you think I lied?" He leaned forward suddenly. She thought she saw something in his face, but she wasn't sure; in the next instant, he just looked angry. "What did he tell you?" he demanded. Then, before she could answer, he leaned back again, waving his hand scornfully. "Whatever it was, it wasn't true. Barry always did have an imagination, and what reality ever intruded was diluted by all the alcohol he drank."

Carlotte said quietly, "He didn't have much to say at all, Nigel. When I saw him, he wasn't in . . . very good shape."

He made a rude sound. "Well, that figures. By the time he disappeared, he was so sodden with vodka that I'm surprised he was still able to stand upright. In fact, come to think of it, it's even more astonishing that he's still around. I thought he died in the gutter long ago."

"No, he's not dead, Nigel," Carlotte said. She sounded so strange that he looked at her sharply.

"Then why won't you tell me where he is?"

"I told you, he asked me not to say."

"Well, fine, I don't give a damn *where* he is. He's the one who walked out on *me*, not the other way around!"

"So you say."

"Yes, I do say!" he shouted suddenly. "Why are you inferring that I'm lying? He was a drunk, and you know it! He'd say anything to get another drink; you can't trust him for a minute!"

She flushed. "How can you be so callous and unfeeling? We all started together, you and Barry and I. We all came to Broadway at the same time, all those years ago. How can you just . . . dismiss it like it never happened?"

"Is it my fault Barry Archer is a drunk?"

"Is it your fault your wife is an alcoholic?"

For a second, he looked angry enough to hit her. In response, her own fists clenched. Now that she was no longer dependent on him, she was a more formidable opponent than Valeska was, and she stood her ground without flinching, glaring at him eye to eye. Finally, with visible effort, Nigel controlled himself. Forcing himself to sit down on one of the bar stools under the counter, he smoothed his hair with one hand.

"All right," he said. "Tell me where he is, and I'll go talk to him." His lip curled. "For old times' sake, if nothing else."

It seemed for an instant that Carlotte might tell him. Then she shook her head. "No, I can't. I promised him."

He banged his fist on the counter, making the coffee cups rattle. "Then why the hell did you bring up the damned subject? Just what do you want me to do, Carlotte? Get down on my knees and beg you to tell me where he is, or how to reach him? What makes you think I care?"

She looked at him for a long moment. Then she said quietly, "I don't want you to do anything, Nigel. I just thought you'd be interested."

"Well, I'm not." He sat there, frowning for a moment, then he looked up. "And if you know what's good for you, you'll stay away from him, Carlotte. I mean it, you can't trust him. Now promise me you'll keep your distance."

"I—"

"Promise me!"

"All right!" she exclaimed angrily. "I promise! Does that make you happy?"

He didn't know what would make him happy. The news about Barry had disturbed him more than he wanted her to know. He left soon after, promising to call her the following week. He was still so upset that he lighted another cigarette in the cab, but when he noticed that his hands were shaking, he angrily stubbed it out. Damn it all! he thought furiously.

With an effort, he thought it out. He really didn't have a thing to worry about, did he? If worst came to worst, who would believe a down-on-his-luck drunk like Barry, even if he had once been on top? He was Nigel Aames, still a force to be reckoned with, so he put it out of his mind. If Barry surfaced again, he'd worry about it then.

Once he decided to forget about Barry, Carlotte's remark about hitching his wagon to the wrong star began to rankle. Was that what people were thinking? Feeling his pulse begin to pound, he told himself to calm down. If he didn't watch it, he'd have a heart attack.

His jaw tightened. He'd lied to Carlotte when he'd said Valeska's voice was fine. The doctor had recently told them that she had to have the operation, but she was terrified by the idea, and had absolutely refused even to discuss it. To his fury, she had remained stubborn no matter how he threatened or cajoled. At his wits' end, he had even taken the unprecedented step of calling her old bitch of a mother, who had about as much told him to go to hell.

"Valeska never listens to me anymore," Edra had said bitterly to him. "In fact, we don't even speak. Even before her grandmother died, things were strained between us. Since then, she's become impossible. Becoming a big star changed her, and no one should know better than you. You're responsible for all this; I blame only you!"

He was so infuriated he hung up on the old bag. Next he went to the doctor alone, but that was even less helpful than the brief conversation with his mother-in-law had been. Muelrath insisted the decision had to be Valeska's. There was a chance—slim, but possible—that surgery could alter, if not destroy, her voice, and only she could take that chance. Because he'd been afraid of that happening himself, he hadn't insisted on going ahead with what they all knew should be done.

But he wasn't going to sit back impotently anymore, he decided as the cab headed toward uptown. Valeska was going to have the surgery whether she wanted it or not. He had coddled her long enough; it was time to take charge. He smiled grimly. He knew how to make her do something she didn't want to do. He had done it before.

———— ✍ ————

CHAPTER TWENTY-TWO

Valeska awoke frightened, totally disoriented, and in terrible pain. Petrified, she tried to call for help, but a fire burst into life in her throat, and the only sound she could make was a harsh croak that brought tears of agony to her eyes. Gasping—which caused another spasm—she lay back weakly on the pillow propped behind her, trying not to cough or to cry.

Slowly, it came back to her: the arguments with Nigel, the assurances of Dr. Muelrath, her reluctance, indecision, finally her capitulation . . . and the surgery. Mild discomfort, Dr. Muelrath had said. If this was discomfort, what did they call pain?

Now that she knew where she was and what had happened, she cautiously opened her eyes again. But if she'd thought her husband would be sitting anxiously beside the bed, she was mistaken: except for herself, the room was empty. Nigel had gotten her a private room—to assuage his guilt, no doubt, she thought bitterly. But what had seemed a good idea at the time just made her feel even more lonely and abandoned, and she wished she weren't alone. Now that she was awake, she felt the night would never end. A glance at the bedside clock told her it was after midnight, but she couldn't remember what day it was. Had she been here one day, two, four? Gingerly she touched the bandage on her throat. It was too well padded for her to feel much, but she imagined that underneath, the incision on her neck was still raw and red. Dr. Muelrath had promised that the surgery wouldn't leave a noticeable scar, but at the moment, she didn't care about marks on her throat: what she wanted to know was if she'd be able to *sing*.

Hysteria clawed at her, and she knew she couldn't give in to panic. If she wanted someone to be with her, she reminded herself, all she had to do was reach over and summon the nurse. She wasn't alone in the hospital; people were right outside the door. But they couldn't—wouldn't—give her what she really wanted right now, and the thought made her feel even more helpless and afraid.

Oh, why was this happening to her? she wondered pitifully. She thought she was done with it. She had tried so hard to give it up, to put it out of her life or, having failed so badly, at least not to make it so much a *part* of her life. But the need was growing in her, so it seemed she had failed at that, too, as she had so many other things these past few years.

She couldn't remember when she had first started needing her little something "extra," she who had always disliked the taste of alcohol. She had never understood people who needed something to get through the day—oh, how superior she'd been! Well, she wasn't feeling superior now. Weak tears came again, and she willed herself fiercely not to cry. You don't need a drink, she told herself. It was what she had been saying for months now, over and over again, even as she poured just one more little, tiny shot. *You don't need a drink.*

But she did. Every waking moment of every day, it seemed, a drink was all she could think about. All that lovely vodka. It made her feel warm and fuzzy, and no one even knew a thing. Whoever had first developed the stuff should get a medal, she'd thought: odorless, colorless, practically tasteless once you got used to it; who would have thought potatoes could be put to such good use?

Another thing she'd never understood was why people drank every day, why they got drunk and stayed that way—until she tried it herself. There was something so ... soothing ... about going through the day in a daze. Nothing intruded, no problem seemed too big to cope with, things just ... went along. When she'd had a drink or two, she didn't have to worry about anything—her career, her voice, her marriage, even the baby she didn't have anymore. Everything just faded into the background, lost in the haze.

She hated herself, but now that she'd started thinking about it, the urge that rarely went away these days surfaced again, and she found herself longing just for one shot. Trying to distract herself, she wondered if she should call for pain medication instead. It seemed worth a try until she remembered the flask she had brought with her. It was hidden in her makeup case; all she had to do was climb out of bed and get it.

Slowly, not remembering if she was supposed to be out of bed or not, Valeska sat up and pushed the covers back. The guardrails were raised and she couldn't figure out how to get them down. She shook one a little, but it made such a noise that she glanced hastily toward the doorway. When no one came rushing in, she decided that if she couldn't lower the rail, she'd just crawl to the end of the bed and get out that way.

But first maybe she should get a drink of water. The act of sitting up had made her feel a little dizzy, and she didn't want to fall and make a real noise that would bring a nurse running. A plastic glass with a straw stuck in it was on the table by the bed; carefully she maneuvered it over the rails and took a sip.

If she could have, she would have screamed. Sharp agony blossomed like evil in her throat the instant the water started down. She wasn't expecting it, and she started to choke. The convulsion of her throat muscles made the pain even worse, and she grabbed the bed rails involuntarily. The glass fell, spilling water all over the sheets, but she didn't notice. Her hands to her throat, she was trying not to gasp in pain.

At last, just when she thought she couldn't stand it any longer, the burning sensation began to die down. Forcing herself, she tried the tiniest of swallows. Echoes of the earlier agony arose like warning bubbles, but she willed the new pain to go away. If she couldn't swallow, how was she going to take a drink?

After a moment, it was better, and she tried another cautious swallow. Then another. And another. It still hurt, but the pain wasn't quite as bad. Carefully, she made a sound. It was little more than an agonized hiss of a whisper, but at least she could speak if she tried. Exhausted, she lay back again. For a few horrible seconds, she'd been sure she couldn't make a sound.

She didn't want to contemplate what her life would be if she lost her voice. It was the thing that terrified her the most. Not to be able to speak, to sing. Squeezing her eyes shut, she thrust away the images that rose like gargoyles in her mind. If she couldn't sing, life wouldn't be worth living. She wouldn't want to go on.

Remembering the bandage at her throat, she carefully touched it again. The thick padding wasn't reassuring; panicked again, she wondered what it really hid. Oh, she felt so bad, so sick and confused and in pain, she didn't know what to do. She needed to talk to somebody—no, not just *some*body, she thought mournfully; she needed to talk to Keeley.

Brushing away her tears with the backs of her hands, she looked at the phone by the bed. Was the switchboard open this time of night? Would it put a call through? Before she could think about it, she picked up the receiver. Even though she'd never completed the dozen calls she'd tried before, she knew the number by heart. As she dialed, she felt her stomach tighten, and she held her breath when it began to ring on the other end. It wasn't ten o'clock in California, and Keeley had always been a night person. If she was home, she'd still be up, Valeska was sure of it.

Oh, please let her be home, she prayed, jerking upright when she heard the click of the receiver on the other end being picked up.

"Hi, this is Keeley—"

Relieved and delighted and suddenly feeling like laughing at the sound of Keeley's voice, Valeska forgot about her painful throat and started to say, "Hi, Keeley. This is—"

But the recorded message, sounding so like her friend, went blithely on. "If you'll leave a message, I'll call you back. Otherwise . . . I won't."

There was a few seconds of silence, then that unfriendly *beep*. Valeska was so disappointed that she couldn't even speak. Her eyes tearing again, she fumbled as she tried to hang up the phone. It dropped from her hand and clattered to the floor, caught on the rail by the cord. She started to retrieve it, but fell back to the pillow again. She was too tired to fight it. I need a drink, she thought. Oh, God, I need a drink. Why wasn't Keeley home?

The urge for vodka's solace was driving her as it never had before, so she got up again, maneuvering shakily to the end of the bed before putting her feet over the edge. The floor seemed an impossible distance down, and she put a hand to her head. Only the thought that she had to get to her stash before the nurse came in made her put her feet on the floor; she felt so wobbly and sick that she just wanted to fall back into bed again.

Somehow, she made it to the closet where her makeup case was. Covered in clammy sweat, so weak it was a struggle to open the closet door, she dropped to her knees when she saw the case on the floor and pulled it feebly toward her. It wasn't locked, and she brushed her forearm across her damp face before she opened the top. The perfume flagon she was looking for was at the bottom of the case, and when she found it, she snatched it up with relief. Shaking with eagerness, she twisted off the ornate cap and put the vial to her lips.

The water had burned, but the vodka going down was like a river of lava. Tears sprang into her eyes at the liquid fire in her throat, and she would have cried out if she'd had the voice. The pain was so bad she didn't think she could stand it; black spots appeared before her eyes, and she knew she was going to faint. She was gasping for breath when the door opened and a nurse appeared. When the woman saw her on the floor, she rushed forward.

"Mrs. Aames!" she cried in dismay. At Nigel's insistence, Valeska had signed into the hospital using her married name. For privacy, he had claimed, but she knew he was more concerned about negative publicity. She hadn't cared at the time if he'd signed her in as Morticia Addams; she'd been so terrified all she wanted to do was get it over with.

"Mrs. Aames, what happened?" the nurse cried, dropping down beside her. "Oh, my, what are you doing out of bed?"

Despite the pain, Valeska wasn't going to admit what she'd been doing. Taking a breath, she put the flagon back in her makeup case. Her voice a dense croak, she whispered, "I wanted some perfume. . . ."

"Perfume! Oh, but—"

Seeing that Valeska was in pain, shaking from fatigue and drenched in perspiration, the nurse wasn't going to argue. "You're not supposed to be talking yet, Mrs. Aames," she said quickly. "And you're certainly not supposed to be out of bed."

Practically lifting her limp patient off the floor, the nurse half carried Valeska back to the bed, where she discovered the wet sheets. Quickly she changed the bed, then briskly helped Valeska into a fresh nightgown before tucking her in again. The sensation of dry sheets and warm blanket was so gratifying that Valeska was almost asleep before the nurse left the room. Leaving a night-light burning, and an admonition to press the call button if she needed anything, instead of trying to get it herself, the nurse slipped out. But the door had barely whispered shut behind her before Valeska bit her lip. Alone in the dark, all she could think of was that she still wanted that drink.

Nigel came the next morning. Sometime about three A.M., Valeska couldn't stand it anymore; using the call button, she'd asked for pain medication, and a new nurse had brought a syringe of something that was better than vodka had ever been. Valeska didn't just drift away; she was gone, waking up the next morning with the burning in her throat subsiding to a bearable pain that Dr. Muelrath assured her would get better.

"I hope so," she rasped.

"Now, now, no strain," he commanded. "If you're a good patient, I'll release you by the end of the week. But you must rest. Absolutely no singing for some time yet. In fact, I'm going to limit your speaking as well, to—let's say, ten words a day at first."

"Ten!" she exclaimed hoarsely. "But—"

"Be careful, you've just used two," he said with a smile. "Don't worry, now, you'll be fine." Then he sobered. "I wanted to talk to you about something else, Valeska. Your drinking." He took her hand as she looked quickly away. "You don't have to defend yourself or try to explain. I know you've been under pressure lately, what with the problems with your voice and trying to do the show at the same time. But—" Gently, he forced her to look at him again "—but we both know that drinking isn't the answer, don't we?"

She felt helpless, pinned in a horrible spotlight of accusation and blame. She didn't know what to say, so she nodded.

"Good," he said, his smile returning. "Now, when you're better, we have some excellent rehabilitation programs—"

She could help herself. "I'm not an alcoholic!" she rasped. "I don't need—"

"Shhh," he soothed. "Didn't we agree just now that I'd talk? I'm not accusing you of anything, Valeska, but I think you need help."

She shook her head violently. "Has Nigel—?"

"Nigel hasn't spoken to me. Beyond expressing his concern, of course. But we did a blood alcohol level when you were admitted, and . . . well, I'm afraid it was pretty high."

She couldn't hold his level gaze. She hadn't known about a blood test, but when she remembered her condition when she arrived for surgery, she cringed. She'd had a few before coming in—to quiet her nerves, she'd told herself. She was sure it hadn't been noticeable, but obviously it had, and she felt ashamed. Still, she couldn't prevent herself from holding up one finger, shoving it at him again and again, to indicate she'd only had one. A lie, like so many she'd told lately, to salvage what was left of her pride.

He looked at her sadly for a moment; then he gave a resigned shake of his head. "All right, Valeska. I can see it's a little too early to talk to you about it. We'll discuss it another time, all right?"

She turned away without answering, thinking that as far as she was concerned, the discussion was finished. Nigel came in a few minutes later, kissing her perfunctorily on the cheek. He saw her rebellious expression and stood back. "What's the matter?" he asked. "Hasn't Muelrath been in?"

Her lips tight, she nodded.

"He had good news, I thought."

She shrugged, still not looking at him.

Nigel had never had much patience. "All right, if you're going to act like this, I'm going to leave. I have better things to do—"

She didn't want him to go. Quickly, she reached for his hand, indicating the chair the doctor had vacated, pleading with her eyes for him to sit down. After a moment, he did. Then, to her surprise, he said, "I've been thinking. What do you say about the idea of us going away for a while? I thought Europe, but if that's too much for you now, maybe the Virgin Islands, or the Bahamas. What do you think? Would you like to go?"

She couldn't believe he was serious. They'd never taken a vacation; the only time they'd been away had been to Las Vegas, where they were married. Completely forgetting about her word limit, she said eagerly, "Do you really mean it? We can go away somewhere, together?"

The doctor had given Nigel good news about her progress; he was in an expansive mood. She didn't know it, but Muelrath had also advised a complete change of scene, to hasten her recovery, and Nigel was all for it. "Anywhere you like. You choose."

Any place in the world! she thought. It was incredible. She knew he'd think her silly, but she knew just where she wanted to go. She had always heard how romantic it was, and she thought maybe they could recapture what they'd lost. So, before he could change his mind, she said, "I want to go to Hawaii."

They left soon after she was released from the hospital. Nigel insisted on first class all the way, and Valeska was delighted when she climbed aboard the big L1011 and was greeted by the flight attendant who smiled warmly and said, "Oh, yes, Miss Szabo! Right this way, please." Everyone in first class looked up; even to those few who didn't know her, she was obviously a celebrity.

But there were drawbacks to being recognized; whether she imagined it or not, she was certain that all the other passengers were counting the glasses of champagne she had and keeping track of the number of drinks she ordered. She tried to ignore the stares by concentrating on the superb first-class service, always a treat in any circumstances.

It was a morning flight, and she could have had anything she wanted for breakfast. But while Nigel feasted on croissants and fresh strawberries and eggs Benedict, all she could manage was a piece of dry toast and a glass of orange juice. If she hadn't been sure people were watching, she would have added a shot of vodka to her juice, but she didn't dare take a chance. Nigel had been in such a good mood that she didn't want to do anything that might destroy it. They'd had some bumpy times during their marriage, but she loved her husband, and she knew he loved her. She was counting on this vacation to put them back on track, again.

They stopped in San Francisco for a short while, then took off again for the islands. Three hours into the flight, with the cabin darkened for the movie, and Nigel fast asleep in the window seat beside her, she couldn't stand it anymore and got up to go to the bathroom. She took her makeup case with her, smiling brightly at the flight attendant who immediately jumped up, but refusing any assistance. She'd had so much to drink already that she couldn't ask for anything else, but she still had her own supply, and she couldn't wait to be alone so she could take one last stiff shot.

In the cramped lavatory, she shot the bolt for privacy. The fluorescent lights immediately came on, and in the orange-gray illumination they cast, she looked at her reflection and hardly recognized herself. She was twenty-five years old and looked a haggard forty.

"What's happened to you?" she whispered. Leaning closer to the mirror, she stared at herself. Where was the fresh-faced, clear-eyed innocent young girl she'd been? In her place was someone she didn't even recognize. Even taking the unflattering light into account, her once-glowing complexion had an unhealthy pallor, and she didn't look slender so much as . . . gaunt.

As Dr. Muelrath had promised, the scar on her neck was barely noticeable; right now, it was a thin reddish line that he'd told her would eventually disappear entirely. Two weeks after surgery, she was allowed to speak if she didn't raise her voice, but practice was forbidden, and she didn't know yet if she'd be able to sing.

"The voice is like a muscle," her teacher, Madame LeDuc, had told her again and again. "You must use it to keep it supple. But to strain . . ." And she would dolefully shake her head.

Whimpering at the memory, Valeska put her hands over her eyes. She hadn't listened to her teacher, and now she regretted it. Trying to please Nigel by playing *Maggie* night after night, she had strained her voice to the point where she couldn't sing anymore. Worse, she had been replaced in the role even before anyone knew she had to have surgery.

Humiliated at the thought, she dropped her hands. Two feet from her face, her reflection stared back at her in the cramped lavatory, wide-eyed and strained. She knew what people were saying about her, what her last director had said, what the cast had whispered. She knew what the rumors and the gossip and the conjecture was, and it made her ashamed.

"Poor Nigel," she had heard her understudy say to someone one day, when she thought Valeska was out of hearing. "Imagine! Being married to *that*. Why, she can hardly remember the words to the songs at times, much less the dialogue! I understand she was pretty good once, but not anymore. Everyone knows she's turned into a lush. And you know what I think? I think Nigel is a saint. Just a saint, for putting up with her . . ."

Recalling it now, Valeska clenched her hands on the edge of the polished aluminum sink. She'd wanted to confront the little bitch, she remembered, but she had been too mortified. Creeping back to her dressing room, she'd had a couple of shots to give her courage to go out on stage that night.

But it had gotten worse. Paranoid or not, she became certain that everyone was looking at her, talking about her, gossiping and conjecturing and wondering how long the long-suffering Nigel would stay in his marriage. She'd been so terrified, so preoccupied and possessed that she'd even forsaken her old friends at Hildredth—another source of shame. She knew she should go and visit even if she couldn't sing, but she couldn't face them. What if they guessed about the drinking? No, she couldn't go to Hildredth.

I can't lose him, she thought. Shakily, she sat down on the covered commode and rested her forehead against the cool edge of the sink. Every time she thought of Nigel leaving her, she felt sick. She knew she should be stronger, but she just wasn't. Everything else was falling apart, crumbling into pieces at her feet, but she had told herself that as long as her marriage was intact, she wasn't a complete failure. Nothing else mattered as much to her, not the star she had been, the roles she'd had, the records she'd cut, the awards she had won. Nigel was her one success story. If it hadn't been for him, she never would have accomplished anything.

But what about Keeley, a voice whispered to her. *Didn't Keeley do more for you than Nigel ever could?*

A sob escaped her, and she looked quickly at the door, afraid someone had heard. She wasn't going to think about Keeley, who had gone off to California and changed into someone she didn't even know anymore. It was Nigel who had helped her; it was her husband to whom she owed everything.

"Miss Szabo?" came a voice from outside the lavatory. "Are you all right?"

Valeska jerked her head up at the sound. Quickly she gathered herself together. "Yes, I'm fine," she said. "Just fine."

"If you need anything . . ."

"No, I'm perfectly all right," Valeska said, willing the woman to go away. She forced a laugh. "Just fixing my makeup. You know how it is. . . ."

A smile in the attendant's voice. "Yes, I do, I'm afraid. Well, if you need anything, just press the button and one of us will come."

"Thank you, but that won't be necessary. I'll be right out."

Valeska looked at her watch. She couldn't believe it; she'd been in here almost an hour. Oh, what would everyone think? she wondered, quickly opening her makeup case. For the trip, she'd not only filled the perfume flagon with vodka, but added another opaque bottle as well. Nigel had never seemed interested in her makeup, but you never knew, and she didn't want to take any chances. Quickly unscrewing the cap from the new bottle, she took a deep swallow, grimacing as the undiluted vodka went down. But the glow in her stomach felt so warm that she took another shot before capping the bottle again.

There, that was better, she thought, looking up at her reflection. She had a little color in her cheeks now, and she felt much better than she had when she came in. Pinning a smile to her face, she unlocked the lavatory door and went back to her seat.

Hawaii was everything Valeska thought it would be—at least when they got there. She had chosen Kauai, the "Garden Island," because it was supposed to be so romantic, and it was.

She loved the thousand and one shades of green, and the white sand beaches, and the craggy mountains with all the waterfalls, but they hadn't been there a day before Nigel complained about how boring it was. Alarmed at the thought that he might cut their vacation short, she agreed to go to Oahu, where the action was. She didn't care where they were; she just wanted to be alone with her husband. But after the short, half-hour flight back to Honolulu, they had barely checked into a new hotel when Nigel disappeared.

"I need some cigarettes," he'd said. "I'll be right back."

When he hadn't returned at the end of an hour, she went looking for him and found him deep in conversation with a beautiful young blonde by the pool. Tanned and gorgeous, the girl was wearing an almost nonexistent bikini that showed off her perfect figure and had the nerve to pretend confusion when Valeska came up to where they were sitting, knee to knee in two lounge chairs.

"I've been looking all over for you, Nigel," Valeska said, trying not to notice that the girl was only in her teens, with very adult eyes.

Nigel looked up without a trace of guilt on his face. "Oh ... hello, Valeska," he said vaguely. "Meet Barbi, won't you? We ran into each other and got to talking."

"So I see," Valeska said. Controlling herself with an effort, she put a proprietary hand on Nigel's shoulder. "You've been gone an hour, darling. I thought we were going to have a drink before dinner."

Nigel looked up at her again. While waiting, she'd had another nip or two from the bar in the room, but she hoped he wouldn't notice. It was only a few, she told herself, trying not to sway as she stood there. And he *had* been gone a long time.

"I think you've had enough, don't you?" Nigel said evenly.

Despite herself, Valeska flushed. She cast a quick glance at Barbi, who was watching curiously, then back to her husband. Intending to teach him a lesson, she said distinctly, "No, I don't." There was a bar poolside, and she turned toward it, catching the eye of the bartender. "I'll have a vodka martini," she told the man, adding for good measure, "Make it a double."

Nigel got up. "Valeska," he said warningly.

"I ... uh ... I think I'd better go," Barbi said, standing up. She smiled winningly at Nigel, displaying a mouthful of brilliant white teeth. "It was *so* nice meeting you," she murmured. "I hope we get a chance to talk again."

As soon as she was out of earshot, Nigel turned to Valeska. "Well, that was a nice little scene! What's the matter with you? She was a nice girl!"

"She was a tart," Valeska said flatly, grabbing the martini the bartender conveniently brought at that moment. Without looking, she scrawled her name across the bill he presented, defiantly adding a generous tip. Before he had moved away two steps, she had tossed down the entire drink.

Nigel clenched his jaw. "Is this how it's going to be?"

With the vodka glowing inside her, Valeska looked at him angrily. "I don't know. You tell me!"

"I told you, I went to get some cigarettes."

"And came back with a blonde young enough to be your daughter?"

Her thrust went home. Reddening, he grabbed her arm and started in the direction of their bungalow. "I'm not going to argue about it out here," he said, in her ear. "I thought we came here to have a good time!"

"I thought so, too," she said. "Nigel, you're hurting me!"

His answer was to grip her arm harder. "This is nothing compared to what I'll do if you pull a stunt like that again," he told her, propelling her down the path and into their room. Inside, he threw her away from him with such force that she stumbled and fell against the bed. "Do we understand each other?"

From her awkward position, half on the bed, half on the floor, she looked at him accusingly. The red marks of his fingers were visible on her arm. "You promised!"

"And you promised not to get drunk anymore!"

"I'm not drunk!"

He took a step toward her. "For God's sake, keep your damned voice down!"

"Why? Because someone might hear me, or because I might ruin it?"

He looked so furious it was all she could do not to cringe away. But instead of coming closer, he muttered something disgustedly and turned again toward the door.

"Where are you going?" she cried.

A slam was her answer, and when she realized he was gone again, she threw herself on the bed and burst into tears. Nigel didn't come back until after two that morning, but by then, she wouldn't have heard him come in if he had announced himself with a brass band. Alone the entire night with only the bar for company, she'd found solace in a fifth of vodka and drank herself to sleep. Her head pounding and her stomach roiling, she apologized the next morning.

To her surprise, he forgave her without any wheedling on her part. They even made love—or what passed for lovemaking. Nigel was always perfunctory with her, but it had been so long since he'd paid her any attention that she didn't care. Lounging afterward on the lanai with the sun beating down through the trees, dappling her body with that wonderful light peculiar to the islands, she just knew everything was going to be all right—until Nigel told her at dinner that night that he was going out again.

"I ran into an old buddy this afternoon while you were taking a nap," he said casually. "He's invited me to a key club downtown. Do you mind if I take off for a couple of hours?"

She tried to hide her dismay. "Can't I go, too?"

"Sorry," he said, not sounding apologetic at all. "It's men only." He sat back again. "If you don't want me to go—"

"No, no, it's all right," she said quickly. She didn't want to upset things again. But she couldn't help asking, "You won't be gone longer than that, will you?"

"Cross my heart," he said, getting up. "You're an angel."

He didn't get back to the hotel until nearly four A.M., but this time she was waiting up for him. A lot of good it did her, she thought bitterly. He'd been drinking and wasn't in the mood to explain where he'd been. She knew the signs, so she left it alone, promising herself he wouldn't do it again. But the next night he went out, and the next, and the next, until finally she had to say something.

"Don't question me, Valeska," he said when she demanded to know where he'd been. "You wanted to come to Hawaii, so we did. This is where *you* wanted to be, so you can't blame me for wanting to go out and have a little fun."

"But why can't you take me with you?"

"Because you wouldn't enjoy it. It's just a bunch of men sitting around playing poker and drinking. Not your style at all."

She was too angry and upset at being left alone so much to care what she said. "How can I be sure that's what you're doing? For all I know, you could be out humping that damned blonde!"

"You want proof?" he said, digging into his pockets and producing two wads of money that he threw at her. "Here it is! I won this these past two nights, so get the hell off my back!"

With money raining down around her, she was contrite. "I'm

sorry," she wept. "It's just that I'm so lonely here all by myself. I thought we'd be together—"

"You want to be together?" he said angrily. "Fine. Let's be together then!"

Before she could react, he threw her onto the bed. She was wearing a satin nightgown, held up by thin straps. Holding her down, he put a hand on the front of the gown and jerked. The satin ripped as though it were tissue, and she cried out.

"Nigel, what are you doing?"

He was struggling out of his clothes, excited now, already erect. "You wanted to be together?" he repeated, climbing on top of her while he pinned her to the bed. Shoving her legs apart with his knees, he entered her so roughly that she cried out again and tried to get out from under him. Her struggles only excited him more.

"You can't get any more together than this, can you?" he panted, thrusting away.

"Nigel, you're hurting me!"

It was as if she hadn't spoken. Weighing her down with his body, he grabbed her face and held her still while he thrust his tongue deep into her mouth. She almost gagged, but he wouldn't release her. Lost in his own sensations, he pounded at her until his thrusting became frenzied, pinning her under him even though she begged him to let her go. Finally, she couldn't struggle any longer; unmoving, she lay still until he climaxed. Sweat poured off his body, sticking them together, making her feel more unclean and dirty and used than she'd ever felt in her life. When he finally rolled off of her, she hauled herself up, grabbed the tattered edges of her nightgown, and ran into the bathroom. She didn't come out until the next morning when she heard him moving around getting dressed.

As soon as she appeared, he came toward her with his arms out. She turned away, but he caught her anyway, forcing her to look at him. "I'm so sorry, darling," he said. "I . . . I don't know what came over me. Can you ever forgive me?"

She didn't want to talk about it. In the bathroom mirror, she could see the marks he'd made when he ripped her nightgown off her the night before. She felt stiff and sore and ashamed, as if what had happened had been her fault.

Suddenly, she couldn't take it anymore. Her wonderful, romantic vacation was ruined; maybe her marriage was, too. If she'd been any kind of woman, she would have walked out on him the first time he forced himself on her; if she'd been any kind of woman, she would never have permitted the abuse. Without warning, she looked at him and hated him—almost as much as she despised herself.

"You think you're such a big shot, Nigel," she said. She could hear the hoarseness creeping in and knew she shouldn't be using her voice like this, but she couldn't help herself. "But I know who's been carrying whom these past few years, and it—"

She never finished the sentence. He was holding her arm tightly with one hand, but out of nowhere came the other, his fist a hard ball that struck her violently, exploding stars behind her eyes. The blow was so vicious that she was thrown off balance and out of his grasp. Stumbling across the room, she hit the big television console, bounced off, almost fell, and landed against the wall, her hand to her face. Under her fingers, the mark of his fist could clearly be seen along her cheek.

"Don't look at me like that!" Nigel commanded belligerently, although he looked a little frightened himself. "You deserved it and you know it."

"Deserved it . . ." She looked at him in shock. He had hit her before, had grabbed her and slapped her and pushed her down. But he had never struck her with his closed fist. Suddenly, she was scared, actually frightened of him. What would he do next?

If a man ever laid a hand on me—just once—I'd never forgive him, no matter how much I thought I loved him. No woman deserves to be treated like a possession, and I don't care what a man says to excuse it. Do you hear me, Val? No woman!

From out of the past, Keeley's voice came to her. She could remember the night they'd had that conversation, how fierce Keeley had been, how proud and independent. She'd been telling Valeska about having to fend off her oldest half brother, a boy named Louis, who thought he had a right to do what he wished. Keeley had taken a bread knife from the drawer the first and only time he'd tried to lay a hand on her, and from then on, he'd given her a wide berth. Keeley wasn't proud of what she'd done, she told Val, but no one else would defend her, so she had to do it herself.

Remembering Keeley gave her strength. She looked at Nigel again, really seeing him, for the first time. Lifting her head, she said, "I want a divorce."

"A divorce!" he exclaimed, as though she'd said something funny. "Not in a million years."

She didn't know why he was laughing, but she said, "I mean

it. You've . . . hit me for the last time, Nigel. I won't put up with
it anymore."

"You won't put up with—" He couldn't finish; he looked at
her incredulously. "You really think it would be so easy? I'm
not going to divorce you, Valeska. Never!"

Had the blow she'd taken shaken her brain? She couldn't believe his reaction. Her lips stiff, she said, "Why not?"

"Why not?" He looked at her as though she were a simpleton,
which, in that moment, she believed she was. "Well, there are
several reasons, my dear."

"Name one."

"All right. For one thing, if your voice does return—"

"*If?*"

He looked at her calmly. "There are no guarantees, remember? And if you find you can sing again after the surgery, you
still have a few lucrative years ahead of you. Providing, of
course, that you stay out of the bottom of the bottle long enough
to perform. I still get my cut of anything you do, you know. So
even if you're reduced to the occasional guest appearance, or
charity event, well, I'll collect, as well."

His cruel remark about her voice had staggered her, but she
couldn't allow herself to be distracted. "It's not your choice,
Nigel. I'll divorce you."

"Oh, no, you won't."

"Yes, I will!"

"No . . . you . . . won't."

She had never heard such menace from anyone. Despite herself, her own voice shook. "You can't stop me."

"Oh, yes, I can," he said, coming a step closer. She backed
away, her body tense. "And believe me, I will stop you. If you
think I'll give up my convenient marriage—"

"Convenient! Is that what it is to you?"

"Well, of course, don't be tiresome, my dear. My staying married assures that I won't have any future . . . entanglements—"

"From your affairs, I presume!" she cried.

"Naturally. Man wasn't meant to be monogomous, no matter
what women insist. Besides, I have to look out for my interests.
Or don't you remember the contract you signed?"

She didn't remember signing a contract. How could she have
signed something and not recall? But she had trusted him, she
thought desperately, and over the years there had been so many
documents—contracts, agreements; she couldn't keep track of
them all. Nigel had always handled the financial details. She had

never paid any attention. And before him, her mother had control of whatever she had earned. The manager she had hired had taken over for a while, but Nigel had fired him when they got married, and she had never bothered to ask why. He was her husband, and she had trusted him!

Don't worry your pretty little head about it, Nigel had told her over and over again. I'll take care of everything.

Her lips shaking, said, "You won't get away with it."

"Oh, but I already have." He looked at her suddenly, evilly. "And don't think you're going to get me out, my darling, because I have weapons I haven't even used yet. I can break you if I choose. I can make sure you never sing again. It would be so simple, really—a blow to the throat, a crushed larynx. Who would question it? After all, everyone knows that drunks fall down." His eyes met hers. "Don't they?"

She looked at him in horror. "You . . . wouldn't!"

He smiled. "Try me."

So frightened she could hardly think, she said frantically, "But if . . . if something like that happened to me, you'd lose out, too."

He laughed. "I have a tremendous insurance policy on you, darling. It would . . . keep me quite comfortably."

She couldn't stop staring at him. "You're a monster!"

"Yes," he agreed blithely, and lit a cigarette.

Valeska booked the first flight home. She was too upset to care who saw her drinking or how many people noticed that she had already been looped when she boarded. After a while, the flight attendants in first class started plying her with coffee, to which she only added her own generous measures of vodka from the flasks she'd replenished in the airport lounge. Finally, she passed out.

She was too drunk to manage by herself when the plane landed; aware of who she was, an airline representative discreetly bundled her into a cab. By then, she was awake enough to give her address, but as the cabby headed uptown, she changed her mind.

"Wait a minute," she said. "Take me to Broadway first."

The driver's glance met hers in the rearview mirror. "Whatever you say, lady." But as they started off, he couldn't seem to keep his eyes off her. His continued scrutiny penetrated even her sloshed state. When she caught him staring at her for the fourth time, she demanded belligerently, "What are you staring at?"

He shifted his glance quickly to traffic. "Nothin', sorry, ma'am. It's just—"

"What?"

He shook his head. "I was sure I knew you. . . ."

Through her vodka-driven haze, she drew herself up haughtily. "I doubt it."

He shook his head again. "You're probably right, but I know I've seen you someplace."

They were coming to the famed street, where she had played to so many packed houses, standing room only. "Well, it's possible—" she started to say. Just then they started to pass the theater where she'd performed in *Maggie the Cat*. Trying to focus, she looked out and noticed that the poster of her and the show had a big black band slapped across it: CANCELLED.

They were stopped in traffic, so she had a chance to get a good long look at it, and she was just thinking with self-pity how high she'd once flown, when the driver snapped his fingers.

"I've got it," he said triumphantly. "That poster just reminded me."

Valeska sat forward avidly, her puffy face and dulled eyes beginning to sparkle, as they once had, entrancing audiences and anyone else who had ever seen her in her glory. "Yes?" she said eagerly.

The cabby turned around, grinning. Proud of himself, he said, "I'm right, aren't I? I know I am. You used to be Valeska Szabo, didn't you?"

CHAPTER TWENTY-THREE

"You have to make a decision," George Weaver told Keeley one smoggy Tuesday morning in her office at Charbonne Films. He was her accountant, and he was flanked by her investment counselor, Peter Dietz. Paid to watch out for her interests, the two men had come to see her—not only as employees, but as friends. She had been expecting them. She had been preoccupied, but she wasn't stupid, and she knew the disastrous state of her finances. But how could she think about investments or taxes or profit and loss sheets when Fitz was so sick? Barely six months after the AIDS diagnosis, his condition had deteriorated to the point where every time she saw him, she was almost afraid his next breath would be his last.

"You have to sue," Peter said, interrupting her thoughts. "If you don't, you'll be bankrupt."

She knew she should pay attention, but she was thinking about Lindsey Grosvenor, who had promised to stand by Fitz. Where was he now, when Fitz needed him the most? The day was coming—too soon, from what Fitz's doctor had told him—when he wouldn't be able to stay home by himself. He was getting too weak; he needed too much help. Tearfully, Fitz told her that he'd kill himself before dying in the hospital, and she didn't doubt it. She knew about his fear of medical centers: both his parents had gone into one when he was a teenager and hadn't come out. In Fitz's experience, people didn't get well in hospitals; they died there.

George could see that he didn't have Keeley's attention, and he leaned forward, causing his chair to creak in protest. He was a big man, broad more than tall, with a fringe of light brown hair and concerned gray eyes. "I know this is a difficult time for you, Keeley," he said, "but you have to pay attention to what's going on in your own life. That business with Noel was a big loss— too big for you to carry, what with all the money you've loaned your family."

Peter spoke up. Unlike George, who was so big and bulky, Peter was tall and thin, always impeccably dressed, his dark hair styled, his eyes keen behind sparkling wire-frame glasses. "George is right," he said firmly. "And if I can put my two cents in, I think that at the very *least* you have to take action against Noel Harrington for breach of contract. Keeley, are you listening to what we're trying to tell you?"

Keeley tried to concentrate. "I'm listening, but what good would it do? Noel is somewhere in Europe, and after what Raleigh Quinn did to him for walking out on the studio, I doubt he's ever coming back."

"Well, you have to do *something*," Peter insisted. "We're talking about a lot of money here. You can't take that kind of loss, not without initiating legal action."

"What are you suggesting?" she asked. "That we extradite him? No, Peter, I've accepted that the money is gone forever."

"I wouldn't be so complacent if I were you. We're not talking nickels and dimes here, after all."

Keeley sat back in her chair and closed her eyes. She felt tired, drained, worn out. She couldn't deal with this, not today, maybe not ever. What did she care about money, when Fitz was at home this very minute, gasping for air, in terrible pain that no medication could alleviate?

"Suing means lawyer's visits, court appearances, God knows what," she said. "I can't get involved with it all right now."

"But—"

She was tired of arguing. There were more important things than money, and Fitz was one of them. "Look," she said, trying to be patient when she felt like screaming—not at them, but at the world in general, "I know you've got my best interests in mind, but I can't cope with it right now. I don't want to take that much time away from Fitz."

They exchanged quick glances. Then Peter started to say, "Fitz is *dying*, Keeley—"

She slammed her hand down on the desk top. "Don't you think I know that?"

The torment in her voice silenced the men, who looked awkwardly away from the naked pain on her face. She turned away, too, telling herself fiercely she wouldn't break down. She had too much to do, she reminded herself, and turned back to her advisers. "You're going to have to take charge. Do what you have to do. Right now, I don't care if I lose everything. . . ." Despite her control, her voice broke again. "I'm about to, anyway."

They glanced covertly at each other again, obviously debating how much to say. George had known her longer, and with a sigh, he leaned forward again. "Have you talked to Mr. Harrington?"

Her lips tightened. She had talked to Noel, all right: about the time her family had descended on her, and she'd found out about Fitz. As though she didn't have enough on her mind, Noel had called one night, sounding like a little boy who knew he'd done wrong. She had quickly discovered that he hadn't called to apologize, but to blame everyone else for his mistakes. She had listened for a few minutes to the self-serving litany, then she had cut him off.

"I don't want to hear about it, Noel," she'd told him. "Just tell me when I'm going to get my money back."

He'd been shocked and hurt that she could even ask. "You

think *I* have that kind of money? I'm going to lose a bundle just like everyone else!"

Somehow, she couldn't muster up the sympathy he seemed to expect. "Not like everyone else," she reminded him. "You're conveniently forgetting the fact that we all invested more than you did—"

"I'm not forgetting," he said defensively. "But I'm the star. I had more to lose, don't you see?"

"I guess it depends on your point of view," she said flatly. "If you really feel you've got so much to lose, maybe you'd better go back to work and save us all a big headache."

He couldn't have sounded more self-pitying if he'd tried. "You don't know how hard it is to try to work with assholes!"

She was out of patience. Pointedly, she'd replied, "Yes, I do."

It was the last she'd heard from him. Two months later she found out that the Wyatt Earp project had been shelved indefinitely because of continuing legal problems with the director. While the heat died down, Noel had gone to Italy to star in a low-budget spaghetti Western with the hot new French actress, Debusette something-or-other, but when that picture failed, too, Noel returned to Charbonne Films, hat in hand. Thinking he had only to express the wish to be admitted back into the fold, he came to ask for his old job back. Raleigh's answer had been to tear up his contract.

Noel hadn't expected this unfeeling response, and with his investors hot on his heels, he'd fled to Europe again. When Keeley heard about it, she knew she'd never see her money. Noel might look the part of a hero, but he was a coward at heart, and he'd never be able to face angry creditors demanding their investments back. The only good thing about it was that the director had dropped all his lawsuits. At least, she thought angrily, she wouldn't have to go to court about *that*.

"This thing with Noel is bad enough, Keeley," George said, breaking into her thoughts again. "But these loans to your family are pretty heavy. I don't mean to be critical, but they've been a big drain."

Keeley didn't want to talk about the money she'd lent to her family, especially since in the case of her father, "loan" was a euphemism for "gift." She hated being put in the position of benefactor, but she didn't see any way out. She didn't give a damn about the rest of them, but she loved Jewell, and she couldn't just abandon her half sister because their father was a loser. In the six months since she'd kicked them out, they had

found an apartment up in Van Nuys, but Joe Cochran's main oc-
cupation since then had been coming to visit her with his hand
out. In vain she had begged both her father and Phyllis to let
Jewell live with her; they refused. Her expression turned bitter.
They knew what a lever Jewell was, and they weren't about to
lose her.

"Taking advantage of a good thing, you mean," Peter said. He
saw Keeley's face and added, "You don't have to look at me
like that. *I'm* not the one who has been spending your money
faster than you can make it. In fact, I'd like a chance to get my
hands on some of it so I can invest it for you before you're
completely broke."

She knew they were right, and that she should have put her
foot down with her father long before now. "I know," she said.
"But you don't understand—"

"Yes, we do," George interrupted. He leaned forward again,
intent on getting through to her. "But I'm not sure you do. If
you don't put a lid on things and soon, my best advice is going
to be to sell the house."

"Sell the house!" She looked at them in disbelief. "But I
thought houses were good investments!"

"They are," George said. "But not when you have the mortgage payments you have along with everything else. When it
was just you, things were different. But now you've taken this
big loss with Noel, and you've loaned your family so much
you're going through your reserves like a hot iron on ice."

"I know. But I just don't see any other way."

Both men looked at each other. Then George said, "You can
always just say no."

She looked meaningfully back. "*That's* a big help."

George flushed. "I'm sorry, but it's true, Keeley. You hired
Peter and me to advise you, and we're trying to do it. If you
think we're getting too personal or—"

"No, no. I know you're trying to help. It's just . . ."

She didn't know how to explain. Sitting here with them in the
light of day, she knew that nothing she could say would make
sense. She'd reviewed her finances lately herself and knew the
score. But every time she told herself she wouldn't loan her father any more, she thought of Jewell, who was trying so hard.
Her younger half sister was the only one who seemed to be trying to make something of herself; she was pulling down straight
A's in school and holding a job after classes, as well, to help out.

No matter what she felt about her father, Keeley couldn't let her down.

"I want to pull my own weight," Jewell had told her, when Keeley asked about her new job. "You've been so good to all of us when you didn't have to be. I don't want to take advantage . . . like everybody else."

A pity, Keeley thought as she looked at the two serious men in front of her, that the rest of her family didn't feel the same way.

"I'll talk to them," she said. "I know I've let it go too long."

"Well, it's your business of course," Peter said smoothly. "But we both feel that you've overextended yourself. If you could just pull back for a little while, until I can get together a new portfolio for you, maybe you can scrape by this quarter. Do you think you can do that?"

"I'll try—" she started to say, and stopped. She'd just had a thought. She had never really cared about the house; she'd only bought it as an investment. She needed so little for herself, after all, and with the financial beating she'd taken this year with Noel and everyone else, it would be a relief to divest herself of unnecessary burdens and do what she'd wanted to do in the first place. Ever since she'd heard Fitz's diagnosis, she'd been driving herself crazy wondering what to do about him, how to help. The whole time the answer had been staring her in the face.

"You're right," she said, making a sudden decision that had been at the back of her mind for months. It seemed so clear now; she wondered why she hadn't thought of it before. "I'm going to sell the house."

"Sell the house?" George looked concerned all over again. "Keeley, when we said—"

"I know, it's all right." She felt relieved, as if she'd dropped a heavy weight she hadn't wanted to carry all this while. It felt so right that she took it a step further. "And I'm going to take a leave of absence."

"A leave of absence?" George looked even more startled at that. He glanced quickly at Peter. "What for?"

"Selling the house I can understand," her investment counselor said carefully. "But taking a leave . . . Don't you think it's a little drastic? I'm not sure just how you think it's going to help."

She couldn't sit still; she got up to pace. Now that it had come to her, it seemed so obvious. Fitz was afraid of ending up alone in a hospital ward, cared for by nurses who might be kind and compassionate, but who had too many other patients to pay much attention to him. Round-the-clock care at home had been one answer, but it seemed so sterile, so cold. He'd be in his own bed, but he'd still be tended to by strangers, a poor compromise at best.

But he wouldn't be alone, and he wouldn't be in the hospital, if she took care of him, she thought triumphantly, and turned to look at her startled advisers.

"It's not going to help my situation," she said, "but it is going to help a very dear friend. I'm going to take care of Fitz."

Peter stood up. "Keeley, I admire what you're trying to do, but you have to think of yourself, too—"

Hauling himself to his feet, George joined the plea. "I agree with Peter. It's noble of you to want to help, Keeley, but—"

"It's not noble, and there's nothing admirable about it," she denied quickly. "It's what I'd want if I were in Fitz's place—a friend to care for me, like I'm going to care for him." She smiled, happy and relieved to have come to the decision. "That's all, you two. Do what you have to do, you have my complete confidence. And when this is over—" her voice cracked slightly, as it did whenever she thought of what Fitz had ahead of him, but she made herself continue "—when this is over, I'll think what to do then. Until that time, you can handle it for me, can't you?"

No one could resist Keeley when she was like this. As petite as she was, there was something so valiant and indomitable about her that both men found themselves promising to take care of whatever needed doing; then they left. Keeley went with them to the door, giving each a handshake and her thanks. Now that she knew what she wanted to do, she had a few preparations to make, and the first one was to see Raleigh. What she had to say was too important to discuss over the phone, so she called his secretary and asked if she could drop by his office.

Five minutes later, she was sitting in front of Raleigh's marble-topped desk, telling him what she had decided. He wasn't happy to lose her even for a short while, but Fitz was one of his favorites, too, and he agreed to give her as much time as Fitz needed.

"I admire what you're doing, Keeley," he said, when she was on her way out after thanking him. As a friend, he put his hands on her shoulders and gazed into her eyes. "You know it could be a long, tough haul, don't you?"

She was trying not to think of it. "Yes, I do. But Fitz has been like a brother to me, and I want to be there for him as long as he needs me."

"Let me know if there's anything I can do."

"You've already done more than enough," she said gratefully. "Thanks, Raleigh. I won't forget it."

Impulsively, he gave her a hug. "Fitz is lucky to have a friend like you."

"No, I'm the lucky one, to have had a friend like him," she said sadly, and went out to Van Nuys to talk to her family.

It was a worse scene than even she had anticipated. Before she pulled into the driveway of the apartment complex where the Cochrans lived, she could hear the music blaring from inside. The door stood open as usual, the stereo blasting away in the living room, while two televisions—one in the kitchen turned to Phyllis's soap operas, the other in the bedroom tuned to sports on cable—competed in volume. As she came in, she saw Sid, the youngest, sitting in the hallway, busily taking the telephone to pieces. Parts were strewn all over the floor around him, and he looked up with a grin when she came in, a circle of dried chocolate around his mouth.

"Hi, Keeley," he said, unaware—or not caring—about the damage he'd done.

She was glad she hadn't tried to call. "Hi," she said. "Is Dad here?"

He shrugged, already bored. Her jaw feeling tight, Keeley glanced into the living room and grimaced. Papers and magazines and abandoned fast-food cartons were scattered around; it was more of a mess than it usually was. Thanking her stars that she had kicked them out of her house when she had, she headed toward the kitchen. Phyllis was there, glued to the TV set on the counter, oblivious to anything going on around her, so she went into the bedroom.

As she had expected, her father was here, asleep on the bed, with this TV going and a half-dozen crushed and empty beer cans on the floor beside him. He didn't stir even when she crossed the room and shut off the set; dead to the world, she had to shake him twice before he opened his eyes and groggily looked up.

"Wha'?" he asked. "Izzit time for dinner?"

"No, Dad, I've got to talk to you," Keeley said.

"Not now, I'm busy," he muttered, heaving his bulk over so that his back was to her. He pulled one of the pillows over his head and, before she could shake him again, began to snore. She stood there a moment, her face expressionless. Then, without trying to wake him again, she went back to the kitchen.

"Phyllis, I want to talk to you," she said, over the loud volume.

"Not now," her stepmother answered, her eyes on the screen. "This is a new talk show, and they're doing a segment on transsexuals who used to be prostitutes but who are now beauty queens."

Keeley shut her eyes for a moment, gathering strength. Then she reached out and pulled the plug to the set. Phyllis looked over angrily. "What'd you do that for?"

"I have to talk to you," Keeley said. "Right now."

Even Phyllis heard something in her voice. Snatching a pack of cigarettes from the counter, she lit one with a snap of a throwaway lighter. "All right, go ahead. Talk."

Keeley decided not to pull punches. "I'm selling the house."

Phyllis looked up with a grin. "Well, that's great news. I hope you're buying a bigger place, because we're sure getting tired of this little place now that Lila's had her baby."

Lila had recently given birth to a baby girl she named Dakota. Keeley had dutifully sent a baby gift, but she couldn't help wondering what kind of life the child would have, with Lila as her mother and a family like this.

But Lila's little girl wasn't her responsibility any more than the rest of the family was, she told herself firmly, and said, "You don't understand. I'm selling the house. I'm not buying another one."

Phyllis looked shocked. "But we were counting on being able to move back in with you!"

Keeley looked at her incredulously. "I can't imagine why you thought such a thing, but I'm telling you right now, it's impossible. And while we're on the subject, I came to tell you that I'm not going to loan you and Dad any more money, either."

Her face instantly distorted with anger . . . and fear, Phyllis looked at her in horror. "You can't do this! We're your family!"

"I know, and that's why I'm in this fix," Keeley said, trying to hold on to her temper. "I've loaned you so much money I'm in danger of bankruptcy myself."

"What lies!" Phyllis cried, red-faced. "That house alone makes you rich! Oh, it's just like you. You only think of yourself, you always have! We counted on you. You can't let us down!"

Keeley clenched her fists. "Louis can get a job. And so can Dad."

Phyllis looked at her as though she'd just grown another head. "Your father can't work! What about his back?"

She couldn't afford pity; it was what had gotten her into this mess. Coldly, she said, "He'll get over it."

"Oh, you selfish, selfish person!" Phyllis cried. "First you abandoned us when you went to New York, and now you want to throw us out into the cold when your sister—your *sister*—has just had a baby and your father can't work! Oh, how can you be so cruel and heartless?"

"Hey," Joe's voice came from behind Keeley. "What's going on? What's all the shoutin' about?"

Keeley turned and saw her father in the doorway. Phyllis saw him, too, and rushed over to his side. "Keeley came to tell us that she won't loan us any more money!"

Joe's puffy eyes turned in Keeley's direction. Rubbing a hand over his mouth, he grunted, "Who asked you for more?"

Thinking that he was lucky she hadn't come to call in the loans, Keeley said, "No one, yet. But I just wanted you to know I can't do it anymore."

"Is that right?" He looked at Phyllis, saw the fear in her eyes, and turned back to Keeley. "We're going to talk about this, little girl. I don't like your attitude."

"That's—" Phyllis started to say, falling silent when Joe looked at her again.

Determined not to be intimidated, Keeley waited until Phyllis left the room before continuing. "We can talk," she said, "but I'm not going to change my mind."

"We'll see about that," Joe said, crossing his arms over his big belly and glaring at her. "What's going on here?"

"There's nothing complicated about it," she said evenly. "I have to sell the house because my expenses have been so high, and because of that, I can't loan you any more money."

His eyes narrowed. "You're doing this to get back at me, aren't you?"

"Get back at you?" She looked at him in surprise; then she shook her head. "No. It has nothing to do with you."

He shifted his weight. "I know you, Keeley. You never had any respect for me and still don't. You think I've been a lazy, good-for-nothing bastard. Well, fine, we both know where we stand, because I think you're an arrogant little bitch. But remember, your sister just had a baby. Do you want her on welfare?"

"No, I don't," she said. She looked him in the eye. "She's your daughter. Do you?"

His face reddened. "She's your sister, damn it!"

"She's my half sister, to be accurate, and she's never given a damn about me or anyone else. Yes, I care, but I'm not responsible for her. Not anymore."

He couldn't have looked more disbelieving if she'd taken a bazooka and blasted out one of the walls. "What's the matter with you? You've never said such things before!"

Thinking of Fitz, of the pain in his eyes and in his heart, she said, "Maybe I should have, Dad. God knows, I've thought about it enough times."

"But we're family!"

"Family!" She looked at him with scorn. "When have I *ever* been part of this family, except for what I could bring in?"

"But I was always on your side—"

"You were never on my side, ever," she said. "After Mom died, it was as if I didn't exist."

His face changed. "You don't understand how hard it was for me after your mother died," he whined. "I loved your mama, Keeley. I was lost when she passed away!"

"She didn't *pass away*, she *died*! And I was lost, too, Dad! For God's sake, I was only seven years old!"

Looking increasingly desperate, Joe pleaded, "I didn't know how to take care of a little girl. I had to work; what was I supposed to do?"

Keeley didn't answer right away. As she looked at him in his baggy trousers and stained undershirt, she finally allowed herself to see him as the weak, selfish man he was, and at that, the last of her pity ran out.

"I don't know, Dad," she said, breathing hard. "But back then, I was too young to take care of myself."

He whimpered, "What's wrong with you, Keeley? You've never been like this."

"How would you know?" She couldn't believe how cold she felt. "You've never paid attention to anything I've ever done in my life. When did you ever mention my music, or even ask me to play a song I'd composed?"

As though she'd thrown him a lifeline, he said eagerly, "You can play one for me now!"

She looked at him for a long moment. She saw the slyness in his eyes, the weakness, the dependence. Sadly, she shook her head. "No, I can't, Dad," she said. "I'm sorry, but I've done all

I can. You're just going to have to make it on your own from here on out."

"You can't do this!" he cried, realizing she meant it. Frantically, he seized on the one thing that had always worked. "What about Jewell? Are you going to abandon her?"

She couldn't believe even he could stoop so low. Contemptuously, she said, "Don't worry about Jewell, Dad. She'll be taken care of."

He drew himself up in a last, ineffective attack. "So, you'll *take care* of Jewell, and the hell with the rest of us, is that it? Well, it's not fair! You've got all that money, all those things! You have to share. You're a success!"

She didn't even want to look at him anymore. He hadn't asked her why she had to sell the house, why she couldn't loan him any more money. He didn't know anything about her, and he didn't care. Reaching for the door, she looked up into his heavy, unshaven face and said, "How would you know what I am, Dad? How would you know what I've done?"

As she opened the door, Phyllis stood nearby, looking frightened. It was obvious she'd been listening, but for once Keeley didn't care. She had never felt so free in her life as she did at that moment. Without looking back, she grabbed her purse and went out to the car.

She took Fitz down to the beach. She knew he loved the ocean, and during the next two months they both found solace there. Tux came with them, and to Keeley's surprise, abandoned his independent, standoffish pose. The fearless hunter with the white fur bow tie no longer went out to scout; instead he spent hours lying beside Fitz, purring mightily while Fitz, increasingly weak, rested his hand on Tux's back.

The house they rented had a deck where they would sit for hours, Fitz on a chaise wrapped in blankets, the cat in his lap, Keeley beside them in a chair. Fitz's favorite time was sunset, and every night he was able to, they sat outside, watching the lowering sun cast a beaten gold path on the endless waves coming in. Sometimes they'd talk; sometimes not. Once Fitz turned to her with tears in his eyes. By then, his once round and rosy face was ravaged by his disease, his eyes sunken in bruised sockets, the bones of his head standing out in sharp relief.

"Everyone else abandoned me when they heard I had this damned disease," he said, his voice choked. "But not you, Keeley. I don't know how to thank you. . . ."

"Then don't," she said simply. Reaching for his skeletal hand, she squeezed it gently, mindful of his pain. Turning her head, she looked out at the sea.

They were on the deck, and the last rays of the sun bronzed her skin and turned her eyes an even more vivid green. A slight breeze ruffled her short, dark hair, and although she didn't realize it, she had never looked more beautiful to him than she did in that moment. Everyone on the beach had gone home; the only sounds were a sharp, lonely cry of a seagull overhead, the never-ending muted pounding of the surf, and Tuxedo, purring away beside Fitz. Aware that Fitz was watching her, she turned her head and smiled at him again.

"You'll do the same for me next time," she said. Her strong gaze held his, giving him courage and peace. "Won't you?"

He was almost too exhausted to answer, too tired even to smile. But he managed to hold her hand a little tighter, and when he put his head back and closed his eyes, she looked at him tenderly for a moment before staring out at the sea again. She wouldn't allow herself to cry; no matter how deep the ache she felt inside, she didn't want him to see her tears.

Another time, when he was so weak and in pain and ill from all the medication that only prolonged his agony, not assuaged it, he wanted to go out on deck again. When he was settled, wincing despite himself at the weight when Tux jumped lightly into his lap, he asked her to go back inside and play something for him. Keeley had rented a piano because she knew the music soothed him and helped him rest, and she often played for him, making up melodies as she went along.

"What would you like to hear?" she said, tucking the blankets gently around him, and giving Tux a grateful stroke. She hardly needed the day nurse now; Fitz was so frail that she could lift him in and out of the wheelchair by herself.

Even the short trip from the chair to the chaise had exhausted Fitz; she tried not to show her alarm at the increasing translucence of his skin. His cheekbones were prominent, stretching his flesh like parchment; she could see tiny blue veins in his eyelids.

"I don't care," he said, sounding sick to death, but smiling at her with an effort that made her heart constrict. "You choose."

She opted for something original. It was the opening number she had planned for *Beauty and the Beast*. As the haunting, unforgettable melody drifted out to the deck, he turned his head. Gasping between words because he was so weak, he said, "I've never ... heard that ... before. Is it ... new?"

She was so attuned to him that she heard every faint word. "No, I wrote it long ago," she answered, feeling a strangeness in the air. She wanted to go out on deck and reassure herself, but she couldn't. Something compelled her to keep playing.

He was silent for so long she thought he'd fallen asleep. Just when she was about to stop for a moment and tiptoe out to see, he said, "It's . . . beautiful, Keeley. The best thing you've ever done. But then, you always were the talented one. What do you call it?"

She could hardly answer. There was something in his voice. . . .

"It's called 'Living in Time,' " she finally managed over the tears that were threatening to choke her despite her fierce vow not to cry. "It's what you're going to do, my friend."

He made a sound, like a cry or a moan, she couldn't tell which, and she lifted her fingers from the piano, intending to go to him. "No, don't stop," he begged her, his voice barely above a whisper. "I want to hear the whole thing again. Play it through for me, will you, one last time?"

She obeyed, spasms of grief already shaking her body, hot tears falling from her eyes to the piano keys in spite of herself. She finished as the last arc of the vanishing sun settled into the sea, far away on the horizon. Just for a moment, it seemed to her that the world held its breath. Even Tux had stopped his comforting purr. Then the wind lifted, and the waves renewed their endless chant. A pain stabbed through her heart as she played the last note, and she put her face in her hands, trying not to sob. After a moment, she quietly closed the keyboard and stood up from the piano bench.

Fitz's lounge chair faced the beach; when she came to the doorway, all she could see of him was the back of his head. She knew from his position what had happened while she'd been playing the song, and she walked slowly past him, out onto the deck. Another spasm shook her, and she gripped the railing. Tuxedo came and pressed against her legs, and she bent down and picked him up. Putting him on the rail in front of her, she put a hand on his back, but for once, he didn't purr.

She stood there a long time without looking back toward the chaise, until it was full dark and the moon had come up, gilding the restless waves with pale, cold light.

Finally, speaking to the night sky and the sea and the stars overhead, to wherever Fitz rested now in peace, she whispered, "Good-bye, my friend. I hope we meet again."

She didn't realize until she went inside to make the call, that the music no longer played in her head. Sometime between the last note she had played, and the realization that her friend was gone, the music had died.

Everyone at the studio came to the funeral, it seemed. People she knew and those she'd never seen, assembled by the grave site to pay tribute to Fitz, who had been more loved than even Keeley realized. Raleigh himself gave a moving eulogy after she realized she wouldn't be able to do it; even though she'd had some time to get used to the fact that Fitz was gone, she was barely able to hold herself together through the brief service. She wanted to cry and scream and throw herself down on the ground, but she was only able to stand with everybody else in strained, frozen silence.

"Don't wear black, Keeley," Fitz had said to her once. It was after they had stopped pretending he wasn't going to die. "It's really not your best color," he'd added solemnly, but with a last twinkle in his eye. "I've always thought funerals were sober enough without everyone trailing around draped in black, so promise me you'll wear something bright."

At times like those, she'd felt her heart would break, but for his sake, she joined in the game with him. He hated to feel sad and depressed and sorry for himself, and he wouldn't let her do it for him. So when she'd felt like crying, she had forced a smile and said, "Maybe we should have clowns, too, and balloons. Would you like that?"

He had laughed—or tried to. His strength by then was almost gone, and it was more like a whisper of mirth. "I said funerals were too somber," he gasped. "I didn't say I thought you should be having a party. But now that I think of it, a balloon or two would be a nice touch. Just make sure they're safe for wildlife, all right?"

So here she stood, dressed in green, holding her biodegradable balloons, too locked in her overwhelming grief even to care about the strange looks she got. The only thing she could think of as the service went on was getting through it. Dry-eyed, she stared down at Fitz's flower-covered casket and counted off the people who were gone: her grandmother; her friend, Nina; Barry; Val. They had all left in one way or another; now it was Fitz.

From somewhere, she realized that the minister had concluded the service and people were drifting away, but she couldn't seem to make herself join them. Raleigh came up and said something to her; so did several others. She didn't know what they asked her; she couldn't answer. She just kept shaking her head. Fitz loved her red Mustang, so she had come in that instead of the limousine.

"I'll be fine, Raleigh," she said when the studio head insisted she come with him. She didn't know it, but with her pallor and her shadowed, bruised eyes, she looked ill herself. She'd lost so much weight that the green suit hung on her body, but it had been Fitz's favorite, so she hadn't thought of wearing anything else.

"I don't want to leave you here alone," Raleigh said. He was concerned, as was everyone else. No one had ever seen Keeley like this, and some had speculated that the strain had been too much even for her. People wondered if she was headed for a nervous breakdown.

"I'll be all right," she said, forcing a faint smile. Even then, her face felt like it would crack. "I just want to stay a few minutes longer. You understand. . . ."

At last, she and Fitz were alone. She hadn't cried since he'd died; her eyes felt filled with sand, her throat clogged with dust, her heart dead.

"Oh, Fitz," she whispered, knowing he would understand. "What am I going to do?"

Her music still hadn't come back to her; the only thing she could feel inside was a stone cold silence. It had never happened to her before; always, ever since she could remember, music had been a part of her—of her self, her soul, her spirit. Now it was gone, and she was afraid she'd never get it back again. It was as if an essential part of her had been cut off, cauterized, destroyed. If she didn't get the music back, she knew she would die.

She couldn't cry; a frozen, hard knot had formed inside her, and sometimes she felt she couldn't even breathe, it had such a tight hold. The day was warm, but she had never felt so cold; she was shivering so much her legs would hardly hold her, and yet she couldn't seem to move. She could only stand there, staring at the box that held her dearest friend, hating a fate that gave with one hand and snatched away with the other.

"Oh, God!" she cried, and put her hands over her face.

"Keeley," someone said quietly behind her. Dropping her hands, she whirled around and looked up into Gabe's face.

"You came!" she exclaimed. Relief almost overwhelmed her,

and for a moment, she didn't allow herself to believe he was really here. She had called the foundation and left a message; when he called back it was from some place in Indonesia, and she could hardly hear him. But even the sound of his voice, as far away as it was, gave her something to cling to, and for the first time in her life, she had admitted her need.

"I'll be there as soon as I can," Gabe had promised without hesitation. Now, miraculously, he was.

Her tears burst forth at last as he reached for her and pulled her close. She clung to him with all her might. The hard knot that had been inside of her began to dissolve now that the only person who could, had come to comfort her, and she finally was able to let go of the pain that had kept her frozen. Fitz had been her best friend, her partner, one of the dearest people in the world to her. But Gabe was her other half, her soul mate, her lover, the best part of her.

"Oh, Gabe," she wept, burying her face in his broad chest, "it hurts so much!"

"I know, I know," Gabe murmured, holding her in his strong arms. She could feel the steady pounding of his heart. "I know. . . ."

Wildly, she shook her head. She couldn't look up. "No, no, you don't. Oh, Gabe, Fitz has died, and so has the music!"

Gabe let her cry until she couldn't cry any longer. The front of his white shirt was soaked by the time she was finally able to look up into his calm blue eyes, but at last she felt a glimmer of peace—the first she'd known since losing her dear friend.

"What am I going to do?" she whispered. Then she said something she'd never said to anyone else in her life. Clutching his arm, she said, "Oh, Gabe, help me."

"I will," he said calmly. He put his arm around her. "Come on, let's go home."

"Home?" She didn't know what that meant. She couldn't go back to the beach house just yet; the memories were too poignant so she'd been staying in a motel that took pets. Sometime in the past month, she couldn't remember when now, the house had finally sold, so she couldn't go there. She hadn't realized it before, but she didn't have a home to go to.

As he always seemed to, Gabe knew what she was thinking. His arm tightened around her, and he smiled tenderly. "My home," he said, looking down at her. "I'm taking you to Montana."

She didn't care where they went, as long as they were together. Allowing him to take her arm and lead her toward the car, she looked up suddenly at the balloons bobbing over her head.

"Wait," she said.

"What is it?"

She hadn't trusted herself to hold on to the balloon bouquet; she had been shaking so violently before and during the service that she had tied them to her wrist. But like Fitz, it was time to let the balloons fly away, and she knew he would think it a fitting ending to the day.

Gabe helped her untie the knot, then stood back a little as she looked first at the balloons, and then up at the clear blue sky. Before she released them, she reached for Gabe's hand and held it tightly.

"This is for you, my dear partner, my collaborator, my wonderful friend," she whispered, letting go of the string. Then, as the bright bouquet lifted up and disappeared high overhead, she bowed her head and said good-bye.

CHAPTER TWENTY-FOUR

For once in her life, Keeley gladly gave up control to someone else. She was so drained emotionally and physically that she was relieved when Gabe said he'd make all the decisions about going to the ranch in Montana—except for one. He thought it would be less traumatic for Tuxedo if they boarded the cat, but on that she was adamant.

"He goes where I go," she declared. She couldn't—wouldn't—leave him behind, especially after the comfort he'd given Fitz. Gabe didn't argue; he took out the cat carrier, and Tuxedo boarded the plane in style, spitting and hissing at being confined.

Gabe had bought first-class tickets because he thought Keeley would rest better on the flight, but as exhausted as she was, she couldn't sleep. Her eyes burning, she held Gabe's hand tightly as the jet took off, and he left her alone until she turned to him and started talking.

"I thought I was prepared for Fitz to die," she said, her eyes filling. "We talked about it. He was ready. But I wasn't, no matter what I tried to believe."

"He was your friend, Keeley," he said. "You'll grieve for him for a long time. There's nothing wrong with that."

"But I don't want to feel this way!" she cried. "It hurts too much!"

Smiling tenderly, he touched her face. "My poor Keeley," he said. "I know it hurts ... you, especially. You feel things so deeply."

Squeezing her eyes shut, she said, "I always have, and I hate it. I wish I didn't feel anything!"

"If you didn't feel anything, you couldn't write such beautiful music. It comes from your heart, Keeley, and—unfortunately for you, but lucky for us at times—hearts like yours can swell with joy, or break in a minute. Your music reflects that; it has emotion no one else can put into it."

She looked away, tears filling her eyes again. "It doesn't matter anymore. I told you, the music is gone. . . ." Despite herself, her voice shook, and he took her chin in his hand and made her look at him again.

"Listen to me," he said, his intense blue gaze holding hers. "You've just been through a terrible experience. You've lost a friend who meant a great deal to you. The music will come back, I know it."

She wanted to believe him; she wanted it with all her being. But she couldn't stop herself from asking plaintively, "But when?"

He smiled again, drawing her close. "When it's ready," he murmured. "Until then, you just ... rest."

His voice was so soothing that she closed her eyes again. Exhaustion finally took over and, still holding his hand, she slept the rest of the flight. She awoke briefly when the plane landed, and tried to keep awake long enough to appreciate part of the drive through some of the most beautiful ranch land in the state. Smiling tenderly, he put her to bed as soon as they arrived, and she fell asleep again halfway through her protest.

Keeley woke the next morning to sounds of galloping hooves and whoops of delight. Groggy and disoriented, she stumbled out of bed and went to the window to see what was going on.

For a moment, she didn't believe her eyes. Was that Gabe in the corral outside, astride a bucking horse? In confusion, she pushed her hair out of her eyes. It looked like a scene from a movie, she thought, until Gabe gave another whoop and she realized it was real life. Instead of dramatically waving one hand in the air, while spurring the horse's sides, as she'd seen movie cowboys do, it was obvious even to Keeley that he was just trying to stay on. The horse—a wildly spotted red-and-white paint with a big circle of white around one blue eye—spun and whirled, clearly determined to get his unwelcome rider off. As Keeley watched, transfixed with horror, the horse gave one last spirited leap. Gabe went flying straight up into the air and then down again—hard—right on the ground.

"Oh, no!" she exclaimed, clutching the windowsill. She waited for him to get up, but when he just lay there, she looked around in a panic. Spying a terry-cloth robe on the end of the bed, she grabbed it and headed for the door. The robe was miles too big for her, the sleeves dragging practically to her knees, but she belted it on as best she could. She ran down the stairs, through a rustic-style living room she barely remembered, and then out the front door and around to the side of the house. When she got there, Gabe was still on the ground.

"Oh, Gabe, are you hurt?" Terrified, she dropped to her knees in the dust beside him. She was reaching out to touch his shoulder when he sat up, spitting out dirt. Glimpsing the blood on his lip, she drew in a breath. "Oh, no! You've broken something!"

"Aw, he ain't broke nothin', not with a head as hard as that," someone said.

Keeley whirled around. A young man who looked to be in his twenties was coming toward them, grinning at the sight of Gabe on the ground, battered and bloody. Instantly and fiercely protective, Keeley looked up accusingly. "He's bleeding!"

"It's just a scratch," the young man said. Reaching down, he hauled Gabe to his feet. "I told you not to sit back like that," he scolded, squinting up at the much-taller Gabe. "You pinched his kidneys, and he didn't like it."

"Yeah, so I found out," Gabe said, spitting out more dirt. Realizing that Keeley was watching anxiously, he tried to smile, wincing a little when he touched the cut on his lip. "I'm all right. Hit hardest in my pride, honest."

The other man laughed, but Keeley didn't think it was funny. "What were you doing? You could have been hurt . . . killed!"

"Oh, I wouldn't have let *that* happen," the young man said.

Keeley whirled around on him again. "You were watching the whole time, and you didn't try to help?"

The young man held up his hands. "Hey, if you know Gabe, you know you can't talk him into or out of anything. You think he'd listen to me? Hell, no. Nothing would do but he had to ride that old paint."

"Yes, well, obviously I've still got a lot to learn," Gabe said wryly, touching the hip he'd landed on. "Keeley, I'd like you to meet Billy Six Horses, my ranch manager. He's part Sioux Indian and all horseman, thank God. He's the man who breaks the horses for the tenderfoot owner. Billy, meet Keeley Cochran, a friend."

"Pleasure," Billy said, sticking out his hand.

Beginning to wonder if she were dreaming, Keeley automatically held out a hand in response. The sleeve of the robe fell over her fingers, and as she dragged the material back again, she wondered if she should call him Mr. Six Horses or Mr. Horses. Unable to decide, she muttered, "Hi, Mr. . . . er . . ."

"Call me Billy," the young man said with a grin, solving her problem. He was much smaller than Gabe, strong and compact, with smooth brown skin, the blackest hair Keeley had ever seen, and eyes so dark they could have been ink. He winked. "Or call me anything you like, just as long as you call me for dinner. Welcome to the Fallin' GT."

"The Fallin' GT?"

"It's the name of the ranch," Gabe said, laughing at Keeley's expression. He held up his hands. "Hey, I didn't choose it. Blame Billy, with his perverted sense of humor. He's seen me fall off horses before."

Now that she knew Gabe wasn't really hurt, Keeley smiled, too. To Billy, she said, "I'm sorry I shouted at you like that. I guess I'm just not used to seeing a rodeo going on outside."

"Well, it doesn't happen every day," Billy said innocently. "Only when the boss comes home."

Deadpan, Gabe replied, "We'll see if you're so cocky after we sell the cattle and concentrate on raising and breaking horses."

Keeley glanced pointedly at Gabe's dusty jeans—and the drying spot of blood on his lip. "I can see why you want to get into that. It's obvious you've got a real flair."

Billy laughed, but Gabe looked indignant. To Keeley, he said, "You're so smart maybe you'd like to ride old Holler yourself."

"Me? I've never been on a horse in my . . . Holler? What kind of name is that?"

"A perfect one for a cayuse who doesn't give a hoot or a holler about anyone or anything else," Gabe said with a glare in the paint's direction. "Come on, Billy, maybe we'd better catch him and get him untacked before he reaches around and takes the saddle off with his teeth."

"While you two are occupied, I think I'll get dressed," Keeley said hastily. She wasn't sure what they had to do to catch the horse again, but she knew she didn't want to be involved. The red-and-white animal was roaming around the corral, looking as though he owned it. Giggling, Keeley headed back to the house. In a way, she thought, he did.

Keeley spent most of the day watching the two men catch and ride various horses—none of which put on the show that Holler had—but by afternoon, she was yawning again and went to take a nap. Mortified, she woke up with a conked-out Tux beside her at sunset.

"I didn't mean to sleep so long!" she exclaimed when she came out and saw Gabe in the kitchen. "I'm sorry! I don't know what got into me."

He came and put his arms around her. "You're worn out, Keeley," he said, giving her a kiss on the forehead.

She looked up into his handsome face. "Yes, I know, but—"

"No buts," he said. "You need some time, that's all. And in the meantime, why don't you go do something else while I get dinner."

She couldn't laze around when he was working, and she shook her head. "I can help."

"Not tonight," he said, giving her a little push toward the door. "Go on, go out and enjoy one of our Montana sunsets. I'll call you when it's ready."

Since she was barred from the kitchen, Keeley did as she was told. Thinking that it was nice to have someone else taking over for a change, she wandered out to the corral where Holler was. The horse was eating his own dinner, but he lifted his head as she approached, one ear forward, one back, munching on a mouthful of hay. Cautiously, not knowing if she would startle him, she climbed up to the top rail of the corral fence and swung a leg over. He snorted and backed away a step.

"Relax, fella," she said. "Here's one person who has no intention of trying to ride you. I just came out to enjoy this time of day. You don't mind, do you?"

Apparently he didn't, for after a moment, reassured when she just sat there, the horse went back to its dinner, leaving Keeley to contemplate her surroundings. Thinking the nap had done her good, she rested her elbows on her knees and perched contentedly alone on the fence as the long Montana dusk began to fall. The air was warm and still, and when she looked around, she felt the first peace she had known in quite awhile.

"Hi," Gabe said softly, interrupting her thoughts. She had been so preoccupied that she hadn't heard him come out of the house, but when she turned, he was right behind her. "You want to sit out here by yourself a while longer, or would you like some company?"

"Is dinner ready?"

"It can wait."

"Then some company would be nice," she said. She had been sad for so long that it was a relief to feel like smiling again. With a deliberate drawl, she added, "Why don't you come up here on this fence rail and sit a spell?"

Gabe obeyed, reaching up and grasping the top rail, swinging one long leg over first and then the other. In the golden dusk, his tanned face looked bronzed, his eyes more indigo than blue. He nodded to the horse, who had stopped eating again and was watching them warily.

"Thinking about riding?" he asked with a smile.

"Not on your life," she said with a shudder. "I promised old Holler there I wouldn't get within ten feet of him unless it was to give him a carrot or two. He's got nothing to worry about from me, I guarantee it."

"You sound adamant."

"I am."

He smiled, his eyes sparkling in the fading light. "We'll see."

"We'll see ... what?"

"Well, you can't visit the Big Sky country without sitting a horse just once."

"Watch me."

He turned his head to stare deeply into her eyes. "And you can't properly be welcomed to the ranch without a kiss," he said, his voice suddenly husky.

"Oh, Gabe—" she started to say.

Concern darkened his eyes. "Too soon?" he asked.

She looked at him mutely, not knowing what to say, or even how she felt. But as she gazed into his eyes, she felt a need of a different kind rising in her, and she said softly, "For a moment, I felt guilty, as though I'd be betraying Fitz's memory." Her voice shook a little with emotion—and something else—as she went on. "But he wouldn't want that. More than anything, he wanted to celebrate life."

Gabe stared at her a moment longer. Then, wordlessly, he swung down off the fence. Reaching up, he lifted her off the rail as though she weighed no more than her cat. "Then let's celebrate," he said hoarsely, and carried her into the house.

Keeley didn't realize how tight a lid she'd kept on her emotions until Gabe took her into the bedroom. Dinner forgotten, he set her on her feet and closed the door. The moon had come up while they were outside, and a shaft of it entered the window and fell across his face. His eyes looked like they held the secrets of eternity.

"Are you sure?" he asked her softly.

In answer, she put her arms around his neck and drew his head down to hers. Until a few minutes ago, she hadn't even thought of making love to him; the strain of all she'd endured with Fitz had pushed everything else out of her mind. But when his lips touched hers, something sprang to life again inside her, and as their kiss deepened, and desire for him began to blossom and then demand release, she had never wanted him more. When they finally broke apart, they were both breathing hard. Then Gabe grabbed her again and pulled her body hard against his. She responded with such a fierce need that even he was surprised.

"Keeley—" he said.

"Don't talk," she said, reaching for the buttons on his shirt. She unbuttoned them quickly, ripping the tails out of his jeans, pulling his shirt off, throwing it to the floor. "Don't talk," she said again, tugging at his jeans. She was in a frenzy now; she wanted to mold his body to hers. Pulling him to the bed, she pushed him down and started undressing while he jerked off his boots. Naked, she stood before him. With burning eyes, she stared into his face. Her voice shook as she said, "I need you, Gabe. I need you like I've never needed you before."

He responded by pulling her down on top of him. What he gave her that night was more than she could have asked for, more than she'd ever dreamed. He took her, and she took him, and together they reached a place they'd never been. By the time they collapsed, exhausted, drenched in sweat, on top of the disheveled bed, they were still gasping for breath. Gabe felt like he'd been in a dream, but for Keeley, it had been a release of an intolerable tension she hadn't even known she was holding inside. She had never felt like this, drained and filled at the same time, and in that moment, she loved Gabe more than she could ever say. Pushing back wet tendrils of hair from her damp face, she turned to look at him.

"Thank you," she said hoarsely.

He was still breathing hard. In the moonlight, his broad chest heaved, and she could see the powerful muscles of his shoulders and arms as he pulled her into his side. "Any time," he panted. "Just let me catch my breath. . . ."

Keeley was up early the next morning, already fixing breakfast by the time Gabe staggered out. Dressed only in jeans, he gripped the doorjamb in pretended exhaustion. "Lord, woman," he said, "what did you do to me last night?"

Ruefully, she looked at the remains of the meal he'd cooked. "I think I ruined dinner."

He shook his head as if to clear it. "It was worth it, believe me."

Abandoning her place at the stove, where she'd been cooking an omelette, she went and put her arms around his trim waist. Looking up into his eyes, she said seriously, "Yes, it was. I don't know how to thank you, Gabe. I . . . I needed that more than I realized."

He turned serious, too. Putting his arms around her, he drew her close. "I'm glad I was here to oblige," he said, burying his nose in her hair. He breathed deeply, then sighed. "Why is it that you always smell so good?"

"Oh, you're just—" she started to say, and then gave a shriek when she smelled smoke. Turning, she saw the bacon burning and pulled away to run back to the stove. "Oh, rats!" she exclaimed, staring down at the pan when she'd taken it from the burner. "Look at this!"

"Tux will eat it," Gabe said, as the cat magically appeared, nose in the air. He wound himself sinuously through Gabe's legs before sauntering over to Keeley, where he looked up expectantly.

"Well, I see *you've* settled in," she said, gazing down at him. She looked at Gabe. "I told you, he'd fit in. He's very adaptable, you know. In fact, down at the beach—"

The words were out before she thought. Helplessly, she looked at Gabe, who came over and took the bacon pan out of her hand. "Go get dressed," he said softly, giving her a kiss. Then he grinned. "After breakfast, I've got a surprise."

"What kind of surprise?" she asked, immediately wary.

"You'll see."

She knew him pretty well by now. "I'm not going riding," she warned, seeing the look in his eyes.

"We'll see," he said.

"I'm not!"

"Okay, whatever you say," he agreed.

But right after breakfast, she found herself sitting astride a little bay mare named Jessie, who had seemed very dainty and pretty while standing still in the corral, but who instantly grew in size when Gabe told her this was the horse she was going to ride.

"I told you, I don't know how." she started to say.

Ignoring her shriek of protest, Billy took one side, and Gabe the other, and they literally picked her up and tossed her into the saddle. She saw a round thing in front of her and grabbed on to it for dear life.

"You're going to have to let go of the saddle horn sometime," Gabe said, swinging up easily onto his own mount. Holler was being left behind today; Gabe was riding a big black horse while Billy climbed aboard a brownish one with spots over its rump that Keeley knew from the Nez Percé movie was called an Appaloosa.

"Why?" she gasped. She was sure the little mare had grown a foot taller while she'd been sitting here, and after one quick glance, she refused to look down.

"Because you have to pick up the reins," Gabe told her.

"What reins?" She couldn't have let go of her death grip on the saddle horn to save her life at this point. Pleadingly she looked at him. "Won't she just follow you?"

Gabe laughed. "I doubt it. Unlike some women I know, horses like to be told what to do."

"Very funny," Keeley muttered, but she forgot her fear long enough to sit up. At that moment, the patient horse shifted its weight from one foot to the other. It was the slightest of movements, but to Keeley, it felt like an avalanche moving under her, and she grabbed quickly for the saddle horn again, crying, "I can't do it!"

"Yes, you can," Gabe insisted. Reaching over, he picked up her reins, pried one of her hands off the horn, and closed her fingers around the leather straps that led to the bridle. "Ready?"

"No!" she cried, panicked, but it was too late. The two men—she'd get them both for this, she thought direly, glaring at their backs—turned their mounts and started out, and she was left with the choice to stay or to follow. Her voice failing her, she shook the reins over the mare's neck and paled when the horse put her ears back.

"She hates me!" she cried.

Gabe looked over his shoulder. "She just doesn't know what you want her to do. Squeeze with your legs to move her forward and cluck to her a little."

"Cluck?"

"Like a chicken," he said helpfully.

Keeley didn't know if he was kidding her or not, but she knew she couldn't just sit here or she'd never live it down. Tentatively, remembering how easily Gabe had been thrown yesterday, she squeezed her legs as he'd told her, and made a tiny clucking sound with her tongue. To her amazement, the horse moved forward. She was so startled she nearly fell off.

"I did it!" she cried triumphantly, and promptly bit her tongue as the horse began to jog, trying to catch up.

Billy had chosen her mount well. As they rode sedately along, the men looking for the last of the range cattle left behind, Keeley concentrating on not falling off her horse, she began to relax despite herself. The mare was a good trail horse, carefully picking her way over fallen logs and branches in the trail, calmly going around moss-covered rocks and over the occasional shallow gully washed into the hillside from the rain. Once when a hawk took off right over their heads with a shrill shriek at being disturbed, Jessie only pricked her ears, not nearly as startled as her rider.

After a while, lulled by the desultory conversation of the men riding ahead, and by the gentle sway of the horse under her as they walked along, Keeley loosened her grip on the saddle horn and began to look around. Overhead, the sky was a brilliant blue as far as the eye could see, and she began to realize why this was called the Big Sky country. It was beautiful, with hills blue in the distance, and tall trees, pines and firs and hardwoods, moving gently in the warm breeze. Meadow after meadow stretched ahead, some dotted with cattle, others postcard pretty. Even the air had a different quality, and she was just breathing in deeply when she heard a tremendous bellow somewhere to the right. It startled her so badly she grabbed on to the saddle horn again.

"What is it?" she asked fearfully.

Unconsciously she had pulled tight on the reins, causing the obedient mare to stop. When Gabe saw her sitting there, he turned and came back. "It's nothing to be scared of—" he started to say, but another loud bellow came, making Keeley jump. Smiling, he assured her, "It's just two mountain bulls staking out territory. They're probably in one of those hills nearby, where sound carries."

With all the noise, they seemed to be right over the next rise. "Are they dangerous?" she asked with a gulp. At this moment, she much preferred New York's subways, where gangs had knives. At least she knew the danger there; here, she was completely out of her element.

"Only to themselves," Gabe answered. He nodded toward Billy, who had spurred his horse and was disappearing through the trees. "Don't worry, Billy's going to go check on it. We can stay right here if you like."

Keeley had no intention of moving an inch. But she could see by Gabe's expression that he wanted to be in on the action, so she swallowed and said bravely, "Go ahead. I'll be all right."

He was obviously torn. "Are you sure?"

"I'm positive," she said, forcing a stiff smile. She patted the mare's neck. "Jessie will take care of me."

"Well, all right. You just wait here, we'll be back in a minute."

He was gone before she could reply, spurring his horse after Billy. As he, too, disappeared into the trees ahead, she tried not to feel deserted. They aren't far away, she told herself. If she called, they'd come running. All she had to do was sit here and—

But just then, a bobcat, or a lynx, or—Keeley didn't know what it was, only that it was a wild, spotted cat—bounded out of the bushes to her left. It had obviously been disturbed by all the noise and had rushed out into the path before seeing the horse. Startled, it skidded to a stop right in front of Jessie, immediately bristling to twice its size, sharp teeth showing in a snarl.

Keeley didn't know what happened next. The wildcat appeared, and the horse stiffened. Keeley felt the mare's muscles go rigid, and she grabbed the saddle horn, dropping the reins in the process.

"Ga—!" she started to shout, but the spotted cat snarled again and swiped a paw through the air, right at Jessie's nose. Before

Keeley could finish her cry for help, the horse bolted, turning in one motion and leaping into a gallop, back the way they had come.

Before she knew it, they were going so fast she didn't have breath to yell. The wind flying past brought tears to her eyes, and she squinted, bending low over the saddle horn, trying not to panic. She had to think what to do, and cringed when she happened to glance down. The ground rushing by made her realize the folly of trying to jump off, but she couldn't just sit here; she could be killed.

"Jessie, Jessie, it's all right," she said over and over again. She didn't know if the mare heard her or not. Panicked by its own flight, the horse was running full out, leaping over the rocks it had gone around before, jumping over branches, flying across the ground. From somewhere at the back of her terrified mind, Keeley remembered the hill they had climbed when they'd left the ranch behind. It was coming up, and she squeezed her eyes shut. She had to stop Jessie before they reached the hill; if she allowed the mare to gallop down that steep incline, they'd fall for certain.

Forcing her eyes open, she looked down again. Gabe had tied her reins together so they weren't flying loose but hanging from a knot off the mare's neck. All she had to do was let go of the horn and grab the reins, she thought. Then she would have some control.

"Jessie's the best we have," Billy had assured her. "But if you get into trouble, all you have to do is circle her one way or the other. Just remember—circle, and you'll stop her."

She had no choice but to try. Praying the horse would respond if she got her hands on the reins, she made herself let go and reach for the flopping straps. Almost sobbing with relief, she grabbed the leather. It was now or never, she told herself and sat up, tugging at the same time with all her might, trying to pull the horse's head to her right.

For a few awful seconds, nothing happened. She's too strong for me! she thought desperately, and she knew they'd never make it. But she'd never given up on anything in her life, so she clenched her teeth and pulled harder.

"Come on, Jessie," she gasped. She couldn't think what she'd do if it didn't work. "Come on . . . come on . . ."

The miracle happened. Just as they came to the crest of the hill, Jessie started to turn to the right. She was still going fast, but at least they were heading away from the slope. Letting out a whoop, Keeley forgot she didn't know how to ride and brought the mare's head almost around to her knee. In such a constricted position, Jessie couldn't run full out; the mare began to slow from a full gallop to a canter and then finally to a trot. When Keeley finally pulled her to a halt, they were both drenched in sweat—but safe.

"Oh, Jessie!" she cried, flinging her arms around the mare's neck. "We made it!"

At that moment, Gabe and Billy came galloping up. Keeley had forgotten all about them, and she looked up in surprise as Gabe pulled his horse to a sliding stop right beside her. Blue sparks shot from his eyes, and he looked scared and angry at the same time.

"What the hell are you doing?" he demanded. "Don't you know you don't run a horse up here like that?"

"Oh, really?" She'd nearly been killed, and he was accusing her of stupidity? She forgot how afraid she'd been and became angry. "Well, ask the wildcat we met on the trail when you abandoned us! It took a swat at poor Jessie and scared her half to death!"

"Wildcat! You saw a mountain lion?"

"I don't know what it was! It was a spotted—"

"A bobcat," Billy said, with relief. "Heck, nothing that small would hurt you."

"No?" Still pumped up from her frightening experience, she looked at them indignantly. "Well, you could have fooled me!"

Too late, Gabe realized his mistake. "Keeley—"

Keeley's eyes flashed. "Don't you Keeley me! This is all your fault, Gabe Tyrell! If you hadn't wanted to play cowboy, I wouldn't have had to go through such a terrifying experience!"

"Aw, Keeley—" Billy tried to say.

She looked at him furiously. Right then, she hated all men. "And you! What do you mean, a bobcat wouldn't hurt me? What do you know? It was as big as a . . . as a lion!"

And with that, she whirled Jessie around and headed down the hill to the ranch. She kept her back straight and her pride intact, but long before she reached the barn, her entire body was one giant ache. Muscles she hadn't even known existed were screaming; even her teeth hurt. All she wanted to do was figure out a way to get off her horse without breaking something and go soak in a long, hot bath. She obviously wasn't meant to be a horsewoman, and as far as she was concerned, today she'd had enough riding to last a lifetime.

*   *   *

Gabe waited to apologize until she emerged from her bath. She'd hoped the hot water would absorb all her aches and pains, but they were still with her when she came out of the bathroom. He met her in the hallway and saw her limping.

"Are you hurt?"

She glared at him. She wasn't ready to forgive him yet, and she pushed him away when he tried to see what was wrong. "Just sore. Do you have any aspirin?"

"In the kitchen," he said, watching her worriedly. "But let me get it. Maybe you shouldn't be walking around. Maybe you broke something."

"Don't be silly," she said curtly, limping off. "I didn't fall, after all. I'm just not used to riding." She glared at him over her shoulder as he followed anxiously. "Not that kind, anyway. I never bargained for a wild gallop down the mountain."

"Keeley, I swear, if I'd dreamed . . ."

She still wasn't ready to absolve him. In the kitchen, she found the bottle of aspirin on the windowsill; as she shook two pills out into her palm, she glared at him again. "Why are you concerned *now*? You weren't so worried when it happened."

He looked at her disbelievingly. He opened his mouth to speak, forgot what he was going to say, and tried it again. "If I live to be a hundred, I'll never understand you, Keeley. How can you say I wasn't concerned?"

Filling a glass with water, she popped the aspirins into her mouth and washed them down. "You blamed me. You made it sound like the whole thing was my fault." She looked at him irately. "As if I *enjoyed* having my horse run away with me! I was terrified!"

"So was I! When I saw Jessie take off like that, my heart just . . . stopped. I thought I was going to lose you, and I—" He stopped, running his hands through his hair. "Damn it, Keeley. I love you. If something happened to you, I don't know what I'd do!"

Damn it, Keeley. I love you. Just like that, her anger vanished, and her voice softened. "Nothing's going to happen to me. You said you wouldn't let it, remember?"

"Oh, Keeley." With a groan, he put his arms around her and drew her to him.

She could feel his arms trembling. "It wasn't your fault, Gabe," she said, feeling a little tremulous herself. "It just . . . happened."

In answer, he buried his face in her hair. "I can't protect you from everything," he said painfully. "God knows I'd like to, but I just can't."

"You're not supposed to protect me from everything," she said. She held him tightly, breathing in deeply of his scent. She loved the way he smelled, clean and masculine, with just a hint of sweat. She looked up at him again, searching his face. "You just promised to be there when I needed you, and you always have been, Gabe. I don't know how you do it, but you do."

His arms tightened around her. "I wish—"

But she never knew what he wished, because she stopped him before he could say. Completely forgetting how sore she was, how every muscle in her body was protesting the wild ride that morning, she kissed him. His arms tightened around her, but now they were trembling with a different reason. Their kiss deepened, their tongues met, and when they finally broke apart, they looked at each other for a long moment; then they went upstairs.

Gabe didn't mention riding the next morning; Keeley was still asleep when he left the bed and returned some time later with a tray of coffee and hot breakfast rolls. When she smelled the coffee, she sat up with a smile.

"If this is the treatment I get, I think we should fight and make up every night," she said.

Grinning, he put the tray over her knees and then took his own cup and sat down on the side of the bed. Teasing, he asked, "Are you saying that last night wasn't reward enough in itself?"

She pretended to consider it while she buttered a hot roll. "Well, I'm not sure. Maybe we'll have to try it again and see."

His eyes gleamed. "You don't have to ask me twice!"

He was already dressed, but as he shucked off his jeans and reached to undo the buttons on his shirt, she smiled slyly into her coffee. "Maybe this isn't a good idea," she murmured. "What will Billy think?"

"Billy who?" he asked, sliding into bed beside her.

By the time they got back to it, breakfast was cold. It didn't matter; they ended up drinking cool coffee and munching hard breakfast rolls side by side in bed.

"I never thanked you," she said.

Smiling, he put his arms around her and brought her close. "Yes, you did."

"No, I mean for bringing me here. For doing everything

you've done." She paused. "For being you. It's just what I needed."

His expression tender, he touched her bare shoulder, enjoying the softness of her skin. "It's what I needed, too," he said quietly. "Keeley, I've been thinking—"

She drew back. "I'm not sure I like the sound of that."

"I'm serious," he insisted. Shuddering slightly, he said, "I keep thinking about what could have happened yesterday."

"Nothing happened, except that I was scared out of my wits."

"So was I. And that's just the point. It made me think about how much time we spend apart. When I realized I could have lost you, I wanted to . . . I don't know what I wanted to do."

"Gabe—"

"Hear me out, please," he said, looking into her eyes. "I don't need to be roaming all over the world, Keeley. I could find a job in New York—open a photography studio . . . something. It doesn't matter what right now. The point is, we could be together, and—"

"Oh, yes. But for how long?" she said gently. "Even if you had your own studio, you'd go stark, raving mad in a week. I know you, my darling. You need to be out where the action is, doing dangerous things, taking your pictures and making your films. If you tried to stay with me, you'd end up blaming me—"

"I'd never do that."

"Not consciously, no. But I think we both know it wouldn't work. We're too independent. We're too involved in our work." Reaching out, she touched his face, running her finger down his straight nose, over his wide, sensuous mouth, down his lean jaw. The scar from the tiger had almost disappeared; it was only a faint line disappearing into his throat. Bending over, she kissed him lightly. "I love our time together, Gabe. I cherish it. But we both have to be free to do what we do. Otherwise . . ."

He reached for her. "I don't want to lose you, Keeley."

"You won't lose me," she said, taking his hands and holding tightly. "How could you? You're part of me, Gabe. You always will be. You're with me every minute, every second, every day of my life, even when we're not together physically. But what we are is—what we do. You have a gift, my love, the gift of making people see what you want them to. I won't be responsible, even indirectly, for making you give it up. It's too much a part of what I cherish about you, too."

His bleak expression told her he knew she was right. Swallowing, he said, "So, what are we going to do?"

"We're going to go on like this, as long as it lasts," she answered, holding his eyes. "And if I have anything to say about it, forever won't be too long for me."

Again he put his arms around her and drew her close. "Oh, Keeley," he sighed. "I'm not sure this is the answer."

"I'm not either. But for now, it will have to do."

Gabe didn't realize it, but in the days following their talk, he seemed relieved. Keeley felt relieved, too. She loved Gabe with all her heart, and she knew he loved her, too. But she also knew theirs wasn't a conventional relationship, and that to try to make it one would destroy the close bond they shared.

She'd thought once that she could tell him anything, and he'd understand, but as time went by, she couldn't talk about her music, and, wisely, he didn't ask. She wanted to tell him it hadn't come back, but every time she tried, her throat closed. She just couldn't make herself say aloud that the music she had always heard, the melodies that had always been so much a part of her, were silent now. To distract herself, she talked Gabe into taking her sightseeing. She'd heard from Billy about Montana's history, and she wanted to explore.

As he was with her that entire summer, Gabe was indulgent. "I didn't think of you as the sightseeing type, but what would you like to see?" he asked immediately.

She had already made her plans. "Yellowstone," she said promptly. "And maybe, if we have time, Glacier National Park."

"Well, that's ambitious. Anything else, madame?"

"You won't laugh?"

Dramatically he crossed his heart. "I promise."

"All right, then," she said, "I'd like to learn to fish."

He broke his promise by bursting into delighted laughter, but she didn't mind. She had diverted him from the dangerous subject of her music—or so she thought. Yellowstone and Glacier Park were too far away for casual day trips, but the next morning they set out for another national monument, twelve miles from Hardin, in the southeast part of the state.

"Where are we going?" she asked, as they emerged from the verdant ranch land into an area that could only be described as bleak. For miles around, the only thing to be seen was flat, featureless prairie, so stark it made her eyes hurt.

"You'll see," Gabe said mysteriously.

He took her to the Valley of the Little Bighorn, where General

George Armstrong Custer and over two hundred of his men had been wiped out by the Sioux and the Cheyenne.

"I thought you might like to see it because of the other film you worked on," Gabe explained, as he parked the car.

Keeley didn't want to think about scoring that film. *I Will Fight No More Forever*, Raleigh's epic story of the last battle of Chief Joseph and the Nez Percé Indians, had won all sorts of awards, not only for hers and Fitz's best score. What should have been a fond, proud memory was still too painful yet, and she couldn't think of it without thinking of Fitz.

As they walked up the path toward the fenced monument, Keeley couldn't describe her feelings. For miles around the only thing to be seen was the open prairie. Only a few other people were there, wandering around the visitor center and the museum, and as she stood on top of the small rise and listened to the absolute stillness and quiet, she tried to picture in her mind the furious conflict that had raged here. Just for a moment, she could almost hear on the wind the war cries of Crazy Horse, and Gall, and Two Moons, as they led their tribes into battle, but as it had been since Fitz died, the music was silent.

She was silent on the way home, feeling lost and alone even though Gabe was so near. He glanced at her several times as he drove, obviously debating whether to break in on her thoughts, finally deciding that she looked so unhappy he had to ask.

"The monument," he said carefully. "It's quite a place, isn't it?"

She felt tears stinging again and quickly looked out the side window. "Yes, it is," she agreed painfully. "I can't imagine sometimes what drives men to destroy one another."

Gabe was silent another moment. "Is that what's wrong? The place affected you so deeply—or is it something else?"

As always, he knew—or had guessed—too much. When she turned to him, the tears that had been threatening were starting to spill over. "I thought . . ." she started to say, and had to stop. Trying to control the desolate wail that rose up inside her, she swallowed and tried again. "I thought that if any place could make me hear the music, it would be there, but it didn't happen. Oh, Gabe, I didn't hear anything. What am I going to do?"

Reaching out with one arm, he drew her close. Holding her tightly, he said, "You're too tough on yourself, Keeley. As I said before, you've been through a painful experience. You're just going to have to give it time."

"Time!" she cried. "How much?"

Smiling sadly, he kissed the top of her head as she huddled against him. "However much it takes."

It took all summer, and then some. They didn't speak of it again, but she knew Gabe was aware the music was still lost to her, for the piano he'd had delivered before they got there remained untouched. Thoughtful as always, understanding too much and far more than she wanted him to at times, he kept her busy. She learned how to fish, grimacing as she baited the hook for the first time, watching in horror as the worm squirmed, using bread or hamburger afterward, even though Billy and Gabe told her she wouldn't catch anything. She proved them both wrong but threw everything back that she caught, unable to watch the poor fish suffer, gasping for air on the creek bank. After she saw Billy gutting and cleaning the trout he'd hooked, she gave up fishing altogether and looked at the men so sadly that they didn't go out again either.

She and Gabe explored a beaver dam close by, carefully working their way in through the tangled branches the beavers had woven, until they were only a few feet from the mound in the center of the pooled creek. They sat uncomfortably on a log for hours, hoping to spot one of the elusive creatures, and Keeley was so excited when one finally popped its head up, saw them, and slapped its flat tail on the water to warn the others before it disappeared, that she almost fell into the water. Sunburned, mosquito-bitten, they returned to the ranch and Billy's look of amusement, but Keeley was happy—and proud.

"So that's how you get all those beautiful pictures," she said admiringly to Gabe at dinner. "You just wait and wait until something happens, and then—*voila*! There's the shot!"

"Not quite, but close," he said, smiling. "It's like the service—a lot of hurry up and wait. All it takes is patience."

There was more to it than that, of course, and Keeley was aware of it. She never objected when he excused himself after dinner to work in his studio for a couple of hours, and because he never told her what he was working on, she didn't ask. She respected his privacy, as he did hers. As summer progressed, every time he went to work in the darkroom, Keeley glanced at the piano. The halcyon days were coming to an end, and she hadn't even touched it.

When? she wondered painfully. When would this awful silence end?

She had no answer, but she knew she had to make some kind

of decision soon. Despite the laughter she shared with Gabe, the fun they had, the lovemaking they enjoyed, she felt some vital segment of her was missing, as though part of her spirit had died. And as summer headed inexorably toward autumn and her music still remained lost to her, she began to believe she'd never hear it again. If she didn't, she wondered, how would she exist? Gabe had his work; Billy had his. But she . . . she had nothing inside; it was as if her soul was dead.

It was September, and a new crispness had just begun to creep into the air. The summer was over, and soon the leaves would turn. Gabe had been putting off leaving for his new assignment, but the foundation was pressing him for a departure date, and finally he couldn't avoid it any longer. He was going to Belize, in Central America, to do a series on an endangered monkey. After that, it would be somewhere else, and somewhere else. . . .

"I'm sorry, Keeley," he said again the morning he was leaving. "If I could delay, I would."

"You've already delayed far too long for my sake," she said, smiling bravely. "Now, stop worrying. You have work to do, and I'm grateful we've had this time together. It's been wonderful."

He took her in his arms, staring down at her with worry in his eyes. "Stay as long as you like," he said, repeating what he had told her several times already. "Billy will be here to get you whatever you need."

She didn't tell him that Billy—nor anyone else—could ever get her what she needed, but she nodded anyway. "I know, and I'd like to stay," she said. "But I've got work to do, too, you know. As much as I want to, I can't linger, either." She went on quickly, before he could ask her. "But I'll never forget this time, Gabe. You've been wonderful, and so has Billy." Despite herself, she could feel tears pressing against her eyelids, and she ended hastily, with a poor attempt at jocularity, "Maybe we can do it again someday."

He looked as bleak as she felt. "Promise me something."

Looking up into his face, aching at how handsome he was and how much she loved him, she asked, "What? You know I'll promise you anything."

Holding her tightly, he said, "No matter where we are, or what we're doing, we'll meet here, a year from today. Promise?"

She couldn't imagine anything longer than a year, she who once had believed twelve months wasn't long enough for what she wanted to do in a particular show. But she didn't hesitate. Softly, she said, "I promise."

"You won't forget?"

"No," she said, holding his eyes, "I won't forget."

He kissed her then, long and hard, breaking away at last as though if he stayed longer, he wouldn't be able to leave. As he climbed into the truck, Billy driving, he called out, "I left you something in the studio."

She was waving from the porch. "What?"

"You'll see," he said, and, with a final wave, disappeared in the Montana dust.

She found the reel of tape on the projector. For a long moment she just stared at it, wondering if she had the courage to play it now. She had never felt so lonely and alone; the moment the truck had disappeared around the curve of the road, silence had descended on her. With the sound of the engine fading away, the meadows surrounding the ranch screamed with the quiet, the trees seemed to vibrate with it. She couldn't even hear the wind.

She looked at the reel again. When Gabe had spent so much time working in the studio this summer, she'd thought he was working on something for the foundation. Now it seemed he had been doing something for her.

"Oh, Gabe," she whispered. "What have you done?"

Before she could think about it, she switched off the lights and turned on the projector. Instantly, even without sound, there sprang to life on the wall screen a scene of such incredible beauty that Keeley felt her heart constrict. It was Africa, and the shimmering grasses of the savannah seemed to stretch into infinity, snow-capped Kilimanjaro rising majestically in the blue-shrouded distance, clouds massing overhead like huge balls of mousse. The picture was so stunning that Keeley fumbled for a chair without taking her eyes off the screen. Transfixed, she sank down as a cheetah appeared at the top of the frame—but a cheetah the likes of which had never been captured before on film. It was running, stretching its long limbs in ecstatic flight, a creature so sure of its power and majesty that it seemed to emit its own light. Dead on, the camera followed the cat's awesome trajectory as it leapt into the air and came down again in another frame—

As a tiger stalking the jungles of India. The transition was so smooth, so unexpected that Keeley drew in a quick breath. She'd never seen such a magnificent beast, and for the barest instant, she thought she heard a cymbal clash. Then the noise was

gone with the movement of the tiger as it glided through a glade
of bamboo. Born of strength and power, every muscle rippled,
and the tiger's coat looked so luxurious she wanted to reach out
and touch it. As though it sensed her desire, the big cat stopped
suddenly and turned toward her. It seemed so close that the
white tips of its ears stood out in sharp contrast to the green behind it. Then with a silent roar that made Keeley's hair stand on
end, even though there had been no sound, the tiger turned and
vanished into the bushes just as—

A snow leopard appeared, filling the screen with a defiant
snarl. It was so close to the lens that Keeley could see the sharp
points of the cat's incisors and the icy green of its eyes as it
drew back its ears. Silvery sparkles of ice crystals dotted the
cat's glorious coat; they shimmered in the camera flash like a
million diamonds as it moved, wraithlike, through the night. The
effect was eerily beautiful, and once again, Keeley heard, for the
merest instant, a few delicate notes from a woodwind, like a
chime in her mind. Then, too soon for such a glorious creature,
the cat passed out of sight and became—

Polar bears lumbering majestically out on the ice packs—

A jaguar hunting with intense concentration through the rain
forest—

A herd of antelope bounding like sprites across the plain—

A flock of brilliant pink flamingoes taking flight from a lake.

There was more, too many images to absorb at once. Keeley
watched, transfixed, until the last few frames when the white
Arctic wolves filled the screen. On the hunt, at play, howling to
the sky, the last of these magnificent animals called to something
primal inside her every time one threw back its head and emitted
its ghostly, silent cry.

The whole film was so beautiful Keeley was overcome. The
only thing it needed—and she wasn't sure it needed even that—
was a score to make it leap even more to vibrant, vivid life.

Without thinking, she knew the instruments that would follow
the cheetah's wild, exuberant flight; she knew the sounds that
would accompany the tiger on his hunt, and the snow leopard
padding its way through the night. And suddenly, it all burst to
life inside her, the music that had been silent so long. She heard
it all, the violins, the brass, the piano, the harp, the drums.

"Oh, Gabe, thank you, thank you," she murmured brokenly,
watching the film again and again. Her eyes shining, she
reached for a piece of paper and slashed four lines in pairs
across it until she'd filled the page. Her hand couldn't move fast

enough; it was as though floodgates long closed had suddenly opened, and she could hear the music bursting forth, demanding release. With the beautiful images Gabe had created for her dancing on the screen, she bent over the paper. Her face alight, she began composing the music for his film.

---&---

CHAPTER TWENTY-FIVE

Keeley wrote through the night. She didn't hear Billy return with the truck after taking Gabe to the airport; she didn't see him when he came in to tell her he was back. She didn't notice when he crept out again with a smile on his face, or realize what time it was until she looked up and saw that dawn had come.

Exhausted, she glanced at the sheet music scattered around. Pages were everywhere, covered with hastily written notes and sidebars about arrangements. At some point she had carried the projector out to the living room where the piano was, but she'd been in such a frenzy to get it all down that she hadn't bothered to bring the screen in with it. Jerking a picture down, she had used the wall for projection instead. After being silent for so long, the music was filling her, demanding release. It surged upward, spilling out, creating itself. She couldn't stop for an instant; she was driven to complete what she had started.

She didn't discover until she shoved the piano into a better position that Gabe had thought of everything. Tucked behind the instrument was an expensive synthesizer, the kind of thing she had once scorned. When she found it, she exclaimed with delight. Once she programmed it to provide orchestral background, it was just what she needed to finish the work. With the equipment, she would record the full sound she heard in her mind, more than the piano itself could provide.

With the score already complete in her mind, she sat down and didn't look up until she was finished. When she was finally able to play the music back in conjunction with the film for the last time, the thrill went all the way to her bones. She knew without doubt that it was the best thing she had ever written.

She was too jubilant to sleep, even though she hadn't slept—or eaten, she realized—since the previous morning. Elated at what she had done, she didn't want to wait for coffee to perk; needing to be outside, she made a quick cup of instant and went out to the porch. She had never felt so tired, or so satisfied, or so content with her soul, and she wanted to share it with the morning.

Dawn was just breaking over the hills when she came out of the house. The rising sun gold plated the tops of the trees, driving away the last of the mauve and magenta clouds. As she stood there, breathing in the sweet morning air with its tang of autumn, the last of the night gave way to day. In those few precious moments the magic light that photographers treasured suffused everything with a golden glow, and she breathed in deeply and sent a silent thanks to Gabe.

To her right, a songbird awoke and trilled into the morning hush; down in the corral, she could see the paint horse looking at her, and she smiled at the sight. Gabe had worked all summer, but Holler was still half-wild, and he and Billy doubted the horse would ever be tamed. She almost hoped not; with his wild spirit and vivid coat and startling blue eye, she thought he was beautiful just the way he was.

"It's the eye," Billy had said solemnly. "You see the white circle around it? It means that this horse is a Medicine Hat stallion, with powerful medicine."

Keeley took Billy at his word, but Gabe had laughed. "I thought Medicine Hat stallions had *brown* circles around one eye, not white," he'd said.

Billy gave him a disdainful look. "Those are the *good* medicine stallions," he answered, glancing around carefully, as though the horse might overhear and cast a dire spell. Solemnly, he added, "The ones with the white circles are bad medicine."

Nostalgically, Gabe had rubbed his backside. "Yes, I remember."

Smiling again at the memory, Keeley went down the front steps and around to the corral. She'd made friends with the horse over the long summer, and he came up to her as she leaned against the rail.

"Sorry, fella," she said, scratching behind his ears as he butted her shoulder. "I was so excited I forgot your carrot. I'll bring it out later."

The horse snuffled as though he understood—or more likely, was disappointed—then he moved off, searching for a wisp of hay he might have missed from dinner. Left alone, Keeley stretched her tight muscles and looked around appreciatively. She loved it here; it had been the perfect medicine, exactly what she had needed after Fitz died. Now that she'd had a summer of healing, she could even think of Fitz now and smile. Not too much, but a little, and that was progress she couldn't have foreseen three months earlier.

He would have loved it here, she started to think, and then laughed to herself. It wasn't true, she realized; she was romanticizing it because she so loved the place. City boy to the last, Fitz would have hated it. But he would have loved the music she'd just written; that she knew with certainty. She just wished he were here to listen to it.

When Billy emerged from his little house down by the creek a few minutes later, she was still standing by the corral, absently watching Holler pace while he waited for his breakfast. Yawning, Billy brushed back his thick black hair, put on his hat, and came up to greet her.

"Hi," he said.

"Hi, yourself," she answered. "When did you get back? I didn't hear you come in."

"I'm not surprised. You looked like you were pretty busy when I got home from the airport, so I left you alone."

She had been obsessed, she knew. "I'm sorry, Billy. I . . . you've just never seen me work, I guess."

"It was quite a sight, I grant you that. Can I ask what you were doing?"

"I was—" she started to say, and then looked at him. "It's better if I show you. Do you have time?"

"Now that the boss has gone again, I've got all the time in the world."

"Then come on," she said eagerly. "I'll fix you breakfast, and you can tell me what you think."

But for once even Billy's prodigious appetite vanished when they went inside and she fixed the projector and the recorder to run at the same time. When her music rose in triumph like a burst of sunrise over Gabe's first shot of the Serengeti, Billy looked stunned. Fumbling for a chair, he sat down, instantly entranced. He didn't move, or look away, or even appear to breathe, until the film was over. Then, his expression dazzled, he looked at Keeley.

"It was—" he started to say, and stopped. He shook his head in wonder. "That was the most beautiful thing I've ever seen.

Those shots of the animals, and the music!" He looked at her in awe. "Is *that* what you do?"

Keeley laughed in relief at his reaction. "It's what I do," she said. "And that's what Gabe does," she added with a grin. "We make a pretty good team, don't you think?"

Billy still looked amazed. "I'll say." He got to his feet and started out.

"Don't you want breakfast?"

He looked at her blankly, his mind obviously still on what he had just experienced. "Breakfast? Uh . . . no thanks, I'm not hungry. I think I'll go out and feed the stock . . . or something."

Keeley had never known him to turn down food, even if he'd just eaten. "Are you all right?"

At the door, he turned to look at her again. "You have been here all summer, and yet I've never even heard you play the piano."

She hesitated. But he was a friend, so she said, "I lost my music for a while, Billy. Last night I got it back again."

He looked at her a moment longer. "I'm glad."

"So am I, Billy," she said fervently. "So am I."

Still he hesitated. "You'll go now, won't you?"

She hadn't consciously thought about it yet, but she knew it was time. "I think so, yes," she said, hearing as she said it the music for *Beauty and the Beast* rising at the back of her mind. Now that the barrier had fallen, it was demanding a voice she had denied it too long. "As wonderful as it's been here, it's time for me to get back to work."

"I'm going to miss you."

She smiled fondly. "I'm going to miss you, too."

For the second time in a week, Billy made the trip to the airport at Billings, this time with Keeley in tow. She had always hated good-byes, and she insisted he leave long before her flight was called.

"Just in case Gabe comes back sooner than expected," she said to Billy before he reluctantly departed, "tell him I left something for him in the recorder."

Billy's dark eyes lit up. "The music?"

Smiling, she nodded. "The music."

Then she kissed him good-bye and pushed him toward the door. She was feeling teary enough; she didn't want him to see her cry.

*   *   *

Now that she had chosen to go back, she couldn't get there fast enough. Deciding that whatever she had left behind in Los Angeles could either stay or be sent for later, she and Tux flew directly to New York. The music for *Beauty*, so long dormant, had sprung to vivid life inside her again, and she wrote during the flight, barely taking time out to gulp down coffee and toast for breakfast before getting back to work.

Keeley didn't watch much television, but she'd heard there was a series called "Beauty and the Beast." Apparently it had inspired quite a following, but as she'd planned the Broadway show, she was aware that if television fans came to the musical expecting their version brought to life, they'd be disappointed.

Keeley's *Beauty and the Beast* was taken from Madame Leprince de Beaumont's original fairy tale. It was the story of a merchant, who, having lost all the ships carrying his wealth, stumbles upon an enchanted castle during a storm. There, he meets a fierce Beast who demands his life as payment for a rose he plucks to give to his daughter, Beauty. When the merchant pleads with him, the Beast relents, saying he will accept the merchant's daughter if she will take her father's place.

Beauty, who loves her father, honors the debt. Even though she is horrified at first by the Beast's terrible countenance, she eventually comes to be fond of him for his kindness. When he asks her to marry him, she gently refuses, saying she can't marry someone she doesn't love. Then, one day, she learns that her father is ill, and she asks Beast to release her from her obligation long enough to go home for a while. The Beast consents, extracting her promise to return in three weeks because he can't live without her. Beauty stays longer than she intended, until one night she has a terrible dream about the Beast. Remembering her promise to return in three weeks, she rushes back to the palace to find him dying. Guilt-stricken, realizing that she does love him, she agrees to become his wife. As soon as she accepts his proposal, the Beast changes into a handsome prince. Released from his enchantment because of her promise to marry him, they live happily ever after.

As Keeley wrote out the story, she could hear the music again rising inside her. And, as the music came forward, she knew—as she had always known—that the only singer who could bring Beauty to life was someone who wasn't speaking to her. Valeska had the delicate, haunting quality this Beauty required; Val had the right range and color and timbre to sing it as she intended it to be written. Val *was* Beauty, and she . . .

With a sigh, Keeley threw down her pen. After checking on Tux, who had finally gone to sleep after yowling indignantly for almost an hour, she looked out the plane's small oval window. She hadn't spoken to Valeska since she'd left New York; they were so out of touch that she wasn't sure she knew Val's address any longer. The several calls she had made these past three years remained unanswered; it seemed clear that her old friend didn't want anything to do with her, and yet ... and yet ...

She remembered the last time she had called. To her displeasure, Nigel had answered. When she heard his voice, she almost hung up, but she was determined to talk to Val.

"She doesn't want to speak to you, Keeley," he'd said coldly, after she had identified herself.

"If it's true, she can tell me herself," she said. "Now, put her on, please."

"No. You're hearing it from me, and I'm her husband."

"But not her keeper," she'd retorted sharply. "Let's stop dancing around, Nigel, all right? I don't like you and you don't like me, but it has nothing to do with Val. If you don't put her on the phone, I'll—"

"You'll what? Do you really think you can threaten, Keeley? You might be big stuff in California, but you're a has-been ... excuse me, *never was* ... in this town. As far as we're concerned here, you've gone Hollywood. No, you won't find any sympathy here."

"That's baloney and you know it, Nigel," she'd said angrily. "You've been seeing too many spy movies."

To her annoyance, he had picked up on the reference immediately. "You should know, my dear. I was just reading in the trades about your relationship with Noel Harrington, of Jason Cross fame. It seems you're the one who's been seeing too many spies."

"Even if it's true, it's none of your business," she retorted, trying to hold on to her temper. "Now, will you call Val to the phone?"

"No," he said, to her fury. "I don't want her upset. You upset her, Keeley, so don't call again. Good-bye."

He had hung up on her. Seething, she had replaced her own phone. But despite his warnings, she had tried again, only to learn that he had changed to an unlisted number. Undaunted, and determined to get through to Valeska somehow, she had written a letter. It had been returned to her. She had written another. There had been no reply. Then Fitz took a turn for the worst, and she had forgotten all about Valeska. Gazing unseeingly out the plane window as the jet sped toward New York, Keeley thought of it and frowned. Had Nigel been speaking for Val? What would she do if Valeska wouldn't sing for her?

Aren't you getting a little ahead of yourself? she wondered. *What will you do if you can't even get the backing for the show?*

She shifted position. She'd put off thinking of her financial state, but she had to deal with it sometime, especially now that she was going to try to bring *Beauty* to Broadway. Even after setting up a trust fund for Jewell, she still had quite a bit left over from the sale of the house; it would be enough to get her started, but not nearly sufficient to take her to opening. Even so, she didn't begrudge the money she'd set aside for her younger half sister; since her father wouldn't allow Jewell to live with her, it was the least she could do to help out.

"I'm sorry, Keeley," Jewell had wept before the family pulled up stakes again and went back to Detroit. "I wanted to stay with you, I did, but Dad just won't let me."

She'd tried her best to comfort Jewell when she'd felt like crying herself. "Maybe someday," she said. "In the meantime, I've started a trust for your college education."

Jewell had been overwhelmed. The sight of her face lighting up with hope had been all the thanks Keeley needed, and when Jewell threw her arms around her, they hugged fiercely.

"I won't let you down, Keeley," Jewell said tearfully.

"You never have," Keeley told her. "And don't worry. I've set up the trust so that no one but you will get it." Briefly, she held Jewell away from her so she could look directly into her eyes. "Don't let them talk you out of it, honey," she said. "You're the only one who has ever said she wanted to go to college, and the money is yours, no matter what they say—promise?"

Tearful again, Jewell nodded. "I promise," she said, then her face crumpled again. "But you're wrong about one thing, Keeley."

"What?"

"I'm not the only one who ever wanted to go to college. You did, too, remember?"

Keeley remembered all too well. The local college at night had been a poor substitution for Juilliard, but she had always known that. Forcing a smile, she said, "Yes, well, now you're going to have to go for the both of us."

"Oh, I will, I will!" Jewell had looked like a dream had come true before her face had clouded over again. "But Keeley, what about you? What will you do?"

"I don't know," she's said, thinking at the time of Fitz, who was dying of AIDS. "Right now, I'm taking it one day at a time."

And now? she wondered, as the plane droned on, taking her back home. What was she going to do now? She had scoffed at Nigel when he'd said she wouldn't be welcome on Broadway if she tried to return, but suddenly she wondered if he was right.

"Don't borrow trouble," she muttered to herself. She would find financing; she would get backers for the show. After paying off her debts and setting up Jewell's trust and taking the long leave of absence without pay from the studio—at her insistence, not Raleigh's—things might be a little tight for her financially, but she wasn't entirely without connections, and if she really needed him, she could always swallow her pride and ask Raleigh for his help. If he didn't want to invest, he knew people who might. It would all get resolved somehow, and she wasn't going to worry about it. Right now her priority was getting Valeska to sing. Once she did that, everything would fall into place. She hoped.

Keeley was so shocked by Valeska's appearance that she almost didn't recognize her. As long as they'd known each other, Val had been fastidious; baths or showers twice a day, her long blond hair kept clean and shining. She had always looked younger than she was; with her childlike innocence and wide blue eyes, Keeley had thought Valeska could have continued playing ingenue roles for years.

But the woman who opened the door at Keeley's increasingly insistent knocking was no ingenue, and what innocence she had once possessed had vanished. As they stared at each other in mutually surprised silence for a moment, Keeley knew her face registered her shock and couldn't help it. For a few seconds, she actually thought she'd made a mistake. The woman leaning drunkenly against the door frame, wearing a soiled silk wrapper over a long, torn nightgown with a dirty hem, couldn't be Valeska. With her bloodshot eyes and tangled, dirty hair and slack mouth, this woman bore no resemblance to the friend Keeley had known and loved.

"I'm sorry," she started to say. "I must have the wrong ap—"

"Well, Keeley," Valeska slurred. "Fancy you showing up. What are you doing here?"

Now that she was here, she couldn't go back. Wondering

what could have happened, she tried to control her expression. "I came to see you, Val."

"What for? Oh, I know. You came back to gloat after all these years, right?"

Keeley became aware that she was still standing in the hallway. Deciding she'd rather the neighbors didn't hear, she didn't answer, but said, "I've come a long way, Val. Do you mind if I come in? Or is Nigel here?"

Hardly able to keep her balance, Valeska had pushed herself away from the door frame, intending to . . . Keeley didn't know what. Open the door wider so she could come in, or get out of the way so she could slam it in her face? When she asked about Nigel, Valeska's puffy, distorted face suddenly crumpled.

"Nigel isn't here," she said pitifully. "If you want to know the truth, he hasn't been for some time." She sniffed, passing a finger under her nose in lieu of a tissue. "He left me."

Leaving Keeley standing there, she turned and staggered away. The apartment had an entry that extended to hallways on either side, opening onto a living room with a view of Central Park. She headed directly toward the window, where a smudged crystal decanter sat precariously atop some magazines on a table. Misjudging the distance the first time she reached for the decanter, she almost knocked it off the table. Involuntarily, Keeley started to lunge forward to catch it.

"I can get it," Valeska said peevishly, trying again. She was more successful on the second attempt, grabbing the decanter by its neck and sloshing whatever it contained into an equally smudged and dirty-fingerprinted glass beside it. Raising the glass in a mocking toast, she turned and saluted Keeley.

"Here's looking at you," she said. It sounded like "heerz lukin atchu."

"Don't you think you've had enough?" Keeley asked. She didn't know whether to reach out and try to steady Val or not; she was swaying on her feet and looked ready to fall down any second.

"Let me tell you something, Keeley," Val said owlishly. "There isn't enough booze in the *world* to fill me up. So there."

She raised the glass again to drink, but Keeley shut the door, set Tux carefully on the floor in his carrier, and crossed the living room. Grabbing Valeska's hand, she looked into her bloated face. "What's happened to you, Val? You never used to—"

Anger flared in Valeska's reddened eyes. "Let go!"

"No. You don't need any more to drink!"

"How do you know what I need?" Valeska cried, trying to take the glass back. Keeley wouldn't release her grip and they struggled for a moment, the vodka that had been inside sloshing out and spilling over their hands.

"Now look what you've done!" Valeska wailed, when she realized they'd spilled it all. She looked down at the decanter. "All right, if that's the way you want to be, I'll just drink it straight!"

She made another grab for the decanter, but this time Keeley got there first. "No!" she said, snatching it up and holding it out of Val's reach. "I said you don't need any more!"

"And *I* said you don't know *what* I need! Goddamn it, Keeley, give it to me!"

"No!"

"Well, fine!" Valeska cried, whirling away. She almost lost her balance again and stumbled against the edge of the couch. Before Keeley could reach out to help her, she dragged herself up and headed toward a cabinet not far away. "You can't stop me, Keeley! If I want a drink, I'm going to have one."

"Oh, no, you're not!" Keeley said determinedly. Setting down the decanter, she went after Val.

Valeska screeched when Keeley grabbed her by her belt and tugged her back. Whirling around, she curled her fingers, obviously intending to attack. Keeley was so shocked she lost her advantage and stepped back, causing Valeska to lose her balance. They crashed to the floor, Valeska screaming her head off.

"Stop it, stop it!" Keeley commanded, trying to get free. "People will think someone's being murdered."

"I want a drink!"

"No!"

Valeska hurled herself at Keeley again, but because of her drunken state, her aim was off, and she crashed against the back of the couch. Keeley was able to scramble up, and before Valeska could launch another attack, she reached down and hauled her to her feet.

"Where's the bathroom?" she demanded, holding Valeska from the back with her arms pinned to her sides.

Valeska had started to struggle but was thrown off by the question. "What?" she said blearily. "The bathroom? Why?"

"Because you're going to take a cold shower and sober up," Keeley said firmly, beginning to drag her toward the doorway. "Now which way is it?"

"I'm not—"

"Oh, yes, you are," Keeley said. Looking right and left, she started down the hallway on the right because it was closer.

Valeska started to shriek again. "What are you . . . You can't do this! You're a monster! Let me go! Let me go!"

"Not on your life," Keeley panted, trying to wrestle the struggling Valeska down the hallway.

Valeska's howls increased in volume; she tried flailing with her arms and succeeded in getting one free. "Get out! You can't come in here and—Wait a minute! What are you doing? You can't—"

Keeley had found the bathroom. Shoving the door all the way open with her shoulder, she hauled Valeska in and held her with one hand while she reached in for the tap. Grabbing the one marked COLD, she pushed it hard all the way to the right. Instantly a stream of icy water poured out of the shower head. When Valeska realized what she was doing, she screamed.

"I'm not! You can't! Aieeeee!"

Valeska's last cry ended in a shocked wail as Keeley, realizing she could never get the knot on Valeska's robe untied, or her nightgown off without a struggle she might lose, decided to toss Valeska into the shower fully dressed.

"I hate you, I hate you!" Valeska cried, trying to cover her head and climb out of the shower at the same time.

"I know," Keeley said, holding her in. "But you'll thank me when you're sober again."

"I'll never thank you!" Valeska shouted. "Never, never, never, not in a million years. I'll hate you to the end of my life!"

Despite Keeley's firm hold on her, she kept trying to climb out, but the shower floor quickly became slippery, and she was wearing a long gown that tangled around her feet. In seconds, she was a sodden mess, unable even to see, much less to fight Keeley off. Sobbing piteously, she subsided and sat down, resting her head on her drawn-up knees as the icy water beat relentlessly on her.

Keeley didn't turn off the water until she saw Valeska start to shiver. By that time, she was a little damp herself. Because of their struggles, the bathroom floor looked like a lake; there was water all over everything, including the few towels she saw flung carelessly about. The place looked as if it hadn't been cleaned in a month. Her nose wrinkling, she asked where she could find some dry towels.

"I don't have any," Valeska muttered, huddling on the floor, her arms over her head.

"You must," Keeley said firmly. "And you have to get dried off, or you'll catch a cold."

"I don't care!" Valeska cried. "I just want to die."

"Well, you're not going to do it while I'm here," Keeley said pitilessly. "If I have to, I'll cut those wet things off you and wrap you in a blanket. It's your choice."

Valeska lifted her head. Her hair was a sodden mess around her face and shoulders, and she looked like an old crone. "I hate you."

Keeley looked at her uncompromisingly. "At the moment, I hate you, too. Now, where are the damn towels?"

Valeska looked as if she wanted to say something else. But she knew how relentless Keeley could be, and she closed her eyes. "All right, damn it," she muttered. "I suppose there might be some dry towels in that cabinet out there." Opening her eyes again, she glared up at Keeley. "Would you *mind* if I took a *hot* shower now?"

"Not at all," Keeley said briskly. "In fact, it might do you some good."

She went out, found a lone towel stuffed in the back of a cupboard, and brought it back in. "I'm going to make some coffee. Strong. Where's the kitchen?"

Valeska stood up, dripping cold water, beginning to shiver despite her anger. "Find it yourself," she said, pushing Keeley out of the bathroom before she slammed the door.

Keeley was on her second cup of coffee by the time Valeska sullenly joined her. Val had washed her hair but hadn't done anything else with it; the long, blond strands hung down her back, still wet. But she had a towel over her shoulders, and although she hadn't bothered to get dressed, she was wearing a warm-looking terry-cloth robe.

"I hope you're happy," she muttered, flinging herself down at the kitchen table. "I'm probably going to get pneumonia and die, and it'll be all your fault."

"Yes, well, if you do, I'll take full responsibility," Keeley said calmly. "Would you like some coffee?"

Valeska glared at her. "What I'd like is a drink."

Keeley returned her gaze evenly. She'd heard the bathroom door open and had listened carefully for any sign that Valeska was sneaking into the living room for a bottle. To her relief, Val had come straight into the kitchen, but that didn't mean she could relax. Far from it, she thought grimly, and said, "I'd take the coffee if I were you."

"I'd take the coffee if I were you," Valeska mimicked angrily. "Oh, all right, pour me a cup."

Keeley joined her at the table. Carefully, she said, "While you were ... showering, I called a couple of places."

Valeska's head snapped up. "What kind of places?"

"Places where you can get help."

"I don't need help!"

"Yes, you do, Val. We both know it."

Valeska jumped up. "Look, you can't just come in after all these years and take over my life! Who do you think you are, anyway?"

"I'm your friend—"

"My friend!" Valeska laughed shrilly. "Who are you kidding? A *friend* wouldn't have stabbed me in the back! A *friend* wouldn't have gone away without telling me!" She dissolved suddenly into piteous tears. "A *friend* wouldn't have ignored me all these years. I called you, Keeley, but you never called me back. I wrote you letters, but you never answered. A friend! What a joke!"

Keeley had been sitting at the table; slowly, she stood up. "When did you call?" she asked. "When did you write?"

Sobbing into her hands, Valeska shook her head. "I don't remember, but I did. I did!" She lifted her ravaged face. "Why didn't you answer, Keeley? I thought ... after all we'd been through ... that we meant something to each other!"

"We did." Keeley felt stricken. Had Val called when her family was there? She'd never gotten messages when they were living in the house. As for any letters .... She looked at Valeska again. "I called, too."

Valeska looked at her in disbelief. "When?"

"I asked Nigel to tell you." She paused. "I guess he never did."

"No, he never did," Valeska said bitterly. "But then, there were a lot of things Nigel should have done and didn't."

"Were you telling the truth when you said he's left you?"

Valeska's face crumpled again. Beginning to sob anew, she said, "Yes, it's true. But I ... I can't remember when. One day he was just here and the next ... he wasn't."

Keeley was silent a moment. Then she said, "I'm sorry, Val."

"No, you're not! You always wanted him for yourself!"

"Oh, please, you know it's not true."

"It is!"

"It's *not*!" Keeley said. She didn't want to get distracted by Nigel. "Look, let's not argue about it now. We'll have plenty of time later. Let's talk about St. Mary's."

Valeska looked at her warily. "What's St. Mary's?"

"It's a . . ." Keeley hesitated, then decided to tell the truth. No sugarcoating, not anymore. "It's a detox center, right here in Manhattan. I called and—"

"Oh, no, you don't!" Valeska said, her eyes wide and starting to look panicked. She backed up until she hit the counter. "I don't need anything like that!"

"Yes, you do, Val."

"No, I don't! I won't go! I won't!"

"Calm down—"

"I won't calm down! You have no right! You can't make me!"

Keeley was trying to hold on to her patience. She was determined to take Val to St. Mary's if she had to drag her there by her wet hair. She would prefer it if Val agreed to go on her own, but whichever way it turned out, she wasn't going to leave her alone. She hadn't come this far just to leave her friend in the same state she'd found her in, and it didn't have anything to do with the show. Valeska needed her, and this time, she'd be there.

"I don't want to *make* you," she said carefully. "I'd rather you made the decision yourself."

"I have made it! I'm not going!"

Keeley tried another tack. "Val, even *you* have to admit you have a drinking problem—"

Her face white, Valeska shook her head fiercely. "No, I—"

"Val!"

"All right!" Valeska cried. "Maybe I have a problem sometimes, but I can control it! I can control it!"

"And controlling it is what I saw today when I came?"

"You don't know what kind of stress I've been under, Keeley! You just don't know! I'll get a handle on this, I promise! I just need time!"

"Time is what you don't have, Val," Keeley said inexorably. "Now, I promised the administrator you'd be there this afternoon, so why don't you get dressed?"

"I'm not going! You can't make me!"

"Yes," Keeley said evenly. "I can. Now can you get dressed by yourself, or do you want me to help you?"

"I'm not a child!"

"Then stop acting like one." She advanced a step. Caught by the counter, Valeska scuttled around, trying to get away from her.

"Don't make me do something I'll regret!" Valeska cried.

Keeley looked at her. Quietly, she said, "I think you've already done that, don't you, Val?"

Valeska looked at her defiantly for another few seconds. Then, abruptly, she threw herself down at the table again and burst into tears. "It won't do any good!" she wept.

Keeley knew then that half the battle was won. She'd seen the relief in Val's eyes that she couldn't hide, and she knew Valeska was glad she'd come to the rescue. Placing her hand on Valeska's head, she said softly, "Yes, it will, Val. And I'll be with you every step of the way to help."

Shuddering, Valeska raised her tearstained face. "You promise?"

Keeley smiled for the first time since entering the apartment. It was a faint smile, a little tremulous, for she realized how far they both had to go now that they'd taken the first step. But in Val's eyes, teary and bloodshot as they were, and in her face, bloated and puffy and older than her years, she still saw her Beauty. Even more, she saw her old friend. Together they'd make it work; she was sure of it. "Cross my heart," Keeley said.

CHAPTER TWENTY-SIX

Valeska's first thought when she opened her eyes was a weary, Oh God, why did you let me make it to another day?

She couldn't muster the energy to turn her head to see what time it was, but when she looked at the dim light beyond the closed draperies in her private room, she knew it had to be close to wake-up call. Here at St. Mary's, everyone was supposed to be on their feet at six A.M., although she had never understood why. There wasn't anything better about the morning than there was the rest of the day, and getting up so early left too many empty hours to fill and too many thoughts to avoid. At six A.M., the whole day spread out before her, ready to trip her up when she least expected it. Groaning at the idea, she pulled the covers over her head, willing it all away.

The buzzer sounded in the hallway at that moment, and with a heavy sigh, she pushed the covers away. She knew from past bitter experience that if she wasn't out of bed in the next five minutes, someone would come in to make sure she was. Despising the place, she got up.

She had a private bath, and as she headed toward it, she muttered to herself; cursing the hospital, the nurses, the doctors, Keeley for putting her here, and herself most of all. She was just deciding that if she didn't get out soon, she'd lose her mind when she caught sight of her reflection. The way she looked, maybe she already had.

She had been here almost a month now, but even after four weeks of being off the booze, she still couldn't stand looking at herself. She hardly recognized the person staring back at her. She looked ten years older than she was, there were dark shadows under her eyes, her skin was pasty and pale, and her hair . . .

Grimacing, she touched her hair. It was starting to grow out now, but it would be a long time before it attained its former length, and she had only herself to blame. She'd cut it all off her first day here in a misguided attempt to teach everyone a lesson. That's what she thought at the time, she guessed. She really didn't remember now. The only thing she recalled clearly about the incident were the people knocking and pleading on the other side of this locked bathroom door while she hacked away at her hair, pulling up fistfuls and cutting it off close to her scalp, letting the long strands fall on the floor. She'd succeeded in cutting it all off before someone came with the master key; God knows what she would have done if they hadn't unlocked the door when they had. Would she have started on some more vulnerable part of herself? She shuddered to think. The nurse from whom she'd taken the scissors had been fired, and every time she looked in the mirror, she felt sick. What had been in her mind? What had she been thinking?

Leaning over the sink, she stared into her haggard face, as if her reflected self could give her the answer. Aside from isolated memories, hazy and dim, she didn't remember much of anything for months before she came, and she hardly remembered anything right after. Despite all the coffee Keeley had forced down her the day of her arrival, she had still been so out of it that she barely remembered checking in. She did recall having a lot of tests she didn't want to take: blood pressure and blood tests and a weigh-in, after which the two nurses holding her up had looked at each other and just shook their heads. She hadn't cared that she was dangerously thin; all she'd wanted was a drink. When she realized no one was going to provide her with one, she started shouting that she'd made a mistake. She didn't want to be here after all; she wanted to go home.

No one had listened; no one had cared what *she* wanted, not even Keeley, who just looked at her calmly and kept insisting she had to stay because it was for her own good.

A vague memory stirred. Had she attacked Keeley? She couldn't remember, or maybe she just didn't want to. She had a confused impression of grabbing Keeley to make her understand, and of Keeley trying to pull away and both of them shouting at the attendants who seemed to rush in from nowhere to separate them. She had been hauled away, kicking and screaming, and the last thing she saw was Keeley's pale face. Keeley's green eyes had been enormous; they seemed to fill Valeska's head with her look of hurt. Then someone produced a needle and syringe; she felt the quick sting in her arm, and everything went . . . dark. When she woke up, Keeley was gone, and she was tied to a bed.

Bending down, she rested her forehead on the edge of the sink. She thought she had been humiliated before . . . all those times with Nigel, then coming to this place, and finally having Keeley see her drunk. But nothing compared to the debasement of being put in restraints. She might not be able to remember much of anything else; she might have forgotten too many things. But one thing she would never forget was the feel of leather cuffs on her wrists and the sensation of being tied down, unable to move, even to go to the bathroom.

Shakily, she reached for a washcloth and held it under running water until it was soaked. Suddenly she was drenched in sweat, and as she squeezed out the cloth and dabbed at her face and neck, she thought about Keeley and felt like crying. She didn't know how she felt about Keeley. There had been times these past few weeks when she had hated her, when she'd been sure that if Keeley had come near her, she would have tried to do damage. Being here had been awful, the worst experience of her life; even now she couldn't think about those first few days without starting to shake.

At first all she could remember was screaming and screaming for a drink, a pill—anything to help her make it through the night. She had asked at first, then demanded. Then—after they had taken the restraints away—she'd gotten down on her knees to beg for release. When no one would help, she'd become furious. Words had come out of her mouth that she hadn't even realized she knew; the things she'd said had shocked even her.

But she'd had to endure it because no one gave in, no matter what she said or how she threatened. It had been a nightmare, a time of twisted sheets and night sweats and bad dreams and tremors. She shook so bad at times she thought her teeth were going to fly right out of her head, and she was sure her bones would shatter into pieces.

Just when she thought she couldn't stand it any longer, someone in white would come at her through her darkness with a syringe in her hand. At first, she had welcomed the relief from the drugs, whatever they had been. It was like drinking, she'd thought dreamily; she could just float off. But the sensation lasted only the first few nights; after that, the sleep she craved eluded her, and she would awaken, shrieking, from horrible dreams. She'd never had such nightmares; she would be jolted awake, terrified and drenched in perspiration, her head filled with murky images all the more awful because she couldn't remember what they'd been. It got to the point where she didn't want to go to sleep. She would fight it—and the nurses who came armed with new medication, insisting she had to get her rest or she'd make herself sick. She had laughed hysterically at that; oh, how she had laughed. Didn't anyone realize she was already sick to death?

Her teeth clenched, Valeska let go of the wash basin and held the cloth under the running tap again, squeezing it until water spurted between her white, shaking fingers. The psychologist, or psychiatrist, or therapist, or whatever the hell he was, wasn't any help, she thought. On the days when it was her turn to go in and talk to him, all he did was sit in his big leather armchair, his pad on his lap, watching her while she sat in front of him, unable to control her shakes.

"How are you feeling today?" he'd always ask.

And she would respond, invariably, "How the hell do you think?"

She wasn't in the mood to cooperate, not when she felt as if fire ants were crawling under her skin; right then, she couldn't think beyond wanting a drink. She didn't remember when she had started smoking; she knew she shouldn't be doing it because of her throat, but she just didn't care. What did it matter now?

she thought drearily, reaching for one of the cigarettes in the holder on the coffee table between them. Without comment, the psychiatrist gave her a light. She took a deep drag and exhaled, looking at the glowing tip of the cigarette with resignation.

"Something wrong?" he asked.

Something *wrong*? She almost laughed again. There he sat, perfectly composed and groomed in his three-piece suit, his shoes glossily polished, his hair styled and carefully cut, while *she*, former Broadway star who had once brought audiences to their knees, was sitting on his couch in a dingy hospital gown, with slippers too big for her on her feet. Something wrong? She was disgraced, debased, and humiliated. Her voice was gone, her career was in ruins; all she had to comfort her was a damned cigarette. Something wrong? Where did she start?

She wouldn't answer; it was all too much. So she'd sit, smoking one cigarette after another, not saying a word, until the hour was up. Since then, they'd spent many similar sessions. Even after the hallucinations had stopped and all she had to contend with were the nightmares and the shakes, she still refused to talk. What did he know, this pompous man in his big chair with his pad on his lap? Even if she told him what she really thought, it wouldn't matter. Her story wasn't special or unique. She was no different from millions of other women who had been foolish enough, and stupid enough, to fall in love with the wrong man. It happened all the time, didn't it?

Then she would think: *But not to Keeley,* and she would feel depressed all over again. Keeley had tried to warn her, she remembered, way back when. Keeley had tried to tell her she was making a big mistake. *Too late,* Valeska would think, and feel resentful again.

"You're going to have to talk to me sometime, you know," the psychiatrist had said to her one day during a session.

She looked at him dully, from behind her comforting cloud of cigarette smoke. She smoked so much now that her voice was hoarse, but she didn't care. Her career was over anyway; what did it matter?

"Oh?" she'd said disinterestedly. "What will happen if I don't?"

"Absolutely nothing," he said with irritating calm. "You just won't be able to leave here until we get a few things straightened out. But you realize that, of course."

She hadn't. "Why can't I leave when I want?"

"It's a matter of regulations and rules, and other things we don't need to go into. The important thing is that I'm here to help you."

"No one can help me," she declared, folding her arms over her waist. She looked at him defiantly. "And I don't want anyone to."

"I see," he said. He looked down at his empty pad. "Well, that's too bad. It's your decision, of course. I just thought you might like to get out of here and resume your career."

"What do you know about my career?"

"I've heard you sing. Several times, in fact. I think it would be a shame to deprive future audiences of such a glorious experience."

She glanced away. Sullenly, she said, "I'm never going to sing again."

"I see. I'm sorry to hear that. May I ask why?"

"Because I . . . Because I . . ." Suddenly agitated, she got up and went to the window. Wrapping her arms around her small waist—she might have stopped drinking since she'd come, but she still had no appetite—she stared out at the hospital grounds. It was almost October now, and the leaves were changing. The trees were aflame with crimson and gold and henna, but she barely saw them. Without warning, she felt a misery so profound she couldn't begin to express it.

"Valeska?" the psychiatrist said softly..

She didn't look at him. After all this time, she knew that he was waiting for her answer, that he would wait patiently for her response until her hour was up today, and that he would still be waiting when she came the next time. He was tenacious, she thought angrily, and she hated him.

"It's all gone," she muttered. "It's all finished. I just can't do it anymore. It's too much. To get out there every night . . . To pretend that everything is all right when it isn't . . ." She stopped, shuddering. "They all expect too much, more than I can give. I can't give it anymore. I can't, and I don't want to."

"I see," he said.

Angrily, she turned to look at him. "Why do you always say that?" she demanded. "Don't you know it doesn't help? Why do you always ask question after question until I don't know what I think?"

Calmly, he said, "I am here to help, Valeska. But only you have the answers. All you have to do is look inside yourself."

"I have!"

He met her glance evenly. "Have you?"

Without answering, she whirled away again. "Isn't the hour almost up?" she muttered.

Was that the merest sigh she heard behind her? She turned to look at him, but he was as bland as ever. "You're right," he said. "Our time is gone for the day. By the way, you have a visitor."

Instantly, she tensed. She didn't want to see anyone, not now, maybe not ever. "I . . . I can't have visitors," she said, clutching at the front of her robe. Her voice rose. "You said I couldn't! Remember? You said no visitors for a while!"

"Yes, but it's been awhile, Valeska," he said soothingly. "And I think it's time for you to—"

"I don't want to!" she cried, backing toward the door. Her eyes were wide and strained and pale, pale blue. "I . . . I can't see anyone now!"

For the first time she could remember, he got to his feet and came to her. She hadn't realized he wasn't very tall; sitting in his chair, judging her, he'd seemed ten feet high, at least. Taking her arm, he gently led her away from the door.

"It's time," he said quietly. "You can't hide in here forever, you know."

"Why not?" she wailed.

"I remember when you first came you couldn't wait to get out," he said with a smile. "In fact, as I recall, you accused us of holding you prisoner. Have you changed your mind?"

"Yes! *Yes!* Oh, Doctor, I don't want to see anyone." Unconsciously, her hand stole to her head, to feel her short hair. It had grown enough to be styled into soft curls, but she still felt naked without her shield of long hair. "Please don't make me, Doctor," she pleaded.

He thought about it for a moment. "You haven't asked who's come to see you."

She hardly knew what she was saying. "Who?"

"Keeley Cochran."

"Keeley!" she exclaimed. Then she caught herself. Her mouth turning down, she said, "I don't want to see her most of all. She's the one who brought me here."

"Yes, that's true."

She was sure she heard something in his voice. "You think I should be grateful to her, don't you?"

"It doesn't matter what I think. I'd rather know what you think about it."

He was confusing her, and she snapped, "I don't know what

to think! Sometimes I hate her, and sometimes I . . . Oh, I don't know. What does she care, anyway?"

"She cared enough to bring you here. She cares enough to come and visit."

"So what?" she cried, beside herself. She didn't know why she didn't want to see Keeley, but she didn't. He was still watching her, and she looked at him accusingly. "Now I suppose you're going to try to make me feel guilty if I don't see her."

"Will you feel guilty if you don't?"

Exasperated, she clenched her fists. "Why don't you ever answer *my* questions?"

Smiling, he said, "It's the nature of the business. She's waiting in your room if you want to see her."

Then he ushered her out.

As the doctor had indicated, Keeley was waiting in her room when she got back. As soon as Valeska opened the door and saw her standing by the windows, she stopped, not sure how she felt. She'd been so drunk and sick and suicidal the last time they'd met that she hadn't noticed Keeley's appearance. Now she saw a new maturity about Keeley, a different look. It wasn't only in the way she was dressed, in wool slacks and flats and a long-sleeved silk blouse the color of the autumn leaves; it was something in her profile, in her posture. Even facing away from her as Keeley was now, Valeska saw she had changed. How beautiful she is! she thought, wanting to rush over and say how glad she was to see her.

Sensing Valeska's presence, Keeley turned and looked at her. She couldn't hide her look of shock at her appearance, and Valeska's own expression turned bitter again as she came in and shut the door.

"Pretty awful, huh?" she said, sitting down on the edge of the bed. She looked up almost defiantly, waiting for Keeley's answer.

Keeley didn't say anything for a moment. Val had always thought Keeley was as close to perfect as you could get, but if she had one flaw, it was that she never could hide what she was thinking. She knew Keeley would have to comment, and she did. After all, they both knew her hair had always been her pride and joy.

"Did you do that, or did they?" Keeley finally asked.

"This isn't the Snake Pit," she retorted. "Although, I admit there have been nights when I've had my doubts. No, this is all my doing. I thought I'd try for a new look. Why, don't you like it?"

"It looks . . . fine." Slowly, Keeley came away from the windows, toward the bed. She looked a little wary, and Valeska suddenly remembered what had happened the last time Keeley had been here.

"You don't have to worry, I won't attack you again," she said. She was still angry—at Keeley, at herself, at everybody, it seemed; all she wanted to do was lash out and hurt whomever she could. Deliberately, she added, "Thanks to you, they've got me on enough medication to tranquilize an elephant. I couldn't harm a flea now, so you're safe."

"I wasn't worried," Keeley said quietly. "I was just thinking how pale and tired you looked." She came close enough to reach out and touch Valeska's short hair. Involuntarily, Valeska jerked back, and Keeley dropped her hand. "Are you sure they're treating you right? Because if they aren't, we'll find some other—"

"They're treating me fine. What do you want?"

Backing away a step, Keeley sat down in the room's only chair. "I'm sorry, Val," she said. "I know you must hate me."

"Now, what makes you think that?"

Flushing, Keeley continued, "If I'd known things would turn out like this, I—"

"You what?" She couldn't seem to help it. "You would have married him yourself?"

When Keeley didn't reply, Valeska felt the first twinges of shame. It wasn't Keeley's fault, she thought, and felt so agitated and uncertain that she reached into her pocket for her cigarettes. They allowed her a lighter now—but not matches, figure that, she thought—and with shaking hands, she managed to pull out a cigarette and get it lit. She saw Keeley's surprised expression when she'd taken a puff.

"It never ends, does it?" she said, feeling increasingly ashamed—and angry because of it. She gestured with the cigarette before taking another quick puff. "I just keep finding new ways to feed my addiction."

She was sure Keeley, of all people, would have something to say about the dangers of smoking, especially for her voice, but all Keeley said was, "I understand. There have been times this past year when I wanted to run away myself." She paused. "Sometimes I even envied you your drinking."

She grimaced. "Never envy that. I wish I'd never started."

"So do I."

Feeling increasingly ashamed at the way she was acting, she forced herself to say, "I was sorry to hear about Fitz Cowan. It must have been awful for you."

"It was."

Ashamed, she heard the note of pain Keeley couldn't hide in her voice. What was she doing? she wondered suddenly. Why was she trying to hurt Keeley, who had only tried to help? Guiltily, she said, "I was going to send a card, or flowers, or something."

"It's all right."

"No, it's not," she insisted. "I should have acknowledged it. I'm sorry, Keeley. I am."

"We both should have done things differently, Val."

"Yes, I know," she said, looking down to hide her eyes. It was more true than Keeley knew. Bitter memories rose in her mind, and to distract herself, she asked, "Have you seen Gabe?"

Keeley smiled for the first time. "Yes, I have. We ... spent the summer together in Montana."

"You did?" Without realizing it, Valeska sounded wistful. "It sounds wonderful."

"It was," Keeley said, her eyes faraway. Then she looked at Valeska again. "But he's off on assignment now, and I ... I came back to New York to do something I've been wanting to do for years."

"What?" she asked. Then she saw Keeley's face, and suddenly she knew. "Not *Beauty and the Beast*!" she exclaimed. They had talked about *Beauty* so many times during their early years that she knew all about it. Despite herself, she leaned forward. "Are you finally going to do it? Oh, I can't believe it!"

Looking relieved at her reaction, Keeley said, "You remember."

"Of course I remember. It was all we used to talk about! You were going to write and compose *and* direct, while I—" Abruptly the light died from Valeska's face, and she jerked back. "No," she said. "You can't be thinking what I think you're thinking."

"Why not? You're the perfect Beauty, Val, and you know it. We've talked about it for years."

Valeska put up her hands, as though in defense. "That was before. I can't do it anymore."

"What do you mean?" Keeley scoffed. "Of course you can. You just need a little time to pull yourself together, to get back to—"

"No, you don't understand!" Valeska was so agitated she jumped up. "I . . . I gave it all up! I can't sing anymore!"

Keeley stared at her disbelievingly for a moment, then she shook her head. "That's ridiculous. Of course you can sing! And when you do Beauty—"

"No, no, I can't!" Without warning, Valeska dissolved into tears. Sinking down on the bed again, she put her hands over her eyes, sobbing. "I can't do Beauty, I can't do anything! I'm never going to sing again. I just can't go back to the stage!"

Alarmed at this extreme reaction, Keeley reached out and pulled Valeska's hands down. "Tell me why not."

"I just can't, that's all!"

"Why not?" Keeley repeated. Her eyes were very green.

Valeska knew that Keeley would never let her go until she answered. She was worse than the psychiatrist. Feeling trapped and cornered, she gave in to the desperation she'd been holding back for far too long. The words started to pour out; once begun, she couldn't stop.

"I . . . it was all a sham, don't you see?" she cried. "Broadway was never something I wanted to do! From the beginning, it was my mother, always my mother—pushing, prodding, telling me I had to be a success!" Even through her growing hysteria, her tone took on a harsh note, mimicking Edra to a T. "Once you get to Broadway, everything will be perfect. You'll be a star—a star! People will adore you; audiences will clamor for more! Your name will be in lights as the greatest singer who ever . . . who ever . . ." Valeska's voice broke, and she burst into renewed tears. Jerking away from Keeley, she threw herself down on the bed, weeping hysterically.

Keeley stood where she was for a moment, wondering what to do. Uneasily, she glanced at the call unit built into the wall, debating about summoning someone to help. Then she looked at Valeska again. To hell with it, she thought. Reaching down, she grabbed Valeska by the shoulders and jerked her upright.

"Do you *hear* yourself?" she demanded, looking hard into Valeska's face. "I've never heard such whining, puling excuses in my life! If I didn't know better, I'd think all that alcohol had pickled your brain!"

Shocked, Valeska stopped crying long enough to look at Keeley. No one here had ever talked to her that way, least of all her psychiatrist. "What . . . what . . . how can you say such a terrible thing?" she wailed. "You just don't understand!"

"Oh, yes, I do!" Keeley shot back. She knew it was now or

never, and she had to make Valeska see she was lying to herself. Giving her a shake for emphasis, she let her fall back. "You make me sick!"

Startled out of her self-pity, Valeska shot up again. "How dare you!"

"I dare because I'm your friend! Don't you think it's about time you stopped blaming your mother for something you wanted all along?"

Valeska couldn't have looked more astounded if Keeley had taken out a machete and began hacking at all the furniture in the room. "Something *I* wanted! Are you crazy? You know how it was."

"No, I only know *your* version of how it was."

Valeska was so angry, she clenched her fist. Looking as though she wanted to strike, she cried, "I hate you!"

"Fine!" Keeley grabbed Valeska's arm. "Hate me! Go ahead! But tell me you'll do Beauty!"

"No, I won't! I won't!" Valeska shouted, trying to free herself. Panting from the struggle, she said desperately, "You don't know anything about me. You think you do, but you don't!" Abruptly, she stopped fighting. "You know what? You make *me* sick! Oh, it's so easy for you to judge, isn't it? You never let anything stand in *your* way. You're always so determined, so unafraid! Nothing shakes you up, nothing terrifies you, except—"

"Except what?"

Valeska didn't know what came over her, but it felt good to shout and scream and say just what she thought without worrying about anybody else. She'd kept everything inside for too long, she thought; it was tearing her up.

Looking as if she did hate Keeley, she drew back. Her eyes glittered like bits of blue glass. "You think you have all the answers to everyone else's problems, don't you, Keeley? You never have any of your own—oh, no, not you, Miss Perfect. Well, let me tell you what *I* think!"

"Go ahead!"

"I will! You talk about success all the time, you know that? But what you're *really* talking about is how afraid you are to fail! Oh, yes, that's right, don't look at me like that! If it's not true, tell me why you never look back, why you never stop for one second to enjoy your success! You never have, you know that? And don't tell me you changed while you were in California, because I won't believe you. I know you, Keeley, you

barely get one thing done before you're on to something else."
She stopped, breathing hard. "I'll bet you never even celebrated
that Music in Film award you won, did you? Well? Did you?"

Despite herself, Keeley looked uncomfortable and angry.
"How did you know about the award?"

"Never mind, I know. Besides, it isn't the point. Answer the
question, Keeley. Are you afraid of failure? Are you?"

"Of course not! Don't be ridiculous!"

Angrily, Valeska tossed her head. "That's right, act like *I'm*
the simpleton! You do that when you don't want to admit something, did you know that? You always did believe you were better than anybody, Keeley. You never had any patience for
weakness. You scorn people who aren't as strong, but the only
problem with that outlook is that no one can be as strong as you.
Not when you won't admit you're weak at times just like the
rest of us!"

Gasping, Valeska paused for breath. Her face pale, Keeley
reached for the chair and sat down. For a moment, there was silence. Then Keeley muttered dazedly, "I . . . I never thought of
it like that. There have been a lot of times when I needed help—
when Fitz died, when the music went away. . . ." She looked up.
"Do you really think of me like that, Val?"

Now that she'd emptied herself of all her hateful feelings,
Valeska felt ashamed. "No, I don't," she muttered. "Not really."
Then she felt resentful again. "But you *do* expect a lot of people, Keeley! No one can ever measure up to your standards,
ever!"

Keeley looked even more stricken. "That's not true!"

"It is!" Valeska insisted. Then she saw Keeley's face. She
didn't know why, but something compelled her to add, "But it's
okay. It's just the way you are. You can't help yourself."

To her dismay, Keeley's eyes filled with tears. "Don't make
fun, Val. I know you hate me, and I don't blame you. I . . . I
think I'd better go now."

She got up, but suddenly Valeska was on her feet, too.
Quickly, she reached for Keeley's hand. "Don't go," she said.
She felt awful now. She didn't want to hurt Keeley, who had
been so good to her. "I don't hate you, how could I? I hate myself, if you want to know the truth. I'm *glad* you came back. If
you hadn't come when you did . . ." She shuddered, remembering the wreck she'd been the day Keeley came to the apartment.
She hated to think what might have happened if Keeley hadn't
shown up when she had.

Keeley looked into Valeska's blue eyes. Her fingers tightened on Val's. "I want to be friends again, Val," she said softly. "Not because of *Beauty*, but because I value our friendship. I've hated it these past few years, not being in touch, not knowing where you were, or what you were doing, or how you felt."

"I hated it, too, Keeley," Valeska said, her own eyes filling. "You don't know how much!"

They stood looking at each other for a few seconds; then they reached for one another at the same time and embraced.

"Oh, Val," Keeley said fervently.

"Oh, Keeley!" Valeska sighed, holding tight.

When they parted, they smiled shakily at each other before sitting down side by side on the bed. They were silent for a few moments, then Keeley said carefully, "Tell me about Nigel."

"Nigel?" Valeska pulled back. "Why? Why do you want to know about him?"

Keeley's gaze was direct. "He's really the reason you're here, isn't he?"

"No! You brought me here!"

"You know what I mean."

Valeska looked away. She couldn't admit, even to Keeley, how afraid she was even after all this time that Nigel would leave his current mistress and come back. Even after she'd lost the baby, he had refused to give her a divorce, and she was too frightened of him to file on her own. So she had let it go, hoping . . . She didn't know what she had hoped. That he would go away if she didn't think about him, perhaps. That she could drown all memory of him in drink.

She glanced at Keeley. She knew she could never explain her true feelings about Nigel because she was so ashamed, so she shook her head. "I don't know," she said. "There are a lot of reasons why I started drinking. I think Nigel was just one of them. Everything seemed to pile up on me at once: Granny dying, losing the baby—"

Startled, Keeley exclaimed, "You were pregnant?"

Valeska nodded sadly. "I miscarried."

"Oh, Val, I'm so sorry!"

Valeska couldn't force herself to meet Keeley's eyes. "It was for the best, I guess," she said. "It . . . wasn't time for us to have a baby."

Hearing something in her voice she couldn't disguise, Keeley asked, "How did Nigel feel about the baby? Was he happy?"

She still couldn't look up. "No, he wasn't . . . pleased."

"I'm sorry," Keeley said again. She reached for Valeska's hand. "It must have been awful for you."

"It was." Shakily, she looked up. "We've had some rough times, haven't we?"

"Yes, we have." They sat there in silence for a moment, then Keeley said, "But maybe it's all behind us now. When we start rehearsal—"

"Rehearsal? Oh, no—"

"Oh, yes," Keeley said, as if it were all settled. "I know you didn't mean it when you said you were never going to sing again."

Valeska tried to pull back. "Yes, I did!"

"No, you didn't."

Agitated again, Valeska stood. "I did mean it. Keeley, I can't." Seeing Keeley's expression, she rushed desperately on, not realizing she was committing herself with every word. She didn't know that her longing, her yearning to sing was evident in every line of her face. "Even if I wanted to, I'm not sure. I mean, I'd need so much practice, so many lessons. . . ." Suddenly realizing what she was saying, she stopped, her hands to her cheeks. "No! I told you! I can't!"

"You know you want to," Keeley said. "We've talked about it so many times—"

"That was before!"

"Before what? The part is tailor-made for you, Val. I know, because I wrote it myself. If ever there was a Beauty, it's you."

Torn, Valeska clenched her hands. "I told you! I can't!"

Keeley saw her indecision, the struggle that was going on between the terrified woman and the artist inside. Because she had to, she pushed her advantage. "What's the matter, Val? Don't you think we can pull it off?"

Eagerly, Valeska seized on the excuse. "You're wonderful, Keeley, but even you can't put together something like this by yourself. You'd need backers—"

"I'll get them."

"And we'd need a place to rehearse—"

"I'll find one."

Feeling increasingly desperate, Valeska rushed on. "And we'd need a book writer and a choreographer and stage manager and a producer and—"

"I'll take care of it," Keeley said, her face shining. She knew she was close. "All you have to do is sing, Val. I'll do what I do, and you do what you do best."

Agonized by indecision, Valeska sank down onto the edge of the bed. She was thinking about all that had happened, wondering if she had the courage, or the stamina, or the energy, or the talent to make the future take place. Terrified at the thought, she looked down at her hands, clasped tightly in her lap. *I can't do it,* she thought. *I don't know if I have the voice.*

Afraid to take the step, afraid not to, she sat there until Keeley reached down and covered her hands with her own. When Valeska looked up into those green eyes, Keeley was smiling, the self-confident, assured smile that always had made everything seem right. Wordlessly, they interlocked fingers, as they used to do to wish each other luck.

"You can do it, Val," Keeley said softly.

Valeska wasn't sure. She knew that when Keeley had that look anything was possible. But could she really manage? She didn't know. Shakily, she said, "I'd have to give up smoking."

Keeley's grasp tightened on her hands. "You never did look good as a vamp. Is it a deal?"

"Oh, Keeley," Valeska said mournfully. "I don't know!"

"I do," Keeley said.

Valeska tried one last time. "Why are you always so sure of yourself? It isn't fair!"

"It's because I'm just the composer, Val," Keeley said with a beatific smile. "You're the star."

Rehearsals for Keeley Cochran's *Beauty and the Beast* began eight months after Valeska was released from the hospital. Keeley had found her backers, and, by using the money from the sale of her house, and the royalties from the songs she'd composed, they got by. Valeska didn't know whether to be pleased or not when she was cast in the starring role, but by then things had gone too far for her to back out even if she'd wanted to. She became a shaky Beauty, determined to do her best.

It was Keeley who convinced her to try, but it was her friends at Hildredth who restored her confidence. After so long an absence, she finally found courage to visit the convalescent home to try to explain why she'd been gone so long. Her hair had barely grown down to her shoulders by then, and she still needed to gain weight. But when they all welcomed her without question, without judgment, worried and anxious about where she'd been, she felt warmed in the circle of their unconditional love, and it was then that the true healing began.

Bettina said it for the rest. Drawing her aside for a moment after the gratifying excitement of her arrival had died down, she looked into Valeska's face with the wise eyes of one who has seen it all in her lifetime. Softly, she asked, "Why didn't you come to see us, dear? We were so concerned."

Valeska couldn't hold Bettina's calm blue glance. "I was ashamed," she muttered, glancing away. "I . . . I didn't like what I'd become, and I didn't want any of you to see me like that."

The old woman sighed, patting her hand. "You don't live to be this age without knowing how hard life is, my dear," she murmured. "We all stumble and fall, every last one of us. The important thing is to get up again." She put a papery-thin, veined hand under Valeska's chin and turned her head before adding quietly, "And to trust in your family, your loved ones . . . and your friends."

"Oh, Bettina!" Val said contritely. "I'm sorry. I was so confused, so . . . afraid. I didn't know what to do. Can you ever forgive me?"

But with the wisdom of age and experience, Bettina and the others already had. Once again, Valeska was welcomed into their little circle, and despite her terror of appearing on stage again, no one was more pleased than she when the Thursday sing-along sessions resumed.

CHAPTER TWENTY-SEVEN

Gabe was notified of his brother's accident while he was in Guatemala. The foundation called him at the hotel on his first night back in civilization, just before he headed out for a wild night on the town—or what passed for it there. At that point, he'd been out six months, and any entertainment was going to be welcome. But when he heard that Frank had been in a serious car accident and might not live, he immediately booked the first plane home.

He didn't want to, but he couldn't stop thinking of Frank the entire flight. Scenes of their childhood came back to him—things he hadn't thought of in years and didn't know why he was remembering now. One particular memory from when he was nine stood out from the rest. The family hadn't yet moved to posh Holmby Hills; they were living in the San Fernando Valley, near a lake that was long since gone, bulldozed over to make room for yet another shopping mall. He and Frank had to pass by the lake going to and from school, and one day he'd found part of an old gate that had been carelessly abandoned. He had immediately seen its rafting potential, but Frank had taken one look at the trash and garbage floating in and under the murky water and had forbidden him to go near it. Naturally that only made him more determined to try, and before Frank could stop him, he'd grabbed a piece of board for an oar and jumped aboard. He still didn't know why Frank had joined him, but they were pretty far out when the makeshift raft began to sink. It was impossible to get it back to shore; the only choice was to jump and swim back. Gabe wasn't worried: he was a good swimmer, and so was Frank. What he hadn't counted on was a rusting piece of machinery lying just under the place where he decided to jump off. He'd snagged his arm when he bailed out, and by the time they both struggled out of the algae-ridden water, he was bleeding and beginning to wish he'd never had the idea of playing Captain Hook.

Frank had been furious, of course, and even Gabe couldn't blame him. He could still remember their homecoming: both of them stinking to high heaven from their dip in the muddy lake, Frank's pants ripped, Gabe's arm bleeding, their schoolbooks sodden. Explaining was out of the question: their horrified mother was sure they'd contract tetanus or some other dread disease; Ellis had been furious. They had been grounded for weeks, and for a long time, Gabe couldn't pass by the lake without his arm tingling in memory of the stitches and the shot the doctor had given him.

Other memories came to him during the long, seemingly endless flight: the time pacifist Frank had waded in to help him during a school fight; the time Gabe had "borrowed" a horse from some farmer's field during a trip to Big Bear and then couldn't get it back again without his indignant brother's assistance.

As he thought about their childhood, Gabe realized there were too many times to count when Frank had stood by him, had stepped in to help, or gotten him out of a jam he'd thoughtlessly gotten himself into. Why had it taken him so long to realize just how good a brother Frank had been to him?

The more he thought about it, the more ashamed he felt that

he hadn't appreciated Frank more. He loved Frank; he did. But why hadn't he ever said so?

The sun had come up during the long flight home, and as he strode into the airport after the plane landed, he remembered when Frank had come to get him for their mother's birthday and felt a pang. Was that to be the last time?

Stop it! he told himself angrily. He was going to drive himself crazy if he kept imagining all these terrible things, so to distract himself, he shifted the duffel he'd brought and glanced around for signs. He had to rent a car, and when he saw the arrow telling him where to go he started off, only to stop again. He should call Keeley, he thought, and then dismissed the idea as premature. He had to find out what was going on first. But as he stood there indecisively, he suddenly felt such a need just to hear her voice that he forgot about the car and started toward the wall of pay phones.

He had her new number; after she'd left the ranch in September, she'd called and left a message at the foundation. The first chance he had, he'd called her back from Benque Viejo when he and the team had come in to replenish supplies. He wasn't surprised that her new number started with a New York area code; he was relieved. Grateful that his ruse with the film had worked, he was delighted to hear that she and Valeska were friends again and would start work on her new show as soon as Val got out of rehab.

The call had been going through while he stood there, and when the phone began to ring at the other end, he felt himself tense. He knew he'd have to call back if she wasn't there; this wasn't the kind of message he could leave on a machine.

"Hello?"

He was so relieved to hear her voice that he let the wall hold him up. "Hi," he said weakly.

"Gabe!" she exclaimed immediately in delight. "Where are you? Are you in town?"

Now that he'd reached her, he didn't know what to say. "No, I just flew into L.A."

He hadn't intended to, but even he heard something in his voice. She picked up on it right away. "What is it? What's wrong?"

He couldn't tell her; his throat felt tight, and he had to close his eyes for a second. "I'm sorry, Keeley. It's just . . . It was a long flight."

Worry sharpened her voice. "Gabe, what's wrong?"

He couldn't keep her in suspense. "It's Frank," he said. "He's been in . . . an accident."

He heard her quick intake of breath. "Oh, Gabe, I'm so sorry. Will he be all right?"

"I don't know. I haven't been home yet; I'm calling from the airport. But it . . . it doesn't look good."

She didn't hesitate. "I'll catch the first flight out."

"You don't have to do that."

"I want to. I want to be there with you."

He wanted her with him, too, but he couldn't ask. He knew how much time and effort went into mounting a production, and he didn't want her to drop everything and fly out here to hold his hand—not yet, at least.

"I appreciate the offer, Keeley. But you're busy with the new show—"

"It can wait."

Despite his state of mind, he smiled weakly. He knew how much her music meant to her; for her to offer to make such a sacrifice meant as much to him as her actually being here herself.

"No, it can't," he said. "Now, promise me, Keeley. I didn't call to upset your schedule. I just—"

"You're not upsetting my *schedule*, Gabe! For God's sake!"

"I didn't mean it that way. Look, I just wanted to tell you and . . . to hear your voice. There's nothing you can do here."

"I can be with you."

Never had he wanted her with him more than he did this minute. But she had her own responsibilities and obligations, and he didn't know what he was facing himself. So he pushed away his longing to hold her, to see her expressive face, to look into her eyes and make believe that everything was going to be all right, and said, "Let me get my bearings first. When I find out what's happened, I'll call you, and we'll talk about it then."

There was a silence. He knew he'd hurt her when she said, "All right, Gabe. If that's the way you want it."

It wasn't, but he didn't know what else to do. "I'll call you as soon as I can, I promise," he said awkwardly, and hung up.

Fifteen minutes later, he headed out of the airport in a rented car, entering the freeway with the accelerator pressed hard to the floor. He calmed down a little and slowed to the speed limit when he spotted two highway patrol cars in the space of a minute; the last thing he needed was to be delayed for a ticket. It seemed forever until he turned into the driveway at home, and when he saw Laveda standing in the doorway, watching him drive in, he rocked the car to a stop and jumped out. Bounding up the steps, he took one look at her face and knew the worst.

"Oh, Gabriel Lee!" Laveda said mournfully, throwing open her ample arms. "Thank the Lord you've come!"

Despite Gabe's hurry to get to the hospital where everyone else seemed to be, he stayed to talk to Laveda. She had been with the family so long that he felt she was one of them, and he trusted her to tell him the truth. They went to the kitchen, where they had shared so much time over the years, Laveda always fussing over something at the counter, he sitting at the big kitchen table eating the treats she fixed. He had no appetite today, but he did accept a cup of coffee from her, insisting she join him and tell him what had happened.

Sorrowfully, Laveda shook her head. "No one's really sure right now. The police are still investigating. The only thing anybody knows is that Frank was coming home when he was hit head-on by a man who just . . . just lost control of his car. The other driver was killed, while Frank—" her voice broke. "Oh, Gabriel Lee, I'm so sorry to tell you, but Frank has bad head injuries. He's on that life support, and they don't—"

Seeing Gabe's white face, she reached across the table and took one of his hands in hers. "I know you, Gabriel Lee. You're like a son to me. I know you'll want the truth."

He wasn't sure he did. Stiff-lipped, he said, "Go ahead, Laveda."

She took a deep breath. Holding him with her strong gaze, she said, "The doctor has said that even if Frank lives, he'll never be the same again. I don't know what they call it now, some fancy name. But it means the damage was so bad that he'll never walk, or talk, or speak, or see."

Gabe couldn't listen anymore. Pulling away from her, he stood up, trying to put some distance between him and the horrible news. "I don't believe it," he said, his face pale despite his tropical tan. "It's a mistake. They can't know this soon."

Quietly, ignoring his outburst, Laveda said, "There's something else you should know."

He didn't know what it could be. He'd already heard the worst news possible, hadn't he? Suddenly, he thought of his mother. How was she holding up? And his father. And Frank's wife, and his two little girls? He had to get to the hospital.

"I don't have time—" he began. He didn't want to hear what Laveda had to say.

"Yes, you do, Gabriel Lee," Laveda said. Reaching for his hand, she made him sit down again. "Did you and Frank ever discuss what . . . what his final wishes might be?"

At that moment, Gabe knew he hadn't heard the worst. The nightmare was only beginning, he thought numbly, and he wanted to fade away. "He . . . he told me that if something happened, he'd never want to be maintained on machines, if that's what you mean," he managed. He made himself say it. "*Is* that what you mean, Laveda?"

She looked down at her hands again, and as he stared at her bowed head, he had an image of his father and knew what he had ahead of him.

"It's Dad, isn't it?" he said.

Laveda looked up with tears in her eyes. "Don't blame your father, Gabriel Lee. Frank is his son, and it's—"

"It's not his decision," Gabe said flatly. He felt as if he were holding on to his sanity by a very fine thread. "If that's what we're facing, it's something only Amy can decide."

Biting her lip, Laveda glanced away. "Amy wants to please your father."

"And Mother? Where does she stand in this?"

Laveda met his eyes. "Your mother has always supported your father, Gabriel Lee. You know that."

No, it's too much responsibility! Gabe thought, feeling an intolerably heavy burden descending on him, crushing the very breath out of him. "So you're saying it's up to me?"

When he heard the pleading note in his voice, he felt ashamed. Before he could recall the words, Laveda took his hands. The scar he'd received so long ago from the man-eating tiger in India had almost faded to invisibility. Tenderly, she reached up and touched it.

"Sometimes the hardest thing in the world is to be strong for someone when they need you the most," she said, her voice breaking, but her grip strong. "It's a terrible thing to take responsibility for another person's life. But you have to think who's important here, Gabriel Lee. Is it you or your family, with your pain and your grief? Or is it Frank, who needs the help only you can give him? You're the one he needs now, and I know that whatever decision has to be made, you'll make it with Frank in mind. You'll be strong for him, won't you?"

Gabe couldn't speak. Wishing he were anywhere but here, he

stood up. Time was wasting and he had to leave. As much as he might want to, he couldn't postpone his responsibility to his brother any longer. Wordlessly, he leaned down and kissed Laveda good-bye.

With the exception of Frank's two girls, who Laveda had said were staying with Amy's mother, the entire family was at the hospital when Gabe arrived. Her eyes dull, Amy was too deep in shock to notice him, but as soon as Audrey glimpsed him through the glass doors to Intensive Care, she got up and rushed to his side with a small cry.

Of Ellis, there was no sign. Audrey saw his glance and knew who he was looking for. "The nurses told your father they had to . . . to take Frank's vital signs, so they sent him to get some coffee," she said. "Otherwise, he's not left your brother's bedside since . . ." She couldn't finish. Shaking her head, she sat down again, covering her eyes with one hand.

Unsure what to do, Gabe looked at Amy, who was still pre-occupied, then back at his mother. He wanted to comfort her, but he wanted to see Frank, too.

"Mom, I—"

"Go ahead," Audrey said, reading his mind. She looked up with sorrow-filled eyes. "I know you want to see Frank, but—" She swallowed convulsively. "Prepare yourself, darling. Frank isn't . . ." She couldn't finish. Shaking her head again, she looked away.

His heart pounding with fear and dread, Gabe went to see his brother.

Despite his experience with accident victims as a police photographer, he was still shocked when he pulled aside the curtain and saw Frank for the first time. For an awful moment, he wasn't sure the figure in the bed was his brother. Frank's head was so heavily bandaged that his swollen and bruised face beneath was barely visible, and what Gabe could see was covered by tubes and lines that seemed to run from every orifice. IV's were plugged into each of Frank's arms; more lines ran out from under the sheets. The collection of machines by the bed softly beeped and hissed and flashed various green and red numbers, and every time there was a faint *whoosh*, Frank's chest rose and then fell, like a tired wave expending itself. As he stood for a few moments trying to adjust to the sight, Gabe found himself counting the beats; it was mesmerizing, and he had to make an effort to look away.

Telling himself fiercely to get a grip on, he saw a chair and pulled it closer. The rails were up on the bed, and it was difficult to lean across, so he reached for Frank's pale, flaccid hand and gently held it.

"Frank, it's Gabe," he whispered, staring hard at his brother's swollen, misshapen face. Frank's eyes were so bruised and puffy that they had nearly disappeared into his cheeks; the sight almost brought him to tears. He had tried to prepare himself, but as he looked at his brother, he knew nothing could have fortified him for the reality of this. Bowing his head, he rubbed his free hand hard across his eyes. He'd seen too many accident victims not to know the outcome of this one.

"Oh, Frank," he murmured, holding his brother's hand tight.

The only response was the beep and whoosh and hiss of the machines that were now performing all the vital functions that Frank could no longer manage to do on his own.

He stayed until he could control himself. Finally, wiping his eyes, he lifted his head and looked at the motionless figure on the bed again. He knew Frank couldn't hear him, but he said it anyway.

"I let you down so many times when we were kids," he whispered, staring at the poor, bandaged head, the swollen nose and lips. "I won't let you down again, Frank. I swear it."

Carefully replacing Frank's hand on top of the blanket, he left Intensive Care in search of the doctor. When he met the man in his office, he learned that the situation as Laveda had explained it to him was essentially unchanged. He hadn't believed it—or wanted to believe it—but he couldn't deny what the doctor himself related. After seeing Frank hooked up to the machines with the relentless rows of numbers that never changed, he didn't have to be told Frank's condition was listed as "persistent vegetative." Laveda might not have known the words, but by whatever name it was called, it meant the same thing. For all practical purposes, Frank, as they had all known and loved him, was already gone.

Audrey and Amy were still in the waiting room when he returned. He hadn't noticed when he first arrived, but he realized suddenly that his mother had aged.

"I'm so glad you're here, darling," Audrey said, when he sat down beside her. Her voice shook, and she put a hand to her mouth, looking up helplessly at him.

Glancing quickly in his sister-in-law's direction, he said in a low voice, "We have to talk, Mother. I just saw the doctor, and—"

Audrey looked ready to cry again. "I know. It doesn't look good, does it?" She seemed so lost and vulnerable that Gabe reached out and held her for a moment. But it didn't change his mind; he had to say it.

"No, Mom. It doesn't look good. That's what we have to talk about. Is Dad back yet?"

Audrey cast an unhappy look toward the cubicles on the other side of the glass wall. There were about a half dozen, each sequestered with drawn curtains to separate one patient from the other. Frank was lying behind the third one, Gabe counted, and had to wrench his glance away.

"Yes, he came back after you left and went right in to sit with Frank again," Audrey said, answering his question. She looked down at her hands, which were worrying a crumpled lace handkerchief. "I've tried to talk to him, but he . . . he won't listen."

Trying to control the unreasonable anger he was beginning to feel toward his father, Gabe said, "I know. That's what we have to discuss. Someone has to make a decision, and I—" he dropped his voice lower "—and I don't think Amy is capable of it by herself right now."

Audrey glanced worriedly in her daughter-in-law's direction. "I think Amy might come to terms with it if your father would . . . would . . ." A shudder ran through her, but she controlled herself with a visible effort. Lifting her eyes to Gabe's, she said, "The doctor told us that there's no hope, but your father just won't believe it. He says that if we have to, we'll fly Frank to the Mayo Clinic, to New York, to Europe. I don't know what to do, Gabe. I've tried talking to him, and to Amy, but . . ."

Gabe thought of what the doctor had said in parting.

"I've spoken to your brother's wife," he'd explained. "But she insists on deferring to your father, who at the moment is . . . er . . . unable to fully comprehend the reality of Frank's condition. I've tried to make it clear, as gently as possible, that there are decisions to be made here. We have your brother on life support at present, but if we have to intubate him for nutrition, things become a little more complicated. I . . ." He hesitated, searching Gabe's tense face. "May I be candid, Mr. Tyrell?"

Tight-lipped, Gabe had said, "I'd appreciate it, Doctor. I've only just arrived, and I'd like to be apprised of my brother's situation, as fully as possible. Please don't spare my feelings. I must know what we're facing here."

The doctor nodded approvingly, then launched into a technical explanation of Frank's condition that made Gabe's head reel. He didn't understand all the jargon, but it wasn't necessary. According to the doctor—and the two other specialists who had been consulted—the only thing keeping Frank alive right now were the machines.

"I'm very sorry, Mr. Tyrell," the doctor concluded unhappily. "I know how difficult this is to absorb, never mind accept. But I assure you, if there were the least hope of your brother regaining any function—"

"I understand," Gabe had said. He didn't need to be told again and again. Forcing himself to focus on the present instead of how the world would be if Frank were gone, he had asked, "What are our options?"

"We can keep him alive indefinitely, if that's what you wish. But I'm afraid it's the best we'll be able to do. His condition will remain constant."

"There's no hope he'll get better? You're certain?"

The doctor nodded. "I'm certain. So are the other two specialists whom I called in. But of course you're free to seek other opinions."

"No, I believe you. It's just . . ." Despite himself, tears filled his eyes, and he turned away. "It's just so hard to think of Frank, like this."

The doctor gave him a chance to compose himself. Finally, when he was able, Gabe said, "I know Frank wouldn't want to live on machines. If there's no chance he'll improve or get better . . ." He could feel tears pushing at the back of his throat again and fiercely willed them away. "I know he wouldn't want it like this."

The doctor searched his face. "You're sure of his wishes?"

"Yes. We . . . we talked about it before. I used to be a police photographer, and whenever I talked about my work with Frank—about the accidents I'd witnessed, and what had happened to the people I'd seen—he always said that if something like that happened to him, he wouldn't want to be maintained on machines. If there was no hope—" Despite himself, his voice cracked and he had to work to steady it "—if there was no hope, he told me he'd trust us to do the right thing and let him go."

"You're certain about this," the doctor said again.

Gabe nodded; his throat felt so constricted that it was difficult to speak. "Yes, I'm sure."

"Unfortunately, we still have a problem. It's customary in situations like this to seek permission from the next of kin. In Frank's case, that would be his wife. But as I said, Mrs. Tyrell—"

"It's not Amy," Gabe said. "It's my father. I'll talk to him."

The doctor hesitated. "Perhaps it's not my place to say so, but as I indicated, your father is having a difficult time accepting the irreversibility of your brother's condition. It could be that he just needs a little more time."

But Gabe knew that nothing would change even if they waited until the *end* of time. As far as he was concerned, the decision—if it had ever really been theirs to make—had been taken out of their hands. Frank deserved more than this; if his life as he'd known it had been so quickly and cruelly snatched away from him, the least his family could do was give him peace and preserve his dignity to the end. Existing on machines was not *life*, no matter what Ellis believed. Gabe knew there was no sense prolonging this agony for them all, not when the solution was available and theirs to take.

Remembering what the doctor had said about tube feeding, Gabe had said, "Thank you, doctor. I appreciate your being honest with me."

Somberly, the physician had held out his hand. "I'll be in my office if you or any of your family need me."

Recalling the conversation, Gabe looked down at his mother. Quietly, he said, "You know what Frank would want, don't you, Mom?"

Dissolving into tears again, Audrey nodded. "I know," she said, her voice muffled behind her handkerchief. "But your father—"

"I'll take care of Dad," Gabe said grimly, and steeled himself as he went to find his father.

Ellis didn't even glance up when Gabe came in; he sat beside Frank's bed, staring down at his elder son, so locked in misery he might have been a stone sculpture. In the greenish light cast by the dim fluorescent at the head of the bed, his skin looked pasty and pale. Like Audrey, he seemed to have aged a great deal.

"Dad?" Gabe whispered. Ellis didn't seem to hear.

"Dad!" Gabe said again, reaching out this time to give his father's shoulder a slight shake. With a start, Ellis broke out of his trance and looked up. When he saw Gabe, his expression hardened.

"What are you doing here?"

Gabe felt the old, familiar tightening in his gut. But he wasn't about to argue at a time like this, so he said, "Dad, we have to talk."

Ellis shrugged away from his grasp. "There's nothing to talk about. Leave me alone with my son."

Despite himself, Gabe felt a flash of anger. He was Ellis's son, too, he thought. Reaching down, he grabbed hold of his father's shoulder again—hard.

"*Now*, Dad," he said.

"There's nothing to talk about," Ellis insisted. But even he saw the implacability in Gabe's eyes, and he glanced quickly toward the still figure on the bed, as though Frank were listening. Gabe was sure he saw a look of fear on his father's face, and for an instant he felt pity. Then he looked at Frank, too, and hardened his heart. This wasn't about Ellis, or Audrey, or Amy, or the girls, or him. It was about Frank, and he had to make his father understand that.

Just when he was about to insist again, Audrey pulled the curtain back and came in. She looked at Gabe for an instant, then she went to her husband. "Please, darling," she whispered. "Come away, just for a moment. We'll ask one of the nurses to sit with him."

"No, I—"

"You must, darling. We have things to discuss."

Ellis's answer was to groan and put his head in his hands. Alarmed, Gabe stepped forward, but Audrey lifted her hand. "We'll meet you in the waiting room, Gabe," she said. "Please, wait for us there."

Gabe glanced at his father, then at his mother again. He was surprised by the look in her eyes, but then he felt ashamed. He had always known how strong his mother was, and he realized that the family had never needed her strength more than now. Nodding wordlessly, he went out to sit with Amy.

Frank's wife was still sitting as Gabe had left her, staring blindly at the floor. She looked blankly at him when he sat beside her, but she didn't speak. Gabe wasn't sure what to say, but finally he said, "Amy, we have to—"

"Don't say it, Gabe!" He didn't know how, but he had broken through her trance. Her head snapped up, and she said, her voice shaking, "You can't come in here and tell us what to do, not when you've been gone so long! It isn't right; it isn't fair, and

I don't care what Frank would say! You've got no right to interfere!"

"I don't want to interfere. But Frank is my brother—"

"And he's my husband! I'll decide what's right, only me!"

"All right, fine," he said soothingly. He could see that she was near hysteria, and he didn't want to be the one who gave her the last little push over the edge. "This is between you and Frank and the doctor—"

"The doctor! I don't believe what the doctor says! Papa Tyrell says it will be all right. We just have to give Frank time."

Gabe didn't know how to proceed. Cautiously, he said, "I know what the doctor told me, Amy, but what did he tell you?"

Amy's lip trembled violently, and she looked ready to cry. Silently, Gabe reached for her hand. To his surprise, she grabbed his fingers and held on tightly. "I can't believe the doctor, I can't!" Her voice rose in a wail. "Oh, Gabe, all I want is my husband back!"

When she burst into tears, Gabe reached out and pulled her close. Her entire body was shaking, and he held her tightly. "I know, Amy, I know," he said, stroking her hair. "I want him back, too." Tears filled his eyes, and he blinked hard to send them away. "But the decision has been taken out of our hands now—"

"No!" she wailed, burying her head in his shoulder. "Oh, Gabe, no!"

He forced himself to say, "Yes. And the best thing, the most loving thing . . ." he held her away from him, forcing her to look into his eyes. "The most loving thing," he repeated, "is to let him go."

Amy shook her head. Burying her face in her hands, she sobbed as though her heart were breaking. Gabe was wiping his own eyes as best he could when his parents appeared. Already tense, Gabe felt as though years had passed. Overhead, the fluorescent lights were harsh, the gray and coral color scheme of the waiting room seemed much too garish. He seemed to see everything in sharp, agonizing relief: the dog-eared magazines, months out of date, the Styrofoam coffee cups scattered around. It reminded Gabe of a cheap hotel lobby, not a hospital waiting room, and he fought an impulse to rip open the door and run outside. He felt suffocated, unable to breathe, and the hard knot in his gut wouldn't go away.

When he met his mother's eyes, she nodded slightly. Ellis didn't even look his way; jerking his arm away from Audrey's grasp, he sat in one of the chairs across the room, distancing himself physically, as well as emotionally, from his family.

Seeing her husband's expression, Audrey said, "Ellis, we have to discuss what's happened. We need to help Amy make a decision—"

Ellis's head snapped up. "There's no decision to be made!" he said sharply. He glared at his younger son. "I don't understand why you're in such an all-fired hurry to get rid of your brother! What did Frank ever do to you?"

Even Amy drew in a sharp breath at that; Gabe's face paled. A muscle leapt out on his tight jaw, and it was only because his mother was present that he didn't tell his father to go to hell. Deciding that he couldn't say anything without the two of them coming to blows right here in the waiting room, he clenched his fists and turned away.

It took Audrey a moment to recover from her shock. "What a terrible thing to say, Ellis! You apologize to Gabe this instant! He's only trying to help, to make us all face the reality we have to face sooner or later!"

"Reality?" Ellis scoffed. "What does *he* know about *reality*? Traipsing all around the world like an itinerant tramp, avoiding responsibility!"

Despite the situation, Gabe couldn't let it pass. "Is that what this is all about, Dad?" he asked. "The fact that I wouldn't go to work at your damned company?"

"I *asked* you to come to work for me! I *begged* you to do it. I wanted it to be Tyrell and *Sons*, but no! Not you. You had to go your own way. Well, think about this, Gabriel. Maybe if you'd done what I asked, what your *brother* wanted as well, Frank wouldn't be lying in there now, fighting to . . . to . . ."

Ellis couldn't continue; sobbing, he put his face in his hands. For a few seconds, the only sounds were the harsh noises coming from his throat.

Gabe was the first to speak. Quietly, he said, "That's not true, Dad, and you know it. But even if it were, now is hardly the time to argue about it." His expression hardened. "Not when Frank needs our—"

With a shout, Ellis came to his feet. "Don't you talk to me about Frank!" he bellowed. "Don't you talk to me about my son!"

"I'm your son, too, Dad, in case you can't remember. And Frank is my brother. I know what he'd want, and this isn't it!"

"You don't know shit!" Ellis shouted. "I'm Frank's father, *I* know what's best for him! You have nothing to say about it!"

"No, but Amy does!" Gabe snapped.

"Amy listens to me!"

Gabe finally lost his temper. "And what makes you so sure you're right?"

Ellis's face was suffused. "Oh, I see! You know better than me!"

"I know what Frank would have wanted!"

"The hell you say!"

"I do! He told me! For God's sake, Dad, are you deliberately blind? Can't you see—"

"How *dare* you talk to me that way! I'll—"

"Gabe's right," Amy said then, her voice so small that they almost didn't hear it. As though caught in freeze-frame, they all turned to stare at her in astonishment. "Gabe's right," she said again. "This isn't what . . . what Frank would want." Tears filled her reddened eyes again as she looked at Gabe. "I couldn't say it before because I didn't want it to be true. But Frank wouldn't want to be . . . to be *kept* this way, I know it. He was always so proud of his mind. . . ." Her voice trailed away for a moment before she looked at Gabe again. Her expression bitter, she said, "So, you're right, Gabe. You're *always* right, aren't you?"

Gabe didn't want to be right; he only wanted to do the right thing by his brother. But before he could speak, Ellis turned to him. His father's eyes were bloodshot; his voice shook. "I'm not going to let you do this thing, do you hear me, Gabriel? I'm not!"

Gabe faced him fearlessly. Long ago, he had stopped being afraid of his father. "Try to think of someone besides yourself for a change, will you?" he said, his voice relentless. "Frank needs us to be strong right now, all of us."

At that moment, Ellis lost control. Shouting, he pulled back his arm, his hand clenched tight. But just as he started to strike, Gabe grabbed his fist. Toe to toe, father and son engaged in a struggle that had been coming for years.

"I'll kill you!" Ellis cried, his face crimson with fury. "So help me, God, I'll—"

"Stop it, Dad, stop it! Do you think this is what Frank would want—us fighting each other?"

As suddenly as he had erupted, Ellis disintegrated. Tears spurting from his eyes, he collapsed against Gabe with a sob. "I love him, I love him," he wept brokenly. "It's so hard to let him go. I'm not ready!"

Gabe held his father tightly, lifting his head so his own tears wouldn't spill over. "None of us are ready, but neither was Frank," he said. "And we have to do this last thing for him, Dad. We *have* to."

It was a long moment before the broken father nodded. Beside them, Amy and Audrey were weeping quietly, and as Gabe looked at them for agreement, Ellis held out his arms, and the women ran to him. Leaving the group holding on to each other tightly, Gabe took a deep breath and went to find the doctor.

The hours following seemed endless. Gabe thought that once the decision was made, the procedure would be over with quickly, but there were forms to fill out and arrangements to be completed, and the doctor had to speak to each of them again. At last, when he thought he was going to pass out from sheer exhaustion, the doctor came into the waiting room one last time. It was afternoon by then, and everyone but Gabe had been in to say good-bye to Frank. At some point during the past hours, they had agreed that Gabe would be the one to give the final word. Amy was sedated; Ellis looked near collapse. Audrey was white and strained, wanting it to be over.

"It's time," the doctor said quietly.

Gabe knew that if he looked at Amy or either of his parents, he wouldn't be able to go through with it, so he got up and followed without looking back. Two nurses were in Frank's cubicle when he entered; both gave him empathetic looks and tactfully turned back to the machines they were tending. They all stood silently for a moment, then the doctor touched his arm.

"Whenever you're ready," he said.

Gabe nodded, his eyes on the still figure on the bed. He felt overwhelmed by the responsibility; he literally held his brother's life in his hands, and for a moment, he panicked. *I can't go through with it,* he thought, and wanted to bolt for the door and never come back. Instead, his heart pounding, he took a seat by the bed and reached for Frank's hand.

"I wish—" he started to say, and he knew he'd never get through it if he began that way. He tried again. "Well, I guess this is it," he said, his voice breaking despite himself. "I didn't want it to be this way, but neither did you. There are a lot of things I wish I'd said, but knowing you, you already know them anyway. You always were the thinker, I just sort of barreled through."

His voice failed him again at that point, and he bowed his head, thinking again that he couldn't do it. Somehow he forced himself to look up. "You saved my life many a time, big brother," he whispered painfully. "And now, in a strange way, I guess I'm here to do the same for you. I . . . I hope this is what you want, Frank, because if I had my choice, I'd . . ."

He had to stop again. His voice barely audible, he ended with, "I know Mom and Dad will watch out for Amy and the girls, but I promise I'll be there for them, too. So . . . go in peace my friend, my brother, and . . . and remember that I love you."

He gave Frank's hand one last squeeze. Then, before he lost courage, he looked up at the doctor and the two nurses. He couldn't find the words, but when he nodded, the doctor came to his side of the bed and suggested he leave.

He shook his head. "I . . . I want to stay. He shouldn't be alone."

Nodding, the doctor moved away. He reached down, and Gabe thought the tiny rip of the tape holding the breathing tube in place was the most wrenching noise he had ever heard—until Frank made a harsh gasping sound. Panicked again, he looked up at the doctor, who shook his head.

"It's all right," the man said. "It's just a reflex."

Gabe looked down again. His heart was pounding so hard he thought it would leap out of his chest; his eyes were swimming with tears, and he could hardly see Frank's face. He tightened his grip on his brother's hand, and thought—must have imagined—a returning pressure as the nurses shut down the machines. One by one, the beep and the whoosh and the ticking died into profound silence. The doctor waited a moment before he leaned over Frank with a stethoscope. He listened for a few seconds, then he straightened. As the nurses silently filed out, he looked at Gabe.

"Your brother is at peace now," he said in a low voice. "I'll leave you alone with him for a few moments while I tell the family."

Gabe couldn't speak. He nodded as the man gave his shoulder a comforting squeeze before he went out; then he looked one last time toward the still figure on the bed. A kaleidoscope of memories flashed into his mind: his brother as a child, a boy, a young man, the man he'd been. Had he done the right thing? It was a question he'd have to live with the rest of his life, and

right now, he didn't know if he had the strength. Despite his
family outside, he had never felt so lonely, so alone. A sob escaped him, a hoarse, harsh sound filled with pain.

"Gabe?"

He jerked his head up at the sound of her voice. For a moment, he thought he was hallucinating, that his desire to have
her with him had conjured her out of his mind. Without realizing
it, he stumbled to his feet. When he turned and saw her, he was
sure he was dreaming.

"Oh, Gabe, I'm so sorry," Keeley said, holding her arms out.
She was wearing a coat over slacks and sweater—the first things
she'd grabbed before rushing to the airport and taking the first
flight she could get out. She looked pale and worried and anxious for him; her green eyes swam with tears. Tenderly, she
reached for him.

He hadn't imagined her; she was really here. With a strangled
sob, he grabbed her to him and buried his face in her sweet-
smelling hair.

CHAPTER TWENTY-EIGHT

Keeley stayed with Gabe for three days. On the third day,
right after Frank's funeral—at which Gabe delivered a touching
eulogy—they had a terrible quarrel she would never forget.
Hurt, angry, and telling herself she'd never really known him,
she was on a plane back to New York before she knew it. It was
all over between them, and she was so despondent she couldn't
even weep.

She had been so glad to see him, so relieved that she had
dropped everything to come. His expression when he first saw
her at the hospital was all she needed, and despite what happened later, she knew she would never forget how he had
reached for her when he saw her standing there, and how his
tears had wet her hair.

She didn't know what hospital to go to when she got into
L.A., so she had called his parents' home and talked to someone

named Laveda, who had given her directions. Outside in the waiting room, she had spoken briefly with the devastated parents, and when she found out the agonizing decision the family had made, her heart went out to all of them. She knew how numb she had been after Fitz had died, and after her reunion with Gabe, she offered to help. Gabe protested, but she was insistent.

"You've always helped me when I needed you," she said. "I'd look up and you'd be there. It's my turn, Gabe. Let me do this one thing for you, please."

So she comforted Audrey, and Gabe's sister-in-law, managing to get them out of the hospital and into the car for the trip home. She'd thought vaguely about getting a hotel room someplace close, but when Audrey heard of her plans, she insisted Keeley come to the house instead.

"Please," Gabe's mother said, taking her hands. Her eyes were reddened from crying, and her face was lined and sad. "It would mean so much to Gabe, and to me. He's told me about you, but I can see it wasn't nearly enough." She tried to smile. "I know the circumstances aren't . . . right, but I would like a chance to get to know you a little better, my dear. Please say you'll stay. It will make us both so happy."

It would have been churlish to refuse such a gracious invitation, and the first night she was glad she'd agreed to stay. It was late afternoon by the time they finally left the hospital, and Laveda, whom Keeley had spoken to over the telephone earlier, welcomed them home with soup and sandwiches. No one was hungry, but it was obvious that the housekeeper felt the loss deeply, too, and the food was her way of showing it. Ellis disappeared into his den, and Keeley, feeling the family had a right to privacy, excused herself early and went to bed.

As she had thought he would, Gabe came sometime later. She had guessed that of all nights, this was one time he would especially need to be with her. In normal circumstances, she would never have abused Audrey's hospitality by welcoming Gabe to her room, but she felt instinctively that Gabe's mother would have understood.

At first, she just held Gabe in her arms as he spoke of Frank—happy memories even though at times his voice shook. She knew that the guilt and recriminations would come later—but in what form, and with what effect, even she hadn't guessed that night. Unable to foresee the future, she had listened and stroked his hair, and when he had finally turned and kissed her, and kissed her again, and she felt the urgency rising in his body, she knew he needed to prove to himself that even though someone close had died, he was still alive. It was a perverse feeling, hard to understand, difficult to explain, but as his lovemaking took on almost a savage intensity that wasn't like him at all, she didn't hold back.

The climax came and he collapsed by her side, his arm covering his eyes. His body felt the physical release, but he still craved something else, and when he turned to her again and buried his face against her breasts, she wasn't surprised when he began to cry. Rocking him slightly, murmuring soothing meaningless sounds, she held him until he fell asleep.

He slept as though drugged, a deep sleep punctuated with dreams. She was too attuned to him to do more than doze; every time he groaned, she came awake in case he needed her. Once or twice he cried out, but she soothed him until he fell back again. He didn't wake again until it was almost dawn.

"How did you know?" he asked, looking at her with a wondering expression.

Tenderly, she touched his cheek. Thinking of the summer after she'd lost Fitz, she answered, "How did you know that I needed you?"

Reluctantly, he left her before anyone else in the house got up. If Audrey suspected that they'd spent the night together, she never said, but Laveda gave her a quick hug that morning, whispering, "You're good medicine."

Funeral arrangements were made, and Frank's two young daughters arrived with their grandparents. Keeley was captivated by the little girls; thinking they were too young to attend, she offered to stay home with them while the rest of the family went to the cemetery. But Amy tearfully insisted she wanted them with her, and in the end, everyone went.

It wasn't until after the funeral, when Keeley and Gabe escaped from the many mourners who had come back to the house, that Gabe told her of his decision to leave the foundation and go to work for his father.

They had gone outside to be alone and were wandering through the huge parklike backyard. Incredibly, it was September again, and Gabe made a weak joke about how they were going to have to forego the promise they had made to each other about meeting at this time of year at the ranch in Montana.

"I don't think we're going to make it, are we?" he said, as they walked in the garden.

Keeley put her arm through his. "We'll try again next year."

He put his hand on hers. "I'll hold you to it."

"I'll be there."

He told her of his plans then, and she was so dismayed that she pulled away from him. She couldn't have been more shocked if he'd said he had decided to leave the secular life to become a Trappist monk.

"You don't mean ... for good!" she exclaimed.

He looked away, suddenly finding an interest in a spreading maple tree. "Yes, I do. Dad needs me, and I owe it to him."

They had walked out to the middle of Audrey's extensive garden, still fragrant with the scent of the roses she cultivated, although their season, too, was almost over. A sudden light breeze wafted through, scattering petals. Blankly, Keeley looked at the rose-colored confetti. He can't mean it, she thought.

He saw her stunned expression and smiled—a bitter little smile that alarmed her even further. "I know what you're thinking."

Presence of mind came flooding back in a rush. "Do you?" she said. "Well, that's good, Gabe, because I certainly don't. I can't believe you mean it. Leave the foundation? You love it there!"

His eyes sought the maple tree again. "I don't want to argue about it, Keeley. My mind is made up."

She knew him so well, enough to see that he wasn't completely comfortable about his decision, although he pretended to be. But she also heard the stubbornness in his voice, and she took a different tack. "Have you told your father yet?"

"Yes."

Her heart sank. She knew how Gabe's father felt about his sons and his company; Gabe had told her long ago about the problems he'd caused by refusing to work at the family business. She didn't have to think about it to know how happy Ellis would be, especially now that Frank ...

A sudden thought occurred to her, and she looked at Gabe. "Have you really thought about this?" she asked carefully.

He glanced at her irritably. "Of course I have. Do you think I would have made the decision otherwise?"

Wisely, she didn't say he might not be thinking too clearly at this point, so soon after his brother died. Instead, she said, "What did your father say?"

"Just what I expected him to. He was pleased—or as pleased

as he's ever going to be with anything I do. He's always wanted me to join the company. Like Frank."

It was the opening she'd been seeking. Putting her hand on his arm, she said quietly, "You're not Frank, Gabe. You don't have to try to take his place."

Instantly, she knew she'd made a mistake. Hot color flooded into his face under his tan, and he turned to her furiously. "Is that what you think I'm trying to do?"

She had never seen him so angry, and it flashed across her mind to apologize, to say she hadn't meant it, to smooth things over and pretend it hadn't happened. But she was his friend, as well as his lover, and she couldn't make herself do it. "You tell me, Gabe," she said. "You're the one who knows."

As suddenly as he'd turned angry, his face became cold. He looked as if he despised her. "I don't have to answer to you, Keeley. I've made my decision. I start work on Monday."

"As what?" she demanded. "Tell me, Gabe. What are you going to do at your father's company that couldn't be done by someone else?" She saw his face change, saw the fury darkening his eyes, and rushed on before he could say anything. She was desperate to make him see what he was doing—what he would do—to himself if he chose this path. "Don't you see?" she continued urgently. "What you do is too precious and valuable to give up! How can you even think of abandoning it for an office? You've told me over and over again how much you love your work, how satisfying it is!"

Gabe's jaw was so tight she could see the muscles stretched along the bone. "I'll be satisfied at Tyrell. And it won't be an office. I'll be flying all over the country."

"You already fly all over the world!" she cried. "Doing what you love to do, doing what you do best! Oh, Gabe, please think about it again. You'll never be happy; it will never work! It's just not right!"

"Yes, it is. It's what I should have done a long time ago. I told you, I've made my decision."

"Well, unmake it then!" she shouted, beside herself. She felt like beating at his chest to make him understand. "Gabe, don't you remember what you've always told me—"

"That was before."

"Before what? Before Frank died? Gabe, you're not thinking clearly. You don't have to make a decision now!"

Savagely he turned to her. Tears glittered in his eyes. "Frank was my brother!"

She nearly flinched at the look on his face. She had never seen such naked pain in anyone's eyes. But she had to press on; she had to make him see that whatever guilt he felt, he couldn't atone this way. "Yes, he was your brother! But he wouldn't have wanted you to make it up to him this way!"

"Oh, yes, he would have! He was on my case for years—for *years*—to join him and Dad at the company. But no, I wouldn't listen. I had to go my own way. Well, maybe if I *had* listened, this wouldn't have happened. Maybe if I'd done what I should have, Frank would be alive right now!"

She couldn't believe he meant it. "You can't know that, none of us can. Frank made his own decisions—"

"Did he? Did he make his own decisions? Who was the one to pull the plug, Keeley? Who? It wasn't Frank, *it was me!*"

In a flash, she knew why Gabe was giving up so much, why he was willing to sacrifice the rest of his life to make up for his brother's loss. She knew he was upset, but she hadn't realized his guilt ran so deep, or was so senseless. Horrified, she reached for him. She had to tell him the truth even if he hated her for it, even if he never spoke to her again.

"Gabe, listen to me," she said. "You're not responsible for Frank's death. You're not."

He wrenched his arm away. "Easy for you to say. You didn't pull the plug. I did."

"Will you stop saying that!" she cried. "No one *pulled the damn plug!* The machines keeping him alive were stopped, that's all. That's all! The doctor said that Frank died in the accident, at the scene!"

"No!" Gabe turned away. His eyes were dark with horror and the memory of what he'd had to do. "He was alive with those machines, and no one in the family wanted to turn them off but me. It was my decision, Keeley—mine alone."

She was beside herself. "It wasn't your decision. It was Frank's! He told you what he wanted a long time ago."

"I still forced my family to let go of him. And now I have an obligation to make it right!"

"Oh, Gabe!" She didn't know what else to say. Why couldn't she make him see he was wrong?

Gabe turned to her. His eyes were like blue steel, his voice suddenly as cold. "You know, I thought you, of all people, would understand. I was wrong, wasn't I?"

She looked at him unflinchingly. She knew she had lost, but she had to say it anyway. "You're wrong, Gabe, but not about that. You can't take Frank's place, just as he couldn't have taken yours. You can try the rest of your life, but you'll never get what you seek because it isn't where you're looking."

Gabe stiffened. He seemed to tower over her, a statue that had turned to ice. "Fine. You've said what you think. Now, I'd appreciate it if you would leave. It's obvious we have nothing more to say to each other—ever."

She was shocked. "You don't mean it!"

He looked at her as if he hated her. "I do. Now, get out."

She'd been too concerned about him to think of herself, but now, because she felt so frustrated and agonized and helpless, her temper erupted with a vengeance. Her voice beginning to shake with rage and pain, she said, "Don't worry, I will! If that's how you feel, I'm on my way." She lifted her chin, her green eyes ablaze. "And don't worry—I won't come back. But before I go, I want to tell *you* something. I thought I knew you, but I was wrong, as well. I thought you were someone strong and talented and independent—a real man who knew his own worth. But you're not, Gabe. What you are is a daddy's boy, just like Frank!"

She shouldn't have said it; she knew by the look on his face. But she had said too many things she shouldn't have said, and so had he. Without waiting to hear his reply, she turned around and went back to the house.

Somehow she managed to leave without breaking down entirely. Fiercely she held back her tears until she made her apologies to her hostess and departed for the airport. Without knowing the real reason for her abrupt departure, Audrey begged her to stay awhile longer. Fortunately, she was too dazed by grief to question Keeley's taut excuse that she had to get back to New York, for Keeley knew she couldn't have explained further. Laveda's eyes were more knowing when Keeley sought her out in the kitchen before she left. Her face sympathetic, she gave Keeley a quick hug.

"Gabriel Lee was always one to take the hard road," Laveda said, sighing. "It's his nature. Always was, and always will be."

Keeley looked into her wise eyes. "Then you know about his decision to go to work for his father."

"I know, but it's something he's going to have to work out, honey. We can tell him what we think, but he's the only one who can find what he's looking for."

As she headed back to New York, Keeley wished she could be as sanguine as Laveda seemed to be. Would Gabe ever find out he couldn't take Frank's place, or would he spend the rest of his life fighting a ghost?

"Oh, Gabe!" she thought sadly. She'd been angry when she left the house, furious with him for cutting her out of his life, enraged with herself for letting him down. She'd told herself she hated him, but as the plane climbed out of Los Angeles International and made a wide turn over the ocean before heading east, she knew he was the last person in the world she'd hate. The idea that she might never see him again caused her real pain; she felt as though a piece of her heart had been cut away. It was really over, she thought, dazed. It was hard to believe that what she and Gabe had had together had been irrevocably destroyed. After what had happened, he'd never forgive her because he couldn't forgive himself.

Her hurt so deep she couldn't even cry, she put her head back against the seat. Closing her burning eyes, she tried to sleep.

Keeley came back to more problems than she'd left. No matter how well planned, complications arose like weeds while putting a show together, and she had dropped everything to be with Gabe at a critical point. Never mind that the book still wasn't done, and that sets and costumes couldn't be designed fully until it was. Never mind that the choreographer couldn't do her work until the set design was done, and that Keeley still had to find an arranger and finish the score. Gabe had been more important to her than anything else; even the show had taken second place.

As the plane touched down at JFK, she was glad she was going to be so preoccupied with the show. Dealing with all the problems still ahead would help take her mind off Gabe—or so she hoped. Now that six hours and a continent separated them, she felt even more desolate than she had when she left; the urge to call him and apologize nagged at her, but she knew it wouldn't do any good. The show was the important thing now, she told herself tearfully. She had to forget her personal problems and get on with it.

Since Nigel was long gone, doing God knew what, Keeley and Tux had stayed on with Val at the apartment. Normally she would have preferred her own place, but she had been absorbed in all the details of getting the show together and it didn't matter to her where she stayed. What with one thing and another, she was rarely home anyway. Staying with Valeska was a simple solution, and although she didn't want to admit it, a good excuse to keep an eye on her.

She frowned, thinking of Val. Valeska had been out of treatment for months now, but there were times she was so shaky that Keeley wondered if she'd be able to hold it together to perform. The doctor at St. Mary's had told her Val needed time and a gentle touch. He'd warned her not to rush her too much, so she had waited weeks before suggesting it was time to start voice lessons. Valeska had been spending all her time on the couch watching TV, and finally Keeley felt she had to put her foot down. If she didn't get busy soon, Valeska wouldn't be ready when the time came.

"Go ahead, get someone else!" Val had screamed at her during one of their fights. "Go ahead, see if I care! I never wanted to do it anyway! I was completely happy as I was, so there!"

Keeley was trying hard to hold on to her temper. What had begun as a discussion had rapidly escalated into a shouting match. Between her teeth, she said, "You weren't happy, you're kidding yourself. When I first came, you were dead drunk; the place was a mess; God knows when you'd eaten last or taken a bath—"

"I don't want to hear it!" Valeska screeched, clapping her hands over her ears like a child. "You can't make me listen, Keeley, you can't! I've done everything you wanted, everything you made me do, but I can't do this. I'm just not ready to sing again!"

Keeley could feel herself rapidly approaching the boiling point. Speaking slowly and distinctly, enunciating every word because she was furious enough to start screaming herself, she said, "All right, Valeska. And just when *do* you think you might be able to sing again?"

"I don't know! I don't know, and I don't care! Maybe I'll *never* sing again, what do you think of that, huh? What do you think of that?"

Keeley didn't say anything for a long moment. As she looked at Valeska, she was thinking that maybe she didn't know Val after all. Maybe too much time had passed; maybe the past years had changed them both too much.

"I think," she said after a silence, "that I've made a mistake. You're not Beauty, Val—maybe you never were. I guess I'm just going to have to cast someone else."

She started out of the room, but she hadn't gone two steps before Valeska ran after her.

"Wait!" she cried. "Where are you going?"

"I don't know. Away from here."

"But you . . . you can't leave me!"

Keeley remembered the doctor's warning. He'd said that Val might test her, and that if—when—the moment came, she had to be strong and make a stand. Addictive personalities could be manipulative, he'd cautioned; she mustn't give in. Steeling herself, she said, "Why not? You've just said you don't need me, and I don't want you to do *Beauty* if you feel I'm forcing you. I guess I'm wasting my time. I've got better things to do than baby-sit you."

"But . . . but . . ." Panic in her eyes, Val was stuttering. Her grip on Keeley's arm tightened, her fingers like claws. "But I can't make it without you!" she cried.

Calmly, although her heart was pounding, Keeley pried the fingers off her arm. "You're going to have to. I can't fight you anymore. I've tried to give you all the time you said you needed, but I'm beginning to think that time isn't the problem." Forcing herself, she looked into Valeska's staring eyes. "Maybe you're right; maybe you won't ever sing again." She paused. "Maybe you just don't have it in you anymore."

The next day, the voice coach came. Valeska had begged Keeley to stay, and she had agreed after Val promised to start her lessons. Madame LeDuc had died, but Mr. Josiah Trevelyan was a dapper little man whose chubby cheeks and pencil mustache belied the martinet underneath. He took complete charge of the apartment for several hours a day at first, then for longer and longer stretches of time. When Keeley was home, she and an increasingly lazy Tux retreated to the den to work, but even through closed doors, she could hear Trevelyan putting Val through scale after scale, regaining control of her voice. He never shouted, he never screamed; he never even raised his own voice, but she could hear him as clear as a bell.

"Some singers put the sound in the nose," he'd pronounce. "It's wrong, wrong, wrong! It comes from the *breath*, the sound is on the *breath*. Now, try it again, please."

Or, "Always use the *entire* voice, even when singing softly. Remember, the center of the tone must always be there. Pianissimo, crescendo. The increase starts with the *mind*, and the body follows. It is a matter of technique. Now, try it again, please."

And still another: "The middle voice should be taken up as high as possible to preserve the quality. The break between *your* middle and high voices comes higher than for most sopranos, you see? Let me test a moment . . . Sing it please. Yes, as I thought. Now *here*—" a crash of piano keys "—is how we take advantage of it. Try it again, please."

Keeley didn't know what he was talking about half the time, but Val did, and Keeley didn't have to understand theory to hear the steady improvement as the daily lessons went on. Soon, Val's high, soaring soprano was filling the apartment with glorious sound, and Keeley was writing better and better herself. In the den behind closed doors, she would write, listen, write again, and then want to dance around the room in elation.

"Yes!" she'd exult, picking up her indignant cat and whirling him around with her. "Oh, yes!" For the first time since she'd dragged Valeska, kicking and screaming into the shower before taking her to the hospital, she was sure that together they could bring *Beauty and the Beast* to life.

But that was before she went to California to be with Gabe. Four months later, when January's icy winds were whipping down the canyons created by Manhattan's skyscrapers, she was delayed coming to rehearsal by a subway accident. Hours later, she hurried into the studio loft she had rented and knew instantly something was wrong. The cast was supposed to be working, but everyone was standing around looking nervous. Her first thought was that something awful had happened to Valeska. "What's wrong?" she demanded at once.

One of the group, a tall, lanky, young dancer named Tony, spoke up. "Uh . . . there's a problem."

"What kind of problem?"

Unable to look her in the eye, he said, "We've been shut down."

"Shut down? What do you mean, shut down? Who told you that?"

"Uh . . . the rumor is that the backers have backed out."

Her voice sharpened. "And just where did you hear that?"

Tony looked uncomfortable. "I . . . don't remember."

"Everybody stay here," she commanded. "I'll find out what's going on."

She had a cubbyhole of an office next to the broom closet. It had a desk and a telephone, which she picked up as soon as she slammed the door behind her. One of the people she had convinced to invest was a man named Cleve Williams, whom she had met when she was working on *Sequins*. Cleve was a theater groupie, and he loved her music. He'd said that if she ever did a show to come to him for money. When she decided to do

Beauty, he was one of the first people she'd contacted. He had not only come through but had brought in other investors with him.

She'd known right from the beginning that they were shaky; he and his friends had never backed a show on their own, and they wanted guarantees she couldn't give. She'd spent a lot of time over the past few months assuring them they'd get a return on their money. Wondering what could have happened in the short time she'd been gone, she dialed Cleve's number, her expression grim.

"Ah ... er ... Keeley," Cleve said when she finally had him on the line. "How are you?"

"Not good," she said flatly. "What's this about the show being shut down?"

"Ah ... we were going to talk to you about it, Keeley."

Her lips tightened. "When?"

"Uh ... maybe we could meet in my office. Tomorrow about three?"

She wasn't going to spend an entire night in a state of dread anticipation. "We'll talk now, Cleve. What's the problem?"

"I really didn't want to do it this way, but since you insist. . . . I'm sorry, Keeley, but Pryor and Jasko and I have decided to pull out of the show."

"What!"

"I'm sorry," he said again, quickly. "But it's a lot of money to be betting on. I mean, I know how talented you are, Keeley, but after all, this is big business. A lot of money is involved, and I—we—well, we decided we can't afford to bet it on someone so inexperienced."

Keeley's head was reeling; she had to grab on to the edge of the desk for support. It was worse than she had expected. She had never dreamed they'd *all* pull out. Fiercely, she pulled herself together. "You didn't feel that way yesterday, Cleve," she said. "What made you change your mind?"

"I ... uh ... nothing, really. We just sat down and talked about it and—"

"Who did you talk to, Cleve?" She knew he was lying; she could hear it in his voice. "You thought I was a 'good bet' before!"

"We didn't talk to anyone," he said, so quickly that she knew he was lying again. "We just had a meeting and decided the risk was too great."

"I see." She was holding on to her control by a thread, trying to think. Her mind felt like it was stuffed with steel wool.

"I'm sorry, Keeley."

"So am I, Cleve. But you're not the only backers in town. I'll find someone else."

"Don't you think it might be better just to . . . put the show on hold for a while?"

"No, I don't," she said. Her voice sharpened. "Why do you say that?"

"You don't really want to go through it, do you?"

"Talk to me, Cleve," she said inexorably. "You owe me this, at least."

He was silent a moment. Then, sighing again, he said, "I don't know who started it, but the word is that the show's going to be a flop. That you're just too inexperienced; that the book is too long; the choreography isn't that great—"

"What are you talking about? We've barely started rehearsals, for God's sake! The book's too long? The whole thing isn't even written yet! And as for choreography—"

"Calm down, Keeley. *I* didn't say it."

"Then who did? Oh, never mind, you don't know, right? Or, you don't remember, is that it?" Her voice dripped contempt. "Well, fine, at least I know who my friends are now. You'll be hearing from me one way or another, but as of right now, you got what you wanted. You're out!"

She managed to hang up without crashing the phone down, but as soon as she broke the connection, she put her face in her hands. What was she going to do? Cleve and his friends had been her major backers; as soon as the other investors heard about the pullout, Keeley had no doubt they'd back away, too. She knew this town; if word had gone around, no one would touch her. What was she going to do?

She'd hang on somehow, she thought fiercely, dropping her hands. She still had some money left—not much, but enough to pay the crew and keep things going until she found other investors. If worse came to worst, she thought with a wince, she'd call Raleigh. She didn't want to do it because she knew how he felt about the theater now, but if she had to, she'd ask his help. There wasn't anything she wouldn't do for this show. She'd bring it to life if she had to sell everything she had.

Squaring her shoulders, she went out to tell the crew they were still working. She didn't know how long she could pay them and felt even worse when a relieved hubbub arose. Feeling a headache coming on, she let them go for the day. Things had to look better in the morning, she thought, and decided to hang it up herself. Calling for a cab, she went home.

The apartment was dark when she arrived, and as soon as she stepped inside, she had a premonition. She had left a message on the machine to say when she'd be home; she thought Valeska would be here, since she hadn't been at rehearsal. *Something's wrong,* she thought, her heart starting to pound. Nervously, she called out, "Val?"

"Good evening, Keeley."

The disembodied voice came from the living room in front of her. Her eyes had adjusted to the darkness enough to see the outline of a man's head and shoulders against the window. He'd been sitting on the couch, but even before he stood and she snapped on the entry light, she knew who it was. She hadn't heard his voice in years, but she would recognize Nigel anywhere.

"What are *you* doing here?" She looked around. "And where's Val?"

Calmly, Nigel stood up. She saw at once how much he had changed. His hair had thinned and silvered; his paunch had grown. But more startling were the lines around his eyes and down the sides of his mouth. He looked at least ten years older than she knew him to be, and she was shocked despite herself.

"Despite what my sweet wife might have told you, this is still my home," he said. "And as for Valeska—" he shrugged, although his eyes momentarily gleamed "—she's in the bedroom, having a . . . nap."

Keeley turned immediately in the direction of the bedroom. She didn't know what he was doing here, but she wanted to make sure Valeska was all right. She knew how afraid Val was of Nigel, but she wasn't sure exactly why. Valeska wouldn't talk about him, or her marriage; every time Keeley pressed her, she'd burst into tears and refuse to discuss it. Thinking now that she should have pushed a little harder, she said, "You stay here. I'm going to check—"

"I think we should talk," Nigel said.

She stopped. "We have nothing to say to each other."

"Oh, I think we do. For instance, I was so sorry to hear that your backers . . . er . . . backed out on the new show. It must have been quite a blow."

She knew at that moment he was responsible—not only for putting pressure on Cleve and his friends, but probably for spreading the other rumors as well. "Yes, it was," she said coldly. "But Cleve and the others are only three. I can get other backers."

"You think so."

"I do."

"A pity you're going to be disappointed."

Her eyes narrowed. "If you came to gloat, you can leave right now. In fact, I don't even know what you're doing here. How did you get in? We changed the locks, so I know you don't have a key."

"Valeska let me in, of course," he said smoothly. "But let's not quarrel, Keeley. I came to rescue you."

"Rescue me? You?" She laughed aloud.

"Now, now, there's no need to be unkind. We go back a long way, after all, you and I. I thought, as friends—"

"We were never friends, Nigel," she said. "Let's stop wasting time. Why are you really here?"

"Always direct and to the point," he said, sighing. "How tiresome you can be."

"I'm going to be even more tiresome when I call security and have you thrown out."

"Of my own apartment?" He made a *tsk*ing sound.

"This hasn't been your apartment since before you walked out and left Valeska high and dry," she snapped.

"You have always misjudged me, my dear. I confess that when I left, my sweet wife was high, but she certainly wasn't dry. We both know what a . . . a problem she has."

"Not anymore," Keeley said, her voice steely. "And stop calling Valeska your wife. She told me you were divorced."

"Oh, dear, I'm afraid that, as she is in so many things, Valeska is confused about our matrimonial state. We're not divorced, Keeley. We're still husband and wife."

Keeley didn't believe him. She knew Valeska had told her she and Nigel were divorced. But suddenly she wondered why she'd never seen any decree. Was that why Valeska was so afraid of him? Because he still had a hold on her? "You're lying," she said. "You'd say anything to cause trouble."

"Ask her. She wouldn't divorce me, you see. And I certainly wouldn't divorce her—not my little nightingale."

"Your meal ticket, you mean!"

"Well, yes, but that was before. My songbird hasn't been singing so much as of late, but it was all about to change, wasn't it? Until ... disaster. Which brings us back to our original topic."

"I've forgotten what the original topic was, Nigel," Keeley said. She reached for the door. "I think it's time for you to leave."

"No, I don't think so. You haven't heard my offer yet."

"I'm not interested in anything you have to say."

"Not even when I have a solution to your problem?"

"Not even then."

"Oh, come now, you always were afflicted with foolish pride. We both know what a bind you're in without backing; that is, if you want to put on your little play. As it happens, we've come to a point in our lives where we each have something to offer the other. Now, if I were directing—"

"Directing! Are you out of your mind? *I'm* directing the show! It's *mine*, and no one's going to take it away from me!"

"Noble sentiments from someone lacking finances," Nigel said. "Now, as I was saying before I was so rudely interrupted, if I were directing, the money would come in. I'm not without influence in this town, as you have recently experienced. The money I took away I can easily get back again."

She had opened the door, intending to show him out. Slowly, she shut it again. Fascinated despite herself, she asked, "Why are you so interested in being involved with *Beauty*?"

For the first time, he looked uncomfortable. Stretching his neck slightly, he said, "Well, it's no secret that I ... haven't had a hit in some time."

"You can say that again. The last one was—what? I can't even remember."

"Yes, well, I find it's futile counting back over the past," he said hastily. "The point is what we're going to do *now*."

"*We're* not going to do anything, Nigel. I've told you—"

"You'll never get the money without me, Keeley," he said. "But since you're too stubborn to realize that now, I'll just have to let you flounder awhile longer, until you come to your senses. In the meantime, there are other things to discuss."

"What things?"

"I'll only say this to you, Keeley—no one else. In fact, I'll deny it if it comes back to me. But you and I have known each other a long time, and I'll tell you this. *Beauty and the Beast* can be a success. I've seen the book, and I've had a glimpse of the score. ..."

Keeley didn't ask how he'd seen these things; it was obvious he had his spies everywhere. "Go on," she said tightly.

He took a step forward until they were only inches apart. She could smell the strong scent of his cologne, and her nostrils contracted. "I'm going to be involved in this project in some capacity, Keeley, make up your mind about it," he said. "I *need* it; I won't pretend otherwise to anyone but you. Now, I left you alone when you were enjoying all your success in Hollywood—"

"You had no choice!"

"True, true. But you're back here now, Keeley, and I'm afraid your contract with me is still in force. If *Beauty* is the success I think it's going to be, you're going to make me a rich man. Oh, so rich again."

Keeley clenched her fists. She had never despised anyone so much as she despised him right now. "*Assuming* you can get away with stealing royalties from me, why the insistence on being involved with the show?" she asked. "Why waste your time directing, when you can just sit home and collect all the loot?"

"Because I want to be involved, my dear," he said. "I want to see *my* name up there again. You can understand that."

"Oh, I understand, all right," she said, her eyes blazing. "I understand that you're nothing but an opportunist who thinks he's going to hitch a ride on my coattails! Well, let me tell you, Nigel, I'm not—"

"Careful, Keeley," he said, his face reddening. "You don't want to make me use my other ace, do you?"

She looked at him contemptuously. "What other ace?"

Glancing in the direction of the bedroom, he smiled. Keeley felt a chill run up and down her back. He looked so evil she believed he'd do anything to get what he wanted. Anything.

"I know you wrote the part of Beauty for Valeska," he said softly, menacingly. "And I know no one but she can possibly sing it as it should be sung." He looked at her again. "But we both know the past few years haven't been kind to our little songbird. Alas, she's lost her confidence."

"She didn't *lose* her confidence; you destroyed it!"

"Be that as it may," he said calmly, "the point is, that if she doesn't sing Beauty, she'll never sing again. We both know this is her last chance, but she's so shaky. *So* shaky. One . . . little . . . push . . . and she could just tip right over, don't you agree?"

Keeley was so angry—and so frightened for her vulnerable friend—that she took a threatening step toward him. "You leave

Val alone, Nigel, do you hear me? If you do anything to undo all the progress she's made—"

Nigel put up his hands. "Oh, my dear, how you misjudge me. Would I do anything to stop the golden goose from singing?" His smile disappeared again. "Unless I was forced to, of course." Stepping around her, he reached for the door. "Just remember, Keeley, I know Valeska, and it wouldn't take much. In fact, I've already talked to her about it, and she agrees we should all work together, just like in the old days. When you come to your senses, call me. I'll be waiting."

"It'll be a long wait!" she shouted. But he was already out the door, scuttling down the hallway like the insect he was. She was tempted to go after him, but she halted on a sudden, awful thought. What had he meant, he'd already talked to Valeska?

Slamming the door shut, she headed down the hall toward the bedroom. Valeska wasn't home, she assured herself. If she had been, she would have come out, wondering what all the shouting was about.

"Val?" she called.

Valeska's bedroom door was closed. "Val?" she said again.

When there was no answer, she took a deep breath and opened the door. When she saw what was inside, she knew why Valeska hadn't heard anything.

"Oh, Val," she whispered, leaning against the door, wondering where she was going to get the strength.

Valeska was lying facedown on the bed. She had almost finished the pint of vodka Nigel must have brought before she passed out, and as Keeley watched, the bottle slipped from Valeska's nerveless fingers and fell to the floor. She didn't even stir.

CHAPTER TWENTY-NINE

When Valeska woke up, the apartment was dark. Groaning, she rolled over and put a hand to her head. *Jesus God,* she thought, what happened?

Cautiously, she opened one eye and tried to see the bedside clock. She thought it read two-thirty, but she was so groggy she couldn't be sure. Was it night or day? The last thing she remembered was leaving rehearsal early. She'd felt so guilty that she decided to fix dinner for her and Keeley.

Keeley! At the thought, she sat up, wincing when a hammering began behind her eyes. She didn't care; she couldn't have Keeley find her like this. Keeley would think she'd been drinking, and . . .

Her foot touched something on the floor. It felt like glass, and she bent down to see what it was. The room pitched and rolled with her sudden movement, and for a moment, she thought she was going to be sick. Her hand to her pounding head, she sat up again. What was wrong with her? She felt like someone had been beating her with big sticks.

Wondering if she had the flu, she dragged herself off the bed. She started toward the bathroom, where she knew she could find some aspirin, but her foot touched the glass on the floor again. Squinting, she looked down and was surprised to see a bottle. A *pint* bottle. Instantly, she recoiled. What was it doing here?

Recollection came flooding back, and she remembered her visitor. Fearfully, she looked around the room, her eyes straining in the dark. Was he still here? Was he watching her from the shadows, sitting in a chair, wearing the calculating expression that had always unnerved her? Before they went their separate ways, she used to think that if she woke up one more time from a binge and saw him sitting there, just *watching* her, she'd go mad. She never knew what he was thinking; she had never asked. She knew she didn't want to know.

Quickly, she reached for the bedside lamp. The room shifted violently again with her sudden movement, but she managed to grab on to the bedside table and switch the light on. The glow was welcome, but she looked fearfully around again. To her relief, she was alone.

The relief was short-lived. The bedroom door was closed, but at the thought that he was still in the apartment, she paled. The bottle on the floor caught her eye again and she was wondering how much was left before she caught herself.

"Oh, God!" What was she thinking? She hadn't had a drink in over a year. Keeley was so proud of her; she was proud of herself. Why was she thinking about drinking now? What was the matter with her? Why did she feel this way?

Her head in her hands, she tried to think. Rehearsals hadn't been going well, and it was her fault. Even after all this time off the booze, she still felt so shaky at times that she could hardly make it through the day. If Keeley wasn't there to prop her up, she started making mistakes. The more mistakes she made, the more nervous she got. The more nervous she became, the more on edge everyone around her felt. It was like a spiral, with herself spinning at the bottom, and she was sure everyone in the cast was wondering if she'd be able to perform when the time came. She was wondering it herself. Today, when Keeley had been so late, they'd decided to start without her, but it had been such a nightmare that she'd known it was hopeless. Using the excuse that she had a terrible headache, she'd left rehearsal and come home, trying to tell herself it would be all right.

But would it? Over the past months, she'd felt herself crumbling around the edges, and there was nothing she could do but grit her teeth and endure. The only time she felt the terror even begin to subside was when she visited the people at Hildredth. But then she was Valine, *not* Valeska Szabo, and when she sang, it was with everyone else. There, she didn't have to think about being on stage, pinned in the unforgiving spotlight; at Hildredth, it was just her and the old people, having their little sing-along.

"But I don't understand, my dear," Bettina had said to her in puzzlement, when she tried once to explain why she was so afraid. She knew by then that she could say anything to this kind, gentle woman and she wouldn't be judged, but Bettina didn't understand.

"You said yourself that you love the stage," Bettina pointed out gently. "And when we went to see you in *Florentina*, you were ..." She had stopped for a moment, her eyes taking on a faraway glow as she remembered the night Valeska had invited them all to the show. Sighing with pleasure, she shook her head. "You were *magic*, my dear. Simply *magic*."

"But that was a long time ago," she'd said, feeling panicked just at the thought. "I'm not sure I can do it anymore!"

"Then you shouldn't," Bettina said at once. "If the thought is so terrifying, you shouldn't put yourself through it."

"But I can't let Keeley down!" she'd wailed.

Bettina took her hand. Softly, she asked, "Is it Keeley you're afraid of disappointing, my dear? Or is it yourself?"

She still wasn't sure of the answer, but as time went on, she was glad she had the people at Hildredth to fall back on. Keeley was wonderful, but she had a vision. All she, Valeska, had was her voice, and sometimes she wasn't even sure she had that. Today at rehearsal had been the perfect example; with all the flubs and lapses and mistakes she'd made because Keeley wasn't there, she'd been so exhausted when she came home that she had to take a nap. The short rest must have done her good, because when she got up, she did feel better—so much so that she decided to make dinner. She hadn't cooked in longer than she could remember, and she was in the kitchen reading recipes to Keeley's cat when the doorbell rang. Tux hated the sound; he immediately streaked off to his bed in Keeley's closet, while she went to answer the door. Keeley had left a message saying she'd be home early, and she thought it was Keeley ringing because she'd forgotten her key. But when she pulled back the chain and opened the door, an eager welcome on her lips, Nigel was standing there. She tried to slam the door in his face, but he put a hand out and held it open.

"Now, Valeska," he said reproachfully. "Is that any way to greet your husband?"

Before she could stop him, he pushed his way inside. "Well, the place certainly looks different than the last time I saw it," he commented. "Have you hired a housekeeper, or does Keeley do the cleaning?"

She didn't know what to say to him. She hadn't seen him for over a year, but just being in the same room with him made her flesh crawl. The sight of him made her want a drink, and that frightened her even more. She didn't know what he wanted, and she didn't care. She just wanted him to leave.

"Keeley will be home soon," she said stiffly, "so I think you'd better go."

"Oh, I don't think so, my dear. In fact, this is just perfect. I really came to talk to Keeley, you see. You're just incidental."

She didn't know where she found the courage, but the words were out before she thought. Bitterly, she said, "Wasn't I always?"

He raised an eyebrow. "Very good, Valeska. I see your . . . er . . . rehabilitation helped you to come to grips with a few facts. How nice. You always were so naive."

She knew she could never beat him in a game of wits. Or anything else for that matter. "You said you came to talk to Keeley. Well, she's not here. I'll have her call you—"

"Oh, no, I'll just wait."

Before she could figure out a way to stop him, he went into the living room. Realizing her hands were shaking, she balled them into fists and followed. "I don't know when she'll be home. I really think—"

"I said, I'll wait."

The cold tone in his voice made her afraid again. It was even worse when he smiled and sat on the couch, patting a spot beside him. "In the meantime, why don't you and I have a little chat?"

"I don't want to have a little chat, Nigel. I want you to go."

"Oh, you don't really mean it. After all we've meant to each other?"

Briefly, Valeska closed her eyes. She needed Keeley, she thought. But Keeley wasn't here right now; she had to handle this herself. "We don't mean anything to each other now, Nigel," she said, looking at him again. "Maybe we never did. Now, please—"

It was as though she hadn't spoken. "You know, I was really pleased to hear that you had turned yourself in for treatment," he said. "God knows, you needed it. Tell me, how long has it been since you've had a drink?"

"A long time. Now, please, Nigel—"

"Long enough for you to have forgotten your manners, I see."

"What?"

"Just because you no longer partake, Valeska, doesn't mean that no one else does. Don't you think you should offer me something?"

Valeska knew that if he'd said it to Keeley, she would have told him he wouldn't be staying long enough to have a drink. But as she had already proved so many times, she wasn't Keeley, and she wasn't brave enough to stand up to him. She didn't trust him in this mood; she had learned from bitter past experience how quickly he could change. Instead of telling him off, as she longed to do, she said resignedly, "All right. What would you like? We don't have any liquor, but I'll fix you a soft drink, and then you'll have to leave."

"You really are testing my patience tonight, my darling," Nigel said. "You know I detest soft drinks, so it's fortunate I brought my own bottle."

Calmly, he pulled a pint bottle of vodka from his pocket and held it out. "You don't mind, Valeska, do you? There aren't many things I can say about you, but you always did make a better martini than I."

Valeska didn't even want to touch the bottle. She and Keeley had never discussed it, but when she'd come home from the hospital, everything remotely connected with alcohol had disappeared from the apartment. Even the cough medicine and the rubbing alcohol were gone from the bathroom, and she knew without looking that Keeley had found all her hiding places, too. She'd been relieved not to have to deal with it, and now here was Nigel, holding out a pint to her and asking her to make him a drink.

You can handle it, she had told herself. All she had to do was remember what she'd been through, and she'd be okay. Keeley would be home soon, and Nigel would leave, and it would be all right.

"I can't make you a martini," she had said. "We don't have any vermouth. I know you don't like it straight, so—"

To her dismay, he said, "Straight would be fine. Why don't you join me?"

"No, thank you," she said. Forcing herself to take the bottle from him, she started toward the bar.

"Ice would be nice," he called after her. "You might try some, too. I heard you in rehearsal, and you sounded hoarse."

"That's because—" She whirled around. "What do you mean, you heard me in rehearsal? You couldn't have! I would have seen you."

"Oh, I have my ways—you, of all people, should know that. I've also had a glimpse of the show's book, and the score, as well." His eyes gleamed maliciously. "Not bad . . . for an amateur."

Valeska rushed to her friend's defense. "Keeley's no amateur!"

"Not in talent, no," he conceded. "But as far as getting a show together, she is."

She knew he was leading up to something. "What have you done?"

He laughed, not fooling her at all. "Why, darling, what makes you think I've done anything?"

Afraid he'd engineered something awful, for once she forgot her fear of him. "Because I know you. You've always been jealous of Keeley, always!"

His face darkened. "I? Jealous of Keeley? Don't be absurd."

"You can deny it all you want, but I know it's true. And now that we're involved in the new show—" She stopped abruptly. "What do you want, Nigel? Why are you here?"

He abandoned his cultured pose. "You know why I'm here, my dear," he said nastily. "I came to get what's coming to me."

"What's coming to you! What do you mean? Keeley doesn't owe you anything!"

"Yes, she does. Oh, she definitely does. I left her alone when she went Hollywood, but now she's back, and she and I have a few contractual obligations to straighten out."

Suddenly she remembered his bragging about the contract he'd gotten Keeley to sign. He'd told her about it in the early days of their marriage, when she had been so in love with him he could do no wrong. Because she'd been so angry at Keeley at the time, she'd actually thought it served her right. Ashamed of herself, she didn't think so now. Picturing Keeley, and how much her friend had done for her, how hard she was working to put the show together, she looked angrily at Nigel.

"You didn't leave her alone, you had no claim on what she did in Hollywood," she said bitterly. "But if you had, I've no doubt you would have been right there, with your hand out! God knows you did it to me enough times during our marriage!"

Nigel came off the couch like a serpent. Before she could move back, he had lifted his hand and slapped her hard right across the face. The blow rocked her back, and as she raised her hand to cover the red marks his fingers had made on her cheek, she looked at him with as much contempt as she could.

"Well, I see you haven't changed," she said. He raised his hand again. She flinched in spite of herself, but she said, "Go ahead. It's how you resolve everything, isn't it? Oh, if everyone knew what you were really like!"

He took another step toward her. She cringed back, but not quickly enough, for he grabbed her by the shoulders and shook her so hard her head snapped back on her neck. "I can be sure my secret is safe with you, can't I, my dear?" To make his point, he shook her again, so violently that her teeth clamped down, and she bit her lip. "Can't I?"

When she didn't answer, he made a face and pushed her toward the wall. She didn't have time to brace herself, and when she hit with her shoulder, she barely prevented herself from crying out with pain. Breathing hard himself, Nigel straightened his tie. "Now, then, let's carry on. As much fun as this has been, I don't intend to wait all night for our Miss Cochran to show up. You may give her a message from me."

She just wanted him to leave. "What message?"

"You may tell her I want a piece of the new show."

She looked at him in shock. "That's crazy," she said, not caring at the moment what his reaction might be. "Keeley will *never* give you part of the show, not in a million years! There's no threat you can make that will force her!"

"Don't be too sure," he said, preening. "I'm afraid that Miss Keeley had some bad news today. Much to her dismay, I know, her investors have mysteriously backed out. Now, if I'm so inclined, I might be able to get them back. But the price won't be cheap."

Her mouth was suddenly so dry she could hardly speak. When she thought of all the hard work Keeley had done to put the show together, she wanted to scream. "You didn't! You couldn't have! Oh, Nigel, why?"

"Various reasons," he said. "For one thing, I felt it would convince her I was serious about coming in as director."

"Director! But Keeley's directing the show!"

He gave her a reproachful look. "As I was saying, I want to direct, with slightly more than the usual percentage, of course."

"She'll never give it to you," Valeska said, but inwardly, she wasn't so sure. Was he telling the truth? Had he really convinced the financial people to back out? He was capable of anything, but if he had, how had he done it? Cleve and the others were friends, she thought. They'd never let Keeley down, would they?

Panic-stricken, she looked at Nigel again. There was no doubting his self-satisfaction, and she blurted, "Even if she has to shut down until she can scrape up new money, she'll never let you direct, or be involved in any way. I know Keeley. It's her show, and she'll do it without you!"

"Is that so?" His eyes gleamed as he approached her again. In spite of herself, she shrank back until the wall was behind her and she couldn't go any farther. "Is that so?" he said again, his breath hot on her face. "Well, you listen to me, my darling little wife. Even if by some miracle Keeley manages to overcome all the obstacles I've thrown in her path, I've still got you."

With him so close, Valeska felt faint and sick and dizzy with renewed fear. Only his body pressing against hers held her up; she didn't have the strength to push him away. "What do you mean?" she whispered, unable to take her eyes off his leering face.

He pressed into her. "You'll help me, won't you, my darling?" he said softly. "Oh, yes, you will. We're still married, and I have control of almost everything—the money, the assets." He grabbed a fistful of her hair, twisting it so painfully that tears came into her eyes. "But most important, I have control of you."

Despite the pain, she gasped, "I won't betray Keeley; I won't!"

He tightened his fist. "I've allowed you to do what you wanted these past months," he said, his breath hot on her face. "I haven't bothered you at all, now, have I? But all that could change in a flick of an eye." To demonstrate, he reached up with his other hand and flicked her cheek with a fingertip, making her cringe. "And you won't sing if I don't want you to, will you, my love. Will you?"

With each word, his grip on her hair tightened. His body was pressing her so hard against the wall that she could hardly breathe, and the combination made her feel completely helpless. "Nigel, please—" she gasped. Weakly, she grabbed at his hand; his grip was like iron. "Please don't do this," she begged, tears streaming down her cheeks. "Haven't you done enough?"

"Oh, I haven't begun if Keeley refuses to give me what I want, my dear." He gave her hair one last savage twist. "You know I mean it, too, don't you?"

He released her so suddenly that she fell forward before she caught herself. She was still trying to catch her breath and her balance when he said, "Now, I think you'd better go freshen up. You look a mess. I'll be waiting right here when you come back. We'll have our drink and discuss our plans. What do you think?"

Valeska didn't answer him. Sidling by, afraid he would grab her again, she ran toward the bedroom and slammed the door. Locking it behind her, she leaned against it for a few seconds, her heart pounding. Pushing herself away with an effort, she ran into the bathroom. She'd never told Keeley, but she had hidden a couple of Valium in the bottom of an aspirin bottle—for emergencies, she'd told herself, trying to believe she'd never use them. She felt comforted knowing they were there, and as she grabbed the bottle out of the medicine cabinet and tried to open it, she thought that if ever there was an emergency, it was now.

"Come on, come on," she muttered, struggling with the top. Her hands were shaking so much she nearly dropped the whole thing into the sink. Catching it in midair, she held it against her chest with a sound of relief. Carefully, she tried it again.

The beautiful, round yellow tranquilizers were at the bottom of the bottle, just where she'd put them. She hesitated only an instant before she took two pills and swallowed them dry. She knew it was impossible for the drug to work so fast, but suddenly she felt calmer. Lifting her head, she looked at herself in the mirror. Her lip was bleeding where she'd bitten it, and her face was pale, her hair a mess. Her scalp hurt, and she turned away from the mirror, her face in her hands. She didn't care about herself, but what about Keeley? She had to stop Nigel somehow, but how? *How?*

The tranquilizers must have taken effect quickly, for she didn't remember anything until she woke up and found the empty vodka bottle by the bed. Wondering again how it had gotten here, she reached down—mindful of her head—and picked it up. Slowly, she looked toward the door. She realized then that it wasn't closed all the way. Fear raced through her. Hadn't she locked it? She was positive she had. She looked down at the empty bottle again. She didn't remember bringing the vodka in here, and she certainly hadn't drunk it. She *knew* what a booze hangover felt like, and this wasn't it. The grogginess she felt had to be from the tranquilizers she had gulped down; after all this time, she wasn't used to the effects, and she'd just . . . passed out.

"Oh, God," she muttered. Where was Keeley? If she had come home and found her like this . . .

Pushing the awful thought away, she went to the door. "Keeley?" she called. "Keeley!"

Silence greeted her; the rest of the apartment was dark. Staggering down the hall, she reached the living room and switched on the light. Nigel was gone. The living room was empty, and she headed to the kitchen, hoping that Keeley had been delayed, or was still working—something! She needed a strong cup of coffee, and then she could think.

She was just reaching for the coffee beans when she saw the note. Snatching it up, she read it quickly. Of course it was from Keeley.

"Came home and saw what you'd been doing while I was gone," the note read. "Am staying with a friend until I can think what to do now. I thought you'd conquered it, Val. I'm sorry I was wrong."

"Oh, no!" Valeska cried. Bursting into tears, she crumpled the note and threw it down. What was she going to do? She didn't know where Keeley was so she couldn't tell her she hadn't been drinking. It was all a ghastly mistake, and now she had to wait until rehearsal tomorrow to straighten it all out. Then she stiffened. If Nigel had told the truth, there might not *be* a rehearsal tomorrow! Oh, this was even worse! If they closed down until Keeley could find more money, and she didn't know where

Keeley was staying, she couldn't tell her that Nigel had been here. How could this have happened? Panicked, she looked around, intending . . . she didn't know what. She wanted to run, but there was no place to run to. She was all alone, and—

"Stop it!" she said aloud. "Pull it together and *think* for a change!"

She couldn't think; she was too scared. Every time she thought about Nigel trying to interfere with *Beauty*, she just went blank. Keeley had worked so hard; the show was going to be so good—for all of them. Beauty was the role of a lifetime, and Keeley had written it just for her. Despite her terror of appearing on stage again, despite her fear that she wouldn't be able to perform, she still wanted more than anything to do justice to the part. It was as though everything in her life had been leading her up to this—that somehow she was destined to be Beauty, and to meet her Beast.

Only in her case, she thought, increasingly panicked, her Beast wasn't a disguised prince waiting to be released from a spell. It was something else, something she hadn't figured out yet, something she still had to face before things came out right after all.

Alone in the kitchen, she clenched her hands to stop herself from screaming aloud. What was she thinking? What Beast did she have to face? She was rambling when she had to stop and think. She had to stop Nigel from—literally—stealing the show. She had to do it, but how? It would take someone far stronger than she, maybe someone stronger even than Keeley. But who?

She knew what Nigel was like when he was determined, and she knew he wouldn't be deterred now. After the flops of the past years, since Keeley had left and she'd struggled through *Maggie* herself, he needed a successful vehicle as much as she did. Maybe more, she thought, remembering the gossip she'd heard, the rumors about how washed up he was, and how he was only as good as the talent he currently went to bed with. When she had been so in love with him, she hadn't realized, or wanted to see what he really was, but she saw him clearly now—now that it was too late!

"I never give up control of what is mine," Nigel had said to her again and again, and she had seen for herself it was true. He always held something on the people he dealt with, just in case he needed a favor—or more—from them again one day. He'd done it with Keeley, making her sign the contract giving him rights to her songs; he had done it to her, his own wife, forcing her to surrender all control. Like an evil monster, he had trapped everyone he'd ever come into contact with into a dark cave with no exit. He'd probably, she thought bitterly, even done it to Barry.

She hadn't thought of Barry Archer in years. Without warning, she remembered an argument she'd overheard between Barry and Nigel, just before Barry went away. She didn't remember what the quarrel was about after all this time, but she definitely recalled the tone. She had thought at the time that Barry was afraid of him, but now she wondered if it hadn't been the other way around. Nigel had refused to discuss Barry in any way; in fact, even the mention of his name enraged him. Was it because he was angry—or scared?

Maybe Barry had something on him, she thought hopefully. Then she realized how ridiculous that was. If Barry knew something, why was *he* the one who had disappeared?

She tried to dismiss it, but again and again, she came back to it, worrying it like a dog with a bone until she convinced herself that if she could find Barry, he could help in some way. It was probably a false hope, but she had to do something. She couldn't just sit here and let Nigel steal the show. Keeley meant more to her than her fear of Nigel Aames, and she'd never forgive herself if she didn't try to help.

Once she had decided on her course of action, the next problem she faced was who to call. Even if she knew where Keeley was, she couldn't tell her what she planned; Keeley had enough problems right now. Maybe she should hire a private investigator, she thought, then recoiled at the idea. She didn't know anything about such people; she needed someone she could trust.

Suddenly she thought of Gabe. He'd be perfect! she thought, clasping her hands. Then she shook her head again. She couldn't bother him now; in addition to the fact that he was mourning his brother, she was sure something had happened between him and Keeley in California. Keeley wouldn't discuss it beyond saying they'd had a disagreement, but the fact that she became so fierce whenever his name was mentioned convinced her it was more serious.

She shouldn't call him, she thought, biting her lip. She looked at the phone. She thought about Keeley, and about Nigel trying to take over the show. She looked at the phone again. She had Gabe's number in California because he'd called once after he'd moved to his new place and left a message on their machine. She'd been surprised that he had taken an apartment and had asked Keeley if he was still working for the foundation, but Keeley had gotten angry. Keeley hadn't returned his call, but Val had kept the number, just in case. She never imagined she'd be the one to use it first.

Trying not to think if she was doing the right thing—or what she would do if he didn't want to help—she looked up the number in her address book. Her hand was shaking as she found the page, but she felt desperate, with no where else to turn. She had always liked Gabe, and before their breakup, if that's what it was, she'd thought he and Keeley were perfect for each other. She knew he had loved Keeley—once. But she had never done anything like this, and for a moment, she nearly lost courage. What if he refused? What if he laughed at her?

What if he did, she thought. She had to do something, and this was it. Before she could change her mind, she picked up the phone and dialed the number.

CHAPTER THIRTY

When the phone rang just after midnight, Gabe rolled over and reached for it before he knew what he was doing. Still asleep, he mumbled a hello. Even after Valeska said her name twice, it took him a moment to realize who was calling, but when he recognized her, he came awake with a jolt. Bolting upright, his first thought was that something had happened to Keeley.

"Is it Keeley?" he asked anxiously.

Valeska sounded as disjointed as he felt himself. "No, no, it's not Keeley—at least, I mean, nothing's happened to her," she stammered. "I'm sorry to be calling so late, but—"

"It's okay, it's okay." Now that he knew Keeley was all right, he could breathe again. "What is it, Valeska? What's wrong?"

"Everything," she cried. To his alarm, she burst into tears. "Oh, Gabe, I'm sorry to call you out of the blue like this, but I need your help! *Keeley* needs your help, whether she'd admit it or not. I just don't know what to do."

Trying to remember that things always sounded worse in the middle of the night, Gabe switched on the bedside lamp and swung his legs to the floor. Running a hand through his hair, he said, "It's okay, we'll figure out something—whatever it is. Just tell me what's happened."

She calmed down at his matter-of-fact tone. "I'm sorry, Gabe. I guess I . . . well, it's not important. The reason I called—" her voice shook a little despite herself "—is because we're in trouble, Keeley and I. Well, Keeley more than me, I guess, because she's got more at stake." She paused again, trying to get herself under control. "I know I'm not making any sense, Gabe, but I'm so upset. Nigel came to see me tonight to tell me that he wants a piece of the new show—do you know about the new show? Keeley is finally going to do *Beauty and the Beast*! Did she ever tell you about the show, Gabe?"

Gabe put a hand over his eyes. Keeley had told him about *Beauty and the Beast*, long before it started to become a reality. Clearly, painfully, he suddenly remembered the first time she'd told him about her dream. It had been the night at the house in Benedict Canyon, after their swim. Wrapped in a big towel, her hands clasped around a cup of coffee they were sharing, she described the musical drama she had envisioned of a young woman and the enchanted prince who had been disguised as a beast. As she'd told him about the songs she had written and intended to write, about the book she wanted, and the score she would compose, it was as though the musical had leapt to life before his own eyes. He could see lonely Beauty in the splendid castle; he could see Beast lurking outside, afraid to show himself for fear she would reject him. Surrounded by everything she could wish for, Beauty longed for her prince, never realizing that he was hidden beside her in another guise.

Keeley intended to remain true to the original fairy tale, which was a love story set in a parable. Gabe had thought at the time that it would be as beautiful a piece of work as anything she had ever done or would do. She hadn't mentioned Valeska as Beauty, but he had known without her saying it that she would write the role as only Valeska could sing it, and it turned out later, she had.

"Gabe? Gabe, are you there?"

"Yes, I'm here," he answered. But suddenly he was wondering how he could have forgotten Keeley's face when she told him about the show. He had never seen her so . . . illuminated. She had had a glow from within, and he didn't doubt that night—or ever after—that she would one day bring her vision to life. He had loved her more than he could express right then. With an almost physical pain, he wondered what had happened to them since that magical time.

Shaking his head to rid it of memories better left forgotten, he forced his mind back to Valeska. "I know about the show," he said. "But I don't understand why Nigel wants a piece of it. What kind of piece? And what right does he have to muscle in?"

"He doesn't have a right, that's the problem!" Valeska exclaimed, agitated again. "Oh, Gabe, it's so complicated, but I think the reason he's pushing so hard is that he needs something like this show, to put him on top again. He hasn't had anything since *Maggie*, and he wants to direct *Beauty*, to prove he hasn't lost his touch. He's persuaded the backers to withdraw unless Keeley lets him in, and if she doesn't, no one will advance her any more money."

"Can he do that?" Gabe asked sharply.

"He already has! He might be a little down on his luck right now, but he's still got lots of friends in this town. And if Keeley still refuses, I . . . I don't know what he'll do." She began to cry again. "He's an evil man, Gabe! I know he'd do anything to get back on top again—anything! We have to stop him somehow!"

"Don't cry," he said, trying to think while Valeska made a vain attempt to control her sobs. His mind was a blank, and he asked, "Do you have any suggestions?"

Gulping back tears, she said, "Only one."

"Well, let's hear it. At the moment, I'm fresh out of ideas."

"We have to find Barry Archer," she said. "I don't know how I know it, but—"

"Who's Barry Archer?"

"You don't know? Never mind, of course you wouldn't. He's a composer. He and Nigel used to work together all the time."

Something was swimming to the surface in the fog of his brain. "I remember. Keeley told me about him. Wasn't he the guy who disappeared six, seven years ago?"

"Yes, yes, Barry Archer! That's him!"

It was coming back slowly now. "But Keeley tried to find him right after he left, and she didn't have any success. What makes you think we will?"

She was near tears again. "I don't know, I guess I thought . . . maybe you could use your police connections or something. You used to be a police photographer, didn't you? Oh, Gabe! If you can't help, I don't know what to do!"

"Now, now, don't cry," he said again. He was already thinking rapidly, wondering whom he could call. It had been a long time, but there were still a couple of guys who owed him. "I can't promise anything," he said finally. "But I'll do what I can and give you a call back."

"Oh, Gabe, I *knew* you'd help! I knew you wouldn't let us down!"

"Don't thank me yet," he warned. "Remember, Archer's been gone a long time. Maybe something happened to him—"

"Oh, no!"

"Or maybe it's just that he didn't want to be found. If that's the case, I really doubt we can find him now. And even if we do, what makes you think he'll be able to help?"

"I don't know," she wailed. "I just know we have to try."

"Well, we'll try, but I have to know a little more than I do now. Do you have any suggestions about where to start? I have some friends I can call, but they'll want me to be a little more specific than that this guy went to ground somewhere in New York City."

Her voice small, Valeska said, "Yes, I see what you mean." She hesitated. Then, her tone taking on an edge despite her concern, she said, "Maybe you can start with a woman named Carlotte Basile. Nigel never knew I knew it, but he was seeing her all along—the whole time we were together. She and Barry and Nigel go back a long way. I remember Nigel saying once that she and Barry started out in strip joints together. He'd play piano, and she'd do . . . whatever it was she did there. Maybe she'll have some ideas."

Making a note, Gabe said, "I'll see what I can do. But remember, I'm not promising anything."

"No, no, I know, but Gabe . . ." She paused, swallowing. "Thank you so much. I don't know what I would have done if you hadn't agreed to help."

"You knew I wouldn't refuse."

"I . . . I wasn't sure. I know something happened between you and Keeley while she was in California—and it's all right, you don't have to tell me what, it's none of my business," she added quickly. "I just want you to know that whatever it is, I really think Keeley's sorry now."

His voice turning hard, he asked, "If she was so sorry, why didn't she ever return my call?"

"You know Keeley and how stubborn she can be. It's not an excuse, but . . . it's just Keeley."

"Yeah, well . . ."

"I hate seeing you estranged, Gabe," Valeska said urgently. "I always thought that if ever two people were meant for each other, it's you and Keeley. Don't you think you could—"

"No, I don't. And you're right, it's none of your business. What happened between Keeley and me is something that won't ever be repaired. So just leave it, okay?"

"If you feel like that, why did you agree to help?"

He didn't want to talk about it anymore. "Let's just call it one for old times' sake, all right? I'll call you when I've found out something."

Gabe regretted his curt good-bye the instant he hung up. He debated about calling back to apologize, but let it go. He couldn't explain the situation between him and Keeley, and things were complicated enough. Wishing Valeska hadn't called and dragged him into this just when he thought he'd put Keeley out of his mind for good, he sighed. He knew he wasn't going to sleep again, so he got up and headed toward the kitchen to make coffee. While it was percolating, he opened the doors to the balcony and went outside, trying to think of anything but Keeley Cochran.

The January night was cold, but even though he was wearing only his shorts and a T-shirt, he barely felt the chill. He was thinking that the past four months had been a more difficult adjustment than he had anticipated. After quitting the foundation and going to work for his father, he had needed a place to live, so he had rented this place down by the beach. Fortunately, it had come furnished; he couldn't be bothered shopping for couches and chairs and things. It was okay as it was; at least he could go running on the sand when things got too tense, he thought. But even though he lived here, it wasn't home, and he knew it never would be. Right now, he didn't know where home was. A jungle? The African veldt? The Falling GT in Montana?

Neither of his parents had questioned his decision to get his own place. He knew his mother had wanted him to live at the house for a while—at least until he got his bearings. But he couldn't live under his father's roof and work for him, too; it was too much. Besides, he was a man, not a child to be supported by his parents. Or at least, he was supposed to be a man. There had been nights, too many to count now since Frank's death, when he had questioned himself and his motives. What was he doing here? What was he doing, period? During his moments of self-doubt, he always thought of the quarrel he and

Keeley had had. Was she right? Maybe he was searching for something here he'd never find. Maybe he couldn't make up for Frank's death. Maybe, as Keeley had told him, he wasn't meant to.

"Damn you, Keeley Cochran," he muttered. It had taken him weeks to beat down his pride long enough to call her and apologize. When her answering machine had picked up, he'd been so disappointed that he had just left his name and number and nothing else. Was it any wonder she hadn't called him back? When she hadn't, he was too stubborn to call her; now he felt he was at an impasse. What a stupid mess, he thought, angry with himself. If he felt like this, why had he agreed to help Valeska?

But it wasn't Valeska he had agreed to help, was it? As the coffee reached boiling point and bubbled over onto the stove, Gabe remained oblivious, on the balcony, wondering why he loved Keeley so much even when she was at her most exasperating. He'd been furious the day of Frank's funeral—but not for the reasons he'd said. What had enraged him was her disconcerting habit of holding a mirror up to his face and forcing him to take a hard look. He hadn't wanted to look that day, and so he had pushed her away, saying all those hurtful things to make sure she left. He'd needed to do what he'd done—or so he'd convinced himself at the time. But less than a week of working for the old man, he knew he'd made a mistake it was too late to back out on.

"Well, tough," he muttered. He'd made his decision, and he wouldn't let his father down. Since Frank had died, he'd seen Ellis age twenty years. The company had always been his father's lifeblood, but now it just seemed something to do to fill his days before he went home, had dinner, went to bed, and started the whole dreary cycle all over again. Gabe tried to tell himself it was grief—he felt the same way at times, dragging himself through one day after another, hoping it would get better soon—but he wondered if his father would ever recover. With that in mind, he couldn't think of leaving; even he could see that the old man depended on him.

So did his mother, Gabe thought with a sigh. Audrey wasn't herself, either, although she tried. It just wasn't the same, and he was getting to hate the weekly family occasions where they all gathered for dinner. Sometimes the only thing that kept him sane, he thought, were his two nieces. He had always enjoyed the little girls, never more than now, when they were so solemn and wide-eyed, unsure of themselves because the grown-ups had changed. Recognizing how confusing it was for them, he always brought presents for the family occasions. Sometimes it was books; at others, stuffed animals. They always seemed to enjoy the presents, but no matter what he brought, they clamored for his attention. At eleven and twelve now, they were getting a little old to read to, something he had always enjoyed doing, but he had interesting conversations with them instead, sitting together on the living room couch, a niece on each arm. For a while they could all pretend it was like it used to be, their uncle Gabe reading a story to them, or asking about school or piano practice, before he headed off to parts unknown again.

Sighing again, Gabe doubted that he'd ever be "heading off" any more, unless it was on company business. Now that they'd lost one son, both his parents seemed to need him too much. It disturbed him, too, that his mother seemed to sense his disquiet no matter how he tried to hide it.

"Are you all right, darling?" she'd ask every time she saw him. Anxiously, she'd reach up to touch his face, his hair, trying to reassure herself that what she was seeing wasn't there.

Invariably, because he didn't want to hurt her, he'd take her hand in his and answer with a smile, "I'm fine, Mom. Now, stop worrying."

Audrey would search his face a moment longer; then she'd sigh and leave him alone until the next time. But unlike her employer, Laveda wasn't so easily soothed—or wouldn't pretend to be. Her gaze was too sharp for him. Knowing he couldn't fool her, he avoided the kitchen as much as he could, but there were times when she still sought him out.

"Are you trying to avoid me, Gabriel Lee?" she'd ask.

"Never," he'd reply, giving her a hug so he could avoid her eyes.

"Well, you look peaked to me."

"I'm fine, just tired," he'd say. Sometimes, because he could feel her knowing glance on him, he'd force a smile and add, "It was a long day at the office, I guess."

"Longer than sittin' out there in the jungle, or those hills of yours?"

He never knew what to answer. She knew too much, and anything he could think of to reply, she'd know was a lie. "Now, Laveda," he'd say with a sigh. "Don't make trouble, okay?"

"All right, Gabriel Lee. I said I wouldn't say anything, and I won't. But one day, you're going to have to face up to it, you know."

He knew she was right, but he wasn't ready. Maybe he never would be. But the remark stayed with him, and the call from Valeska had stirred up his discontent just when he'd thought he had it under control again. Wishing he hadn't agreed to help, he went inside, wiped up the boiled-over coffee, and made his plans. When he realized he had to fly to New York, he frowned. It was a bad time to be gone from the office, but the absence didn't give him pause. The question was, would he see Keeley when he was there?

He still hadn't decided when he called a friend of his at the Twentieth Precinct, Manhattan, early the next morning. By then, he had already formed a plan. After debating a while, he made a second call, to Raleigh Quinn.

It took a month to find Barry Archer, and it only happened then because of a fluke. Gabe never got the whole story: it had something to do with a snitch needing a fix; he didn't want to know the details. But when his detective friend called him one morning about six to tell him where Archer could be found, Gabe immediately made reservations on a flight going right out. As he had expected, his father wasn't too pleased; they were in the middle of negotiating for a major government contract, and he needed Gabe at the office. Insisting it couldn't be helped, and that he'd be back as soon as he could, Gabe caught his plane and arrived in New York in the middle of the night. His friend had told him Barry was working in a dive near the waterfront called Cimino's, and when he got there and saw the place, he was glad he knew how to handle himself.

Cimino's was a bar with some rough clientele. When Gabe walked in, an altercation erupted in the back room over a dart game. As he hesitated in the doorway, he could hear sounds of struggle and a round of violent cursing. Before he could decide whether to go and come back again, the obvious loser in the fight reeled toward him and out the door. The man had a dart sticking out of his neck, but nobody seemed to mind, including the victim.

"Nice place," Gabe muttered to himself, looking around. He'd never met Barry Archer, but Raleigh Quinn had sent him a picture from his Musicians' Guild files. As soon as he saw the bartender, he knew he'd found his man. Archer looked about twenty years older than Gabe knew him to be; it was obvious, with his bloodshot eyes, that he was an habitual drinker.

Gabe decided he'd better sit down at the bar. He'd already attracted attention; having been forewarned, he was wearing old jeans and a worn leather bomber jacket, but even so, in this sparse crowd, he stood out. Everyone else had on heavy boots and torn sweatshirts and woolen caps on their heads; the bar was a place where longshoremen gathered before hitting the docks at four A.M.

A cigarette dangling out of his mouth, Archer came down to where Gabe sat. "What'll it be?" he asked, trailing ashes all over the counter. He looked down, saw the flakes, and gave the bar a desultory swipe with a rag from his back pocket. His voice was hoarse, and he didn't meet Gabe's eyes directly.

"I'll have a beer," Gabe said, trying to decide how best to play it. He'd never liked such places, dark and smoke-filled and stinking of stale sweat. He could feel his nostrils contracting and hoped everybody would just leave him alone long enough to do his business and get out.

Barry shuffled down to the tap and poured out a beer. When he came back and set the glass down, Gabe said casually, "Are you Barry Archer?"

Archer drew back. "Who wants to know?"

"My name's Gabe Tyrell. I'm here for a friend."

The bloodshot eyes narrowed. "Well, whoever he is, he ain't no friend of mine. You want anything else, Mr. Tyrell? 'Cause I got customers need my attention."

"I know somebody who needs your help, too," Gabe said. "Her name is Keeley."

Archer had turned away. Despite himself, he turned back. "I don't know any Keeley Cochran."

"I never said her name was Cochran. How did you know?"

Fear flashed in Archer's reddened, rheumy eyes. "Come on, mister, I don't want any trouble. It was a long time ago—another life. It doesn't concern me now."

Gabe reached out and grasped Archer by the arm. "I think it concerns you more than you know. You see, my friend Keeley is having a little problem with someone else you're acquainted with—Nigel Aames. Aames wants a piece of a show that isn't his. Sound familiar? I came to see what I could do about it. I could use your help."

"I don't know what you're talking about," Barry said. "I told you, it's none of my business."

"I think it is."

"Yeah, well, I—" Archer's brief spurt of bravado collapsed under a sudden spasm of coughing. Once started, he couldn't seem to stop. The paroxysm became so bad that his face turned red, and he had to grab on to the bar for balance. The cough was hard and dry with an underlying sound Gabe didn't like. *Cancer?* he wondered, regarding the man in a new light.

"Sorry," Barry gasped, when the attack finally passed. He was gasping for breath, but Gabe noticed that the cigarette still dangled out of his mouth. As though suddenly remembering he was still smoking it, Barry reached up and took the butt in nicotine-stained fingers. His mouth turned down, he crushed it out in an overflowing ashtray behind the bar before immediately lighting another. Noticing that Gabe was watching, he shrugged. "No sense stopping now, I figure."

Gabe waited until the man had puffed a few times. He still hadn't touched his beer, and when Archer noticed it, he jerked his chin at the glass. "You're not drinkin'. You want somethin' else?"

Gabe shook his head. "I want to talk. When does your shift end?"

Barry squinted up at the clock hung haphazardly behind the bar. It had a cracked face and was missing a few numbers, but the hour hand was pointing at four. "In about ten minutes, not that it matters. I said you and I got nothin' to talk about, Mr. . . . Tyrell, was it? Well, that's it. I think you'd just better get back uptown where you came from and leave me alone."

Pulling out his wallet, Gabe took a five out and put it on the bar. "That's for the beer," he said, and then, aware the man was watching, deliberately put a hundred dollar bill on top. "And that's for you if you'll meet me outside. I'll be waiting."

Barry licked his lips. His glance flicked from the money to Gabe's face and back again. "I'm not comin'," he said. "You can wait all night, for all I care."

"Whatever it takes," Gabe said. He pulled another hundred out and held it so only Barry could see. "There's three more where these came from. All I'm asking is five minutes. You haven't made this kind of money since you left Broadway, Archer. And even in these inflated days, five hundred still buys a lot of booze and butts, isn't that right?"

Slowly, the other man's eyes met his. "Five minutes? That's all you want?"

"Five minutes and what you know about Nigel Aames," Gabe

said, getting up off the stool. He was almost half a foot taller, and when he leaned forward over the bar, Barry flinched and involuntarily moved back. Holding Archer's eyes, Gabe said quietly, "No funny business, Barry. I don't like it when other people try to interfere in something that's none of their affair. Do we understand each other?"

Archer seemed mesmerized. His glance flicked to the other men in the bar. Wordlessly, he nodded. Gabe nodded back. "I'll be waiting outside," he said. Then he escaped gratefully out into the cold. After the stale air in the bar, it was like breathing ambrosia.

They went to an all-night coffee shop away from the docks. Gabe was too keyed up to eat, but he told Barry to order what he wanted. As they waited for the waitress to amble over, he looked covertly at his table companion and wondered if he'd made a mistake. Even to his eyes, the man looked sick.

"I don't want nothin'," Barry said, when the woman finally came. "Just coffee."

"Make it two," Gabe said, leaning forward when the waitress went away. Instantly, Barry looked wary.

"I don't want any trouble," Barry said, anticipating him. "I told you, I turned my back on Broadway long ago."

"Did you turn your back on your friends, too?"

"If you mean Keeley, she's done just fine without me being around."

"You've followed her career, have you?"

"I said I'd left Broadway. I didn't say I'd stopped reading the paper."

"So you know about *Beauty and the Beast*."

"Look, mister—"

"Why don't you call me Gabe?"

Archer narrowed his eyes. "Why? 'Cause you think it'll make us friends? Look, what's all this to you? If Keeley sent you—"

"Keeley doesn't know I'm here. She doesn't even know I'm in town."

Exasperated, Barry said, "Well, what, then?"

"Let's just say that she and I go back a few years, too. She tried to do something for me awhile ago, but I . . . I wouldn't listen. I feel I owe it to her to try and help now."

Just for an instant, Barry's expression softened. It was as if he were remembering some of the things Keeley had done for him, too. Then the barrier went up again. Beginning to rise, he said, "Well, great, it's your trip, then. It has nothing to do with me."

Calmly, Gabe reached out and gripped his arm again. His fingers tightened, forcing his guest to wince and sit down again. Staring into Barry's blotched face, he said quietly, "She tried to find you when you disappeared. She haunted your place for weeks. She even called the police because she thought something had happened to you. And when you never showed up again, she put your things in storage."

"She did that for me?" Barry said, before he caught himself. Quickly, he looked down at the table. "Look, even if I wanted to, I don't know what I could do to help. I told you—"

"I know what you *told* me, but don't you think Keeley deserves more than a brush-off? She tried to help you."

"She shouldn't have! I didn't ask her to."

"No, she didn't have to," Gabe said evenly. "But she was your friend. She thought you were her friend, too."

Barry couldn't meet his eyes. "I . . . was."

"And now?"

Barry suddenly looked up. "Look, Gabe, or whoever you are, I don't know what you want from me. I told you—"

"I know what you told me. But what I want you to do is simple, even for you. You don't have to do anything, but if you know of any way to get Nigel Aames off Keeley's back, I want you to tell me. I'll take it from there. Just tell me."

"What makes you think I know anything?"

"Two reasons. The way you're acting, and Aames himself. If he's not above using threats and intimidation now, he wasn't above it back then. You worked with him for a long time before Keeley ever came into the picture, so if you know something, tell me. I'll leave you alone, and you'll be five hundred bucks richer."

"It's not the money."

Gabe was positive then that Barry knew something. Hiding his relief, he waited. Barry sat still for a long minute. Despite the fact that he had wrapped both hands around his coffee mug to hold them steady, Gabe saw him shaking. Reminding himself that he couldn't afford pity—not yet, anyway—he just sat there drinking the awful coffee. Finally, Barry sniffed, raised his hand to wipe his nose, then reached into his pocket for a crumpled cigarette. Toying with it for a moment, he studied Gabe. At last he came to a decision.

"I don't know why I'm telling you this," he said, putting the cigarette into his mouth and lighting it from a crushed pack of matches he got from another pocket. "Comin' from me, it's probably not going to make much difference. But Keeley was good to me." He stopped, peering at Gabe, smoke curling up around his head. "What do you know about the theater?"

Gabe shrugged. "Just what Keeley's told me. Maybe a little more than the average person, I guess."

Impatiently, Barry shook his head. "No, I mean about what goes on behind the scenes—*way* behind the scenes. You know that Nigel used to produce, don't you? In the good old days, when he was in his glory. Do you know why he became a producer?"

"I imagine because he had an interest in the theater."

"Oh, yeah, he had an interest all right. Not too many people realize that producing is what we in the business call an easy entrance. To get in, all you have to do is option something—pay a sum for the rights to a property for a negotiable number of months, and bingo, you're in the producing business."

"If it's so simple, why doesn't everybody produce?"

" 'Cause there's a catch, of course. In *theory*, a producer gets nothing until a show is out of the red and paying off. Then he splits any profits with the backers, fifty-fifty. But if the show loses money, he gets nothing."

"So it's a gamble."

"Only for the innocent and unwary."

"Of which Nigel is neither, I presume."

"Never was," Barry said. "Remember what I said about theory? The fact is that a show doesn't have to make a profit for a producer to earn money. All it has to do is run for a while."

"But you said—"

"It's simple. If they work it right—and Nigel was always a master—a producer gets a flat percentage of a show's weekly gross, maybe one percent, maybe more. And, to cover office expenses, he also gets what we call a cash office charge, which could vary from, say, five hundred a week for a straight play, to upwards of a thousand a week for a musical. Now, say it's a musical we're talking about—"

"Something like *Beauty and the Beast*?" Gabe said, his gut tightening.

"That, or any other," Barry said with a shrug. "We can use *Beauty* for an example. Let's say it has a million dollar investment—a little low these days, but for argument's sake, I'll use round numbers. Okay, let's say it runs a year and loses half of its investment."

"How could a show run that amount of time and still lose five hundred thousand dollars?"

"In the theater? Easy. But let's stick to our producer for a minute, all right? In our little scenario, with a loss of half a million, the producer doesn't get any money because he's working a percentage. Zero of zero is zip, right?"

"Right," Gabe said slowly. "In *theory*, anyway. I've got a feeling you're about to tell me differently."

"Well, yeah, because remember, for the fifty-two weeks of the run, our man has received a thousand a week for office expenses. That's already fifty-two thousand, right up front. A nifty piece of change just because he's got his name on a door somewhere, don't you think?"

"But still not enough to make him rich," Gabe pointed out.

"No, but I haven't finished. We haven't counted in the percentage of the show's weekly gross, remember? Let's say that for the year, *Beauty* does three-quarters of capacity—not unreasonable—and let's say the capacity is—oh, we'll make it a little low for these days, somewhere around a hundred thousand a week. It's usually higher, but I was never good at math. So let's see, at the end of the year, the grosses could net even a reasonable man another forty thousand, give or take, which brings him up to a take-home pay of around a hundred thousand. Not bad for a show that's *losing* half a million dollars—and that's just for a reasonable man, not one who's greedy."

Gabe was silent. It didn't seem possible, but it was obvious that Barry knew what he was talking about. "I'd hate to think what a producer could take home on a smash hit," he said.

Barry smiled, his first of the evening. "Or if he fiddled a little more than average with all those lovely percentages." Barry continued, "Oh, hey, what I just told you is only the tip of the iceberg. Any fool can do it. But it takes someone with real finesse, like Nigel—" his smile vanished when he said the name "—to work what we call the 'take.' "

Barry lit another cigarette. "I'm not saying that all producers take, mind. I'm not even saying that those who do, do it all the time. But there's all sorts of ways to do it, and believe me, Nigel was—probably still is—one of the best."

And so, with Gabe listening intently, disbelieving at first, then with growing disgust, Barry proceeded to educate him about "the take." One method involved submitting names of family members—real or not—to the musician's union, which required payments every week from theater management for four musicians—whether the show was a musical or not. Additionally, if the producer listed himself as a publicity adviser, and some other family member as a stage manager, or lighting assistant, or anything else, he earned money for those people, too, whether they were actually there or not.

Then there was the "wall" scam, in which a producer with a show coming in rented space for billboard ads. Thousands could be made per year if the space being rented was already owned or leased by the producer himself and charged back to the show. Some producers had rented space all over town just for that purpose.

In the kickback business, various companies bid to make sets, or costumes, or do the lighting or staging. The company who "won" the business had already paid the producer a previously agreed-upon price. With the advertising gimmick, a producer might have two shows running, but pay out less than twice as much for the advertising as with one show, charging both shows as if advertising them separately—and pocketing the difference.

"And of course, the *major* taking done by producers is in the area of ticket sales," Barry concluded. "But that's a little more complicated, and we can go into it later, if you need it. If you want to, you could send Nigel to jail until he's got a beard down to his knees with this other stuff I've already told you."

Gabe had let his coffee grow cold. Pushing it away, he said, "Let me get this straight. Aames has done everything you've just told me?"

"And more," Barry said, lighting another cigarette. The ashtray near his hand was full by this time; neither noticed.

"I suppose it's too much to hope that you have proof."

Barry smiled. "Thanks to Keeley, I do. If she stored all my stuff, I've got records there that go back years, if you're interested."

"I'm interested," he said grimly, and then had a sudden thought. "Or maybe I should leave it up to you."

"Me?" Barry thought about it. "I don't know. Even so, there's a price."

Gabe sat back. He'd expected this. "How much?"

Something flashed in Barry's eyes—longing? Regret? Quietly, he said, "You didn't even quibble. Keeley must mean a lot to you."

"She does," Gabe said briefly. "You said you had a price. How much?"

Barry had seen Gabe's earlier look of disgust. Smiling again, he said, "Not *how* much. *What*."

"I don't understand."

Staring at his nearly spent cigarette, Barry rolled the cylinder back and forth between his fingers and said, "You were right when you said that a long time ago Nigel and I worked together a lot. In fact, we used to be partners." He looked across the table. "I doubt you remember—or even knew—these names, but three of the shows we did together, which Nigel produced, and for which I wrote the music, were called *Torchlight*, *Miss Fortune*, and *Preacher, Preacher*. We had a lot of successes over the years, but these three were all solid hits. Nigel made a lot of money on those shows—" his eyes met Gabe's briefly again "—a lot more than any of the other people involved did." He paused. "Including me."

Gabe was silent a moment. "I see. So it's revenge you want."

Barry shook his head. "No, what happened was my own fault. I could have stopped him. I should have stopped him. But I wasn't . . . I wasn't man enough to do it. I had something else on my mind at the time."

Gabe didn't know whether to ask or not. "You want to tell me about it?"

Barry took a breath. He looked as if he were about to start coughing again, and Gabe tensed. The one paroxysm he'd witnessed had been enough to convince him that Archer needed hospitalization—or at the very least, to see a doctor. But he said nothing, and after a moment, Barry controlled the impulse and started to speak. His voice was so low that Gabe had to strain to hear him.

"It doesn't matter anymore, and it's not important anyway," Barry said, "but when I first started, I was talented, just like Keeley." He smiled sadly. "Maybe not quite as good as she is, but definitely in the running. In those days, I could make anything sing; there seemed nothing I couldn't do. Songs flowed out of me like sweet wine; words and music wrote themselves as if in a dream. Then I met Nigel, and we teamed up, and suddenly we had all those hit shows—one after the other. I thought I'd died and gone to heaven, no kidding. I was young, I was successful, I was making money, and I was doing what I loved to do. I couldn't have asked for more. And then one night, I saw the books Nigel was keeping and realized what he'd been doing."

Barry stopped to take a sip of coffee. Gabe saw the waitress resignedly grab the coffeepot and start over, but he signaled her to leave them alone. Now that Barry had started talking, he didn't want any interruptions. Gladly, the waitress put the pot back on the burner and picked up her tabloid newspaper again.

Setting down the cup, Barry looked up with a weary smile. "Confession is supposed to be good for the soul, right? Maybe that's what's been wrong with me all along. Anyway, when I realized all the stuff Nigel had been pulling—all the things I've told you about tonight—I didn't know what to think. I knew it was illegal, and I was terrified at the thought of what could happen if he was caught. So I confronted him."

"What did he do?"

Barry's mouth twisted. "He laughed at me, can you believe it? He told me I was a baby, that I didn't understand, that everyone did it. When I told him I didn't, he laughed again. We were in it together, he said. Because we were partners, I was just as liable as he was. And if I told anyone, whatever might happen to him would happen to me."

"So you didn't do anything."

His expression bleak, Barry shook his head. "No, I didn't, God help me. I wanted to, but . . . It's hard to explain. I knew it was wrong, that I should tell someone, but I just couldn't. You have to understand. Nigel had been mentor, partner, confidant . . . friend. We were closer—I thought—than most married couples. Oh, not sexually, I don't mean that. I mean in everything else we did. We had the same concept of the shows we were doing and wanted to do; we knew what music worked and what wouldn't. If you're not involved in theater, it's hard to comprehend, but it's the . . . the *vision* of a show that's the most important thing. And when you share it with someone, without words to explain it, well . . . There's no feeling in the world like it."

"I think I understand," Gabe said. A pained expression flashed briefly across his face; he was thinking of all those times out in the field when everything came together for the perfect picture. Oh, he understood, all right, he thought, and looked at Barry again.

"There's more, isn't there?" he asked.

Barry nodded. "I started drinking after that," he said, his voice low. "It was the only way I could handle it. I didn't realize until too late that Fate gives with one hand and takes with the other." He looked bitter. "I didn't know that unless you take care of what you've been given, you can lose it forever."

Gabe looked at him uneasily. "Are you saying that you lost your ability to compose?"

"No, I still had the technique, the ability. But the . . . the brilliance was gone." He shrugged. "Maybe it was guilt; maybe it was retribution. I knew what I should have done, but I didn't do it, and so I was being punished. Deservedly so, maybe, but not easy to accept. After a string of flops, I was desperate. So was Nigel, as you can imagine. What I couldn't compose, he couldn't produce, and we were at each other's throats out of frustration. He turned to directing to save his ass. Then along came a boy named Leo Sargeant."

Barry paused to take another sip of his cold coffee. His hoarse voice had grown hoarser, and he looked ready to collapse. Gabe wanted to tell him he didn't need to go on, but he was too fascinated to stop him. After a moment, Barry continued.

"Leo wanted to write songs, he told me," Barry said. "He wanted to be a composer. He'd heard of the great Barry Archer, and he had come to New York to sit at my knee and learn from me. Imagine. I took him on as an apprentice after hearing one song he'd written." Without warning, Barry crushed the cigarette he was holding to pieces. Looking down as he dribbled the mess into the ashtray, he murmured, "I took everything he had, and then I destroyed him."

Gabe wasn't sure what to say. Was he being dramatic, or did he mean it? Cautiously, trying to think if he'd ever heard Keeley talk about anyone named Sargeant, he asked, "What do you mean, you destroyed him?"

"I mean, I destroyed him. When Leo realized what I was doing, that I was stealing his songs and claiming I'd written them, he was so bitter and unhappy and . . . disillusioned that he committed suicide."

Gabe sat back. "And you blame yourself."

"Wouldn't you?" Barry asked. "I know I'm responsible, no matter what anyone else thinks." He looked up at Gabe with tear-filled eyes. "Why do you think I've been trying to kill myself all the years since?"

Gabe was preoccupied as the big jet lifted off from JFK and turned west, toward California. Things hadn't turned out in quite the way he had expected, and he had a lot to think about as he flew home again. After promising to confront Nigel with the evidence he'd saved all these years, Barry had asked if Gabe wouldn't come with him when he went to see Keeley.

"No, it's not a good idea," Gabe had said immediately, backing away. "Keeley and I . . . well, it's just not a good idea," he'd finished weakly. It was no excuse at all, but he couldn't go into it.

Barry had searched his face before nodding wisely. "I see I'm not the only one with a demon on my shoulder," he had said. He held out his hand. "All right, have it your way. I'll do what I can for her, and the rest she'll do herself. She has a talent like none I've ever seen, and as hard as it is to get a hit in this town, or even break even, she'll do it if anyone can. Grit, genius, guts, it's a hard combination to beat, and she's got it all. It'll see her through, Gabe. I know there's nothing she can't do."

"I know it, too."

"I can see how much you care for her, Gabe. I hope someday you two work things out."

Gabe didn't know what he thought. "I don't think there's much chance."

"You never know. Look what you've done for me. You gave me a reason to live again, when I didn't think there was one. I'm going to enjoy confronting Nigel. God knows, I should have done it years ago."

Gabe had smiled for the first time. "I'm glad I could help. Take care."

"And you, my friend. I hope you find what you're looking for as well."

He hadn't replied to Barry's last remark, but it stayed with him all the way back to California. He returned in time for the weekly family dinner, and although he was tired and feeling drained from the long session with Barry, he decided to drive out to the house and get it over with. If he didn't show up, his mother would worry, and he had enough on his mind without adding additional guilt. He was feeling depressed despite what he had accomplished, and the thought of seeing his two young nieces made him feel better. As always, they were waiting anxiously by the front windows when he arrived, and they ran to meet him with cries of delight.

"What did you bring us, Uncle Gabe? What did you bring us?" they demanded, as he bent down and gave them each a hug and kiss. They were too old now to be swung into the air, but he whirled them around just the same.

As he'd hoped, they were good medicine. Trying not to think

how much he had longed to see Keeley, he teased, "Is that the only reason you're glad to see me, because I might have brought you something?"

With kisses and hugs in return, they assured him it wasn't, but they weren't disappointed when he produced two books he had purchased on the way out.

"Come into the living room and talk to us for a minute, Uncle Gabe," they begged. "We have time before dinner, Grandma said we did."

So Gabe went with them into the living room. As they had on so many occasions, they all sat on the couch, one on each side of him. But before he could ask them about school, Sarah, the older, looked at him and said, "Uncle Gabe, why don't you take pictures anymore?"

Despite himself, he felt a pang. "Because I work for Grandpa now, that's why," he answered. Forcing a smile, he added, "I don't have time for it anymore."

On his other side, Melissa, always the solemn one, put her small hand over his. "That's too bad, Uncle Gabe," she said seriously. "I used to love your pictures. I thought you were the best picture-taker in the whole world."

He smiled at her. "You did?"

She nodded. "So did Daddy. He used to tell us so, whenever he saw one of your pictures in a magazine."

Would he always feel such a sharp pain when Frank was mentioned? "Did he really say that, or are you trying to make me feel good?"

"He really did," Melissa assured him. "He used to tell us all the time how good you were. He said that after all these years, you had finally found what you were best at."

Gabe looked at her in surprise. "Your dad said that?"

"He was proud of you, Uncle Gabe," Sarah said shyly. "I remember. He used to tell us all the time how proud he was of you."

Over the growing lump in his throat, Gabe said, "I was proud of him, too. In fact, I always wished I was more like your dad. But no matter how hard I tried, I just couldn't seem to manage."

Sarah looked at him wonderingly. "But why would you want to be like Daddy, when you were so good at being you?"

Gabe had no answer. Giving both his nieces a hug in lieu of a reply, he started talking about something else. None of the three saw Ellis Tyrell standing out in the hallway, listening. Gabe's father had come down the stairs just as Gabe and the girls went into the living room, and although he didn't mean to eavesdrop, he couldn't pass by. As the three talked, Ellis watched his handsome son, his own expression unreadable. Then, silently, he turned and went to his study. Closing the door behind him, he crossed to his desk and switched on the desk lamp. In the pool of light that shone down, he sat in the chair and unlocked the bottom drawer of the desk. A scrapbook was inside, and he took it out and put it on the desk top.

Long ago, when Gabe had started working for the foundation, Ellis had privately started the scrapbook. Not even his wife knew he had it. But carefully pasted inside was a copy of every one of Gabe's published pictures, some of which he'd gone to a great deal of trouble to obtain. Slowly, he began leafing through the book, stopping at one page or another as a particularly vivid or beautiful shot caught his eye. When he reached the last page, he silently closed the book and put it away. When he looked up, there were tears in his eyes.

CHAPTER THIRTY-ONE

Keeley sat in her theater office, her head in her hands. Rehearsal had gone so badly again that she had stopped it an hour before and sent everyone home before she began screaming. Then she'd locked herself in her office, trying to think. She was so depressed all she could do was stare into space.

She didn't know where to turn. She had exhausted all her money, and she didn't know where to get more. Feeling frantic again at the thought, she pulled out the account books, hoping she'd made a mistake, or missed something, or that she'd miraculously find more money where none had been before, but no— everything was in the same dismal state it had been. Creditors were calling; people had to be paid. She had staved off disaster as long as she could, but she had to accept it now. The best she could do without additional help was to keep rehearsals going a week or so more. Then . . .

She didn't want to think beyond that point. A week wasn't

long enough to get ready, even for a preview out of town. She had tried her best and failed. The reality was, she had not only run out of money, she'd run out of time.

Wanting to shout, or curse, or jump up and yell that it wasn't fair, she looked down at the account books scattered across the top of the battered desk. Resisting the impulse to reach out and sweep them all into the wastebasket, she clasped her hands and tried to work it out. But no matter which way she tried to approach it, the result was the same. At a critical juncture where she needed things to fall into place, she was broke.

She didn't even have the solace of rehearsals going well; today had been such a nightmare that she despaired just thinking about it. After months of working and planning and spending every waking minute thinking of the show, everything was wrong. Several of the songs weren't working; some of the sets didn't seem right; costumes weren't ready; and the lighting was so awful the show might as well be staged in the dark.

To make matters worse, she'd had a quarrel with her stage manager, whose only crime had been to remind her of something she'd forgotten, and she was still feeling badly about yelling at him when Linda Swan, her choreographer, told her she needed three bars more, or less, to stage the last second-act number or it wouldn't work. She was trying to deal with those problems when her lighting director complained that he needed Valeska on stage so he could light the opening number. Ready to scream with frustration at that point, she had angrily told him to go get Valeska himself. That was when he had apologetically relayed the news that their star had locked herself in her dressing room and refused to come out.

"Oh, for Christ's sake!" she had exclaimed, aggravated beyond endurance. Throwing down the pencil she'd been using to make quick changes in the sheet music for Linda, she stormed down the cramped hallway backstage to the warren of dressing rooms. Enraged, she banged on the door with her fist, demanding to be let in.

"Valeska, you open this door at once, do you hear me?" she shouted. "If you don't, I'm going to get Charlie to come and break it down!"

Charlie was one of the stagehands, a big block of a man with a huge appetite and enormous strength. Keeley had seen him carry sets easily by himself that would have flattened two ordinary men.

"I mean it, Val!"

There was a short silence. Just as Keeley was turning away to yell for Charlie, she heard the tiny click of the lock. Not giving Valeska a chance to change her mind, she flung the door open. Val had backed up to the dressing table, tears running down her face. She looked terrified.

As well she should, Keeley thought grimly, coming in and slamming the door behind her. "What is it *now*, Val? I swear to God, if you get temperamental on me once more today, I'm going to—"

To Keeley's annoyance, Valeska burst into sobs. Covering her face with her hands, she wept, "Don't yell at me, Keeley. Can't you see I'm upset enough as it is?"

Thinking she didn't know the meaning of upset, Keeley took a fierce grip on her temper. She knew from experience that shouting at Valeska only made things worse, but she was so infuriated that she had to speak between clenched teeth. "I won't yell if you won't cry. Now, what is it? Things are going bad enough around here today without you playing prima donna!"

Sniffling, Valeska reached for a tissue. Wiping her eyes, she said weakly, "I'm sorry, Keeley. It's just that I'm so scared."

Trying to control herself, Keeley counted to ten. Before she said anything, she reminded herself that Valeska had been on the verge of a nervous breakdown ever since Nigel's visit to the apartment, and that she'd had to handle her carefully. She didn't want to destroy her good work with a few ill-chosen words, especially since she still felt badly about that incident herself. The one good thing about it was that they seemed to have learned from past mistakes; after she'd had a chance to cool down, they had gotten together and talked it out. When she found out that Nigel had planted the empty vodka bottle after Valeska had taken the Valium and conked out, she'd felt so guilty about her prejudgment that she had vowed never to do it again. Nigel's attempt to drive a wedge between them had failed, but if his goal had been to undermine Valeska's shaky confidence, Keeley thought, he'd certainly succeeded.

Valeska seemed even more fragile emotionally than she ever had been—so much so that Keeley wondered at times if she knew the whole story. They'd been friends for a long time, and she knew when Valeska was hiding something. Val denied it, but Keeley was sure something was wrong. Whatever it was, it was affecting her performance. Valeska couldn't concentrate, and while her voice was soaring after all the past months of retraining, she couldn't seem to put the feeling into the role of Beauty that Keeley envisioned. They'd had battles about it before but had always worked it out. Hoping for the same result today, Keeley tried to think of another approach.

"You don't have to be scared, Val," she said encouragingly. "You're doing just fine. Now, come on. All Dick wanted to do was check lighting."

Valeska looked at her agitatedly. "It's got nothing to do with the *lighting*! I'm scared because Nigel just called!"

She didn't want to believe it. They hadn't heard from Nigel for weeks now, ever since the night he'd made his threatening visit to the apartment. As time went on with no further action, she had convinced herself that he wouldn't bother them again. More disturbed than she wanted to admit by the news, she wondered what he was up to. Why now? Why had he waited this long? Was he desperate—or did he think *she* was?

"What did he want?" she asked. She didn't intend to be intimidated by Nigel Aames at this late date, no matter what he tried.

Valeska reached for another tissue. "He said that you've ... put him off long enough about directing the show. He's coming over to talk to you about it, and that you—" she shuddered "—that you better have the right answer for him if you know what's good for you."

If the situation hadn't been so serious, Keeley would have laughed. Scornfully, she said, "He sounds like something out of a bad gangster movie."

Collapsing on the seat in front of the dressing table, Valeska looked at her fearfully. "You don't understand. If you did, you'd be as afraid of him as I am."

"Don't be silly," she said boldly, for her own confidence as much as Val's. "Nigel can't hurt either of us. We both know he's just a big bully."

Valeska shook her head wildly. "You don't know him like I do, Keeley. You don't know what he can do!"

"For heaven's sake, Val! If—"

"No, no, Keeley, you don't understand! He's capable of anything!"

No matter what she'd said, she hadn't been able to calm Valeska, so in the end, she had finally just sent her home to rest. Rehearsal had gone from bad to worse afterward, so she ended up sending everyone else away as well. Alone in her office, she sat back and rubbed her eyes. She had deliberately acted confident with her star, but she didn't believe what she'd said any more than Valeska did. They both knew the harm Nigel could do. Neither of them doubted for an instant that he would do it, either.

Trying not to panic at the thought, she wondered what had ever made her think she could pull this off by herself. It really had been a dream—nothing but pure fantasy on her part. Her vision had been so clear; she knew what she wanted. She just hadn't realized how difficult—no, how impossible—it might be to bring it to life.

Her chin came up. She wasn't going to give in, she told herself fiercely. She'd find an answer somewhere or die trying. She hadn't come this far to be defeated—at least not by a sleaze like Nigel Aames.

With loathing, she looked at the account books on the desk. Why couldn't they lie, for once? Every time she thought about all those people depending on her to come through, she felt the noose tighten. She was at the end of her financial rope with nowhere to turn and no help in sight. What could she tell them? Sorry, gang, but I can't pay you after all? She clenched her fist at the thought. She'd kill herself first. Every one of the cast and crew had worked long hours with no overtime, taking pay cut after pay cut on her promise that she'd pay them all back, plus a big bonus, when the show finally opened. Now it seemed a question of "if" rather than "when," and she had to face the fact that she had some tough choices ahead.

Angry and frustrated, she pushed the books away. She didn't need the ledgers to tell her that the way things stood now, she'd never be able to mount the production without new backers. The die had been cast as soon as Nigel had convinced the money men she wasn't a good risk by spreading gossip all over town about her inexperience and inability. It didn't matter that it wasn't true; she knew that once he'd sown the seeds of doubt no one was going to help her. Too proud to admit defeat, she had pressed on, sure that grit and determination would see her through. But no amount of determination could change reality, and the reality was that Nigel had boxed her into a corner. He'd made damn sure that the only escape was through him.

"Hellfire," she muttered. The way things stood now, she needed a miracle to save the show. It was either that or face two equally unpalatable choices: agreeing to let Nigel direct so he could bring in more money, or abandoning the project completely.

At the last thought, her chin lifted again. She wouldn't give up. The thought of abandoning her dream when she was so close to making it was not an option, no matter what.

Brave thoughts, she told herself sarcastically, especially when she was in this fix. But she still wouldn't let Nigel take what was hers and make it his own—as he would, if he ever got his hands on it—she'd destroy it completely first.

But how was she going to prevent it?

She looked at the phone. She did have another option, one she didn't want to take. But with her back pushed to the wall, it was time to consider it.

She'd thought of calling Raleigh Quinn to ask his help several times, but she hadn't been able to make herself do it. She couldn't ask him to bail her out. He'd told her over and over when she was in Hollywood that he didn't want anything to do with Broadway again.

"I've left Broadway for good," he'd said to her. "There's too much corruption."

That had been in better days. Smiling, Keeley had reminded him that Hollywood was just as bad in its own way.

"Yes, it's true," Raleigh had agreed, a twinkle in his eye. "But at least I understand the process here."

He'd been inflexible about severing all his ties with Broadway, and as she debated about calling him to ask for his financial help now, she remembered his stand with a grimace. Did he still mean it?

There was only one way to find out, and since she seemed to have run out of options, she had no choice. She was just picking up the phone when Nigel walked in.

She hadn't heard him coming, and when she looked up, he was standing in the doorway, looking completely in charge and superior as hell. It was obvious that he believed he had her where he wanted her, and as they stared at each other, she felt weary enough to wonder, just for a second or two, if it might not just be easier to give in. *There will be other shows,* she thought, before she realized what she was thinking. Angrily, she straightened. There might be other shows, but there was only one *Beauty and the Beast*, and it was hers—hers alone. Nigel Aames wasn't going to have anything to do with it, not if she had to sell everything she had to keep going—not if she had to beg, borrow, or steal . . . or throw herself on the mercy of friends.

"Well, Nigel," she said, calmly replacing the telephone receiver she was holding. "What brings you here?"

He was surprised. "Didn't Valeska tell you I was coming?"

"Now that I think of it, she might have mentioned it. I really don't remember. I've been so busy."

His face darkened; he didn't like being thought inconsequential, and he came in and shut the door. Hiding the sudden, hard pounding of her heart, she looked blandly up at him.

"No matter," he said. "I came to see if you've reached the right decision yet."

She sat back without answering. There was no other chair in the tiny office; he was forced either to stand or perch on the edge of the desk, which had no space for him, either. She was enjoying the power play and let him simmer a moment.

"You think you have it all figured out, don't you?" she said. "If the show's a hit, you'll be in clover. If it's not, well, you did your best to help a . . . friend. It couldn't be your fault, if you came on board too late to rescue a sinking ship. People will say how unselfish you are. Such a prince. How very clever."

Preening, he said, "Right you are, my dear Keeley. Everybody in town knows that you were once my protégée, so of course you would come to me for help, advice, my expertise. I'm so glad you've listened to reason. Now we can get on without this posturing."

Thinking that he was the one guilty of striking poses, she said calmly, "You know what your problem is, Nigel? You think you still have influence."

His eyes narrowed. "Defiant to the last, is that it? Well, it won't do you any good, Keeley. We both know the inevitable outcome."

"Oh, the outcome is inevitable, all right. I just don't think it'll be the one you want. Please shut the door on your way out, Nigel. I'm busy now—putting together my show."

"I always knew you were an arrogant little bitch. I didn't think you were stupid as well!"

"You're the one who's stupid, Nigel, if you think I'm going to give in to your puny little threats."

Deliberately, she turned her back to him, reaching for something on the desk. She saw him out of the corner of her eye a split second before he reached her, his arm upraised. She jumped up from the chair, her eyes blazing.

"Don't you even *think* about it, you pitiful excuse for a man!" she cried. At her sides, her hands were clenched into fists. She looked ready to fight. "I mean it! You hit me and it will be the *last* thing you ever do!"

Surprised by her counterattack, Nigel took a step back. At her fierce expression, he lowered his arm, but tried to save face by blustering, "No one talks to me that way! No one!"

"Then maybe it's about time someone did. Is this how you get your way?" She had a sudden thought, and her eyes blazed a fiery green again. "Is this why Valeska is so afraid of you, because you hit her when she didn't do as you asked?"

His face was a mask of hate. "Why don't you ask her, you bitch! Oh, I knew you'd be trouble the first day we met! You'll be sorry for this, Keeley. I swear it!"

"Is this a private party, or can anyone join in?" someone said behind him.

Recognizing the voice, Nigel spun around with a gasp. As soon as he moved out of the doorway and Keeley saw who was standing outside, her jaw dropped.

"Barry!" she exclaimed, wondering if she dared believe her eyes. "I can't believe it!"

Barry Archer stepped into the office. He looked much older than when she'd last seen him, but it had been years, she thought—nearly seven—since he had disappeared. He looked frail, so thin it seemed a light breeze would blow him over. His eyes were bloodshot, his skin an unhealthy color. But it was Barry, and despite the tension, she was thrilled to see him.

"Barry! Where have you been?"

"Later, Keeley, okay?" he said. As though Nigel were a snake, Barry didn't take his eyes off him. "Right now, we've all got a few things to discuss."

Her predicament came back to her with a rush, and she looked quickly at Nigel, who was staring at Barry as though he were the phantom come to life. When she saw his eyes drop to the books Barry was holding under one arm, she looked down, too. They seemed to be journals, or ledgers of some kind, just like the ones she'd been working on herself earlier. Or maybe not, she thought. These looked older, more worn, as though they'd been around a long time.

Barry smiled when he saw Nigel looking at what he held. "Remember these?" he said.

"Why should I?" Nigel replied. He was doing his best to act nonchalant, but Keeley had seen the flicker of fear in his face, and she moved closer. What was going on?

"I'd think they'd be hard to forget," Barry said. "But just in case, think of it this way. Remember the saying about your chickens coming home to roost?"

Nigel paled. His glance flicked to the books, then back to Barry's face again. "Those can't be—"

"They are."

Abruptly, Nigel's bravado deserted him. Fascinated, Keeley watched as he reached behind him and grabbed on to the edge of the desk. "You told me they were stolen."

Smiling again, Barry said softly, "I lied."

Nigel looked again at the ledgers, then up at the composer. "What . . . do you want?" His voice sounded strangled; two red slashes of color had appeared on his cheeks.

"What do you think?"

"If you think you can come back here after all these years to blackmail me—"

"Blackmail! Such an ugly word. Besides, why does everything have to be about you? I'm here to help Keeley."

Nigel glanced quickly in Keeley's direction; she was staring in blank surprise at her old friend. He looked at Barry again. Between his teeth, he said, "Why?"

Barry's smile disappeared. "It's a concept you never learned, Nigel. Call it friendship, loyalty . . . poetic justice, whichever you choose. You've gotten away with so many things over the years that you believe you're invincible."

Nigel lifted his head. "I *am* invincible! If you think you can threaten me with—"

"It's no threat," Barry denied. "You know as well as I do what these ledgers contain. You should; they were yours. I'm afraid it's time to reflect on all your misdeeds, my friend. If you've forgotten any, or conveniently choose not to remember the details, it's all in here—" he patted the books "—which are soon to be on their way to all the right people."

"If you think I believe any of this tripe—"

"Of course you believe it. Otherwise, you wouldn't be standing here, trying to remember just what you wrote in here."

"Why don't you let me see them and satisfy my curiosity, then?"

Barry started to laugh. It changed to a cough instead, which he controlled with an effort that made his face red. His voice sounding hoarse, he said, "You haven't changed, I see. You can't honestly believe I'd let you get your hands on these so you can destroy them." He coughed again, once more controlling the spasm with difficulty. "You'll see them again soon enough. When you're trying to explain what it means to people who could do you damage. Like the police, for instance. Or the—"

"I know what you're up to here!" Nigel said, his face darkening. "But even if the statute on this kind of thing hasn't run out, I doubt anyone is going to believe—or care. You could have found them. You could have written them yourself!"

"But I didn't."

"So you say. Do you think any authority is going to believe you—you, a drunk down on his luck?"

Keeley involuntarily stepped forward, but Barry didn't even flinch. "I might be a drunk, as you so eloquently put it," he said with another cough, "but I'm sure someone will be interested, either downtown at police headquarters, or at one of the Guilds." He hefted the ledgers. "My drinking doesn't have anything to do with the proof here, written in your own hand."

Despite his bravado, Nigel looked shaken. Keeley saw his expression, and even though she'd been around long enough to hazard a good guess about what the ledgers contained, she was avid to see them. It had to be incriminating, she thought, or Nigel wouldn't be reacting like this.

As if he'd read her thoughts, Nigel glanced in her direction before he looked at Barry again. "I would have preferred to do this privately, Barry, but since you've dragged Keeley into it—"

"I didn't *drag* Keeley into it," Barry corrected him, wheezing. "She's directly concerned. This time it's *her* show that's at stake."

Recovering a little, Nigel retorted nastily, "You mean instead of the *other* time when Leo was involved?"

For the first time since he appeared, Barry looked shaken himself. Instinctively coming forward when she saw him sway, Keeley stopped when he raised a hand in her direction.

"Barry, don't you think . . ." she started to say, but subsided at the look he gave her. Moving back reluctantly again, she tried to remember if she'd ever heard of a Leo. She couldn't recall, not at this point, when the tension already in the room seemed abruptly to sizzle and thicken.

"You're right, Nigel," Barry said, his wheezing increasing until he could hardly speak without gasping. "Maybe this is about Leo. If it is, it's about time, don't you think?"

Nigel seemed somehow to have climbed to safer ground. "Leo was your problem, not mine. If anyone is to blame, we know it's you. After all, *you* were the one who stole 'Mystified,' and all the other songs from *Torchlight* from him, not me."

Despite herself, Keeley gasped. She had suddenly remembered who Leo was. She'd read about Leo Sergeant long ago—a brilliant talent who had burned out at a young age. Depressed and despondent over his career, he had killed himself by jumping off a bridge. He'd left no note behind, no family, no music—at least none that had ever been found. Swiftly, she looked from Nigel to Barry. Without warning, doubt rose like an ugly cancer in her mind.

Barry saw the doubt written on her expressive face. "Some day I'll tell you about it," he said hoarsely. "Until then, don't judge me too harshly, okay?"

"I don't judge you at all, Barry," she answered. "I—"

"Well, well, isn't this cozy," Nigel interrupted. "If you don't mind, you two can have your little reunion without me."

He started to push his way out of the office, but Barry held his ground. "We're not finished yet, you and I," Barry said. He began coughing again and reached for a handkerchief to cover his mouth.

Nigel looked at him contemptuously while he struggled to control the spasm. "You won't carry out your threat. You've always been a weakling, Barry. It's only one of the flaws in your character."

"I admit I've always avoided trouble," Barry gasped. "But this is one time I'm going to set the record straight. I'm going to do what's right, as I should have long ago."

"Oh, really? And what's so different about this time?"

"I know what I owe. I've been carrying guilt around too many years. It's a heavy burden, Nigel, and I want to put it down."

"You're a fool, Barry. You always were. You never knew how to deal with consequences."

Barry put away his handkerchief. Taking a wheezing breath, he looked Nigel in the eye. "And you do, I suppose. Well, that's nice to know, since now you're going to have to deal with a few consequences yourself."

Despite his control, Nigel looked ready to strike. His eyes flashing, he said, "You won't get away with it. You forget, you're in this as deep as I am."

"I know," Barry wheezed. "But this time I'm willing to pay the price."

As worried as Keeley was about Barry's condition, it was obvious to her that Nigel was finally beginning to believe Barry meant what he said. "If you bring me down, you'll destroy yourself, too."

"It would be a relief, believe me," Barry rasped. "I've been trying to do it myself and not succeeding for years now. I'll welcome the chance."

Clearly feeling trapped, Nigel started to sound a little frantic. "I can't believe you mean it. We go back a long way, Barry. We can work it out, can't we?"

Standing silently by, trying to stay out of it, as Barry had asked, Keeley looked at Barry with growing concern. She could see the lines of exhaustion deepening in his face and knew he was almost at the end of his endurance. His breathing sounded more harsh with every breath, and it was obvious he was holding back another coughing fit with an effort. His pasty color frightened her, and she wanted to beg him to sit down, or even better, allow her to call a doctor. Biting her lip, she told herself not to interrupt. This was between him and Nigel, and she couldn't interfere.

Barry must have realized how worried she was, for he looked at her and forced a weak smile. When she instantly came to his side, he grasped her arm and held on tightly. She tried not to show it, but she was even more alarmed when she felt his body trembling. She knew what a terrible effort this was for him, and she couldn't prevent herself from saying, "Barry, please—at least sit down."

He didn't look at her. His attention was on Nigel. "In a moment," he said to her. And then, "So, you want to work it out, do you, Nigel? Just what do you have in mind?"

Now that Barry seemed to be relenting, Nigel couldn't take his eyes off the books. "Name your price," he growled. "It's what you came for, isn't it?"

To Keeley's alarm, Barry started to cough again. He controlled it with an effort that practically doubled him over. "I don't want money," he gasped. "I'm past needing it now. In a few more weeks—months, at the most, as you can see—it won't matter anyway. I'm sick, old friend. I doubt I'll last much longer."

Keeley gasped. His grip on her arm tightened. Gazing at Nigel, he smiled ironically before he began to cough again. "Another case of poetic justice, don't you think?"

Nigel didn't answer, but Keeley made a sound of protest. Tears springing into her eyes, she said, "Oh, no! Oh, Barry!"

"It's all right," he said, holding on to her with trembling fingers as he tried to control another spasm. "I've known it for a long time now, and I've accepted it. As I said, it'll be a relief in a way." His eyes sought Nigel's face again. "But before I go, I want to make things right."

It was clear that Nigel finally believed Barry meant it. After all, he had nothing to lose now. "You won't make it right this way," he said quickly. Beads of sweat had appeared on his face, making him look shiny and greasy. "Nothing is going to bring back Leo now."

"You're right," Barry said with a rasping sigh. "Nothing is going to bring him back. But if I can stop you from exploiting someone else, maybe things won't go so badly with me. So I'm giving these to Keeley—" he handed her the books, which he had refused to relinquish until now "—for safekeeping."

"Safekeeping! Just what is that supposed to mean?" Nigel demanded. His look of fear was back, and he licked his lips.

"I think you know what it means, Nigel," Barry replied, leaning heavily on Keeley. "She can do with them what she likes, but I imagine if you agree not to bother her again with any demands about directing—or producing"—his eyes met Nigel's—"or being connected in any way with the show, maybe she'll agree to keep the contents to herself. Her freedom for yours. Not a bad bargain, don't you agree?"

"You son of a bitch!" Nigel hissed, his face reddening again with impotent fury. "I'll get you for this."

"You're too late, Nigel," Barry said, beginning to cough again. "Someone already has."

Looking as though he wanted to kill, Nigel glanced at Keeley. "Well?"

Keeley looked directly back. The ledgers felt hot in her hands, heavy with evidence. But she was more concerned about Barry. "Well what?"

Nigel's eyes narrowed. "You'd do it, too, wouldn't you?"

She didn't hesitate. To save her show? To get him out of her life? To show Barry that his gesture wasn't in vain? "Yes," she said. "In a minute."

"Damn you! Damn you both to hell!"

"It will be for me," Barry said, reaching for his handkerchief again. To her horror, Keeley saw blood drops appear on it when he put it to his mouth. Containing the spasm, he looked at Nigel. "But we'll see each other there, no doubt, won't we, old friend?"

"You won't get away with it!" Nigel cried, pushing past them. He ran out into the hallway. "You won't get away with it, I swear on your grave!"

Before he had disappeared, Keeley turned to Barry. "Barry, I—"

He lifted a shaking hand. "If you're about to thank me, don't," he rasped. "I did it for me as much as for you. I don't think Nigel will bother you again, at least not about the show."

Wildly, she shook her head. "I wasn't thinking about the show! I'm worried about you. Please, let me call the doctor!"

"Not yet," Barry said. Weakly, he gestured toward the chair. "If I can just sit down . . ."

Hastily, she reached for the chair and helped him sit down. "Barry, please! Let me call . . ."

He tried to smile. She could see blood at the corners of his mouth. "It won't do any good. It's been coming on a long time."

She hardly knew what she was saying. "Please, let me help. Oh, I can't believe you're here! Where have you been all these years?"

"In the bottom of a bottle, I guess," he panted.

"But I tried to find you!"

"You couldn't find me when I'd lost myself." He started to cough again. "But it all worked out," he gasped. "I—"

He never finished the sentence. The fit of coughing overtook him, and when he doubled over with obvious pain, Keeley threw the ledgers on the desk and reached for the telephone. Before she could grab it, Barry collapsed against the side of the desk.

"I think . . . I'm . . . in trouble . . . here," he gasped. To her horror, blood spurted out his nose, and as she reached for a tissue for him with one hand, she grabbed for the phone again with the other.

"I'm calling an ambulance," she said, dialing the emergency number. "You need to get to a hospital."

Barry couldn't stop coughing. It had an underlying bubbly sound that terrified her. She was sure he'd die before the ambulance arrived, and when she thought of all the wasted years of his disappearance, she wanted to cry. Fiercely willing the tears away, she gave the theater address to the operator, then slammed down the phone and yelled for the janitor. When the man came at a run, white-faced and frightened at what he'd heard in her voice, she sent him back to watch for the paramedics; then she bent down and tried to hold Barry in the chair. He was coughing so badly now that his entire body shook with each spasm, but when he looked up once and saw her white, frightened face, he tried to smile.

"You'll . . . be . . . all right now," he gasped.

Panic-stricken, she reached for his hand. Her other arm was around him, and the position was awkward, but she didn't care. She'd keep him alive with sheer force of will, if she had to. "Oh, Barry," she cried, holding him tightly. "Just hang on. Everything will be all right."

When the ambulance came, she insisted on riding to the hospital with him. She held his hand all the way there, willing him to live, but terrified he would die instead. As the vehicles sped through the streets, sirens screaming, she sat tensely, holding on to a life she was sure was slipping away with each beat of his heart.

"Oh, Barry," she said brokenly at one point. "We had so much to talk about!"

He opened his eyes one last time. Smiling faintly, he gestured her closer. It was difficult to hear him with all the noise from the siren and the machines inside, but when she bent over him, he pulled aside the oxygen mask that was covering his face.

"Hey—" the attendant said. But Barry held up one finger.

"Keeley," he said.

"I'm here, Barry," she answered. Bending over him, she clung to his hand.

"I'm proud of you, kid," he said, trying to hold back another coughing spasm. "That show of yours is damn good. It's going to be a hit."

Thinking that even with Nigel off her back, she doubted she could raise enough money to keep it going in time, she tried to smile. She couldn't argue with him at this point, so she said, "Thanks."

"I mean it. I've been watching rehearsals the past few days—"

She looked at him in dismay. "You were there, and you didn't let me know? Oh, Barry!"

He shook his head. Blood was beginning to bubble at the corners of his mouth again. "Doesn't matter now," he gasped. "Just wanted to say . . ."

"What?" She could hardly hear him; he was getting weaker by the second.

"The number opening the second act—the one sung by Beauty's sister?"

She couldn't believe they were having this conversation, not now, not here! "Yes, I know it," she said, intending to beg him to be quiet, to conserve his strength. "But—"

"It's not right, Keeley," he persisted. Every breath looked like an agony, but he held on. "Make her sing it spiteful instead of sweet. If you do, you'll have the whole act."

The instant he said it, she knew he was right. Why hadn't she seen it before? She'd worked so hard on that song, but no matter what she did, she'd known it wasn't right. Now Barry had given her the clue in just a few words, and she looked at him in awe.

"You're . . ." she started to say. At that instant, his eyes closed, and her heart leapt. "Barry?" she cried. Then louder, and more shrill, *"Barry!"*

The attendant gently pushed her out of the way, pulling out her stethoscope and placing it against Barry's chest. She listened a moment, then she reached for the intercom to the driver. She spoke tersely to him, and Keeley felt the ambulance pick up speed.

"Is he . . . ?" She was almost afraid to ask.

The paramedic's expression was somber. "It'll be close," she said, bending over her patient again.

With Keeley holding Barry's hand tightly, the ambulance screamed through the darkness. Every time the driver blared the horn at a vehicle blocking the way, Keeley cursed the careless driver. Didn't they know a man was dying in here?

"Oh, Barry," she murmured, again and again. Her heart felt cold as stone.

By the time Keeley finished talking to the doctor in Intensive Care and learning that the next twenty-four hours would tell the story for Barry, it was long after midnight. Wearily, she took a cab home and found that Valeska had left a light burning in the living room for her, with a note pinned to the shade saying that she had taken a sleeping pill and to wake her in the morning for rehearsal. Thinking glumly that there might not be too many more rehearsals left, Keeley wandered into the kitchen and leaned wearily against the counter. Tux came and rubbed against her legs as if he sensed how depressed she felt; bending down, she picked him up and buried her nose in his fur, thinking how much he'd changed over the years. But then, they both had, hadn't they? Neither of them were so fiercely independent anymore, and at this point, she didn't know whether that was good or not. Deciding she was too tired to think about it, she put him on the counter.

"Do you want some dinner?" she murmured, before she saw that Valeska had already fed him. In answer, he just purred.

She hadn't had dinner, but she wasn't hungry; even her vague notion of making a cup of tea seemed to take too much energy. Her purse seemed to weigh her down even more, so she took the heavy bag off her shoulder. She was just setting it on the counter when she realized she'd brought Barry's journals home with her. In all the fright and confusion after the paramedics had met them at the theater, she must have stuffed the ledgers into her purse without thinking.

Slowly, she took the books out and put them on the table. Hours ago, she had been avid to see what was inside, but when she thought that Barry might be dying, she could hardly bring herself to open them. Still, he'd believed they were important enough to safeguard all these years, so she sat down at the kitchen table, intending to leaf through them.

Sighing, she opened the book on top—and saw that it was blank. Thinking she had chosen an odd one, she reached for another, with the same result. Quickly, she leafed through the rest. Every single one was blank. She didn't realize what Barry had done until then, but once she did, she began to smile.

"He was bluffing the whole time!" she said to herself in amazement. "Damn, it was all one big bluff!"

She began to laugh in sheer delight before she realized she wasn't out of the woods yet. The trick had scared Nigel off—for the time being, at least—but now what? Her smile disappeared when she thought that she still needed money, a lot of it, to keep the show going. After the damage Nigel had done to her reputation, she could prostrate herself, beg, borrow, and grovel, but she still wouldn't get enough money, not now.

Feeling blue again at the thought, she brushed tears from her eyes and got up. She had to get to bed; she was so tired she couldn't think straight. She was just reaching for the light switch when she realized she had a message on the answering machine. Tempted to catch it in the morning, she wondered if the hospital had called after she left and quickly reached for the PLAYBACK button.

"Hi, Keeley," came a voice she knew very well when the tape recycled. "This is Raleigh. Say, listen, I've been waiting for you to call all this time, but I know how stiff-necked and proud you are, so I decided, what the hell, I'll do it myself. Now, I know what I said about never darkening Broadway's door again, but I guess there comes a time when a man just can't help himself. My spies tell me that this *Beauty and the Beast* of yours is going to be a real corker, and you know me—I'm a patsy for a good investment. If you can squeeze me in, let me know. And to show you this is a business offer, instead of just a handshake between old friends, I'll put up the dough if you'll agree to score another film or two for me. Tit for tat, as they say, and we'll call it even. What do you think? Let me know, and we'll do a deal."

The machine cycled off, but Keeley just stood there. She knew Raleigh was serious; he might be a friend, but he was—as he'd said—a businessman, too. A score or two for financing for the show? She felt dazed, so buffeted from the emotional swings she had endured lately that she didn't know whether to laugh or cry or start to celebrate.

Then she laughed aloud, in pure delight. One thing was certain, she thought giddily. She was going to bring *Beauty and the Beast* to life. Together, Raleigh and Barry had given her the keys, and she wouldn't let them down. She had always known what she wanted; she had always believed she could do it. And now, thanks to them, she could write the music as she'd always wanted. Laughing again, she picked up the resigned Tux and began to dance around in glee. Then, stars in her eyes, she went to wake up Valeska and tell her what had happened.

CHAPTER THIRTY-TWO

Six weeks after Barry reappeared and Raleigh Quinn called Keeley with his offer, *Beauty and the Beast* opened in Boston. For Keeley, the time had flown by like a runaway train. By then, Barry, still weak and frail after his bout with pneumonia and assorted other problems, was out of the hospital and convalescing with Valeska's friends at Hildredth. An increasingly phlegmatic Tux was staying with them, too, while Keeley was out of town; it was bending the rules slightly, but by this time, Keeley was a favorite at the home, as well. Laughing, Barry claimed he was a little too old for that lively group, but she knew there were times when he could be prevailed upon to play the piano for them. He was there with the rest of the group waiting anxiously by the phone for her to call with the news of the opening. He was positive the show would be a hit, and she wished she had his confidence. Dressed in glamorous emerald-green floor-length satin culottes and a beaded jacket top for this momentous occasion, she knew that, outwardly at least, she had never looked better. Inside, she was a wreck.

After a year and a half of preparation, she was going to see what she had done. *Beauty and the Beast* would play tonight for the first time to a paying audience, and even though she had two weeks to refine, redefine, and recraft the show if necessary before they went back to New York, she knew that what happened tonight would determine the outcome. If the audience—or worse, the critics—didn't like it, if no one got teary in the right places, or applauded when they were supposed to, she knew there might not *be* a New York opening.

Shivering at the thought, she rubbed her icy hands together, wondering how she was going to hold herself together until it was time. She had been at the theater all day, coming in early to keep herself busy, hoping that time would fly until the curtain went up and she was committed, ready or not.

She definitely wasn't ready. An hour or so before judgment, she was still so keyed up she felt like an exposed nerve ending. Adding to her worries was the storm. Snow had begun to fall about three this afternoon, and she was concerned that the roads would close and no one would be able to come. At this point, she didn't know what would be worse: an empty theater, or a disappointed audience. Maybe there was time to cancel, she thought. She still didn't like that one scene in the first act, and there was a spot in the third. . . .

"Stop it," she muttered between clenched teeth. If she didn't control her nerves, she'd be no good to herself or anyone else. Telling herself to concentrate on what still needed to be done, she went to see who needed help.

At this hour, backstage was a hive of activity. Everyone in the crew was running back and forth; stagehands were moving sets and completing final checks to make sure all was in order. Dancers were stretching, and various cast members were clustered in little groups, rehearsing one another. Wes Abbott, her stage manager, was everywhere, it seemed, clipboard in one hand, a pencil behind his ear, another at the ready. Everyone had started coming in around three, the performers to sing and dance a number or two to loosen up, the orchestra to play a little so they wouldn't open cold.

Thinking of the near crisis with the orchestra, Keeley shuddered again. "We've got a problem," Wes had told her when they started arriving earlier that afternoon. "They didn't raise the pit, as promised."

To Keeley, it had been instant nightmare. In this theater, the floor of the pit was at least fifteen feet below the stage; a couple of weeks ago when the orchestra had first rehearsed, she knew it wouldn't work. If she couldn't hear them when she was standing two feet away, the audience wouldn't even know they were playing. She had arranged to have the floor raised, and she assumed it had been done. When Wes told her it hadn't, she knew with a sinking feeling she should have checked.

"We'll get stools," she said decisively, after going with him and peering down into the pit.

"Stools?" Wes echoed. "But the orchestra can't play perched up like—"

"They'll have to," she said grimly. "It's too late to raise the floor, and we haven't any other options. Get your coat."

"My coat?"

She was so tense she nearly screamed at him to stop repeating everything she said. Grabbing him instead, she pushed him ahead of her and together they went out into the falling snow in search of a furniture rental store. Miraculously, they managed to find what they needed; even better, no one complained when she explained what she wanted them to do. Game to try, the entire orchestra climbed onto the high stools and played the opening number.

"It'll work—but just," she told them, relieved. "Thanks, everybody. I owe you one."

She had barely solved that problem before she was confronted with another, and another. It seemed endless; she thought she'd scream if one more person came to her with a last-minute emergency. Was this what directors went through? No wonder there were collapses and ulcers!

First, the set designer came to tell her that one of the forest backdrops had been damaged in the move to the theater and had to be repainted. Not a big problem . . . until she learned that the paint wouldn't be dry by curtain, so the choreographer had to be consulted. Because of the wet paint, two stage entrances for act two had to be altered, and that meant the actors involved had to be summoned and shown the changes. She had barely taken a breath from overseeing that when Angie, the costumer, arrived to tell her that one of the studded gloves the Beast wore until his transformation in the final act had been lost somehow in all the confusion, and she didn't have time to make another one. Did Keeley have any ideas?

Feeling increasingly beset, wondering why she had ever thought she could pull this off, Keeley tried to think. "You don't have time to make a complete glove, but you can make two studded wrist guards out of leather, can't you?" she said finally. "All you have to do is make a cone that widens as it goes up Dom's arm. It will look medieval enough, and we'll just glue some hair on the backs of his hands until he turns into the prince. What do you think?"

Angie gave her an admiring look. "I think it'll work. Are you *sure* you've never been a costume designer?"

"Jill of all trades, mistress of none. Can you have it done in time?"

"No problem," Angie replied; then she'd laughed. "It's going to be a little difficult getting the hair off Dom's hands for the final act. Knowing him, he's going to scream."

Dominic Kilgore, a handsome young man in his late twenties, was playing the Beast. In addition to his good looks and acting ability, he possessed a rich baritone that blended beautifully with Valeska's soprano. Size-wise, they were perfect for each other. In Keeley's vision, Beast towered protectively over Beauty, and Dom's broad chest and wide shoulders contrasted just right with Val's slender, delicate body. Remembering how Dom had complained about his two-hour makeup jobs as the lionlike Beast, Keeley knew he wasn't going to be pleased at the new addition. Deciding she'd stop in to see him and smooth any ruffled fur if necessary, she'd turned to someone else who had come up with yet another problem for her to fix.

What with one thing and another, afternoon turned into early evening. Various members of cast and crew either went out for a light supper or had something brought in, but Keeley was too nervous to eat. She went to get her hair done instead, then to her office to get dressed. When she was ready, she remembered she hadn't seen Valeska since she came in about four. Val had practiced a few scales and sung a song or two before announcing she needed to rest. The sign on her dressing room door stated that she didn't want to be disturbed by anyone.

Keeley hadn't bothered her. Valeska had been on edge all week, bursting into tears at the slightest provocation, forgetting her lines during dress rehearsal, refusing to sing one of her songs in the second act until it was dropped to another key. Keeley had made the change temporarily, hoping it was just nerves, but as she headed toward Valeska's dressing room to check on her, she felt uneasy. Valeska had been so shaky that Keeley wasn't sure she'd sing tonight.

Trying to tell herself she was letting her own nerves get the best of her, she sidled down the hallway crowded with props and sets to Valeska's closed dressing room door. She was just starting to knock when she thought she heard voices inside. One was a man's voice, she was sure, and she was debating about whether to go in or go away when the decision was made for her. She was still standing there when the door opened. To her stunned surprise, she was suddenly face-to-face with Nigel Aames.

Instantly, she was enraged. She'd thought she was done with this man. Nigel hadn't been seen, even around town, since the night Barry had appeared, and Keeley had finally begun to believe she and Val wouldn't have to deal with him again. As they stared at each other tonight, he stepped into the hallway and shut the door behind him.

Keeley took the initiative, demanding, "What are you doing here?"

He had the gall to look reproachful. "Why, Keeley, I came to wish my wife good luck."

"She's not your wife!"

"Indeed, she is, my dear. You've forgotten; we've never divorced." He smiled, but it didn't reach his eyes, which remained cold and hard, like little pebbles. "I'm also her manager, still. Ah, yes, I see you'd forgotten that inconvenient little detail. What was it I heard? That you've promised Valeska and certain other members of the cast a percentage of the profits in lieu of salary? Well, assuming your little production doesn't open and close right here, I'll definitely be watching the sales. You and I might still do business, my dear—"

"Never," Keeley said coldly. "And as for Val—"

He smiled confidently. "She won't divorce me, if that's what you're thinking."

"Don't be too sure."

He shrugged. "Ask her yourself."

"I will," she said icily, debating about pushing him out of the way so she could check to see what was happening inside. She didn't like it that he'd shut the door behind him; she liked it even less that he was here so close to curtain. She knew how terrified Valeska was of him, and she vowed that if he had upset her star in any way, she'd kill him with her bare hands.

"Let me by, please," she said stiffly.

To her surprise, he stepped aside. "Be my guest."

She reached for the door. "Get out, Nigel. You don't belong here."

"Is that any way to talk to an old friend?"

Flushing angrily, she declared, "You were never my friend!"

"How strange. That's just what Valeska said."

Keeley didn't like the look on his face. He seemed much too . . . satisfied, and her feeling of dread increased. Ignoring him, she flung the door open, expecting to see . . . she wasn't sure what. She knew Nigel was capable of anything, and Valeska had been much too quiet in here.

"Val?" she said sharply, stepping inside the cluttered room.

When she saw Valeska huddled on the couch against the wall, she felt real fear. Val didn't look up when she came in, and when she tried to close the door, Nigel was right there behind her. Deciding that Valeska was more important, she ignored him and went over to the couch. Her hands over her face, Valeska was curled into a tight ball, sobbing uncontrollably.

"Val?" Keeley said. Quickly, she sat down beside her friend. Taking her by the shoulders, she forced her to a sitting position.

Valeska took one look at Nigel and exclaimed in terror. "Don't let him near me!" she cried, her face white, shaking with fear. "Don't let him near me!"

It was all Keeley needed to hear. Whirling around, she said to Nigel, "Get out. Get out before I call security."

His eyes on Valeska, he smiled. "No need for such drastic measures, my dear," he said. "I'm going. But I did want to wish you good luck." He paused. "You're going to need it."

"What do you mean? What have you done?"

He looked at her pityingly. "What do you think I mean? Look at her, Keeley. Do you really believe your 'star' is up to singing tonight? She looks closer to a nervous breakdown than a performance."

It was true; even Keeley couldn't deny it. Under the arm Keeley had put around her, Valeska was trembling like a leaf; she looked feverish and ready to collapse. Accusingly, Keeley turned to Nigel again. "What did you do to her?"

"Why, Keeley, what do you take me for?"

"A monster," Keeley said between her teeth. "Now, tell me, what did you do—or say?"

"Nothing," he said with an elaborate shrug. "You misjudge me. All I did was wish her good luck."

Huddled against Keeley's side, Valeska cried, "That's not true! He told me that if I sang, he'd break my neck."

"Oh, Valeska, how dramatic you are," Nigel drawled. "I certainly didn't say I'd break your *neck*. I *said*, break a leg. It's an old show business expression, remember? It means good luck."

"What it *means*," Keeley said, her hands clenched, "is that if you're not out of here in two seconds, I'm going to have you thrown out. Is that clear?"

To her fury, he gave her a mocking little bow. "Utterly," he said. He gave the shattered Valeska a satisfied look. Then, his malignant glance met Keeley's again, and he added softly, "I told you, didn't I, that you'd be sorry for crossing me."

She was so infuriated she got up and took a step toward him. "You bastard!"

Hastily, he backed out. His hand on the door, he delivered a last salvo. "Would you like me to send the understudy in before I leave? I know my little wifey, and I think you're going to need her."

Keeley's answer was to reach out and slam the door in his superior face. Whipping the lock on, she turned back to Val, who had collapsed again on the couch.

"Oh, Keeley, I can't go on tonight, I can't!" she wailed.

"Oh, yes, you can! You're not going to let Nigel Aames ruin everything with a few stupid threats!"

"They're not stupid! I told you, Keeley, you don't know what he can do!"

"He can't do anything worse to you than *I'm* going to do if you don't snap out of it!" Keeley cried, frustrated. "Come on, Val, pull yourself together!"

"I can't!" Valeska cried. She put her hands over her eyes. "Oh, I need a drink!"

Keeley wanted to shake her until her teeth rattled. "No, you don't! You've been sober now for months and months! You're not going to get drunk a half hour before curtain, not if I have to stand here and watch you until it's time for your entrance!"

Valeska dropped her hands. "I told you, I can't go on! How am I supposed to sing after all this?"

"You're supposed to sing because you're a professional, damn it!" Keeley shouted. "Now, get ready."

"No, I can't!"

"Yes, you can!"

"I won't!"

"You damned well *will*!"

"No, no, you can't make me," Valeska cried, bursting into sobs again. She threw herself back against the couch. "I can't go on. Nigel was right—call my understudy! Let her go on!"

Keeley was so furious she nearly slapped Valeska right across the face. By sheer force of will she kept her hands at her sides, but her fingers itched. "You're not going to do this to me, Val," she said, between her teeth. "I won't let you. You can't be that afraid of Nigel! You can't!"

Too agitated to sit, Val jumped up. Tears were streaming down her red, blotched face; she looked ready to whirl around and run. "I am!" she shouted. "I am! And don't tell me I'm not, because you don't know. You don't know anything, Keeley Cochran, you just don't know!"

"Then tell me, Goddamn it! Tell me once and for all, and get it over with!"

"I can't! If Nigel knew I'd told anybody—"

"*Fuck* Nigel!" Keeley cried in a rage. Pushed beyond endurance, she grabbed Val by the shoulders, shaking her hard. "Now, Goddamn it, tell me! What have you been hiding all these months? What is the cause of all those nightmares? *Tell me,* Val. I can help!"

"No one can help!" Val sobbed. "No one. It's all over with. I lost the baby, and it's all my fault!"

Keeley felt as if she'd made a wrong turn somewhere. Baby? Why was Val bringing that up now? "What do you mean? What about the baby?"

As if she couldn't trust her legs to hold her anymore, Valeska sank down onto the dressing table bench. She had looked ready to leap out of her skin before; her sudden lifelessness was even more alarming.

"It doesn't matter anymore," she muttered dully. "Nigel said I couldn't prove it, and he was right. . . ."

"Prove it? Prove what?" Keeley sat down beside her. She had forgotten they were close to the curtain rising on the most momentous night of her life; she had forgotten that she should be outside in case someone needed her. Valeska was more important than anything at the moment, and she repeated urgently, "Tell me."

Valeska raised tragic eyes to her face. "Remember when I told you I'd . . . lost the baby, Keeley? Well, I didn't just . . . lose it."

Keeley's first thought was that she'd had an abortion. "Well, it was your decision. You don't have to apologize, or explain anything to anybody. It was between you and—" she could hardly say his name "—Nigel."

"No, you don't understand," Val said, wringing her hands. "The reason I lost the baby was because ... because Nigel pushed me one night, and I fell down the stairs."

Keeley gasped. "Oh, Val!"

Valeska looked away bitterly. "Yes. Oh, Val. Now what do you think of me? Not only couldn't I protect myself from my husband, I couldn't protect my own baby."

Keeley didn't know what to say. "Did you ... did you tell anyone what happened? The doctor ... the po—"

"The police?" Val said it for her. "What would the police have done? Nigel told me he'd say I got drunk and fell all by myself. He almost had me believing that's the way it happened, too, except I had the bruises to show for it."

"Oh, Val," Keeley said helplessly. She didn't know how to deal with this; it was beyond her experience.

Valeska didn't notice she had spoken. Lost in sad memory, she said, "You know, when I realized I was going to have a baby, I was the happiest woman on earth. I thought ... I thought it would make things right between Nigel and me, but I was wrong." She shook her head. "So wrong."

"It wasn't your fault that Nigel didn't want a child."

"No, but I knew he didn't. And as soon as he found out, he began pressuring me to have an abortion, but I just couldn't. When I refused, he ... he turned mean." She looked down at her hands. "Even more so, I mean. He'd hit me before, pushed me around. It's how he got me to do *Maggie the Cat*. I knew it was wrong for my voice, but I just couldn't ... fight him." She drew a shaky breath. "Well, it doesn't matter now. The point is that when he found out I was pregnant, he was very angry."

Keeley reached for her hand. "Why didn't you call me?"

"I tried, but you weren't home, and I couldn't leave a message, not about that." Hopelessly, she put her face in her hands again. "I felt so alone, Keeley. I was drinking so much I wasn't thinking clearly. I ... I know now that's *why* I was drinking, so I wouldn't have to think at all."

Keeley was silent. She couldn't comprehend what Val had willingly gone through, or permitted to happen; it was beyond her understanding. She never would have allowed a man to take advantage of her like that; she would have died first—or killed him.

But before she started to feel superior, Gabe's face suddenly flashed into her mind, and she cringed. She hadn't been so successful where men were concerned. Foolish pride had kept her from the only man she had ever loved—or would ever love in her life. Because of her stubbornness and intolerance, she doubted Gabe would ever forgive her, and she couldn't blame him. She had judged him when she had no right to judge him at all, and if he was lost to her now, she was the one at fault.

Fiercely, she pulled herself together. She didn't have time for recriminations; she had to deal with the present. She had always known that she and Val weren't alike; in her heart, she had always accepted that she was the stronger, the one who was more aggressive and determined. But she had felt a special bond with Val since they'd met at the bus station. And just as Valeska had needed her strength at times, she had needed Valeska's softer side, her kindness, her sweetness. She had believed that, together, they were destined for success. Valeska's angelic voice would be lifted in her songs; she would provide the glorious music for Val to sing.

And now? Confused herself, she glanced at her friend. Val looked shattered, distraught, unable to cope. After what she had confessed tonight, how could she insist that Valeska go out and perform? Then she thought: *I have to.* Tonight she wasn't just Val's friend; she was the director of a show that concerned more than just the two of them. People depended upon them; she couldn't just . . . let it go.

"We're quite a pair, you and I, aren't we?" she said. "I thought we'd come a long way since that night at the Port Authority, but right now, I feel like I haven't learned a thing."

"Oh, Keeley, that's not true!"

"Yes, it is. I thought I was so smart, so smug. But even if the show's a success, who are we going home to, you and I . . . each other? You're my best friend, Val, and I love you. But it's not enough."

Valeska looked down at their clasped hands. She was silent a moment; then she said quietly, "I never told you because he asked me not to, but who do you think found Barry for you?"

Surprised at the turn in the conversation, Keeley said, "Found him? What do you mean? He just showed up at the theater that night."

Valeska shook her head. "No, he didn't. Gabe sent him."

Keeley was shocked. "Gabe! That's impossible!"

"No, it's not. I called him, in California. I knew you'd never call to ask his help, so I—"

Keeley jumped up. Suddenly, without warning, she was furious again. "You had no right! You asked Gabe for his help, after he and I . . . Oh, how could you!"

Valeska flushed, but she held her ground. "You always were stubborn, Keeley."

"And you always were a sentimental fool! Oh, I don't believe this!" Angrily, Keeley whirled around, only to whirl back again. "Why did you do it? You *knew* how I felt about Gabe."

"Yes, I knew!" Valeska cried, getting to her feet, too. "I knew you were in love with him."

"Were!" Keeley shouted. "*Were* is the operative word! You had no right to interfere!"

Valeska clasped her hands in distress. "Even if he found Barry, and Barry got Nigel to back off—of you, at least? Oh, Keeley, how can you be so ungrateful? You and Gabe were made for each other, you know it! If only—"

"If we're made for each other, why didn't he come to see me?" Keeley shouted. "Why didn't he call? He had to be in New York, if he talked to Barry. *Why didn't he at least call?*"

"I don't know!" Val cried. "Maybe you should ask him! Maybe for once you should swallow your stubborn pride and think of someone else for a change!"

"You can talk to me like that? You've got your nerve!"

"For God's sake, look what happened here! How can you—"

There was a knock on the door. They both whirled around. "What?" Keeley shouted.

"Uh . . . just wanted you to know we're fifteen minutes to curtain," Wes said, from the other side. There was a pause. "Are you two all right?"

"Never better," Valeska cried. "Now, go away!"

"Uh . . . there's some people out here to see Keeley," Wes said, clearly unhappy at having to deliver the news. "Shall I tell them you'll see them after the show?"

"Oh, for God's sake!" Keeley exclaimed angrily. "No, tell them I'll be out . . . in a minute."

"You got it," Wes said. He went away.

As soon as he was gone, Valeska turned to Keeley again. "I'm not going on tonight," she declared. "Call my understudy; get somebody else to sing!"

"Oh, isn't this just like you!" Keeley said in a fury. "You never could stand up to pressure. You haven't the faintest idea what being a professional means!"

Valeska was outraged. "No, that's something only *you* know

anything about!" she cried. "You're so *professional* all you think of is yourself!"

"That's not true!"

"The hell it's not!"

They glared at each other, breathing hard. Then Keeley said cruelly, "You know what I think? I think you don't want to sing tonight because you're afraid of success."

"Afraid of success! Are you crazy? I was the biggest success on Broadway! Audiences adored me! People *sobbed* when I sang!"

"And what happened? You tell me, Val! For a while, you loved it—when it didn't matter, when you were just getting started. Oh, yes, you loved it then!"

"I didn't love it! I hated it. I always did!"

"Is that why you sabotaged yourself? I always wondered!"

"*Sabotaged* myself!" Valeska was infuriated. "What do you mean?"

"You know damned well what I mean! You never drank until you became a success! You never—"

"I never had to—until Nigel!"

"Oh, don't give me that! You never had to until you realized that the dream might come true! That's when you started falling apart! Don't forget, *Valeska*, I knew you when you were plain little Valine Smits from Noplace, Indiana! You came here just like I did, *wanting* it, *craving* it! Only you couldn't admit it, could you? You had to blame your mother for pushing you, for seeing to it that you got what you wanted all along! It was convenient to blame her—to blame everyone!—until you saw your star rising. But up there on top, you had nobody to blame but yourself, did you? *That's* when you started drinking! *That's* when you couldn't handle it!"

"You lie!" Valeska cried. "It wasn't that way at all!"

"Wasn't it? Remember when you accused me of working so hard, of running all the time, of not looking back at *my* successes because I was so afraid of failure?"

"Of course I remember! But—"

"Well, you think about it, Val, because as far as I'm concerned, we're two sides of the same coin! I might be afraid of failure, but at least I'm not terrified of success! Say what you want to anybody else, but don't lie to yourself. This could be your comeback, tonight. We both know it. So why, suddenly, don't you want to sing? Is it because you're afraid you can't do it—or because you're afraid you will?"

Breathing hard, Keeley reached for the door. Jerking it open, she looked back at the equally furious Valeska. Her voice steely, she said, "If you want your understudy to go on, you tell her yourself. I'm not going to do it and give you an excuse. Not now, not ever, and especially not tonight! You decide, for once, what you really want. And then have the courage to take responsibility for it!"

Valeska looked angry enough to throw something. "And you?" she cried. "What do *you* want?"

Gabe's face flashed into Keeley's mind again. She could see his sun-streaked blond hair that always seemed to need a haircut, but which somehow suited him even in a tux; she could see his intense gaze, bluer than the Montana sky. She saw the scar on his temple and down his cheek, faint now, but still a reminder of the attack by the tiger, and his nose with the aristocratic bump that she loved and he hated. With an almost physical pain, she could hear his voice murmuring endearments, and feel his lips on hers, calling forth something deep inside her, instantly and without effort.

Angrily, she thrust Gabe's image away and looked at Valeska. "You know what I want. I want you to sing. I created Beauty for you. It's yours if you want it. But you have to choose." Despite herself, her expression turned bitter. "Just like I have."

Out in the hallway, alone for a few precious seconds, she leaned against the door, trying to gather strength. She felt drained, exhausted, and the night hadn't even started. Would Valeska sing? She didn't know; at the moment, she couldn't even care.

Why was it that she seemed to hurt the people she loved the most? She didn't mean to; it just happened. Val had been right when she accused her of being arrogant and self-centered, so driven by her need not to fail that she never considered anyone else. It was true, and at the moment, she didn't like herself much.

Involuntarily, she turned back to the dressing room again. She hated to leave it like this; they'd been through too much to say such awful things to each other without apologizing. She was just about to reach for the doorknob when she dropped her hand again. She'd said all she was going to tonight. She had her beast to face, just as Val did. If Valeska was afraid of success, as she had accused her of being, only she could decide what to do about it. Either she would sing or she wouldn't, and after what had just happened, Keeley thought it would be the understudy who went on tonight.

Her steps dragging, she turned and went down the hallway. But as she approached backstage, she straightened her shoulders and quickened her pace. She had responsibilities, obligations to her cast and crew; it wasn't their fault that the night she had looked forward to with such anticipation had suddenly turned to dust for her. She was director, composer, *producer* of the show; it was her vision that people were going to see tonight, and if the worst happened, and Val didn't sing the role of Beauty, she'd just have to live with it.

"Five minutes, Keeley," Wes said, when she came backstage. He gave her an anxious, cautious look, clearly wondering what was going on.

Not wanting to alarm him, she managed a quick, reassuring smile. "Everything's fine," she lied. "Don't look so worried."

He looked ready to collapse. "Is Valeska going to . . . ?"

"I don't know," she said. "But just in case, you'd better tell Roxanne."

"Oh, lord," Wes moaned. But he saw Keeley's tight expression and went off to find the understudy in case she was needed.

Raleigh Quinn came back moments before curtain. Spying Keeley, he took both her hands and gave her a quick kiss. "You look beautiful," he said approvingly.

She felt like she was going to crack. "It's all a facade. Inside, I'm a wreck."

He laughed. "It's a good sign. It's when you're *not* worried that disaster rushes in."

"In that case, we should be a monumental success."

"You will be. I'll see you later for congrats."

Raleigh had no sooner disappeared than Keeley felt a tiny tug at her waist. When she turned and saw Jewell standing there, she gave her a hug. She hadn't cared about the rest of her family, but she had asked Jewell to be there—Jewell, who would be attending San Diego University on a scholarship next year. Lovely in a pale pink dress, Jewell was holding something behind her back. Leaning forward, she gave Keeley a kiss.

"I'm so glad you came!" Keeley said, touched.

"I wouldn't have missed it for the world," Jewell replied, looking ready to burst. "Oh, I'm so proud of you, Keeley!"

"Did the rest of the family come?"

Jewell's smile broadened. "They . . . couldn't make it. You know how it is."

Keeley grinned. "What a shame."

"It is, isn't it?" Jewell said. "I brought something for you."

"You did? What?"

From behind her, Jewell produced the cardboard keyboard Keeley had given her so long ago. Startled because she had forgotten all about it, Keeley laughed. "What's this?"

"Don't you remember? The night you left, you told me to keep it in case you ever needed it. Well, I think tonight proves you won't. You've made your dream come true, Keeley, but I thought you should have it to remind you of how far you've come."

Emotionally, Keeley took the cardboard from her. It still had all the piano keys drawn in black and white, and she ran her fingers along the top. So many memories, she thought, and looked at Jewell. "Thank you," she said, feeling choked.

Just then they heard the orchestra tuning up. Quickly, Jewell gave Keeley another kiss. "I'll see you after the show," she whispered. "And don't worry, the one clapping and cheering loudest will be me."

As Jewell hurried away, Keeley quickly dashed the tears from her eyes. Charlie happened to be passing by, and she stopped him for a moment. "Put this where it won't get lost, will you?" she asked, grinning when he looked at it curiously. "A souvenir from the past. If this doesn't go well, I might need it again after all."

It was time to make her way to the balcony at the back of the theater, where she had decided she'd spend the next nerve-racking hour until intermission. She'd wanted to be where she could see everything—performers and audience, as well. But as the lights dimmed and the theater noises began to die down, she was sure everyone in the place could hear the loud pounding of her heart as she climbed the stairs and shrank back into the shadows, hoping to remain unnoticed. She had rolled the die; whether she was ready or not, it was time to see what came up.

Feeling sick and dizzy and hot and cold at the same time, she rubbed her hands together and tried to get a handle on her nerves. The entire show depended on Val's singing Beauty; the understudy was good, but she wasn't Val. Could Valeska pull it together after everything that had happened? Keeley had bet everything she had that her friend wouldn't let her down. She'd been so sure . . . until tonight. Would Val sing? Like everybody else, she had to wait to find out.

When the curtain went up, the entire stage was in darkness.

Contrary to custom, the show didn't open with the overture, but with Beauty's haunting, longing lament. Val sang an entire quatrain a cappella before the orchestra joined in; the effect was stunning and startling, the show opening Keeley had long dreamed.

In rehearsal it had worked beautifully, making even cast and crew, who had heard the song dozens of times, stop and listen, some with tears in their eyes. Out of the darkness, Valeska's bell-like voice would float out across the theater for three bars before a single spot would click on, illuminating her, as Beauty, on stage right, alone with her song.

That's the way it had been planned. But as the curtain whispered up, Keeley still didn't know which voice she would hear. Would it be Valeska, for whom the role had been created—or Roxanne, singing her heart out, no doubt, but at best, second-best.

"Oh, Val," Keeley murmured, clasping cold hands together. "Don't do it for me, do it for you. You deserve it, after all this."

There was a gut-wrenching silence after the curtain finished drawing up; the entire theater was in darkness, waiting for what might come next. Her nerves strained to the breaking point, Keeley was just thinking despairingly that all was lost . . . when out of the inky blackness came the voice she had longed to hear—so clear and beautiful she thought her heart would break if she heard another note.

Valeska Szabo, née Valine Smits, held the entire audience spellbound with that single first note. It floated out over the theater like gossamer, impossibly gathering strength until it rose to an exquisite pitch, then it slowly faded as another vibrant note took life. As Beauty, Val sang of loneliness and longing, of her yearning to find her handsome prince.

The audience was motionless, mesmerized, entranced. The theater was so silent there wasn't a whisper, a murmur, a cough. Listening, Keeley bowed her head, giving thanks.

"Oh, Val," she murmured, as the orchestra joined in and applause rose and swelled in response. "We did it. . . ." She lifted her head, tears glittering in her eyes as she looked down at the vision on stage. Valeska had never looked more beautiful; she had never sung better. And her voice rose in glorious triumph as Keeley clasped her hands and whispered, "Oh, Val, *we did it at last!*"

Three hours later, after a standing ovation and sixteen curtain calls, Keeley was hauled out on stage with the rest of the cast, to pose between the radiant Valeska and a gallant Dom, who bowed over her hand and kissed it. The applause was deafening, and under cover of the noise, Keeley looked at Valeska and said simply, "You were brilliant."

Valeska, her fears put to rest, smiled joyously and linked her arm with Keeley's. "It was your music," she said. "All I did was sing it."

They smiled tremulously at each other before turning to accept the first of the dozens of rose bouquets that poured in. Everyone in the cast got something, and Keeley was trying to balance the half-dozen bouquets she had received herself when one more was brought out to her. It didn't contain roses. When she saw the white lilacs nestled amid delicate green ferns, she stiffened. Wes handed them to her with a grin.

She grabbed his hand. "Where did you get these?"

The audience, enthusiasm unabated, was still applauding like crazy. Embarrassed to be on stage in his backstage getup, Wes shook his head. "Don't know. They were just delivered."

Keeley knew who had sent them—or thought she did. *It can't be,* she thought, trying to peer out over the glare of the floodlights to the body of the theater. She couldn't see a thing at first, but then as she squinted, she was sure she caught a glimpse of a man in a tuxedo, a black overcoat over his arm and a white scarf tossed around his neck, heading up the aisle. He paused at the door, turning just for an instant to look back. The lobby lights beyond the door glinted on his blond hair, and Keeley's heart leapt. The pungent scent of the flowers filled her nostrils, and suddenly she was remembering a night, so long ago now, when he'd told her she looked like a white lilac kind of woman.

Dom was surprised when she thrust the flowers she was holding at him. "What . . . ?" he said.

She didn't want to explain. She had to get off the stage and out to the front of the theater; if it was Gabe she'd seen, she couldn't let him get away without—what? She didn't know; she only knew she had to stop him.

"What is it?" Valeska asked, grabbing her as she started away. Flushed with triumph and success, having faced and conquered her own beast, she looked thrilled and excited. Dressed in Beauty's medieval costume, with her hair braided and entwined with flowers, she looked every inch the star she had proved herself to be tonight, and despite her hurry, Keeley paused to give her a quick hug.

"I think I just saw Gabe," she whispered.

"Gabe!" Valeska looked delighted. "Oh, Keeley, you mean he came?"

"I'm not sure, I couldn't see," Keeley said hurriedly. The curtain had just come down before it was raised again, and she wanted to get off the stage.

She started to hurry away, but Valeska grabbed her again. "You can't leave, not now! They'll want you here, Keeley! This is your night!"

But Keeley couldn't wait; kissing Val on the cheek, she escaped clutching hands, ran through the cheering crew backstage and around to the front of the theater. When she got to the lobby, it was empty; everyone was still inside, but Gabe—if it had been he—was gone.

She was crushed with disappointment. She had been so sure.

Looking down, she saw with dull surprise that she was still carrying one of the lilacs. With a barely checked sob, she crushed it between her fingers. Released, the spicy fragrance floated up to her nostrils, and she was reminded poignantly of the night he'd given her the lilacs. He had promised he would always be there for her. In triumph or tragedy, he'd said, laughing at himself for sounding poetic. But his eyes had held her, contradicting his laughter, and she had never doubted he meant it.

Had he really been here on the night of her greatest triumph? Had he listened to the exchanges between Beauty and her Beast and realized that, in so many ways, even without her realizing it, Keeley had been using her music to speak of her longing for him?

Thinking of it, she was just deciding to go after Gabe when the double doors leading to the lobby were thrown back and the crowd came pouring out. She had time to see Raleigh, and Jewell, and a couple of others she knew before she was surrounded; after that, her opportunity to follow was lost. A critic from the *Times* approached with a smile on his face; another from the *Globe*, known for not finding anything good to say about anything, came forward with his hand held out. Seconds later she was inundated: congratulations and well wishes followed her as she was wafted to the party backstage on a tide of celebration.

Valeska caught her glance when she came in; they were separated by too many people to talk, but Keeley saw the question in her friend's eyes and she answered with a brief shake of her head. Sympathetically, Valeska tried to reach her, but the party was already too crowded.

Keeley couldn't have confessed her feelings anyway; she was glad she was occupied with the constant stream of people until, sometime very early in the morning, one of Raleigh's contacts phoned to say the reviews had been called in. By then, the noise level was so high that Wes had to shout for attention when he took the details down. Ceremoniously, he handed his notes to Keeley. Suddenly tense, everyone quieted.

"I can't," she said. "I'm too nervous. Someone else do it."

The reviews were unanimous. With a few small quibbles here and there, and a few sour grapes thrown in, the consensus was that Keeley had a hit on her hands. Once again the crowd surged forward to congratulate her, and as she laughed and embraced Valeska and Jewell and Raleigh and a dozen others, Gabe's face flashed into her mind again. He had always said that one day she would fulfill the dream she'd dreamed playing on her cardboard keyboard in that crowded house in Detroit. And tonight, against all odds, it seemed she had.

———— ⸎ ————

EPILOGUE

Keeley flew to Montana in September, exactly two years to the day she and Gabe had last been together at the ranch. She was so nervous about seeing him after so much time had passed that she hadn't called ahead. If he wasn't there, if he hadn't remembered what they'd told each other before they'd had that awful quarrel the day of Frank's funeral—if he didn't care, she didn't want to hear it in advance, even from the tactful Billy Six Horses.

It was the thought of the white lilacs that convinced her to make the trip. Months later, after all her success, she kept thinking of the special bouquet she had received opening night. Even though there had been no note, it couldn't have been a coincidence. Carnations, maybe. Violets, even. But not white lilacs.

"Why don't you call him?" Val had asked ... begged ... pleaded.

When she thought of Val, she smiled. Almost seven months after the Boston preview, Valeska was better than she'd ever been. The wild success of *Beauty and the Beast* had given her enough confidence to divorce Nigel, who, Keeley had heard, was following Carlotte around the country while she tried to make a living for them doing a lounge act.

"And don't think you can scrounge off Keeley!" Val had told Nigel to his face. "If you so much as *think* of trying to hold her to that ridiculous contract, I'll have you arrested for wife abuse! I'm sure the theater community will be interested to know the *real* story behind my so-called miscarriage!"

Although the charge was—and would be—serious, Keeley smiled again, just thinking about it. She never would have believed it of Val, but she had finally stood up to him—another beast faced—and Nigel had scuttled off like the insect he was and hadn't bothered either of them again.

She'd thought for a while there might be something brewing between Valeska and Dom, who night after night created such magic on stage together, but when she had mentioned it, Valeska had been indignant.

"Do you honestly think that, after freeing myself from one man, I'm going to get tangled up with another?" she had demanded. Then she had smiled. "But I *am* going home in a while to see Ned again. He's seen *Beauty* a dozen times, can you believe it?"

Keeley had met Ned Kowalski, Val's old boyfriend from Allentown. She liked Ned, and he certainly seemed to be in love with Val—or "Vallie," as he called her affectionately—whenever he came to town, which seemed to be more often of late. Keeley thought it was great; it was about time Val found herself a good man.

Valeska had even been reconciled with her mother after all these years. She and Keeley hadn't realized it preview night, but Edra had been in the audience. She had traveled all the way by bus from Allentown, and Valeska had been so touched she had cautiously agreed to a new start. Edra was still living above the grocery, but she came occasionally to New York for a weekend now.

"Maybe a new start is what you need with Gabe, Keeley," Val had suggested. "*Please* call him!"

But Keeley couldn't say the things she wanted to say over the phone, and once *Beauty* had moved from Boston to advance sell-out crowds in New York, she hadn't been able to get away. Offers had come flooding in, so many it was hard to choose. And Raleigh was first on the list; after bailing her out of such a tight spot, she owed him his score. Or two, she amended with a grin, remembering the two fingers he'd held up before he left on his plane.

"I know I can't lure you back permanently, not with a hit on your hands," he'd said. "But I am going to hold you to our deal. Two scores, and maybe, if you're feeling generous, a title song or two."

"As a favor for a friend?" she'd teased.

"Well, you certainly don't need the money, not after this."

It was true: she didn't need the money. What she needed was time . . . and Gabe. But if they were going to have any relationship at all, she knew the only way for them was to face what had happened and go on from there. How she would accomplish *that*, when she wasn't even sure he would remember their promise to meet today, she didn't know.

Holding her breath, she drove up the last rise to the ranch and stopped the car before heading down again to the gates. Far down the slope, she could see the house and the barn and corrals. She could even see Holler's loudly marked coat as the paint horse ambled about one of the pastures. What she didn't see was the truck.

"What do I do now?" she muttered, turning to look at Tux, who had inveigled his way out of his cat carrier and who was sitting beside her on the seat. "Do we go for it, or not?"

Tux's response was a slant-eyed look followed by his peculiar *Meerrow*.

"You're right," Keeley said, turning to look down at the ranch again. "We're here, and we're not going to leave without letting him know *we* kept our promise."

Putting the car in gear again, she drove down the hill and up to the house. She was just getting out of the car when she saw the backpack on the porch. She stopped, her heart skipping a beat. She knew that backpack; she knew the camera equipment stashed beside it. Did it mean what she thought it did?

After thinking about it all these long, lonely months, she had come prepared to tell Gabe she'd been wrong—wrong to judge him, wrong to tell him what to do. It didn't matter that her motives had been the best, that she was only concerned about his happiness; she knew she'd had no right to tell him he shouldn't go to work at the family business. It had been such an unhappy time, right after Frank's death; neither of them had been thinking clearly. If she had been, she would have realized it was his decision, and she had no right to interfere—at least, not the way she'd tried. She'd been wrong, and she had vowed never to say another word, not even a silent reproach. All she wanted, all she ever wanted, was just to be friends.

She was just closing the car door when she heard the screen door open. Her hand on the car door, she looked up and saw him. He hadn't changed at all, she thought, a lump in her throat. He was still the man who made her heart race, still the man who haunted her dreams.

As she stared at him, it was as though the past months of indecision, of longing and wondering and trying to forget him, hadn't happened. She would never forget him, she thought, slamming the car door. And she didn't want to be . . . just friends.

"Hi," he said. He stayed where he was on the porch, but his eyes didn't leave her. Even though he didn't move, it was as though he were drinking her in. "I didn't think you were coming. It's almost sunset, the day's nearly over."

Or just beginning, she thought, but she couldn't seem to say anything; her throat felt constricted. She wanted to run up the steps and throw herself at him, but her legs wouldn't move, either.

"I promised, didn't I?" she said unsteadily. "I thought you were the one who'd forgotten. When I didn't see the truck—"

"Billy has it. He went over to Bozeman to sell some horses."

Wondering why they were carrying on this inane conversation when there were so many other things to say, she said, "I see." She had to take her eyes away from him; she felt like she was drowning. Glancing toward the corral, she gestured weakly. "I saw Holler when I was coming over the hill."

"I kept him for you. I had Billy break him last summer."

"You kept him for me?" she said before she caught herself. Her eyes narrowed. "You're pretty sure of yourself."

A look of pained regret crossed his face. "I was," he said. "Then I lost it. Then something happened to help me put things in perspective again."

She felt like she was holding her breath. "What?"

He came down one step, his hands in his jeans pockets, as if he didn't trust himself. Jerking his head back toward the house, he said, "I came up here to think and found the tape you'd left."

"I see," she said again. She sounded like an idiot. She wanted to ask if it had been before or after he'd come to the preview of *Beauty*, but she couldn't make herself say it. Instead, she asked, "Did you like it?"

Amusement showed briefly in his eyes. "You really thought I wouldn't?"

She flushed. Aside from *Beauty*, it was the best thing she'd ever done, and she knew it. "I don't know. It depends on when you listened to it."

"Before, or after I went to Boston, you mean?" he said softly.

Her face lit up. "You did come to the preview!"

"Didn't you get the lilacs?"

"I got them." Her heart was singing. "But there was no note."

"I figured if you didn't know who sent them, it didn't matter."

She had to get hold of herself. She wanted to dance and sing and shout it out. "Just like you figured it wasn't necessary to call me after you found Barry?" she asked.

It was his turn to flush. "I tried to call you once, but you didn't call me back," he reminded her.

He had her there. "I know. I . . . I wasn't thinking too clearly then. I was too angry." Suddenly, she was tired of fencing. She wanted him to know how she felt. "Oh, Gabe, I'm so sorry. It was all my fault—"

He held up his hand, stopping her in midsentence. "No, you were right to tell me off. You were right about a lot of things, Keeley, one of which is that I can't take Frank's place—no, don't say anything, I've had months to work on this speech, and with you standing right here in front of me, looking so damned beautiful, I'm going to forget it if I don't get it out." He took a deep breath. "I'm working with the foundation again—"

She forgot everything else. "That's wonderful!" she said before she remembered his family. Her smile faltered. "But what about your father?"

He looked touched and wry at the same time. "He came to me, if you can believe it. He had a scrapbook filled with photos I'd taken from various assignments. He . . . he said it was about time I got back to doing what I did best."

"Oh, Gabe!"

His eyes held hers again. "Just like you're doing what you do best," he said. "I knew you'd be a success, Keeley. You really have a gift. I was so proud that night in Boston; it was all I could do to leave when I did."

She looked at him, longing and regret deepening the green of her eyes. "Then why did you?"

"Because you weren't ready. No, you weren't," he said, when she began to protest. "You had to follow your dream, to make it happen. You always said that one day you'd compose and direct your own work on Broadway, and you made it come true. I can't tell you how much I admire you for that." He looked at her again. "How much I love you for it." He smiled his crooked grin, the one she'd always loved. "Independent spirit and all."

Fierce, quick, independent, legendary. Sort of reminds me of you, Keeley.

Gabe had written that at the bottom of his splendid snow leopard photograph. But as they stood there looking at each other, Keeley knew she wasn't nearly so independent as she had been. She needed him, and she could admit it now. Their careers kept them at times literally worlds apart, but somehow they'd work around it. They'd have to. He was like her other half, her soul mate, a part of her heart. She could never leave him; it would be like dying. Music soothed her, renewed her, gave her a fierce, deep satisfaction, but it was Gabe who gave her life true meaning, and after this endless, arid separation, she wouldn't let go of him for so long again.

She thought of another photo he'd given her, one of the tiger in India, who seemed to hold the secret of life in her fierce eyes. "She went her way and allowed me to go mine," Gabe had written on the bottom. But as she raced up the steps and into his willing arms, she knew this was where she and the tiger parted company.

Lonely in my castle keep
I dream of you and pine
Release me from this wretched sleep
And let me make you mine. . . .

In the emotional, show-stopping duet between Beauty and the Beast, Beast had sung the song in his misery, believing that Beauty could never love such as he. He didn't know that, alone in her silken prison, Beauty was singing of her own longing, like Keeley.

No man could match the prince of my dreams
None could be so gentle or strong.
But now I see he was here all the time
How can I ever say I was wrong. . . .

"I love you, Keeley, as in Cochran," Gabe said, looking down into her face as he held her tight.

For Keeley, there was no more doubt. "And I love you, Gabriel—as in the Angel," she said with a glorious smile that made his pulse race. Free to speak her true feelings at last, she said it with all her heart.

Left alone in the car, Tux jumped out and sauntered into the house. *Meerrow,* he said, sounding satisfied as he found a comfortable spot on the couch.

Lost in a world of their own, it was a long while before Keeley or Gabe noticed.

trying to do it myse_ _nd not succeeding for years now. I'll wel-